SPEARWIELDER'S TALE

SPEARWIELDER'S TALE

R. A. SALVATORE

ACE BOOKS, NEW YORK

THE BERKLEY PUBLISHING GROUP
Published by the Penguin Group
Penguin Group (USA) Inc.
375 Hudson Street, New York, New York 10014, USA
Penguin Group (Canada), 90 Eglinton Avenue East, Suite 700, Toronto, Ontario M4P 2Y3, Canada
(a division of Pearson Penguin Canada Inc.)
Penguin Books Ltd., 80 Strand, London WC2R 0RL, England
Penguin Group (Ireland), 25 St. Stephen's Green, Dublin 2, Ireland (a division of Penguin Books Ltd.)
Penguin Group (Australia), 250 Camberwell Road, Camberwell, Victoria 3124, Australia
(a division of Pearson Australia Group Pty. Ltd.)
Penguin Books India Pvt. Ltd., 11 Community Centre, Panchsheel Park, New Delhi—110 017, India
Penguin Books (NZ), 67 Apollo Drive, Rosedale, North Shore 0632, Auckland, New Zealand
(a division of Pearson New Zealand Ltd.)
Penguin Books (South Africa) (Pty.) Ltd., 24 Sturdee Avenue, Rosebank, Johannesburg 2196,
South Africa

Penguin Books Ltd., Registered Offices: 80 Strand, London WC2R 0RL, England

PRINTING HISTORY
Ace trade paperback edition / September 2004

Library of Congress Cataloging-in-Publication Data

Salvatore, R. A., 1959–
    Spearwielder's Tale / R. A. Salvatore.
        p. cm.
    Contents: The woods out back — The dragon's dagger — Dragonslayer's return.
    ISBN 978-0-441-01194-0
        I. Title.

PS3569.A462345S64 2004
813'.54—dc22

2004046180

PRINTED IN THE UNITED STATES OF AMERICA

19 18 17 16 15 14 13 12 11

CONTENTS

LAND OF

TIR NA N'OG

GNOM

OVER

DILNAMARRA

DROCHIT

RIVER OSTLE

FIRTL

BRAEMAR

TO CONNACHT

TO CANCARRON
MOUNTAINS &
BRETAIGNE

LOCH DEVENSH

CONNACHT
(KING KENNIMORE)

YNIS GWYDRI

A SCALE OF MILES

0   25   50   75

FAERIE

the
FIVE SISTERS

GONDABUGGAN

MAL

LORE

the CRAHGS

LOCH TULLAMORE
(DRY)

the Witch's
Teats   GIANT'S THUMB

EN DRUITCH

RUINED FOREST

DREADWOOD

N

W   E

S

Ann Myer Maglinte

THE
WOODS OUT BACK

To the memory of J.R.R. Tolkien and to Fleetwood Mac,
for giving me elfs and dragons, witches and angels,
and for showing me the way to find them on my own.

Prelude

"YOU were caught fairly and within the written limits of your own rules," Kelsey said sternly. His sharp eyes, golden in hue and ever sparkling like the stars he so loved, bore into the smaller sprite, promising no compromise.

"Might that it be time for changing the rules," Mickey the leprechaun mumbled under his breath.

Kelsey's golden eyes, the same hue as his flowing hair, narrowed dangerously, his thin brows forming a "V" over his delicate but angular nose.

Mickey silently berated himself. He could get away with his constant private muttering around bumbling humans, but, he reminded himself again, one should never underestimate the sharpness of an elf's ears. The leprechaun looked around the open meadow, searching for some escape route. He knew it to be a futile exercise; he couldn't hope to outrun the elf, standing more than twice his height, and the nearest cover was fully a hundred yards away.

Not a promising proposition.

Always ready to improvise, Mickey went into his best posture for bargaining, a leprechaun's second favorite pastime (the first being the use of illusions to trick pursuing humans into smashing their faces into trees).

"Ancient, they are," the leprechaun tried to explain. "Rules o' catching made for humans and greedy folk. It was meant for being a game, ye know." Mickey kicked a curly-toed shoe against a mushroom stalk and his voice held an unmistakable edge of sarcasm as he completed the thought. "Elfs were not expected in the chase, being honorable folk and their hearts not being held by a pot o' gold. At least, that's what I been told about elfs."

"I do not desire your precious pot," Kelsey reminded him. "Only a small task."

"Not so small."

"Would you prefer that I take your gold?" Kelsey warned. "That is the usual payment for capture."

Mickey gnashed his teeth, then popped his enormous (considering his size) pipe into his mouth. He couldn't argue; Kelsey had caught him fairly. Still, Mickey had to wonder how honest the chase had been. The rules for catching a leprechaun were indeed ancient and precise, and, written by the wee folk themselves, hugely slanted in the leprechaun's favor. But a leprechaun's greatest advantage in evading humans lay in his uncanny abilities at creating illusions. Enter Kelsey the elf, and the advantage is no more. None in all the land of Faerie, not the dwarfs of Dvergamal nor even the great dragons themselves, could see through illusions, could separate reality from fabrication, as well as the elfs.

"Not so small a task, I say," Mickey iterated. "Ye're looking to fill Cedric's own shoes—none in Dilnamarra that I've seen are fitting that task! The man was a giant . . ."

Kelsey shrugged, unconcerned, his casual stance stealing Mickey's rising bluster. The human stock in Faerie had indeed diminished, and the prospects of finding a man who could fit into the ancient armor once worn by King Cedric Donigarten were not good. Of course Kelsey knew that; why else would he have taken the time to catch Mickey?

"I might have to go over," Mickey said gravely.

"You are the cleverest of your kind," Kelsey replied, and the compliment was not patronizing. "You shall find a way, I do not doubt. Have the faeries you know so well do their dance, then. Surely they owe Mickey McMickey a favor or two."

Mickey took a long draw on his pipe. The fairie dance! Kelsey actually expected him to go over, to find someone from the other side, from Real-earth.

"Me pot o' gold might be an easier barter," the leprechaun grumbled.

"Then give it to me," replied a smiling Kelsey, knowing the bluff for what it was. "And I shall use the wealth to purchase what I need from some other source."

Mickey gnashed his teeth around his pipe, wanting to put his curly boot into the smug elf's face. Kelsey had seen his bluff as easily as he had seen through Mickey's illusions on the lopsided chase. No leprechaun would willingly give up his pot of gold with no chance of stealing it back unless his very life was at stake. And for all of the inconvenience Kelsey had caused him, Mickey knew that the elf would not harm him.

"Not an easy task," the leprechaun said again.

"If the task was easy, I would have taken the trouble myself," Kelsey replied evenly, though a twitch in one of his golden eyes revealed that he was nearing the end of his patience. "I have not the time."

"Ye taked the trouble to catching me," Mickey snarled.

"Not so much trouble," Kelsey assured him.

Mickey rested back and considered a possible escape through the meadow again. Kelsey was shooting down his every leading suggestion with no room for argument, with no room for bargaining. By a leprechaun's measure, Kelsey wasn't playing fair.

"You shall accept my offer, then," Kelsey said. "Or I shall have your pot of gold here and now." He paused for a few moments to give Mickey the chance to produce the pot, which, of course, the leprechaun did not do.

"Excellent," continued the elf. "Then you know the terms of your indenture. When might I expect my human?"

Mickey kicked his curly-toed shoes again and moved to find a seat on the enormous mushroom. "Suren 'tis a beautiful day," he said, and he was not exaggerating in the least. The breeze was cool but not stiff, and it carried a thousand springtime scents with it, aromas of awakening flowers and new-growing grass.

"Too beautiful for talking business, I say," Mickey mentioned.

"When?" Kelsey demanded again, refusing to be sidetracked.

"All the folk o' Dilnamarra are out to frolic while we're sitting here arguing . . ."

"Mickey McMickey!" Kelsey declared. "You have been caught, captured, defeated on the chase. Of that, there can be no argument. You are thus bound to me. We are not discussing business; we are . . . I am, establishing the conditions of your freedom."

"Suren yer tongue's as sharp as yer ears," mumbled Mickey quietly.

Kelsey heard every word of it, of course, but this time he did not scowl. He knew by Mickey's resigned tone that the leprechaun had surrendered fully. "When?" he asked a third time.

"I cannot be sure," Mickey replied. "I'll set me friends to working on it."

Kelsey bowed low. "Then enjoy your beautiful day," he said, and he turned to leave.

For all his whining, Mickey was not so unhappy about the way things had turned out. His pride was hurt—any self-respecting leprechaun would be embarrassed over a capture—but Kelsey was an elf, after all, and that proved that the chase hadn't really been fair. Besides, Mickey still had his precious pot of gold and Kelsey's request wasn't overly difficult, leaving plenty of room for Mickey's own interpretation.

Mickey was thinking of that task now as he sat on the mushroom, his legs, crossed at the ankles, dangling freely over its side, and he was thinking that the task, like everything else in a leprechaun's life, just might turn out to be a bit of fun.

"IT cannot be," the sorceress declared, pulling away from her reflecting pool and flipping her long and wavy, impossibly thick black hair back over her delicate shoulders.

"What has yous seen, my lady?" the hunched goblin rasped.

Ceridwen turned on him sharply and the goblin realized that he had not been asked to speak. He dipped into an apologetic bow, fell right to the floor, and groveled on the ground below the beautiful sorceress, whining and kissing her feet piteously.

"Get up, Geek!" she commanded, and the goblin snapped to attention. "There is trouble in the land," Ceridwen went on, true concern in her voice. "Kelsenellenelvial Gil-Ravadry has taken up his life-quest to forge the broken spear."

The goblin's face twisted in confusion.

"We do not want the people of Dilnamarra thinking of dead kings and heroes of old," Ceridwen explained. "Their thoughts must be on their own pitiful existence, on their gruel and mud-farming, on the latest disease that sweeps their land and keeps them weak.

"Weak and whimpering," Ceridwen declared, and her icy-blue eyes, so contrasting her raven-black hair, flashed like lightning. She rose up tall and terrible and Geek huddled again on the floor. But Ceridwen calmed immediately and seemed again the quiet, beautiful woman. "Like you, dear Geek," she said softly. "Weak and whimpering, and under the control of Kinnemore, my puppet King."

"Does we's killses the elf?" Geek asked hopefully. The goblin so loved killing!

"It is not so easy as that," replied Ceridwen. "I do not wish to invoke the wrath of the Tylwyth Teg." She winced at the notion. The Tylwyth Teg, the elfs of Faerie, were not to be taken lightly. But Ceridwen's concern soon dissipated, replaced by a confident smile. "But there are other ways, more subtle ways," the sorceress purred, more to herself than to her wretched goblin.

Ceridwen's smile only widened as she considered the many wicked allies she might call upon, the dark creatures of Faerie's misty nights.

ONE

The Grind

WHRRRR!

The noise was deafening, a twenty-horsepower motor spinning eight heavy blades. It only got louder when a chunk of scrap plastic slipped in through the creaking hopper gate and landed on that spinning blur, to be bounced and slammed and chipped apart. In mere seconds, the chunk, reduced to tiny flakes, would be spit out the grinder's bottom into a waiting barrel.

Gary Leger slipped his headphones over his ears and put on the heavy, heat-resistant gloves. With a resigned sigh, he stepped up on the stool beside the grinder and absently tipped over the next barrel, spilling the scrap pieces out before him on the metal table. He tossed one on the hopper tray and pushed it through the gate, listening carefully as the grinder blades mashed it to ensure that the plastic was not too hot to be ground. If it was, if the inside of the chunks were still soft, the grinder would soon jam, leaving Gary with a time-consuming and filthy job of tearing down and cleaning the machine.

The chunk went straight through, its flaky remains spewing into the empty barrel beneath the grinder, telling Gary that he could go at the work in earnest. He paused for a moment to consider what adventure awaited him this time, then smiled and adjusted his headphones and gloves. These items were his protection from the noise and the sharp edges of the irregular plastic chunks, but mostly they were Gary's insulation from reality itself. All the world—all the real world—became a distant place to Gary, standing on that stool beside the grinder table. Reality was gone now, no match for the excitement roused by an active imagination.

The plastic chunks became enemy soldiers—no, fighter jets, variations of a MiG-29. Perhaps a hundred of the multishaped, dark blue lumps, some as small as two inches across, others nearly a foot long, though only half that length, lay piled on the table and inside the tipped barrel.

A hundred to one, both bombers and fighters.

Overwhelming odds by any rational estimate, but not in the minds of the specially selected squadron, led by Gary, of course, sent out to challenge them.

An enemy fighter flashed along the tray and through the hopper gate.

Slam! Crash and burn.

Another one followed, then two more.

Good shooting.

Work blended with adventure, the challenge being to push the chunks in as fast as possible, to shoot down the enemy force before they could get by and inflict damage on your rear area. As fast as possible, but not so fast as to jam the grinder. To jam the grinder was to be shot down. Crash!

Game over.

Gary was getting good at this. He had half the barrel ground in just a couple of minutes and still the blade spun smoothly. Gary shifted the game, allowed for a bit of ego. Now the enemy fighters, realizing their enemy, and thus, their inevitable doom, turned tail and ran. Gary's squadron sped off in pursuit. If the enemy escaped, they would only come back another time, reinforced. Gary looked at the long line of chunk-filled barrels stretching back halfway through the large room and groaned. There were always more barrels, more enemies; the reinforcements would come, whatever he might do.

This was a war the young man felt he would never finish.

And here was a battle too real to be truly beaten by imagination, a battle against tedium, against a day where the body worked but the mind had to be shut down, or constantly diverted. It had been played out by the ants of an industrialized society for decades, men and women doing what they had to do to survive.

It all seemed so very perverted to Gary Leger. What had his father dreamed through the forty-five years of his working life? Baseball probably; his father loved the game so dearly. Gary pictured him standing before the slotted shelves in the post office, pitching letters, throwing balls and strikes. How many World Series were won in that postal room?

So very perverted.

Gary shrugged it all away and went back to his aerial battle. The pace had slowed, though the enemy still remained a threat. Another wide-winged fighter smashed through the creaking gate to its doom. Gary considered the pilot. Another man doing as he had to do?

No, that notion didn't work for Gary. Imagining a man being killed by his handiwork destroyed the fantasy and left him with a cold feeling. But that was the marvel of imagination, after all, for to Gary, these were no longer pilot-filled aircraft. They were robot drones—extraterrestrial robot drones. Or even better, they were extraterrestrial aircraft—so what if they still resembled the Russian MiGs—piloted by monster aliens, purely evil and come to conquer the world.

Crash and burn.

"Hey, stupid!"

Gary barely heard the call above the clanging din. He pulled off the headphones and spun about, as embarrassed as a teenager caught playing an air guitar.

Leo's smirk and the direction of his gaze told Gary all that he needed to know. He bent down from the stool and looked beneath the grinder, to the overfilled catch barrel and the pile of plastic flakes on the floor.

"Coffee man's here," Leo said, and he turned away, chuckling and shaking his head.

Did Leo know the game? Gary wondered. Did Leo play? And what might his imagination conjure? Probably baseball, like Gary's father.

They didn't call it the all-American game for nothing.

Gary waited until the last banging chunks had cleared the whirring blades, then switched off the motor. The coffee man was here; the twenty-minute reprieve had begun. He looked back once to the grinder as he started away, to the piled plastic on the dirty floor. He'd have to pick that up after his break.

Victory had not been clean this day.

The conversations among the twenty or so workers gathered out by the coffee truck covered everything from politics to the upcoming softball tournament. Gary walked past the groups, hardly hearing their talk. It was too fine a spring day, he decided, to get caught up in some discussion that almost always ended on a bitter note. Still, louder calls and the more excited conclusions found their way through his indifference.

"Hey, Danny, you think two steak-and-cheese grinders are enough?" came one sarcastic shout—probably from Leo. "Lunch is almost an hour and a half away. You think that'll hold you?

". . . kick their butts," said another man, an older worker that Gary knew only as Tomo. Gary knew right away that Tomo, and his bitter group were talking about the latest war, or the next war, or the chosen minority group of the day.

Gary shook his head. "Too nice a day for wars," he muttered under his breath. He spent his buck fifty and walked back towards the shop, carrying a pint of milk and a two-pack of Ring Dings. Gary did some quick calculations. He could grind six barrels an hour. Considering his wages, this snack was worth about two barrels, two hundred enemy jets.

He had to stop eating so much.

"You playing this weekend?" Leo asked him when he got to the loading dock, which the crew used as a sun deck.

"Probably," Gary spun about, hopping up to take a seat on the edge of the deck. Before he landed, an empty milk carton hopped off the back of his head.

"What'd'ye mean, probably?" Leo demanded.

Gary picked up the carton and returned fire. Caught in a crosswind, it missed Leo, bounced off Danny's head (who was too engrossed with his food to even notice), and ricocheted into a trash bin.

The highlight of the day.

"I meant to do that," Gary insisted.

"If you can plan a throw like that, you'd better play this weekend," remarked another of the group.

"You'd better play," Leo agreed, though from him it sounded more as a warning. "If you don't, I'll have him"—he motioned to his brother, Danny—"next to me in the outfield." He launched a second carton, this one at Danny. Danny dodged as it flew past, but his movement dropped a hunk of steak to the ground. He considered the fallen food for a moment, then looked back to Leo.

"That's my food!"

Leo was laughing too hard to hear him. He headed back into the shop; Gary shook his head in amazement at Danny's unending appetite—and yet, Danny was by far the slimmest of the group—and joined Leo. Twenty minutes. The reprieve was over.

Gary's thoughts were on the tournament as he headed back towards the grinding room. He liked that Leo, and many others, wanted him to play, considering their interest a payoff for the many hours he put in at the local gym. He was big and strong, six feet tall and well over two hundred pounds, and he could hit a softball a long, long way. That didn't count for much by Gary's estimation, but it apparently did in many other people's eyes—and Gary had to admit that he enjoyed their attention, the minor celebrity status.

The new skip in his step flattened immediately when he entered the grinding room.

"Now you gonna take a work break?" snarled Tomo. Gary looked up at the clock; his group had spent a few extra minutes outside.

"And what's this?" Tomo demanded, pointing to the mess by the catch barrel. "You too stupid to know when to change the barrel?"

Gary resisted the urge to mouth a sharp retort. Tomo wasn't his boss, wasn't anybody's boss, but he really wasn't such a bad guy. And looking at his pointing hand, with three fingers sheared off at the first knuckle, Gary could understand where the old plastics professional was coming from, could understand the source of the bitterness.

"Didn't teach you any common sense in college?" Tomo muttered, wandering away. His voice was full of venom as he repeated, "College."

Tomo was a lifer, had been working in plastics factories fully twenty years before Gary was even born. The missing fingers accentuated that point; many older men in Lancashire were missing fingers, a result of the older-design molding machines. Prone to jams, these monstrosities had a pair of iron doors that snapped shut with the force (and appetite, some would say) of a shark's jaws, and fingers seemed to be their favorite meals.

A profound sadness came over Gary as he watched the old man depart, limping slightly, leaning to one side, and with his two-fingered hand hanging freely by his side. It wasn't condescension aimed at Tomo—Gary wasn't feeling particularly superior to anyone at that moment—it was just a sadness about the human condition in general.

As if sensing Gary's lingering stare, Tomo spun back on him suddenly. "You'll be here all your life, you know!" the old man growled. "You'll work in the dirt and then you'll retire and then you'll die!"

Tomo turned and was gone, but his words hovered in the air around Gary like a black-winged curse.

"No, I won't," Gary insisted quietly, if somewhat lamely. At that point in his life, Gary had little ammunition to argue back against Tomo's cynicism. Gary had done everything right, everything according to the rules as they had been explained to him. Top of his class in college, double major, summa cum laude. And he had purposely concentrated in a field that promised lucrative employment, not the liberal arts concentration that he would have preferred. Even the general electives, courses most of his college colleagues breezed through without a care, Gary went after with a vengeance. If a 4.0 was there to be earned, Gary would settle for nothing less.

Everything according to the rules, everything done right. He had graduated nearly a year before, expecting to go out and set the world on fire.

It hadn't worked out quite as he had expected. They called it recession. Too pretty a word, by Gary Leger's estimation. He was beginning to think of it as reality.

And so here he was, back at the shop he had worked at part-time to help pay for his education. Grinding plastic chunks, shooting down enemy aircraft.

And dying.

He knew that, conceded that at least that part of Tomo's curse seemed accurate enough. Every day he worked here, passing time, was a day further away from the job and the life he desired, and a day closer to his death.

It was not a pleasant thought for a twenty-two-year-old. Gary moved back to the grinder, too consumed by a sense of mortality and self-pity for any thoughts of imaginary battles or World Series caliber curve balls.

Was he looking into a prophetic mirror when he gazed upon bitter Tomo?

Would he become that seven-fingered old man, crooked and angry, fearing death and hating life?

There had to be more to it all, more reason for continuing his existence. Gary had seen dozens of shows interviewing people who had come close to death. All of them said how much more they valued their lives now, how their zest for living had increased dramatically and each new day had become a challenge and a joy. Sweeping up the plastic by the catch barrel with that beautiful spring day just inches away, beyond an open window, Gary almost hoped for a near-death experience, for something to shake him up, or at least to shake up this petty existence he had landed himself into. Was the value of his life to be tied up in memories of softball, or of that one moment on the loading dock when he had unintentionally bounced a milk carton off of Danny's head and landed it perfectly into the trash bin?

Tomo came back through the grinding room then, laughing and joking with another worker. His laughter mocked Gary's self-pity and made him feel ashamed of his dark thoughts. This was an honest job, after all, and a paying job, and for all his grumbling, Gary had to finally admit to himself that his life was his own to accept or to change.

Still, he seemed a pitiful sight indeed that night walking home—he always walked, not wanting to get the plastic colors on the seats of his new Jeep. His clothes were filthy, his hands were filthy (and bleeding in a few places), and his eyes stung from the dark blue powder, a grotesque parody of makeup, that had accumulated in and around them.

He kept off the main road for the two-block walk to his parents' house; he didn't really want to be seen.

TWO

The Cemetery, the Jeep, and the Hobbit

A cemetery covered most of the distance between the shop and home. This was not a morbid place to Gary. Far from it; he and his friends had spent endless hours in the cemetery, playing Fox and Hounds or Capture the Flag, using the large empty field (the water table was too high for graves) in the back corner for baseball games and football games. The importance of the place had not diminished as the group grew older. This was where you brought your girlfriend, hoping, praying, to uncover some of those "mysteries" in a Bob Seger song. This was where you sneaked the *Playboy* magazines a friend had lifted from his father's drawer, or the six-pack someone's over-twenty-one brother had bought (for a 100 percent delivery charge!). A thousand memories were tied up in this place, memories of a vital time of youth, and of learning about life.

In a cemetery.

The irony of that thought never failed to touch Gary as he walked through here each morning and night, to and from the grind of the grinder. He could see his parents' house from the cemetery, a two-story garrison up on the hill beyond the graveyard's chain-link fence. Hell, he could see all of his life from here, the games, the first love, limitations and boundless dreams. And now, a bit older, Gary could see, too, his own inevitable fate, could grasp the importance of those rows of headstones and understand that the people buried here had once had hopes and dreams just like his own, once wondered about the meaning and the worth of their lives.

Still, it remained not a morbid place, but heavy with nostalgia, a place of long ago and far away, and edged in the sadness of realized mortality. And as each day, each precious day, passed him by, Gary stood on a stool beside a metal table, loading chunks of scrap plastic into a whirring grinder.

Somehow, somewhere, there had to be more.

The stones and the sadness were left behind as soon as Gary hopped the six-foot fence across from his home. His tan Wrangler sat in front of the hedgerow, quiet and still as usual. Gary laughed to himself, at himself, every time he passed his four-wheel-drive toy. He had bought it for the promise of adventure, so he told others—and told himself at those times he was feeling gullible. There weren't a lot of trails in Lancashire; in the six months Gary had owned the Jeep, he had taken it off-road exactly twice. Six months and only three thousand miles clocked on the odometer—hardly worth the payments.

But those payments were the real reason Gary had bought the Jeep, and in his heart he knew it. Gary had realized that he needed a reason to go stand on that stool and get filthy every day, a reason to answer the beckon of the rising sun. When he had bought the Jeep, he had played the all-American game, the sacrifice of precious time for things that someone else, some make-believe model in a make-believe world, told him he really wanted to have. Like everything else, it seemed, this Jeep was the end result of just one more of those rules that Gary had played by all his life.

"Ah, the road to adventure," Gary muttered, tapping the front fender as he passed. The previous night's rain had left brown spots all over the Jeep, but Gary didn't care. His filthy fingers left a blue streak of plastics' coloring above the headlight, but he didn't even notice.

He heard the words before his mother even spoke them.

"Oh my God," she groaned when he walked in the door. "Look at you."

"I am the ghost of Christmas past!" Gary moaned, holding his arms stiffly in front of him, opening his blue-painted eyes wide, and advancing a step towards her, reaching for her with grimy fingers.

"Get away!" she cried. "And get those filthy clothes in the laundry chute."

"Seventeen words," Gary whispered to his father as he passed him by on his way to the stairs. It was their inside joke. Every single day his mother said those same seventeen words. There was something comfortable in that uncanny predictability, something eternal and immortal.

Gary's step lightened considerably as he bounded up the carpeted stairs to the bathroom. This was home; this in his life, at least, was real, was the way it was supposed to be. His mother whined and complained at him constantly about his job, but he knew that was only because she truly cared, because she wanted better for her youngest child. She couldn't imagine her baby losing fingers to some hungry molding machine, or covering himself and filling up his lungs with a blue powder that was probably a carcinogen, or a something-ogen. (Wasn't everything?) This was Mom's support, given the only way Mom knew how to give it, and it did not fall on deaf ears where Gary Leger was concerned.

His father, too, was sympathetic and supportive. The elder Leger male understood Gary's realities better than his mom, Gary knew. Dad had been there, after all, pitching World Series into the letter sorters. "It will get better," he often promised Gary, and if Dad said it was so, then to Gary, it was so.

Period.

Gary spent a long time in front of the mirror, using cold cream in an attempt to get the blue powder away from the edges of his green eyes. He wondered if it would be there forever, vocational makeup. It amazed him how a job could change his appearance. No longer did his hair seem to hold its previous luster, as though its shiny blackness was being dulled as surely as Gary's hopes and dreams.

Much more than blue plastic washed down the shower drain. Responsibility, tedium, and Tomo all went with the filthy powder. Even thoughts of mortality and wasted time. Now the day belonged to Gary, just to Gary. Not to rules and whirring grinders and cynical old men seeking company in their helpless misery.

The shower marked the transition.

"Dave called," his father yelled from the bottom of the stairs when he exited the bathroom. "He wants you to play for him this weekend."

Gary shrugged—big surprise—and moved to his room. He came back out in just a minute, wearing a tank top, shorts, and sneakers, free of his steel-toed work boots, jeans thick with grime, and heavy gloves. He got to the stairs, then snapped his fingers and spun about, returning to his room to scoop up his worn copy of J.R.R. Tolkien's *The Hobbit*. Yes, the rest of the day belonged to Gary, and he had plans.

"You gonna call him?" his father asked when he skipped through the kitchen. Gary stopped suddenly, caught off guard by the urgency in his father's tone.

As soon as he looked at his dad, the image of himself in forty years, Gary remembered the importance of the tournament. He hadn't really known his father as a young man. Gary was the youngest of seven and his dad was closer to fifty than forty when he was born. But Gary had heard the stories; he knew that Dad had been one heck of a ball player. "Could've gone pro, your father," the old cronies in the neighborhood bars asserted. "But there wasn't no money in the game back then and he had a family."

Ouch.

Play by the rules; pitch your World Series in the post office's slotted wall.

"He's not home now," Gary lied. "I'll get him tonight."

"Are you gonna play for him?"

Gary shrugged. "The shop's putting a team in. Leo wants me in left-center."

That satisfied Dad, and Gary, full of nothing but respect and admiration for his father, would have settled for nothing less. Still, thoughts of softball left him as soon as he stepped outside the house, the same way thoughts of work had washed away down the shower drain. The day was indeed beautiful—Gary could see that clearly now, with the blue powder no longer tinting his vision—and he had his favorite book under his arm.

He headed off down the dead-end road, the cemetery fence on his right and neighbors he had known all his life on his left. The road ended just a few houses down, spilling into a small wood, another of those special growing-up places.

The forest seemed lighter and smaller to Gary than he remembered it from the faraway days. Part of it, of course, was simply that he was a grown man, physically larger now. And the other part, truly, was that the forest was lighter, and smaller than it had been in Gary's younger days. Three new houses cut into this end of the wood, the western side; the eastern end had been chopped to make way for a state swimming pool and a new school; the northern edge had been cleared for a new playground; even the cemetery had played a role, spilling over into the southern end. Gary's forest was under assault from every side. Often he wondered what he might find if he moved away and came back twenty years from now. Would this wood, his wood, be no more than a handful of trees surrounded by asphalt and cement?

That thought disturbed Gary as profoundly as the notion of losing fingers to a hungry molding machine.

There was still some serenity and privacy to be found in the small wood, though. Gary moved in a few dozen yards, then turned north on a fire road, purposely keeping his eyes on the trees as he passed the new houses, the new trespassers. He came up to one ridge, cleared except for the remains of a few burned-out trees and a number of waist-high blueberry bushes. He kept far from the ridge's lip, not because of any dangerous drop—there were no dangerous drops in this wood—but because to look over the edge was to look down upon the new school, nestled in what had once been Gary's favorite valley.

The fire road, becoming no more than a foot-wide trail among the blueberries, dipped steeply into a darker region, a hillside engulfed by thick oaks and elms. This was the center of the wood, too far from any of the encircling roads to hear the unending traffic and packed with enough trees and bushes to block out the unwelcome sights of progress. No sunlight came in here at this time of the afternoon except for one spot on a west-facing, mossy banking.

Privacy and serenity.

Gary plopped down on the thick moss and took out his book. The bookmark showed him to be on one of the later chapters, but he opened the book near the front, as he always did, to consider the introduction, written by some man that Gary did not know named Peter S. Beagle. It was dated July 14, 1973, and filled with thoughts surely based in the "radical" sixties. How relevant those ideas of "progress" and "escape" seemed to Gary, sitting in his dwindling wood more than fifteen years later.

The last line, "Let us at last praise the colonizers of dreams," held particular interest for Gary, a justification of imagination and of his own escapism. When Gary read this introduction and that last line, he did not feel so silly about standing by the grinder shooting down alien aircraft.

His sigh was one of thanks to the late Mr. Tolkien, and he reverently opened the book to the marked page and plowed ahead on the great adventure of one hobbit, Mr. Bilbo Baggins.

Time held no meaning to Gary as he read. Only if he looked back to see how many pages he had flipped could he guess whether minutes or hours had passed. At this time of the year, the mossy banking would catch enough sun to read by for two or three hours before twilight, he knew, so when his light ran out it would be time for supper. That was all the clock Gary Leger needed or wanted.

He read two chapters, then took a good stretch and a good yawn, cupped his hands behind his head, and lay back on the natural carpet. He could see pieces of the blue sky through the thick leaves, one white cloud lazily meandering west to east, to Boston and the Atlantic Ocean fifty miles away.

"Fifty miles?" Gary asked aloud, chuckling and stretching again. Here with his book, it might as well have been five thousand miles. But this moment of freedom was fleeting, he knew. The light was already fading; he figured he might have time for one more chapter. He forced himself back up to a sitting posture—he was getting too comfortable—and took up his book.

Then he heard a small rustle to the side. He was up in an instant, quietly, crouching low and looking all about. It could have been a field mouse or, more likely, a chipmunk. Or maybe a snake; Gary hoped it wasn't a snake. He had never been fond of the slithery things, though the only ones around here were garters, without fangs or poison, and most of them too small to give even a half-assed bite, certainly not as nasty a nip as a mouse or chipmunk could deliver. Still, Gary hoped it wasn't a snake. If he found a snake here, he'd probably never be able to lie down comfortably on the mossy banking again.

His careful scan showed him something quite unexpected. "A doll?" he mouthed, staring at the tiny figure. He wondered how he could possibly have missed that before, or who might have put it here, in this place he thought reserved for his exclusive use. He crouched lower and moved a step closer, meaning to pick the thing up. He had never seen one like it before. "Robin Hood?" he whispered, though it seemed more of an elf-like figure, sharp-featured (incredibly detailed!), dressed in woodland greens and browns, and wearing a longbow (a very short longbow, of course) over one shoulder and a pointed cap on its head.

Gary reached for it but recoiled quickly in amazement.

The thing had taken the bow off its shoulder! Gary thought he must have imagined it, but even as he tried to convince himself of his foolishness, he continued to watch the living doll. It showed no fear of Gary at all, just calmly pulled an arrow from its quiver and drew back on the bowstring.

Oh my God! Gary's face crinkled in confusion; he looked back to his book accusingly, as though it had something to do with all of this.

"Where the heck did you come from?" Gary stuttered. Oh my God! He glanced all around, searched the trees and the bushes for something, someone with a projector. Oh my God!

It seemed like the trick of a high-tech movie: "Help me, Obi-Wan Kenobi, you're my only hope."

Oh my God!

The doll, the elf, whatever it was, seemed to pay his movements little heed. It took aim at Gary and fired.

"Hey!" Gary cried, throwing a hand out to block the projectile. His reality sense told him it was just another trick, another image from the unseen projector. But he felt a sting in his palm, as real as one a bee might give, then looked down incredulously to see a tiny dart sticking out of it.

Oh my God!

"Why'd you do that?" Gary protested. He looked back to the tiny figure, more curious than angry. It leaned casually on its bow, looking about and whistling in a tiny, mousey voice. How calm it seemed, considering that Gary could lift one foot and crush it out like a discarded cigarette.

"Why'd . . . ," Gary started to ask again, but he stopped and tried hard to hold himself steady as a wave of dizziness swept over him.

Had the sun already set?

A gray fog engulfed the woods—or was the fog in his eyes? He still heard the squeaky whistling, more clearly now, but all the rest of the world seemed to be getting farther away.

Had the sun already set?

Instinctively Gary headed towards home, back up the dirt road. The . . . the thing—oh my God, what the hell was it?—had shot him! Had fricken shot him!

The thing, what the hell was it?

The smell of blueberries filled Gary's nose as he came up over the embankment. He tried to stay on the path but wandered often into the tangling bushes.

The sudden rush of air was the only indication Gary had that he was falling. A soft grassy patch padded his landing, but Gary, deep in the slumbers of pixie poison, wouldn't have noticed anyway, even if he had clunked down on a sheet of cement.

IT was night—how had he missed the sunset?

Gary forced himself to his feet and tried to get his bearings. The aroma of blueberries reminded him where he was, and he knew how to get home. But it was night, and he had probably missed supper—try explaining that to his fretful mother!

His limbs still weary, he struggled to rise.

And then he froze in startlement and wonderment. He remembered the pixie archer, for the sprite was suddenly there again, right before him, this time joined by scores of its little friends. They danced and twirled around the grassy patch, wrapping Gary in a shimmering cocoon of tiny song and sparkling light.

Oh my God!

Sparkling. The light blurred together into a single curtain, exuded calmness. The fairie song came to his ears, compelling him to lie back down.

Lie back down and sleep.

THREE

Sylvan Forest

IT was day—what the heck was going on?

Gary felt the grass under his cheek. At first, he thought he had simply fallen asleep, and he was drowsy still, lying there so very comfortably. Then Gary remembered again the sprite archer and the dance of the fairies, and his eyes popped open wide. It took considerable effort to lift his head and prop himself up on his elbows; the poison, or whatever it was, weighed heavily in his limbs. But he managed it, and he looked around, and then he became even more confused.

He was still in the blueberry patch; all the trees and bushes and paths were in the places he remembered them. They were somehow not the same, though—Gary knew that instinctively. It took him a moment to figure out exactly what was different, but once he recognized it clearly, there could be no doubt.

The colors were different.

The trees were brown and green, the grass and moss were green, and the dirt trail a grayish brown, but they were not the browns, greens, and grays of Gary's world. There was a luster to the colors, an inner vibrancy and richness beyond anything Gary had seen. He couldn't even begin to explain it to himself, the view was too vivid to be real, like some forest rendition by a surrealistic painter, a primordial viewpoint of a world undulled by reality and human pollution.

Another shock greeted Gary when he turned his attention away from his immediate surroundings and looked out over the ridge, at the landscape beyond the school that had stolen his favorite valley. He saw no houses—he was sure that he had seen houses from this point before—but only distant, towering mountains.

"Where did those come from?" Gary asked under his breath. He was still a bit disoriented, he decided, and he told himself that he had never really looked out over that ridge before, never allowed himself to register the magnificent sight. Of course the mountains had always been there, Gary had just never noticed how large and truly spectacular they were.

At the snap of a twig, Gary turned to look over his shoulder. There stood the sprite, half a foot tall, paying him little heed and leaning casually on its long-bow. "What are you?" Gary asked, too confused to question his sanity.

The diminutive creature made no move to respond; gave no indication that it had heard the question at all.

"What . . . ," Gary started to ask again, but he changed his mind. What indeed was this creature, and this dream? For it had to be a dream, Gary rationally told himself, as any respectable, intelligent person awaiting the dawn of the twenty-first century would tell himself.

It didn't feel like one, though. There were too many real sounds and colors, no single-purposed visions common to nightmares. Gary was cognizant of his surroundings, could turn in any direction and see the forest clearly. And he had never experienced a dream, or even heard of anyone else experiencing a dream, where he consciously knew that he was dreaming.

"Time to find out," he muttered under his breath. He had always thought himself pretty quick-handed, had even done some boxing in high school. His lunge at the sprite was pitifully slow, though; the creature was gone before he ever got near the spot. He followed the rustle stubbornly, pouncing on any noise, sweeping areas of dead leaves and low berry bushes with his arms.

"Ow!" he cried, feeling a pinprick in his backside. He spun about. The sprite was a few feet behind him—he had no idea how the stupid thing got there—holding its bow and actually laughing at him!

Gary turned slowly, never letting the creature out of his glowering stare. He leaned forward, his muscles tensed for a spring that would put him beyond the creature, cut off its expected escape route.

Then Gary fell back on his elbows, eyes wide in heightened disbelief, as a second creature joined the first, this one taller, at least two feet from toes to top, and this one, Gary recognized.

Gary was not of Irish decent, but that hardly mattered. He had seen this creature pictured a thousand times, and he marveled now at the accuracy of those images. The creature wore a beard, light brown, like its curly hair. Its over-coat was gray, like its sparkling, mischievous eyes, and its breeches green, with shiny black, curly-toed shoes. If the long-stemmed pipe in its mouth wasn't a dead giveaway, the tam-o'-shanter on its head certainly was.

"So call it a dream, then," the creature said to him "and be satisfied with that. It do not matter." Gary watched, stunned, as this newest sprite, this leprechaun—this fricken *leprechaun!*—walked over to the archer.

"He's a big one," the leprechaun said. "I say, will he fit?"

The archer chirped out something too squeaky for Gary to understand, but the leprechaun seemed appeased.

"For yer troubles, then," the leprechaun said, and he handed over a four-leaf clover, the apparent payment for delivering Gary.

The pixie archer bowed low in appreciation, cast a derisive chuckle Gary's way, and then was gone, disappearing into the underbrush too quickly and completely for Gary to even visually follow its movements.

"Mickey McMickey at yer service," the leprechaun said politely, dipping into a low bow and tipping his tam-o'-shanter.

Oh my God.

The leprechaun, having completed its greeting, waited patiently.

"If you're really at my service," Gary stuttered, startled even by the sound of his own voice, "then you'll answer a few questions. Like, what the hell is going on?"

"Don't ye ask," Mickey advised. "Ye'd not be satisfied in hearing me answers. Not yet. But in time ye'll come to understand it all. Know now that ye're here for a service, and when ye're done with it, ye can return to yer own place."

"So I'm at your service," Gary reasoned. "And not the other way around."

Mickey scratched at his finely trimmed beard. "Not in service for me," he answered after some thought. "Though yer being here does do me a service, if ye follow me thinking. Ye're in service to an elf."

"The little guy?" Gary asked, pointing to the brush where the sprite had disappeared.

"Not a pixie," Mickey replied. "An elf. Tylwyth Teg." He paused, as if those strange words should mean something to Gary. With no response beyond a confused stare forthcoming, Mickey went on, somewhat exasperated.

"Tylwyth Teg," he said again. "The Fair Family. Ye've not heard o' them?"

Gary shook his head, his mouth hanging open.

"Sad times ye're living in, ye poor lad," Mickey mumbled. He shrugged helplessly, a twittering, jerky movement for a creature as small as he, and finished his explanation. "These elfs are named the Tylwyth Teg, the Fair Family. To be sure, they're the noblest race of the faerie folk, though a bit unbending to the ways of others. A great elf, too, this one ye'll soon be meeting, and one not for taking lightly. 'Twas him that catched me, ye see, and made me catch yerself."

"Why me?" Gary wondered why he'd asked that, why he was talking to this . . . whatever it was . . . at all. Would Alan Funt soon leap out at him, laughing and pointing to that elusive camera?

"Because ye'll fit the armor," Mickey said as though the whole thing should make perfect sense. "The pixies took yer measures and say ye'll fit. As good yerself as another, that being the only requirement." Mickey paused a moment, staring reflectively into Gary's eyes.

"Green eyes?" the leprechaun remarked. "Ah, so were Cedric's. A good sign!"

Gary's nod showed that he accepted, but certainly did not understand, what Mickey was saying. It really wasn't a big problem for Gary at that moment, though, for all that he could do was go along with these thoroughly unbeliev-able events and thoroughly unbelievable creatures. If he was dreaming, then fine; it might be enjoyable. And if not . . . well, Gary decided not to think about that possibility just then.

What Gary did think about was his knowledge of leprechauns and the leg-ends surrounding them. He knew the reward for catching a leprechaun and, dream or not, it sounded like a fun course to take. He reached a hand up behind his head, feigning an itch, then dove headlong at Mickey and came up clutching the little guy.

"There," Gary declared triumphantly. "I've caught you and you have to lead me to your pot of gold! I know the rules, Mr. Mickey McMickey."

"Tsk, tsk, tsk," he heard from the side. He turned to see Mickey leaning ca-sually against a tree stump, holding Gary's book, *The Hobbit,* open before him. Gary turned slowly back to his catch and saw that he held Mickey in his own two hands. "Sonofabitch," Gary mumbled under his breath, for this was a bit too confusing.

"If ye know the rules, ye should know the game," Mickey—the Mickey lean-ing against the tree—said in response to Gary's blank stare.

"How?" Gary stuttered.

"Look closer, lad," Mickey said to him. "Then let go of the mushroom be-fore ye get yer hands all dirty."

Gary studied his catch carefully. It remained a leprechaun as far as he could tell, though it didn't seem to be moving very much—not at all, actually. He looked back to the leaning leprechaun and shrugged.

"Closer," Mickey implored.

Gary eyed the figure a moment longer. Gradually the image transformed and he realized that he was indeed holding a large and dirty mushroom. He shook his head in disbelief and dropped it to the ground, then noticed *The Hob-bit* lying at his feet, right where he had left it. He looked back to Mickey by the tree trunk, now a mushroom again, and then back to the dropped mushroom, now a leprechaun brushing himself off.

"Ye think it to be an easy thing, catching a leprechaun?" Mickey asked him sourly. "Well, if it was, do ye think any of us'd have any gold left to give out?" He walked right next to Gary to scoop up the strange book. Gary had a thought about grabbing him again, this time to hold on, but the leprechaun acted first.

"Don't ye be reaching yer hands at me," Mickey ordered.

"'Twas me that catched yerself, remember? And besides, grabbing at the likes o' Mickey McMickey, ye just don't know what ye might put them hands in! Been fooling stupid big folk longer than ye've been alive, I tell ye! I telled ye once . . . what did ye say yer name was? . . . don't ye make me tell ye again!"

"Gary," Gary answered, straightening up and taking a prudent step away from the unpredictable sprite. "Gary Leger."

"Well met, then, Gary Leger," Mickey said absently. His thoughts now seemed to be fully on the book's cover, "Bilbo comes to the huts of the raft elfs," an original painting by Tolkien himself. Mickey nodded his approval, then opened the work. His face crinkled immediately and he mumbled a few words under his breath and waved a hand across the open page.

"Much the better," he said.

"What are you doing to my book?" Gary protested, leaning down to take it back. Just before he reached it, though, he realized that he was putting his hand into the fanged maw of some horrid, demonic thing, and he recoiled immediately, nearly falling over backwards.

"Never know what ye might put yer hands into," Mickey said again absently, not bothering to look up at the startled man. "And really, Gary Leger, ye must learn to see more the clearly if we mean to finish this quest. Ye can't go playing with dragons if ye can't look through a simple illusion. Come along, then." And Mickey started off, reading as he walked.

"Dragons?" Gary muttered at the leprechaun's back, drawing no response. "Dragons?" Gary asked again, this time to himself. Really, he told himself, he shouldn't be so surprised.

The fire road, too, was as Gary remembered it, except, of course, for the colors, which continued with their surrealistic vibrancy. As they moved along the path towards the main road, though, Gary thought that the woods seemed denser. On the way in, he had seen houses from this point, the new constructions he always tried not to notice. Now he wanted to see them, wanted to find some sense of normalcy in this crazy situation, but try as he may, his gaze could not penetrate the tangle of leaves and branches.

When they came to the end of the fire road, Gary realized beyond doubt that more had changed about the world around him than unnoticed mountains and dense trees and strange colors. This time there could be no mistake of perception.

Back in Lancashire, the fire road ended at the dirt continuation of the main road, the road that ran past his parents' house. Across from the juncture sat the chain-link cemetery fence.

But there was no fence here, just more trees, endless trees.

Mickey paused to wait for Gary, who stood staring, open-mouthed. "Well, are ye coming, then?" the leprechaun demanded after a long uneventful moment.

"Where's the fence?" Gary asked, hardly able to find his breath.

"Fence?" Mickey echoed. "What're ye talking about, lad?"

"The cemetery fence," Gary tried to explain.

"Who'd be putting a graveyard in the middle of the forest?" Mickey replied with a laugh. The leprechaun stopped short, seeing that Gary did not share in the joke, and then Mickey nodded his understanding.

"Hear me, lad," the leprechaun began sympathetically. "Ye're not in yer own place—I telled ye that already. Ye're in me place now, in County Dilnamarra in the wood called Tir na n'Og."

"But I remember the blueberry patch," Gary protested, thinking he had caught the leprechaun in a logic trap. Surprisingly Mickey seemed almost saddened by Gary's words.

"That ye do," the leprechaun began. "Ye remember the blueberries from yer own place, Real-earth, in a patch much like the one I found ye in."

"They were the same," Gary said stubbornly.

"No, lad," Mickey replied. "There be bridges still between yer own world and this world, places alike yer blueberry patch that seem as the same in both the lands."

"This world?"

"Sure that ye've heard of it," Mickey replied. "The world of the Faerie."

Gary crinkled his brow with incredulity, then tried to humor the leprechaun and hide his smile.

"In such places," Mickey continued, not noticing Gary's obvious doubt, "some folk, the pixies mostly, can cross over, and within their dancing circle, they can bring a one such as yerself back. But alas, fewer the bridges get by the day—I fear that yer world'll soon lose its way to Faerie altogether."

"This has been done before?" Gary asked. "I mean, people from my world have crossed . . ."

"Aren't ye listening? And have ye not heard the tales?" Mickey asked. He grabbed his pipe in one hand, plopped his hands on his hips, and gave a disgusted shake of his head.

"I've heard of leprechauns," Gary offered hopefully.

"Well, where are ye thinking the stories came from?" Mickey replied. "All the tales of wee folk and dancing elfs, and dragons in lairs full o' gold? Did ye not believe them, lad? Did ye think them stories for the children by a winter's fire?"

"It's not that I don't want to believe them," Gary tried to explain.

"Don't?" Mickey echoed. "Suren ye mean to say 'didn't.' Ye've no choice but to believe the faerie tales now, seeing as ye've landed in one of them!"

Gary only smiled noncommittally, though in fact he was truly enjoying this experience—whatever it might be. He shook his head at the thought. Whatever it might be? Oh my God!

He asked no more questions as they made their way along footpaths through the marvelous colors and aromas of the sylvan forest. He did stop once to more closely regard the leprechaun, shuffling up ahead of him. Mickey crossed over a patch of dry brown leaves, but made not a whisper of a sound. Gary moved up behind as carefully as he could, noting his own crunching and crackling footsteps and feeling altogether clumsy and out of place next to the nimble Mickey.

But if Gary was indeed an intruder here, the forest did not make him feel so. Birds and squirrels, a raccoon and a young deer, skipped by on their business not too far from him, paying no attention to him beyond a quick and curious glance. Gary could not help but feel at home here; the place was warm and dreamy, full of life and full of ease. And to Gary, it was still entirely in his mind, a fantasy, a dream, and perfectly safe.

They arrived many minutes later at a small clearing centered by a huge and ancient oak tree—Gary figured it to be located on the spot normally occupied by downtown Lancashire's Dunkin' Donuts. Apparently the leprechaun had set out with this destination in mind, for Mickey moved right up to the tree and plopped down on a mossy patch, pulling out a packet of weed for his pipe.

"A rest?" Gary asked.

"Here's the place," Mickey replied. "Kelsey's to meet us here, and then ye're on with him. I'll take me leave."

"You're not coming with us?"

Mickey laughed, nearly choking as he simultaneously tried to light his pipe. "Yerself and Kelsey," he explained. "'Tis his quest and not me own. Rest and don't ye be testing. I'll give ye some tips for handling that one." He paused to finish lighting the pipe, and if he went on after that, Gary did not hear him.

A song drifted down from the boughs of the great oak, high-pitched and charmingly sweet. It flittered on the very edges of Gary's hearing, teasing . . . teasing.

Gary's gaze wandered up the massive oak, seeking the source.

Teasing . . . teasing.

And then he saw her, peeking around a thick lower branch. She was a tiny thing by human measures, five feet tall perhaps and never close to a hundred pounds, with a pixieish face and eyes too clear and hair too golden.

And a voice too sweet.

It took Gary a moment to even realize that she was naked—no, not naked, but wearing the sheerest veil of gossamer that barely blurred her form. Again, that edge-of-perception tease.

"What are ye about?" Gary heard Mickey say from some distant place.

The melody was more than a simple song, it was a call to Gary. "Come up to me," the notes implored him.

He didn't have to be asked twice.

"Oh, cobblestones," moaned Mickey, realizing then the source of Gary's distraction. The leprechaun pulled off his tam-o'-shanter and slapped it across his knee, angry at himself. He should have known better than to take so vulnerable a young human near the haunting grounds of Leshiye, the wood nymph.

"Get yerself down, lad," he called to Gary. "There's not a thing up there ye're wanting."

Gary didn't bother to reply; it was obvious that he didn't agree. He swung a leg over the lowest branch and pulled himself up. The nymph was close now, smelling sweet, singing sweet, and so alluring in her translucent gown. And her song was so inviting, promising, teasing in ways that Gary could not resist.

"Get yerself gone, Leshiye!" Mickey yelled from below, knowing that any further appeals he might make to Gary would fall on deaf ears. "We've business more important than yer hunting. Kelsey'll be here soon and he won't be pleased with ye. Not a bit!"

The nymph's song went on undisturbed. Gary tried several routes through the branch tangle, then finally found one that would lead him to his goal.

A huge snake appeared on the branch before him, coiled and hissing, with fangs all too prominent. Gary stopped short and tried to backtrack, eyes wide, and so frantic that he nearly toppled from the branch.

Still, Leshiye sang, even heightened the sweetness of her song with laughter. She waved her hand and the snake was gone, and as far as the entranced Gary was concerned, the serpent had never appeared. He started up the tree again immediately, but now the branches began to dance under him, waving and seeming to multiply.

Gary looked down at Mickey, guessing both the serpent and now this to be more of the leprechaun's illusionary tricks.

"What are you doing?" he called down angrily. "Are you trying to make me fall?"

"Leave her be, lad," Mickey replied. "Ye're not for mixing with one of her type."

Gary looked back at the nymph for a long, lingering while, then turned back sharply on Mickey. "Are you nuts?"

Mickey's cherubic face twisted in confusion over the strange phrase for just a moment, but then he seemed to recognize the general meaning of the words. "And block yer ears, lad," Mickey went on stubbornly. "Don't ye let her charms fall over ye. Ye must be strong; in this tree, her home, I've no magics to outdo her illusions."

The leprechaun's warnings began to make some sense to Gary—until he looked back at the nymph, now reclining languidly on one stretching branch. Gary looked all about helplessly, trying to sort some safe way to get through to her.

Leshiye laughed again—within the melodic boundaries of her continuing song. She drew her powers from the tree—this was her home base—and she easily defeated Mickey's illusionary maze, leaving the correct path open and obvious before Gary's eager eyes.

Mickey slapped his tam-o'-shanter against his knee again and fell down to the moss, defeated. He could not win the attention of a young human male against the likes of a wood nymph. "Kelsey's not to be liking this," he muttered quietly and soberly, not thrilled at facing the stern and impatient elf with still more bad news.

Leshiye had taken Gary's hand by then, and she led him higher into the tree, just over the second split in the thick trunk area to a small leafy hollow.

"Oh, well," Mickey shrugged as they disappeared from sight. "I'll just have to go out and find another one fitting the armor." He tapped his pipe against the tree and popped it into his mouth, then took out Gary's book and sat down for a good read.

FOUR

The Elf

THE elf's expression soured as he neared the small field surrounding the giant oak tree. Mickey was there, as arranged, sitting against the tree, intently reading a book. But Mickey was alone, and that was not according to the plan.

"Just like a bunch o' dwarfs to go off chasing some long-lost treasure," the elf, with his sharp ears, heard Mickey mutter lightheartedly. "Never could resist a gem or bit o' gold and always claiming that it was their own from the start!"

Mickey looked up then, sensing the elf's approach. "And a good day to ye, Kelsey!" he declared, not bothering to rise.

"Where is he?" Kelsey demanded. "I have gone to great trouble to make all the arrangements in time and Baron Pwyll is not a patient man. You agreed to have him here today."

"And so I did," Mickey replied.

There came a high-pitched giggle from above. Kelsey knew the forest at least as well as Mickey, and seeing the leprechaun holding the strange book and hearing the call from above, he looked up at the towering oak and quickly figured out the riddle.

"Leshiye," Kelsey grumbled.

He turned back to Mickey, still absorbed by the book. "How long has he been up there?"

Mickey put a hand over his eyes to regard the position of the sun. "Two hours, by now," he said. "He's a scrapper, this one!"

Kelsey didn't appreciate Mickey's lightheartedness; not where his life-quest was concerned. "Why did you not stop him?" the elf demanded, his golden eyes flashing with anger.

"Think what ye're asking," Mickey shot back. "Stop a healthy young man from getting at a nymph's offered charms? I'd as soon try to catch a dragon in me hat"—he pulled off his tam-o'-shanter and held it out upside down in front of him—"and make the beast warm up me dinner stew."

Kelsey couldn't argue against the leprechaun's claims of helplessness. Nymphs were a powerful foe where young men were concerned, and this one, Leshiye, was as skillful at her seductive arts as any in all Tir na n'Og. "Is he the proper size to wear the armor?" Kelsey asked, obviously disgusted.

On Mickey's nod, the elf dropped the longbow off his shoulder and began scrambling up the tree. Mickey just went on reading. If Kelsey could handle it, then fine, that would mean less work for the leprechaun. And if not, if Gary was too far gone to be rescued, then Kelsey certainly couldn't blame Mickey for the failure, and Mickey would at least be able to get the elf to give him more time in his hunt for another suitable man. Either way, it didn't bother the leprechaun—very little ever truly bothered any leprechaun. It was a sunny warm day, with good smells, good sights, and good reading. What else could a leprechaun ask for?

He settled back against the tree and found his spot on the page, but before he could begin reading again, a sneaker plopped down upon his head and bounced to the ground next to him.

"Hey!" he cried, looking up. "What are ye about, then?" A second sneaker came bouncing down, straight at Mickey, but he quickly pointed a finger and uttered a single word and the shoe stopped in midair a foot above his head, and hung there motionless.

There came the sound of scuffling up above, a complaint, which Mickey recognized as Gary's voice—the scrapper was still alive, at least—and suddenly Leshiye's singing sounded not so happy. Nymphs held little power over the Tylwyth Teg, the leprechaun knew, for the elven folk were not taken by enchantments and illusions as easily as were humans. Mickey nodded and shook his head helplessly, in sympathy with the nymph—it was that same resistance that had allowed Kelsey to catch Mickey and start this whole adventure in the first place.

A moment later, Gary came over the lip of the leafy hollow, followed closely by Kelsey. Gary cast a mournful look at what he was leaving behind, but the pointy sword tip at his back overruled Leshiye's pull on him. He moved slowly, picking his way down the tree, and kept looking back over his shoulder. Kelsey, obviously agitated and knowing that he had to get Gary as far away from the nymph as quickly as possible, prodded him along none too gently each time.

Leshiye came out behind them then, singing still.

"Get back in your den!" Kelsey yelled at her. He spun about, his gleaming sword up high and ready.

Leshiye, naked and vulnerable, stubbornly held her ground.

"Don't hit her!" Gary snapped at Kelsey. "Don't you dare!"

Kelsey turned and calmly slipped his foot across Gary's. A subtle twist sent Gary tumbling from the branch, the last ten feet to the ground. Without giving the human another thought, the elf spun back on Leshiye and warned again, "Get back in your den!"

Leshiye laughed at him. She knew, and Kelsey knew, that the elf's threat was a hollow one. No member of Tylwyth Teg would ever strike down a creature of Tir na n'Og, and Leshiye the wood nymph was as much a part of the forest as any tree or any animal.

Kelsey slipped his sword back in its gem-studded scabbard, scowled once more at the nymph, just for good measure, then skipped down the tree so lightly and easily that Gary, recovering down below, blinked in amazement.

Almost immediately, Leshiye's singing started up again.

"Be quiet!" Kelsey yelled up at her. "And you," he growled at Gary, "straighten your clothes and come along!"

Gary looked at Mickey, who nodded that he should obey. He picked up one shoe, then bumped his head on the other, noticing it for the first time. It remained hanging in the air where Mickey had magically held it. Gary expected to find some invisible wire supporting it, but it came freely into his hand when he tentatively grasped it.

"How?" Gary started to ask, but he took Mickey's sly wink as the only explanation he would ever get.

"Hurry along!" Kelsey demanded.

"Who the hell is he?" Gary asked Mickey. Kelsey swung about immediately and stormed over, his clear eyes shining fiercely, and his shoulder-length hair, more golden than the eyes even, glistening brightly in the sunlight Kelsey was fully a foot shorter than Gary, and a hundred pounds lighter, but he seemed to tower over the young man now, enlarged by confidence and open anger.

"There I go again," Mickey said, slapping himself off the side of the head. "Forgetting me manners. Gary, lad, meet Kelsey . . ."

Kelsey showed Mickey a look that bordered on violence.

"Kelsenellenelvial Gil-Ravadry," Mickey quickly corrected. "An elf-lord of the Tylwyth Teg."

"Kelsen . . ." Gary stuttered, hardly able to echo the strange name.

Mickey saw the opening for a good taunt at his captor. "Call him Kelsey, lad," the leprechaun said with obvious enjoyment. "Everyone does."

"Sounds good to me," Gary said pointedly, realizing the elf's renewed glare. At that moment, anything that bothered the elf—the elf who had interrupted Gary's pleasure—would have sounded good to Gary. "Who invited you up the tree, Kelsey?" Gary asked evenly.

He realized at once that he was pushing his luck.

Kelsey said not a word; his hand didn't even go to the hilt of his exquisite sword. But the look he gave Gary silenced the young man as completely as that sword ever could.

Kelsey let the stare linger a bit longer, then turned about sharply and strode away.

"He's a good enough sort," Mickey explained to Gary. "Ye can get a bit o' fun outa that one, but be knowing, lad, that he saved your life."

Gary shot an incredulous look the leprechaun's way.

"She'd not ever have let ye go," Mickey went on. "Ye'd have died up there— a pleasing way to go, I'm not for arguing."

Gary did not seem convinced.

"Ye'd have been a goner," Mickey went on. "In the likes of Leshiye's clutches,

ye'd have forgotten to eat or drink. Might that ye'd have forgotten to breathe, lad!
Yer mind would've been set to one task only, until yer body died for the effort."

Gary slipped his sneaker on his foot and quickly tied it. "I can take care of
myself," he declared.

"So have sayed a hundred men in that nymph's embrace," Mickey replied.
"So have sayed a hundred dead men." The leprechaun chuckled and moved off
after the elf, pulling out *The Hobbit* as he walked.

Gary stood for a while shaking his head and considering whether or not he
should go back up the tree. Just to make things more difficult for him, Leshiye
appeared again over the edge of the hollow, smiling coyly. But the nymph
looked out towards Kelsey, not so far away and with his longbow in hand, and
she did not call out to the human this time.

Gary saw Kelsey, too, and he figured that if he started up the tree, the elf
would surely put an arrow into his wrist, or perhaps somewhere else, somewhere more vital. "Time to go," he prudently told himself, and, casting a quick
glance Kelsey's way, he zipped up his shorts. He gave more than one lamenting
glance back at the tree as he wandered away, back at Leshiye in her translucent
gown reclining comfortably on the branch beside the hollow.

Even Kelsey didn't blame him.

THE elf set a swift pace through the forest, following no trail at all as far as
Gary could discern. But Kelsey seemed to know where he was going, and Gary
thought the better of questioning him. Mickey proved to be little comfort on
the journey. The leprechaun skipped along, his footsteps impossibly light, with
his face buried in *The Hobbit,* laughing every now and then or muttering a "begorra." Gary was glad that the leprechaun was enjoying the book. Even though
Mickey, by the leprechaun's own admission, had kidnapped him, Gary found
that he liked the little guy.

Another laugh from Mickey sent Gary over to him. He peeked over the leprechaun's shoulder (not a difficult thing to do), trying to see what chapter
Mickey was on.

"What?" Gary babbled when he saw the open book. What had once been
ordinary typeset was now a flowing script, in a language totally unrecognizable
to Gary. Great sweeping lines had replaced the block letters, forming runes that
did not resemble any alphabet Gary had ever seen. "What did you do to it?" he
demanded.

Mickey looked up, his gray eyes turned up happily at their edges. "Do to
what?" he asked innocently.

"My book," Gary protested, reaching down to take back the copy. He flipped through the pages, each showing the same unintelligible script. "What did you do to my book?"

"I made it readable," Mickey explained.

"It was readable."

"For yerself," replied Mickey, yanking the book back. "But ye can read it anytime—who's knowing how long I've got with it? So I made it readable for meself, and quit yer fretting. Ye'll get it back when I'm done."

"Forget the book," said a voice up ahead. The two looked to see Kelsey, stern-faced as usual, standing by a fat elm. "The book does not matter," the elf went on, talking to Gary. "You have more important concerns than casual reading." Kelsey cast Mickey a suspicious glance. "Have you informed him of the quest?"

"I been meaning to," Mickey replied. "Truly I have. But I'm wanting to break the lad in slowly, let him get used to things one at a time."

"We have not the time for that," said Kelsey. "The arrangements have already been made in Dilnamarra. We will soon be there to collect the artifacts, and then the quest begins in full."

"Very well, then," Mickey conceded, closing *The Hobbit* and dropping it into an impossibly deep pocket in his gray jacket. "Lead on and I'll tell the lad as we go."

"We will break now," Kelsey replied. "You will tell him before we go."

Mickey and Kelsey eyed each other suspiciously for a few moments. The leprechaun knew that Kelsey had only ordered a break in the march so that he could better monitor the story that Mickey laid out to Gary. "Suren Tylwyth Teg's a trusting bunch," Mickey muttered quietly, but Kelsey's smile showed that he had heard clearly enough.

"I telled ye that ye were bringed here to serve an elf," Mickey began to Gary. "And so ye've met the elf, Kelsenel . . ." He stumbled over the long name, looked at Kelsey in frustration, and said, "Kelsey," gaining a measure of satisfaction in the insulted elf's returned scowl.

"Kelsey catched me to catch yerself—that, too, ye know," Mickey continued. "He's got himself a life-quest—the Tylwyth Teg take that sort o' stuff seriously, ye must understand—and he's needing a human of the right size to see it through."

Gary looked over at Kelsey, standing impassive and proud, and truly felt used. He wanted to shout out against the treatment, but he reminded himself, somewhat unconvincingly, that it was only a dream, after all.

"Kelsey's to reforge the spear of Cedric Donigarten," Mickey explained. "No easy task, that."

"Shouldn't you have caught a blacksmith?" Gary asked sarcastically.

"Oh, ye're not here to forge . . . ," Mickey started to explain.

"The blacksmith will be next," Kelsey interrupted, aiming his words at Mickey. They had some effect, Gary saw, for the leprechaun stuttered over his next few words.

"Ye're the holder," Mickey managed to say at last. "The spear must be in the hands of a human—one in the armor of Cedric Donigarten, which is why ye were measured—when it's melted back together."

Gary didn't see the point of all this. "Who is Cedric Donigarten?" he asked. "And why can't he just wear his own armor?"

"Who is Cedric Donigarten?" Kelsey echoed in disbelief. "Where did you get this one, leprechaun?" he growled at Mickey.

"Ye said ye needed a man that'd fit," Mickey snapped back. "Ye did not say anything more for requirements." He looked back to Gary, thinking he had properly put Kelsey in his place. "Sir Cedric was the greatest King of Faerie," he began reverently. "He brought all the goodly folks together for the goblin wars—wars the goblins would suren have won if not for Cedric. A human, too, if ye can imagine that! All the goodly folks of all the lands—sprites, elfs, men, and dwarfs—speak the legend of Cedric Donigarten, and speak it with respect and admiring, to their children. Suren 'tis a shame that men don't live longer lives."

"Some men," Kelsey corrected.

"Aye," Mickey agreed with a chuckle, but his voice was reverent again as he continued. "Cedric's been dead three hundred years now, killed by a dragon in the last battle o' the goblin wars. And now Kelsey's to honor the dead with his life-quest, by reforging the mighty spear broken in that last battle."

Gary nodded. "Fine, then" he agreed. "Take me to the armor, and to the smithy, and let's go honor the dead."

"Fine it is!" laughed Mickey. He looked to Kelsey and cried, "Lead on!" hoping his enthusiasm would satisfy the elf and relieve him of the unpleasant task of finishing the story.

Kelsey crossed his slender arms over his chest and stood his ground. "Tell him of the smithy," the elf commanded.

"Ah, yes," said Mickey, pretending that he overlooked that minor point. "The smithy. We'll be needing a dwarf for that. 'Greatest smithy in all the land,' commands the spear's legend, and the greatest smithy in all the land's ever been one o' the bearded folk."

Gary didn't appear the least bothered, so Mickey clapped his hands and started towards Kelsey again.

"Explain the problem," the elf said sternly. Mickey stopped abruptly and turned back to Gary.

"Ye see, lad," he said. "Elfs and dwarfs don't get on so well—not that dwarfs get on well with anyone. We'll have to catch the smithy we're needing."

"Catch?" Gary asked suspiciously.

"Steal," Mickey explained.

Gary nodded, then shook his head, then nearly laughed aloud, silently praising himself for a weird and wonderful imagination.

"Are ye contented?" Mickey asked Kelsey.

"Tell him of the forge," the elf replied.

Mickey sighed and spun back on Gary. This time the leprechaun's face was obviously grave. "The spear's a special one," Mickey explained. "No bellows could get a fire hot enough, even could we get two mountain trolls to pump it! So we're needing a bit of an unusual forge, so declared the legend." He looked at Kelsey and frowned. "I'm growing tired of that damned legend," he said.

"Tell him," Kelsey demanded sternly.

Mickey paused as if he couldn't get the explanation past his lips.

"An unusual forge," Gary prompted after a long silence.

"I telled ye before that ye'll be playing with dragons," Mickey blurted.

Gary rocked back on his heels and spent a long moment of thought. "Let me get this straight," he said, wanting to play all of Mickey's meandering words in a straight line. "You mean that I have to hold some dead King's spear while a dragon breathes fire on it and some captured dwarven smithy puts it back together?"

"There!" Mickey cried triumphantly. "The lad's got it! On we go, Kelsey." Mickey started along again but stopped, seeing that Kelsey hadn't moved and sensing that Gary wasn't following.

"What now, lad?" asked the exasperated leprechaun.

Gary paid him no heed. He slapped himself softly on the cheek several times and pinched his arm once or twice. "Well, if this is a dream," he said to no one in particular, "then it's time to wake up."

Kelsey shook his head, not pleased, then glowered at Mickey. "Where did you get this one?" he demanded.

Mickey shrugged. "I telled me friends to bring one that'd fit the armor, just as ye telled me," he replied. "Are ye getting particular?"

Kelsey regarded Gary for a while. He was big and well muscled—bigger than any of the people in Dilnamarra and probably as big as Cedric Donigarten himself. Mickey had assured him that Gary would fit the armor and Kelsey didn't doubt it. And Mickey was right with the remark about "getting particular." The legends said nothing of the subject's demeanor, just that he be human and wearing the armor. Kelsey walked over to Gary.

"Come along," the elf ordered to both of them. "You are not dreaming, and we want you here as little as you apparently wish to be here. Complete the task and you shall return to your own place."

"And suppose that I refuse to go along?" Gary dared to ask, not appreciating the elf's superior tone.

"Uh-oh," Mickey muttered, his grave tone making Gary wonder again if he had overstepped the bounds.

Kelsey's golden eyes narrowed and his lips turned up in a perfectly wicked grin. "Then I will declare you an outlaw," the elf said evenly. "For breaking the rules of capture. And a coward, deserving a brand." He paused for a moment so that Gary could get the full effect. "Then I shall kill you."

Gary's eyes popped wide and he looked to Mickey.

"I telled ye the Tylwyth Teg take their quests seriously," was all the comfort the leprechaun could offer.

"Do we go on?" Kelsey asked, putting a hand on the hilt of his fine sword.

Gary did not doubt the elf's grim promise for a minute. "Lead on, good elf," he said. "To Dilnamarra."

Kelsey nodded and turned away.

"Good that that's settled," Mickey said to the elf as he strode past "Ye've got yer man now. I'll be taking me leave."

Kelsey's sword came out in the blink of an eye. "No, you will not," the elf replied. "He is your responsibility and you will see this through for the time being."

Gary didn't appreciate the derisive way Kelsey had said "he," but he was glad that the leprechaun would apparently be sticking around for a bit longer. The thought of dealing with Kelsey alone, without Mickey to offer subtle advice and deflecting chatter, unnerved Gary more than a little.

"I caught you, Mickey McMickey," Kelsey declared. "And only I can release you."

"Ye made the terms and I've met them," Mickey argued.

"If you leave, I will go to all lengths to catch you again," Kelsey promised. "The next time—and I will indeed catch you again—I will have your pot of gold, and your word-twisting tongue for good measure."

"The Tylwyth Teg take their quests seriously," Gary snorted from behind.

"That they do," agreed Mickey. "Then lead on, me good elf, to Dilnamarra, though I'm sure to be ducking a hundred pairs of greedy hands in the human keep!"

Kelsey started away and Mickey took out *The Hobbit* again.

"Worried about the dragon?" Gary asked, coming up to walk beside the diminutive sprite.

"Forget the dragon," Mickey replied. "Ye ever met a dwarf, lad? Mighten be more trouble than any old wyrm, and with breath nearen as bad!

"But make the best of it, I always say," Mickey went on. "I've got me a good book for the road, if the company's a bit lacking.

Gary was too amused to take offense.

"I do not tolerate failure!" Ceridwen snarled. "You were given a task, and promised payment for that task, yet the stranger walks free."

The nymph giggled, embarrassed. Leshiye did not fear Ceridwen, not here in Tir na n'Og, the source of the nymph's power but a foreign place to the sorceress.

Ceridwen stopped talking and fixed an evil stare on Leshiye. Her icy-blue eyes narrowed and widened alternately, the only clue that she was calling upon her magical energies.

Dark clouds rolled in suddenly, the wind came howling to life.

Leshiye had a few tricks of her own. She let the sorceress fall deeper into her spellcasting, waited for Ceridwen's eyes to close altogether. Then Leshiye looked into her oak tree, followed its lead into the ground and along its long and deep roots. Other nearby oaks reached out their roots in welcome and the nymph easily glided through the plant door out of harm's way.

Ceridwen loosed her storm's fury anyway; several bolts of lightning belted the giant oak in rapid succession. But, furious though they were, they barely scarred the ancient and huge oak, still vital and with the strength of the earth coursing through its great limbs. Ceridwen's satisfied smile evaporated a moment later when she heard Leshiye's giggle from beyond the small field.

The witch did not send her storm in pursuit, realizing that she was overmatched and out of her place in Tir na n'Og. "You would be wise to ever remain in this wood," she warned the nymph, but Leshiye hardly cared for the threat; where else would she ever be?

The sorceress huffed and threw her black cloak high over her shoulder. As it descended, Ceridwen seemed to melt away beneath it, shrinking as the cloak moved closer to the ground. Then garment and sorceress blended as one and a large raven lifted off from where Ceridwen had stood.

She rose high over the enchanted wood, racing away towards Dilnamarra, scanning as she flew to see if she could discover the progress of the elf's party. Ceridwen wasn't overly disappointed by Leshiye's failure; she never really believed that stopping the life-quest of an elf-lord of Kelsenellenelvial Gil-Ravadry's high standing would be as easy as that.

But Ceridwen was a resourceful witch. She had other, if less subtle, plans set into motion, and even in light of her first failure, she would not have bet a copper coin on the success of Kelsey's quest.

FIVE
Dilnamarra

AS soon as they emerged from the wood, the land, even the air, seemed to change before them. Tir na n'Og had been bright and sunny and filled with springtime scents and chattering birds, but out here, beyond the forest, the land lay in perpetual gloom. Fog hung low on the dirt roads, human-crafted roads, and along the rolling farmlands and small unadorned stone-and-thatch cottages.

Fields, bordered by hedgerows and rock walls, rolled up and down the hilly region, thick with grass and thick with sheep and cattle. Copses of trees spotted the landscape, some standing in lines like silent sentinels, others huddled in thick but small groups, plotting privately. By all logical measures, it was a beautiful countryside, but it was shrouded in melancholy, as if the gloom was caused by more than the simple mist.

"Watch yer footing," the leprechaun offered to Gary.

Gary didn't seem to understand; the road ran straight and level.

"Ye're not wanting to step into the heeland coo left-behinds," Mickey explained.

"Heeland coo?" Gary asked.

"A great hairy and horned beast," Mickey replied. Gary glanced around nervously.

"All the farmers keep them," Mickey went on, trying to calm him. "They're not a dangerous sort—unless ye set to bothering them. Some o' the lads go in to tip them over when they're sleeping, and some o' the coos don't take well to that."

"Tip them?" Now Gary was starting to catch on, and he was not overly surprised when Mickey pointed up to a distant field, to a shaggy-haired brown cow grazing contentedly. Gary rolled Mickey's description over in his thoughts a few times.

"Highland cow," he said at length.

"Aye, that's what I said," answered Mickey. "Heeland coo. And ye've not seen a left-behind to match the droppings of a heeland coo!"

Gary couldn't bite back his chuckle. Mickey and Kelsey exchanged curious looks, and Kelsey led them off.

Whatever romantic thoughts remained to Gary of the forest Tir na n'Og or the melancholy countryside were washed away an hour later by the harsh reality of mud-filled Dilnamarra. To the unsuspecting visitor, the change came as dramatically as the shift that had brought him to the land of Faerie in the first place, as if his dream, or whatever it was, had taken a sidelong turn, an undoubtedly wrong turn.

A square stone tower set on a grassy hill dominated the settlement, with dozens of squat stone shacks, some barely more than open lean-tos clustered in the tower's shadow. Pigs and scrawny cows ran freely about the streets, their dung mixing with the cart-grooved mud and their stench just one more unpleasant ingredient in the overwhelming aroma.

People of all ages wandered about, hunched and as dirty and smelly as the animals.

"Pick me up, lad," Mickey said to Gary. Gary looked down to see not the leprechaun, but a small human toddler where Mickey had been standing. Gary studied the toddler curiously for a moment, for the youngster held his book.

"Look through it, I told ye!" the toddler said somewhat angrily when Gary gave him a confused look. Gary peered closer, reminded himself who should be standing beside him and not to believe what his eyes were showing him. Then he saw Mickey again, behind the façade, and he nodded and scooped the leprechaun into his arms.

"I caught you," Gary whispered, smiling.

"Are ye to start with that nonsense again?" Mickey asked, and the leprechaun, too, was wearing a grin. "I'm yer brother, lad, for any what's asking. Ye just hope that none o' the folks see through me disguise as ye have done. Suren then Kelsey's sword'll be cutting man flesh this day."

Gary's smile disappeared. "Kelsey wouldn't," he said unconvincingly.

"The Tylwyth Teg have fallen out of favor with the men about," Mickey said. "Kelsey's here only for reasons of his life-quest; he has not a care, one way or th'other, for the wretches of Dilnamarra. Woe to any that get in Kelsey's way."

Gary looked back to Kelsey, worried that Mickey's prophecy would come true. Where would Gary stand in such a fight? he wondered. He owed no loyalty to Kelsey, or even to Mickey. If the elf took arms against people of Gary's own race . . .

Gary shook the dark thoughts away, reminding himself to play through this experience one step at a time.

Every pitiful inhabitant of Dilnamarra turned out to see the strange troupe as they passed along the dung-filled streets. In this town, Gary was no more akin to the wretches as was Kelsey, for he carried no scars of disease, no open sores, and his fingers were not blackened by years of muddy labors. Angry glares came at them from every corner of every hut, and beggars, some limping, but most crawling in the mud, moved to block their way with a tangle of trembling crooked fingers and skin-and-bone, dirt-covered arms.

Gary held his breath as Kelsey reached the first of this group, deciding at that moment that he wouldn't let the elf strike the pitiful man down; if Kelsey's sword came out, then Gary would tackle him, or punch him, or do whatever he could to prevent the massacre. Not that he gave himself any chance of surviving against the grim elf—he just could not sit back and watch helplessly.

It never came to that, though, for Mickey's estimate of Kelsey proved to be a bit exaggerated. The elf obviously didn't appreciate the interference, but his sword did not move an inch out of his scabbard. Kelsey simply slapped the reaching hands aside and continued straight ahead, never looking the beggars in the eye. The wave of wretches did not relent, though. They swept along behind the strangers, groaning and crawling to keep pace.

Mickey, too, avoided the pleading gazes, nestling deep in Gary's clutch and closing his eyes. It was a common sight to the leprechaun, one to which he had long ago numbed his sensibilities.

Gary saw the beggars, though, could not block them out, and their desperate state stung him in the heart. He had never seen such poverty; where he grew up, poor meant that your car was more than ten years old. And dirty was the term Gary used to describe his appearance after a day at the plastics shop. Somehow, looking at these people, his usage of that term now seemed very out of place.

If this, then, was Gary's fantasy, his "twilight fancy," as that Mr. Peter Beagle had described it in the introduction to *The Hobbit,* then in Gary's eyes, the light around reality was suddenly burning a bit brighter.

The crowd dispersed as Kelsey neared the stone keep. Two grim-faced guards stood at either side of its single, iron-bound door, and the glares they shot at the trailing lines of beggars were filled with utter contempt.

"The heights of royalty," Gary heard Mickey mutter softly.

Crossed pikes intercepted Kelsey as he neared the door. He stopped to regard the guards for a moment.

"I am Kelsenel . . ."

"We know who ye are, elf," one of the guards, a stout, bearded man, said roughly.

"Then let me pass," Kelsey replied. "I have business with your Baron."

"It's on 'is order that we're keepin' ye here," the guard answered. "Stand yer ground now, an' keep behind the spears."

Kelsey looked back at Gary and Mickey, his expression hinting at explosive anger.

"I'd thought the arrangements made," Gary said, or at least it appeared as though Gary had said it. In truth it was Mickey, using ventriloquism to keep up his toddler façade.

"As did I," Kelsey replied, understanding the leprechaun's trick. "I spoke with Baron Pwyll just a week ago. He was more than willing to agree, thinking that the reforging of Donigarten's spear during his reign would assure his name in the bard's tales."

"Then another has spoken with him," Mickey said through Gary, cutting off Gary's own forthcoming response. Gary gave Mickey a stern look to tell him that he didn't appreciate being used this way, but Mickey continued his conversation with Kelsey without missing a beat.

"Who wishes ye stopped?" the leprechaun asked.

Kelsey shook his head to dismiss the possibility, but he, too, was beginning to have his concerns. They hadn't even really yet begun their journey, and they had already run into two unforeseen obstacles.

The iron-bound door creaked open and a cleaner and better-dressed guard appeared. He whispered a short exchange with the other two, then beckoned for Kelsey and company to enter the keep.

The hazy sunlight disappeared altogether when the heavy door closed behind them, for the one window in the ground level of the squat tower was too tiny to admit more than a crack of light. Burning torches were set in the four corners, their shadowy flickers giving spooky dimension to the tapestries lining all the walls, morbid depictions of bloody, smoke-filled battles.

Across from the door, in a gem-studded throne, sat the Baron, wearing clothes that had once been expensive, but had worn through in several places. He was a big, robust man, with a bristling beard and an expressive mouth that could equally reflect jollity and outrage. Behind him stood two unremarkable guards and a lean figure carrying the mud of the road on his weathered cloak. This man's hood was up, but back enough for Gary to see his matted black hair and suspicious, darting eyes. He wore a dagger on his thick belt, and his hand rested on it as though that was where his hand always rested.

Gary followed Mickey's stare to the side of the throne, to an empty stone pedestal and an iron stand.

"So says King Kinnemore," Mickey said derisively under his breath, and Gary realized that the empty pedestal had probably been the resting place for the armor and spear. Kelsey, too, seemed less than pleased, focusing more on the pedestal and the road-worn figure behind the Baron than on Pywll himself.

The elf kept his composure, though. He walked proudly up to the throne and fell to one knee in a low respectful bow.

"My greetings, Baron Pwyll," Kelsey said. "As arranged in our previous meeting, I have returned."

Pwyll looked back, concerned, to the cloaked figure, then to Kelsey. "Things have changed since our last meeting," he said.

Kelsey stood up, fierce and unblinking.

"Our good Prince Geldion here—long live the King—" (there was something less than enthusiastic about the way Pwyll said those words) "has brought word that the armor and spear of Cedric Donigarten are not to leave my possession."

"I have your word," Kelsey argued.

Pwyll's eyes flashed with helpless anger. "My word has been overruled!" he retorted. The Baron's guards bristled behind him, as though expecting some sudden trouble.

Prince Geldion did not try to hide his superior smile.

"Are you a puppet to Kinnemore, then?" Kelsey dared to ask.

Pwyll's eyes flashed with anger.

"Oh, begorra," Gary heard himself moan.

Pwyll jumped up threateningly from his seat, but Kelsey did not blink and the blustery Baron soon settled back. Pwyll could not refute Kelsey's insult at that time, in these circumstances.

"Where is yer edict, good Baron," Mickey said through Gary. Gary looked down angrily, but the toddler appeared fast asleep and did not return his stare.

Pwyll's angry glare fell over Gary. "And who are you, who speaks unannounced and without my permission?" he demanded.

"Gar—" Gary started, but Mickey's thrown voice cut him short.

"The armor wearer, I be!" Gary heard himself proclaim, and he wondered why no one noticed that his lips were not moving in synch with the words. Or were they? It was all too confusing.

"He who will fulfill the prophecies, come from distant lands," Mickey's ventriloquism went on. "The spear carrier to look a dragon in the eye! A warrior who will not return until the legends and me task are complete. So where be yer edict, I say? And what King dares to stand against prophecies of Sir Cedric Donigarten's own wizards?"

Pwyll sat in absolute disbelief for a moment, his mouth hanging open, and Gary thought the man would surely kill him for his outburst. But then a great blast of laughter erupted from the large man's mouth. He held an open hand behind him, to the Prince, and was given a rolled parchment, tied with the purple ribbons that served as the exclusive seal of King Kinnemore.

"And your name, good Sir Warrior?" Pwyll inquired through a grin.

A long moment of silence passed and Mickey nudged his carrier. "Gary," Gary replied hesitantly, expecting to be interrupted at any moment. "Gary Leger."

Pwyll scratched his thick beard. "And where did you say you came from?"

"From Bretaigne, beyond Cancarron Mountains," Mickey's voice answered. Both the Baron and the Prince appeared to catch the abrupt change in accent, but the Prince seemed to care more about it than did Pwyll.

"Well, Gary Leger from Bretaigne," Pwyll said. "Here is my edict, from King Kinnemore himself." He untied and unrolled the parchment and cleared his throat.

"To Baron Pwyll of Dilnamarra Keep," he began regally, articulating carefully in the proper language of royalty. "Be it known that I, King Kinnemore, have heard on good authority that the armor and spear of Cedric Donigarten, our most esteemed hero, will soon go out from Dilnamarra Keep on an expedition that might surely bring its destruction. Therefore, by my word—and my word is law—you are not to release the artifacts from your possession." Pwyll blinked and smoothed the parchment suddenly, as though it had in it a crease he had not noticed before.

". . . unless you, in your esteemed judgment, determine that said artifacts are given into the proper hands as spoken of in the prophecies." Pwyll blinked again in amazement, and before he could react, Prince Geldion reached down to tear the parchment from his grasp.

Pwyll resisted, though, and he held the parchment up for the Prince to see. "Below the fold," he instructed, his voice reflecting confusion as profound as that marked on Geldion's face. "I did not see the fold before, nor the clause."

The Prince's lips moved as he read the words—words he, too, had not seen before.

"Right above your own father's signature," Pwyll said pointedly. "Well, that does put things in a different light, I say."

"What treachery is this?" Prince Geldion demanded, starting at Kelsey and Gary. He stopped before he ever rounded the throne, however, for though his hand remained on the hilt of his belted dagger, Kelsey's had now gone to his fine elven sword. Geldion had heard enough tales of the Tylwyth Teg to know better than continue his futile threat.

"What treachery?" he said again, this time spinning on the Baron.

Pwyll shrugged and laughed at him. "Get the armor," he instructed his guards. "Put it on Gary Leger of Bretaigne. Let us see how it fits."

"The armor is not to leave Dilnamarra Keep," Geldion protested.

"Except by my own judgment," Pwyll calmly replied. "So says your own father. You remember him, do you not?"

"There is some magic here!" Geldion protested. "That was not in the edict; I penned it myself . . . under my father's word," he added quickly, seeing the suspicious stares coming at him from all directions.

"Magic?" Mickey's voice, through Gary, quickly put in. "Me good Baron o' Dilnamarra. A stranger I am to yer lands, but was it not by yer own King's edict that magic be declared an impossible thing? A tool of traitors and devil-chasers, did yer King Kinnemore not say? It may be that I've heard wrong, but I came across the mountains thinking that I'd left all thoughts o' magic behind."

"No," answered Baron Pwyll, "you have not heard wrong. There is no magic in Dilnamarra, nor anywhere else in Kinnemore Kingdom, so proclaimed King Kinnemore." He looked wryly at Geldion. "Unless the Prince is privy to more than the rest of us."

"You tread along dangerous shores, Baron Pwyll!" Geldion roared, and he crumpled the parchment and stuck it in his cloak pocket. "Hold the armor, I say, until the King may address the situation."

"We have a deal," Kelsey interrupted, his golden eyes boring into Geldion's dark orbs. "I shall not delay my given quest in the week it will take a messenger to get to Connacht, and the week it will take him to return. You have the edict of your King," he said to Pwyll. "Do you find this Gary Leger fit to bear the weight of the prophecies?"

"The armor first," Pwyll said, giving Kelsey a wink. "Then I will give my decision."

Outraged beyond words, Prince Geldion kicked the empty pedestal, then limped out of the chamber.

"YOU really expect me to walk around in this suit?" Gary asked as the attendants fit the heavy, overlapping plates and links of metal onto his chest. His legs were already encumbered by the mail and he felt certain that when they were finished with him he would weigh half a ton.

"The weight is well distributed," Kelsey answered. "You will become comfortable in the suit soon enough—once your weak muscles grow strong under its burden."

Gary flashed an angry glare the elf's way but held his thoughts silent. He was twice Kelsey's weight and no doubt much stronger than the elf, and he didn't appreciate Kelsey's insults, particularly when the elf wore a finely crafted suit of thin chain links, much lighter and more flexible than the bulky armor of Cedric Donigarten.

"Cheer up, lad," Mickey offered. "Ye'll be glad enough o' the weight the first time the mail turns a goblin's sword or a troll's weighty punch!"

"How I am supposed to keep taking this off and putting it back on if we're going to be out on the road for days?" Gary reasoned. "You can't expect me to sleep in it."

"The first time is the most difficult for fitting the armor," Kelsey explained. "Once the attendants have properly designed the padded undersuit, you will be able to strip and don the armor much more quickly."

"Yeah," Mickey snickered. "Only an hour or two for the lot of it. Kelsey and meself will hold back any foes 'til ye're ready."

Gary was beginning to appreciate Mickey's sarcasm less and less.

"It is finished," one of the attendants announced. "Shield and helmet are over there." He pointed to the wall, where several shields and helmets lay in a pile. "You will have to see the Baron if you desire the spear."

It was not difficult to determine which items in the jumble matched the decorated armor, for only one shield bore the griffon-clutching-spear insignia of dead King Cedric, and only one helmet, edged in beaten gold and plumed with a single purple feather from some giant bird, could appropriately cap the decorated suit.

Mickey picked out the helmet right away, and as the attendants left the room, it came floating from the pile, hovering near Gary's face. Gary reached out to take it, but his attempt was lumbering at best and the leprechaun easily levitated the helmet up and out of his reach.

Again, Gary glared at the leprechaun, but it was Kelsey that put an end to Mickey's antics.

"You wear the guise of a human child, but still you act the fool," Kelsey growled. "If the Baron or the Prince were to enter now, how might we explain your trick? There is no magic here, they say, unless it is magic spawned in Hell. They burn witches in Dilnamarra."

Mickey snapped his fingers and the helmet dropped. Gary, his hands on hips and his arms weighted in metal, could not react quickly enough to get out of the way, or to block the descent. The helmet thumped onto his head and slipped down over his ears, settling backwards on the armor's steel collar. Gary teetered, dazed, and Mickey's voice sounded distant, hollow.

"Catch him, elf!" the leprechaun cried. "Suren if he falls we'll be needing six men to pick him up!"

Kelsey's slender fingers wrapped around Gary's wrist and he jerked the young man straight. Gary reached for the helmet, but Kelsey beat him to it, roughly turning it about so that the man might see. Gary felt as if he was sporting a stewing pot on his head, with a small slit cut out in front for viewing. The helmet was quite loose—Gary wondered just how big this Cedric Donigarten's head actually was!—but better loose than tight, he figured.

"You look the part of a king," Kelsey remarked. Gary took it as a compliment until the elf finished the thought. "But you, too, act the part of a fool." He handed Gary the huge and heavy shield and moved back to join the leprechaun. Gary slipped his arm into the shield's belt and, with some effort, lifted it from the floor. It was wide at the top, tapering to a rounded point at the bottom—to set it in the ground, Gary realized—and more than half Gary's height.

"Baron Pwyll will have to agree," Kelsey said to Mickey. "The suit fits properly in body if not in stature."

Tired of the insults and wanting to make a point (and also wanting to give his already weary arm a break), Gary dropped the shield tip to the floor. Unfortunately, instead of clanging defiantly on the stone, as Gary had planned, it came to rest on top of his foot.

Gary bit his lip to keep from screaming, glad for the masking helmet.

Kelsey just shook his head in disbelief and walked past the armored man and out of the room, back to see Baron Pwyll.

"Ye'll get used to it," Mickey offered hopefully, giving Gary a wink as he followed Kelsey.

"THE Lady will gives usses gifts, eh?" a big goblin croaked in Geek's face.

"Many gifts," Geek replied, bobbing his head stupidly. "M'lady Ceridwen wantses usses not to hurts the elf, but stops them, we will!"

The big goblin joined in the head-bobbing, his overgrown canines curling grotesquely around his saliva-wetted lips. He looked around excitedly at the host behind him, and they began wagging their heads and slapping each other.

"No like," said another of the band. "Too far from mountains. Too much peoples here. No like."

"You no like, you goes back!" Geek growled, moving right up to the dissenter. The big, toothy goblin moved to support Geek and all the others fanned out around them, clutching their crude spears and clubs tightly.

"Did Lady send usses?" the dissenter asked bluntly. "Did Lady tells Geek to kill 'n' catch?"

Geek started to retort, but the big goblin rushed to Geek's defense, stepping in front of Geek and cutting his reply short.

"Geek know what Lady Ceridwen wantses!" the brute declared, and he curled up his crooked fist and punched the dissenter square in the mouth.

The smaller goblin fell over backwards but was caught by those closest to him and hoisted roughly back to his feet. He stood swaying, barely conscious, but, with typical goblin stubbornness and stupidity, managed to utter, "No like."

The words sent the already excited band into a sudden and vicious frenzy. The big goblin struck first, slamming his huge forearm straight down on the dissenter's head. This time, the smaller goblin did fall to the ground, and those around him, rather than support him, fell over him, jabbing with their spears and hammering with their clubs. The fallen goblin managed a few cries of protest, a few pitiful squeaks, which quickly turned to blood-choked gurgles.

The band continued to beat him long after he was dead.

"Geek know what Lady Ceridwen wantses!" the big goblin declared again, and this time, not a single voice spoke against him. The host respectfully circled Geek to hear his forthcoming commands.

"They goes in town," Geek explained. "But come out soon, they will. Lady says they goes to mountains. We catches them on road in trees; catches elf and killses humans."

The other goblins wagged their fat heads and hooted their agreement, banging their spears and clubs off trees and rocks, or the goblins standing beside them or against anything else they could find.

Convincing goblins to "kill 'n' catch" was never a very difficult thing to do.

GARY did find the armor growing more comfortable as he loped along beside Mickey on the road leading east out of Dilnamarra. The suit was also surprisingly quiet, considering that more than half of it was of metal and it hadn't been used in centuries.

They had set right out from the keep after Baron Pwyll had tentatively agreed, over Prince Geldion's vehement protests, that they could take the artifacts. The sunlight was fading fast even then, but Kelsey would not wait for the next morn, not with the Prince so determined to stop him and the Baron caught in a dilemma that ought soon lead him to second thoughts. Now the sun had dipped below the horizon, and the usual wafting mist off the southern moors had come up, drifting lazily across the road, obscuring their vision even further.

Kelsey would not relent his pace, though, despite Mickey's constant grumbling.

"We should've stayed the night in the keep," the leprechaun said repeatedly. "A warm bed and a fine meal would've done us all the good."

Gary remained silent through it all, sensing that Kelsey was on the verge of an explosion. Finally, after perhaps the hundredth such complaint from Mickey, the elf turned back on him sharply.

"We never would have gotten out of Dilnamarra Keep if we had stayed the night!" he scolded. "Geldion meant to stop us and he had more than one guard at his disposal."

"He'd not have gone against us openly," Mickey argued. "Not in Pwyll's own keep."

"Perhaps not," Kelsey conceded. "But he might have convinced Pwyll to hold us until the matter of the edict was properly settled. I applaud your actions in the audience chamber, leprechaun, but the illusionary script would not have fooled them forever."

"Don't ye be thinking too highly of humans," Mickey replied, then he cleared his throat, embarrassed, as the insulted Gary turned on him.

But the events in the keep had left Gary quite confused, and he had too many questions to worry about Mickey's unintentional affront. "What illusionary script?" he asked Kelsey.

"Ye see what I'm saying?" Mickey snickered, throwing a wink Kelsey's way.

Now even Kelsey managed a smile. "The Prince did pen the edict, by his own admission," the elf explained to Gary. "Mickey simply added a few words."

Gary turned his incredulous stare on the smug leprechaun.

"And that fact make us outlaws," Kelsey continued, more to Mickey than Gary. "The road is now our sanctuary, and the more distance we put between ourselves and Prince Geldion, the better our chances."

"*Yer* chances, ye mean," Mickey muttered.

Kelsey let it go. For all the leprechaun's complaining, the elf could not deny Mickey's value to the quest. Without Mickey's illusions, Kelsey would never have gotten the armor and spear out of Dilnamarra Keep.

"Three more hours, then we may rest," the elf said, picking up the leather case that held the ancient spear. The weapon had been broken almost exactly in half and the pieces were laid side by side, but the case was still nearly as tall as Kelsey.

Gary was more than a little curious to view the legendary weapon—only

Kelsey had seen it back at the keep—but he did not press the elf at that time. He hoisted the heavy shield and unremarkable spear he had been given and trudged off after Kelsey.

Mickey stood alone for a few moments, kicking at a rock with one curly-toed shoe. "Ye landed yerself in it deep this time, Mickey McMickey," he said quietly, and then he shrugged helplessly and tagged along.

SIX

Crossroads

THEY set camp far from the road, fearing that the Prince and his men might be out looking for them. Kelsey took the watch, and said he would keep it for all the night, sitting grim-faced and stoic, his thin sword lying ready across his lap. No sense of chivalry bubbled up in Gary to argue. He was thoroughly exhausted from the weighted hiking and he was ready, too, after the mud-filled spectacle of Dilnamarra, to put this entire crazy fantasy behind him. Dilnamarra was unlike any town Gary had ever fantasized about, with so much suffering and true poverty, and after that sight, he figured he would never look upon Lancashire and upon his own existence in quite the same negative way.

But how to get back there? It seemed only logical, Gary tried to convince himself, that if he went to sleep in the middle of a dream, he would wake up in reality.

"Go to sleep," he whispered quietly to himself, "if you want to wake up."

Mickey heard the private conversation as Gary laid out the blankets and stripped off the bulkier parts of his armor. "As it always is and always will be with big folk from Real-earth," the leprechaun chuckled, and took a deep draw on his long pipe.

Gary knew that Mickey was laughing at him and his hopes of returning home, and he knew, too, that those hopes had no foundation in this situation. For all of his logical denial, Gary was beginning to catch on to the truth of his very real situation. Still, he turned sharply on Mickey and stubbornly held on to his previous perceptions of reality.

"You'll be gone soon," he assured the sprite.

Mickey chuckled again, conjured a small globe of light, and opened *The Hobbit*. Gary stared at him a moment longer, then dropped to the blankets and tried to put the leprechaun out of his thoughts.

Every time the mist thinned, Gary got a too-brief glimpse of the evening canopy. A million stars dotted the sky, an enchanting view, but Gary rarely got to see more than a fraction of it through the opaque veil. The mist was stubborn, hanging like a pall over the land, dulling the crisp and wonderful sights that would indeed have made this a world of twilight fancies.

It hadn't missed the mark by far. Tir na n'Og was bright and cheery and warm and song-filled, a fitting forest indeed. Such places of enchantment could not be found in Gary's world—at least, not as far as Gary knew. And the Faerie countryside, if a bit plain, was untainted and undeniably lush.

But the harshness of Dilnamarra overshadowed the wood and the fields, brought a grim reality to steal the harmony of the forest song and country road.

Gary washed it all from his thoughts. He focused on his Jeep and the cemetery and the stool by the grinder, and hoped that he would not wake up too late for at least a cold supper, that his parents weren't too worried.

Then he saw the mist again, silvery in the starlight, and Kelsey keeping silent watch, and Mickey busy reading. How many hours had he been here? Not broken and episodic but real hours, filled with experiences both exciting and mundane, with all the little details that he never considered a part of the realm of dreams.

Gary knew that this was no dream. Plain and simple. He wondered if he had died, or gone insane. Had his love of fantasy novels and daydreams consumed his mind? Had his disappointments with life's realities driven him mad? He thought of a Jack Nicholson movie, of psychotics wandering aimlessly, hopelessly lost, and he wondered if they, too, had entered their own land of Faerie.

And what now for him? What "realities" now awaited Gary Leger? Would he find a long line of dreary towns like Dilnamarra, or a world of enchantment, a world of Tir na n'Og and leprechauns and stern elfs and wood nymphs?

The mist cleared again and Gary got his best view yet of the twinkling stars. Then it faded as his physical exhaustion overcame the turmoil in his mind and he drifted off to sleep.

GARY knew as soon as he opened his eyes that he was outdoors. He thought—hoped—for a brief moment that he was in the familiar wood back home, between the school and the cemetery and the intruding houses, but that hope died as soon as he smelled the breakfast cooking and heard Mickey's flavored voice.

"Mushroom stew'll fill yer belly fine," the leprechaun said to Kelsey.

"Prepare it quickly," Kelsey replied. "We have many more miles to go this day, and it will be hot. I expect our friend will need to stop and rest every few minutes." Kelsey's tone was not complimentary.

"Ye're too hard on the lad," Mickey said. "Ye'd be wanting rest yerself if ye had to walk around in that man-sized bucket."

"I, too, wear metal mail," Kelsey reminded him.

"Chain crafted by the Tylwyth Teg?" Mickey balked. "Suren yer whole suit's weighing less than Donigarten's helmet alone!"

"Prepare the stew quickly," Kelsey ordered again, his snarling tones revealing that he had run out of arguments. "I wish to be on the road before the sun has come fully over the horizon."

"Ah, ye're up, then!" Mickey greeted Gary, seeing Gary sitting on the blankets and stretching. "Good for that; now ye'll get a fine meal in yer belly."

Gary looked all around in continued disbelief, his expression a mixture of confusion and budding anger.

"I told ye that ye can go home after ye finish the task," the leprechaun explained, honestly sympathetic, "I told ye that ye were not dreaming; I'd not be lying to ye."

Still unable to come to terms with all of this, Gary shook his head slowly and nibbled his upper lip.

"Call it a dream if it makes ye feel better," the leprechaun advised. "And whatever ye might call it, enjoy it!"

"I didn't find the town so enjoyable," Gary said grimly.

"Then think o' Leshiye in the wood," Mickey offered with a sly wink. "I know ye liked that part."

That notion did bring a smile to Gary's face, and the mushroom stew proved truly delicious and did fill his belly. They were back on the road soon after, Kelsey leading them at a swift pace and Gary struggling to keep the loose-fitting helmet on straight and the heavy shield from dragging its tip along the ground.

Soon, Gary didn't even try to keep the shield aloft. The day was hot and dreary, damp with the mist and painfully bright. Sweat soaked the under-padding of Gary's suit and stung his eyes. He kept stopping and poking his fingers through the eye slit of the helmet to wipe the moisture away, but it hardly helped, since his fingers were as wet as his face.

"Take the helmet off and hang it on yer spear," Mickey offered to him, seeing his distress. Kelsey, up ahead, spun about.

"Oh, let him!" the leprechaun spouted, cutting short the elf's forthcoming argument. "He'll drop dead in that suit in this heat, and what good'll he be to yer quest then?"

Kelsey turned back and started away and Mickey smiled smugly. He helped

Gary get the cumbersome helmet in place on the spear and they set off again with Gary feeling much better.

His brightened mood sustained him through most of the morning, but near noon they came to a crossroads, two intercepting muddy trails in the otherwise unremarkable rolling fields. Four high poles had been set into the ground, one at each corner of the intersection.

Men were hanging from them, by the neck, long dead and bloated, twisting slowly in the gentle breeze.

Gary dropped his spear and shield and clutched at his turning stomach. Even Kelsey, halting his determined march to state unblinking, seemed affected by the gruesome sight.

"Poor wretches," Mickey remarked. "Cut them down, will ye?" he asked Kelsey.

Kelsey's hand went to his sword hilt, but he stopped and shook his head.

"Cut them down!" Gary shouted suddenly, though he nearly lost his breakfast for the effort.

"I cannot!" Kelsey shouted back at him. "None in all of Faerie would dare to do so but the Tylwyth Teg, and if I cut them down now it would surely tell Prince Geldion that we passed this way. As surely as if I signed my name on the road. I do not want the Prince anywhere near to us."

Gary and Mickey couldn't really argue against the practical reasoning.

"What did they do?" Gary asked somberly. "Were they criminals? And why would they be hung out here, so far from the town?"

"Probably couldn't pay their taxes," Mickey spat in reply. "Or said something the Prince didn't like hearing. Or stole a piece o' bread for feeding their children. Get yerself used to the sight, lad. Ye'll be seeing it at many crossroads."

"They always hang them at crossroads," Kelsey explained. "That way, if a dead man's vengeful spirit comes back seeking justice, it will not know which way to go."

"Vengeful spirits," Mickey grumbled. "The poor wretches hadn't the strength to fight in life, never mind in death."

"Let us get far from this place," Kelsey offered, and the others did not disagree.

Long after they had put the crossroads behind them, Mickey noticed that Gary's visage had not softened.

"Don't ye let it trouble ye, lad," the leprechaun offered. "Suren 'twas a terrible sight, but it's behind us now."

Gary's expression did not change. "'Call it a dream,' you said," he replied evenly. "But should I call it a dream or a nightmare?"

For the first time, Gary's words had left the leprechaun without reply.

"You said that I had heard of this land of Faerie," Gary went on, trying to hold his voice steady and hide his rising anger. "And so I have, in old folktales—fairy tales. But according to those stories, the world of elfs and leprechauns was supposed to be an enchanted place, peaceful and beautiful, and not a place where a man is left hanging by the neck at a crossroads for stealing bread to feed his hungry children."

"Aye," Mickey agreed somberly. His gray eyes misted over sorrowfully and took on a faraway look. "And so it once was," he went on, "before him named Kinnemore found a seat on the throne . . ."

"Enough!" shouted Kelsey, who had come back to join them and had over-heard their conversation. He glared at Mickey, then turned on Gary. "The poli-tics and ways of the land are not your concern," he growled. "You were brought here to play a small part in a quest, and nothing more. Whether the sights of Faerie please you or turn your stomach is of no concern to me."

Gary accepted the elf's berating without question, understanding that his and Mickey's observations had struck a sensitive nerve in Kelsey. He could not help but notice Kelsey's helpless frustration. The sight of the hanging men had stung the elf as deeply as any, maybe more so, and Gary knew that such images as that and as the huddled wretches of Dilnamarra were not in agreement with Kelsey's high-browed views of how the world should be.

Mickey and Gary exchanged shrugs as Kelsey started off again and they said no more as the miles passed. For Gary, it was hot and lonely and dreadful. His thoughts drifted back to his own world, back to Tir na n'Og, or to nowhere at all, and in his blank trance, he didn't even notice that Kelsey had stopped, crouching low as though he was inspecting something in the road.

Fortunately Mickey managed to grab Gary before he walked right into the bending elf.

"What've ye found?" the leprechaun asked.

"Tracks," Kelsey replied quietly. He looked up at Mickey and Gary, his face grave. "Goblin tracks."

"Goblins here?" Mickey asked. He put a hand above his eyes and peered at the distant mountains. "Five days yet," he muttered. "Too far for goblins to be wandering." He looked to Gary as though he expected the inexperienced man to confirm his suspicions.

"Goblin tracks," Kelsey said again, this time with a tone of finality.

Mickey looked all around, to the mountains and back to Kelsey. Then he understood. "Ye're thinking it's no coincidence?" he asked.

Kelsey didn't immediately respond, though his expression revealed that he considered Mickey's guess right on target. They were barely into the second day of the quest, yet they had met interference at every turn. First the nymph, then the Prince, and now recent evidence of a band of goblins (and no small band, judging by the number of tracks) nearly a hundred miles from their mountain holes.

"We'll know soon enough," Kelsey replied, studying the westering sun. "If the goblins are still about, the night will likely reveal them."

"And with us sitting open in the middle of the plain," moaned Mickey.

"Not so," said Kelsey. "The wood, Cowtangle, is but a few miles down the road. We must hurry to get there before all the daylight is gone."

Gary didn't like the thought of hurrying, but he liked the thought of meeting goblins even less. He put his helmet back on and started off as quickly as he could go. Kelsey and Mickey helped him as much as possible; Kelsey even took turns with Gary carrying the heavy shield.

By the time they reached their destination, it was so late that the trees seemed no more than a darker silhouette against a deep gray background. With his keen eyes, Kelsey led them into the thicket easily, though, and soon found a clearing where they could set camp in relative safety.

"Set no fires," Kelsey ordered, then he looked pointedly at Mickey. "And light no enchanted globes." To Gary, he added, "Keep your armor on and your spear close. If we are forced to flee, do not forget a single piece of the ancient and priceless suit."

Kelsey seemed to be trying to convince himself as much as the others as he added quietly, "The wood will hide us."

Both Mickey and Gary couldn't help thinking that the thick trees of Cowtangle might be hiding other things as well.

FROM the shallow depths of a fitful sleep, Gary heard Kelsey's startled cry. He opened his eyes just in time to see a form go crashing back into the brush away from the elf.

A ghostly light encircled the area—Mickey's doing, Gary knew—and everything seemed to be moving too slowly.

"Run!" Kelsey yelled, turning back towards Gary, and Mickey added, "For all yer life, lad!"

Gary's mind was wide awake now and alert, but his body moved sluggishly as he tried to rise in the bulky armor. Kelsey ran over to him; there was movement and shouting now from every direction, wild hoots and croaks.

Gary accepted the elf's free hand and started to rise, pausing just long enough to notice that Kelsey's sword dripped of blood. As if sensing his horrified hesitation, Kelsey jerked him upright with surprising strength, plopped his helmet on his head, handed him both spear and shield, and pushed him off behind Mickey.

Gary knew that the elf had joined battle right behind him only a split second later. He tried to turn back and look over his shoulder, but the helmet was not properly strapped on and it did not turn with his head.

"This way!" Mickey yelled up ahead. "Don't ye be fearing for Kelsey!"

It was all a shadowy blur to Gary when they came out of the clearing and out of Mickey's magical light. He stumbled and crashed through many small branches, desperately trying to keep up with the nimble leprechaun. The fine armor easily deflected the weight of the blows, and Gary did finally catch up to Mickey, the leprechaun casually sitting on a low branch, peering back the way they had come.

Mickey absently waved Gary by, and the frightened man stumbled on blindly, not daring to slow. Every tree seemed an ominous form; he imagined branches as sword-wielding goblin arms, reaching out to cut him down. Every bush seemed a crouched demon, poised to leap up in his face and swallow him. He tried to reason through the terror, he tried to catch his breath.

He tried.

MICKEY carefully considered his next moves. If Kelsey was too distracted to see through the deception, then the leprechaun might bring him harm. But goblins were everywhere, scrambling and shouting, and goblins could see in the dark.

Kelsey might escape, Mickey surely would, but unless Mickey took some prompt action, Gary Leger was doomed.

"Tisk, tisk, trees in the mist," the leprechaun chanted, waving his hands to create the most common trick used to deter would-be leprechaun hunters. A simple illusion but a nasty one.

Every tree between Mickey and the clearing appeared to move three feet to the left.

IT didn't take Kelsey long to figure out what had happened. He saw a goblin darting to the side of him run face-first into a thick oak and drop in a dizzy heap. Another goblin, a big toothy one, came straight at Kelsey, but veered to the right at the last moment and got collared by a low branch. The creature's neck snapped with a horrible *crack!* and it lay quite still.

At that moment, Kelsey came to consider again that having a leprechaun around might not be such a bad thing. He started off on a circling route, but stopped as another goblin rebounded off yet another tree. The creature stood staring in confusion and scratching its head, and Kelsey, not worrying about fair play where goblins were concerned, promptly stuck it through the exposed ribs.

Then the elf slipped into the brush, carefully picking his way past Mickey's splendid illusion.

FOR the first time in his life, Gary Leger truly knew fear. He heard the goblins, many goblins; they seemed to be nipping right at his heels, and now he had lost his friends! What would he do if the goblins caught up with him? He didn't know how to fight with a spear and he could hardly move about in the armor.

Gary was far beyond the area of Mickey's deception, but that hardly mattered, for he could not see in the dark anyway, particularly with his loose helmet bouncing all about his shoulders, and could hardly think above his paralyzing terror. He hooked his shield on some brush and stumbled. He caught his balance quickly, but the jerk sent his helmet spinning right about, the eye slit facing behind him.

Gary realized that he was in trouble and tried to reach up and turn the thing back right, but the continuing goblin snorts and shouts overruled his rational decision to slow down. A root tripped him up and he lurched forward. Somehow, he kept his footing.

A rush of relief came over him as he stood up straight and finally maneuvered the helmet back aright, but his sigh lasted only the second it took him to register the low and thick branch directly crossing his path. Gary actually wished he hadn't turned the helmet; he would have preferred not to see it coming.

He heard the dull thud and felt the sudden jolt, and the next thing he knew, he was lying on his back thinking how pretty the stars were this night. Strangely he could still see the stars, a million stars, even though the jolt had turned his helmet back around to cover his eyes.

"Lie still and stay that way!" he heard Mickey say a few moments later. Gary managed to lift his head and tilt his enormous helmet back far enough to see the leprechaun running past, slowing to mutter a few soft chants and wave his small but plump hand Gary's way.

"Lie still and stay that way!" Mickey said again, more forcefully, and then he disappeared into the thick brush.

Gary hardly comprehended anything at that dazed moment—until he heard the croaks and hoots and floppy footfalls and remembered the monstrous pursuit. His first instinct was to jump up and flee, but he could tell from the proximity of the hoots that the closing goblins would surely catch him before he went very far, probably before he ever got to his feet. Mickey's words rang in his thoughts and Gary was wise enough to understand that he had no practical choice but to put his trust in the leprechaun. He lay back flat, very still.

THE goblins, grouped together again, gained confidence with every step and every tree safely passed. They had gone beyond the area of Mickey's first illusion, though they had lost track of the nimble elf completely. It didn't trouble Geek and his surly friends, though, for they knew the general direction the fleeing human had taken—and there was just one footpath through the heavy brush in this area. Goblins could see in the dark, as could elfs, but humans were quite helpless in a thick and gloomy forest after sunset.

But it was that very night vision that betrayed the goblins again. Geek led them on wildly, hooting and beating at any hiding places in the bushes beside the trail. They skipped over roots and ducked under low branches, and scrambled across one unremarkable mound.

GARY, the unremarkable mound, tried hard to stifle his grunts as the goblin troupe thudded over him. One goblin hooked its foot between helmet and breastplate and crashed headlong onto Gary's legs. Gary thought he was surely doomed, but the creature simply got back up, brushed imaginary dirt off its filthy tunic, and continued down the path.

Then they were gone, their hoots trailing away in the distance. Gary didn't even try to stand. He lay quite still and helpless, his chest heaving as he tried futilely to calm himself. He had no idea what to do, where to go, and above everything else, he feared that his companions were surely dead or lost to him.

"Get up!" came a harsh cry a moment later. Gary recognized Kelsey's voice, then heard some light footsteps and sensed that the elf was bending over him.

Kelsey's sigh reflected as much anger as sorrow. "What mighty beast did this to you, poor soul?" Kelsey moaned, staring at Gary's backwards helmet. "Twisted your neck so completely . . ."

Gary reached up to straighten the great helm and the elf fell back in horror.

"I'm all right," Gary tried to explain, finally managing to turn the cumbersome thing.

"He's been stepped on, that's all," Mickey added, coming out of the underbrush to Kelsey's side. "Just a bump in the road to the stupid goblins' eyes."

"Then get up," Kelsey growled, embarrassed and angry. He reached down and roughly pulled Gary back to his feet.

"They'll not be gone long," Mickey remarked.

"Why were they here at all?" Kelsey replied grimly.

Mickey nodded, understanding where Kelsey's question was leading. Too many things seemed to be interrupting them to be explained away by coincidence. Alone, the nymph, the Prince, even the goblins, could be brushed aside as one of the many dangers of undertaking such a journey, but together, those ingredients added up to a conspiracy.

"And who might be talking to them all?" Mickey asked.

"To who?" Gary asked, trying to get included in the vague conversation.

"Who has the ear of kings and goblins alike?" Mickey went on, ignoring Gary. "And who in all the world might be making any suggestions to Leshiye?"

Kelsey didn't need to respond, for they both knew that there was only one possible solution to Mickey's questions.

"Then ye've got yet answers," Mickey snarled, suddenly gruff and dark. Gary looked at the leprechaun curiously, never having seen this side of the normally cheery sprite.

Still, Kelsey said nothing. He led them off silently to find a new place to camp.

They settled under the low-hanging boughs of a huge pine tree, quite removed from the forest outside. Despite the relative safety, though, neither Kelsey nor Mickey grew at ease. Mickey called up a tiny spot of light and took out the book, but Kelsey was on him in a blink.

"Dispel it!" the elf commanded in a soft but harsh whisper.

"It cannot be seen outside the branches," Mickey argued. "Ye mean to sit here in the dark?" He looked over to Gary. "Suren that one'd not get through the night without hurtin' himself."

Gary was more concerned with the tension in Kelsey's face than with Mickey's words. The elf seemed barely able to respond; the lines of his angular face creased under the strain of his clenched jaw. He looked at Gary and started to speak, but his golden eyes widened and he grinned weirdly, shaking his head.

"Just a bit o' reading?" Mickey asked, realizing what Kelsey had noticed and hoping the humorous sight—muddy goblin-sized footprints running down the front of Gary's armor—would bring some much-needed relief.

Kelsey moved to the natural wall, pushed aside some branches, and peered out through the tangle. Mickey took that as permission and he quickly popped his pipe in his mouth and found his place in the book.

Gary wanted to talk to the leprechaun or to Kelsey, to find out what they had decided concerning this unknown conspiracy, but he dared not say anything as the night deepened. He sat down against the tree trunk and tried to get as comfortable as possible, though he now knew better than to take off anything more than his helmet. He hoped that he would find sleep again and hoped that this time it would bring him back awake in his proper place.

He didn't believe it, though. Whatever this was—insanity, death, or perhaps a wild but very real journey—Gary was now fully convinced that it was not a dream.

He had just begun to nod off when Kelsey prodded him. Looking up into the elf's stern visage, Gary at first wondered what he had done wrong this time.

"You take this," Kelsey explained, handing Gary the long leather case that held the legendary spear. Kelsey untied it at one end and slid out the marvelous weapon. It was pitch-black, shaft and head, and even in the dim light, its polished tip gleamed as though it held some inner brooding light.

Gary couldn't pull his gaze from that crafted spearhead. Its basic shape was triangular, as long and nearly as thick as his forearm. Small barbs ran along the edges of the front tip, and the back two points were elongated and curled up towards the front. Runes, ancient and wonderfully crafted with swirling images of noble warriors and fearsome beasts, canvassed the black metal of the head and shaft.

"When it is forged whole, it will stand half again your height," Kelsey said. He gave the bared weapon to Gary to let the man feel the strength of its iron.

Gary grasped it tightly. It appeared as though it would weigh a hundred pounds, but when Kelsey let go, Gary found it to be surprisingly light.

And incredibly balanced—Gary felt as though he could heave the thing a hundred yards.

"The magic," Kelsey explained, understanding Gary's confused expression. For perhaps the first time since he had met Gary, the elf truly smiled. He took the weapon, slid it back into its case, and retied the end.

"You want me to carry it?" Gary asked him.

"Our trials are not ended," Kelsey replied. "Even if we elude the goblins, I know now that there will be other dangers along our path. I remain dedicated to my quest, but, on my word, I must keep safe the artifacts of King Cedric. If the goblins fall upon us, I will lead them away. You must then get the spear and armor back to Baron Pwyll." There was no compromise in Kelsey's tone.

"Give me your word of honor," he demanded.

Gary nodded and Kelsey walked away.

Gary was glad that Kelsey had entrusted him with so important a task, but the elf's uncharacteristic behavior only made him more uncomfortable with the events at hand. Something very dangerous was going on around him, something that even his new friends, who seemed so superior, greatly feared.

Mickey did not alleviate Gary's concerns a moment later, when the leprechaun threw *The Hobbit* off of Gary's chest and gave a resounding "Oh, pooh!"

"What's the matter?" Gary asked, scooping up the book.

"Calling himself an historian, is yer J.R.R. Tolkien fellow?" Mickey asked incredulously. "And what a pretentious sort to be calling himself by his initials like that! Afraid to use his whole name?"

"What?" was all that Gary could sputter.

"Read at the folded page!" Mickey replied. Gary found the mark easily enough, but he could hardly read the flowing runes that Mickey had placed where the typeset had once been.

"Sunlight turning trolls to stone?" Mickey spouted, seeing Gary at a loss. "Bag o' blarney! Every fool's knowing that to be a rumor started by the trolls alone. They're the ones carving troll statues, making people think it's trolls turned by sunlight. How many stupid travelers have turned back on the trolls chasing them, pointing a finger and laughing when the sun peeked over the rim? How many stupid travelers then found themselves stuffed into a troll's hungry mouth?"

"What the hell are you talking about?" Gary cried.

Kelsey jumped in between them, his flashing eyes reminding them that silence was their ally.

Mickey waved his hand furiously, his magic pulling *The Hobbit* from Gary's grasp and levitating it back to his waiting hand. "Mr. J.R.R. Tolkien, Historian," he muttered sarcastically. "How many stupid travelers will get eaten after reading yer bag o' blarney?"

Gary just looked at Kelsey and smiled sheepishly.

The nervous elf did not smile back.

SEVEN

Wet with Blood

THE three unlikely companions ate a meal of berries and bread and started off just before dawn, Kelsey leading them through the tangle of underbrush far from the main road. Both the elf and the leprechaun covered the rough ground with little trouble and not much more than an occasional rustle, but Gary, in his heavy armor, stumbled and crashed with every step, broke apart branches and committed wholesale slaughter on the many unfortunate plants in his path.

"We'd best get him to the road," Mickey said after only a short while.

"The goblins may be watching the road," Kelsey answered grimly.

"Better that the goblins kill him than he kills himself," Mickey retorted. "Besides, with the clamor that one's making, all the wood'll know of our passing!"

Kelsey gave Gary yet another of his increasingly common derisive stares. Gary wanted to argue back, to ensure the elf that he could make it through, but unfortunately he picked that moment to hook his toe on yet another snag. Down he went heavily and noisily, and the exasperated elf announced, before he even bothered to pick Gary up, that the road seemed the safer course.

For all of his wounded pride, Gary did have a better time with the flat road than the thicket, though the day grew hot, particularly so under the thick padding of the armor. Gary had thought that his body was getting used to the weight, that, except for the heat, he was actually beginning to feel somewhat comfortable in the stuff. But a short while later, he came to believe that the armor felt even heavier and less balanced than it had the day before. Gary didn't understand the change until Mickey abruptly appeared, comfortably perched on his shoulder.

"You've been sitting there all along," Gary accused him.

"Ye did not even notice," Mickey replied. "I weigh but a pittance next to that armor ye carry. If I'd stayed invisible, ye'd have carried me all the way to Dvergamal without a word o' complaint!"

"Dvergamal?" The strange word deflected Gary's ire.

"Voice o' the dwarf," Mickey explained. "A name given to the stony mountainsides where we'll find the buldrefolk, the dwarfs."

Gary considered the revelations for a moment, wondering if he had heard those curious names somewhere back in his own world. "Well, why didn't you stay invisible?" he scolded Mickey, halfheartedly trying to push the bothersome leprechaun from his shoulder—a quite impossible feat given Mickey's uncanny agility and the restricting shoulder plates of Gary's armor.

"I've some reading to do," Mickey answered calmly, and he promptly produced *The Hobbit.* "Can't do that when me and the book are invisible, now can I?'

Gary was seriously considering diving sidelong to the ground, just to annoy the annoying leprechaun, but Kelsey turned back on them suddenly, ferociously.

"Silence!" the elf commanded in hushed but very firm tones. "We walk in dangerous . . ." Kelsey paused suddenly and Gary could see the elf's fine muscles tighten.

In a movement too swift for Gary to follow, Kelsey snapped his sword from its scabbard and leaped straight up, leading with his deadly blade. There came a squeak from a thick-leafed branch overhanging the road then a goblin tumbled from the thicket to land dead at Kelsey's feet.

Gary felt a jolt on his side and looked down to see a crude arrow lying on the ground, its tip snapped from the impact against his metal armor.

"Mickey," he started to say, but the leprechaun was not to be seen, nor to be felt.

Hoots and shouts went up all about the sides of the road and the goblins were upon them.

For all that he had been forewarned about Kelsey's battle prowess, Gary could not have imagined anything as precise and perfect as the elf-lord's movements. Kelsey danced a ballet, silent except for the swish of his fine sword and the screams of those enemies he encountered.

A large and fat goblin came upon the elf first, wrapping him in a bear hug from behind. As if he had anticipated the move, Kelsey stuck his sword arm far out in front, keeping it from the cumbersome creature's grasp. The sword dipped through the elf's legs and came slicing up between the goblin's legs.

The monster let go, right away.

From across the road, in front of the elf, two goblins charged out, holding a net between them. Kelsey crouched low and let them get right near to him, then leaped straight up, planting his feet atop the net and driving it down beneath him. The overbalanced goblins lurched helplessly and Kelsey's sword flashed left, then right. The gleaming silver blade appeared crimson now, and two more goblins crumpled.

So entranced by the spectacle in front of him, Gary hardly understood his own peril. He could not outrun the goblins, could not even hope to make it to the side of the road and hide in the underbrush.

An arrow bonked off the side of his helmet. He spun quickly to the side (though his loose-fitting helmet did not). Still, he saw enough to be afraid, for the goblin archer was now charging him, screaming wildly and holding a spiked club high above its gruesome head.

Something nicked Gary on the other side of the head, straightening his helmet as it flew by, and Gary registered the scene clearly as the heavy rock soared past him, crashing right into the charging goblin's face. The monster's head snapped back with a loud cracking noise and it dropped straight to the ground.

"Oh, good shootin'!" Gary heard Mickey congratulate himself from somewhere behind.

Three more goblins had surrounded Kelsey, coming at the skilled elf in measured, defensive strides. Time favored the goblins, for they had many allies

lying in wait along this entire area, and hoots and cries echoed from every direction as more of the filthy creatures rushed to join the fight.

"Run!" Kelsey commanded Gary. "Back to Dilnamarra!" Then the elf charged
his three opponents, quickly reversed direction, and broke free, scampering
back towards Gary.

Gary turned and lumbered away, wondering what in the world he would do
when Kelsey, and then the goblins, overtook him.

But Kelsey had other ideas. He had almost caught up to Gary, and had purposely allowed the goblins to keep pace, when he wheeled about suddenly and
threw himself into the goblins' midst.

The startled creatures hadn't even leveled their spears, and they would
never get the chance. A shield smash downed the one on Kelsey's left. He thrust
out to the right with his sword, catching another monster cleanly in the throat,
then buried the third in a tight embrace and bore it to the ground.

Other goblins were coming out of the brush, but they were all farther up
ahead on the road—the trap had been sprung too quickly, before the companions had gotten past the first ranks of the creatures—leaving Gary a clear path
back the way he and his companions had come.

And Gary did run, as best as he could, and it took him a long moment to
wonder why Kelsey hadn't sprinted by. He dared to stop and turn, and he saw
the elf struggling in the dirt with one foe, another dazed goblin nearby trying to
pick himself up.

And a dozen more monsters charging down the road.

"Keep running!" Mickey cried from the brush to the side. "Ye can do nothing for him, lad, but to save the precious items!"

Gary cared nothing for the armor, or even for the legendary spear that
seemed so valuable to the people of the land. His gaze focused only on Kelsey,
not yet truly a friend, perhaps, but one who had selflessly thrown himself back
on the goblins so that Gary could escape. Gary had never considered himself
overly brave, and he most assuredly was scared to death at that brutal moment,
but he could not leave Kelsey to such a fate. He hoisted his spear for a desperate
throw.

"*Do not throw it!*" rang a voice in his head. "*What weapon will thee fight
with when the spear is loosed?*"

Not about to take the time to argue, Gary leveled the spear and charged, a
primal scream that was as much terror as anger erupting from his lips. The
dazed goblin to Kelsey's left started for the struggling elf, then saw Gary coming
and hooted in glee, abruptly changing its course.

"Now what?" Gary moaned, and he tried to veer to the side, but stumbled instead and crashed heavily against a thick tree. As soon as he righted himself, he hoisted the spear again, desperate to stop the charging monster.

"*Do not throw it!*" came that inner voice again.

"Then what?" Gary answered silently.

"*Take it up and fight with it!*" implored the voice.

Gary braced the spear against the side of his heavy shield and wondered how he might maneuver the weapon well enough with one hand to possibly defeat the goblin.

The monster was almost on him; Gary could see the saliva dripping over its thick bottom lip from between its pointy yellow teeth.

"*Not like that!*" screamed the inner voice.

Gary's helpless frustration apparently sufficed as an answer, for the voice quickly explained. "*Against the tree,*" it said calmly. "*Brace the spear's butt end against the tree.*"

Gary considered the words. He was out of time; the goblin was upon him.

"*Now!*" cried the voice. Gary didn't even think about his movements as he followed the undeniable command.

The goblin foolishly barreled in, its own spear leading. Gary's weapon caught fast on the tree; his shield deflected the goblin's spear up high and to the side. Then the monster was up against him, its breath hot and smelly in his face, its bulbous, vein-streaked eyes boring into his.

GEEK led the goblin charge down the road. The elf was gaining an upper hand in his struggles, but the goblin knew that even if the elf won, he could never recover in time to escape the approaching horde. The plan seemed so beautifully executed; wouldn't Lady Ceridwen be thrilled!

Suddenly the road was fully blocked by a huge spiderweb. Geek shrieked (even goblins are terrified of the merciless giant spiders), dropped his spear, and covered up, plunging headlong into the tangle. Those others up in front shared similar fates, and the trailing goblins halted their charge and looked about in confusion.

KELSEY finally got atop the goblin, pinning its spear with his shield. He pushed free of the creature's stubborn grasp, getting into a kneeling position, and put his sword in line.

The doomed goblin whined and frantically threw its arm across its face. Kelsey's fine sword dove right through the arm, and right through the face.

Kelsey looked up the road, expecting to be overwhelmed. What he saw instead brought a smile to his dirtied lips. A dozen goblins thrashed and rolled, caught fast by an illusionary web. A score more stood behind, jostling each other and scratching their fat heads.

Then Kelsey heard a horn, back behind him, and the thunder of hoofbeats rolling down the road.

"The web'll not fool them for long," Mickey whispered from the side. "We should be going."

THE creature's mouth opened wide in a silent, agonized scream. Staring into its gaping, yellow-toothed maw, Gary feared that it meant to bite him. The goblin's features contorted weirdly; a few sudden convulsions brought some blood out of its mouth.

Then Gary truly understood. He still held his spear, out straight, and the goblin's heaving tummy was right against that hand.

"Oh my God," Gary muttered without thinking.

The goblin jerked, showering Gary in blood, then went limp. Gary let go of the spear, watching mesmerized as the dead thing toppled to the side, the front half of his spear protruding from the creature's back, covered in blood and gore and entrails.

The young man stood very still for a long moment, not even remembering to breathe.

"*Well done, goodly young sprout,*" congratulated that voice in his head, but Gary wanted no applause, didn't feel a hero, didn't feel anything except sick to his stomach.

He put his head in his sweaty hands and tried to find the strength to retrieve his stained weapon.

The sound of approaching riders brought him back to the situation at hand. A score of armored knights charged down the road, banners waving and lances leveled. Gary forgot his horror for a brief moment and thought their salvation at hand. He lifted his arm and hailed loudly through the growing tumult.

Something crashed heavily into his back and the surrounding brush seemed to rush up and catch him. His first thoughts were that a goblin had tackled him, but the hand that came up under his chin was not gnarly and scratchy, like a goblin's, but delicate, though strong.

"What?" he started to ask, but found his head jerked back roughly and a fine-edged, bloodstained sword came in against his exposed neck.

"Silence," Kelsey whispered into his ear, but the command seemed hardly necessary with the elf's blade scraping a clear warning against Gary's throat.

"Prince Geldion," Mickey added. "Me thinking's that it should be a fair fight." The leprechaun looked back down the road at the goblins and blinked his eyes. The creatures stopped their thrashing as the illusionary web disappeared, and they gave it no more thought as the new nemesis, Prince Geldion and his guard, charged into them.

The first moments of battle went all the knights' way. Lances struck home and horses trampled helpless, sprawling goblins. But many more of the monsters were still filtering out of the woods to join the battle, and soon the Prince and his company found themselves tangled in a mire of goblin flesh. One rider was borne down under the weight of a dozen creatures, and he and his horse were swallowed up before they even settled to the ground.

"We have to help them!" Gary cried, and he struggled against Kelsey's loosened grasp.

Kelsey slapped him on the back of the helmet and put his full weight over Gary to hold him down. "Whoever wins would indeed be pleased to see us so easily delivered," the elf said grimly.

"The riders came for us?"

"It would seem so, lad," Mickey answered. "What other business would Prince Geldion have on the eastern road? It's no secret in Dilnamarra that we meant to go to the mountains."

Out on the road, the goblin press continued, but the knights were skilled fighters and seemed to be more than holding their own.

"We should be on our way," Kelsey commented. "The goblins could flee at any time, and if the Prince fathoms that we are in the area, we'll not have an easy time escaping." He crawled off of Gary's back and, still crawling, led Gary deeper into the underbrush. Soon they were up and trotting at a cautious pace, heading east and paralleling the road, but deep within the concealing shadows of the thick woods.

"I'm thinking that yer chosen quest might take a bit o' doing," Mickey remarked after the sounds of the continuing battle at last faded far behind them. "Ye've got enemies coming at ye from both sides, it'd seem."

"Why would the Prince . . ." Gary started to ask, but Kelsey cut him short.

"Both seek similar results, I would agree," the elf answered Mickey. "But they do not work in unison—that is our hope."

"Aye," Mickey replied. "One hand tangled the other."

"What are you talking about?" Gary demanded. "And why would the Prince . . ."

"It is of no concern to you," Kelsey interrupted once again.

"If someone's trying to kill me, I consider it my business," Gary replied as forcefully as he had ever spoken to the grim elf.

Unexpectedly Kelsey did not scold him, or even flash him a threatening glare. "You did well in the battle," the elf said sincerely. "Your bravery surprised me, as did your skill in handling the spear."

Gary shrugged, a bit embarrassed. "Thank Mickey," he explained. "He talked me through the whole fight."

Kelsey's look to the leprechaun was no less confused than the leprechaun's own expression. "Did I, then?" Mickey asked curiously.

"Well, you helped anyway," Gary replied, but his own face twisted in confusion as he came to realize that his guess was not correct. "It's curious that your accent changed when you communicated telepathically," Gary went on, trying to resolve the situation logically. "I never thought about it before, but I guess it makes sense. We all think the same way, even if we talk differently, and I didn't really hear words. I heard thoughts, if that makes any sense."

Mickey took a long draw on his pipe and nodded to Kelsey. "It wasn't me in yer head," the leprechaun explained to Gary.

"When did these inner voices begin?" Kelsey asked.

"Only at the battle," Gary replied, now growing concerned.

"And what do you carry on your back?"

"Just the spe—" Gary fumbled around to grasp the leather case, pulling it in front of him. "This thing talks?" he asked, his voice only a whisper.

"*Thing?*" rang a perturbed voice in his head.

"Of course it cannot talk," Mickey explained. "But its magic is strong, among the strongest in all the land."

"Sentient?" Gary reasoned.

"Aye, to its possessor," answered Mickey. "And ye'd be wise to listen to it carefully—that spear's seen more battle than the rest of us."

Gary sent the leather pack swinging back around him as though he was afraid of the thing.

"Be glad," Kelsey said to him. "You have an ally now who will aid you greatly in the trials ahead." A horn blew back down the road, once and then again, and Kelsey spun about. "And the trials behind," the elf added grimly.

"The Prince has won," Mickey remarked. "No goblin'd blow a note so clear."

"Then we must hope that Geldion has suffered too many losses to continue his pursuit," said Kelsey. "Cowtangle will soon end and the land between the wood and the mountains is clear."

An image of running across hedge-lined fields came into Gary's thoughts, with himself stumbling and struggling to get over each barrier, while the great armored knights pursuing him easily jumped their steeds along. Surely this adventure had taken on the dressings of a nightmare, with Gary running slowly, too slowly, to outdistance his determined pursuers.

They came out of Cowtangle Wood a short time later, as Kelsey had predicted. The mountains towered much closer now, seeming far less than the five days away Kelsey had claimed them to be when he had first discovered the goblin tracks. But as the day moved on, Gary understood the illusion. The ground was uneven here, rolling up and down regularly, and often at a steep pitch, and after four hours of walking, the mountains seemed no closer than they had when Gary had first exited the woods.

Kelsey veered north from the road then, explaining that he had no desire to go near to the town of Braemar.

"Probably find more traps waiting for us there," Mickey readily agreed.

They came to the bank of a river, running swiftly westwards from the mountains, a short while later. "The River Oustle," Mickey explained. "It'll take us right near to Dvergamal, though we'll get away from it before we get there, I expect, to keep around the town of Drochit."

Kelsey nodded at the leprechaun's reasoning.

Though this was no road, they made good time, and no evident pursuit, goblin or knight, came down the trail behind them.

GEEK stumbled out of Cowtangle Wood to the southwest, a region of thick mosses and steamy bogs. Not many of his band remained alive, the goblin knew; perhaps he was the only one. He plopped down on a patch of moss and put his pointy chin in his rough hands.

"Drat the luck," he muttered.

He hadn't even considered yet what he might tell Lady Ceridwen, who was sure to be none too pleased.

"Drat the luck," the goblin spat again. "Stupid princes."

He heard a rustle to the side and jumped to the ready, thinking the knights had found him. He saw nothing, though, and figured it to be just the wind in the birch trees.

When he turned back, he nearly swooned. A shimmering blue and white light hovered over the ground he had just been sitting upon, gradually taking shape. Geek gulped audibly, recognizing the spectacle.

Lady Ceridwen stood before him.

"Dear Geek," the sorceress began, her voice sounding as a cat's purr. "Do tell me what happened. Who has harmed my dear Geek?"

"Mens," Geek replied. "Many mens, Prince's mens. What does they be doing in wood?"

"Perhaps," Ceridwen replied, pursing her lips, her flashing eyes staring far away. "Perhaps they were working for me." Her glare fell with full force over the now-trembling Geek. "Perhaps they were doing as I instructed, instead of interfering!"

"Geek did it for Lady," the goblin whined, falling to his knees and slobbering wet kisses all over Ceridwen's delicate hand.

The sorceress pulled away, revolted. "Why were you here?" she asked calmly.

"Geek catches elf and killses man," the goblin sputtered. "For Lady. Geek take armor—for Lady!"

"Did Lady tell Geek to do this?" Ceridwen prompted calmly.

The goblin shook his head. "Geek thinks . . ."

"Did Lady tell Geek to think?" Ceridwen asked, her voice louder, revealing some of her anger.

The goblin found no reply.

Ceridwen stepped back and drew out a thin wand from her sleeve.

"Lady!" Geek pleaded, and then he said no more, for frogs have little command of the common language.

Ceridwen walked over and casually picked up the pitiful creature. She moved to toss him into a nearby pool, then reconsidered and started away, petting Geek and casually promising him all sorts of adventure.

The merciless sorceress carried the goblin-frog to the other side of the small swamp, to a place where she knew a fat snake made its home.

EIGHT

Dvergamal

THEY traveled easily over the next couple of days, though Kelsey set a swift pace and only stopped for camp long after sunset, and had them on the trail again before the dawn. After the battle of Cowtangle Wood, Gary offered no arguments against the elf's haste; Mickey, of course, kept up his steady stream of under-the-breath remarks every step of the way.

The journey to the foothills crossed rolling but not broken land, and after the initial soreness of the unfamiliar armor had worn off, Gary found that he could get along quite well in the bulky suit.

Then they came to Dvergamal.

Sheer and jagged, bare and bony-hard, the mountains seemed a barrier that no man could hope to pass. Cliffs rose up a thousand feet; gullies beyond them dropped a thousand more than that, and all the way seemed a confusing criss-cross of narrow and perilous trails. Kelsey seemed confident enough of his steps as he found a path and started up. Mickey, just a leprechaun's stride behind, never even took his eyes off *The Hobbit.*

Truly Gary felt embarrassed at his own fears, and that gave him the courage to fall in line. Each step out, crossing deep ravines, winding along the sides of mountains, did little to bolster his confidence, though, and he continually found himself wondering how much a suit of mail might cushion so long a fall.

Where Kelsey skipped, Mickey rambled absently and Gary crawled. Short climbs which the elf took with a single leap, grab, and twist, and Mickey by simply floating up, Gary had to be threatened, then hauled and levitated, just to get over.

And all the while for poor Gary loomed death-promising drops, drops that grew ever deeper as the small troupe wound its way ever higher into Dvergamal. Sometimes their trail was open to both sides, sheer drops, left and right. Other times they disappeared into impossibly narrow crevices, twenty feet deep and barely a few feet wide and bordered by high walls of sharp stone.

That first night in the mountains, they camped out in the open (for lack of choice), on the side of a mountain where the ledge was at its widest, and this being only about five feet. The stiff wind bit at them, foiled any fire-making attempts, and threatened to push them over the edge if they did not take care.

When the sky mercifully lightened and Kelsey led them off, Gary's eyes showed the dark rings of a sleepless night.

"Set the pace a might slower this day," Mickey bade Kelsey, seeing Gary's condition. "Weary's not the way for crossing Dvergamal."

Kelsey looked back at Gary and huffed loudly. "The journey is hard," the elf scolded sternly. "Why did you not sleep?"

A helpless expression crossed Gary's face.

"He's not used to such heights," the leprechaun answered for him. "Be easy on the lad; ye've asked a lot of him these past days, and he's answered ye with little complaint."

Kelsey huffed again and started off, but he did keep the pace easier.

————

THE large raven spotted the troupe later that day and marked their surprising progress with some concern. Leshiye, Geldion, and Geek had all failed her, and now Ceridwen, in her black-feathered form, had to find another obstacle to throw in Kelsey's path. She knew Kelsey's destination, and her growing respect for the resourceful elf only heightened her fears that he might get past the next expected barriers—dwarf echoes, hurled boulders, and water slicks.

"But how far will you get if the buldrefolk know that you mean to steal Geno?" the raven cackled. "And where will Kelsey turn if Geno is no more?" Several devious options crossed Ceridwen's thoughts as she sped along the mountain updrafts and began her own search for the reclusive dwarfs.

"WE'LL have no talking from here on in," Mickey whispered to Gary as they crossed one high and sharp ridge. "The mountains have ears all about us, more foe than friend." The leprechaun put a stubby finger over his pursed lips, gave Gary a wink, and skittered up ahead, back in line between Gary and Kelsey.

Long shadows marked the jagged mountains as scattered dark clouds swept along on the wind overhead, or sometimes below. Peaks disappeared in a veil of gray. Crevices and jutting outcroppings cut sharply from every angle, and rivulets of water, from the morning rains and morning mists, slipped down every mountainside, some dark under ominous clouds, others glittering in sunlight, skipping easily across the stones.

Gary wondered what power had shaped this region, what force had so blasted and torn the earth. He had viewed this scene in his imagination, and in the illustrations of imaginative artists, before, while reading books of prehistory, of the violent upheaval that split the continents and raised the mountains. The preternatural edge of stone before the eons of wind and water beat it down and tamed it.

And that primordial, majestic scene spread out all about him, coupled with the interspersed sunlight and Mickey's warning, added greatly to the out-of-place human's trepidation. How insignificant he seemed beside the cliffs of Dvergamal! Gary bent low to the rock along the narrow trail, feeling a strength in the land itself that could blot him out in the blink of his eye.

What creatures might call this land home? he wondered, imagining beasts of incredible might crouched behind every stone, or watching from nearby ledges.

His fears slowed him, and by the time he bothered to notice, Mickey and Kelsey were far ahead, turning a bend that would put them out of sight.

"Wait up!" Gary called, forgetting the leprechaun's words.

"Wait up!" came a response from the side.

"Up," replied another distant stone. "Up . . . up . . . up . . . up . . . up? . . . up!"

Gary looked all about, startled and confused by the suddenness of the echoes and the changes in their inflection.

"I told ye to hold yer words!" Mickey scolded, spinning about.

"Words . . . words . . . wo . . . wo . . . words . . . rds . . . rds," the echoes grumbled back, resonating through every valley.

Kelsey and Mickey scrambled back to join Gary. "What is it?" Gary whispered harshly, seeing from his companions' expressions that these were indeed more than ordinary echoes.

"It," the hidden voices replied. "It . . . itititit . . . it?"

"Dvergamal," Mickey said under his breath. "Voice o' the dwarfs. They're playing with us, as they do with all who speak in their mountains." His voice had risen as he talked and the echoes took up a responsive chant.

"Oh, shut yer mouths!" Mickey shouted.

"Shut yer mouths . . . yer mouths . . . shut them good! . . . yer mouths."

"Shut them good?" Gary asked incredulously.

"Dwarfs like to put their own thoughts in," Mickey explained dryly.

"Come along, then," Kelsey interjected. "And keep silent—or they will follow our every move."

"Yes, do come," answered the echoes that were not echoes. "And keep silent . . . silent . . . silent . . . ssssh!"

Gary's trepidations only increased, but this time he worked much harder to keep close behind Kelsey and Mickey.

DOWN a deep ravine, amidst a tumble of boulders, the dwarven mimickers congratulated themselves.

"A bit of fun, that," Dvalin, the chiseled dwarf with wild black hair atop his thick head, but not a bit of fuzz on his cheeks and chin, clucked to his brother Durin, an ancient specimen, gray-haired and with a beard long enough to tuck into his boots if he so chose. Both dwarfs were overjoyed to hear the passage of strangers in the mountains. It was their month to guard the passes, a normally tedious duty, and playing the echo game with a passing troupe came as a most welcomed diversion.

"If they keep to the high ridges, we will catch them again crossing the north side," Dvalin reasoned, rubbing his stony, stubby hands together (which produced a rocky, grating sound).

"And if they turn down low, their path will bring them right past us," added

Durin, adjusting his wide belt to straighten his beard. "Perhaps we should gather some of the others . . ."

"Dogtail their every step!" Dvalin finished, thinking the idea positively grand. Dvalin turned to leave but stopped abruptly as a large raven flapped down to land on a rock only a foot from his prominent nose.

Both startled dwarfs hooted and rushed about, bumping into each other and into boulders—both types of collision making similar sounds—grabbing wildly for their belted weapons, mattock for Durin, axe for Dvalin.

"Boulders!" howled Durin a moment later, regaining his wits and adjusting his belt once more. "It is only a bird!"

"Only a bird indeed!" Ceridwen retorted sharply, sending the dwarfs into another bouncing dance.

"Brother," Dvalin began very slowly, fingering his small but wicked-looking axe, "did that bird speak to us?"

"You have never met a talking raven?" Ceridwen asked, cocking her little black head. "The memories of dwarfs are not so long as the tales tell!"

"Talking ravens!" the brothers howled at each other, and then the stones rumbled their cry again and again in a true echo.

"A thousand thousand pardons," Durin answered, dipping into a bow that dragged his long silver beard on the ground.

"None of your race has been seen in Dvergamal in a grandfather dwarf's memory," added Dvalin, similarly dipping impossibly low.

"Well, one has been seen now," Ceridwen said a bit more sharply than she intended. "One has come to tell you to ware the elf, the man, and the sprite you so gladly taunt. The elf most of all. His name is Kelsenellenelvial . . ."

"Elfs have such stupid names," Durin remarked dryly.

"And he has come in search of a smith," Ceridwen finished.

"No, no," replied Dvalin. "We cannot have that. Not for an elf; not at any price!"

"He does not mean to pay," Ceridwen explained. "He means to steal. And the smith he has in mind . . ."

"Geno!" the dwarfs hooted together, and they hopped about, rebounding around the boulder tumble until they finally popped free of it.

"We shall see!" insisted Dvalin.

"And thank you, O great speaking raven," added Durin, dipping another bow as he rolled away.

Ceridwen watched them disappear into the shadows, then flew off to further ensure her success.

KELSEY pulled up in a shallow cave a short while later, sheltered, he hoped, from the eyes and ears of the mountains.

"We are close," the elf announced when Mickey and Gary entered. "I have seen the dwarfsign."

"Dwarfsign?" Gary had to ask.

"Scrapings on the stone," Mickey explained. "I never did meet a dwarf who could pass a good piece o' stone without taking a taste of it."

This time, Gary kept his questions to himself.

"They know we are about," Kelsey went on, then he paused and looked at Gary as though he expected Gary to interrupt once again. "Since one of us chose to reveal our whereabouts," he finished a moment later, his golden eyes boring into the bumbling human. "But travelers are not uncommon in Dvergamal, and most go to all lengths to keep clear of the dwarfs."

"They'll not be expecting us," Mickey put in. "No wise folks'd go looking for them."

Kelsey's unrelenting glare settled on the leprechaun. He pulled a parchment, a map, from a pocket in his cloak and spread it on the floor. "We are here," he explained, pointing to one of many mountains on the scroll. They all seemed quite unremarkable to Gary, but he didn't question Kelsey's proclamation.

Kelsey moved his finger a short distance across the map. "Here lies the Firth of Buldre, the falls," he said. "And here, too, somewhere, we shall find Geno Hammerthrower."

"Somewhere?" Gary dared to ask. "How will you know for certain?"

Kelsey didn't blink for a long, long while. He replaced the map and headed toward the cave entrance. "Come," he bade his companions. "We must get to the smith and back out again before the shadows engulf the mountains. I do not wish to be in the region after sunset while holding a captive."

"What happens if we come across some dwarfs other than this Geno?" Gary asked Mickey before the leprechaun could scamper after Kelsey.

"I told ye before," Mickey replied grimly, "elfs and dwarfs don't get on well."

The three had barely gotten back on the open trail when a growling rumble shook the mountainside. It came from within the stony ground, yet it rolled as loudly as a thunderstroke. Kelsey and Mickey exchanged concerned glances, but the elf pressed ahead, picking up the pace. They were terribly exposed now, transversing the top ridge of a double-peaked mountain.

A second trail broke off from the first, diving down between the twin peaks. Kelsey considered the course for just a moment, then plunged ahead, thinking the lower trails safer. He had only gone a dozen long strides, though, when the ground opened up suddenly before his lead foot. Like an animal maw, the earth snapped shut. Kelsey's uncanny agility saved him, for though he was startled by the sudden break, he managed to twist around to the side to stay his momentum.

The earthen mouth opened again and snapped shut, like some hungry child straining to reach a morsel that had dropped to his chin.

"Might that they know why we're here?" Mickey asked.

Kelsey didn't answer. He rushed around the snapping maw and down the path, drawing his sword and muttering with every step.

"Come along, lad," Mickey coaxed. "And don't ye get too close to the mouth!"

Gary watched the snapping earth for some time before he mustered the courage to continue. He couldn't imagine any power that could bring the ground to life like that, and he suspected the maw to be an illusion. His suspicions, however, did not give him the courage to march across the opening and prove his theory.

As they continued on, Gary tried his best to keep up, but in the heavy armor he was no match for Kelsey's frantic strides. Worse than his fears of separation, Gary now heard his clanking and thumping echoing back at him from every direction.

And he was certain that those echoes were not from any natural formations. He thought he heard giggling from one side, but all that he saw there was a broken cluster of fallen boulders. He shook his head, telling himself that it was just his imagination.

Then one of the boulders rose off the ground.

"Mickey!"

Gary's yell came just in time. The boulder went soaring through the air, and would surely have smashed in the back of Kelsey's head, but the leprechaun spun about and pointed a finger at the approaching rock, countering the magic and holding it still in midair.

"Run on!" Kelsey ordered, and he rushed away. More boulders shuddered, as if to life, then rose up, and the three companions scrambled furiously to find some cover or simply to get out of range.

Gary felt better this time when Mickey appeared perched on his shoulder.

"Keep going, lad," the leprechaun prodded, waving one finger about in the air. "I'll catch any that's coming from behind!"

To Gary's dismay, they were soon back on an exposed ledge, with a deep gorge to their left. The ground sloped more gradually to Gary's right, and he considered running down that way. But Mickey, apparently understanding Gary's thoughts, told him to keep in line behind Kelsey and trust in the elf's judgment.

Soon they heard a dull, continuous roar, and then the perpetual mist from the towering waterfalls, the Firth of Buldre, came into sight, not so far to the left of the fairly straight trail. Gary didn't dare look behind him; he could tell from Mickey's grumbling and wild, jerking movements that flying rocks were still in pursuit.

Up ahead, Kelsey stopped suddenly and whacked his fine sword against a boulder on the side of the trail. Gary didn't understand until he got up close enough to see that the rock had reached out an arm to grab at the passing elf!

"Dwarf magic," Mickey muttered, then he yelled, "Duck, lad!"

Gary lurched forward and stumbled, unable to break his weighted momentum.

The boulder shot by him, a near miss, then continued on to slam heavily into the rock holding Kelsey. Both stones split apart and the shocking jolt sent the elf sprawling to the ground.

Gary lumbered by, fighting for his balance, reaching for the downed elf. Another rock skipped alongside him, clipping his shin. The earth roared and trembled, and Mickey tumbled from Gary's shoulder.

"Kelsey!" Gary called, and he finally skidded to a halt on the edge of the trail. He turned about to regard his elven companion, then found his own troubles as the rocks broke away under his feet.

"Catch him!" he heard Kelsey yell to Mickey, but the leprechaun, already holding two large stones motionless in the air, had no magic left for Gary.

The air rushed past him; his shield twisted painfully behind him, holding hostage his strapped arm. He felt the fine mist as he descended below the level of the waterfalls, several streams of water eagerly rushing and diving over the ledge.

That horrible moment did not feel like any dream to Gary Leger. The blur, the rush of air, was too real; he knew that he would not awaken safely in his own bed. The continuous thunder of the Firth of Buldre drowned out his pitiful screams.

And then he hit with force enough to rattle every bone in his body, in a pool protected from the tumult of the falls by a rock jetty. Everything seemed to move in slow motion as Gary floundered, not comprehending which way was up. His helmed head clanked against rocks; the current, the aches, and the weight of his armor fought against his every move. Then his foot hooked on a chunk of stone, and his momentum, as he rolled his body back over the leg, brought his head and shoulders clear of the cold water.

Gary gasped and sputtered as the water drained from his helmet. He kept enough wits about him to throw his shield arm over some nearby rocks, hooking the bulky item securely. He hung there for what seemed like many minutes, finally dragging himself half out of the pool, getting enough of his weight onto the rocks to keep him from sliding back in, at least.

He could hear nothing above the thunderous falls, could feel nothing beyond the hard stone and the chilling bite of the water, and his long wet hair hung in his eyes. Somehow he managed to get a numbed finger into the helmet's eye slit and brush the hair aside.

And then he glimpsed a wondrous sight indeed.

All about him, the water cascaded down the hundred-foot cliff face in dozens of separate falls, barely visible through the perpetual mist. Huge chunks of rock stuck up out of the basin pools, stubborn sentinels against the relentless onslaught, defying the pounding water. In this basin, many of the mountain streams created by the seasonal melt came together, collecting below the falls to form the birthplace of the River Oustle.

From the angle where he was lying, Gary could also see behind the largest of the falls. Instead of the expected stone wall, though, there loomed a cave, lighted within from the blazing fire of an open hearth. Gary struggled a bit to the side to get a better view. There was a table in the little room, with an empty platter and a large flagon atop it, and a bench filled with ironworking tools: tongs, hammers, and the like.

The single occupant, bandy-legged but broad-shouldered, stood before the hearth, swinging a huge hammer easily at the end of one of his lean, sinewy arms. His sandy-brown hair hung straight under a tall knitted cap and he continually flicked his head, as if to move some strands from in front of his face. The creature could not have been more than half Gary's height, half again taller than Mickey, but there was a solidness about this one, a powerful presence that Gary could sense clearly, even from this distance.

Gary knew it was a dwarf, though he couldn't be certain if it was *the* dwarf. But what if this was the famous Geno? Gary pondered. What might arrogant Kelsey say if Gary walked right in and captured the smithy? Gary realized then that he had lost his spear in the fall. He twisted about to look up the long cliff—was amazed that he had even survived such a dive—and realized, too, that he had lost all trace of his companions.

"He can't be that tough," Gary told himself, sluggishly dragging himself farther up onto the rocks. He meant to sneak in and make the capture barehanded, but he stopped before he had even cleared the water, watching curiously as a large raven swooped in around the thunder of the waterfall and landed inside the little room, behind the oblivious dwarf.

Gary grew truly amazed as the raven shifted form, flattening out as it slipped down to the floor, transforming into a long black snake. It started for the dwarf, then seemed to change its mind and made for the table instead. It coiled and curled its way up the table's single central leg and slithered over the flat rim to the flagon.

"What the hell?" was all that the disbelieving Gary could mutter as the snake hooked its considerable fangs over the lip of the mug and began milking venom into the dwarf's drink.

Gary finally managed to get his legs under him. He tried to rise, but wound up crawling instead, knowing that he had to get behind the falls. He stumbled down with a loud clang and held very still. But neither the dwarf nor the snake apparently heard him—of course they didn't with the continual roar.

The snake had finished by then and it slithered back to the floor and across the room, disappearing into a crack in the wall.

The dwarf, too, had finished. He turned about—his face was clean-shaven and his eyes wide and blue-gray—and headed for the table.

Gary called out to him, but he didn't seem to notice.

"Can't let him drink that!" Gary growled at himself, and he picked up a stone and threw himself forward, scrambling and rolling the last few yards to the edge of the room, his fear for the dwarf overruling his sincere respect for the powerful falls.

The dwarf had hoisted the flagon by the time Gary got in range, but the man launched the large stone anyway, praying for luck. The missile bopped off the side of the dwarf's head, causing little damage, but it did manage to knock the poisoned flagon to the floor on the rebound.

"What?" the dwarf roared, and Gary, sheltered somewhat from the roar of the falls by the rim of the cave, heard him clearly. Gary got up to his feet, finally, and he fell back against the cave wall, bruised and exhausted, and knowing that he owed the diminutive smithy an explanation.

The dwarf, seeming not even dazed by the rock, turned on Gary and planted his stubby knuckles against his hips, against the leather sides of a wide and jeweled belt.

"Poisoned," Gary rasped helplessly against the growling echoes, and the steely-eyed creature didn't blink.

Gary started forward from the wall, figuring he couldn't be heard well enough to explain.

Then he learned how Geno Hammerthrower had earned his name.

"You spilled my mead!" the dwarf roared, and he launched the hammer so effortlessly that Gary didn't even realize it had been thrown—until it popped him square in the faceplate of his helm. He grunted and bounced back against the wall.

When his eyes stopped spinning, he saw a second hammer spinning end over end his way, and then a third and fourth, before the second even reached him.

"Wait!" Gary shrieked, trying futilely to get the heavy shield up to block. The hammers bonked in—one, two, three—again right between the eyes.

Waves of dizziness rolled over Gary, the clangs echoed over and over in his ears. Another hammer struck home, and then another—did this infernal dwarf have an endless supply?

Gary realized that he was sitting now. He looked out the helm's small slit—it wasn't running straight across anymore—and saw the diminutive dwarf hoisting an impossibly huge hammer. Even Cedric's magical helm wouldn't stop that one, Gary realized, but there was little the dazed man could do to stop the dwarf from finishing him off.

There came a splash from the side and Kelsey swung into the cave at the end of a rope. His momentum carried him right into the dwarf, sending both of them tumbling across the floor.

Mickey came into the room then, floating right through the falls at the end of an umbrella! The leprechaun landed easily, snapped his fingers to make the umbrella fold up again and disappear up his sleeve, and tossed Gary a casual wink.

Kelsey came up first, putting his sword in line with the dwarf's face. "I have you!" the elf declared. The dwarf, still kneeling, spat in Kelsey's eye. His gnarly hands seemed to actually grab hold of the floor and he jerked it as a maid might snap a carpet. The ground rolled under Kelsey, sending him head over heels backwards. He rolled right back to his feet, but without his precious sword, and then he crashed against a wall.

Gary felt a tug on his back. He watched curiously as a leather strap across his chest untied itself. The tug came again, and the case holding the spear of Cedric Donigarten slipped out from under him. Gary understood what was causing the strange events when he noticed Mickey holding his hand out towards the case, magically pulling it in.

Kelsey was still standing, leaning, against the wall, and Gary thought the stunned elf would surely be crushed as the wild dwarf dipped his rock-hard head and barreled in.

But Mickey was the next to strike. The spear case shot across the room, just a few inches from the floor, and cut in between the dwarf's pumping legs. The creature pitched in headlong, and Kelsey found a hold above his head and lifted his legs high and wide.

With a tremendous *crack!* the beardless dwarf hit the wall face-first. He bounced back several feet, but somehow managed to hold his balance.

"I have you, Geno Hammerthrower!" Kelsey cried again, and he jumped out, pulling a chain, shackles at its ends, from under his green cape. The stunned dwarf still did not move as Kelsey looped the chain over him and snapped the shackles around his wrists.

NINE
Rules Is Rules

"I have you," Kelsey said again. "And you must fulfill my wish before you shall regain your freedom."

The dwarf considered the shackles and the loosely looped chain for a moment. He had relative freedom of movement, for the chain dragged long on the floor behind him. He looked at Kelsey and smiled widely, showing one large hole where a tooth had once been.

Kelsey seemed to read his thoughts. "*Biellen*," the elf whispered, even as Geno's legs started to move. Geno had hardly taken a step before the magical chain suddenly shortened, pulling his arms tightly behind his back. His gap-toothed smile disappeared along with his balance, replaced by a wide-eyed look of disbelief as he pitched headlong to the floor.

"Now we are leaving," declared the victorious elf, scooping up his sword and laying its blade to the side of Geno's stubby neck. "By the lawful rules of capture, you are bound to me. I'll not tolerate any more resistance." He pulled the dwarf to his feet, while Mickey went to see about Gary.

"Nasty dents in the helm," the leprechaun remarked. "I'm hoping yer head isn't the same."

"Yes . . . er, no," Gary replied, somewhat absently. He had watched the capture from afar, his thoughts still filled with spinning hammers and pretty stars— there seemed to be so many stars in this wondrous land!

With Mickey's help, the young man managed to get unsteadily back to his feet, and once there, Gary realized just how sore he was, from the fall and the hammers, and just crawling across the jagged rocks. Every joint in his body seemed as if it had been pulled and stretched beyond its limits. There was not time for whining, though, not with Geno captured and many other crafty dwarfs nearby no doubt already spinning devious spells to block their escape.

Kelsey quickly collected Geno's hammers, and some heavy gloves the dwarf kept near the burning forge, and the troupe prepared to depart.

"I've lost my spear," Gary remarked as Mickey started away. Three sets of eyes turned to him.

"In the fall," he explained. "It's probably in the river, a mile away by now."

Mickey looked to Geno. "Spear?" he asked. The dwarf nodded to a cubby, barely a crack in the wall. Mickey cast him a suspicious glance, then wagged a finger the crack's way. A dozen different weapons came tumbling into the room to the leprechaun's magical call: swords, axes, a tall halberd, and one spear. "Better than the one ye lost," Mickey muttered and he floated the iron-shafted weapon into Gary's hands.

Feeling the balance of the dwarf-crafted weapon, Gary couldn't disagree.

"Now we must be on our way," Kelsey demanded. He looked straight into the dwarf's gray-blue eyes. "Which way?"

Geno nodded towards a narrow tunnel on the far side of the little chamber. Gary regarded it curiously for a second, mentally comparing this image to the one he had seen when first he gazed upon the hearth-lighted room.

"That opening wasn't there before," he started to protest, fearful of this newest trick, vividly recalling the biting maw in the earth up along the high trail.

Mickey looked to him, then nodded to Kelsey. Then, to Gary's disbelief, Kelsey continued straight ahead, leading the way to the tunnel.

The elf had barely crossed the threshold when the walls snapped shut, jagged stone teeth closing about the elf.

Geno Hammerthrower squealed with glee.

"No!" Gary shouted, and started forward.

Mickey intercepted him. "Haven't ye learned yet to look through the mist?" Gary didn't understand until the real Kelsey, still standing next to Geno, slapped him on the shoulder.

The dwarf's devious grin disappeared, replaced by a stone-face grimace.

"Rules is rules," Mickey scolded the dwarf.

"You reject the rules of capture?" Kelsey added angrily. "You disgrace your people and your trade? You are the finest smithy in all of Faerie, Geno Hammerthrower; you should understand your responsibilities in these matters."

"Not a fair capture!" the dwarf huffed. He stomped one heavy boot and tried to cross his arms over his thick chest, but of course, the shackles wouldn't allow for that.

"How so?" Kelsey and Mickey asked together.

"You caught me," Geno said to Kelsey. "But you were not the first attacker. Rules is rules!" he snarled, imitating Mickey's accent. "And by the rules, only the first attacker is entitled to make the capture!"

"Who . . . ," Mickey started to ask, but then he realized the answer as he looked at Gary, the only one who had been in the chamber before Kelsey.

"You have ruined everything!" Kelsey roared at poor, confused Gary. "By what authority did you take it upon yourself . . ."

"I didn't do anything!" Gary protested.

"Stonebubbles!" Geno yelled, thrusting his chiseled chin Gary's way. "He hit me with a rock—right in the face!" The dwarf took a step to the side and kicked the same rock, lying conspicuously next to the fallen flagon in the middle of the floor.

"Explain your actions!" Kelsey demanded of Gary.

"I wasn't trying to catch him," Gary stammered.

"To kill me, then?" Geno huffed. "That, too, denies the elf the right of capture . . ."

"No!" cried Gary. He looked helplessly to Mickey, the only possible supporter in the room. "I just tried to stop him from drinking the mead."

"Worse than killing me!" Geno roared.

"It was poisoned," Gary explained,

"Poisoned?" Mickey balked. "Come now, lad. How might ye know such a thing?"

"I saw it," Gary replied, and now everyone, even the outraged dwarf, was listening intently. "The raven . . . I mean the snake. Well, it was a raven when it flew in, but it became a snake, and it crawled up the table to the mug. It had started for you," he said, pointing to the dwarf. "I don't know, maybe it didn't think it would like the taste of dwarf."

"That's believable enough," Mickey put in with a snicker.

"Then it went to the cup," Gary continued. "I saw it, I swear. The snake hooked its fangs on the top of the cup and pumped venom in. I swear it."

"Fairy tales!" Geno snarled.

"Look who's talking," Gary retorted.

Kelsey and Mickey stared long and hard at each other. If their suspicions about the source of their continuing problems were correct, Gary's story was not so unbelievable.

The issue became almost irrelevant a moment later, though, when the wall at the back of the small chamber split wide and a dozen bandy-legged dwarfs charged in, wielding all sorts of nasty-looking cudgels. They surrounded the companions in the blink of an eye, and one of them, a hunchbacked, gray-haired, and gray-bearded creature, asked Geno casually, "Which one shall we kill first?"

"Hold, Durin," Geno replied, not so quick to risk his reputation, though he hardly believed Gary's tale.

Kelsey clutched his sword hilt tightly, inching it closer to Geno's exposed neck. But Mickey, pulling out his long pipe, seemed well at ease.

"And tell me," the leprechaun bade, suddenly putting all the pieces of this puzzle together, "Who telled ye that we were about?"

Durin and his black-haired brother exchanged curious glances. "We saw you ourselves," Dvalin replied honestly—and purposely dodging the question. "Crossing the high trails."

"And do ye always attack wandering travelers?" Mickey asked. "For, to be sure, me and me friends were attacked, and attacked by dwarfish magic."

"Thieves!" Dvalin snapped angrily.

"And how did ye know our intent?" Mickey replied, taking a deep draw, appearing not at all concerned. "Who telled ye that we came for Geno?"

The dwarven brothers looked to each other again and shrugged, wondering what could be the harm. "It was a great speaking bird," Durin replied.

"A raven?" asked Mickey, and he looked to Gary and nodded.

Both the dwarfs bobbed their heads.

Mickey waggled a finger, retrieving the fallen flagon. "There's a bit o' mead left inside," the leprechaun explained, holding the flagon out to Geno. "Would ye care for a drink?"

Geno kicked the stone at his feet clear across the room. "Damn!" he spat.

"What is it, rock-kin?" Durin cried, and all the dwarfs took up their weapons. "Who must we kill?"

"None!" Geno growled back. "I am caught fairly, it would seem, indentured to this elf"—the word did not sound like a compliment—"and owing my life to this wretched human thing."

"No!" came several dwarven voices all at once, and the dwarfs took up their weapons and advanced another step towards the companions. But Geno knew well the rules of capture, a responsibility that the finest smithy in Faerie often found dropped upon his rock-hard shoulders.

They left the Firth of Buldre a short time later, accompanied by an armed guard of twenty none-too-happy dwarfs. The bandy-legged warriors did not try to hinder Kelsey's departure at all, though, even though the elf had Geno firmly in tow.

Gary did not quite understand it all, and his continued ignorance bothered him even after the other dwarfs had departed and the companions were once again out on the open trails.

"Why did they let us go?" he asked Mickey, who was perched comfortably on his shoulder again, reading *The Hobbit*.

"Why did this hobbit feel guilty about gaining the ring from the wretch in the cave?" Mickey answered without missing a beat. He held the open book Gary's way.

Gary thought about it for just a moment; he knew the tale as well as any. "Bilbo didn't play fairly at the riddle game," he replied. "He cheated, and his keeping the magic ring could have been considered stealing. Although," Gary quickly added, in defense of his favorite character, "if he had given it back, he would have been invited for supper, if you know what I mean."

"And there ye have it," Mickey said. "For still, he felt guilty. Faerie, too, is a land of ancient rules. And rules is rules, lad. To break them would bring ye dishonor in the eyes of all. What are ye without yer honor, I ask? Even the wretch, this Gollum thing, a murderer and thief a hundred times over and a heap bit worse than our Geno, thinked twice about cheating in the riddle game."

Gary considered the answer, wondering how many people of his own world would have given in to the capture merely for the sake of an intangible thing such as their honor, as had Geno, with so obvious an advantage in the fight.

"Just one more question," he begged Mickey, who had gone back to his reading. The leprechaun looked up.

"You said that illusions wouldn't work on dwarfs, but in Geno's room, you fooled him completely with the image of Kelsey walking into the phony tunnel."

"Indeed, illusions do not work well on dwarfs," Mickey replied. "But I showed Geno just what Geno most wanted to see. Tricks work much the finer when they play on yer target's heart. Even if yer target's a dwarf."

Gary nodded; it seemed logical enough. "Where now?" he asked, looking ahead to Kelsey and the dwarf.

"Ye said one question," Mickey reminded him.

Gary gave him a pleading look.

"Straight through the mountains to the east," Mickey replied. "The trails are flat and not to be so tough with Geno talking to the stones. Then north to Gondabuggan, to buy a gnomish thief—second best thieves in all the world are the gnomes."

Gary suspected that he knew which race ranked above the gnomes, but he kept his thought to himself.

"Then back to the southern end of Dvergamal," Mickey went on. "And up

the plain and the Crahgs to a place called Giant's Thumb." He dropped his voice
to a mysterious whisper as he finished. "Where ye'll meet the worm."

CERIDWEN looked across the few miles to Dvergamal, where she knew
Kelsey's party was making fine progress. The sorceress had left the stronghold
of the dwarfs soon after the companions had set out from the falls. With the
dwarfs on their guard and in their mountain homeland, Ceridwen knew that
she could do little against Kelsey. She had to somehow turn the party back, get
them out on the plain west of the mountains, and buy herself some time.

She stood under a holly tree beside an unremarkable gray stone, surrounded by lifeless dirt, a spot she had marked well in ages past. "Come awake,
Old Wife," the sorceress demanded softly. "I know your guise and need you now."

A long uneventful moment passed.

"Come awake, Old Wife!" Ceridwen called again, more loudly. She reached
into a pocket of her black robes and took out a small bag, passing it quickly
back and forth from hand to hand, for it was deathly cold.

"Summer has passed, autumn wanes," the sorceress lied, and she opened
the bag over the stone, sprinkling icy magical crystals. The stone began to trem-
ble almost immediately. Its hue shifted from dull gray to icy blue, and then it
began to grow and re-form.

Soon it towered over the sorceress, twenty feet high and still growing. Its
shape became that of an old woman, white-haired, one-eyed, and with skin as
blue as winter ice on a clear day. Despite her height, the giantess appeared a
meager thing, incredibly lean and wrapped in a tattered plaid.

"Cailleac," Ceridwen whispered, obviously impressed by the spectacle.

The giantess looked about curiously. "Allhallows has not passed," she said
through her brown-stained teeth. "What trick is this?" She looked down then,
and seemed to notice Ceridwen for the first time.

"Ah, sorceress," the Cailleac said, as if those words explained everything.

"I need you," Ceridwen explained.

"My time is not come," the Cailleac replied sternly.

"Just in Dvergamal," Ceridwen quickly added. "In the mountains where the
chill wind blows even in the high days of summer. A small favor is all that I ask,
and then you may return to your slumbers."

The Cailleac looked around at the new-blossomed flowers and the green
summer canopy, feeling uncomfortable. Ceridwen tossed another handful of
chilling dust at her and that seemed to comfort her.

"Do this for me and I will have your bed tended throughout the season,"

Ceridwen promised. "My minions will keep it cold for you and signal you when Allhallows is passed."

"Just in the mountains?" the Cailleac tentatively agreed.

Ceridwen smiled and nodded, confident that she had just bought herself the time she needed.

THE companions camped on a flat stone in a gully between towering peaks. The wind was stiff this night, their second from the Firth of Buldre, and a bit chill, but it seemed refreshing to the weary troupe. Gary, Mickey, and Geno sat around the fire, with Gary glad for the break from wearing his cumbersome armor. Kelsey thought them safe enough in Dvergamal with a dwarven guide, and with the other dwarfs sworn to leave them be. The stones would tell Geno of the approach of any enemy long before the creature became a threat. The elf had even removed Geno's shackles, knowing that the bonds of responsibility would hold the dwarf tighter than any metal ever could.

Gary never took his gaze off the dwarf. Geno was much different from his kin (at least from those that Gary had seen), younger looking, almost boyish, despite his obvious strength. His unkempt hair was lustrous and his gray-blue eyes shone clear and bright and inquisitive. His missing tooth reminded Gary of a mischievous nephew back in that other world, a boy whose smile inevitably signaled trouble.

"How long have you been a smithy?" Gary asked, surprising even himself with the words. He had been silently trying to determine the curious dwarf's approximate age.

Geno snapped an unblinking glare upon him and did not respond. Mickey, too, paused in his reading to look up at Gary.

"I mean," Gary stammered, suddenly uncomfortable, "is that all you do?"

The dwarf rose and walked out of the firelight.

"What?" Gary asked, looking back to Mickey.

The leprechaun chuckled and went back to the book.

"What did I say to offend him?" Gary pressed, not willing to let this issue slip past.

"Ye think he'd be one for talking?" Mickey replied. "He's catched, lad."

"So were you, but you seemed friendly enough," Gary replied indignantly, brushing his black hair out of his eyes.

"I'm a leprechaun," Mickey answered. "I'm supposed to get catched. Makes everyone's life a bit more exciting, don't ye see?"

"Bull," said Gary. "You were as miserable as Geno—probably still are—but at least you had . . . have . . . the decency to talk to your companions." He said it loudly, purposely wanting Geno to overhear. "I'm a captive, too, when you get right down to it."

"Geno's owing to ye," Mickey explained. "It's not something he's comfortable over."

Gary didn't understand.

"Ye saved his life," Mickey went on, chuckling softly at Gary's continuing confusion. The young man couldn't quite seem to catch on to anything in Faerie. "Rules is rules," Mickey explained. "And, sure enough, there be rules for saving lives, too."

"He's coming with us; I thought that was my repayment," Gary replied.

"He's come to answer for Kelsey's capture, not for yerself," Mickey explained. "This is the elf's quest, and not yer own."

Geno walked back into the firelight then, still staring unblinkingly at Gary.

"I don't want any favors!" Gary snapped suddenly, sick of that stare.

Geno hooted and charged right through the dancing flames. He was on top of Gary in an instant, easily pinning the young man flat on his back.

"Ye shouldn't've said that," Mickey remarked, and he went back to his book.

Gary couldn't believe the strength of the dwarf's iron-like grip. He struggled and wiggled to no avail, and all the while, Geno leered at him, showing the gap in his shiny teeth.

"Let me . . . ," Gary started to say, but Geno head-butted him and shut him up.

"What is going on here?" Kelsey demanded, storming into the camp, his sword drawn.

"The boy insulted the dwarf," Mickey replied absently.

Geno hopped off Gary, growled at Kelsey, and went back to his place opposite the fire, again walking straight through the glowing embers. He spun about and plopped down, dropping his accusing, threatening stare fully over Gary once again.

He kept it up interminably; Gary fell asleep with that uncomfortable image full in his thoughts.

Gary awoke sometime before dawn, shivering, for the wind had grown wickedly chill. Mickey and the others were also up and about, trying to get the fire back to life in the whipping breeze.

"Are we that high up?" Gary asked, moving to join them.

Geno and Kelsey ignored him, as usual, and as usual, Mickey tried to explain.

"Not so high," the leprechaun replied. "And a bit cold for the season even if we were among the tallest peaks of Dvergamal. But not to fear; we'll get the fire up in a bit, and a bit after that we'll find the morning sun."

Dawn did come soon after, but it was a gray and unwarming one, shrouded by a heavy overcast. The wind relented somewhat, but the air hung cold about the companions, their breath coming out in visible puffs.

"It smells like snow," Mickey remarked. Kelsey seemed not to appreciate the grim observation. He led them off without even a breakfast.

The first flakes drifted down around them less than an hour later.

Kelsey looked to Geno—this was the dwarf's homeland, after all—for some explanation, but the smithy offered nothing and seemed as confused as the rest of them.

"Do we go on or go back?" Mickey asked. "We've a week o' walking before us, but just two days behind."

"The weather cannot continue," Kelsey insisted. "Summer is upon us—even Dvergamal warms under its gentle breath."

As if in response, the wind groaned loudly throughout the mountain valleys.

By noon, snow was beginning to collect and many rocks grew dangerously slick with nearly invisible ice. It was then that the companions found their answers.

Geno bolted straight upright, as though some unknown voice had spoken to him. He rushed back to a high point the party had just passed and peered through the still-gathering storm into the far distance.

"Cailleac Bheur!" the dwarf cried, the first words he had spoken since they had left his waterfall home.

Mickey and Kelsey nearly fell over at the unexpected revelation. When they finally recovered, they rushed to join the dwarf, with Gary right on their heels.

Gary peered through the storm to the distant peaks. He thought he saw something, but simply couldn't bring himself to believe it.

"Cailleac Bheur!" Geno cried again.

"The Old Wife," Mickey translated for Gary.

Gary looked harder, beginning to understand that his vision was no trick of the weather. Drifting on the wind from mountaintop to mountaintop, barely visible through the snowy veil, was a huge woman, leaning on a giant staff and trailed by several large herons.

"Suren ye've heard of the Blue Hag," Mickey said to Gary. "'Tis she that brings the winter, withers the crops, and freezes the ground. Her touch is death, lad, to men and to the land."

"It is months before her time," Kelsey argued.

But the elf's words rang hollow, for the Blue Hag drifted on towards them, leaving in her deathly wake snowcapped peaks where there had been, only moments before, bare stone.

TEN

Winter Frolics

"WE shall stay to the lower trails," Kelsey insisted, leading them on stubbornly against the gathering storm.

Mickey and Geno exchanged looks that did not comfort Gary Leger. He thought he had heard of the Blue Hag before, in a fairy tale, perhaps, and he vaguely remembered that what he had heard had not been pleasant.

The temperature continued to plummet. Kelsey took them down to the lower trails, but even there, the snow was fast piling. They plodded and struggled, slipped on ice-covered stones, and fought hard against the stiff and freezing wind. Finally even the elf realized that he could not keep to his determined course.

"We're getting deeper into her storm," Mickey remarked. "Even if the Cailleac is out on a confused wander, ye're taking us right to her killing feet!

"And, Kelsey," the leprechaun added ominously, "we're both knowing that she's not out on any confused wander."

Kelsey turned to Geno. "Get us back to the west," he instructed. "Through the swiftest trails you know."

"You go beyond the bounds of my indenture," the dwarf replied, somewhat hiding his relief.

"To save us is to save yourself," Kelsey promptly reminded him. "Dwarfs fare no better than elves in the Cailleac's wake."

Geno's grunt was filled with hatred, but the dwarf rushed back to the end of the line and turned them about. Geno moved along at a tremendous, rolling pace, and once again, poor Gary found himself hard-pressed to keep up. Mickey perched upon his shoulder and whispered grim reminders of what would happen to him if he lagged too far behind.

At first, the small party seemed to be outrunning the storm, for the trails were flat and smooth. But then as they began to tire and cross rougher ground, the winds caught up to them, nipping at their backsides, howling like a pack of hungry wolves, and promising doom. Snow swirled all about them, limiting their vision to only a few feet. At one point, they came sliding and slipping down a steep and narrow decline, the stones slick with ice and a sheer drop to their right.

Kelsey shouted warnings, Gary screamed, and the leprechaun, holding on for all his life, nearly choked the young man, as they neared the bottom, for the trail took a sharp right turn that seemed as if it would leave them flying headlong over the drop.

Geno knew the area well, though, and he listened to the promises of the stones rather than depending on his vision. The dwarf called to the mountain, and a curving and smooth slab rose up from the lip at the turn, blocking the fall and deflecting the out-of-control companions safely along the trail. Every time the trail wound sharply, dwarven magic lifted a stone banking to guide them along.

Their pace continued to slow, though, as the snow deepened. Gary's feet and legs went numb and many times he thought he would simply fall down and wait for the blizzard to bury him.

Then Geno made a most welcomed announcement.

"Cave!" the dwarf shouted, and he slipped around a boulder and into a narrow opening.

"We can only rest for a moment," Kelsey said.

"My legs are numb," Gary retorted. "I won't make it if we go back out there."

"I, too, would prefer to rest," the elf replied. "To build a fire and sit in here until the storm abates." He looked at Mickey, who nodded his agreement. "But the Cailleac is out with a purpose, I fear. The trails this deep in the mountains will be blocked before nightfall and then we will have nowhere to go."

"We cannot stay and wait," Mickey agreed.

"Who said we would?" Geno, who had been sniffing around the back of the cave, huffed. "But I'll not go back out there," he declared, pointing to the whiteness beyond the cave entrance.

All three looked at him curiously.

"Get a fire going," Geno commanded. He walked to the back of the shallow cave again, braced his shoulder against a rocky spur, and heaved with all his strength. To the amazement, and relief, of his companions, the rock slid away, revealing a dark tunnel winding down into the west. "You might as well warm yourselves while we rest," Geno said nonchalantly.

Kelsey always kept some kindling in his pack, and he soon had a small fire burning. It wouldn't last long, they all knew, so they huddled about it, stealing every bit of warmth they possibly could.

"How far does the tunnel go?" Kelsey asked. With the immediate danger passed, the elf was more concerned with what the future might hold. This would be a temporary stay indeed if they came out still many miles from the edge of Dvergamal with the Cailleac's storm deep about them.

"Long way," Geno replied.

"You saved us all," Gary remarked honestly.

"Shut your mouth!" the dwarf snapped back. "I saved myself."

"We just happened to be along to get saved with ye," Mickey added, understanding the dwarf's feelings.

Geno briskly rubbed his thick hands together, brushed his hair from in front of his face, and stormed away from the fire.

"Keep quiet, lad," the leprechaun whispered to Gary. "Ye'll find no friendship with that one, and if ye anger him too much, he'll suren leave us lost in the dark."

"Time to go," Kelsey said, realizing before the others that Geno had already disappeared into the tunnel. The elf considered the dying fire, wondering if he might salvage a brand large enough to use as a torch. There wasn't much left, though, so Kelsey gave an uncomfortable grimace and a helpless shrug.

"Just keep close to the dwarf," Mickey reassured him.

Kelsey looked to his longbow and to the glowing embers.

"It'd only burn for a few minutes," Mickey quickly reminded him. "Then ye'd be without light and without yer bow."

Kelsey shrugged, obviously uncomfortable, and rushed into the darkness.

"Elfs aren't overly fond of caves," Mickey explained to Gary as he floated to his regular position atop the young man's shoulder.

"I knew that," Gary replied quietly.

DEEP and dark, so dark that Gary couldn't see his hand if he waggled it just inches in front of his face. Not even a shadow of it.

Deep and dark.

Gary's sigh was audible when Mickey, perched upon his shoulder, conjured some light to read by.

"Put it out!" Geno roared from up ahead.

"We're not all dwarfs, ye know," Mickey retaliated. "Our eyes don't show us much through the dark. If ye want . . ."

Geno stormed back, nearly toppling Kelsey, and hopped up on his toes to put his face right up to Mickey's knees. "Put it out," the dwarf growled.

Kelsey, also very glad for the light, started to interrupt, but Geno would hear none of it.

"There are dark things sleeping down here," the dwarf warned. "Big and dark. Would you want to wake them?"

Mickey and Gary looked to Kelsey, who was sweating and obviously uncomfortable in the tunnel. To Gary, this hardly seemed the imposing elf he had come to know. When Geno, too, turned about and snapped a glare on the elf, Kelsey only shrugged and turned away.

Reluctantly Mickey extinguished his light.

"Good enough," grumbled Geno. "Now keep close to my back; if you get lost down here, you will never find your way out."

They trudged on slowly, Gary, even agile Kelsey, stumbling often. Gary thought that Geno must surely be enjoying all of this. On one occasion, Gary came down an abrupt decline and slammed his helmet into a low-hanging stone. Mickey squeaked and dropped heavily from his shoulder.

"Duck your head near the bottom," Geno said, a bit late with the warning. Mickey lit another globe, just long enough to find his way back to Gary, and the dwarf, too amused to even scold him, continued on, hardly hiding his snickers.

Gary had never been this far underground before. He had never suffered claustrophobia of any kind, but every step now came hesitantly to him as he became conscious of the thousands of tons of stone above his head. The air grew comfortably warm again—that was something, at least—but Gary's breathing came in terror-filled gasps; he felt he would just scream out, or plunge blindly into the darkness.

"Are ye all right, lad?" Mickey asked, hearing the labored breaths.

When Gary didn't even respond, Mickey lit a globe of light.

"Put it out!" came the expected roar from up front.

"Wait," said Kelsey, who had also seen—or felt—enough of the blackness, "Hold the enchantment." He turned to Geno. "I would rather awaken a horde of demons than continue on blindly. I do not care much for your dwarven realm, good smithy."

"Good enough for you, then," Geno growled back. "And when we do awaken the dark things, I'll gladly step aside that you alone might battle them!"

"Hold the enchantment," Kelsey said again to Mickey, and the leprechaun shrugged and pulled out *The Hobbit*, thinking, as usual, to make the best of the situation.

As they at last continued on, Gary wasn't certain if he liked the light better or not. Whenever the walls and ceiling came tight about them, he felt as though they would surely be smothered, and whenever the passage opened up wide and high, stalactites leered down at him, and stalagmite mounds resembled those demons that Kelsey had made mention of.

They made better progress, though, not having to shuffle blindly, not stubbing their toes every other step. Even Geno grew more at ease, particularly when the tunnel at last began to slope upwards once more.

How many miles they walked as the hours slipped by only the dwarf knew for certain, but the passage was almost arrow-straight and all of them, except for Geno, were quite surprised when they finally saw the waning light of day up ahead and came out on the western fringes of Dvergamal, not too far from the foothills.

"We've covered near to two days of trail walking in half a day," Mickey remarked with obvious admiration.

The leprechaun's claims proved true enough, but the danger was not completely behind them. The leading edge of the Blue Hag's storm had passed even this point and the snow lay deep about the tunnel exit, and still more tumbled down from the thick gray sky.

"We'll gain nothing by waiting," Kelsey said. "Move ahead and quickly, before the cold weakens us once more." Unfamiliar with their exact location, the elf let Geno continue in the lead.

The new-fallen snow was no match for the heavy footsteps of Geno Hammerthrower. The dwarf put a hammer in each hand and plowed ahead wildly, bursting through drifts more than twice his height and smashing away patches of ice wherever he found them. In his wake, the others had an easier time of it, though the blizzard grew stronger and the wind bit at them and forced lithe Kelsey to take a step to the side for every one he took forward. Mickey prudently put the book away (the pages would have gotten soaked anyway) and clamped both his hands around Gary's helmet.

With the lower foothills in sight and Geno cutting a path for them, the group made great progress and their hopes soared. Perhaps it was that strong pace and budding confidence that made Gary a bit less cautious, and on one slick descending trail, disaster struck.

Sheltered by a high mountain wall from the brunt of the wind, the trail was not so deep with snow. The companions trotted along anxiously, Geno leading, then Kelsey, then Gary, with Mickey more relaxed on his shoulder.

The leprechaun regretted loosening his grip when Gary slipped to his back and skidded down the slope, gaining momentum. Like a turtle on its shell, the young armored man flailed helplessly. Kelsey nimbly hopped out of harm's way; Geno, busily calling up a blocking stone, as he had done on the earlier winding trails, noticed Gary only at the last moment.

The dwarf swung about and braced himself, his muscles snapping taut as Gary barreled into him. The force of the impact sent Mickey head over heels. They all came to a skidding stop, Mickey atop Geno now, and Geno's heels hanging out over a deep ravine.

"You nearly killed us both!" the dwarf roared at Gary.

"All three, ye mean," Mickey quickly added. He started to say something else, but his words turned into a shriek as a gust of wind slammed him and knocked him from Geno's back.

"Mickey!" Gary cried, rolling about to get his head over the lip of the ravine. He saw the leprechaun spinning down, his tam-o'-shanter flying away, and then an umbrella opened, offering some hope.

But the wind whipped and swirled in the narrow ravine, and Mickey's umbrella twisted and turned, then folded up on itself. The sound of a renewed shriek and the image of plummeting Mickey died away, buried in the wind-whipped, deadening snow.

"Mickey," Gary whispered again.

"The leprechaun has many tricks," Kelsey offered, though there was little confidence in his tone.

Gary just continued to stare blankly into the chasm.

"How can we get down there?" Kelsey asked Geno.

The dwarf pointed across the narrow ravine. The path continued on after the ten-foot expanse; the ravine was really just a sharp crack where the ancient mountain had split apart.

Without saying a word, the dwarf coiled his bowed legs under his boulder-like torso and leaped out. He slammed face-first into the cliff across the way, but found a solid grip with his powerful hands and easily scrambled back up to the path.

Kelsey went next—two short strides and a graceful leap that cleared the ravine with several feet to spare.

Gary looked at them in wonderment, then turned his gaze back to the deep fall. He knew that the expanse was barely ten feet across, but he was amazed at how far that distance appeared with a drop of several hundred feet between the ledges. Without the snow, and without the armor, he probably could have made the jump—if he could have summoned the courage to even make the attempt.

"You must come across," Kelsey yelled to him, the voice seeming distant through the blizzard, "If we are delayed, the Cailleac's storm will bury us."

"You forget what I'm wearing," Gary shouted back. "I wouldn't make it halfway!" He heard Geno and Kelsey conversing, though he couldn't make out the words.

"I will throw you a rope," Kelsey said after what seemed to Gary to be a long, long while. "Tie it about you securely."

Gary didn't really see how that would be of much help; if he leaped and came up short, he would just swing down into the side of the cliff, probably breaking every bone in his body.

"Wait for the wave!" came Geno's gravelly voice.

"Wave?" The tone of Gary's question did not reflect an abundance of confidence.

"You will know when to leap!" the dwarf promised, and then Gary heard him chanting softly, as softly as Geno could with his grating, thunder-rumbling voice. The ground came alive under Gary's feet, swaying and rolling like an ocean.

Gary felt the momentum building, each surge stronger than the last, the ice cracking and sliding away. The stone groaned for the effort and Gary blinked in amazement as he watched one tall wave speeding at him from behind. Understanding now the dwarf's instructions, he waited until it bucked the ground behind him, then, knowing that it would surely toss him into the ravine if he did not act, he summoned his courage and leaped with all his strength.

His timing was perfect; he sailed high and far, easily clearing the expanse, even clearing Kelsey and Geno. So relieved to be over the chasm, Gary didn't even consider his new problem.

Landing.

He came down stumbling and scrambling. Realizing that he could not stay on his feet, he quickly veered for a pillowy-looking snowbank. Appearances can indeed be deceiving, as Gary learned when he crashed through the scant inch of snow covering the boulder.

He lay very still on the hard ground, not noticing the cold, or even the whiteness of the snow-filled sky.

Just the stars again.

After what seemed like an hour, he felt a small hand roughly clasp his arm and he was flying again, back up to his feet. He had no choice but to fight away the dizziness, for by the time he even realized that he was standing, Kelsey and Geno had already started away.

The three charged along for just a few minutes, then Geno stopped suddenly and put an ear to the mountain wall. The dwarf stepped back, as though he was considering what the mountain had told him. He reached for a loose slab of stone, somewhat bowl-shaped, and hoisted it from its position beside the wall. Gary shook his head at the feat, for though the slab must have weighed several hundred pounds, powerful Geno handled it easily.

"Get on," the dwarf ordered, laying the slab out before him. "The trail is ice-covered from here on down."

Kelsey jumped right aboard, but Gary wasn't so certain about tobogganing down a narrow mountain trail, especially not with a sheer drop looming on one side.

"Stay if you choose," Geno said, and he started to kick the sled away. "I will not promise that I'll come and retrieve your frozen body when the storm abates."

Gary caught him three strides down, diving to the sled and holding on for dear life. They had gone a hundred feet by the time Gary managed to get his whole body on the slab, taking a tight seat between Kelsey and the dwarf.

Geno remained in the back, hardly able to see over Gary. Since Gary considered the dwarf their pilot, he wasn't too confident of that arrangement, but the dwarf had his eyes closed anyway, concentrating and calling to the mountain to guide them.

They gained speed with every passing foot, plummeting along the steepening winding trail. They climbed several feet up the mountainside for every right-hand turn, and the trail conveniently (purposefully?) banked upwards to keep them from flying out on the left bends.

The wind roared inside Gary's loose helmet, and the eye slit did not offer enough protection to stop the windblown tears from flying freely. All the world became a surrealistic blur, mountain peaks blending together and rushing past. Sometimes the trail cut in from the ledge, sending the sledders rushing into darkness between towering walls of stone. Then the light returned in the blink of an eye as the sled zipped back out the other side.

As they flew through one tumble of boulders, Gary could only imagine that someone had turned a strobe upon them. The fight flashed and flickered as they weaved in and out, under a small arching natural bridge and through a short and narrow tunnel.

"Hold tight!" Geno cried, a perfectly unnecessary order, as they came up on another ravine. Then they were flying in open air; the mountain seemed to disappear behind them. Gary hadn't yet found his stomach when they bounced back to earth, now speeding along an open and smooth rock face. The wind buffeted them fiercely, threatening to flip them right over.

"Lean!" Geno roared, and together they put the slab right up on one edge, letting their angled weight fight back against the stubborn wind.

All the world rushed back up around them as the trail dropped suddenly. With the counterbalancing wind suddenly blocked, their lean sent them along sideways, spinning out of control. Gary slid free, saw Kelsey jump clear, and watched in terror as Geno and the bouncing slab whipped down toward an empty stone wall.

The dwarf curled and kicked out ferociously, launching the slab into the air. *Crack!*

The slab hit the wall and broke apart into a thousand pieces. Geno skidded in after it, but hit feetfirst and was back up before Gary or Kelsey had even recovered.

"A fine ride," Kelsey commented.

Gary gave him a disbelieving look.

"How long would it have taken us to walk those icy trails?" the elf asked in reply. "We are near to the bottom now, and soon to be out of Dvergamal."

"What about Mickey?" Gary asked, looking at both his companions.

"The trail doubles back on itself," Geno answered. "We will soon go near to where the leprechaun fell."

Kelsey looked up at the gloomy sky and his doubting expression told Gary that he did not think they would have an easy time finding their lost friend. The sun did not set early this time of the year, but so thick was the overcast that the light in late afternoon was growing meager.

The snow was deeper down here, but the trails were fairly even, and with Geno chopping out a path, the companions made good time. Kelsey found Mickey's tam-o'-shanter after an hour or so, but they saw no other sign of the leprechaun, and their calls were hopelessly buried by the storm.

A dark twilight fell over them; Gary had almost lost hope. And then they saw a bright glow to the side of the trail—not the flicker of a fire, but the steady glow of a magical light. They rushed over and found a snowdrift—a glowing snowbank with a leprechaun-shaped depression in its side.

"Mickey!" Gary yelled, and he and Kelsey, though their hands were again numb, began digging furiously at the snow. More than two hours had passed since the leprechaun's fall and they didn't need to voice their concerns that Mickey could not have survived engulfed in snow.

"Ye think I'd stay in there?" came a voice behind them. In a shallow cubby on the wind-protected side of the mountain wall, the leprechaun came back from invisibility into view. "Suren I'd be a month in the thawing!" He dropped his gaze to Kelsey's belt and smiled widely. "Ah, good, ye found me hat!"

"Unbelievable" was all that Gary could mutter, and his remark was the only response at all forthcoming from the three amazed companions.

They soon realized that they had put the worst of the storm behind them. They came out of the foothills a short while later, walking from winter into summer, it seemed, for even the Cailleac had little power over the lowlands in this season. Gary could only equate it to the time he had flown from Boston to Los Angeles on a December day.

They set a comfortable camp and Kelsey went off with his bow, returning a short time later with several coneys.

"You saved me up there," Gary mentioned to Geno, looking back to towering Dvergamal.

Anger flashed in Geno's blue-gray eyes. "I saved myself," the dwarf insisted.

"No," Gary corrected. "Not at the ravine where Mickey fell. I had no way across, and you could have gone on without me. But you didn't. You used your magic to help me across."

Geno mulled over the words for a moment, then spat on Gary's sneaker and stalked away.

Kelsey came up and glowered at the confused young man. "Take care that you do not release him from too many bonds!" the elf growled right in Gary's face, the words sounding clearly as a threat. And then Kelsey, too, charged off.

Gary looked helplessly to Mickey, who sat with arms crossed and not looking too pleased.

"Now ye got yer wish," the leprechaun scolded. "Ye released the dwarf from yer responsibility and he's owing ye nothing. I wouldn't be talking with Geno overly much, lad—he'll likely rip yer tongue from yer mouth."

"Why is he so miserable?" Gary snapped back.

"He's a dwarf," Mickey was quick to answer, as though that explained everything. "Dwarfs don't like peoples who aren't dwarfs!" the leprechaun added, seeing that Gary still did not understand. "Besides, he's been catched, and that's not an agreeable state."

Gary silently denied Mickey's claims. For whatever reason, Geno had taken the trouble to save him, to save them all, and the "he's a dwarf" argument simply didn't hold up against that fact.

ELEVEN

Trolls

THE snake's muscles rippled, slowly drawing the helpless frog deeper into its mouth. The frog struggled pitifully, but it was just a harmless, weak thing and no match for the great black serpent. This was the natural way of things, but to Geek, the goblin-turned-frog, it did not seem natural at all.

He knew that soon the unhinged jaw would slip beyond his bulbous eyes, and then all the world would be darkness. He had seen engorged snakes before and knew that it would be a long time before he was fully digested. How long would he live in that awful state?

"Dear Geek," he heard someone—was it Lady Ceridwen?—say. "We have no time for such play!"

"Play!" he wanted to scream back at the wicked sorceress, but his cry came out as no more than a breathless croak as the snake clamped down on its fairly won quarry.

Then Geek saw the tip of a wand dip down before his bulging eyes. The snake started to wriggle away, dragging the helpless frog with it. Ceridwen uttered a few words and there came a *pop!* and a ripping sound, and Geek was a goblin again, lying facedown on the swampy ground.

"Bless you, me lady!" he groveled, trying to crawl to Ceridwen's feet. He found himself encumbered by the body of the ten-foot snake, its head and upper torso torn apart by the transformation, but still stubbornly clinging to Geek's waist and legs. The goblin whimpered and thrashed to get free, thoroughly disgusted.

"Will you please stop playing with that snake?" Ceridwen said calmly. "We have much business to attend. And get up out of that mud! You are the personal attendant of Lady Ceridwen! Do try to look the part!"

Geek bit back the curses he wanted to spout at the sorceress and instead resumed his groveling, slobbering kisses all over Ceridwen's muddy feet. She kicked him in the face and he thanked her over and over.

"I have turned them back from Dvergamal," the sorceress explained. "We must catch them on the plain, before they get south around the mountains, heading up towards the Crahgs." Her deadly, icy gaze fell fully over the goblin. "You must catch them."

Geek nearly toppled, realizing the price of failure. He looked back to the shredded remains of the black snake and knew that many more such creatures, and even worse creatures, lived in the swamp.

"Geek go get goblins for help," he stammered.

"Goblins?" Ceridwen laughed. "You would be defeated, as you were defeated on the road." Those icy-blue death-promising eyes flashed again. "We'll need bigger things than goblins to stop Kelsenellenelvial and his friends—and they have a dwarf with them now."

"Bigger?" Geek dared to ask, though he truly feared to hear the answer.

"You will go into Dvergamal for me," Ceridwen explained. "To a northern valley feared by travelers and even by the dwarfs."

Geek paled, beginning to understand why he was saved.

"I have some friends there which you must enlist," the witch said calmly, as though it was all no more than a minor task.

"Lady . . . ," Geek began, thinking then that he preferred being a frog.

"They are big enough to catch the likes of that troublesome elf," Ceridwen went on, totally ignoring the whining goblin. "And cunning enough to resist the foolery of that leprechaun." Her description was unnecessary at that moment; Geek knew that she was talking of trolls. Horrid trolls, which even mighty Ceridwen did not wish to face.

"Lady . . . ," he gasped again.

"Promise them a hundred gold pieces and a dozen fat sheep," Ceridwen went on. "A purse and mutton, that should bring them running. Two hundred gold pieces and two dozen sheep if they do not kill the elf or any of his friends. Just catch them and bring them to me."

"Trolls will eats me!" Geek cried.

"Oh, Geek," Ceridwen laughed. "You are always thinking of play! You will not be eaten, not if you promise them enough."

"Geek bring gold?" the goblin asked hopefully.

Ceridwen laughed again, louder. "Bring gold?" she echoed incredulously. "*Promise* gold, dear Geek.

"Oh, very well," Ceridwen said after Geek did not relinquish his pouting expression. Geek smiled hopefully, a grin that dissipated as soon as Ceridwen handed him a single gold piece.

"Give them this," the sorceress explained. "Promise them the rest."

Geek looked to the west, to the towering, snow-covered mountains, then back to the torn snake behind him, honestly wondering which fate he preferred.

It wasn't his choice to make.

Ceridwen uttered a few words and made a hand gesture or two, and in the blink of the astonished goblin's eye, Geek found himself far from the swamp and the plain. Jagged snow-packed mountains surrounded him, stretching as high up as he could see.

"No, lady, no," he whined through chattering teeth, though he realized that Ceridwen couldn't hear him, and wouldn't care anyway.

He inched along the trail in a secluded dell on the southern side of Dvergamal. The Cailleac Bheur's storm had diminished and the temperature had grown more seasonable, but still the paths remained deep with snow. Poor Geek's progress slowed even further with each step, hindered as much by valid fears as by the icy trails. Somehow, Geek almost found himself homesick for the snake's unhinged jaw. He rarely dealt with trolls, especially huge and nasty mountain trolls who were always hungry and not particular about what, or who, they stuffed into their yellow-fanged mouths.

The pitiful goblin came around a ridge, trying to be as stealthy as possible. He heard the trolls grumbling and arguing (trolls were always grumbling and arguing) in the distance and saw the flickering light of their campfire. Then the world went dark for poor Geek as a sack dropped over his head. In a second, he was hoisted feet-up and slung over a huge shoulder.

"Ten thousand golds and a million sheep!" Geek cried in terror, smelling disgusting troll breath right through the dirty sack. He managed to poke one hand out of the sack, presenting the troll with a single gold piece, the coin Ceridwen had enchanted with promises of splendid riches.

THE companions broke camp early the next day. An uncomfortable stillness engulfed them, fed by silent fears of their powerful nemesis and by the heightened surliness of the gruff dwarf. No one dared to ask Geno to help in breaking down the camp, and the dwarf did not offer.

Stern-faced and without saying a word, Kelsey led them off. The elf had barely gone a dozen feet when Mickey trotted up ahead of him and turned back sharply.

"Where're ye going, then?" the leprechaun asked. "Ye're needing a gnome, and Gondabuggan, the gnome burrows, are to the north, not the south."

Kelsey stared unblinkingly at the sprite.

"Gnomes're the second best of thieves," Mickey went on, somewhat hesitantly, for he was beginning to catch on.

"Second best will not suffice," Kelsey replied evenly.

Mickey's sparkling gray eyes narrowed to dart-throwing slits. "Ye're beyond the bounds," he muttered.

"Then run," Kelsey offered, his tone unyielding and his stare promising that he could make Mickey's life much more unpleasant.

Mickey wasn't overly surprised. He had suspected that Kelsey would force him along from the very beginning. Elfs were usually cheerful folk, especially towards sprites, but life-quests had a way of stealing their mirth.

The leprechaun pulled a long drag on his pipe and let Kelsey pass him by. He fell into line beside Gary without saying a word and a short time later had resumed his perch on the young man's shoulder, book in hand.

Gary didn't mind the leprechaun's familiarity. After his mistakes of the previous night and the anger both Kelsey and Geno had shown him, he was glad for the company.

They trudged on through that day with few words being exchanged. Kelsey kept the point position, far out in front, his hand often resting on his sword hilt, with the others following in no particular order. Geno grumbled every now and again, and spat often, usually in Gary's general direction. It all seemed unremarkable and quite boring to Gary, except that on several occasions, he noticed Mickey put something resembling a whistle up to his lips. No sound, at least none that Gary could hear, emanated from the little silver instrument when Mickey blew into it, though, so Gary did not question the leprechaun about it and let it fall from his thoughts.

He tried to concentrate on his own predicament instead. He had no remaining thoughts whatsoever that this might be a dream. But what, then? The only answer that came into Gary's mind, the only possible solution, he decided, was that he had gone quite insane. Several times, he tried to look through the guises of his companions, to see them as people from his own world.

He gave that up quickly enough, seeing no hint that anything was any different. If he had gone insane, then he obviously could not consciously push that insanity away.

So he decided to continue to play it out and made a vow to at least try to enjoy the adventure.

He kept thinking of his parents, though, and of the distress he was no doubt causing them.

GARY suspected that something out of the ordinary was up as soon as he saw Mickey slip out of camp later that night, that curious silver whistle in hand. He followed the leprechaun in a roundabout way, not wanting to be noticed but not wanting the elusive Mickey to get out of his sight. Mickey did, though, as usual, and, Gary suspected, without too much difficulty. The young man found himself out alone, peering helplessly into the dark tangles of a tree copse.

Gary was about to give up and head back to camp when he heard a curious buzzing noise followed by the leprechaun's voice. He crept slowly in the direction of the noise, and his eyes grew wider when he saw, under the light of a full moon, Mickey's companion—the same sprite who had stuck Gary with the poisoned arrow and started this whole adventure.

"Ye know what's to be done," he heard Mickey whisper. The sprite's high-pitched reply came too fast for Gary to decipher any of the words.

"A loss it is," Mickey agreed. "But I've no way to get out of it without angering the likes o' the Tylwyth Teg, and I've no desire to walk into Robert's lair without having a few scoring cards tucked up me sleeve."

Gary silently mouthed the name Robert thinking that Mickey couldn't be referring to the dragon.

Again the sprite buzzed a response that Gary couldn't understand.

"I'll be getting it back, don't ye doubt!" Mickey insisted as forcefully as Gary had ever heard him. "But me first concern's getting meself back with me skin still on."

The sprite buzzed and bowed, and disappeared into the brush. Mickey stared ahead for a few moments, then sighed loudly and took out his pipe.

Gary thought it best not to question Mickey about the strange encounter, so he said nothing later that evening when Mickey strolled back into camp, nor all the next day, hiking along the roiling hills east of the mountains.

The weather was fine, if the company was not, and they continued to make steady progress that day, and then the next. When the southern edge of Dverga-mal at last came into view, Kelsey picked up the pace.

But then Geno stopped suddenly and sniffed the air. Mickey uncrossed his ankles and looked up from his book; even Kelsey spun about curiously on the dwarf. Geno didn't seem to notice either of them. He stood very still, head back and nose up, sniffing at the air.

"What is it?" Kelsey asked, drawing his sword.

Gary could feel the tension growing.

"Uh-oh," he heard Mickey whisper.

Geno glanced right, then left, then spun right around, his wide and round blue-gray eyes darting every which way.

Kelsey's golden orbs flashed with mounting anxiety. "What is it?" the elf de-manded again.

Geno met his stare head-on. "Trolls," the dwarf announced.

"Uh-oh," Mickey said again.

Gary turned on the leprechaun. "That's enough," he growled. "Ever since we left Dilnamarra, I've had the feeling that you and Kelsey know more than you're telling me. What's going on? Who's after us, and why?"

"Ye wouldn't understand," Mickey replied. "'Tis of no concern . . ."

"You tell me now or I'm done with this adventure and you can send me right back to my own world," Gary snapped. He threw his spear to the ground, looped the case with Donigarten's spear over his shoulder and let that fall, too, and crossed his armored arms defiantly over his chest.

"Tell him as we run," Kelsey bade Mickey. Geno was still standing, sniffing the air, his expression growing more and more alarmed,

Seeing even the steady dwarf so obviously unnerved, Gary lost the momentum for his argument. He scooped up his belongings and off they went, Geno leading them away from the mountains.

"'Tis Ceridwen, we're thinking," Mickey started to explain to Gary, the leprechaun taking his usual seat.

"You have angered the sorceress?" Geno cried, overhearing. He skidded to a stop and spun around, eyes flashing and his jaw clenched tight. "And it was she who roused the Cailleac," he said angrily.

Mickey nodded gravely.

Geno turned on Kelsey. "You said nothing about battling the likes of Ceridwen!" he roared. "You did not mention the witch at all!"

Gary listened to the conversation distantly, his thoughts tied around the name of the witch. So many names in this enchanted land seemed somehow familiar to him, and he was certain that he had heard of Ceridwen before, back in his own world.

"I did not know that the witch was involved," Kelsey answered honestly. "Only when I spied the Cailleac drifting across the peaks of Dvergamal did I come to truly believe that the dangers we have encountered have not been random chances. "

"For only she could rouse the Cailleac," Geno reasoned grimly.

"And the trolls?" Mickey put in, prodding them all to the realization that this might not be the best opportunity to sit and discuss the matter.

The reminder sobered Geno. He spun all about, sniffing anxiously at every direction. "Trolls," he replied. "And not too far."

As if on cue, the others suddenly caught the disgusting scent.

"Run!" Kelsey cried, and he and Geno led them on wildly, Kelsey stopping every few feet to encourage Gary to keep up. Now more comfortable with the armor, Gary was up to the great pace, but still the stench of trolls deepened around them, from every side.

Geno led them up a small, bare hillock. "They are all about!" the dwarf declared, taking up his two favorite throwing hammers and arranging the others for easy grabbing off his wide belt. "Set for defense!"

Kelsey pulled his longbow off his shoulder and quickly strung it, while Mickey hopped down from his perch and surveyed the area, wondering what tricks he might play. Gary tried hard to appear busy, though he had little idea of what to do. He clasped his spear tightly in both hands, feeling the balance, and foolishly ran a finger along (instead of across) its metal tip, drawing a line of blood. With Kelsey, Geno, and even Mickey so worried about the trolls, Gary could only pray that the enchanted weapon on his back would aid him when the fighting started.

And then Gary watched and waited, wondering what a troll looked like.

It wasn't long before he found out. A huge, humanoid shape appeared over the rolling hills behind, lumbering towards them on legs as thick as the trunk of a mature oak. Another troll appeared behind it, and a third behind that.

"Three of them to the north," Gary remarked, squinting through the eye slit on his helmet.

"Three that way," Mickey corrected. Following the leprechaun's motion, Gary turned left and saw another troll, this one close enough for him to get a better view. The creature stood fully ten feet tall, maybe more, and wore filthy hides over its green, wart-covered skin. While its legs and torso were unbelievably thick, its arms were long and lean, made for snatching fleeing prey with long curling fingernails. Scraggly hair, yellow eyes, and even yellower teeth completed the gruesome picture. When he was finally able to pull himself from the approaching spectacle, Gary completed his visual circuit. Two more trolls had gotten ahead of the companions and now came in from the front, the south, and a seventh creature, accompanied by a smaller form, approached the hillock from the east.

"Have ye noticed the sunlight?" Mickey asked sarcastically. "When ye get back to yer own world, ye go and tell yer Mr. Tolkien that ye seen trolls moving about in the sunlight!"

"No regular hunting band," Geno remarked, regarding the engulfing formation. "This group is skilled in catching quarry."

"As part o' that quarry, I'm not pleased to be hearing ye," Mickey put in.

"They have not caught us yet," Kelsey declared, shooting the sarcastic leprechaun a dangerous glare. He took a bead on the closest troll, the one to the west, and his great bow twanged in rapid succession, sending a line of arrows at the monster.

If Gary had been impressed with the elf's swordsmanship against the goblin raiders, he was even more amazed now. Kelsey had his fifth arrow in the air before the first hit the approaching troll.

The elf's aim was near perfect, though the thin darts seemed to have little effect. One snapped in half against the troll's shoulder; another nicked the creature's neck, drawing a bit of blood. But the troll slapped it and the others away as though they were but a minor inconvenience, showing them no more heed than Gary might show a few stinging gnats.

But then Kelsey went from near perfect to perfect, driving an arrow into the troll's eye. The creature howled in agony, swerved to the side, and went down in a heap, screaming and thrashing, its clawing hands and kicking feet digging wide holes on the grassy plain.

Geno went to work on the two trolls charging in from the north. Hammers spun in, bonking against the attackers with tremendous force.

"Ow!" cried the first, catching a hammer squarely on the tip of its stubby thumb.

"Me nose!" snuffled the other. "'E breaked me nose!" Even twenty yards away, Gary could hear the cartilage cracking as the monster grabbed its prominent proboscis in both hands and twisted it back trying to stem the flow of gushing blood.

Both of those trolls ducked and dodged, suddenly more concerned with keeping away from the continuing stream of hammers than with attacking the hillock.

Gary looked at his spear and at the trolls closing from behind and from the east. The three behind were not an immediate threat, having taken up a zigzag route around a wide crack that had suddenly appeared in the ground between them and the hillock. Gary had just crossed that same ground, running in an unhindered straight line. He didn't have to spy out the concentrating leprechaun to know that Mickey's illusions had caused the crack.

The troll from the east, having left its smaller companion (which Gary now recognized as a goblin) far behind, was not deterred, though, and with Kelsey and Geno deep in their own fights and Mickey busy with his illusion, only Gary stood to block the monster's way.

He looked again at his spear.

"*Do not even think of throwing it,*" came the voice in his head.

"I wasn't!" Gary retorted aloud.

"*A thousand pardons,*" answered the silent voice. "*Take heart, now, young warrior. I will guide thee.*"

Gary was glad for the help, but hardly taking heart. The troll hadn't even started up the side of the hillock, but its evil yellow eyes were even with Gary's. Up, up, came the monster, holding a huge club at its side.

"*Strike before it finds even footing!*" the spear of Cedric Donigarten implored, and Gary did, thrusting straight out, driving the point of his dwarf-forged spear against the troll's massive chest. The weapon dug in just an inch, then its long tip bent over to the side.

"Blimey!" screamed the troll, stopping its ascent and looking down in surprise.

Gary didn't hesitate. On his own instincts, he curled his legs under him and leaped out, slamming his heavy shield into the troll's face and chest.

The foolish young man bounced back, stormed, without his breath, and with every metal plate of his armor singing a vibrating tune.

"Never shield-rush a mountain troll!" scolded Cedric's spear.

Down to his knees, Gary hardly comprehended the call. He noticed his spear lying beside him, and then noticed impossibly huge feet and impossibly thick ankles on either side of him. He understood, somewhere in the back of his spinning mind, that the troll straddling him held its club up, ready to squash him.

"Up! Up!" cried the sentient spear on his back.

The call could have meant several things, Gary noted, but he again went with his instincts, grabbing his dwarven spear in both hands and thrusting it straight up above his head. He heard a sickly squishy sound and watched the monster hop up to its tippy-toes. The troll groaned weakly, then toppled, pulling the spear from Gary's grasp as it went.

A relieved Gary knew that he had done well, but when he looked around for applause, he realized that he could hardly afford to stop and congratulate himself.

Geno had run out of throwing hammers and now met the two trolls head-on. A larger hammer in each hand, the dwarf scooted every which way, between the trolls' legs, around to the side, slapping and smacking wherever he found an opening.

Kelsey hadn't joined the dwarf, though, for two of the trolls from behind had found their way through Mickey's maze and pressed in on the elf.

"Two trolls?" Gary muttered. "Only two?" He got a terrible feeling and spun about, bringing his shield up more as a matter of reflex than conscious thought.

There, right behind him, he found the missing troll, and saw, too, its arcing club. The heavy weapon slammed the top of Gary's shield, snapping the straps and nearly breaking Gary's arm, then clipped the young man on the side of the head. Gary's helmet spun about several times, finally coming to a stop facing backwards.

Donigarten's spear implored him to action, crying for him to dive and roll, or fall back and tumble down the hillock.

None of it mattered, for Gary wasn't seeing anything or hearing anything at that moment. The ground rushed up to catch him, but he didn't know it.

KELSEY'S sword spun and swirled, cut teasingly wide arcs, then darted straight ahead at troll hands or troll faces, or whatever target the elf could find. The two trolls trying to get at Kelsey had a dozen wounds each, but these were minor nicks, for the elf's sword was a slender weapon, more designed for battling smaller, less mountain-like foes.

Still, Kelsey, fighting in a purely defensive manner, managed to keep them at bay for many minutes, though he knew that something dramatic had to happen if he and his companions were to prevail. Two trolls were down—the one Kelsey had blinded with an arrow and the one Gary had pierced through the groin—but five others remained. One was busy now, wrapping Gary in a crude net; Geno had the remaining two fully engaged.

The time had come for Kelsey to strike hard.

"Circle 'im!" one of his opponents cried, slipping around to Kelsey's side. The other, after a moment's consideration, moved the other way, getting opposite the elf from his companion. Kelsey worked hard to keep them on his sides, where he could watch their every movement. They stepped towards him and back out, lifted their clubs and waved them about menacingly, looking for an opening.

Kelsey dipped under a clumsy club swing, but instead of backing away to keep his defensive posture, he leaned forward under the blow and charged straight in. The surprised troll had no way to get its club back in line for any semblance of defense. It waved its free arm frantically, trying to keep Kelsey at bay.

The elf drove in fiercely. His crafted sword bent nearly double as he thrust it into the rock-like troll's chest, but it was a magical blade and it did not break. He heard the troll wheeze as the blade slipped through its ribs, then it fell back, grabbing at its chest.

The doomed creature's companion bellowed and hurled his club, but Kelsey, hearing the roar, was not caught unawares. He tucked his head and rolled to the side, barely dodging the heavy missile. The troll came on, diving after Kelsey and grabbing him by the leg in one huge hand. Quickly the troll scrambled back to its knees and tugged with all its strength, meaning to spin Kelsey around and around.

The elf did come off the ground under the troll's incredibly powerful pull, but Kelsey, veteran of a hundred battles, kept his composure and bent over double against the momentum, hacking at the troll's hand with all his might. Troll fingers fell to the ground and Kelsey, free of the grasp, went spinning through the air. Agile as any cat, he landed easily and started right back in for the fight.

But then a boot fell over his back and he was flattened to the grass. Kelsey felt as if a mountain had fallen on him; he couldn't even squirm about under the tremendous weight.

"Squish 'im, Earl!" yelled the troll that had thrown him. "He cut off me fingers!"

GENO Hammerthrower was no novice to troll fighting. The trolls were the very worst enemy of the dwarfs of Dvergamal, and every time one of their hunting parties went anywhere near the thunderous spray of the Firth of Buldre, Geno had personally led the charge.

The odds had always been better than this, however. For the first time, Geno found himself outnumbered by trolls two to one, and outweighed by at least twenty to one. Undaunted, the dwarf growled and spat, and used every trick he had ever been taught about fighting giant-kin.

"I'll puts ye in a sandwi—" one of the beasts started to say, but it stopped abruptly when Geno's hurled hammer put out two of its teeth. The troll spit the hammer out, and Geno was quick to reclaim it, preferring to fight with both hands.

The other troll, seeing Geno going for the hammer, went for Geno, both its hands outstretched.

"Stupid!" Geno laughed, spinning about, and he laughed even louder as he realized that the troll's reaching fingers were straight out and rigid.

"This will hurt!" Geno promised, and he smashed both his hammers, one after the other, straight into the tips of the monster's fingers. Suddenly the troll had little desire to grab at the dwarf—or grab anything at all.

Geno wasn't quite finished, though. He scooted through the troll's wide-spread legs, but reversed his direction and came right back out the front. His ploy worked perfectly and the stupid monster was still looking over its shoulder as Geno cracked a hammer into its kneecap.

KELSEY stared blankly as his own arms became writhing tentacles, horribly tipped by barbed claws. The troll standing over him jerked back in surprise, its foot coming up enough to allow the elf to draw breath.

Then Kelsey noticed Mickey standing beside the massive body of the troll that Gary had downed. The elf mouthed a silent thank-you, then started to cry out an alarm as he noticed a goblin creeping up behind the leprechaun, sack in hand.

But Kelsey had his own problems. The sack went over Mickey and the tentacle illusion was no more. The troll growled and pressed down again, even more forcefully.

"Squish 'im, Earl!" screamed its wounded companion, and Kelsey surely thought that his life was at an end. But then Earl reached down and grabbed him in both hands, plucked his sword away, and tossed him into the same net that held Gary.

"I gots him, I gots him!" Geek squealed in glee, holding up the leprechaun-filled sack by its drawstring. But then the bag went limp, giving the illusion that the leprechaun had somehow vanished. Stunned, the goblin grabbed at the sack, stupidly pulling it open.

A long-stemmed pipe whipped out and cracked into Geek's eyes, and the sack fell free.

Mickey thought himself quite clever—until a huge hand plucked him out of midair.

"No, ye don'ts, ye trickster!" growled the nearby troll, holding its sliced groin in one hand and wrapping the other about the leprechaun. The troll gave an uncomfortable squeeze.

"Any more o' yer tricks, and I'll squash ye good!" it warned, and Mickey didn't have to be told twice.

THE troll clutched its busted knee and hopped up and down on its good leg. Every time it came down, though, Geno slammed a hammer onto its toes.

The gap-toothed troll crept up behind the dwarf, club in hand.

"Quiet as a thunderstorm!" Geno chided, rolling out of harm's way just as the sneaking troll launched its swing. The swinging club took the troll's hopping companion on the side of the good leg and sent the poor monster tumbling down the hillock like an avalanche.

The gap-toothed troll flew into a rage, swatting and clubbing frantically, putting huge dents in the soft ground, but never, for all its fury, getting anywhere near to hitting Geno. The dwarf scrambled and dove, appearing desperate, but using each maneuver to better his position for counterstrikes. He came up alongside the club one time and smacked the troll's hand; another time, he used the down-cutting club to great advantage, tossing a hammer right over it as it descended. The stupid troll never even saw the missile until it rebounded away from its face, taking another tooth with it. Geno was upon the weapon in a split second, coming back up, both hands ready to continue.

Then the troll got more cautious. It bent low to the dwarf, keeping its club raised defensively between its face and Geno.

Geno shrugged and hurled a hammer into the club, which in turn smacked the troll in the face. The monster roared and lifted its weapon high, just as the dwarf had anticipated. Geno leaped right into its face, grabbing a handful of scraggly hair and flailing away furiously with his remaining weapon. Geno understood and even anticipated the stupid creature's every move, and he leaped away just as the heavy club came swatting in.

The troll's head snapped over backwards; the club fell to the ground. The monster stood very still for a long moment, regarding Geno through crossed eyes, then fell like a cut tree.

But now Earl came stomping over, followed by his seven-fingered companion, and by a gingerly walking troll holding a small sack.

"Sorry to leave you," Geno called to his captured companions. "But fair is fair!" The dwarf figured his indenture to be at an end; he had never agreed to die beside the elf. When Geno turned to go, though, he found that retreat would not be so easy a feat. Another troll, with a broken arrow protruding from one eye and a murderous look in its other eye, had come around behind the dwarf, and the first troll Geno had felled was also back up, limping and still holding its knee, but blocking that route.

The chase and fight went on for several minutes. Geno whipped a hammer here, smacked a hammer there, and put each of the trolls down more than once. But there were too many enemies, and finally Earl put a bag over the stubborn dwarf's head.

TWELVE

Ynis Gwydrin

IT was a long time before Gary Leger opened his eyes again. He was tangled up with Kelsey, hanging in a net supported by poles slung over the shoulders of two trolls. The first thing that struck Gary, aside from the throbs of a terrible headache, was the condition of his captors, for the trolls, though victorious, had not come away unscathed. There were six of them now, not seven, and each one of these showed fresh and vicious battle scars. The one carrying the net up front was missing fingers on its right hand; the one behind Gary had a bandage wrapped about his head, angled to cover one eye.

Trolls flanked the net on either side. Gary recognized the one to his left, walking gingerly, as the one who had caught his spear between the legs. The troll across on the right sported an even more pronounced limp and it reached down often to clutch its kneecap. The remaining two monsters walked up front, along with a scrawny goblin. From his tangled position, Gary couldn't see this group very well, but he noticed that one of the trolls carried a large sack, which it banged against a tree whenever they passed one along the side of the road. From the sputtering, cursing, and thrashing that inevitably erupted from inside the sack after each hit, Gary soon understood that Geno's ride was even less pleasant than his own.

"We didn't win, huh?" he groaned as soon as he felt able to speak. His mouth felt as though it had been stuffed with cotton and his throat was sorely parched. How long had he been out?

Kelsey twisted about, which turned Gary's leg in a very uncomfortable way.

"We fared better than most against the likes of trolls!" the proud elf growled angrily.

"'Ere, shut yer mouth!" snarled the troll behind and it shook the poles roughly, jostling the net. Scratchy cords dug at Gary from every angle, finding creases in his armor and cutting at his skin.

"At least Mickey got away," Gary whispered hopefully after a few minutes had passed.

Kelsey shook his head. "He did not," the elf explained. "The large troll up front has him."

"Earl's got 'im!" snarled the troll on the right, having overheard. "In his pocket. Even the little trickster won't get outa Earl's pocket!"

The troll behind gave another rough shake on the poles and Gary fell silent, feeling thoroughly miserable. Was he to be cooked in a large pot? And what would death in this land of Faerie mean back in the real world? Gary had heard that people who died in their dreams really did die, from the shock. He had never believed that, but he wasn't anxious to try out the theory.

And worse still, Gary absolutely did not believe this adventure to be a dream. The little details, like the rope now digging at the back of his knee, were too complete and too real—and how long could a dream last anyway? Were these trolls, then, hospital attendants, the proverbial "men in white coats"?

Gary shook the absurd thoughts away, replaced them with his heartfelt belief that all of this was as it seemed, that he was actually in this magical land of Faerie.

Talk about your absurd thoughts!

The trolls bumped along at a great pace—even wounded trolls could cover wide expanses with their long-legged strides—across the rolling plain region, through a small wood, and then over many more miles of open lands. They set no camp, ran right through the night, and the next morning, they went up into yet another mountain region. Gary, lost though he was, was certain that these peaks were not part of Dvergamal, though. They were less jagged and foreboding, though rugged enough.

"Penllyn," Kelsey muttered grimly, and the name meant something to Gary, though he couldn't exactly place it. Kelsey fell silent as the trolls lumbered on, through tight passes, through a tunnel once, and over ridges that Gary would have spent half an hour climbing, but that the trolls merely stepped across. Poor

Geno continued to get the worst of it. At one point, the troll carrying him dropped the sack to the ground and jerked and dragged it along with a lead rope, purposely bouncing it among the sharpest stones while the troll and its companions shared a wicked laugh.

Geno kept up his muffled stream of stubborn curses throughout the ordeal, promising retribution and revealing no pain.

"Gwydrin! Gwydrin!" Geek the goblin squealed a short while later. The trolls got noticeably nervous at the proclamation, but it was Kelsey, up tight against Gary, who seemed the most afraid, more afraid than Gary had ever seen him.

"What is Gwydrin?" Gary whispered, but the elf offered no reply.

The troupe came around a jutting stone then, and a wide mountain lake spread before them, reflecting the surrounding peaks on its crystalline surface. In the middle, far away and barely visible, loomed an island that, despite its tiny size, filled Gary with dread. Somehow he knew that to be their destination, as though the island itself was emanating some evil, beckoning energies.

"Gwydrin!" Geek squealed again. He rushed down to the shoreline and led the trolls to several small craft hidden in tall weeds.

"Puts them in the boatses," Geek squeaked. "We takes them to the Lady."

"Where's me pay, goblin thing?" croaked Earl, casting a not-so-fond stare at the rowboats—small boats indeed by a troll's estimation!

"Lady pays," Geek promised.

"Goblin pays!" Earl corrected. "Or Earl eats goblin!"

"Two hundreds?" Geek replied squeamishly.

"Ten thousands, ye says!" howled the seven-fingered troll, dropping its end of the net with a thump. Geek shied away from the brute but had nowhere to run.

"Yeah," added Earl, poking the goblin in the back hard enough to send him flat to his face. "An' a millions sheeps!" Earl reached down and grabbed poor Geek up by the head, giving him just a little shake for the fun of it. "Where's me sheeps?"

The goblin didn't even try to fight back. Earl's hand fully covered Geek's head and he knew well that one little squeeze from the mighty troll would pop his skull.

There came a shriek from far out on the lake, the cry of a large bird. Trolls and captives alike watched a black speck soaring high into the clear sky, growing larger as it sped towards them. The great black bird went into a curl-winged stoop, plummeting for the glassy surface of the minor lake. At the last second, it leveled out and let its momentum carry it quickly to the shore, where it landed right before Earl and his captive.

"What's . . . ," Earl started to say, but he was interrupted by a sudden and blinding flash of light. When the big troll's vision returned, Lady Ceridwen stood before him, cold and stern and incredibly beautiful in her shimmering black gown.

"What's . . . ," Earl started to say again, but truly the troll forgot what it wanted to ask and the words stuck in its throat.

"Good," purred Ceridwen. "You have brought them alive." She looked more closely at Kelsey and Gary, trying to fathom if any more forms were caught up in that tangle of ropes and limbs. Then she looked to the large sack and the blood staining its side.

As if on cue, the troll holding the bag gave a quick shake and Geno set into bitching again.

"And the leprechaun is in there as well?" Ceridwen asked.

"'E's in me pocket," grumbled Earl, growing more suspicious and less impressed by the moment.

"Alive?"

"Fer me to know," Earl retorted. "And fer yous to find out when ye pays me me gold and sheeps!"

"Two hundred gold and two dozen sheep," Ceridwen offered.

"Ten thousands, 'e says!" Earl corrected, poking Geek hard.

"An' a millions shee—" the seven-fingered troll started to assert, but Ceridwen's icy gaze froze the words in its mouth.

Ceridwen looked sternly at her goblin slave. "A hundred gold and a dozen sheep was my bargain," she explained, as much to the terrified goblin as to the trolls. "Twice that if they are all alive. That was my offer; that remains my offer."

The trolls blustered and grumbled, each looking to the other to make the first move against the impertinent witch. Ceridwen's reputation was not something to be taken lightly, though, not even for a group of mountain trolls.

"Ten thousands!" one of the monsters, the one Gary had stuck, growled finally. "Or we eats yous all!" The troll took one step towards Ceridwen, but the witch uttered a simple phrase, and the troll found itself hopping instead of walking.

"She turned 'im into a rabbit!" the seven-fingered blusterer peeped. Indeed, where a moment before had stood a twelve-foot-tall mountain troll now sat a lop-eared bunny-troll, no bigger than Earl's fat thumb.

Gary blinked in sheer amazement as the trolls grumbled and milled about in confusion. The monsters were not amused.

But neither were they making any moves towards the raven-haired witch.

"Is the leprechaun alive?" Ceridwen asked Earl again.

Earl shoved his hand into a pocket and pulled out a very shook-up, but very alive, Mickey McMickey. Earl held the stunned leprechaun high between his thumb and index finger and gave Mickey a rough shake, telling him to "Squeak out."

Mickey couldn't find the words to respond and Earl went to shake him again, but Ceridwen stopped the troll with an outstretched palm. "Two hundred pieces of gold and two dozen plump sheep," the witch agreed.

"Ten . . . ," the seven-fingered troll started to complain, but a look from Earl and its three other remaining companions put an end to that.

"We gets to keep the dwarf?" Earl asked. "Me friends be wantin' a pie."

"Keep the dwarf," Ceridwen replied, and Earl smiled wide. Nothing tasted better than dwarf pie, after all, not even two dozen plump sheep.

But then the witch abruptly changed her mind, considering the benefits of having the finest smithy in all the world at her disposal, a prisoner on her island. "I take the dwarf," she insisted.

Gary knew what was coming, but he cringed anyway when Earl begged on, "We keeps the man?"

"Oh, no," Ceridwen said. "Not the man, nor the elf, nor the leprechaun, I am afraid."

"What about me pie?" Earl grumbled.

Ceridwen thought for a moment, cast a look at Geek that made the goblin faint dead away, then came up with a solution. "Rabbits make fine pies," she offered.

With typical troll loyalty, the four monsters behind Earl fell murderously over the lop-eared troll-bunny.

"Not big enough!" grumbled the seven-fingered troll, and a moment later, it, too, found itself hopping along the ground zigging and zagging desperately to get away from greedy troll hands.

"Big enough now?" Ceridwen asked Earl when the second troll-bunny was at last scooped up by its floppy ears, kicking wildly.

Earl blanched, managed a smile, and nodded stupidly.

Ceridwen snapped her fingers and two boats drifted out from the weeds. "Put the prisoners in the square one," she instructed. The trolls looked all around, waiting again for another to take the lead.

"Now!" Ceridwen cried, and the monsters fell all over themselves getting to the prisoners. Geno went flying in first with a crash, followed by Gary and Kelsey, and finally Mickey, who managed to produce an umbrella at the last second to slow his descent.

Ceridwen waved her hand, and lines of blue light, a magical cage, shot up around the boat's perimeter.

"And put their equipment in the other boat," Ceridwen said.

Earl shrugged, quite a heave for the square-shouldered giant, as if he did not understand. "Equip—?" the troll stuttered, hoping to get away with the precious items.

"Hop, hop," Ceridwen promised. A sword, two shields, a spear, a leather case, assorted packs, and a dozen hammers went flying into the boat.

"And be throwin' in the trickster's hat!" Ceridwen heard herself say, though it was neither her thought nor her voice. Before she could say anything, Earl flipped Mickey's tam-o'-shanter into the boat.

Ceridwen's icy-blue eyes flashed in Mickey's direction, but the sprite only shrugged in reply and the witch's visage softened, revealing almost admiration for the clever trick.

The companions didn't even try to get out of their boat prison as Geek towed them far out on the lake.

"Caught again," Geno grumbled. "And now I am working for that wretched witch."

"The burdens of fame," Mickey put in, drawing a scowl from the dwarf.

"We'll not be long on Ceridwen's isle," Kelsey vowed.

Gary let them ramble on without him, more interested in the island. A castle sat upon it, walls glistening in the sunlight as though they were made of glass. Gary sat and stared at the magnificent structure for a long while, mesmerized by the beauty.

"The Isle of Glass," Mickey explained, shifting beside him.

"Ynis Gwydrin," Gary replied offhandedly. Only Mickey's sudden startled movement reminded the young man that his knowledge of the place was unexpected.

"Where'd ye hear of it?" the leprechaun asked.

"Folktale," Gary replied. "I must have read it in some book. It's like many of the things and places around here, yourself included." Gary's brow crinkled as he tried to sort it all out, his green eyes reflecting the sparkle of the glistening waters of Loch Gwydrin.

"The names are strange to me," he explained after some time, "but I know that I've heard them before." He looked to Mickey for answers. "Does that make any sense?"

"Aye," Mickey replied, to Gary's relief. "Many from yer own world have crossed to Faerie and returned with 'folktales,' as ye call them."

"And Penllyn," Gary went on. "That name, too, is familiar, but I think it is an actual place in my world."

"Not to doubt," replied the leprechaun. "Many are the places that share borders, and many more that share names, between Faerie and yer own world, though not nearly as many as there used to be. 'Tis a sad thing."

"And what have you heard of Ynis Gwydrin?" Kelsey asked, hearing the conversation.

"Just the name, that I can recall," Gary answered. "And that it was an enchanted place."

"*Is* an enchanted place," Mickey corrected. "But not as it used to be. The isle is Ceridwen's now, and that's not a good thing for the likes o' me and yerself."

"We'll not be long on Ceridwen's isle!" Kelsey said again, more forcefully, but the vow seemed lost on all of them at that moment, for Geek's boat had already scraped bottom and the dreary beach loomed just a dozen feet away.

Ceridwen met them as they landed. With a wave of her delicate hand, both boats climbed right up on the sand. A second wave brought down the cage of blue light, and the companions filtered out onto the shore.

"Welcome to Ynis Gwydrin, Kelsenellenelvial Gil-Ravadry," the witch said with a polite curtsy. "You may retrieve your belongings; the isle is yours to enjoy."

"You would give me my sword?" the elf asked suspiciously.

"It won't be bringing her harm," Mickey explained, "No weapon forged by mortal hands, even elvish hands, can wound Lady Ceridwen."

"How true," purred the witch. "And how convenient for me!"

Kelsey said nothing, but thought of the many ways in which he might cause havoc on Ynis Gwydrin and escape the island. Ceridwen smiled as though she had read the elf's thoughts. In a burst of movement, she twirled about and waved her arms, her voice crackling as she cried:

> *"Elf and dwarf and man and sprite*
> *By any day and any night*
> *If you swim the water blue*
> *As acid it will be to you.*
>
> *And any boat you seek to take*
> *Upon the waters of my lake*
> *Will fall apart and splinter thin*
> *And in the acid drop you in!*

And if you find a way to fly
Across the lake up in the sky
Let a wind come rushing down
And push you in to burn and drown!"

"Not very good," Mickey commented dryly.

Ceridwen stopped laughing and shot a glare at the impertinent leprechaun. "But effective, do not doubt!" she promised, and none of them, not even Geno, wanted to go and try the water.

"How long are we to be held here?" the dwarf growled. "I have work to do, many contracts to fulfill."

"A hundred years," Ceridwen replied. "Or until that one"—she pointed to Gary—"has died. Ynis Gwydrin is your home now. Do make yourselves comfortable. There are caves, which should please you, good dwarf, and my resourceful slaves have even managed to construct some small huts. With your fighting skills, mighty elf-lord, you should be able to claim one or two structures as your own."

"Why have you interfered?" Kelsey demanded. "This was no business of yours, witch Ceridwen!"

"But it was," Ceridwen replied. "I cannot allow you to reforge the spear and stir up thoughts of ancient heroes."

"Yer puppet strings're not so tight on Kinnemore?" Mickey asked slyly.

"On the King, yes," Kelsey reasoned, remembering Prince Geldion's interference. "But not on the common people. She fears that they will look back to find their heritage and their way out of the mire."

"You are a fool, Kelsenellenelvial Gil-Ravadry," Ceridwen spat.

"Call him Kelsey," Mickey offered, but the witch paid the leprechaun no heed.

"Ever were the elf-lords of Faerie fools!" Ceridwen went on. "You sing old songs and play with legends while I . . ." She stopped suddenly, realizing that she might be revealing too much—even to prisoners.

"Come along, Geek!" Ceridwen growled, and she grabbed up the case containing Cedric's spear and rushed away, the cowering goblin close behind.

There was really very little that the companions could do. Geno retrieved a hammer from the goblin's boat and hurled it Ceridwen's way, but it turned into a crow long before it ever reached the witch and simply flew off into the sky.

So the weary companions set a camp and sat down in the sand, and stared glumly at the shore. It did not seem so far, with the mountains rising up sharply beyond the water's edge, but the trip in the boat had taken many minutes, covering a half mile, at least. Given Ceridwen's spell, the shore might as well have been a world away.

The break gave Gary time to consider his fate, and the consequences of this strange adventure. He slid over to sit by Mickey, who was just about done with *The Hobbit.*

"Too bad I don't have the rest of the series," he offered. "You'd have a way to spend the next week or two."

"Fine with the words, is yer Mr. Tolkien," the leprechaun agreed, never looking up from the book.

"Mickey," Gary started again somberly, and he put a hand on the leprechaun's shoulder. Mickey looked up and knew at once that something was deeply troubling his captured man.

"How many days . . . I mean, I've been here a while . . ."

Mickey's sudden burst of laughter put Gary a bit at rest. "Not to worry, lad," the leprechaun explained. "Time's running different in Faerie. When the sprites danced about ye, they danced against the turn o' the clock."

"Against the turn?" Gary did not understand.

"If they go against the turn, then the time in Faerie runs quicker than time in yer own world," Mickey explained. "If they go with the clock, then the other runs true. A day here'd see a dozen years pass in yer own world. But they went against the clock in bringing ye; ye'll not be missed in yer home for a long, long time."

"But what happens . . ." Gary stuttered on, searching for the right words. "I mean, if I die here, do I wake up there? I hadn't really thought about it before . . . well . . . maybe in the goblin fight, and just for the moment when I fell over the cliff. But what happens?"

Mickey's comforting smile faded. "No, lad," he replied quietly. "If ye die here, then die ye do. They'd not find yer body—unless I can think of a way to bring ye back to the woods where me pixie took ye. This is no dream, I telled ye before."

Gary spent a few minutes considering the grim possibility that he would die here, and the pain it would bring to his parents. He imagined them looking over his sword-hacked body in the woods out back, totally perplexed, and with half the Lancashire police force standing right beside them, having no explanations.

How many unexplained deaths . . . ? Gary dismissed the seemingly limitless possibilities of the confusing notion, preferring to concentrate on his own predicament

"Suppose Ceridwen keeps us, for a year or ten years," Gary reasoned, "and then you get me back?"

"As I said, in yer world, ye'll have been gone just a short time, even though ye been ten years in Faerie.

"But will I have aged?" Now Gary thought he saw some intriguing possibilities here concerning immortality. Mickey dashed them immediately.

"Aye," the leprechaun replied, and he chuckled as he thought about it. "Ye'd be showing the ten years. Many's the ones who've gone back to yer world after long years in Faerie, trying to explain how their hair turned all gray overnight."

"But it won't be ten years, or a hundred," Gary prompted, looking over to Kelsey, sitting a short distance away and staring into the darkening sky. "You'll get me out of here."

"Ceridwen's a mighty foe," Mickey began, not at all convinced. It wasn't hard to see, though, that Gary needed some comforting. "Aye, lad," the leprechaun finished as cheerfully as he could. "Kelsey'll find a way to beat the witch."

Gary smiled and motioned for Mickey to go back to his book, then joined Kelsey in the silent stare to the twilight sky.

THIRTEEN

Island Boss

THEY spent a quiet night—almost. Sometime before dawn, Gary awakened from a fitful sleep to find yellow eyes staring at the camp from every direction. Kelsey and Geno were already up; Gary could make out their dark forms nearby in the gloom.

The yellow eyes slowly advanced.

"Give us some light," Kelsey whispered, and with a snap of a leprechaun's fingers, the whole area was bathed in a soft glow. The grubby slaves of Ceridwen's island jumped back, startled, then began thumping crooked clubs against their makeshift shields and throwing sand into the air. Not even Kelsey or Mickey had ever seen such a mixture of rabble. Dirty humans, goblins, a troll, and even a dwarf stood shoulder-to-shoulder (or shoulder-to-hip) in the threatening ring about the camp. Gary wasn't sure whether they wanted a fight, or if they had come to enlist the newest slaves in their ragtag army, and he wasn't certain which of those choices he would prefer.

The rabble calmed and quieted as the initial surprise of the light wore off and once again they tightened their ranks. They looked around to each other, hesitatingly, and finally one ugly, powerfully built man, fully armored (though his armor was quite rusty), strode out boldly from the ranks.

"Jacek," he proclaimed, thumbing his barrel-like chest. In a proclamation of superiority, the large man chopped his heavy sword against the soft ground. "This is Jacek's island."

"Seems this one's for Kelsey," Mickey mentioned, and the grim elf nodded his agreement. Without the slightest trepidation showing in his determined strides, Kelsey stepped out to meet Jacek squarely.

"I had been told that this was Ceridwen's island," the elf replied to the boast.

"Castle is Ceridwen's," Jacek retorted without a second's hesitation. "Island belongs to Jacek."

The grubby dwarf stepped out of the ranks then, eyeing Geno fiercely and stroking his thick blue beard.

"Ye know him?" Mickey asked.

"Not of my clan," Geno replied, never taking his eyes from his counterpart. Like Geno, the stranger had several hammers hanging from his wide belt. Deliberately Geno pulled two hammers out and sent them spinning into the air above him. After just a few catches, he added a third. The other dwarf did likewise, and added a fourth as soon as Geno had, then put a fifth up before Geno could respond.

"Dwarfs have their own types o' challenges," Mickey explained to Gary.

"Well, Jacek," Kelsey said evenly, "it seems that you must now share your island, for Ceridwen has trapped us here."

"You join with Jacek!" the ugly man roared. "You serve Jacek and Jacek lets you live."

Kelsey looked at Mickey and Gary and the two could tell from his smirk that Jacek was about to get a lesson.

"I think not," Kelsey replied. Jacek started to turn towards his own troops, but Kelsey's sword flashed up and nicked him on the ear. The ugly man spun back and wetted his finger in his own blood, his face contorted in budding outrage.

Gary realized that Kelsey could have killed the man as he had turned away, but he understood the elf's caution, and his plan. Kelsey didn't want the whole rabble force, particularly the troll, to get into the fight, and the elf was betting that defeating Jacek fairly would put an end to it all.

The nick on the ear had worked. Too angry to care about his allies, Jacek roared and launched a mighty swing Kelsey's way.

Kelsey was too nimble for the heavy weapon. He easily stepped back, then came in with a straightforward thrust that cut a strap on Jacek's crude breastplate, leaving a vulnerable hollow. Kelsey couldn't finish the move, though, for Jacek, incredibly strong, reversed the lumbering swing and came across again, driving the elf backwards.

Jacek advanced, holding his sword by both hands straight out in front of him. Kelsey moved to the side and Jacek turned to follow, wisely keeping the swift elf out at sword's length.

A fierce thrust had Kelsey spinning to the side. He slipped down to one knee and Jacek roared in, cutting an overhand chop. Gary screamed, thinking Kelsey doomed, but the elf dove and rolled towards Jacek, inside the angle of the blow, and came up beside and then beyond the man, slashing him in the leg as he passed.

Jacek growled, but seemed not to care about the wound. From his scars, Gary could see that he had suffered many worse hits in his fighting days.

To the side of the main action, Geno and the grubby dwarf continued their five-hammer juggling. In the blink of an eye, the grubby dwarf, seeing his leader in trouble, launched one of his weapons Kelsey's way. Fully engaged, Kelsey never saw it coming.

But Geno did. He, too, hurled a hammer, his catching the grubby dwarf's missile in midflight and deflecting it harmlessly away from Kelsey.

Gary and Mickey, even Kelsey and Jacek, turned to regard the dwarfs. In a flurry of movement that none of them could truly follow, the half-sized opponents whipped their hammers at each other. Sparks flew as hammers connected in midair; Geno grunted as he took one off his chest; the grubby dwarf grunted as one of Geno's connected.

Then from the midst of the confusion there came a sharp *crack!* and both dwarfs stood facing each other for a long, silent moment, each holding his last remaining hammer. Gary wasn't sure what had happened, but he came to understand when he noticed the line of blood rolling down the grubby dwarf's forehead. Without a sound, the little creature fell facedown on the sand.

A goblin started out from the ranks, but Geno waved his hammer the creature's way and it promptly retreated. Gary knew the rabble forces, wouldn't hold back for long, though; all of them began shifting uncomfortably and looking about.

"Get ready for a fight," Mickey said at Gary's side.

"I will kill you and kill your dwarf next!" Jacek promised. He launched a series of wild, straight-across cuts that kept Kelsey up on his toes and backing, but in no serious trouble. Jacek continued the vicious assault, swinging and slashing and muttering curses. Soon, though, Kelsey tired of the game. The heavy sword came across a bit low and the nimble elf hopped right above it, coming back down and charging ahead, slamming his shield into the side of Jacek's head before the man could possibly recover.

Kelsey went right by the man, just ahead of Jacek's fast-approaching back-hand sword cut. The elf fell low to his knees, reversing his grip on his sword as he dropped. Jacek's heavy sword waved dangerously close above Kelsey's head, but Kelsey expected it, and knew it would miss, and didn't even flinch. He doubled his own weapon back under one arm and thrust it straight out behind him, driving it deep into the self-proclaimed island boss's lung.

Jacek heaved for air and started to bring his sword back in. Kelsey came up and about, throwing his shield against Jacek's arms to stop the dangerous weapon from coming back around. Kelsey was face-to-face with the man now, barely an inch apart, close enough to smell Jacek's hot breath.

Kelsey grimaced and pulled straight up on his sword hilt, further tearing the man's insides.

"Kill you," the big man promised, but his threat was lost in a breathless wheeze and a spout of blood. He shook violently a couple of times, then Kelsey unceremoniously pushed him back to the ground, where he lay quite still.

"Are there any others who claim ownership of the island?" Kelsey asked evenly. The goblin reappeared from the ranks, looking the troll's way, and started to mutter something. Geno had seen enough of that one. The dwarf's hammer went spinning, catching the ugly goblin on the side of the head and cleanly snapping its neck.

"Pretend ye got more," Mickey whispered to Geno, and the dwarf laughed in reply and began pumping his (empty) arms. Illusionary hammers spun out at the rabble. They dove and ducked, and turned and fled, the hammers chasing them out impossibly far into the night.

Soon the whole force was in wild flight, running with all speed to the south. Geno kept up his laughing, Mickey joined in, and Kelsey flashed a satisfied smile as he wiped the blood from his sword on Jacek's pants.

"Shut up," Gary demanded, his green eyes narrowed as he regarded the wildly amused dwarf. Geno turned on him sharply.

"You got a real one?" the dwarf growled at Mickey, holding one hand out as though he expected the leprechaun to give him a real hammer to heave at Gary.

"They're dead," Gary replied, thinking that those words explained everything.

"They asked to die," Kelsey cut in. "Would you feel better if it were my own body and Geno's lying in the sand?"

"You don't have to enjoy it so much," Gary protested.

"He was just a human," Kelsey spat. "If you care so much for him, then give him to the lake, or bury him." Never releasing Gary from his golden-eyed gaze, the elf walked away, Geno in tow. Gary looked to Mickey, but the leprechaun had no answers for him this time.

So Gary did bury Jacek, and the dead dwarf and goblin as well. He thought of his parents throughout the task and wondered what pain they would suffer if he never returned to them. He imagined his picture on telephone poles and milk cartons, fliers handed out at malls, as his parents sought desperately some information about what had happened to him.

When he got back to the others the next morning, Gary's eyes were blood-shot. None of them asked him about it, though, and he was beginning to believe that they didn't even care.

The day passed without incident, without anything but the small, wind-driven waves lapping on the forlorn beach and the mountains hovering just out of reach. The next night, too, showed no excitement, no noises in the dark or yellow eyes staring at the encampment.

By the morning after that, Gary came to realize that boredom would be their biggest enemy, boredom that led to ambivalence, ambivalence that would lead the companions to the same state as Jacek and his wretched band.

Gary feared that many, many days and nights would pass quietly. He had seen Kelsey in dire straits, outnumbered by goblins and by trolls, but the elf had fought with fire in his golden eyes, slashing and battling fiercely even when all seemed lost. Now, though, Kelsey truly appeared defeated. He sat on the beach, staring.

Just staring.

Mickey finished *The Hobbit* that day. "Fine tale," he muttered as he handed it back to Gary, but when Gary tried to respond, tried to get the leprechaun to elaborate, Mickey only walked away.

Geno was the noisiest of the group, stomping and cursing, throwing ham-mers at any target that presented itself. But the dwarf would not talk directly to Gary, or to Kelsey or Mickey, and every time Gary went anywhere near him, he lifted a hammer threateningly.

Gary snorted at him and spun away, angry and afraid. He felt as though a cage had been built around him. He almost wanted to test Ceridwen's spell and jump in the water, but he couldn't find the courage. "Can't I go for a walk?" he asked Mickey some time later.

"Go north," the leprechaun advised. "And ye might want to put yer armor back on." The leprechaun nodded to the pile, lying on the beach.

Something odd struck Gary Leger then. Ceridwen had pointedly taken the broken spear from him, though she cared nothing for his dwarf-forged spear and allowed the others to keep their weapons as well. Why hadn't she taken the armor? It certainly was as valuable as the spear.

"Ceridwen's got slaves all about, and most're nasty things like the ones we fought, would be me guess," Mickey went on, not noticing Gary's perplexed expression.

Gary nodded but started away, leaving the armor in a pile on the beach.

"And keep from the castle!" Mickey shouted a warning. "It's warded, don't ye doubt!"

Though the glassy-sided castle did intrigue Gary, he had no intention of going anywhere near the place at that time. He stayed along the beach, studying the shore, looking for some solution to Ceridwen's riddle, and thinking, too, of the mystery surrounding the missing spear. The distance across the lake was much less north and west of the island, but Gary saw no chances for escape in those directions. Sheer mountain walls ran down right into the lake, and even if Gary and his friends managed to get across the shorter expanse of the water, they'd have an impossible time trying to get up from the lake. The only way out was back in the same direction they had come, Gary knew, but he had no idea of how they might get across.

An hour later, Gary found himself scrambling over the sharp rocks of a jutting jetty, dangerously close to the water. Too frustrated to really care, he just spat at the lake that would burn like acid and continued on, stubbornly inching ever closer to the edge. Then Gary dropped flat to his belly, suddenly, wide-eyed and staring ahead to the lagoon beyond the rocks. Many yards from shore, but only waist-deep in the water, stood a monster that would have towered above the mountain trolls, a giant three times Gary's height.

It was lean, though still huge, and apparently fishing for a meal, slapping its thick hands into the water but coming up empty each time.

Gary watched for several minutes, filled with a combination of amazement and terror, then dared to get back to his knees and began backtracking the way he had come. He knew it was only a matter of time before the behemoth looked his way, and he felt naked indeed out on the rocks without his spear and armor (though he didn't know what good the puny weapon, dwarven-forged or not, would do against the likes of this monster!).

He had almost made it to the sand, and was thinking that it was a good thing that he did not have the bulky armor on, when the giant saw him.

"Duh, hey!" it cried, a booming baritone voice.

Gary didn't stop to reply. He scrambled and kicked his way across the remaining stones of the jetty, jumped down to the sand, and sprinted away, spurred on by the approaching splashes as the behemoth lumbered its way across the lagoon.

Sand dragged at Gary's legs, slowing him—again he felt as if he was in that dream state unable to outrun his pursuer. An image of his parents flashed in his mind, the two of them staring down in disbelief at their son, squashed in the blueberry bushes in the woods out back.

Then the sound of splashing stopped and Gary dared to look back, hoping that the monster had changed its course. But the giant hadn't given up its pursuit; to Gary's surprise and dismay, the huge thing had already made it to the beach and was almost across the rock jetty.

"Stupid to come out here," Gary berated himself. He put his head down and ran on, knowing that the giant's long strides would surely overtake him before too long.

His breath came in labored gasps. He veered to the water, then prudently remembered the curse and realized he would find no escape that way. Now his weary feet dragged even deeper in the sand. He heard the heavy footsteps closing, inevitably closing.

They were right at his back!

Gary swung about to meet his doom. The giant towered over him but made no immediate moves, its heaving breaths coming nearly as labored as Gary's. "Duh, you run fast," the monster commented.

"Not fast enough," Gary muttered under his breath as he glanced all about for some possible escape. He pointed suddenly back to the water, cried out, "A whale!" and took off as soon as the dim-witted monster turned about.

"Where?" the giant asked, oblivious to the trick. By the time it turned back, Gary was way ahead. "Hey, wait!" the monster called, and the chase was on once more.

Gary knew that his only hope was to find some cover, so he veered away from the water's edge, heading for the bare stones farther inland.

The giant plodded behind, its wide feet unhindered by the soft sand. "Duh, hey!" it called out several times.

The first of the huge stones was barely twenty feet away.

Out in front of Gary stepped Kelsey, sword in hand. Geno came around the other side of the rock, juggling three hammers. Gary nearly fainted in sheer relief. He turned back to consider the giant. It still approached, but at a walk, more cautiously.

"Duh, hey," it said again.

Geno whipped a hammer off its shin.

"Du . . . ow!" the behemoth roared, grabbing at the leg. Another hammer bounced off its shoulder, and both Kelsey and Geno circled to opposite sides and steadily advanced.

Great birds shrieked and rushed down from the skies to peck at the giant's head; huge-clawed crabs dug themselves out of the sand and snapped at its bare toes. The monster squealed and cried, kicking and slapping.

Gary was only confused for the second it took him to realize that Mickey must also be in the area. "Where are you, Mickey?" he demanded.

The leprechaun materialized, perched upon a stone off to Gary's right. "This kind's bigger than trolls," he remarked. "But not so hard to fool. Ye're lucky we came out to get ye, lad."

Gary wasn't so sure about the leprechaun's assessment. Another hammer bounced off the giant's head and it howled again. Behind it, Kelsey stood with leveled sword, lining up a vital area for a critical strike. The pitiful giant was too engaged and confused by Mickey's illusions and Geno's missiles to even know that the elf was behind it.

"Stop it!" Gary yelled at Mickey. The leprechaun shot him a curious glance. "What're ye about?"

Again Gary found himself without the words to answer. The giant hadn't harmed him; he had the feeling now that he was not so vulnerable, that maybe the giant hadn't meant to harm him at all. "Just stop it!" he screamed in Mickey's face, loud enough to get Kelsey and Geno's attention as well, and he swung around and rushed towards the combatants. Gary silently congratulated himself as Mickey's illusions disappeared, but the giant wasn't out of danger yet.

"Behind you!" Gary heard himself yell, to his own disbelief, as Kelsey again leveled the sword and started his thrust. The giant spun about and Kelsey reversed his attack and hopped back defensively, turning a murderous stare upon Gary.

Gary didn't care. He ran right up to the giant and skidded to a stop in the sand, standing with his arms out wide. Geno raised yet another hammer for a throw, but Gary poked a finger the dwarf's way and warned, "Don't!" Amazingly the gruff dwarf lowered the weapon and scratched at his hairless chin.

Gary and the giant regarded one another for the second time.

"What are you doing?" Kelsey demanded of Gary.

"I don't think he meant to hurt me," Gary replied. "He was just fishing when I found him. He's a prisoner, too, isn't he?"

"But a dangerous one, don't ye doubt," Mickey answered, strolling up to a position a few cautious feet behind Gary. "Giants been known to make meals of ones such as yerself."

"Duh, eat him?" the giant balked, a disgusted look crossing his thick but almost boyish features: dimpled checks, thick lips, and bright eyes the color of a crisp and clear winter sky.

"I thought so," Gary said, noting the expression and relaxing visibly.

"How come I have not seen you before?" the giant asked in its slow, deliberate voice. "Elf and dwarf?" The giant scratched at its wild black hair.

"We haven't been here for very long," Gary replied. "I'm Gary Leger and these are . . ."

"Enough!" Kelsey demanded. Then to the giant, he said, "Your life has been spared. Now be gone, before you feel the sting of my blade."

"I've more hammers yet!" Geno added, putting three more up in a juggling routine.

"Forget them!" Gary growled, commanding the behemoth's attention. "What's your name?"

"Duh, Tommy," the giant replied, glancing around nervously from elf to dwarf. He held up his huge hands, showing a missing digit on one. "Tommy One-Thumb."

"Well, Duh Tommy," Geno muttered sarcastically, "I believe that you should be leaving now."

"Greetings, Tommy One-Thumb," Gary said, more at the obstinate dwarf than at the giant. "I'm sorry for the fight."

"He's a giant, lad," Mickey warned. "A rogue, a killer, don't ye doubt. Giants aren't evil like the trolls, but they can be a nasty lot and a mighty enemy. Let him go and come along—for everyone's good fortune."

When Gary looked upon Mickey, he saw only sincere concern in the leprechaun's gray eyes.

"Maybe ye should go back to yer fishing, Tommy One-Thumb," Mickey offered.

"Where is whale?" Tommy asked Gary. "Tommy did not see any whale."

"There wasn't any whale," Gary apologized. "I was just trying to trick you. I was afraid."

"Duh, oh," mumbled Tommy. "Most people are afraid of Tommy."

"Well, can ye blame them?" Mickey asked.

The giant shrugged and turned, and started slowly away. Gary began to protest, but Geno and Kelsey rushed up to stand right before him, Geno purposely stomping his heavy boots down on the tops of Gary's sneakers.

"You ask him along, and my next hammer kisses you good!" Geno promised, poking a stubby finger against Gary's nose to accentuate his point. Gary tried to push the dwarf away, but Geno shoved off first, and Gary, his feet hooked under the dwarf's boots, fell down to the sand. He jerked aside to avoid a stream of Geno's spittle.

Kelsey said nothing, but the elf's narrow-eyed stare revealed similar sentiments and, as with the fight of the previous day, Mickey had no answers for Gary.

Ceridwen was waiting for them, or more particularly, for Kelsey, when they arrived back at the camp.

"So you have defeated Jacek," she purred at Kelsey, placing her hand familiarly on the elf's shoulder. Kelsey brushed her away but would not look her in the eye.

"I had hoped that would happen," Ceridwen went on. "Jacek was such a brutish beast. The slaves will perform better with you leading them."

"I'll not lead your wretched slaves," Kelsey replied.

"We shall see," Ceridwen said calmly. Her hand went back to Kelsey's shoulder and she stroked the long strands of his sparkling golden hair back from his face.

"And I'll not serve you in any capacity!" the elf screamed at her, verily running away from her undeniably alluring touch.

"I could not let you complete your quest," Ceridwen explained, and it seemed to Gary that the witch was almost apologizing. "You understand that, of course."

"I understand more than you believe," Kelsey countered slyly.

"Not so," Ceridwen retorted, stubbornly walking back to stand beside the elf. "You have no idea of how long a hundred years can be on an empty island, Kelsenellenelvial Gil-Ravadry. Your people will not come for you—not here. You have only me." Ceridwen's hand went back to Kelsey's golden locks, petting delicately. Kelsey tried to pull away again, but this time the witch grabbed tightly to his hair and pulled him to her as easily as if he had been made of paper.

Gary was horrified at Ceridwen's bared power; Kelsey seemed so insignificant against her. Both Mickey and Geno had turned away, but Gary could not avert his eyes.

Ceridwen had Kelsey's head bent at an awkward angle, as though she meant to snap his neck. "Draw your sword and strike me down!" the evil witch hissed in Kelsey's face.

Kelsey's hand went for his sword hilt, but he backed it off immediately, his whole body slumping in despair.

"You are my slave," Ceridwen growled, a voice that seemed unearthly, demonic. "My plaything. I will do with you as I please, and when I please!" With just the one hand, Ceridwen tossed Kelsey into the air, towards the shore. He landed in the sand, dangerously close to water's edge, and as he rolled about, his elbow touched the lake.

Kelsey howled and rolled back, clutching at his burning arm. If Gary or any of the others had doubted Ceridwen's spell, they knew better now, for Kelsey's sleeve and fine armor were burned right through at the elbow from barely brushing the deadly water.

"I will have some work for you soon," the witch said to Geno, paying no heed to the wounded elf.

"As you wish, my lady," the brown-haired dwarf replied with a low bow. Ceridwen cackled and threw her black cape high about her shoulders. As it descended, her form shifted and she was again a raven, soaring back to her castle of glass.

FOURTEEN
Tommy One-Thumb

THE meals were tasteless, the sun hot, the days long, and the nights empty.

Every day that went by deepened the feeling of solitude for Gary. He couldn't remember the last joke Mickey had cracked, or even the last time the leprechaun had spoken to him without first being asked a direct question. Even beyond their obvious dilemma, something seemed to be bothering Mickey. Gary could only think back to the first night after they had left Dvergamal, when he had seen Mickey making some secret deal with the pixie. Whatever it was, Mickey wasn't talking.

And Kelsey. When Gary had first met the golden-haired elf, in Leshiye's tree, he had looked upon Kelsey with awe, a sincere admiration that had only grown throughout their first few ordeals. But now Kelsey seemed quite an ordinary being to Gary, helpless and forlorn, accepting defeat. Kelsey sat and watched the water and the sky, sat and did nothing to facilitate their escape. Also, Gary couldn't forget, would never forget, the carefree manner in which Kelsey had killed Jacek, had killed a human being without the slightest hint of remorse.

Of all his companions over those next few days, Gary found that he actually preferred Geno's company. The gruff dwarf more often responded with spit than words to Gary's questions, and once Geno had even launched a hammer Gary's way (though Gary had seen enough of the dwarf's hammer-throwing proficiency to know that if Geno had really meant to hit him, he surely would have been smacked). But Geno, at least, was not complacent about their situation, not willing to surrender. Despite his feigned subservience to the witch a few days before, the dwarf promised that he would somehow find a way to pay Ceridwen back.

Gary didn't doubt him for a minute.

Finally one gray but uncomfortably hot day, Gary Leger had seen enough. "What's our plan?" he asked Kelsey, sitting in his usual position on the shore.

The elf looked up at him blankly. Gary noticed how pallid Kelsey appeared, and how thin and dirty. Kelsey had been barely eating enough to keep himself alive.

"What's our plan?" Gary asked again.

"Our plan for what?" Kelsey replied absently, going back to his distant stare.

"Our plan to get off of this island!" Gary retorted, more sharply than he had intended.

"Ye don't understand the nature of our enemy," Mickey, sitting to the side, put in. "Ceridwen's got us, lad. We'll no find a way through her tight clutches."

"That's it, then?" Gary balked. "You're all giving up? We're just going to sit here until we die?" Gary considered his own words for a moment, then remarked, even more pointedly, "Or should I say, until I die? You'll all live longer than me, right? So you can wait the hundred years . . ."

"I've no desire to sit here a hundred years, lad," Mickey offered half heartedly.

"Nor do I!" Geno roared. The dwarf stood with his bowed legs wide apart, gnarly hands on his wide belt (which sported five more hammers now, taken from the grubby dwarf), and his blue-gray eyes narrowed dangerously. "I'll give it back to that witch!"

"Ah, save yer bluster," Mickey scolded. "Ye cannot do anything against the likes o' Ceridwen, and ye know it well enough."

"I won't accept that," Gary growled, and he poked a finger Kelsey's way. "You owe me!" he declared.

"I owe you nothing." The elf's tone showed more resignation than anger, and that, too, made Gary want to reach down and choke him.

"It was by your command that I was brought here," Gary fumed. "And by your deed," he added, snapping his accusing finger Mickey's way. "You both share the responsibility of taking care of me, of getting me back safely to where I belong."

Kelsey came up in Gary's face, suddenly showing more fire in his golden eyes than he had in many days.

"Strike me down," Gary invited him, and he honestly wasn't sure that

Kelsey wouldn't. "That's how you work, isn't it? Brave Kelsey," he spat sarcastically. "But brave only when he knows that he can defeat his foe."

"You are bound by the rules of cap—" Kelsey began, but Gary didn't want to hear that again.

"Save it," he snapped. "I am bound to you by nothing!"

"Calm ye, lad," Mickey said quietly, obviously stunned by Gary's outburst and fearing that Kelsey would surely kill him.

"You strike him down and the witch might let the rest of us go," Geno reasoned logically.

"You kidnapped me—that's all it can be called," Gary went on, ignoring the leprechaun's condescension and the dwarf's frightening logic. "You can put all the pretty names on it that you want, but you stole me from my world and from my home. So strike me now, Kelsenellene . . . whatever the hell your name is. Strike me down and compound your crime!"

Kelsey's golden eyes flashed, his jaw clenched tight, and his hand slipped slowly towards his sword hilt. But Gary had faced him down, for the elf did indeed feel responsible for their dilemma. Kelsey turned back to the lake and sat on the sand.

"I expected as much," Gary mumbled, and he walked away. Mickey was quick to catch up with him.

"Don't be too hard on the elf," the leprechaun explained when they were some distance away. "Ceridwen's given him a bitter pill."

"We have to fight back," Gary replied.

"If ye think it's that easy, then ye're reading too many of these books," Mickey said, patting Gary's pocket, which held *The Hobbit*. "Not all in Faerie's got such a happy ending; not all the dragons go belly-up to a well-aimed arrow."

"So we don't even try?" came Gary's sarcastic response.

Mickey had no answer.

"I'm taking the armor and my spear," Gary announced. "I've earned that much and you won't need it anyway."

"Ye going somewhere?" Now Mickey seemed truly concerned.

"Away from here," Gary answered. "Maybe Tommy will help me."

"Don't ye be bringing that giant around," Mickey warned. "Forget Kelsey and be worrying about Geno—dwarfs and giants don't get on well."

"Dwarfs don't get on well with anything," Gary reminded the leprechaun, and for the first time in many days they shared a smile.

———

GARY found the giant in the same lagoon, fishing contentedly, but using a pole this time instead of his monstrous hands.

"Catch anything?" Gary called, and Tommy's huge face lit up as soon as he noticed the man.

"Come and fish with me," the giant offered happily. Gary moved to the water's edge and almost hopped in—until he fortunately remembered the curse. He wondered why Ceridwen hadn't similarly cursed the giant. He couldn't imagine one as gentle as Tommy being a willing accomplice to the evil witch.

Gary moved down the rocks towards the beach, and met Tommy there, coming out of the water with an armful of fish.

"Tommy does better now," the giant announced. "Uses a sticky stick!"

"Sticky stick?" Gary echoed, examining the giant's fishing pole. It was thin and hollow, nearly eight feet long, and Gary understood Tommy's description when he saw that its end was covered in a gooey substance.

Tommy smiled and poked the stick down on a nearby rock. When the giant lifted the stick, the rock came up with it, firmly secured to the goo.

"Where did you find that?" Gary inquired, thinking that he might somehow find some use for the substance.

Tommy pointed down the beach to a thick patch of reeds and weeds on the far side of the lagoon. Gary immediately started around the beach and the giant followed. There were two main types of reeds: green ones filled with the sticky substance, and brown hollow ones, like the one Tommy was using to catch fish.

"Tommy will make one for you," the giant offered. "Then we can fish together."

Gary smiled and shook his head. "I can't go in the water," he explained.

"It is not cold."

Gary just smiled again and did not even try to explain.

They spent the rest of the day talking, with Tommy showing Gary all the secrets of the lagoon region he had come to claim as his home. Gary felt quite safe, even before Tommy assured him that no others would dare to come around and bother them.

The talkative giant came as a welcome distraction for Gary, and Gary as even more of one for lonely Tommy. Tommy eagerly told Gary everything he could remember about himself. He told of life as a giant in the world beyond the lake, of how both his parents had been hunted by scared farmers and killed. Tommy had escaped, after losing one of his thumbs, but had nowhere to go, for he was just a young giant at the time. Lost and alone, Tommy had stumbled upon Ceridwen, and she had taken him to the island, where she told him he would be safe.

At first Gary didn't know what to make of the witch's uncharacteristic mercy, but when Tommy continued, recalling the first "soldiers" Ceridwen had asked him to fight beside, Gary came to understand that Tommy was merely meant to be another addition to the witch's slave collection.

"Then Ceridwen gave Tommy a new boss, a man named Jacek and a dwarf—smelly—named Gomer," Tommy continued, his big-featured face souring.

"Not nice people," the giant explained. "Jacek is mean. He hurts things."

"Not anymore," Gary assured him, confident that Tommy bore no friendship at all for the rogues. "He tried to hurt Kelsey, my elf friend, but Kelsey killed him in a sword fight."

Tommy considered the news for a long time, then decided that it was a good thing.

"Now you live all alone," Gary reasoned. "How long has it been?"

Tommy started counting on his nine fingers, but ran out of digits. "Ten years," he decided, though his face crinkled in confusion. "No, twenty." He shrugged helplessly. "Long time."

"Don't you get bored?"

Again the giant only shrugged.

"Then why have you stayed?" Gary asked. "There must be other giants like you out in the mountains beyond the lake."

The giant thought that a ridiculous question. "Tommy can't swim," he explained. "And no boats are big enough for Tommy."

"How convenient for dear Ceridwen," Gary muttered under his breath. Tommy didn't hear him. The giant looked around, as though expecting someone to be eavesdropping, then he put his face right up to Gary's.

"Tommy walked off island once," he whispered, as much as a giant can whisper. "Water go over Tommy's head, but Tommy jumped up real high and breathed, jump up and breathe."

"You made it all the way?" Now Gary was starting to get some ideas.

The giant looked over his shoulder again, then turned back, his grin from ear to ear. "Yes!" he replied. "But Tommy came right back—did not want to make the Lady mad!"

"Of course not," Gary readily agreed, but what the young man was thinking at that time would certainly not have pleased Ceridwen.

Gary slept in Tommy's cave that night, or at least he stayed there, for he hardly closed his eyes. He had learned quite a few things in his single day with Tommy One-Thumb, and he believed in his heart that he could somehow turn that knowledge into escape. When he had heard of Tommy's lake crossing, he had almost asked the giant to pick him up and carry him over. But that wouldn't work. Even if he could get Tommy to agree, which he doubted, the giant's descriptions of jumping "real high" just to get his head above the water didn't bode well for passengers, not when splashes from the lake would burn Gary's skin away!

But the answer was before him, Gary knew. Like pieces of a puzzle, just waiting to be put into proper order.

Gary finally fell asleep, long into the night, with those thoughts in mind.

When he opened his eyes, he found not Tommy, but Ceridwen, waiting for him. Gary's first thought was that the witch had somehow read his mind and that he was about to be turned into a rabbit or some other benign little creature. He realized a moment later, though, that the witch was as surprised to see him as he was to see her. She called to Tommy, who came bouncing back in the cave entrance.

"What is he doing here?" Ceridwen asked the giant sharply.

"I came to visit Tommy," Gary answered before Tommy could blurt anything out. "I've never known a giant before—I was curious."

Ceridwen thought it over, then flashed her disarming smile Gary's way. "It is good that you have made a new friend," she said, that same throaty voice she had tried on Kelsey a few days earlier. "You will be here for a long time—all of your life, in fact. You may as well enjoy your stay."

Gary didn't like the subtle inferences of that last statement, especially not with Ceridwen standing so very close to him. His disdain for her apparently showed in his face, for the witch's expression went from smile to scowl and she pointedly turned away from Gary.

"There is a wall to be fixed at the castle," she mentioned to Tommy. "See to it."

"Tommy will fix it," the giant assured her.

"And get the dwarf," Ceridwen said after a moment. "Let him help you. I want to see if Geno Hammerthrower lives up to his considerable reputation before I give him any of the more important tasks I have in mind."

Tommy started to object, not wanting anything to do with fiery Geno, but Gary motioned for the giant to remain silent. Ceridwen saw the confusion on the giant's face and guessed easily enough that Gary, standing behind her, was the cause.

"Good," she purred, turning back to Gary. "You play the role of ambassador, and make things easier for everyone."

"I do what I can," Gary said evenly.

"A long time," Ceridwen reminded him in her throaty voice, her perfect, lush lips curling up in a lascivious smile. She let her gaze linger on the sturdy young man for a long while, then turned back on Tommy. "I will be away for a few days. I expect that wall to be repaired by the time I return.

"And when I return," she continued, looking coyly over her shoulder at Gary, "perhaps you and I can become better friends."

An old saying about snowballs and hell crossed Gary's mind, but he wisely held his thoughts silent. Again he worried that the witch could read his mind, but then she was gone, in the blink of an eye, a large raven soaring out over the smooth lake.

It took some convincing, but Gary finally had Tommy willing to go with him to get Geno. The giant really didn't want to face the volatile dwarf, or the surly elf, again, but Tommy, desperately in need of some companionship, had already come to trust in Gary, and Gary promised him that nothing bad would happen.

Gary almost wished he hadn't made that promise when they came in sight of the camp, for the first things he and Tommy noticed were Kelsey, bow in hand, and Geno, juggling his hammers and eyeing Tommy with open hatred.

"You'd better wait here," Gary offered, and Tommy didn't have to be asked twice. Even though Gary went the rest of the way alone, Kelsey did not lower his drawn bow.

"Ceridwen wants Geno to go and help the giant fix a wall," Gary explained as he came into the camp.

Geno snorted and spat. "Cold day in a dwarf's forge," he muttered.

Gary blinked and paused a moment to consider the similarities of that curious phrase to one he had been thinking of earlier. He wondered how many sayings from his world had variations in Faerie. How many sayings in his world had actually come from Faerie, and were just adapted to make better sense in his world?

"I think you should go," Gary said at length, reminding himself not to get sidetracked. Mickey moved up, suspicious of Gary's smug tone, and Kelsey finally lowered his bow.

"In fact," Gary continued, "I think that we should all go."

"To the castle?" Mickey asked incredulously.

"That's where Cedric's spear is located," Gary replied, as though the answer should have been obvious. "We wouldn't want to leave Ynis Gwydrin without Cedric's spear."

"What're ye talking about?" Now Mickey's tone was more curious than incredulous.

"If you know of something, then speak it clearly," Kelsey demanded. "What riddles do you offer?"

"I know a way that we can get off the island," Gary said bluntly.

Even Geno moved up then, to better hear. All three—dwarf, leprechaun, and elf—looked to each other and to Gary, waiting impatiently for the young man to elaborate.

"I haven't worked out all the details," Gary said, not wanting to reveal his as yet uncompleted scheme. "But I can get us out of here—I'm sure of it."

Mickey seemed intrigued, but Kelsey and Geno frowned and turned away.

"Cold day in a dwarf's forge," Gary heard Geno say again. Gary growled and rushed around them, cutting off their retreat.

"Do either of you have a better idea?" he demanded angrily. "Have you thought of something wonderful during the hours you have wasted staring at the water?"

Knowing the Tylwyth Teg better than anyone who wasn't of the Tylwyth Teg, Mickey cringed at Gary's bold sarcasm. But Kelsey didn't retaliate, physically or verbally. Both he and Geno stood staring at Gary, neither of them blinking.

"I can get us out of here," Gary said evenly.

Kelsey looked to Geno, who just shrugged.

"We'll go to the castle," the elf agreed.

"And if we manage to steal back the spear," Mickey put in, "and then we don't get off the island, who's going to face Ceridwen?"

"It's my plan," Gary offered.

"I will claim responsibility," Kelsey declared suddenly. "What can she do to me that would be worse than exile on this forsaken island?"

Mickey looked at the elf in blank amazement. "Ye always were a hard one to figure," the leprechaun commented.

For the first time in many days, Kelsey flashed one of his rare smiles. "I am of the Tylwyth Teg," he explained to Mickey. "Am I not expected to be difficult?"

"I always expected that out o' ye," Mickey readily agreed.

FIFTEEN

Ceridwen's Place

THE castle proved to be even more splendid up close than it had appeared from the beach. High crystalline walls gave way to even higher crystalline turrets, spiraling up into the sky, every inch of them glistening and sparkling in the morning sunlight. Intricate angles and many-faceted stones threw the light off in a hundred directions, making Gary and his companions squint their eyes from the stinging brilliance.

This was a castle for a goodly, king, Gary decided then, and not the appropriate palace for an evil witch. How sad for the land of Faerie that Ceridwen had come to call Ynis Gwydrin her home.

Geek met the companions at the front gate, eyeing them suspiciously and casting particularly uncomfortable glances at Kelsey's sheathed sword.

"Lady said to meet Tommy and a dwarf," the goblin asserted. "Just Tommy and a dwarf."

"She asked . . . she told . . . us all to help," Gary replied.

Geek's yellow eyes narrowed doubtfully.

"We refused, except for the dwarf," Gary bluffed. "So Ceridwen probably didn't tell you to expect us. But we thought it over and figured that repairing a wall would be a better thing than facing the Lady's wrath when she returns from her trip."

"And if I don't lets yous in, Ceridwen will punish you?" the goblin asked, and the weaselly little creature seemed to like that idea.

"In that event, we might as well kill you, since we would be doomed anyway," Kelsey reasoned evenly. "At least I might know some enjoyment before Ceridwen's wrath descends over me." The elf's hand inched towards his belted sword.

Geek's face crinkled for a moment, then he nodded stupidly and told them to follow.

"Well done," Kelsey congratulated Gary, but it was Mickey's expression towards the young man, both amused and amazed, that Gary took as the highest compliment.

They moved across a gigantic audience hall and along a maze of mirror-walled corridors. The ceilings were quite high, but Tommy had to stoop anyway, and even crawl in some places, just to get through. Gary went up front for some small talk with the goblin, trying to gain Geek's confidence, but Geek said little, and commented more than once that he hated the smell of humans.

The maze continued, down a stairway, through a few irregular-shaped rooms, up a stairway, and along several corridors. Gary suspected, and he knew that he wasn't the only one with the feeling, that Geek was purposely leading them in a roundabout manner, as if trying to prevent them from getting any bearings about their location in the castle. It made sense—they were certainly less likely to try any mischief if they couldn't even find their way back out.

Finally they came into a room, similarly mirrored as the corridors except for one wall where the glass had all been broken away. The companions were somewhat amazed to see stonework behind the shattered section; from every angle, the castle appeared almost translucent, though undeniably solid. In one area, the stones, too, were broken away—this was undoubtedly what Ceridwen wanted repaired, for the dwarf was no glassworker.

Beyond the hole in the wall lay another room, this one set with braziers and a pentagram design on the floor. Even Gary knew enough about legends of magic to guess this second chamber to be a room for summoning. He couldn't contain a shudder, wondering what beast Ceridwen might have conjured, wondering what hellish beast might have blasted the wall.

"Right there," Geek explained. "Fix the stones. The Lady will put new glass over them." Gary started to ask the goblin something, but Geek spun about and left immediately, giving the distinct impression that he was uncomfortable in this place.

"She brought in a big one," Mickey commented, looking at the blasted wall.

"A big what?" Gary dared to ask.

"Demon, lad," the leprechaun replied. "Ceridwen's always playing with demons."

Gary wanted to claim that he didn't believe in demons, but it seemed a silly thing to say to a leprechaun, since he didn't believe in leprechauns, either.

"So we are in the castle," Kelsey remarked. "Now we must find the spear and be gone. And quickly . . ." He stopped, seeing Gary with a finger over pursed lips, his other hand subtly pointing in Tommy's direction.

Tommy was oblivious to the conversation, though. The giant had already started clearing aside the rubble, while Geno measured the break and pondered the best way to patch it.

Kelsey called Gary and Mickey over to the far side of the room for a private conference.

"Do we let them work on it?" the elf asked. "I fear that the goblin will return to check on our progress."

"I can make the poor thing think he's seeing us fixing it," Mickey replied. "But I'd have to stay here."

"Could you then find your way out?" Kelsey asked. "I would like to have the dwarf, at least, accompany me on the search for the spear."

"I'll go with you," Gary offered. Kelsey gave him a sidelong smirk.

"I will need another fighter," the elf continued to Mickey, "if, as I expect, Ceridwen has the spear guarded."

Gary accepted the insult without comment, thinking that having two friendly—or at least nonenemy—fighters around him might not be such a bad thing.

"Take him," Mickey replied, looking to Geno. "The giant'll think the dwarf's here working, and the goblin'll think so, too, if the stupid creature returns.

"I'll give ye just an hour, though," Mickey went on. "If ye get into trouble or get found out, I've no desire to get catched in this castle!"

"Two hours," Kelsey bargained. "It is a big place."

Mickey agreed.

"The door's locked," Gary reminded them.

Mickey laughed and waved a hand, then called to Tommy. "Ye'd find patching easier if ye used this slab leaning against the wall over here," the leprechaun reasoned. Tommy and the others followed Mickey's leading gaze to the door, or at least, to where the door had been. Now the portal appeared as leaning beams and cross sections, the perfect infrastructure for a wall.

"Yeah, get it," Geno agreed, and Gary wasn't sure if the dwarf understood the illusion or was just happy to see that much of the work was already done.

Gary feared that Tommy would figure out the dupe—they had just come through that same door, after all. But the giant, not a powerful thinker, moved right up to the illusionary beams and searched for handholds along their sides. He tugged, but the illusion didn't move. Tommy set his feet wide apart and pulled mightily, then turned back to the wall holding his prize between his huge hands.

"Door's not locked anymore," Mickey said smugly. Gary looked through the illusion to the gaping hole in the wall; Tommy had yanked out the door, jamb and all.

A moment later, Geno came over to join Gary and Kelsey, though when Gary looked back, he saw Geno working hard beside Tommy, tying to fit the door, which still appeared as beams and planks, into the original hole in the wall. Mickey moved over to the side, plopped down, and popped his pipe in his mouth, folding his chubby little hands behind his head.

"Is dealing with leprechauns always this confusing?" Gary asked helplessly to Kelsey.

"Aye, lad," snickered the real Mickey, standing invisibly behind the elf. "Ye should try catching one sometime."

Gary blinked and looked back to the side, where the illusionary Mickey sat contentedly drawing on his pipe.

"Now off with ye," the real Mickey told them. "Ye got two hours and not a minute more!" He grabbed Gary as the man started away, and shoved something into his hand. "Take this," the leprechaun explained. "It'll get ye back to me and bring ye luck on yer hunt."

When Gary opened his hand, he found a four-leaf clover. He wasn't surprised.

Once again, Gary, Kelsey, and Geno found themselves in the maze, but this time they had no goblin to guide them. Kelsey took up the lead, alternating his turns, left and right, to prevent them from walking in circles. The elf tried to appear assured of his steps, but Gary figured that he was simply guessing.

"I would find our way if this was underground," Geno grumbled more than once. And more than once, the dwarf turned a corner and smacked a hammer into his own reflection, thinking, in his startlement, that the enemy had found them. "Stupid mirrors!" Geno just grumbled as he continued on his way, leaving a spider's web of broken glass behind him every time.

When they did actually come across one of Ceridwen's guards, an unfortunate goblin, it took them a long moment to even realize that it was not some manifestation of the tricky mirrors. The goblin squeaked once and turned to flee, but Kelsey's sword and Geno's hammer sliced and pounded it down before it got two steps away.

Then on they went, blindly, turning corners and crossing identical rooms with identical furnishings. Kelsey's confidence seemed to waver; they came to one four-way intersection and the elf hesitated and glanced one way and then another, before finally deciding to go straight ahead.

"No, left," Gary corrected suddenly. Kelsey and Geno turned on him in surprise.

Gary had no definite answers to their questioning stares; he just, for some reason he could not explain, believed that they had to go left at that point. Kelsey shot him an incredulous look and started straight ahead again, but Gary was certain of his mysterious insight.

"Left," he said again, more forcefully.

"What do you know?" Kelsey demanded. Gary shook his head.

"I know only that we have to go to the left," he answered honestly.

"We have wasted half an hour going your way," Geno reminded the elf.

They went left, and at the next intersection, when Geno and Kelsey looked to Gary for guidance, he quickly replied, "Straight ahead." At each corner, Gary's feelings grew more definite—he only feared that the sensations might be some trick of Ceridwen's to lure them into a trap.

But then, with a profound sigh of relief, he figured it out.

"It is the spear," he announced unexpectedly. "Cedric's spear is calling to me!"

"Good spear," Geno mumbled, and Kelsey did not argue the point, nor did the elf any longer doubt Gary's instincts.

They knew a few turns later that they were nearing Ceridwen's private quarters. No longer did mirrors line the walls, and the furnishings were much richer in this section. There were many more guards, though, marching in tight, well-ordered formations.

The companions came through a set of large double doors, into a spacious room filled with comfortable chairs and a long oaken table. Across from them stood another set of double doors, even more ornate than the ones they had just come through, and corridors ran off both sides of the wide room.

"Meeting hall," Geno reasoned.

"And Ceridwen's chamber beyond," added Kelsey. He looked to Gary for confirmation. Gary closed his eyes and heard the cry of the spear. Very close, straight ahead.

"That's it," Gary announced. He started forward, but Kelsey pulled him suddenly around the door and back into the previous corridor. Geno, too, slipped out of the room, and before Gary could begin to argue, he heard the marching stomp of many boots.

Peeking through the slightly cracked door, they saw two nervous goblins rush into the meeting room from the left corridor, quickly straightening their armor and helmets and taking positions on either side of the ornate double doors. A moment later, the troupe arrived, in ranks three abreast and five deep, marching from right to left through the meeting room and led by one burly goblin and a troll he commanded to keep his ragtag troops in line. The burly goblin paused to consider the two guards, eyeing them suspiciously for some time before he two-stepped to catch up to his still-marching troops.

"We have to take them out quickly," Kelsey whispered, lamenting that he had left his bow back on the beach. In answer, Geno flipped two hammers up into the air.

Kelsey grabbed the door handle and mouthed, "One . . . two . . . three," then yanked the door open and Geno let fly.

The first hammer caught the goblin on the left square in the faceplate of its helmet, hurling the creature back into the wall. The second goblin, breaking into a run, caught the next hammer on the shoulder, a glancing but wicked blow. Still, the goblin managed to keep on going.

Kelsey charged in; Geno readied another hammer. But Gary beat them to it, hurling his spear at the fleeing monster. He got the goblin on the hip and it went down squealing.

The first goblin had recovered by then, but found Kelsey, or more point-edly, Kelsey's sword, dancing right in its face. The creature yanked out its own weapon desperately, then lost all sense of reality. It felt no pain, but saw the floor rush up and the room spin about wildly. The goblin realized its horrid fate in the last instant of its life, as it looked back to its headless body still leaning upright against the door.

The other goblin stopped squealing almost immediately as Geno fired hammer after hammer into its head. Gary figured that the thing was dead after the second hit, but the dwarf hurled three more hammers into it, then rushed up and konked it a few more times just for good measure.

"Fine throw," Geno commented, tearing out Gary's bloodied spear and handing it back to the man. Gary knew that the dwarf wouldn't give him an unconditional compliment, and sure enough, Geno lived up to his reputation.

"Next time, hit it in the lungs so it cannot yell out," Geno growled. "Its screaming will probably bring the whole force back upon us!"

"Next time, you try to hit it right with the first throw," Gary snapped back. Geno shrugged and "accidentally" dropped a hammer on Gary's toe. Gary grimaced and bit his lip, but would not give the dwarf the satisfaction of seeing his pain.

"The door is trapped, no doubt," Kelsey said to them, reminding them that they had little time to waste.

Still fuming, Geno stomped over and inspected the portal. He grunted and scratched his hairless chin, then moved to the other end; grunted and scratched his chin again. He pulled a chisel from his endlessly pocketed belt and went to work, tapping here and tapping there, popping a hinge pin on one side and then the other. Then he walked back three steps, bowed to Kelsey (eyeing Gary all the while), and tossed a hammer into the center of the doors. They fell in like a cut tree, hitting the floor with a tremendous *whoosh!*

"Stealthy," Gary remarked sarcastically, and he prudently hopped away before Geno could have any more accidents concerning hammers and toes.

Ceridwen's room, for this was indeed the witch's private chamber, was among the most remarkable places Gary Leger had ever seen. A huge desk lined one wall, covered with parchments and inkwells, quills and books, some opened and some tightly bound with leather straps. Metal sconces, gracefully designed, though somehow discordant or unbalanced, or something else that made Gary uncomfortable to look at them, were evenly spaced around the room, each holding a torch that burned with a different-colored flame. The witch's bed was centered along the back wall, huge and canopied in purple silk. All three companions breathed a little easier when Kelsey went over and moved the curtain aside, showing the bed to be made up and empty.

The elf spotted the spear case, set on the wall beside a changing screen opposite the desk. He sheathed his sword and went for it immediately, reaching with hungry hands.

"*Trap!*" came a call in Gary's head.

"That's not it!" Gary cried.

The warning came too late. As Kelsey grabbed the case, it broke apart in his hands and an egg fell from a concealed cubby in the wall behind it. The three companions froze, staring at the cracked egg curiously, and with a shared sense of dread.

The egg split in half and a cloud of black smoke burst forth. Kelsey threw his hand over his mouth; Geno dove away; and Gary, too, assumed the vapors to be toxic. But the trap was nothing that simple; as the cloud rose up, it took a definite shape. Glowing red eyes appeared and a huge, gaping maw opened wide, hungrily. Black mist still hung about, obscuring the monster's form, but it seemed to have no absolute form anyway, shifting, growing limbs, almost on a whim, a writhing mass of blackness. Whatever its shape, it was huge and mighty, exuding a horrible power.

And for all his denials and all his logic, Gary Leger would never again make the claim that he did not believe in demons.

A thick black arm shot out at Kelsey from the still-forming cloud. The elf got his shield up to block, though his arm went numb under the sheer weight of the blow, and countered with his sword, the magical blade sizzling and hissing as it struck demon flesh. The demon howled—it might have been a laugh—and another arm appeared, and then a third arm, and a fourth beside that.

"Tylwyth Teg!" the monster bellowed in a voice that Gary could only compare to the grating of a diesel truck. "I have not killed one of the Tylwyth Teg in centuries! Is elf flesh still as tasty as I remember?"

A hammer whipped past Kelsey into the mist, but seemed to float to the floor, finding nothing tangible to smash against.

In an instant, Kelsey was pressed hard, fending against all four demon arms. The elf's shield and sword worked in perfect harmony, parrying and blocking. Kelsey dodged and dove, coming right back up to catch another blow with his fine shield. For all his brilliance, though, Kelsey couldn't hope to slow the attacks enough to get in any more solid hits of his own.

Gary knew that he must go to his companion, his friend, but he found his feet rooted to the floor in terror. He lifted his spear halfheartedly in both hands as if to rush in, but then changed his mind and took aim, thinking it wiser to throw the weapon instead. The demon's red eyes fell over him, and, caught in their hellish gaze, Gary felt as though his weapon weighed a hundred pounds.

The monster continued to stare at him, and continued to battle Kelsey, as though its mind could work easily in different directions at once. Gary noticed Geno dash ahead and slide down to the floor, the cunning dwarf's hammer going to work furiously on the eggshell, smashing it to little bits. For the first time, the demon seemed wounded; its ensuing cry was obviously founded in pain. A huge, clawed foot appeared from the mist and stomped down on Geno, but the diminutive and stubborn dwarf kept on smashing at the bits of egg.

The demon roared again, in pain and outrage, and twin lines of fire shot out from its eyes towards Gary. Gary managed to get a blocking forearm up in front of his face in time, but the searing jets burned into him and their sheer force hurled him backwards across the room. He found himself sitting against something hard, alternately clutching at his arm and at the twin holes burned into the armplate of Cedric Donigarten's fine armor.

DESPITE the distractions of both Gary and Geno, there was no letup at all in the demon's attacks against Kelsey. A heavy arm thumped against the elf's shield, and another battering limb came in the other way at the same time, forcing Kelsey to throw his sword out wide in a desperate parry. A third arm came in between sword and shield, with long horrid claws reaching for Kelsey's heart.

Kelsey threw himself straight backwards into a roll, but the arms, stretching impossibly long, followed him every inch of the way.

GENO was made of the stuff of mountains, but even that dwarfish trait seemed puny under the weight of the demon's huge foot. The dwarf smashed away, and when the pieces of egg were too small to hit anymore, he stuffed as many as he could grab into his mouth and swallowed them. He felt the weight on his back diminish, as though his actions had actually lessened the substance of the monster. Spurred by his success, the dwarf dropped his hammer aside and reached out with both hands, trying to find every last bit of eggshell.

But then the weight returned, crushing him down, pinning him helplessly. In one hand, Geno held a fair-sized chunk of the shell, but he couldn't hope to get that hand anywhere near his mouth.

He bit the foot instead, but that seemed to have little effect. And even Geno, who had eaten more unconventional meals than a billy goat in a junkyard, had to admit that demon flesh was among the most horrid things he had ever tasted.

THE demonic gaze fell over Kelsey, and the elf slumped, knowing he was surely doomed.

Propped against Ceridwen's desk one arm hanging useless by his side, Gary thought again of his parents. Where would he run when Kelsey was gone and Geno crushed? Where could he hide from this hell-spawned monster?

A temporary reprieve came to them as the goblin patrol unwittingly rushed into the room. The demon's head shot up and the creature sent its flaming beams out at the newest intruders. The burly goblin, in the lead, threw its arm up as Gary had done, but it was not wearing armor nearly as fine as Cedric's. The fire bored right through the goblin's arm and then right through its head, and it fell, smoldering and quite dead, to the floor.

Flashes of fire continued throughout the goblin ranks, felling several others. Goblins rushed all about, banging into each other, hacking at each other to get free and get away. The one troll bravely, stupidly, charged ahead, not understanding its foe. A demon arm caught it by the throat and lifted it from the ground before it ever got close to the misty cloud. The great, clawed hand clenched down—Gary heard a resounding *snap*—and the troll suddenly stopped thrashing.

The demon shook the huge form a few times, then hurled it into the midst of the scrambling goblins, crushing one. And then the demon, too, came on, suddenly just a billowing cloud once more. It overtook the goblins in the meeting room and passed right through their ranks. One cloud became three and a monster stood to block every exit.

Hearing the screams from that meeting room, cries of sheer terror and sheer agony, Gary hugged tight to the desk leg and even Kelsey, bravely in pursuit of the monster, stopped in his tracks and backpedaled.

In a moment, the cries diminished and three goblins came rushing back into the room. Jets of flame cut two of them down; the third ran right by Kelsey, hooking the stunned elf's arm and holding tight behind him.

"Pleases! Pleases!" the goblin sputtered. "Kills it! Oh, kills it!"

Kelsey shrugged the goblin away and stood firm to meet his foe. Geno stuffed that last hunk of eggshell into his mouth, retrieved his favorite hammer, and moved beside the elf.

Gary, too, knew that he must go and join his friends, go and die beside his friends. Determinedly he hooked his arm over the desktop and pulled himself to his feet. He meant to tun and go straight over but found himself held suddenly by the images in an open book on Ceridwen's desk.

Gary blinked several times, glancing over his shoulder and then back to those strange images. In the book, he saw Kelsey and Geno, standing as they were now standing in the middle of the room! Cowering in the corner behind them was the goblin.

"It has been an honor to fight beside you," Kelsey said to the dwarf, and Gary blinked again as the spoken words became a flowing script (though in a language he could not read) at the top of the page!

"A journal?" Gary breathed in disbelief.

He continued to stare dumbfounded as the page turned of its own accord. The next scene showed him the demon in the door, advancing on his friends.

Gary grabbed a nearby quill and poked it at the image of the demon, but the instrument snapped apart as it struck the magical book. Desperately Gary grabbed at the pages and flipped them back, hoping beyond reason that he might turn back time.

But the demon came on and the book fought back against Gary's actions, its pages trying to catch up with the events at hand. Gary put all his weight on one side of the book to hold it open where it was, at the two pages depicting Kelsey reaching for the spear case, and the egg coming apart on the floor.

Gary couldn't see the renewed fighting behind him, but he heard a crash by the canopied bed and heard Geno grunt and groan from that direction. Without even thinking of the possible consequences, the desperate man grabbed at the page with the intact demon egg and pulled with all his strength.

Suddenly Gary was in darkness, floating in space, it seemed, but there were no stars and no sun to light the way.

SIXTEEN

Time Unglued

GARY floated in the dim grayness, searching for some bearing, for some reference point in this unremarkable universe. He saw a seam before him, far in the distance, a line, perhaps, in the fabric of existence.

Gary willed himself towards that seam, understood then that this was not some physical place he had been dropped into, but an extra dimension, a place of the mind. He reached for the seam with prying fingers, tried to push himself through it, figuring that anything beyond it could only be an improvement.

One finger slipped through. Suddenly Gary was not so sure of his actions. What if he was at the gates of Hell? Or what if his tearing of this seam unraveled the fabric of the physical universe. But he decided at last that he couldn't just hover in the grayness and wait. Determinedly he drove his hand through the barrier, and then his other hand, and with all his strength began pulling the gray walls apart.

His blood pounded in his head—he could feel that distinctly, the pressure growing, though he was sure that his consciousness was somehow detached from this physical form. Gary steeled his mind and pulled. He feared he wouldn't be strong enough, and indeed, the sides of the curtain, for that is what he now believed it to be, barely moved apart. Through the crack came a blinding light, stinging Gary's eyes and all his sensibilities.

He thought he would surely collapse. He thought all the world would be destroyed if he persisted. He thought that his tear might loose a thousand other demons upon the land of Faerie. He thought . . .

But while he thought, Gary continued to pull, stubbornly held on to his course, and gradually the curtains did begin to move apart.

The light overwhelmed him.

And then he was back in Ceridwen's room, holding a torn page from the magical book. Kelsey and Geno stood side by side in the center of the room beside the burned and broken corpses of several goblins and the troll; the lone living goblin cowered in the corner. The demon was gone, but above the goblin's head, another egg (or was it the same egg?) teetered on the edge of a cubby much too shallow to hold it.

"Egg!" was all that desperate Gary managed to cry out, pointing to the cubby. Kelsey seemed to understand. The elf spun around just in time to see the egg drop.

It landed on the goblin's stooped shoulder. It did not break, though, but started to roll. The stupid creature reflexively caught it. Kelsey rushed in; the goblin squealed and threw the egg at him.

Kelsey's sword and shield went flying to the sides. The elf fell to his knees, juggling the precious egg, his hands moving in a blur to soften the impact until he finally managed to get control of it. Quickly Kelsey inspected the delicate shell, then breathed a sigh of relief to see that it had no visible cracks.

The companions' troubles were not ended, though. The troll body rose up suddenly and flew back through the air to the spot where the demon had thrown it. It shook a few times and dropped to land on its feet, very much alive. One of Geno's hammers, lying on the floor, came spinning back at the dwarf, who kept the presence of mind to catch it. Fire crackled and shot out of the bodies of the dead goblins, and some of them began to stir once more.

"What is happening?" Gary cried, but he had a better guess at the answer than either of his stunned companions. He had torn the fabric of time, at least as far as Ceridwen's magical journal was concerned. He felt himself falling away again, into the grayness, into the void.

He reached over and closed the book.

The dead goblins fell dead again, the troll crashed down in a heavy, broken lump, and the fires died away. And Kelsey, still on his knees, held the fragile egg.

"What have you done?" Geno asked Gary breathlessly.

Gary had no answer, had never seen the tough dwarf so unnerved.

"Pleases! Pleases!" the lone living goblin begged, groveling on the floor before Kelsey. Geno, frustrated and confused, started for it, hammer raised, but Gary stopped him.

"The goblin can show us the way out," he blurted.

"But we have not found the spear," replied Kelsey.

Gary fell within himself, consciously tried to reach his thought out to the spear. He knew that it was in here, that it had been the one who had warned him when Kelsey had reached for the phony case.

"*Up high, above the room,*" came an answer. Gary looked up to the unremarkable ceiling, thinking there must be a concealed trapdoor somewhere. Then his gaze settled on the high canopy of Ceridwen's silk-covered bed.

"The canopy," he explained. "The spear is on top of the canopy."

One of the bottom bedposts was already down, having taken a hit during the fight. Geno made short work of the other bottom post, flinging a hammer through it. The canopy fell diagonally to the floor and the precious spear case rolled off it, coming to a stop just a few feet from Kelsey.

The elf reached for it, but this time, Gary's warning came quickly enough to stop him.

"No!" Gary shrieked. He grabbed a blue-glowing torch from a sconce beside him and rushed over, and to Kelsey's horror, he put the flames to the case. The leather erupted in a sizzling display, sickly green fumes rushing up from the white-hot fires.

"What are you doing?" Kelsey demanded, and he pushed Gary aside. The elf hopped about the blaze, blowing at it, kicking at it, frantically trying to save the legendary spear—though, if Kelsey had not been so badly shaken, if he had taken the moment to calm himself and consider things, he would have realized that no simple torch fire could have possibly harmed the legendary spear.

The fire was gone an instant later, the leather case completely consumed. The spear remained, though, unscathed, and Kelsey thought himself foolish for his fears.

"The case was poisoned," Gary explained. "Contact poison. If you had touched it . . ." Gary let the thought hang in the air as he tentatively moved to pick up the spear. He found it surprisingly cool to his touch.

"Hello again," he said, and then, though he didn't really know why, he added, "I have missed you."

"*My greetings as well, young warrior,*" came the spear's telepathic reply. Gary considered that title and smiled, obviously pleased.

"What are you planning to do with the egg?" Geno asked Kelsey. "I do not believe that we would take it along."

Kelsey paled at that suggestion.

"Give it to me," Gary said, nearly laughing aloud at his plan. Kelsey hesitated for a moment, but then, apparently realizing that Gary had earned his trust, handed it over.

Gary moved to Ceridwen's desk again and took one of the side drawers right out of its perch. With all caution, he placed the egg deep inside the hole, then replaced the drawer, easing it halfway in, but taking care not to crush the fragile egg.

"Ceridwen will have a bit of a surprise waiting for her when she closes that drawer," Gary snickered, letting them in on the joke.

"Again you have proven more valuable than I would have believed," Kelsey remarked, his tone brightened, almost lighthearted. He looked to the book on Ceridwen's desk. "Against the demon, with the spear, and in this matter. Not many, I would guess, could look into one of Ceridwen's tomes and find the strength . . ."

"My thanks," Gary interrupted, reverently sliding the spear through a loop on the side of his belt. "But can you tell me later? Right now, I just want to get the hell out of here."

"That is a curious way to put it," Geno piped in, though the dwarf wholeheartedly agreed. "Do you know the way out?" he barked at the goblin.

The goblin thought it over for a moment, then answered, "No know."

"Kill him," Geno said evenly to Kelsey, and not a person in the room had any doubts about the dwarf's sincerity.

"Knows the way out?" the goblin cried, as though it had misunderstood the original question. "Yesses, oh yesses. Jesper shows you out, oh yesses!"

"I guess you have to know how to talk to them," Gary remarked, and Geno nodded and grinned, his missing tooth again reminding Gary of his mischievous nephew. Their smiles abruptly disappeared, though, and Geno whirled towards the bed and whipped a hammer. Following the hammer's flight, Gary and Kelsey both saw a flash of black dart back under the bed.

"A cat," Gary said, hearing the creature's ensuing cry.

"Witch's familiar!" Kelsey corrected, and he dove down flat to his belly and poked his sword under the bed. But then the cat's meow became a lion's roar and a huge paw shot out, hooking Kelsey under the shoulder blade. A split second later, the elf disappeared under the bed, only his feet sticking out.

Geno roared and charged right into the bed, his cord-like muscles heaving wildly. The bed came up, and so did the lion, bowling over Geno and bearing down on Gary.

The sentient spear cried a hundred different telepathic commands in that one terrible instant, but Gary heard none of them. He fell backwards—he had nowhere else to go—bringing his dwarven spear up defensively as he toppled. Unable to break its momentum, the lion came on, catching the spear in the chest. The dwarf-forged shaft bowed but did not break as the lion's full five-hundred-pound weight fell over Gary. The beast thrashed and roared as it impaled itself.

Unlike the goblin Gary had impaled many days before, though, this enemy kept thrashing, and with its huge claws getting closer and closer to Gary as it slid down the spear pole, the young man thought he was surely doomed. One paw raked at his chest, claws squealing against the metallic armor.

Geno roared again and ran headfirst into the flank of the impaled cat, knocking it over to the side. The lion continued to thrash, but no one was in its range then, the dwarf having gone right over and continued his rolling and Gary quick to scramble the other way.

Kelsey helped Gary to his feet. The elf didn't seem too badly hurt, though one of his sleeves had been torn off and his bare arm showed several fairly deep scratches.

"The spear will finish it," Kelsey said uneasily, obviously shaken from the second or two he had spent under the bed with the lion.

"How many pets does Ceridwen keep?" Gary asked.

"Too many," came Geno's reply.

A moment later, the cat lay still. A gray mist surrounded it and it seemed to melt away. To the friends' surprise, the black house cat sprang out of the mist and zipped into the cubby formed by the overturned bed. Geno started for it, then changed his mind.

"I am thinking that we should be leaving," the dwarf offered, and he found no arguments, not even from the still-cowering goblin.

They had barely gone through the adjacent meeting room, pointedly closing the door behind them, when there came another lion's roar from Ceridwen's chambers.

"Stubborn cat," the dwarf remarked dryly.

SEVENTEEN

Reading Between the Lines

THEY found Mickey some time later, after a dozen wrong turns and close brushes with goblin guards. The leprechaun was sitting against the wall as he— or at least, as his illusion—had been doing when they left him. Tommy was still hard at work on the wall beside the illusionary dwarf.

"Time to go," Kelsey said to the leprechaun. "Has our goblin friend returned?"

"Twice," Mickey replied, drawing deeply on his pipe. "He's thinking everything's as it should be."

From somewhere down the halls, there came the roar of a lion.

"Time to go," Kelsey said again, pulling the frightened goblin prisoner into the room beside him. "We have a guide."

Gary nodded from Mickey to the giant, who was still oblivious to the fact that the missing group had even entered the room. "He won't go unless he thinks he's finished," Gary explained.

"Then let him stay," whispered Geno. "Who wants a giant around?"

"We need him," Gary said firmly, and he feared that he would have to go into a long and detailed explanation of his tentative escape plans, an explanation that he was sure would make little sense to his companions.

Mickey trusted him, though. The leprechaun winked Gary's way and the illusionary dwarf went into a whirlwind of activity that had the hole patched in mere seconds. Tommy blinked at the sight, not quite knowing what to make of it.

"Ye must leave now!" the goblin prisoner heard himself command, though he hadn't moved his lips. He looked questioningly around the room, but Kelsey's sword came up beside him in a flash.

"If you make any more noise than drawing your breath, I will cut off your head," the elf promised.

"Duh, is the wall fixed?" Tommy asked helplessly. He felt around as though he didn't believe his eyes. "The wall is not fixed."

"Now!" cried the goblin with a leprechaun's voice. "The Lady wants ye out o' the house!"

The illusionary dwarf walked over and seemed to blend right in with Geno. "The wall is fixed," Geno answered Tommy, taking the cue, though he gave Gary an angry sidelong glance as he addressed the giant.

"Come on, Tommy," Gary added. "I'll show you something else that will please the Lady." That got the giant's attention, and he shrugged at the somehow-fixed wall, scratched his huge head one final time, and fell into line behind Gary.

"One wrong turn costs you your head," Kelsey promised, whispering into the goblin's ear so that the giant would not hear. But the terrified goblin needed no prodding. It had seen quite too much of the powerful companions already to offer any resistance. It led them on at a great pace, pausing every now and then at an intersection to check its bearings.

They came unexpectedly upon one group of guards, bursting in through open doors before they even noticed that the room was not empty.

"I have to get these wretches outa the castle," Mickey's voice explained from the goblin's mouth, before Kelsey could set his sword into action. Mickey wanted no fights here, not with Ceridwen's pet in pursuit and a tentative and unpredictable giant by his side.

A roar erupted from somewhere behind them and the eyes of the goblin guards went wide.

"The Lady's cat's not too pleased that they're still around," Mickey went on.

"Then gets them out of here!" screamed one of the goblins, and it, and the others, darted out a side passage, scrambling away with all speed from the pursuing cat.

"That is Alice," Tommy said. The others looked at him curiously. "The Lady's cat," the giant explained. "Alice. The Lady lets me play with her sometimes."

"Go and play with Alice now," Geno offered.

"Shut up!" Gary snapped at the dwarf, and he thought himself incredibly stupid for talking that way to the volatile Geno. But Kelsey backed him this time.

"We have no time for bickering," the elf said, and he prodded the goblin along once more. "Let us discuss our differences when we are safely outside."

They ran down one long hallway, the outer doors in sight, but then Geek the goblin turned into the hall behind them. "Where is yous going?" the spindly-limbed goblin demanded. "You comes back here!"

Tommy spun about, confused, but Mickey was quicker, putting up an illusion of an empty hallway behind them.

"Come on, Tommy," Gary prodded, grabbing the giant's thumb in his hand and pulling with all his might.

"Duh," was all that Tommy replied, giving in to Gary's tug.

The distant goblin began shouting again, until a roar silenced his further tirade. "No, Alice," they heard Geek cry as they continued through the doors. "Nice kitty, Alice!"

And then they were outside. Geno closed the doors behind them and popped a spike into the ground at their base for good measure.

"If they have any way of contacting Ceridwen . . . ," Kelsey warned, but he did not finish the thought, seeing Tommy overly interested in his words. He pulled Gary and Mickey aside, and the goblin prisoner, seeing a chance, wasted no time. As soon as Kelsey let go of it, with Geno busy at the doors, the creature ran off.

"How do we get off the island?" Kelsey asked bluntly, paying no heed to the fleeing goblin.

Gary still hadn't actually figured out exactly how they should proceed at that point; retrieving the magical spear and getting out of the castle had come in such a wild rush. Whatever details were yet to be worked out, though, Gary knew what role his companions had to play. "Get back to the camp and retrieve all of our belongings," he instructed. "And bring one boat along. Go north along the beach until you find a rocky jetty. I'll meet you there."

"And what of the giant?"

"He comes with me," Gary replied. He looked to Mickey, trying to think things through, trying to figure out what coaxing Tommy might need. "You had better come with me, too," he said.

Gary had little trouble convincing Tommy to go with him to the lagoon. Thrilled at preparing another surprise for the Lady, the giant even picked Gary and Mickey up and carried them along. Once again, Gary was amazed at the giant's strength, and glad, for he knew that Tommy would need all of it to carry out the plan.

When they got back to the lagoon, Gary instructed Tommy to retrieve weeds, both brown and green. The giant shrugged and did as he was asked, though he had no idea what the man had in mind. Mickey's amused smile showed that the leprechaun was beginning to catch on, though.

Gary found the widest hollow tubes of the bunch and glued them together with the sticky goo from the green reeds.

"Okay, Tommy," he said confidently, "put this in your mouth."

"I do not like to eat the water plants," Tommy explained.

"No, don't eat them," Gary explained. "Breathe through them." Off to the side, Mickey whistled and couldn't contain a chuckle.

Tommy scratched his huge head. "Duh?"

"Don't you understand?" Gary asked, as though things should have been obvious. He had to continue to appear confident, he knew, if he was to have any chance of convincing the giant. "With these, you can walk all the way across the lake."

"That will not please the Lady," Tommy reasoned.

"Oh, but it will!" Gary replied immediately. "If you can go back and forth without having to jump and scramble, you'll be able to carry things for Ceri . . . the Lady."

Tommy scratched his head.

"When the Lady has things to bring across to the island, she will no longer have to go back and forth with puny boats," Gary went on, revealing his sincere excitement. "She will have you to simply carry the things across for her."

"Duh, I do not . . . ," the giant began slowly.

"Just try it," Gary pleaded. "Go across once, and then come back."

Tommy looked at the reed tube sourly and shook his head. Gary knew that his time was running out. And with all the damage they had done back in the castle, and with the spear back in their possession, he had no desire to be on the island when Ceridwen returned.

"You already went across once," Gary said grimly, his tone an obvious warning. "If the Lady finds out, she'll be mad."

"You will not tell her?" Tommy begged.

Gary shrugged his shoulders noncommittally. "If this works, though, you can explain to the Lady that you went across only because you wanted to find some way you could help her. Won't that make her happy?"

Tommy thought for a moment, then took the reed tube.

"Just put the tube in your mouth and your face in the water," Gary explained. "Keep calm and breathe easy."

Tommy walked into the lagoon and did as Gary asked, but brought the whole tube underwater with him and came up a few seconds later, coughing wildly.

"It does not work," he complained as soon as the fit had ended.

"We're in trouble, lad," Mickey remarked.

Gary motioned for Tommy to come back to him, then showed the giant how to keep one end of the tube above the lake, so that the air could go into him. The giant shrugged and went back into the water, ducking his head. Again, he came up in mere seconds, panicked and spitting water.

"We're in trouble," Mickey said again.

Gary realized that Tommy's mouth was simply too big for the tube. He called Tommy back to the shore, then refitted the reeds, this time smearing goo all around them to secure them in the giant's mouth. Using both hands, he pinched Tommy's nostrils to show the giant that he could indeed breathe through the tube.

Tommy shrugged, went back and tried again, and again, and each time he stayed underwater a little longer and came up looking less afraid.

"Long way to the shore," Mickey remarked. "Ye're thinking that the giant can keep calm enough to stay underwater all the way, carrying us besides?"

"Would you rather stay here and take your chances with Ceridwen?" Gary replied dryly.

"Good point, lad," agreed the leprechaun. He looked down the beach past the jetty and saw Kelsey and Geno approaching, Kelsey laden with their belongings and Geno carrying the heavy boat up over his head.

"How does he do that?" Gary remarked, amazed at the diminutive dwarf's incredible power.

"Comes from eating rocks," Mickey replied, and Gary couldn't tell from the leprechaun's tone if he was kidding or not.

Tommy came back to Gary and Mickey at about the same time as their other companions joined them. Tommy eyed the boat suspiciously, wondering what Gary had in mind, what this whole business was about.

"For the test," Gary explained, reading the giant's thoughts (not a difficult task). "You carry the boat high above your head; take care that it does not touch the water!"

"Duh, why are they here?" Tommy asked, pointing particularly at Geno. "The Lady does not want you to leave the island. You should not have a boat."

Tommy stood motionless, perplexed, trying to remember all that he had learned of his companions' dilemma. The giant was slow to catch on, but not nearly as stupid as some people assumed.

"You want Tommy to carry you past the water," he reasoned, his big eyes growing bigger.

"Carry us? Don't be silly!" Gary lied, flashing a disarming smile. "Kelsey and Geno will help me to pile rocks in the boat as you walk underwater past the end of the jetty. We have to see how strong you are, how much you can carry, before you go and tell the Lady your surprise."

"I am strong!" the giant asserted, an obvious fact that none of the companions were about to argue against.

Gary bobbed his head. "But we should know exactly how much you can carry before you tell the Lady about your surprise. The water's deep enough by the jetty's end to get the boat down near our level." Gary could only hope that the slow-to-catch-on giant wouldn't simply reason that it would be easier to fill the boat before he even started out. Tommy stood scratching his head, and looking at the lake and mountains beyond, then at the boat, and then, suspiciously, at Geno and Kelsey. Finally, to Gary's relief, Tommy popped his reed pipe in his mouth and hoisted the boat overhead.

Gary clapped his hands together and beamed at his friends, but Geno and Kelsey didn't seem to share his enthusiasm.

"You want us to climb in the boat as the giant walks past us?" the dwarf balked as soon as the giant moved far enough away. "I have lived too long—and hope to live too long again—for such a stupid trick!"

"You forget that the lake is acid to us," Kelsey added sourly.

Gary motioned to Mickey to give the answer, thinking that the leprechaun's backing might not be such a bad thing at that time.

"Would ye rather stay here and take yer chances with Ceridwen?" Mickey asked.

They were all in place on the end of the jagged jetty as Tommy came walking past, still holding the boat high. This was the trickiest part of the whole plan, for Gary couldn't be sure that the water was deep enough to get over the giant's head and keep him blinded to their real intentions.

It was, but just barely, and the giant's long arms had the boat high up above them, with Gary having no way to instruct Tommy to lower it. They tossed their bundles into the boat, then Gary jumped up and caught the side. He was going to tell his companions to climb up over him, but they hardly needed an invitation. Kelsey verily ran up his back. Mickey, boosted by Geno, barely touched Gary's shoulders as he flew past, and the dwarf came last—Gary was amazed at how much weight was packed into that little body!

They pulled Gary in, and then they all sat tight, fearful that the water, which Ceridwen had promised would burn them as acid, was only about six or seven feet below them. Looking over the edge of the boat, when any of them mustered the nerve to look over the edge, they could see the top of Tommy's head, bobbing along steadily.

As the giant continued deeper into the lake, his head disappeared altogether, and they grew even more afraid, for the dangerous water came closer and closer.

"If he bends his arms, we're done for," Mickey commented, and none of them appreciated the remark.

"Stupid plan," Geno muttered. "And I am a stupid dwarf for going along with it!"

Fifteen minutes later, Tommy was still walking. They were much closer to the mountainous shoreline than the island, and resting a bit easier. Tommy's iron-hard arms did not quiver, and the boat was steadily, if gradually, coming up again, for the giant had passed the lake's deepest point.

"Clever lad, to find a way through Ceridwen's spell," Mickey commented, aiming the remark more at Kelsey and Geno than at Gary. "I feared that the giant'd panic long before he reached the shore, but he's soon to be breathing without help o' yer . . . what did ye call it again?"

"Snorkel," Gary replied, peeking over the side. "When Tommy's head clears the water, stay still in the middle of the boat," Gary warned, "I don't know how he'll react when he finds out we've tricked him."

The lake grew more shallow with each giant step, and soon, not only Tommy's head but the top half of his body were clear of the water. He paused and looked back towards the island, as amazed as anyone that he had come this far.

The boat shifted suddenly as Tommy let go with one hand. It did not tip too far, though, so strong was the giant's remaining grip. The companions didn't know what the giant was up to, but then they heard Tommy pull the snorkel from his mouth.

"Duh, the Lady will be happy with me," the companions heard him say, to their absolute relief. But then, to their surprise and dismay, Tommy grabbed the boat in both hands again, turned around, and headed back towards the island.

"Stop him!" Kelsey mouthed silently at Gary, the elf's face contorted with frustration.

Gary looked around desperately. There was no escape; the land was simply too far away for them to even attempt a jump. Gary took a deep breath and leaned far over the edge of the boat. "No, Tommy," he called. "Get to the shore first, then we can go back."

Tommy spit out his snorkel in surprise. "Duh, what are you doing in my boat?" asked the confused giant.

"I . . . we," Gary stammered.

Mickey started a spell, but before he could get it off, Tommy lowered the boat down by his chest and looked less than thrilled to see the four companions inside. "Hey!" he cried.

"You held the boat up too high when you passed us on the jetty," Gary blurted suddenly. "We couldn't get the rocks inside, so we climbed in instead. The weight is about . . ."

"You tricked Tommy!" the giant roared. "The Lady wants you to stay on the island!" He started to turn back, but Geno, horrified at the thought of going back to face the witch, whipped a hammer into his chest. The weapon bounced off without doing any serious damage, and, as a pointed reminder to the companions, it dropped into the water and dissolved before their eyes.

Kelsey rushed up beside the giant, his sword bared and point aimed in towards Tommy's heart. "To the shore!" the elf demanded.

He almost got his wish. With a great growl, Tommy heaved the boat towards the shore, but it didn't quite make it, landing with a tremendous splash a few feet from the beach. Ceridwen's spell began its wicked work immediately—the boat started to sizzle and sputter, white smoke rising up from its timbers.

Kelsey and Geno went into action, grabbing bundles and hurling them to shore. Geno picked up Mickey and flung him to the beach, then grabbed Gary and, before the stunned man could protest, put him up above his head, spun him about twice to gain momentum, and launched him as well.

Gary landed heavily on the rocky shore. He rolled to a sitting position, spat sand from his mouth, and regarded Mickey, sitting next to him. "From eating rocks, huh?" Gary remarked.

Kelsey leaped across the ten-foot gap with no trouble, but the dwarf did not follow. Geno considered the jump and considered the consequences of not getting out of the fast-breaking boat, but the dwarf knew that his bandy legs couldn't possibly propel his body all the way to the shore.

"Who is the next best smithy in the world?" Kelsey, ever the pragmatist, inquired of Geno.

Geno couldn't jump the ten feet but his spit made it across easily enough.

"Help him, Tommy!" Gary cried. "The water will kill him!"

The giant regarded the boat curiously, scratching his head. Geno couldn't wait for him to make up his mind.

"Come and play, blockhead!" the dwarf roared, and he twirled another hammer Tommy's way.

Of all the insults one might throw at a giant, none could stir such a creature more than "blockhead." Tommy growled and charged and Geno got up on the very lip of the boat closest to shore. When Tommy crashed over the back of the splintering boat, the other end, Geno's end, went high into the air. The dwarf timed his leap perfectly, using the momentum of the tilting boat to send him high and far. As Gary had done with the stone wave back in Dvergamal, Geno easily cleared his friends. He soared past and came down headfirst into a huge chunk of stone, laughing wildly all the way, even after he had bounced off.

Their troubles were far from over, though, for Tommy bounded up onto the shore, his big fists clenched in rage. "You told Tommy that it would please the Lady!" the giant sputtered.

"I'm sorry, Tommy," Gary replied sincerely, making no move to either run or defend himself "But we had to get off that island. Ceridwen would have killed us all."

"She will be mad at me."

"Then go back in the lake and drown," Geno offered. Tommy's next words came out as undecipherable, guttural snarls and he advanced upon the dwarf. For the first time since he had met Geno, Gary sensed that the dwarf was afraid.

"Why, Tommy?" Gary asked simply, leaping up to catch hold of the giant's fist. Tommy looked down at him. "Why?"

"You're free now," Gary explained. "You don't have to go back to the island, or if you do go back, you don't have to tell Ceridwen how we got off the island."

"She will be mad at me," the giant said again.

"No, she won't," Gary insisted. "Not unless she finds out what happened." He and the giant stared at each other for a long while, Gary finally slipping from Tommy's fist back to the ground. Tommy had no further designs on Geno. He went over to the water's edge and sat down, putting his chin in his huge hands.

Kelsey intercepted Gary before he could get near his forlorn friend.

"Leave him, lad," said Mickey, agreeing with the elf. "We cannot wait here, and if we're found near the giant, then all the worse for him."

Gary hated to go, but he couldn't disagree. They scooped up their bundles and set off along the mountain trail, leaving the giant to his staring and his thinking.

EIGHTEEN
Smorgasbord

"WE have come too far to the south," Kelsey explained when they entered a valley that allowed them to look out beyond Penllyn's peaks. The elf pointed back to the north, to the distant towering mountains of Dvergamal. "But we are closer to Giant's Thumb now than before the trolls captured us, and the ground between here and the mountain should be easier traveling once we have broken free of these mountains."

"Not so easy in the Crahgs," Geno remarked, but no one seemed to hear.

"Giant's Thumb?" Gary asked Mickey.

"That's where Robert makes his lair," the leprechaun explained. "Not too big a mountain—not as big as those in Dvergamal—but flat-topped and big enough to keep the dragon comfortable."

"Robert?" Gary asked. "Who is this Robert?" It was the second time Gary had heard the leprechaun speak the name, but he thought it wise not to mention his previous eavesdropping.

Mickey gave him an incredulous stare. "The dragon," he answered. "Have ye not been listening?"

"A dragon named Robert?" Gary had to remind himself of the gravity of their situation, of all that they had come through and could expect to yet face, to keep from bursting out in laughter.

"Robert the Righteous, he calls himself," Kelsey put in.

"Though most others peg him as 'Robert the Wretched,'" Mickey added with a snicker. "It's not his real name, of course, not a name for a dragon. But that's a hard one, harder than Kelsenellelll . . . oh, well, ye get me meaning."

"Only thing harder to pronounce than the name of an elf is the true name of a dragon," Geno clarified grumpily. He gave Kelsey a derisive stare. "At least dragons have the courtesy to give themselves an easier title that people can use when addressing them."

"Afore they're eaten," Mickey had to add.

Gary looked from one of his companions to the other, as lost in the conversation, and all the innuendo he instinctively knew was flying about, as he was in this strange world. For the first time, Gary gave careful consideration to this up-coming beast. When Mickey had first mentioned the quest, and the dragon, Gary had thought this whole adventure a dream and had not given it too much thought. Between then and now, the young man had simply been too busy just keeping himself out of trouble to think about what lay at the end of his road. Now, though, with Ceridwen's island behind them and Kelsey promising a clear road to Giant's Thumb, the dragon—Robert the Righteous, or Wretched, or whatever title best fit the beast—inevitably hovered about Gary's thoughts.

"How big is this dragon?" Gary asked a short while later. Mickey was back on his shoulder, the leprechaun having no chance of matching the elf's eager pace with his tiny legs.

"Read your Mr. Tolkien, lad," the leprechaun replied. "Seems he got the dragon part right, at least. Aye, he's been to Faerie, that one. Not a secondhand account o' that Smaug creature. I'm just a bit surprised that since he seen it, he got back to yer own world to write about it!"

Gary started to say, "You're kidding," but changed his mind, realizing that the leprechaun spoke with all seriousness. And given his own unbelievable situation, how could Gary say with certainty that Tolkien had not visited Faerie? Or so many other of the fantasy writers he loved to read? And what about the common folktales of a dozen different countries, particularly Ireland and Scotland? Might those legends of elfs and sprites, dragons and bandy-legged dwarfs, be based on the actual experiences of simple farmers?

"What're ye thinking?" the leprechaun asked him, seeing his face crinkled in confusion.

"I don't even know," Gary replied honestly, for the notion had overwhelmed him.

"Well, if ye're thinking of old Robert, then don't ye bother," Mickey said, and Gary couldn't help but notice that the leprechaun's tone had taken on a grim edge. "Ye cannot imagine a dragon, lad. Nothing yer mind'd conjure could come close to the truth.

"Read yer Mr. Tolkien again, lad," Mickey went on. "Read and be afraid. Ceridwen's made the day dark for us, but Robert will make it darker still!"

Gary took out *The Hobbit* and considered opening to Bilbo's first encounter with the dreaded dragon. Then he thought the better of it and put the book back into his pocket. No sense in scaring himself, he figured.

Robert would do it for him.

"I told ye they'd come walkin' back from the witch's island," one troll boasted to another, seeing the companions crossing the lower trails near to the edge of Penllyn. "We gots to go tell Earl!"

"Meat fer the table," the other agreed. "Them bunnies was good, but a dwarf pie'll taste better!"

"An' manflesh and elf-on-a-stick!" said the first. "And the little trickster's goin' in me mouth before Earl gets 'is fat paws on 'im!"

The other troll punched him in the eye. "In *me* mouth, ye ogre baby," the troll protested. "I seen 'im first."

"*I* seen him first!" the first troll argued back, but he didn't move to retaliate physically, more concerned with dinner than with fighting at that moment. "But I'll split the trickster with ye—right down the middle!"

The other troll smacked his lips with his big fat tongue and rubbed his greedy hands together. "Let's go get Earl," he offered. "Me belly's growlin' awrful."

THE companions ran on long past sunset, none of them complaining about putting the miles between them and Ceridwen's island and all of them anxious to be out of the dark mountains. When they finally set camp, on a high flat rock with the empty plain in sight and the scattered bumps that were the Crahgs beyond it, they agreed, again without protest (except a squeak from Mickey—and

Kelsey said that didn't count because Mickey was always complaining), that they wouldn't start a fire. The night was chilly for the season, with a cold wind blowing down across the empty miles from Dvergamal—the last remnants of the Cailleac Bheur's summer storm, Mickey reasoned. A full moon made its way up above them, bathing all the land in silvery light.

Gary got up often, rubbing his arms and walking briskly in circles to keep his circulation going. He knew that he would get little sleep that night, but he didn't care. They had come to the last stage of their journey, for better or worse, and he knew that a little weariness wouldn't slow him down.

He felt better, too, about having the sentient spear back on his belt. He sensed that the weapon was communicating with him almost constantly, though not on a level that he could consciously respond to. It was just a feeling he got, a subconscious bonding. Whatever was happening, Gary carried his normal spear with growing confidence, thinking that if it came to blows again, he would know what to do.

Still, he wasn't pleased to find out if his instincts were correct quite so soon.

Kelsey saw the dark silhouettes shortly after midnight, circling the camp at a wide radius, cutting in and out of the shadows of jagged boulders and rocky outcroppings. The elf and dwarf agreed that the big shapes were trolls, and the fact that there were four of them led them all to believe that they had met this particular band before.

"Four against four," Gary whispered, crouching beside Kelsey and Mickey and popping his loose-fitting helmet onto his head. "Even odds."

"Anyone who's ever fought trolls'd tell ye that even numbers don't make for even odds," Mickey was quick to point out.

"We nearly beat them before!" Geno growled. "And there were seven of them then!" As if to further his point, the dwarf sent a hammer spinning out into the darkness, heard a thump, and grunted in pleasure as a troll groaned.

"You see?" the beaming dwarf asked, looking so much again like a disreputable youngster with his one tooth missing and his cat-ate-the-canary smile.

Things didn't follow the exact course that Geno expected. Kelsey cocked back his bow, Geno readied another hammer, but before they began their assaults, several large rocks came bouncing into the small camp. One caught Gary in the chest and blew the air from his lungs, sending him flying over backwards. Kelsey managed to dive around a second throw, but his evasive action took him right into the path of a third. He twisted and rolled, but the rock caught him squarely in the knee and sent him spiraling down to the ground.

Mickey threw up one of his umbrellas. Lying next to the leprechaun, Gary wondered what good it would do, but amazingly a rock heading straight for the sprite hit the umbrella and bounced harmlessly away.

"You got one of those for me?" Gary asked weakly, struggling to get back to his feet.

Geno launched a hammer and scored another hit (at least another troll groaned as though it had been hit), but a second volley of rocks thundered in. The dwarf was the main target this time, and he was struck twice, though the missiles appeared to do little damage and hardly moved him. One soared past Geno, though, and scored another hit on Kelsey, knocking him flat.

And then the trolls were upon them.

Mickey lit up the area with an eye-stinging flash of light.

"Go to Kelsey!" Gary instructed Mickey. The leprechaun seemed hesitant to leave the inexperienced human, but Kelsey, out cold on the ground, seemed in more dire peril. Mickey leaped over to the prone elf and conjured an illusion to make Kelsey appear as a part of the flat rock. Then the leprechaun prudently faded into invisibility, hoping that no trolls had noticed his actions.

Geno went into his customary troll-battle maneuvers, darting between legs, stomping his hammers down on troll toes, and generally making life miserable for the two attacking him.

One of the trolls—Gary recognized him as Earl—went over towards where Kelsey had been lying, sniffing the air and prodding the ground suspiciously. Out of the illusion came Kelsey, sword leading, and Earl got a good cut on the arm for his efforts.

Gary squared off against the fourth of the group. He held his spear and shield in front of him, feeling their balance. The troll came straight in, unafraid, swinging its heavy club for Gary's head.

Gary went down low beneath the blow and countered with a sharp spear jab that poked the troll in the belly and sent it hopping back onto its tiptoes. Gary used the break to circle to the side opposite the troll's weapon hand. The monster turned with him, more apprehensive now.

A second swing from the troll fell harmlessly short. Gary started to counter, then thought the better of it, for the troll was recovering much more quickly this time.

The monster tensed; Gary knew another swing was coming. As the troll's arm came about, Gary dropped forward to his knees, braced his shield against his shoulder, and angled it to deflect the club harmlessly high. At the same time, he got his spear in line with the troll's hand, angled so that the weapon's butt end remained tight against the ground.

The troll howled in pain and its club went flying as it drove its hand deep onto Gary's spear tip. Gary's own clever actions amazed him, but he knew that this was not the time to gloat, nor to pause and consider his fortunes. He came up from his knees, bowling straight ahead, and got two or three good spear pokes in on the troll before it recovered enough so that he was forced to back off.

The creature stood staring at Gary dumbfounded, clutching its wounded hand, and with several trickles of blood running down its filthy shirt.

THE two trolls fighting Geno were growing dizzy indeed as the dwarf, slapping and cursing every step of the way, continued his wild darting. Always, the trolls' counters seemed one step behind Geno, coming crashing down onto the hard rock at the dwarf's heels as he slipped between the monsters or between their widespread legs.

"'Ere, watch where ye're swingin'!" one of the trolls warned the other, having had the misfortune to have battled the cunning dwarf in the previous fight as well. "He's lookin' to get ye to hit me!"

The dwarf charged in on it as it spoke, and the troll, thinking it had its diminutive opponent's tactics figured out, quickly pulled its legs together. Geno's hammer led the way, smashing the inside of the troll's left knee. The legs went back apart and the dwarf darted through, smacking the inside of the right knee as he passed.

The other troll had come around to intercept, and the dwarf spun about, but slipped on the flat stone and skidded down.

Two trolls hovered over him, clubs raised and yellow-toothed smiles wide.

KELSEY fought valiantly for many seconds, spinning his sword about and in too quickly for Earl to launch any counterstrikes. The elf was hurt, though, bleeding from the side of his head and unable to use his legs to keep him out of Earl's reach.

Earl recognized this advantage immediately and tossed the club to the ground, reaching in with both hands. Kelsey nicked one, then the other, then cut a third time at the first arm. Earl seemed not to notice, and wrapped a huge hand about Kelsey's waist.

A dart appeared from nowhere, arcing through the air to find a resting place on Earl's big nose. Kelsey was free again as Earl tried to pull the stinger out.

"Won me championships three years in a row," Mickey boasted, coming visible again and putting another dart into Earl's face. Kelsey smiled and joined in the fun, more than willing to take advantage of the distraction. He stepped right in and drove his sword in and down above Earl's kneecap.

"YE cut me hand," the monster whined.

"More than that," Gary promised. He pumped his arm as if to throw, then leaped ahead instead, dropping his heavy and pointy-tipped shield onto the troll's toe. He knew that he was vulnerable right beneath the towering giant, but knew, too, that quickness was on his side. The troll, after a howl, had just begun to bend low to grab at him, when the spear came rushing up, blasting out a troll tooth and widening the creature's smile.

The troll fell back, staggered, and for some reason, Gary had no doubt at all that he would win this fight. Still, he was surprised when the troll's eyes went wide and the creature turned suddenly and sped away.

If he had not been so self-congratulatory at that point, Gary might have realized that the suddenly terrified troll had looked right past him.

GENO hoped that one of the trolls would pick him up and try to put him in a sack. At least that way, he'd have the satisfaction of getting a few more good strikes in before going out of the fight.

The trolls weren't intent on capturing the companions this time, the dwarf soon realized, and he realized, too, that he had no way of getting away from the great clubs.

But then one of the trolls rose up from the ground and went flying away into the darkness. The other troll stared ahead blankly, its eyes going up, up, up, until it met the gaze of Tommy One-Thumb.

On a troll's list of things to avoid, giants ranked just below dragons, and the terror was obvious in this troll's scream as it whipped its club across at Tommy.

The giant did wince, a little bit, as the club rebounded off his massive chest, but he did not fall back. Tommy came with a backhand response that caught the troll on the side of the head and sent it flying head over heels.

Gary had seen many wondrous things since coming to Faerie, but none of them outdid the spectacle of a twelve-foot-tall troll spinning through the air. He heard the resounding thump as the creature landed, and then heavy footsteps pounding away into the night.

"He's got me darts!" Gary heard Mickey yell, and then Earl loped past him. Strictly on instinct, Gary dropped to the ground, hooking his foot in front of Earl's huge ankle. Without even considering the move, Gary came across with a vicious spear swipe that caught the fleeing troll in the back on the knee (his one remaining good knee) and sent him crashing facedown to the stone. Without the slightest hesitation, Gary ran up the monster's back and dove headlong. His spear caught Earl on the back of the neck and drove up under the troll's thick skull bone.

Earl slumped back to the ground, shuddered once or twice, and expired.

Gary lay on the troll's back for a long time, holding tightly to his spear, hardly believing he had so efficiently dispatched such a powerful creature. When he finally looked back over his shoulder, he saw that Mickey and Kelsey shared his disbelief.

"When did ye learn to fight like that?" the leprechaun asked.

Gary had no answers for him—until a voice rang out in his mind. "*Thou has done well.*"

"You taught me," Gary replied out loud, looking down to the broken weapon on his belt.

"I did no such a thing," Mickey replied.

"Not you," Gary explained.

"The spear led ye through the fight?" Mickey asked.

Gary thought for a moment, then shrugged, unsure of exactly what had happened. In the previous fights, the spear's communications had been obvious, but if the spear had instructed him during this battle, he had not noticed. Still, Gary realized that he could not have fought so well on his own instincts. He wondered how closely he and the sentient spear had bonded, and which one had been in charge during the battle.

"Whatever it was, lad, ye did a fine job," Mickey went on, and Kelsey, wincing in pain again, nodded his head slowly in agreement.

"And Tommy saved us," Gary replied, speaking directly at Geno. The dwarf said nothing, just walked by Gary and spat on his sneaker.

"I'll take that as a thank-you," Gary said, a smile finding his face. He moved quickly (wisely) away from the dwarf and over to Tommy.

"You have our thanks, Tommy," he offered, reaching up to grab ahold of the giant's huge hand. "But why did you follow us?"

"He probably means to take us back to that stupid witch," Geno fumed.

"Tommy had nowhere else to go," the giant answered simply.

An idea came to Gary, but Mickey, seeing his face light up, was quick to squelch it.

"The giant's not coming to Robert's lair," the leprechaun insisted. "And better off he is for not coming!"

"He's a great fighter," Gary replied, confident that he would win this debate. "We might need . . ."

"Not so great against the likes o' Robert," Mickey was fast to interrupt. "If it comes to a fight, lad, he'd go down as quick as the rest."

"What are you talking about?" Gary yelled in reply. "We're going off happily to battle some dragon and you refuse allies? If it's that hopeless, they why are we going? How can we think that we might win?"

"You'll not be fighting the dragon," Kelsey replied evenly. "I will."

"You can hardly stand up," Gary shot back, more harshly than he had intended.

"I must fight the dragon in single combat," Kelsey explained. "And subdue the creature. If we brought the giant—if we brought an army—and killed the beast, what good would it be to us? No, we must get Robert's cooperation, and that can only be achieved in a challenge of honor."

"Then why can't Tommy go along?" Gary asked.

"Because dragons fear giants," Kelsey replied. "And if Robert is afraid, then he will fight us all and kill us before I even offer my challenge." The elf turned to Tommy. "You do indeed have our thanks, noble giant. And you may come with us across the brown plain and the Crahgs as far as the Giant's Thumb, if you are not afraid. But when we go up to the dragon's lair, we go alone."

Tommy just looked at Gary and shrugged again. When they broke camp the next dawn and began their run across the rolling hills, they were five, not four.

NINETEEN
The Crahgs

THE companions passed through the rolling farmlands between Dvergamal and Penllyn without incident, taking shelter at night in ancient stone farmhouses, long deserted and with nothing left at all of their thatched roofs. In better times, when Ynis Gwydrin had been the seat of goodly power and not in the possession of evil Ceridwen, these farms were among the finest in all of Faerie, Mickey explained grimly to Gary.

Gary detected that faraway look in the leprechaun's gray eyes, that distant longing for times long past. Suddenly Gary found himself wishing that he could see Faerie at its magical glory, that he could walk in the land of twilight fancies and walking fairy tales.

This wasn't it, and if Gary doubted that fact for one moment, all he had to do was conjure an image of mud-filled Dilnamarra or of the poor souls hanging at the crossroads, turning slowly in the stench-filled breeze.

As the companions continued east the rolling hills and rock walls gave way to taller, more imposing mounds.

"The Crahgs," Mickey mentioned, obviously not at all pleased by the sight. The mountains appeared as great balled lumps of green grasses, interspersed with stone and plopped down randomly on the rolling fields. They rose up two or three thousand feet, with the tops of many shrouded by low-riding clouds, thick and gray and mysterious. Small but tightly packed groupings of trees sat on the sides of many of the Crahgs, usually huddled in sheltered dells from the unending winds, and every mountainside sported streams of crystalline water, dancing down in trenches of bare stone, leaping over rocky breaks in the otherwise smooth decline.

Gary didn't at first know what to make of this place. It seemed a land of paradoxes, both imposing and inviting, magnificently beautiful yet strangely eerie and untamed. Even the light came in uneven, unexpected bursts. One steep side of two joined mounds disappeared into mist at the top, while only a hundred feet down, the wet grass gleamed and rivulets sparkled in a distinct line of sunny brightness. Just a short distance below the sunshine loomed the shadow of another cloud, dark and foreboding.

Full of life, yet full of melancholy. The paradox of existence itself, Gary thought, of vital life and quiet death.

The companions spoke little as they hiked their way into the Crahgs, for the wind carried away all but the loudest shouts, and none of them felt secure enough to yell out. Silently they climbed and descended, under rushing clouds, in rain showers that lasted but a few minutes and sunshine that shared a similar, brief life.

The first day hadn't been so bad, and Gary had thought that the second would be easier, on his emotions if not on his body. But the Crahgs were no less eerie that second day, and Gary had the distinct feeling that he and his friends were being watched, every step, by eyes that were not friendly.

"Loch Devenshere," Mickey explained on the afternoon of the third day, when the group rounded a rocky outcropping and came in view of a long and narrow lake. The waters continued on beyond sight in the east, cutting between poised and ominous lines of crahgs. All the world seemed a patchwork quilt of green and gray to Gary as he looked out over the sun-speckled landscape. Below him, the waters of Loch Devenshere bristled under the wind, deep and dark—and cold, he could tell from the sudden chilly and moist bite of the breeze.

"Do we feel safe enough to cross?" Mickey asked Kelsey. The elf looked up to the sky, then back to the loch, finally settling his gaze upon Tommy. "The waters of the loch are far too deep for a giant to walk them," Kelsey quickly explained, seeing Tommy taking out his makeshift snorkel.

"We'll save days of walking by going across," Mickey reasoned, and he didn't have to add that all of them, that all of their weary feet, could use a break from the difficult hike.

"So spend a day in strapping a raft that will hold the giant," Geno put in, casting a none-too-happy glance Tommy's way. "Or leave him here—we already decided that he will not go all the way to the Giant's Thumb."

Gary grew alarmed at the resigned looks Kelsey and Mickey exchanged, fearing that Geno's blustery suggestion might actually be accepted. "You can't just leave him," Gary protested.

"There's not much wood to be found, lad," Mickey explained grimly. "I'm not for thinking that we'll get together a boat big enough to hold that one's weight."

Gary really couldn't argue against that reasoning, and he, too, had no desire to continue the brutal hike if it could in any way be avoided. But neither did Gary want to leave Tommy behind, alone in this strange and eerie place. "Compromise," Gary said at length. "Build the boat for us and keep it close to the shore. Tommy will keep up and keep in sight. He can get around these hills faster than us."

Mickey nodded, as did Kelsey, in acceptance of the compromise. Tommy had gotten them over obstacles that would have otherwise turned their path to the side many times in the last two days, and no doubt the giant could have crossed on an even straighter path unencumbered by his diminutive companions.

"Are ye up for it?" Mickey asked the giant. "The ground's sure to be hard going."

"Tommy likes mountains," came the giant's even-toned reply

Kelsey nodded; he would not so quickly abandon their valuable companion. Even Geno did not seem too upset that the giant would parallel them on the shore, and the dwarf returned Kelsey's nod with an uncomplaining shrug of his broad shoulders.

With Tommy's powerful assistance, the group soon had two huge logs snapped together and in place on the waters of Devenshere. Gary and Kelsey worked to flatten the top of the raft and lessen its weight while Geno fashioned oarlocks and a rudder of stone. Thinner logs were soon shaped as oars, and the companions even managed to get a sail up, using Kelsey's forest-green cloak.

Tommy gave them a huge push for a start, and off they cruised, Gary working the sail (which didn't prove too effective) and Geno pulling tirelessly and mightily at the oars (which kept the raft rushing along at a great pace). Their path was smooth and straight, unlike Tommy's, but the giant, striding across sharp ravines and stepping over huge boulders, had no trouble keeping pace.

Gary worried when Kelsey flatly denied his request that they anchor for the night, allowing Tommy some rest. "The giant will keep pace with us," the elf declared, and he would hear no more of Gary's arguments. He didn't have to remind Gary of what they had left behind them, of the pursuit that would surely soon come.

They floated on easily through the night, putting many miles behind them. When the sun came back up, a lighter blur through the gray clouds, Gary was quite relieved to see that tireless Tommy had indeed kept pace with them through the hours of darkness. The giant moved easily, incredibly gracefully, across the trails and rocks lining the shore. There loomed no weary shadows on Tommy's face and he was even singing to himself, Gary noted with some amusement.

With his fears for Tommy eased, Gary's thoughts became as calm and smooth as the cold, dark water below them on the serene loch. He munched his morning meal and purposely kept any thoughts of Robert the dragon from his mind. Instead, the young man from that faraway world concentrated on nothing at all, allowed himself to bathe in the melancholy and majesty of the beautiful land about him. Whatever this adventure might be—even insanity—Gary did not want to lose these incredible images, wanted to engrain them indelibly on his mind and carry them with him for all of his life.

A ripple far to the side of the raft caught his attention away from the drifting mountains. Gary blinked many times, his trance dispelled, as a serpentine head appeared above the waters of the loch, rising up five to ten feet, followed in its meandering course by a dark hump and then a second.

Gary's mouth drooped open; his biscuit fell from his hand and rolled into the water.

"Don't ye be feeding her!" Mickey barked at him suddenly. The leprechaun darted to the edge of the raft and scooped the biscuit from the water. "Suren then she'd follow us all the way across!"

"She?" Gary barely managed to stammer. Continuing their course towards the center of the loch, away from the raft, the neck and humps slipped gently under the surface.

Wide-eyed still, Gary looked to Mickey. "Nessie?"

The leprechaun didn't seem to understand. Mickey's cherubic, bearded face crinkled profoundly.

Gary didn't press the point. He turned back to the open loch, its waters calm again save the bristles from the breeze, and watched, fearful yet intrigued. Too many questions came at him; too many possibilities. Out there, vulnerable on the makeshift raft, Gary desired the predictable days of home.

And yet, there remained in the young man that nagging yearn for adventure, that flickering flame of spirit that sent tingles along his spine as he held his gaze steady on the dark waters, searching for a monster on a deep and dark loch in a remote and untamed land.

He saw no more of the mysterious "she," but the tingles along his spine did not diminish for a long, long while.

As they rounded one bend in the loch, near twilight of that second day, the Crahgs seemed to part before them and Gary was treated to his first sight of the distant, dreaded mountain.

It seemed more akin to an obelisk than a mountain, a great cylinder of rock heaved up from the plain by long-past volcanic pressures. From this distance, Gary couldn't begin to guess how high the Giant's Thumb truly was, but that didn't make the spectacle any less imposing. Suddenly Gary found himself wanting to yell out at Kelsey and Mickey for bringing him along, to shake them good and tell them that there was simply no way they could hope to even get up the sides of that gigantic tower of stone. But he said nothing, and the view disappeared as abruptly as it had come when an opaque veil of gray mist floated past in the distant plain.

None of the companions, except for Tommy, was thrilled when they came to the eastern shore of Loch Devenshere. Reluctantly Gary pulled his sneakers back on his sore and swollen feet and tightened the many belts of Donigarten's armor. They camped before sunset, not far from the loch, and set off before sunrise with just a hasty breakfast.

Up and down, along winding trails, over boulder ridges and cold, dancing streams. Only the knowledge that they were nearing the end of the Crahgs enabled Gary to continue placing one foot in front of the other. Seeing his weariness, gentle Tommy offered to carry him, but Gary declined, thinking that the giant, without even the short reprieve of floating comfortably on the loch, had gotten the worst of this trip so far.

Unexpectedly the ground flattened out soon after, running along the lush and level base of a valley—Glen Druitch, Mickey called the place—for nearly a mile before rising up to form one final barrier to the plains beyond.

"The witch is modest this day," Mickey said grimly to Kelsey.

"Ceridwen?" Gary asked, overhearing.

"Not that witch," Mickey explained. The leprechaun pointed ahead to the visible end of the valley, and the end of the Crahgs: twin conical peaks shrouded halfway up to the top by a thick layer of fog. "The Witch's Teats," said the leprechaun. "She's wearing her veil, and that means trouble for wanderers in Glen Druitch, and in all the Crahgs."

"Can't we go around it . . . them?" Gary asked, suddenly not liking the look of that last obstacle.

"Too steep," Geno answered. "And too mean. There is just the one trail out from this point. Right through the cleft of the Teats."

"Or at least tight to their base," Mickey added grimly.

Kelsey suggested they pause and eat their lunch there in Glen Druitch before continuing, though the morning was barely half over. None disagreed, and so more than an hour passed before they at last came to the steep-sided twin mountains, sheets of rising green disappearing into low clouds, dotted by bare chunks of stone poking through the grass, and lined by several rushing and chattering streams. Kelsey spent a long moment staring up the Crahg, his gaze curious and, it seemed to Gary, just a bit fearful. Gary really didn't see anything different about this mound than the hundreds they had left behind, but he could not ignore the sense of dread that had obviously descended over his more knowlegeable companions.

Still, Gary was quite surprised when Kelsey announced that they would skirt the bottom of both Crahgs instead of clambering up through their cleft.

"That course will cost us two hours," Geno grumbled, considering the wide girth of the Witch's Teats.

"Skirt them," Kelsey said again, casting a sidelong, uncomfortable glance to the concealing cloud high up the slope. Mickey and Geno exchanged worried looks and Geno veered a bit to the side, heading for one small waterfall dancing through a tumble of boulders, as the others started off.

Gary spent more time looking behind, to Geno, than ahead, and he inadvertently kicked his foot against a jut of stone and fell headlong to the ground. Kelsey was upon him in an instant, roughly pulling him back to his feet.

"We have no time for blunders," the elf said in hushed tones, more sharply than Gary expected.

"I didn't mean . . ."

"What you meant does not matter," Kelsey argued as loudly as he dared. "Not here. Here, all that matters is what you did."

Gary's confusion only heightened a moment later when Geno grunted loudly. He and Kelsey turned back and saw the dwarf with his ear pressed against the stone behind the waterfall, a grim expression on his face. Finally Geno came out and looked at his companions, shaking his head resignedly and drawing out two hammers.

The moment seemed impossibly silent; not even the wind could disturb the calm.

Their emergence from the cloud veil was prefaced by a series of bone-chilling shrieks that stole the strength from Gary Leger's body.

"Crahg wolves!" he heard Mickey and Kelsey cry in unison, and he never had to ask what the two were talking about. Down the mountainside charged more than a dozen canine creatures. They resembled hyenas, though were much more slender, with dark gray, bristling fur and long and thick snouts. Their howls were part wolf, part human baby, it seemed, and part something else, something unnatural and evil.

They came down the steep slope at full speed, with front legs twice as long as their hind legs, allowing them to run downhill with complete balance. Long before they reached the companions, small groups of the cunning pack fanned out, left and right, flanking and surrounding their prey.

Geno darted out from the boulders around the waterfall and ran to another slab of rock set into the sloping side of the Crahg. One edge of this rock stuck out from the earth, allowing the dwarf to squeeze in behind it.

Watching the dwarf's movements, Gary at first thought that Geno had gone into hiding. But he dismissed that notion quickly, reminding himself that cowardice was not a part of the sturdy dwarf's makeup. Geno would fight any foe fearlessly, no matter the odds. While he took comfort in that knowledge, Gary had to wonder from the concerned looks on the faces of his other two visible companions (Mickey, of course, was nowhere to be found) just how bad these Crahg wolves might be.

Kelsey wasted no time in setting his bow to its deadly work. Arrow after arrow zipped up the hill, the elf concentrating his fire on the wolves that had circled to the right. One took a solid hit in the shoulder and began a yelping tumble; another caught an arrow right in the head and dropped straight down to the ground, skidding to an abrupt stop.

More shrieks echoed from above and another group of wolves came rushing out of the gray mist.

Gary heard a loud crack behind him and turned to see Tommy holding an uprooted tree. The giant shrugged, almost apologetically, and rubbed his foot across the ground where he had torn out the tree, trying to smooth the great divot.

It struck Gary then that part of Tommy's thick black hair was standing up straight, a curious cowlick, and he soon understood where the invisible, and opportunistic, Mickey had made his perch.

Kelsey continued to pepper the flanking wolf pack, each arrow finding a mark. The more immediate danger would come from straight ahead, Gary soon discerned, from the advance of the main pack.

The largest grouping of Crahg wolves came on fiercely, howling and drooling, eager for flesh. They hopped rocks and dropped over short abutments with ease, hardly slowing, hardly turning from the straight line to their intended victims.

The leading wolves came to one large and flat boulder, pressed against the grassy hillside with a sheer seven-foot drop beyond. On the wolves charged, taking no notice of the diminutive form wedged in the narrow opening between the rock slab and the ground behind it.

Geno, his back set firmly against the stone, let the first few wolves get past, then tightened his powerful legs and pushed with all his strength. The slab shifted out from the hillside so quickly that those wolves coming next could not adjust the angle of their charge.

Long forepaws dropped into the newly created ravine as the first wolf crashed in, slamming the bottom of its neck against the edged lip of stone. The creature's momentum carried it onward, bending it right over backwards as it rolled across the stone lip and down the hill beyond. Three trailing wolves were able to turn enough or duck enough to avoid a similar fate, but they slammed against the back side of the rock heavily and fell into the opened gully right beside the furious dwarf.

Gary shook his head in disbelief at the howl and yelps that came from behind that stone. One wolf clambered over the rock, trying to flee, but a stubby, gnarly hand appeared behind it, grabbing it by the tail and pulling it right back into the fray. Mud flew wildly; hammer-tops came up from behind the lip of the stone, then dove back down ferociously; a wolf paw appeared, sticking out one side of the rock, a wolf tail out the other. One wolf went flying up right above the stone, turning a complete somersault and then dropping back down into the dwarf's playroom.

But even with those four Crahg wolves dead or engaged, and with the pack of four to the right decimated by Kelsey's arrows, the fight was far from won. The third group of the first wave, also numbering four, rushed in from the left, and the ten more of the second wave came at the companions from above, prudently veering to avoid Geno's ravine.

Tommy hoisted his uprooted tree and rushed out to meet the closest attackers.

Up above, ten became nine as Kelsey fired one last arrow before dropping his bow and taking up his sword. The elf looked to Gary and nodded grimly. "These are not stupid beasts—they will work together to separate us," Kelsey explained. "And then they will work to get at you from behind. Keep on the move, and turn often as you do."

Kelsey's predictions rang painfully true as the first wolf rushed in, heading straight for Gary, but then veering at the last moment to leap right between the young man and Kelsey. The creature took a severe hit from Kelsey's swift sword for its efforts, but its maneuver did the intended work, pushing the companions farther apart.

Then the wolves swarmed all about them, four to each, circling and nipping, looking for openings.

"*Thou must take the beasts one . . . ,*" the magical spear began to instruct Gary.

"I know how to fight them," Gary heard himself asserting, with a surprising (even to Gary) tone of confidence.

The spear imparted just one more thought before ending the communication altogether. "*Indeed.*"

IN the tight quarters of the tiny ravine, the stiff-legged Crahg wolves found themselves at a serious disadvantage. The dwarf could not wind up very far with his hammers, but Geno didn't need to, popping the wolves with short and powerful chopping strokes. He had one wolf upside down and wedged low in the stone and earth gully, the creature kicking and howling pitifully. Whenever Geno found the opportunity, he smacked a hammer down on its back side, driving it deeper into the wedge.

One wolf managed to twist about and snap its jaws over Geno's forearm, drawing droplets of blood on the dwarf's stone-like skin. Geno clenched his hand as tightly as he could, flexing his smithy-hardened muscles so forcefully that the wolf's bite could not continue its penetration; the creature might as well have tried to tear through solid stone!

Geno whacked and hammered with his free arm to keep the remaining attacker off of him, then, when the opening presented itself, he used the wolves' own tactic, biting the nozzle of the wolf that was clamped onto his arm.

The beast yipped and thrashed, and let go of Geno's arm.

But Geno, growling every second, held firm his bite, even lifted the creature up before him with his teeth and pressed it against the stone wall, leaning against it with his heavy frame to smother its clawing kicks.

Thinking the dangerous dwarf fully engaged, the last wolf came back in.

Geno's hammer was waiting.

———————

TOMMY One-Thumb was not so fortunate. The giant's lumbering swipes with the uprooted tree could not match the speed and quickness of the darting wolves. They nipped at Tommy's heels, rushed between his legs, and kept him spinning and turning so fully that the giant soon found himself thoroughly dizzy.

Tommy leaned one way and then the other. A wolf threw its body against his thigh, trying to topple him; another leaped up high and bit Tommy on the hand.

Tommy knew that he must not fall. The wolves might cause him pain, but could do no serious damage against his massive legs. If he fell, though, more vital areas would surely be exposed.

He felt a pain in his calf, but ignored it, concentrating instead on simply keeping his balance, on stopping the world about him from turning. Gradually he began to reorient himself. The leaper came up again, snapping at Tommy's palm.

Stupid thing.

Tommy clamped his hand shut around the wolf's nozzle. He spun about and heaved with all his might, pitching the wolf head over heels back up the mountainside. It narrowly missed a rock, though that hardly mattered, for it crashed headlong into the slope, contorted weirdly with its tail end coming right up over the back of its head.

Tommy had no time to congratulate himself, though. There came again the pain in his calf, and then another bite, inside his thigh. The giant frantically tried to catch up with his attackers, but this only sent him spinning about again, and sent the whole world spinning around in Tommy's big eyes.

GARY wheeled and threw up his shield just in time to deflect a wolf charge from his back side. The young man could not take the time to calculate any maneuvers. He had to trust fully in his instincts now, and so far they had not let him down. Turning, thrusting, feinting, Gary continued to keep the four wolves at bay, but likewise, he did no real damage to them.

He knew that time would work against him, that he would tire long before his ravenous attackers.

A shriek turned him momentarily to the side, where a wolf lay dead, its head nearly severed. Now Kelsey, too, faced only four, and one of these was not so mobile, having taken a hit on its flank in its initial charge between the elf and Gary.

But Gary pushed away any hopes that Kelsey might soon come to his aid. Even if the elf managed to win out against the difficult odds, Gary doubted that Kelsey could get to him before the Crahg wolves tugged at his lifeless limbs.

Furthermore, Gary Leger was tired of being the extra baggage on this adventure. For his salvation this time, he would look no further than the end of his own spear.

A wolf snapped in low, but Gary dropped to one knee and dipped his shield sidelong to put it in line with the approaching foe. Sensing the creature's sudden reversal, Gary lifted the shield back upright and thrust straight out under its edge with his spear. The startled wolf, its head up, for it intended to leap over the dipped shield, caught the spear right through the base of its neck and down into its chest.

The creature issued a wheezing sound as Gary, realizing that every hit he made left him vulnerable to the other wolves, ripped the weapon out and frantically tried to rise and spin.

His clumsy shield hooked on the ground, slowing him, and only the fine armor saved his life, for a wolf leaped onto his back and bit at his neck.

WOLF jaws rushed in; Geno punched straight out, driving his hammer right down the creature's throat. The dwarf smiled grimly as he heard the canine jawbones crack and break. He let the wolf pull itself back from the hammer, but let the weapon fly to follow the creature's retreat.

It popped off the wolf's head, blinding it in one eye.

Geno slammed his heavy hand against the wolf he still pressed against the stone, pinning it by the throat. He finally pulled his face away, tearing off a chunk of the wolf's nose in his rock-munching teeth.

"Farewell, little doggie," the dwarf laughed, and, after just a moment to inspect his bitten arm, he nodded his satisfaction that the wound was not too serious and pounded home his second hammer, crushing the creature's skull.

Free again, Geno pulled another hammer from his belt and advanced on the half-blinded wolf. Its jaw broken, the creature had no desire to stick around and it had nearly scrambled over the blocking stone wall before Geno clamped his teeth onto its tail and held it in place. The wolf kicked with its short hind legs and tugged mightily, but then the dwarf's hammers went to work, pounding alternately against its exposed flanks. Wolf bones turned to sand under that brutal beating, and very soon the thrashing stopped.

Geno turned on the lone remaining wolf, still helplessly wedged upside down at the base of the stone.

"I would not want to be you right now," the dwarf said evenly, and steady, too, was his determined advance.

GARY threw himself completely over, throwing his armor-enhanced weight right down on his attacker. The creature yelped briefly—for the split second it had any breath in its lungs—and Gary rolled over it, somehow managing to find his footing before the other two wolves overwhelmed him.

The wolf on the ground kicked and wriggled, but couldn't seem to right itself, indicating that Gary's crunching fall had snapped a vital bone or two.

The other wolves rushed at Gary from opposite sides, though. He flung his shield out to stop one, then tried to turn quickly enough to deflect the second. But again, the heavy shield hooked the ground, leaving Gary vulnerable.

He dove forward instead, narrowly dodging the flying creature's snapping maw.

"How did Cedric ever fight with a spear and this damned shield!" Gary screamed mentally.

"*He did not,*" the sentient spear on Gary's belt answered. "*King Cedric fought with spear alone. The shield was for ceremony, and for those times when Cedric chose to wield his sword.*"

Gary blinked and shook his head. He shook his arm, too, glad to be rid of the cumbersome shield. "Thanks for telling me," came his sarcastic thoughts.

"*I am here to serve,*" the spear answered sincerely, taking no offense.

CRAHG wolves were not overly large creatures, nor were their jaws as powerful as those of normal wolves. Crahg wolves relied on numerical advantage, and also on their speed—jerky movements enhanced by the strange proportions of their legs.

In their fight with Kelsey, though, the Crahg wolves held no advantage at all.

Whenever a wolf came in at the elf's heels, it was met by a blinding backhand of Kelsey's fine sword. And unlike Tommy, Kelsey could spin and twirl endlessly, experiencing not the least bit of dizziness. He kept his balance perfectly, shifting his weight from foot to foot, and always with his sword poised to strike—at whatever angle necessary to turn back the closest wolf.

But Kelsey, too, knew that he could not hold a defensive posture for very long. While the elf did not fear that he would quickly tire, he knew that his less skilled and less agile companions would not likely hold out. And if either Geno or Gary was killed, killed, too, would be Kelsey's quest.

A wolf circled to Kelsey's right. Kelsey spun on it and took one step ahead, but backed off immediately as the creature hopped out of range.

A second wolf came in past the first, circling even farther to the elf's right. This time, Kelsey noticed something that the wolf did not.

He spun and charged, and the wolf hopped away. But Kelsey did not halt. Another bold step sent the wolf hopping backwards again, and this time it crashed into its wounded companion, the one Kelsey had first hit when it dove between him and Gary.

The wounded wolf faltered as it tried to get out of its comrade's way, for its sliced hip did not allow it much maneuverability. The healthy wolf scrambled and kicked but could not get away.

Kelsey's sword came thrusting in, once and then again.

Knowing two more creatures to be closing from behind, Kelsey rushed past his fresh kill, chopping down the wounded wolf as he passed. He spun about just beyond the bodies, lifting his sword in line for the closest attacker. The wolf veered, but too late; Kelsey hacked its long foreleg clean in half.

One against one, the remaining wolf had no heart to continue. It barked an impotent protest, turned, and fled. Kelsey started towards the limping, three-legged beast, but changed his mind and went for his dropped longbow instead.

TOMMY stopped spinning, but the world did not. Nor did the pain in the giant's leg relent as the stubborn wolf held on. The giant started to bend low, thinking to grab hold of the wolf and launch it away.

The world spun too fast; the ground leaped up at Tommy.

Then he was lying on his back, looking curiously at the spinning clouds.

A dark form descended over him. Instinctively Tommy punched out with both hands, connecting solidly enough to knock the Crahg wolf aside. But his arms were out helplessly wide when a second dark form hurtled in at his exposed neck.

The wolf's snapping maw would have surely found a murderous hold had not a dwarven-hurled hammer intercepted its flight, spinning the creature right about in midair. The giant let out a muffled cry of surprise as the gray-furred beast flopped onto his face.

Instinctively again, Tommy's hands came back in together, wrapping the beast in a bear-like hug. The wolf bit at the giant's thick limb; Tommy's great arms squeezed in response. In such tight quarters, it was no contest.

Tommy won.

———

WITHOUT the encumbering shield, Gary became a whirlwind of movement, spinning, thrusting, and slapping with the butt end of his dwarven-forged spear so effectively that the remaining two wolves never got close to biting him.

He didn't think of tiring, didn't wonder if these movements were sentient-spear-guided or not. Gary didn't think of anything at all at that critical moment, reacting on pure instinct, letting his heart guide his movements more quickly than his mind ever could.

He almost stumbled but caught himself. The helm hid Gary's wry smile, for he continued to lean, purposely, and did not show his opponents that he had regained his balance, that he had his legs squarely under him. He even kept his spear out wide, appearing defenseless.

Expectedly a Crahg wolf rushed right at him.

Gary waited for the very last moment, then jumped straight up in the air, folding his legs under him. The startled wolf stopped abruptly and Gary crashed back down atop its back. The creature's legs buckled and flew out wide—was that snapping noise its backbone? Gary wondered.

Gary didn't wait to find out. He brought the spear in close and jabbed it straight down, straight through the wolf's back, with all his weight behind it.

The second wolf wasn't far behind the first. Gary ripped his spear free and reversed his grip on it as he fell over, away from the threat. Like Alice the lion in Ceridwen's chamber, the wolf's momentum carried it on, and in its helpless charge, it impaled itself upon Gary's deadly spear.

Gary kept the presence of mind to force the spear over and down to the side as the wolf slipped down its shaft, the doomed creature's jaws snapping frantically. It thrashed for a few moments longer, then lay very still.

Exhausted, his burst of energy spent, Gary dragged himself to his feet. To his right, Kelsey took careful aim and loosed an arrow, dropping the lone fleeing wolf.

Worried for the lying giant, Gary stumbled over to Tommy and Geno. Tommy held one squashed Crahg wolf close to his chest while the dwarf's hammers worked furiously on the wolf that was still stubbornly clamped onto Tommy's calf.

"It's dead," Gary remarked as he passed by the dwarf. Geno paused long enough to confirm the words.

"And stubborn," the dwarf replied, noting that death had down nothing to loosen the beast's tight jaws. Geno shrugged, put one of his hammers back into a loop on his belt, reached into a pouch, and took out a chisel instead.

"Are you all right?" Gary asked Tommy.

The giant nodded.

Geno's hammer smacked home on the chisel.

Tommy screamed and reflexively kicked, sending Geno soaring straight up into the air.

Thoughts of the Doppler effect flashed in Gary's mind as the flying dwarf, too, let out a rapidly diminishing howl. Gary wisely looked up as the dwarf cry again intensified, and he wisely dove to the side, flat to the ground alongside Tommy's head, as Geno the dwarven cannonball crashed in for a three-bounce landing.

Geno hopped right back up to his feet, glancing all about as though he was confused. Gary stayed on the ground, wondering if the dwarf would launch an explosive tirade.

"Hey, giant," Geno said instead, excitedly, after he spit out a clump of grass and dirt. "Remember that trick." He looked up again and scratched his brown hair, marveling at how high he had flown. "We might be using that one in our next fight!"

Tommy's reply echoed Gary's thoughts perfectly. "Duh?"

Gary started to pull himself back up to his feet, but stopped when he realized that something was odd about Tommy's prone posture. The giant's head was not flat to the ground, though the grass under it was certainly flattened and lying to the side.

Gary remembered then that someone was missing.

Mickey faded into view a moment later, looking thoroughly miserable pinned under Tommy's massive skull.

"Ye'd never guess how much a giant's head might weigh," the leprechaun remarked dryly.

Hearing the sprite, Tommy promptly lifted his head and Mickey slithered out.

"Run on!" Kelsey called to them suddenly, and his warning was surrounded by the distant howls of many more Crahg wolves.

Gary didn't know what to make of it all. The wolves had been formidable opponents, but no more so than many other creatures the companions had faced—and defeated. Why, then, did Kelsey and Mickey, and even gruff Geno, once again wear expressions of such profound fear?

"EEE YA YIP YIP YIP!"

The cry split the air like a chorus of a hundred sirens and a hundred cannons all at once. Gary's backbone seemed to melt away under that blast and he nearly fell to the ground.

"What the heck was that?" he gasped, after he had somewhat recovered.

"Run on, lad," Mickey said to him. "It's better that ye do not know."

TWENTY

Citadel of the Rock

"EEE YA YIP YIP YIP!"

It resounded off of every stone, coming at the companions from every direction.

"What is it?" Gary cried again, more frantically. He pulled and tugged at his spear, but it wouldn't come free from the impaled wolf.

Geno rushed over and pounded on the spear's butt end, pushing it nearly all the way through the gory mass. The dwarf ripped it out of the creature's body the rest of the way and tossed it, covered in blood, to Gary. Gary caught it tentatively and started to bend, to wipe the bloodied shaft on the wet grass, but then Tommy scooped him up and flew off in pursuit of Kelsey.

"EEE YA YIP YIP YIP!"

"What is it?" Gary demanded of Mickey, sitting atop Tommy's massive shoulder just above him.

The leprechaun, his face ashen and his expression more grave than Gary had ever seen it, ignored him and whispered something into Tommy's ear. Without slowing, the giant reached down as he passed Geno and scooped the dwarf into his other arm. Even carrying all three, the giant had no trouble in keeping pace with Kelsey, who was sprinting at a dead run.

Having no time for their original route around the base of both Crahgs, Kelsey scrambled for the pass between the Witch's Teats. The going was rough and the ground broken, but every time Kelsey got to a shelf or sharp ravine that would have slowed him, Tommy came up behind and hoisted him, or even tossed him, across.

"Crahg wolves!" Geno called, peering around the giant's wide girth to look behind.

"Run on!" Kelsey replied. "They cannot climb very well!"

Gary looked back and saw the truth of the elf's claims. The wolves were indeed in pursuit, but were lower down on the mountainside than the companions. With their long front legs, their progress was severely limited; some of them had even taken to trotting backwards up the slope, possibly the most curious thing Gary Leger had ever seen.

Despite their gains ahead of the wolf pack, none of Gary's companions breathed easier. They were not fleeing from mere Crahg wolves, the young man realized, but from something much more powerful.

Something much more terrible.

Up and down, around boulders and across sharp cracks in the weathered stone, they ran and they jumped. They came to the lip of a drop, perhaps fifty feet, above a brown pool of muddy water—or was it just mud? Gary couldn't be sure.

The path wound down to the side, steep and treacherous, and terribly narrow, promising slow going indeed.

"EEE YA YIP YIP YIP!" It came from every rock; the creature sounding that terrible call was behind them, beside them, in front of them—they just did not know!

Kelsey cried out and jumped. Still holding tight to Gary and Geno, and with Mickey holding tight to him, Tommy blindly followed.

They hit in a rush of mud and muck. Filthy water burst right under the lip of Gary's too-big helmet, splattering his face and flushing up his nose. He fumbled out of the helmet and saw Mickey gently descending below an umbrella, tilting the unorthodox parachute to catch the crosswinds and float him clear of the murky pool.

Gary shook his head at the leprechaun, always amazed. But not complaining, for he, too, wasn't really very wet. Nor was Geno, for Tommy continued to hold them up high, out of the muddy pool. Tommy had sunk in deeply, though, with just his head and shoulders up above the water level, and Kelsey, though he had managed to quickly scramble out of the water, was brown from head to foot.

"Keep moving," the elf instructed them. "We are still near to the Crahgs and can afford no delays."

Geno and Gary waited for a moment, then the dwarf looked curiously at Tommy. "Are you going to follow or not?"

Their gigantic friend seemed truly perplexed. "Tommy cannot move," the giant admitted after a brief struggle with the gripping mud.

Without a moment's thought, Gary slipped down from Tommy's arm into the pool. The water was only shoulder-deep to him, which should have put it somewhere around Tommy's knees. Yet, here Gary was, staring the giant directly in the eye.

"Oh, begorra," Mickey moaned, coming to the pool's edge and immediately comprehending their newest dilemma.

"He's ten feet into the mud," Gary reasoned gloomily. "At least."

"Oh, begorra," Mickey moaned again.

Kelsey looked fearfully back up towards the pass, then turned and considered the brown plains looming in the east.

"Not to worry," Geno asserted as Tommy carefully lifted him over to the edge of the water. The dwarf hopped around to the back side of the pool, inspecting the rock wall that formed its western border. "I can get him out," Geno claimed, nodding confidently at Tommy.

With that assurance, Tommy smiled widely as he hoisted Gary to the water's edge.

"Ye'll not pull him from that mire," Mickey replied to the dwarf. "Not if ye had a dozen ropes and a hundred dwarfs."

Geno agreed with the leprechaun's assessment wholeheartedly, but he had no intention of trying to pull Tommy out—not yet. The dwarf grabbed his largest hammer and began pounding furiously on the rock wall behind the pool. Kelsey grimaced at each resounding smack, glancing nervously up to the higher passes.

"The beast'll not come out o' the Crahgs," Mickey said to calm the elf. "The Witch's Teats marks the end of its domain."

"What beast?" Gary demanded.

"Ye heard it," Mickey replied casually.

"Heard what?" Gary shot back, frustration evident in his near-frantic tone.

"The haggis," Kelsey whispered softly.

"Wild hairy haggis," Mickey added grimly.

"Haggis?" Gary echoed incredulously. "Haggis?" The name was not new to Gary. In his bureau back home, he even had a sweatshirt depicting three small caricatures of Scotsmen and proclaiming them to be "Haggis Hunters Unlimited."

"You mean the little hairy creatures that run around the Scottish Highlands?" Gary asked.

"Not so little," Kelsey remarked.

"But more than a little hairy," added Mickey. "And mean, lad. Ye've never seen anything so mean as a wild hairy haggis."

Gary's incredulous stare did not diminish. Several times, he pinched himself on the arm and muttered, "Wake up.

Geno's victorious grunt turned them about. The dwarf had cracked a hole in the rock wall, and the water of the muddy pool was fast draining, leaving behind a quagmire, with the giant buried to the hips.

Kelsey produced some fine cord, while Geno began laying stones around the giant, giving Tommy something solid to use for leverage and giving the industrious dwarf a firm base from which he could begin to dig out the mud trapping his giant companion.

Gary could hardly believe the sight: the taciturn dwarf working frantically and determinedly to free a giant—a giant that Geno not so long ago had considered an enemy. And more than simple pragmatism was guiding Geno's actions, Gary knew, though none in the group would deny that Tommy was a valuable companion. Geno's determination now went beyond what the dwarf would do for a pack mule. Something wonderful had just happened back in dangerous Crahgs and here, now, in the muddy pool.

An undeniable bond of friendship.

Even with the teamwork, it took them more than an hour to get Tommy out of the mud. No more chilling cries came from the Crahgs, though, and no visible pursuit, of Crahg wolf or haggis.

Glad to leave the Crahgs behind, the companions cleaned themselves and their supplies as best they could and set out across the brown and blasted plain, with the Giant's Thumb, the lair of Robert, clearly in sight every step of the way.

In all his life, Gary had never seen such total desolation. The land was scarred, brutally and completely. They passed one long and wide patch of charred tree skeletons, once a teeming forest, and they came down into a flat region, a clay bed dotted with long puddles and small clumps of scraggly grass and weeds poking through at uneven intervals.

Many bleached bones lined the clay bed, fish bones, and before long, Gary realized that this area had once been a huge lake, as wide as Loch Devenshere, perhaps, though not as long.

"Aye, and so it was," Mickey confirmed when Gary asked him about it. "Loch Tullamore, she was called. Full of fish and full of beauty."

"But Robert, he did not like it," Mickey went on, his tone a combination of anger and sadness. The leprechaun paused and again came that faraway longing look in his gray eyes.

"What did he do?" Gary prompted after a while, honestly intrigued. After all, what could any beast, dragon or not, possibly do to a lake?

"He hissed it, lad," Mickey explained. "Breathed his fiery breath upon the waters until they were no more. Day after day, Robert the Wretched came here, steaming the waters of Tullamore away."

Gary had no comment to offer in response. The sheer scope of what Mickey claimed the dragon had done overwhelmed him, and his sense of dread only heightened when he looked up again at the distant obelisk-shaped mountain. Every step came harder to him then, every step towards the lair of Robert the Wretched. Fortunately for Gary's rattled emotions, the sight of the mountain was soon lost, for Kelsey led the troupe into a long and narrow crevice, a great crack in the clay-like ground. The walls, tight about Tommy's shoulders, rose up twenty feet on either side of his companions, and the trail wound on for many miles.

They camped that night on the plains above the crevice, the sheer stillness of the region serving as a testament to the dragon's ultimate desolation. Not a cricket chirped, and the fog came in early and thick, defeating any starlight offered by the evening sky. The next day, like the first, came hot and dreary, and unnervingly quiet. The mountain loomed much larger when the group gazed upon it before descending again into the crevice walkway, but Gary paid it as little heed as he could, preferring to keep his thoughts far away from the dragon and the dangers that lay ahead.

He could not ignore the sight late that afternoon, though, when the group emerged from the crevice, turning a final bend that again put them in direct line with the Giant's Thumb. Directly before them lay a small vale, cluttered by the charred remains of long-dead trees and a few patches of weeds and grass. And beyond the vale loomed the mountain.

Gary had to remind himself to breathe as he scanned up, up, up the side of that obelisk. And if the almost sheer cliffs of jutting and angular stones were not imposing enough, atop the mountain loomed a castle, its stonework walls and towers seeming as if they had grown right out of the natural stones as extensions of the mountainsides.

"We're going up that?" the stunned young man asked to anybody who could give him a rational answer.

"There is a more gradual road around the mountain's other side," Kelsey answered. "But we would find it crossing between the barracks of Robert's slave soldiers. This is our path."

"It must be five hundred feet," Gary protested.

Mickey lifted his tiny foot before him, comparing it to the scale of the enormous cliff. "Oh, five hundred feet at least," the leprechaun remarked. "Twice that'd be me own guess.

"Or just a hundred of his," Mickey added with a wink, casting a glance Tommy's way.

"We can't climb that," Gary asserted, his mood not improved at all by Mickey's attempted humor. "And what if there are guards on those castle walls?" Gary imagined buckets of hot oil rolling down at him, or a storm of arrows plucking him from a cliff that he had no desire to climb even if Kelsey could assure him that no monsters waited atop it. "And what kind of a dragon needs a castle anyway?" Gary protested.

"Our path is up," Kelsey announced, having no time for Gary's obviously terror-inspired rambling. "And the daylight is fast waning." The elf led them on, asking Geno to see what the stones would tell him concerning the swiftest and easiest path.

Tommy stood perplexed at the edge of the small vale. As soon as Gary looked at the pitiful giant, he understood, for Tommy had no chance of scaling the cliff all the way up to the dragon's castle. Even if he did manage to find giant-sized handholds, a climbing Tommy would certainly present an easy and obvious target for any castle guards. With the huge giant hanging out so many feet from the stone, guards up above could hardly miss him, even under the cover of night.

"Come along!" Kelsey instructed Gary sharply.

"Tommy cannot follow," Gary argued.

"Tommy was never meant to follow," Kelsey retorted. "We allowed him to come to the base of the mountain—that is all."

"Kelsey's right, lad," Mickey put in. "We've telled ye already why the giant should not be going near to Robert's lair. It'd make the dragon uneasy and dangerous."

"We can't just leave him out here," said Gary.

"He'll be safer than the rest of us," Mickey reasoned.

Looking up at the imposing cliff and knowing what waited atop it, Gary couldn't honestly argue against the logic. He stared at his huge friend for a long moment.

"Tommy will wait," the giant assured him. He scratched his huge head, then pointed back to the crevice. "In there."

Gary nodded, managed a weak smile, and rushed to catch up to the others.

Kelsey led them through all the cover he could find in the vale. There wasn't much, actually, but the elf was not too worried, for if there were any guards along this side of the castle, the elf's sharp eyes couldn't spot them.

Without incident, the companions, now four again, made the base of the rock wall and started up. They discovered that the wall, which had looked so sheer from across the vale, was lined by many small ledges and walkways, but all of these seemed to lead nowhere and after a half hour of stretching up to reach the next handhold and inching their way along impossibly narrow ledges, they found that they had really made very little progress.

"Do the rocks tell you anything?" Kelsey whispered to the dwarf in frustration. "Is there no way up?"

Geno grunted and put his ear to the stone. He took out a small hammer and gave a series of light taps, which sounded to Gary like some strange code. The dwarf listened for a moment, then tapped again, then listened some more.

"Hmmm," the dwarf grunted, looking up at the distant castle walls and then back to his friends.

"The rock is not solid," he said evenly, though too loudly for Gary's or Mickey's liking. Both glanced nervously upwards to the castle, expecting a shower of arrows to come whizzing down at them.

"It seems sturdy enough to me," Kelsey replied quietly.

"Of course it is," Geno huffed, and he banged his forehead against the stone to accentuate that obvious point. "What I mean is that the mountain is not a solid block. It is honeycombed by caverns and tunnels."

"That would make sense," Gary concurred, his unexpected reasoning turning both Mickey and Kelsey to him.

"From the same volcanic pressures that formed the mountain," Gary explained. "From the steam and the pressure of the hot lava." Mickey and Kelsey looked to each other and shrugged incredulously, then turned back to Geno for an explanation.

"He speaks the truth," the dwarf said, giving Gary a sidelong glance. "I knew that there were caves before we ever started up, but I did not believe that they would aid us much. Now, though, I believe that some of them probably climb fairly high within the mountain. That might be a better path than out here—in the open."

Those words again inevitably turned their attention to the castle. A lamp was burning in one of the towers up above, and even Kelsey had to honestly admit that he felt vulnerable out on the ledge. While the elf was not fond of caverns, he had to admit as well that the climb would be long and handholds would not be easily found in the coming darkness.

"Ye're leading, elf," Mickey said. "But I'm thinking that the dawn will find us hanging halfway up the mountainside."

"Where will we find an entrance?" Kelsey asked Geno.

Geno put his ear to the wall and tap-tapped again, ever so lightly. "Down and around to the south," he announced a moment later.

They had spent the next few minutes clambering back to the ground and working their way along the mountain's base. After crossing one rocky outcropping of tree-like pillars of broken stones, they found themselves on the edge of yet another pool, this one wide and steamy and crimson red, even in the fast-fading light.

Geno and Kelsey, at the lead, did not dare to touch the water.

"Red from the blood of Robert's victims, no doubt," Mickey reasoned, and Gary suspected that a legend had just been born. He knew, too, that there was probably a quite natural explanation for the coloring of the water, an excess of iron oxide, or something like that, but after the looks he had received during his "volcanic pressures" lecture, he decided to keep the thoughts private. Besides, Gary thought, Mickey's explanation seemed more romantic and more fitting for the land of Faerie.

"We have a bit of a problem, elf," Geno said, pointing diagonally across the pool to the mountain wall behind it. "There is your cave entrance."

Kelsey determinedly knelt down and dipped a hand in the ominous water. "It is warm, but not too hot," he said, as though he meant to hop right in and cross over.

"But how deep?" Mickey was quick to ask.

Gingerly Kelsey turned about and lowered one leg into the pool. Up to the hip, he had still not touched bottom.

"We're to have a rough time getting through that," the diminutive leprechaun remarked, aiming his voice mostly Geno's way.

"Tommy could cross it!" Gary piped in, somewhat loudly.

"Hush!" Kelsey scolded him, but the elf's ire faded away as Gary's idea rang true to him. "Go get your giant friend," he bade Gary, and the smiling man didn't have to be asked twice.

Tommy had little trouble carrying the four across the warm-watered pool. He kept his snorkel handy on his wide belt, but he found no need for it, for the water never got deeper than the middle of his chest. Still, the other companions were genuinely appreciative of the giant at that time—Geno even patted Tommy on the head once (when the dwarf thought that no one was looking).

They were at the tunnel entrance in just a few short minutes, and there, a few feet above the level of the pool, they had to say goodbye to the giant once more. Again, Tommy promised to wait back in the crevice. He turned about in the crimson water and strolled away, leaving great ripples in his wake.

The companions watched him for just a moment before he was lost in the gathering gloom, then they turned to their own path, the winding cave.

Already Kelsey, more accustomed to dancing under an open sky, seemed unnerved. He produced a tinderbox from his pack and a torch and quickly lit it, despite Geno's warnings that the light would "bring in every critter in the whole damn mountain!"

Kelsey ignored him and pressed in. The cave was a curious formation, its arcing walls scalloped and winding.

"Like the inside of a worm," Gary muttered under his breath, not wanting the others to hear that rather uncomfortable, though accurate, description.

The light bounced back at them from a dozen angles, flickering ominously, and Gary held his breath around every corner, imagining that a great dragon's treasure hoard, complete with a great dragon, awaited. When he took the time to remind himself that they were still in the outer and lower chambers, not far at all from the cave entrance, Gary thought himself incredibly foolish.

Until he realized that his companions were holding their breath, too.

Still not so far in, the group came upon some bones lying scattered in the corridor.

"Just fish bones," Kelsey assured them on closer inspection.

"But what brought them here?" Gary had to ask, and his answer came not from any of his companions, but from the gigantic crab that rushed at them suddenly from around the next bend.

TOMMY plodded slowly back across the crimson pond, paying little heed to his surroundings and thinking of nothing at all (Tommy was good at that).

Even if he had been alert, though, the giant would have had a difficult time in distinguishing the red-shelled crab moving effortlessly under the red-colored water.

A great vice-like pincer locked around Tommy's waist; another found a stubborn hold on his shoulder. The giant tried to scream out in the hope that his companions were not so far into the tunnel, but before Tommy hardly knew what had happened, he was pulled under the suddenly not-so-tranquil crimson waters.

TWENTY-ONE

Flies on the Wall

IT was surely the stuff of 1950s sci-fi B movies, its clacking hard-shelled legs scampering to keep it balanced in the scalloped, curving walls of the tunnel—a tunnel that the giant crab easily filled. Great jagged-edged pincers swayed and snapped ominously.

Kelsey reacted first, slicing his sword in at the closest menacing claw. The weapon, fine though it was, bounced harmlessly aside and the monster claw came around more quickly than Kelsey had anticipated, opening wide enough to envelop the elf.

Geno saved him. The dwarf slammed into Kelsey, knocking the elf safely aside, then, unexpectedly, rushed straight ahead, into the grip of the snapping claw. The dwarf lifted his arms up high as he wedged in tightly, keeping his hammer-holding hands free to punish the crab even as it tried to crush him.

Gary and Mickey gasped in unison, but the tough dwarf understood his rock-hard makeup better than they. The gigantic crab claw squeezed relentlessly, but it hardly seemed to bother Geno, singing a song now and drumming his hammers against the monster's stubborn shell.

Kelsey, seeing that the dwarf was in no immediate peril, scrambled over the clawing arm to get in close to the crab's face. His fine sword swiped across at a stalk, and a crab eyeball dropped to the tunnel floor.

Any thoughts of quick and easy victory blew away, though, as the wounded monster went into a frenzy, whipping its engaged claw up behind the elf and knocking Kelsey across the way, into the reach of the other deadly appendage. Kelsey skittered down to the floor, rolled to his back, and slashed wildly with his sword, struggling to keep the second claw up above him. He tried to scramble out, but the press of the monstrous limb was too great, and the crab too quick.

"*Now is the time for courage, young sprout,*" came a call in Gary's head. Gary hardly needed the encouragement, and about the only thing in the communication that he took note of was the sentient spear's continuing reference to him as a "young sprout."

He took up his dwarven spear in both hands, leveling its iron tip before him, and as soon as he found the opening, let out a roar and charged straight ahead, between the deadly claws.

MANY minutes passed with the giant crab holding tight to Tommy. Tommy fought against his building panic, forced himself to remain patient. He had popped the snorkel into his mouth soon after the crab had pulled him under, and though the instrument's seal wasn't tight without the extra goo around it, the giant found that he could breathe readily enough.

Tommy wasn't the most powerful of thinkers, but he was cunning enough in battle, having taken care of himself in the wild mountains since his childhood days. He knew now that he could not break the crab's hold, not with one of his arms so tightly pinned, but guessed that the creature would likely loosen its grip when it believed Tommy to be drowned.

Another crab, a much smaller one, pinched hard on Tommy's toe right through his heavy boot. The giant grimaced and sublimated the pain, knowing that to move now would only convince his captor that much more time was needed to finish the drowning. And Tommy was running short on patience. In the trapped and terrified giant's thoughts, the water was beginning to hug him nearly as tightly as the crab.

When the claw finally loosened around Tommy's arm, the giant exploded into action. He pulled his limb free, punched and kicked, and scrambled for the shore. He got free for just a second, but then the relentless crab's claw caught him again, by the ankle. Tommy grimaced and tugged. He lost his snorkel and had to fight, not only to get to the shore but to keep his head above the water.

He nearly turned the wrong way in the sudden confusion, thought for certain that the crab's wicked pincer would tear his foot right off, but somehow, he got within arm's reach of the outcropping of tree-like pillars along the shoreline. When the powerful giant clasped his hands around a tangible support, the crab had no chance of holding him back. The monster came right with Tommy out of the pool, snapping at the fleeing giant's legs every step of the way.

Tommy roared and turned about, grabbing one of the huge claws. Spinning around and around, he soon had the crab up in the air, and then he sent it soaring far out over the small pond. It hit the mountain wall with a resounding crack and splashed heavily into the crimson waters.

Far up above, Tommy heard shouts from the castle guards. He turned to run but found that his wounded ankle would not support his weight. So the terrified giant hopped and crawled, pulled himself any way he could back to the safety of the distant crevice.

THE spear tip, still a bit bent over from Gary's fight with the mountain troll, ricocheted off crab shell, but then hit a fleshy spot near the creature's mouth. Determinedly Gary drove on, throwing all his weight behind the weapon. He smiled grimly as the head of the spear disappeared into the monster's flesh.

Crab claws flew about wildly—one holding Geno and slamming the dwarf off the ceiling, wall, and floor. The creature bucked and thrashed, kicking all of its legs, spinning a complete circle in the corridor, even trying to roll back over itself. The claw waving over Kelsey retreated, focusing on Gary, the more immediate danger. He felt its pinch about his waist, but told himself to hold onto the spear and trust in his armor and in his companions. Gary knew that he had committed himself to the charge; there could be no retreat.

Flecks of shell flew about the corridor as the relentless dwarf continued to batter the claw that was squeezing him. Chunks of flesh followed and soon the claw's iron grip relaxed.

Kelsey came up in an instant, knowing that Gary had helped him, literally, out of a tight pinch, and knowing, too, that now Gary was the one needing the help. The elf thought nothing of his prized quest as he leaped in to fight right beside the human, thought only of aiding a companion, of aiding this man who, unbelievably, had somehow become Kelsey's friend.

His first target was the crab's remaining eye, and in the flash of an elf's magical sword, it, too, bounced to the floor.

The remaining claw let go of Gary's waist immediately, but the crab's thrashing only intensified. Gary's helmet rolled about on his shoulders, blinding him as completely as the eyeless crab; his elbow slammed hard into a wall, sending waves of pain through him, followed by a tingling numbness.

He held on. For all his life, Gary Leger held on.

He was on the floor, a great weight atop him. Something battered the side of his head, but his spear slipped deeper into the monster, and still he held on.

Then it was over, suddenly. Gary couldn't see, didn't know how badly he was injured, but he heard Kelsey and Geno congratulating each other and felt the weight lessening as his friends worked to pull the giant crab off of him.

After what seemed like many minutes, Geno hoisted Gary to his feet and Kelsey straightened his helmet. Gary blinked in disbelief at the toppled monster, and managed a weak smile when he heard Geno smacking his lips and describing a hundred different ways to cook the thing.

"Suren the three of ye have come to fight well together," Mickey said from back down the corridor.

Gary's smile disappeared.

He spun towards the leprechaun, his green eyes narrowed. "And where were you?" he demanded. "That's twice now, two fights in which Mickey McMickey played no part and didn't even try to play a part!"

For the first time since he had met the leprechaun, Gary believed that his anger truly wounded Mickey.

"Tommy almost died against the Crahg wolves," Gary fumed on, holding to his ire. "And you would have let him die—as long as you could keep your hiding spot behind his head!"

"Crahg wolves pay no heed to illusions," the leprechaun explained meekly.

"Be easy, friend," Kelsey said to Gary, putting a calming hand on the young man's shoulder. The elf's words and the gesture struck Gary profoundly, an action he would never have expected from grim and aloof Kelsey.

"And what can I do against the likes of a crab?" Mickey asked, gaining strength from Kelsey's intervention. "Just an animal, and a stupid one at that! I've no weapons . . ."

"Enough!" Kelsey commanded, ending the pointless debate. "We are alive, and we have come far, but our greatest trial yet awaits us."

"Do you think we could stop and have a bit of supper before running off to face that trial?" Geno asked hopefully, smacking his lips again and staring at an exposed area of juicy crab meat.

Kelsey smiled—another action that struck Gary as curious, given their situation and their impending meeting with Robert—and started making his way over the fallen crab to the tunnel beyond. After he had passed the tangle of legs, he motioned for Geno and the others to follow.

"The meat will stay good for a few hours," the dwarf mumbled as he passed beside Gary. "So let us get to Robert and get our business finished quickly."

Mickey strolled by as Gary worked to free his spear. The leprechaun did not even look Gary's way, and Gary, though he now realized his previous ranting about Mickey's contributions to be ridiculous, couldn't find the words for an apology.

The scalloped tunnel wound in and up the mountain, climbing gradually mostly, but so steeply at some points that even Kelsey had a difficult time in climbing. The passage forked only once, and Kelsey led them to the left, deeper into the mountain. Fortunately for the companions, they met no more monsters and no guards, and a short while later they came to a small and square opening, covered by an iron grate.

Kelsey looked out to a flat gravel bed, lined by sheer walls fifteen feet high.

"Dry moat," the elf whispered.

"I can get the grate out," Geno remarked, but Kelsey stopped him as he reached for his hammer.

"Guards outside, no doubt," the elf remarked softly. They waited in the quiet and soon heard the scrape of many marching soldiers on the wall above them.

Geno shrugged and put his tool away.

"We will go back the other way," Kelsey instructed in a whisper, and he swung the group around and headed back for the fork.

When they came to the end of the other passage, they were not so certain that they were any better off. This exit had no iron grate covering, but it came out on the exposed side of the treacherous cliff, still more than twenty feet below the base of the castle wall and several hundred feet from the ground. Kelsey sighed as he looked down, way down, to the tops of tall trees.

"Back to the grate?" Geno asked him when he came back in, the dwarf's gravelly voice diminished by the wind's howl as it entered the tunnel.

Kelsey leaned out again, looking for some path up to the castle walls.

"This way is the better," the elf decided. He unbelted his sword and handed it to Gary, then removed his pack.

Gary leaned out to regard the cliff. Agile Kelsey might make it, he decided, but he wasn't so certain about himself, wasn't so certain that he would even willingly follow. He had never been afraid of heights, but this was insane, with sheer walls and a strong wind and the tops of trees waiting like feathered spikes down below.

Kelsey never hesitated. Sometimes holding on by no more than two fingers, the strong and agile elf picked his careful way up the mountain cliff. The difficulty only increased when Kelsey made the base of the wall, for the castle stones were tightly fitted and wind-beaten smooth. Still, the wall was not that high—no more than fifteen or twenty feet—and Kelsey only needed two well-spaced handholds to get his fingers on top of the parapet.

He heard a commotion, the rasping voices of several guards, not too far to the side just as he was about to pull himself up over the wall. He waited a moment to ensure that he was not the cause of that commotion, then gingerly peeked over the wall.

A group of three guards, scaly humanoids as much lizard as human (Kelsey knew them to be lava newts), huddled together along the wall a short distance from Kelsey. They apparently had no idea that there was an elf nearby, for they continued to peer down to the region of the crimson-colored pond.

Kelsey held his place and held his breath.

The lava newts' excitement soon ebbed, and two of them wandered away, back to their distant posts, while the third began a slow, meandering course back towards where Kelsey was hiding.

Kelsey had nowhere to run, nowhere to hide. He produced a slender dagger from his boot and put it between his teeth, then hung low, just his fingers on the wall.

The barely alert creature passed right by the hanging elf, taking no notice whatsoever. In the blink of an eye Kelsey came up behind it, slapping one hand around its snout and driving his dagger into its throat. The creature, much stronger than Kelsey, struggled back powerfully, bending forward to lift the elf's feet right from the ground and nearly breaking free of Kelsey's stubborn grasp.

Kelsey's dagger ripped in again and again, and finally the creature slumped heavily in Kelsey's arms. The elf glanced around nervously, praying that no other guards had seen.

The night was dark, though, and all the castle remained quiet.

Kelsey carefully rolled the heavy creature onto and then over the wall, letting it drop, to be swallowed up by the darkness and the mournful wind. The elf quickly secured a rope on the parapet above the cave exit, dropping one end down to his waiting companions, then took up a defensive position, hiding tight against the wall, but with his stained dagger drawn and ready.

———————

GARY looked doubtfully at the dangling rope, and even more doubtfully at the deep drop below. This should be easy, he argued against all his instincts. He had seen dozens of adventure movies where the hero simply leaped out onto a rope and scaled hand over hand up impossible distances.

This wasn't easy.

In fact, Gary decided, as he leaned out and gingerly took the rope in his hands, this was damned impossible. He fell back into the tunnel, shaking his head helplessly.

"Ye have to go, lad," Mickey said to him. "Kelsey cannot wait for long."

Again, Gary shook his head.

"Get out of my way!" Geno fumed, roughly shoving Gary aside. The dwarf scrambled out to the edge of the tunnel, and, without the slightest hesitation or any look below, hopped out to the rope and began pumping arm over arm, powerfully and methodically, just like one of those adventure-movie heros.

"Ye see?" Mickey coaxed. "It is not so hard a thing."

"I can't do it," Gary replied. "Especially not in this armor!"

Mickey saw the excuse for what it was. "Ye've gotten used to the fit," the leprechaun reasoned. "And it's not so heavy now, is it?

"Ah, go on, lad," Mickey continued. "Ye cannot fall with me below ye. Ye remember the rocks in Dvergamal? I catched them good, and held them up in the air. Ye think I'd let ye fall?" Mickey held a pointed finger up before him and motioned for Gary to go on.

Gary considered the words for a long moment, then moved again to the tunnel exit, taking the rocking rope in his hands. He couldn't see the top of the castle wall from this distance, but suddenly the rope stopped bobbing and Gary knew that Geno had already made it up.

"I've got to start eating rocks," Gary muttered dryly, and he checked once to make sure that both his spears were secure on his belt, then hoisted himself out onto the rope.

His arms ached every foot of the way; only the knowledge that Mickey was below him, ready to levitate him should he fall, gave Gary Leger the courage to continue.

He heard a sharp hiss from above, followed by a crunch that he knew instinctively to be the result of a dwarf-wielded hammer. Sure enough, just a moment later, another lizard-skinned humanoid form came tumbling over the wall.

"Quickly!" came Kelsey's hushed call from above. Gary tried to respond, but his already weary arms simply did not answer his mental call to pick up the pace. Finally, after what seemed like many minutes, Gary put his first hand onto the parapet. Geno grabbed it up in an instant and hauled the tired man over.

"I wish Mickey could have given me more of a magical push," Gary rasped. "With the leprechaun's magic, I don't even know why we needed that stupid rope anyway."

"The leprechaun's telekinetic powers are limited with regard to living beings," Kelsey replied. "Mickey can lift a rock easily enough, but would have a difficult time in levitating even a frog."

"What's that now?" Mickey asked, umbrella in hand as he floated easily over the wall.

Gary considered the deep drop one more time, then shot the leprechaun a dangerous glare.

Mickey shrugged innocently. "Call it a lie, lad," he said. "But it worked, now didn't it?"

They had crossed the castle's outer wall, but that signaled only the first obstacle in the two-tiered structure. Just a few feet down from the companions lay an open courtyard, encircling a higher cluster of stone buildings. The castle had been built around the natural formations of the mountain, and in many places, bricked walls blended harmoniously with natural jutting stone.

Fortunately the courtyard was not overly busy. The main bustle seemed to be to the companions' right, down a road that went beyond a portcullis out of the castle proper, and through many buildings tightly packed together.

"The side gate," Kelsey explained in a whisper, "Leading to the barracks. And up there"—he gazed at the walls of the structures looming above them— "is where we will find Robert."

Gary didn't like the prospects—even forgetting that a dragon waited at the end of their road. There were but two ways up from this level as far as they could see: a steep stair around the left-hand side of the massive structure directly before them, and a sloping cobblestone path circling up around the same building's right side that forked from the main road, which led out of the castle's side gate.

"The stairs?" Mickey asked softly.

Kelsey nodded. "The gates up the road will likely be closed—and guarded in any event." Kelsey motioned for them to wait, then took his sword from Gary and slipped across the courtyard to the base of the stairway. He didn't go up immediately; rather, he moved along the wall running down the left-hand side of the stair, around the base of the structure and out of sight of his companions.

The elf reappeared almost immediately, waving frantically for the others to run and join him, and Gary knew that trouble was brewing.

Sure enough, several sword-wielding lava newt soldiers intercepted them before they reached the stairs.

At the sight of Geno, leading Gary and Mickey, the monsters howled wildly (like so many of the races of Faerie, good and bad, lava newts hated dwarfs), and charged ahead, taking no note of Kelsey, lying in wait behind the solid handrail a few steps up the stairs behind them.

Three flying hammers preceded the dwarf's answering charge, dropping two of the seven newts. A third tumbled heavily at the end of Gary's hurled spear.

"*Didst thou throw it?*" the sentient weapon on Gary's belt screamed incredulously in Gary's head.

Confident of his actions, Gary didn't bother to answer. He was certain that Kelsey and Geno would make short work of the remaining four, and knew that even if he still held his weapon, he probably would never get close enough to an enemy to use it.

As he figured, Kelsey leaped down into the midst of the remaining group of monsters, his brilliant sword glowing fiercely as it flashed every which way. Geno barreled into the throng a moment later from in front of the group, and in mere seconds of whipping hammers and a slashing sword, all the guard lay dead.

Gary went for his spear but never got there. Around the side of the stair came a host of soldiers, and the blare of horns went up all around the trapped companions.

Gary felt a strong hand—he knew it to be Geno's—grab him by the arm and tug him along. "My spear . . ." he started to protest, but stopped almost immediately when he heard Kelsey, up ahead on the slightly curving stair, engaged in battle once again. Geno released Gary and charged up to join the elf, and Gary reluctantly reached for his belt and took out the tipped half of Cedric's magical weapon. Unbalanced and unwieldy, Gary could only hope that he could find some way to utilize it in battle.

"*Fear not, young sprout,*" came a comforting thought. "*Thou is not alone.*"

KELSEY slashed and fought savagely to gain each subsequent step, but a line of lava newts packed above him, blocking his progress every step of the way. At the back of the party, Geno faced similar unfavorable odds.

Gary trusted in his two warrior companions, and facing the newts one or two at a time on the narrow stair certainly made the situation less catastrophic. But the lines of newt soldiers were long indeed, and were only going to get longer, Gary knew.

Another lizard-like form went over the outside wall of the stair, at the end of Kelsey's sword.

Gary blinked once, even moved to rub his eyes, when he looked back to Kelsey, for he saw not an elf, but a great mountain troll in the place where Kelsey had been. The lava newts up above apparently noticed the change as well, for no longer did they press the attack. Indeed, many of them turned about and fled back up the stairs; others even scrambled over the low wall of the handrail and dropped the fifteen to twenty feet to the outer courtyard.

Guessing the source of the apparent transformation, Gary turned to regard Mickey, standing at his side.

"I do what I can," the leprechaun remarked smugly, reminding Gary once more of how ridiculous his earlier remarks concerning Mickey's value had been.

They made great progress then, the illusionary troll Kelsey leading the charge all the way up to the upper courtyard. This area was more squared than the lower bailey, with a cobble-stoned base laid flat around many lumpy natural stone breaks, and lined by several buildings, some tall and towering, others low and long.

Still, the newts retreated from the troll figure, but many more poured out into the courtyard, threatening to surround the small band.

Kelsey gazed diagonally across the courtyard, to a distant door at the far end of a low-roofed but obviously sturdy structure. If the elf meant to go there, though, he quickly changed his mind as dozens of lava newts rushed out that very door. For lack of a better choice, Kelsey led his companions to his left instead, to the tallest structure. He burst through a door, neatly slicing the throat of the surprised newt standing just inside, and rambled up a narrow spiral stair.

Hearing the continuing battle behind him, Gary was glad that Geno had taken up the rear. The walls of the stair pressed in tightly against Gary's broad shoulders and he did not believe that he could manage to fight in here at all.

Geno, too, was tightly pressed, but the dwarf, with his chopping hammers, did not need much room to maneuver. One newt lunged in boldly, lizard maw snapping, and Geno promptly crushed its skull. Other monsters came on bravely, though, clambering right over their dead companion.

The room at the top of the stairs would have proven disastrous for the companions if the newts up there had been better prepared. Apparently oblivious to what had transpired outside, the undisciplined rabble hadn't even taken the effort to arm themselves.

Kelsey came in first, appearing as an elf again (Mickey's troll illusion wouldn't have been very convincing, given that a troll wouldn't even have fit in this low room!), hacking and slashing at the wildly rushing monsters. He nicked one but didn't bring it down, as it made its way for a magnificently ornamented dagger hanging on the far wall. A single glance revealed to Gary the magic of that ancient, gem-encrusted weapon and he knew that he must not allow the newt to retrieve it. He leaped forward past Kelsey, shoulder-blocked one newt aside, and closed on the one reaching for the dagger.

The evil soldier grasped the weapon and swung about, but Gary got his strike in first as it blindly turned, catching the newt on the shoulder.

It was not a deep wound, nor did the spear hit a vital area, and Gary threw up his arm and ducked aside, expecting a retaliation. The lava newt did not swing or throw the ornamental dagger, though, did not make any move at all, save to open its toothy maw in a silent scream.

"*Taste of blood!*" came an emphatic thought in Gary's head. He felt the power thrumming through Cedric's spear, a power long dormant. Horrified, Gary tried to pull the spear out, but the barbed weapon resisted, holding stubbornly to its enemy's wound. When Gary finally did extract the tip, he felt compelled beyond his control to thrust it right back into the dying newt, this time blasting the creature through the heart.

Telepathic waves of intense satisfaction rolled through Gary's mind and body. Gary couldn't stop and consider them, though, for Kelsey came to him, prodding him towards the small room's other door.

Gary managed to reach out and pluck the dagger from the fallen newt before Kelsey had pulled him too far, and Kelsey, intent on escape, did not even notice the ancient weapon. Hardly giving the dagger a further thought, Gary slid it under the folds of his wide belt.

Then they were out of the room, going down a staircase quite similar to the one that had taken them up the tower. A hallway ran off its side at the ground level and the companions heard lava newts stirring down there. Kelsey took the group right by the corridor, and moving through a door, they came back into the courtyard of the upper bailey just a short distance from the door that had first brought them into the tower.

That short distance gave the companions all the opening they needed to get across the way, for the pursuing newts were still stupidly gathered at the other door.

Mickey scrambled up to perch on Gary's shoulder. Gary started to protest, fearing that he would soon be fighting once again, but then he realized that the leprechaun needed the position to work some more of his magic. Soon Gary, Kelsey, and Geno all appeared as mountain trolls, their footsteps even sounding like the thunder of a troll charge. The newts scrambled furiously to keep out of their way as Kelsey led the charge across the courtyard towards the desired door in the low-roofed and sturdy structure.

Again the elf burst right through, sending two not-so-surprised lava newts fleeing down a small and dark passage directly ahead. Kelsey didn't pursue them. A few steps inside the building, beyond a hanging tapestry, he turned a corner and came into a huge and ornate hall.

Just a few lava newts stood in the hall, and these made no move to intercept the companions. They remained at their posts, spaced in regular intervals along the decorated walls. And those newts outside that had found the courage to pursue the group did not even enter the low-roofed building. Gary had the uncomfortable feeling that this had all been arranged, that he and his friends had been purposely herded to this very chamber.

Hammers ready for more play, Geno started for the closest newt, but Kelsey held him back. To the dwarf's—and to Gary's—amazement, the elf then sheathed his sword and nodded to Mickey.

The troll illusion disappeared. The group was just an elf, a dwarf, a man, and a leprechaun once more.

As if on cue, a huge man, red-haired and red-bearded, with thick and corded muscles, stepped out from behind a suit of plated armor at the far end of the hall. Even from this distance, Gary could tell that the man stood at least a foot taller than he, and a hundred pounds heavier.

"Kelsenellenelvial, how good of you to finally arrive," the red-haired man cried out in a bellowing voice that reverberated off of every wall.

Kelsey's return greeting confirmed what Gary somehow suspected, what Gary feared, though he couldn't sort out the obvious discrepancy in this strange man's appearance.

"My greetings, Robert."

TWENTY-TWO
In Sheep's Clothing

GARY blinked many times in amazement as he scanned the huge torchlit hall. Suits of intricate and decorated armor, both metal and leather, stood at silent attention—why weren't the lava newt soldiers wearing them?—gleaming with new polish. Swords, spears, pole arms, weapons of so many shapes and sizes, lined the walls, joining the many rich-colored tapestries. One group of spears in particular caught Gary's eye. Identical in build, they were lashed halfway up the

wall with their butt ends touching at evenly spaced angles, giving the whole en-
semble a harmonious semicircular design, like the top half of the sun cresting
the eastern horizon.

And one sword in particular held Gary in absolute awe, both for its obviously magnificent craftsmanship and for its sheer size. Unlike the other weapons
in the room, this sword was not fitted to any wall or held by empty, decorative
armor. It leaned easily against the far wall, as if waiting for a wielder, waiting for
battle. Gary couldn't imagine anyone actually lifting the monstrous thing, let
alone wielding it in a fight.

Beyond the armor and weapons and tapestries, and all the other fabulous
decorations, the room itself seemed a spectacular thing. Thick stone walls ran
up straight and smooth, giving way to a dark-wooded ceiling of great interlocking beams. How high were those walls? Gary wondered. Twenty feet? Fifty?
Dimensions seemed out of kilter in here—a room more suited to a giant than a
man—and no matter how high it actually was, the sheer mass of that ceiling
awed Gary and made him feel very small indeed.

"Your friend approves of my meeting hall," the huge red-haired man bellowed, looking from Kelsey to Gary. "Is he the one to fulfill the prophecies?"
Robert walked a few steps closer, studying Gary as he came. His face brightened
suddenly, as if in revelation, and, to Gary's sincere relief, he stopped his advance.

"Yes," Robert answered his own question. "I see that he wears the armor of
Cedric Donigarten, though not as well as dead Cedric once wore it!" He roared
out a laugh that came straight from his belly.

"Is there no one who does not know of your quest?" Geno, obviously not
similarly amused, asked Kelsey snidely.

Kelsey turned on the dwarf sharply, and Gary could see true pain in the elf's
golden eyes. Geno's sarcasm had stung; apparently Kelsey had not expected
Robert to be so well informed.

"I could kill you all right now, you realize," the red-haired man said suddenly,
and from the strength of his voice alone, Gary held no doubts about his claim.

"There's the boasts of a true dragon," Mickey replied dryly, and Robert's ensuing laughter shook the hall like the rumble of thunder.

By this time, Gary was even more confused. When he had first heard the
man referred to as Robert, he had assumed that this was a different Robert, a
human counterpart to the dreaded dragon, perhaps. Or Gary had hoped that
this Robert was different, he realized, for in his heart he had known the truth all
along. Gary could not deny the aura of power surrounding this being, a strength
much greater than any mere human could contain.

But if this was really Robert the dreaded dragon, he certainly did not fit the description of the dragon in Gary's book, or, for that matter, any description of any dragon that Gary had ever heard of. Yet Mickey had told Gary to read those passages concerning the dragon in his book to get an idea of what Robert would be like.

"Well, I know why you are here," Robert said. "Or at least part of the reason. No doubt you have come to steal from me as well—I see that you have brought a dwarf along."

Geno ground his teeth at the insult, but, to Gary's amazement, did not offer any retort.

"We have come for one reason alone, great wyrm," Kelsey said firmly, stepping out in front of his companions and slapping his hand to his belted sword.

"Wyrm?" Gary whispered to Mickey, but the leprechaun motioned for him to keep silent.

Robert, appearing unimpressed by Kelsey's bravado, stalked the rest of the distance across the room to stand right before the elf.

Gary blew a silent whistle. The red-haired man was seven feet tall if he was an inch, with shoulders broad and strong, and corded arms that could tear Kelsey right in half with a simple twist and tug. If Geno got his strength from eating rocks, Gary decided, then this Robert ate mountains—whole.

"In accordance with the rules of our ancestors," Kelsey said, his voice not quivering in the least, "as was done by Ten-Temmera of Tir na n'Og against the dragon Rehir, as was done by Gilford of Drochit against the dragon Wobegone, as was done by . . ." The list went on for many minutes, with Kelsey naming ancient heroes in legendary duels against Faerie's most fearsome dragons.

"The Tylwyth Teg never could get by the formalities," Mickey whispered to Gary, and Geno, standing right beside the leprechaun, snorted his wholehearted agreement.

"Thus, with these precedents in mind and in accordance with all of the stated rules," Kelsey finally finished, "I do challenge you to a fight of honor!"

Through the entirety of Kelsey's prepared speech, Robert did not blink.

"Again, in accordance with precedent and established rules," Kelsey added, "if you are defeated, you must perform one small service to me. And you know the task well, dragon Robert—you must furnish the fire to reforge the ancient spear of Cedric Donigarten."

Robert nodded as though he had fully anticipated that price.

"No fires wrought by mortals could soften its metal," he replied, as if reciting a portion of some ancient verse.

"And you must," Kelsey continued with a nod, "adhere to the rules of banishment and remain in your fortress for a hundred years."

Again Robert nodded casually. What was a hundred years to a dragon, after all?

"And if victorious?" the red-haired giant asked, too nonchalantly, his sincerely calm confidence sending shudders up Gary's spine.

"There are precedents for that possibility . . . ," Kelsey began.

"Damn your precedents, elf!" Robert roared suddenly, and Kelsey, for all his nerve, retreated a step. "You wish me to do battle against you, a battle full of rules that eliminate my obvious advantages." He looked around at his lava newt guards, his smile reminding the companions that he could call in a hundred more loyal soldiers with a snap of his fingers.

"And you have told me of my price," Robert went on. "Irrelevant drivel! Do you truly believe that you have any chance of defeating me?"

Kelsey firmed his angular jaw, narrowed his golden eyes.

"So do not speak of precedents, elf," the dragon went on, nearly chuckling at the spectacle. "Tell me what I gain by accepting your challenge of honor; tell me why I should exert the effort against so pitiful a foe."

"Not so pitiful that ye did not take the trouble to gather his name," Mickey remarked, and Gary nodded, thinking it wise for the leprechaun to lend Kelsey some much needed support at that time.

Robert smirked but did not answer.

"If you win, my life is forfeited to you," Kelsey said at once.

"You state the obvious," Robert replied. "You will not survive the battle."

Kelsey drew out his magnificent sword. "And this," he said. "Forged by the Tylwyth Teg, it can only serve one so designated by its wielder. If you win and my life is forfeit, then I give to you my sword!"

"A pittance." Robert replied, and Kelsey frowned so gravely at the insult that Gary thought that the elf would surely strike out at Robert then and there. Robert turned his head, leading Kelsey's gaze across the room, to the gigantic and magnificent sword leaning against the far wall.

"But I will accept your pittance," Robert said suddenly, turning back on the elf. "Your life and your sword, elf, and the lives of your friends."

Mickey and Geno started to protest, with Gary startled too numb to even utter a single word, but Kelsey simply spoke above them. "According to precedent," he said. "And so we are agreed."

"Don't ye think that we've a word or two to say about it?" Mickey asked.

"No," was Robert's simple and straightforward reply, and while Kelsey did not openly vocalize his agreement, it seemed obvious to the others that he considered the dragon's demands quite reasonable.

The huge man walked easily across the room and casually lifted the massive sword.

"A strong one," Mickey remarked, seeing Gary's gawk, for not only had Robert lifted a sword that Gary thought more appropriate for a Tommy-sized giant, but he had lifted it, so very easily, with just one hand!

"You choose swords?" Kelsey asked, seeming confused. "I had thought . . ."

"I choose my weapons as I choose," Robert replied with an ironic chuckle. "The sword will do nicely—for a start." He moved to the hearth on the back wall. Bending low, the red-haired man, without the slightest hesitation or wince of pain, used his bare hands to push aside the glowing embers.

"Are you coming along?" he asked, and he tugged on one of the hearth's pokers, a concealed lever, which drew open a secret trapdoor. "And I warn you only once," he added, "if you steal a single coin or trinket from my gathered hoard, then the rules are no more, and your lives are surely forfeit! I have not come forth for many decades; perhaps it will be time again for Robert the Righteous to feast upon the flesh of men!"

Gary could hardly find his breath as he looked to Mickey. The leprechaun nodded gravely, not doubting the dragon's threats in the least.

The four companions, Kelsey determinedly at their lead, followed Robert down a long and winding set of stairs, ending in a series of vast and empty chambers. Mickey paused as they passed by one archway, low and covered by a hanging tapestry, the only man-made article they had seen down here under the castle.

"Treasure room," the leprechaun remarked to Gary's inquisitive stare. Gary knew from Mickey's expression that the leprechaun had no intention of trying to steal anything, nor did any of the companions, in light of Robert's warning. But there was a profound and obvious sadness in Mickey's eye as he continued to gaze back at the blocked archway. Gary studied the leprechaun closely, not understanding.

He didn't question the leprechaun about it, though, too concerned with what lay ahead to worry about what might lie behind.

The smell of sulphur continued to grow until it fully filled Gary's nostrils. At first he thought the aroma a relic from the ancient volcano that had raised the Giant's Thumb, but as Robert moved into one room and lit the torches lining the chamber's walls, Gary noticed many scarred and blasted areas, along every wall, the ceiling, and the floor.

Dragon fire?

Gary also noticed many scratches in the stone floor, deep and wide. If a dragon's claws had caused those . . .

That undeniable shudder ran its path again along Gary's spine.

"How did Robert know of our coming?" Kelsey whispered to Mickey as Robert moved far across the room to finish lighting up all of the torches.

"Maybe the witch told him," Gary offered, what he thought to be a logical conclusion. Three skeptical stares showed him differently, though.

"No, lad," Mickey explained. "Ceridwen would not be talking to the likes of Robert. Nor would any of her minions. They don't get on well; it'd be as likely for the witch to side with Kelsey in the coming battle as to side with Robert."

"She doesn't want the spear forged," Gary reminded him.

"Nor does she desire to see the spear and Cedric's armor fall into the dragon's clutches," Geno reasoned. "I would guess that Ceridwen would prefer to deal with Kelsey holding the repaired spear than to deal with Robert at all."

"The two do take pains to keep away from each other," Mickey said with an amused expression. That the leprechaun could find any mirth at all in their dire situation told Gary just how profoundly Ceridwen and Robert hated each other—to the delight of many of Faerie's inhabitants, no doubt.

Kelsey went back to his original question. "How did Robert know?" he asked again, and this time, it seemed to Gary, the elf cast more than a curious stare the leprechaun's way.

Mickey just shrugged and popped his pipe into his mouth. "Ye'd better take the lad's shield," the leprechaun remarked, deflecting the question. "It'd block a dragon's fire, so say the legends."

Kelsey looked again to Robert, now making his deliberate way back across the vast chamber, and knew that his question would have to wait.

He turned to Gary for the shield, but Gary, staring at approaching Robert, did not notice him. The image of this red-haired man spouting flames did not add up to Gary—and who ever heard of a dragon fighting with a sword?

"Well?" Kelsey's impatient tone pulled Gary from his private deliberations. He looked around curiously for a moment, confused, then realized what Kelsey was after and fumbled to get Cedric's great shield off of his back.

"Some of the straps have come loose," Gary explained. "When a troll hit it . . ."

A wave of Kelsey's hand stopped him. "I'll not use it in the battle," the elf said, to Gary's further confusion. "It is too cumbersome for swordplay, and little defense against that mighty sword, especially in the hands of Robert. The dragon would drive his blade right through this shield even if I were quick enough to raise it for a block." Kelsey took the shield then and turned away to begin his challenge, to meet his destiny.

"Then why did he take it?" Gary asked Mickey.

"As I said, the shield'll turn even a dragon's fire," Mickey replied casually, lighting up his pipe. "If Robert decides to loose his breath, then Kelsey'll be quick to pick it up."

"But he's not a dragon!" Gary cried in frustration, more loudly than he had intended.

Geno's laughter mocked him.

"Just watch, lad," Mickey replied. "Just watch."

KELSEY and Robert squared off near to the center of the huge chamber, Kelsey laying the magical shield on the floor beside one decapitated stalagmite and taking up his sword in both hands.

Robert, too, hoisted his weapon in both hands, bringing it into an easy, circular swing above his head. "Do not die too quickly, elf," the great man growled "I have not enjoyed the excitement of battle for many years. A dozen lava newts fall too quickly for me to take pleasure in those jousts!" The monstrous sword whipped around suddenly, an exclamation point for Robert's boasts, and Kelsey barely fell back out of its nearly seven-foot reach.

Despite the momentum of the swing, Robert easily halted the sword's progress and brought it back in the other way. Wisely Kelsey never slowed his backpedaling, even rolling to his back and then to the right to come up facing his enemy, but far out of Robert's reach.

"Ah, very good!" Robert roared. "Hard to catch, if not so hard to kill!"

On came the red-haired monster in a frightening wild rush.

"Get out of there!" Gary heard himself cry out, but Kelsey had other ideas. As Robert charged, so did he, diving to his knees at the last moment and sliding right by the lumbering giant.

Kelsey's sword drove home once and then again into Robert's thick thigh as they passed, and Kelsey came back up before Robert could even spin about to regard him.

The red-haired man looked down to his injured leg, astonishment clear upon his face.

Gary's smile widened at Kelsey's brilliant move but it faded immediately when he looked upon Mickey, who seemed not so confident.

"Ah," Robert roared again. "Very good!" And then he laughed, so loudly and profoundly that it echoed again and again off of every stone in the chamber, sounding as if the dragon had brought along his own invisible cheering section. Giving no more heed to the wounds at all, he advanced upon Kelsey once again, this time slowly, deliberately, his great sword waving out before him.

"At least I'll get to see the damned elf die before it's my turn to face the wyrm," Geno muttered grimly.

TWENTY-THREE

The Fighter and the Wyrm

THE great sword swiped about, then again, and a third time, the momentum of each swing bringing raging Robert just a bit closer to his prey. Kelsey didn't even try to parry the mighty blows, knowing that unless his sword angle was exactly perfect, Robert's powerful cuts would surely blast right through his meager defenses.

Normally in such a fight against a larger foe, the elf would hold a wide advantage of quickness, especially with his opponent wielding so heavy and unwieldy a sword. But not this time; Robert swung the blade as easily as Kelsey maneuvered his slender elven sword, and the giant man proved deceptively quick and always balanced.

Again came a mighty swing, and this time, the elf barely managed to get back out of harm's way. Robert's widening smile mocked Kelsey's continuing retreat.

Kelsey was far from ready to surrender, though—not that vicious Robert would have accepted it anyway. He had gone through many trials to get to this point, and now, so close to realizing his quest, the one great task appointed him for his life, his elven blood coursed through his slender limbs with renewed vigor. Besides, the elf reminded himself as the red-haired giant continued to stalk in, he had known all along that the fight against Robert would be the greatest trial of all his life.

Robert's sword whipped across yet again, and once more Kelsey slipped backwards out of reach. The huge man came on fiercely, suddenly, turning his wrists to send his weapon up high, then reversing his grip to angle the sword for a mighty downwards chop.

Kelsey threw his sword up above him, angled diagonally. In typical combat, the cunning elf would have turned his sword horizontal as the blow came in, catching his opponent's weapon on his own blade to fully stop his attacker's momentum chop. From there, a simple twist would throw the attacking sword harmlessly aside and leave Kelsey's foe vulnerable for a counter.

Wisely Kelsey did not try his usual tactics against the inhumanly strong Robert. As Robert's sword crashed in, the elf, instead of turning his sword to the horizontal plane, twisted it vertically and immediately stepped to his left, away from the deflected blow. Robert was quick to recover, but not quick enough to defeat Kelsey's obvious advantage. With Robert's sword far to the other side, Kelsey rushed by the red-haired man's right flank, launching a rapid series of stinging slashes and pokes as he passed.

"Oh, grand move!" Mickey blurted out around the edges of his long-stemmed pipe, clapping his chubby little hands together.

Every onlooker, and Robert as well, thought that Kelsey would then simply run out of range again, putting the fight back on even ground.

None of them, particularly not the dragon, truly understood the fires that burned in the veins of the noble elf.

As Robert spun to catch up with the passing elf, Kelsey cut around in a tight circle, keeping ahead of Robert's blade and keeping Robert's right flank open and vulnerable. The elf's sword hit home perhaps a dozen times in the next frenzied moments before Robert wisely stopped his futile chasing and retreated a few steps instead.

"Oh, grander move!" Mickey called, adding another series of claps. Robert turned an angry glare upon the leprechaun, silencing Mickey immediately, except for a profound gulp.

Gary thought that the huge man would surely run over and slaughter Mickey—and Gary didn't trust that the monstrous red-haired man would stop at that. The weight of doom suddenly heavy around his shoulders, Gary looked to Geno for support. He was not comforted by what he saw, though, for the dwarf had prudently moved a dozen long steps away from Mickey's other side.

But fears of the attack proved unfounded. Robert was too busy in his battle to take any actions against the others at that time. He turned his glower upon Kelsey, then looked disdainfully at his wounded side. His right arm had been opened in several places—one gash had the brute's corded muscles hanging out right beyond his thick skin.

"I had thought to spare you," Robert spat at Kelsey.

"A lie," Kelsey muttered in reply.

"But now you die!" Robert roared, and he came on wildly, sword slashing back and forth.

Despite Kelsey's previous moments of brilliance, Gary found that he absolutely believed Robert's prediction as the next furious assault began. How could anyone—especially one as slender and delicate as Kelsey—fend off or escape the crushing power of Robert's mighty swings? And even if Kelsey managed to stay away, how could he hope to win? He had nailed Robert with many direct hits—strikes that would have killed, or at least stopped, any real human opponent—to no avail, and Robert showed not the slightest signs of tiring.

Kelsey dropped behind one of the few stalagmite mounds in the room, hoping to diminish the intensity of the attack.

Robert didn't slow, didn't hold back his ringing sword at all. Sparks flew as the great weapon slammed against the stone, and when they cleared, the stalagmite mound stood but half its original height.

To the companions' dismay, Robert's sword had not broken, had not even visibly chipped. On came the red-haired monster, his face contorted with rage, his sword humming as it again began its death-promising sidelong cuts through the empty air.

Kelsey did not fear his constant retreating in the vast room, but neither did he believe that he was gaining any advantage, that the great Robert would tire. The elf knew that he would have to continue his brilliance and his daring, and that one mistake would surely cost him his life.

Kelsey nearly laughed at that thought. His life mattered not when weighed against the successful completion of his life-quest.

Kelsey backed and watched, watched closely the subtle movements of Robert's fingers clenched about the huge sword's leather-strapped hilt.

Gary tried to look away, not wanting to see his friend share a similar fate with the halved stalagmite. He found that he could not avoid the remarkable spectacle, though, and his mouth drooped open in confusion when he looked back to the combatants, back to Kelsey, unexpectedly smiling with apparently sincere confidence.

Gary couldn't know it then, but the elf had found his advantage. For all of Robert's sheer power and uncanny quickness, the dragon was not a swordsman—at least not by the elf's high standards. Robert's attacks were straightforward, his movements, even his feints, becoming more and more predictable to the seasoned warrior of Tylwyth Teg.

Kelsey continued to watch those gnarly, huge fingers, waiting for the telltale turn. A few strides, a few swings later, Robert twisted and sent his sword flying up high—and Kelsey was ready for him.

Just like the first time he had attempted the downwards chop, three quick strides brought the red-haired man rushing towards the elf.

Kelsey, though, did not offer a defense similar to the previous one. He, too, came rushing forward, sword leading, desperate to beat Robert to the quick.

Robert's great sword was still up high over his head when the fine tip of Kelsey's elven blade came in tight against Robert's throat.

"You lose!" the elf cried.

Robert roared and drove his sword down at the elf.

Kelsey could have thrust his sword right through Robert's throat—his instincts almost made him do it. But what good to him would be a slain dragon? He dove aside instead, rolling to his feet and pointing an accusing finger Robert's way.

"Treachery!" he yelled, looking to his companions, the witnesses, for support. "I had you bested."

"I am not down!" Robert roared back. "You had nothing!"

"What fairness is this?" Kelsey cried, pleading his case to Mickey and the others, to the stones of the cavern, to anyone and anything that could hear his voice. He turned back on Robert. "Must I kill you to win? What is my gain, then, in this challenge of honor?"

"You had nothing!" Robert roared back, and it seemed to Gary as if his voice had changed somewhat, taken on a more throaty call.

"My sword was at your throat!"

"And mine at your head," Robert quickly added. "To finish your move would have allowed me to finish mine." Robert poked his finger against his own throat. "Small hole," he spat sarcastically. "Perhaps fatal, but not so surely fatal as an elf cut down the middle!"

Kelsey knew Robert's estimate of the fight was far from accurate. He could have driven his sword right through Robert's neck and still dodged the downwards chop. But Robert's argument was convincing, Kelsey knew, convincing enough for the dragon to avoid the mark of dishonor in the general retelling of the fight.

"He's playing Bilbo's game," Gary muttered under his breath. Mickey looked up at him curiously, remembering the story, then nodded his accord.

"Half-truths," Gary went on. "Kelsey had him."

"Tell that to Robert," Mickey muttered. "But wait long enough for me to get far from yer side afore ye do, lad."

Gary didn't miss the leprechaun's point.

"Enough of this foolishness!" Robert roared suddenly. With one arm, he heaved his huge sword across the room. It hit the wall with a blinding flash, and hung in place, halfway embedded in the solid stone.

Gary thought for a moment that Robert had capitulated, had admitted that Kelsey had fairly won.

Sensing the truth, though, Kelsey raced back to retrieve the magical shield of Cedric Donigarten, working frantically to get it in place on his slender arm.

Gary started to question the elf's movements, but when he looked back to Robert, he came to understand, came to understand so very much.

Robert began to change.

The human coil warped and bulged; red hair wrapped Robert's head and blended with his mutating skin. A great wing sprouted, then another, and huge claws tore the boots from the creature's feet. Great snapping sounds of re-forming bones echoed sickeningly through the chamber; a monstrous, scaly tail slammed to the floor behind the creature and rushed out as it thickened and elongated, seeming almost like a second creature.

"Oh my God!" Gary Leger stammered. "Sonofab . . . Holy Sh . . . Oh my God!" Gary simply ran out of expletives. His mouth worked weird contortions, but no words spewed forth. If Tommy had been standing beside him and had uttered one of his customary "Duhs," Gary would certainly have patted him on the leg for giving him the right word. Nothing in Gary Leger's life, not the volumes of fantasy reading he had done nor any sights he had ever seen, in his own world or in Faerie, could have possibly prepared him for the spectacle before him.

The chamber no longer seemed so large—the dragon had reached fifty feet long and continued to grow, to stretch. Gary remembered the dry lake, Loch Tullamore, and now he understood how the dragon might indeed have "hissed" it away. He clutched at *The Hobbit,* sitting in a pouch on his belt, like it was some protecting amulet, a source of strength and a reminder that others had faced such a creature and lived to tell about it.

But even Gary's amulet could not begin to insulate him from the sheer terror of facing Robert the Wretched. The change was complete then—Robert loomed nearly a hundred feet in length, with spear-like, stone-tearing claws and a maw that could snap a man in half, or fully swallow him, at the dragon's whim.

Gary's knees went weak under him. He wanted nothing except to run away, but knew his legs wouldn't carry him. He wanted nothing except to close his eyes, but he could not, held firmly by the awesome spectacle, the majesty and the horror of the true dragon.

"Enough!" the dragon roared again. If Robert's voice in human form could shake stones, then the power of this blast could surely split them. "The game is ended, Kelsenellenelvial Gil-Ravadry!"

Geno cast a disconcerting look Gary and Mickey's way. "I suppose that the spear will have to wait some time before it gets back in one piece again," the dwarf muttered sarcastically.

"Stupid elf," he added, and his derisive chuckle momentarily freed Gary from his awestricken trance.

"You don't seem too concerned," he muttered Geno's way, his voice cracking several times as he struggled to spit out the words.

Geno gave a resigned shrug. "Robert will not eat me," he replied with some confidence. "Dragons are not overly fond of the taste of dwarfs, and besides, dragons like the pretty things a dwarf hammer might bring." Geno's snort twanged against the marrow of Gary's bones. "He'll eat you, though."

Gary turned his attention back to the fight, which seemed more a prelude to a massacre now. Kelsey's smile was long gone, and so was the elf's look of confidence, even of determination. And who could blame him?

"Can we help him?" Gary whispered to Mickey, though Gary knew that if Mickey told him to charge in beside Kelsey, his quivering legs would betray his noble intentions.

The leprechaun snorted incredulously, and Gary said no more. He finally managed to close his eyes and turned his thoughts inwards instead, calling upon the sentient spear, his most reliable battle ally, for some answers to this nightmare.

KELSEY braced himself and clutched his sword more tightly, trying to remind himself of his purpose in being there, of the fact that he had known from the beginning of his quest what creature he would ultimately face.

Rationale just didn't seem an antidote to the sheer terror evoked by the sight of the unbeatable dragon.

Serpentine Robert slithered, belly low, towards Kelsey. He gave a swipe of his huge foreclaw, almost a playful swing, like some kitten with a ball of yarn. Kelsey threw his weight behind the heavy shield to block, but still went sliding many feet across the stone floor.

"Oh, damn," Geno muttered; and turned away, thinking the fight at its gruesome end.

"Oh," the dwarf corrected weakly when he looked back, looked at Kelsey.

Somehow still standing and somehow undaunted, the elf stepped right back and ripped off a series of three short jabs into the dragon's extended arm.

The wind from Robert's ensuing laughter knocked Kelsey to the floor.

"Do not make it so easy," the dragon growled. "I wish to play for as long as I might. Who knows when another hero might be as foolish as you, Kelsenellenelvial Gil-Ravadry?"

"HOW might I aid my friend?" Gary's thoughts asked the sentient spear.

No answer.

He called mentally to the spear several times, insisting that it communicate with him.

"*The fight is not yours,*" the spear finally answered.

"I must help Kelsey!"

"*You must not!*" came an emphatic reply. "*The fight is a challenge of honor; events go exactly as they were dictated before the elf's quest was undertaken.*"

Gary started to protest, to argue that no one single warrior could defeat such a beast and that the quest must be abandoned for the sake of Kelsey's life. But then he understood. The spear cared nothing for Kelsey. This battle, carried out properly in accordance with ancient rules, was the sentient weapon's only chance of being reforged.

Helplessly Gary Leger opened his eyes.

Kelsey was on the attack again, rushing in beyond Robert's foreclaws and banging away at the dragon's scaly armor with all his strength. The huge horned dragon head bobbed with bellowing laughter, mocking Kelsey. Every now and then, Robert casually dropped a claw near to the elf, knocking him aside.

But stubborn, incredibly stubborn, Kelsey did not relent, and his persistence paid off.

Robert's lizard-like features contorted suddenly in pain as Kelsey's sword slipped between armor plates and dug deep at dragon flesh. The dragon set his wings into a fierce beat, their wind driving Kelsey back while lifting Robert to his towering height.

Kelsey stubbornly kept his balance, using the great shield to somewhat deflect the blasting wind. He nearly overbalanced when the dragon sucked in its breath, countering the force of the beating wings.

"Here it comes," Gary heard Mickey mutter.

And indeed it did, a blast of fire that seemed to swallow pitiful Kelsey and warmed all the vast chamber so profoundly that Gary, standing many yards away, felt his eyebrows singe underneath his loose-fitting helmet. Robert's exhale went on for many seconds, the white-hot fires pouring over Kelsey, scorching the stone all about the elf's feet.

And then it was ended—and Kelsey still stood! Stone bubbled beside him and the outer metal of the shield of Cedric glowed an angry red, but the elf, even his clothes, and the ground in the protective shadow of that shield, appeared unharmed.

"Damned good shield," Geno said in disbelief.

Robert, too, seemed stricken, gawking at the elf who somehow had held his ground against a blast that could melt stone.

"Ye'll have to do better than that, mighty wyrm," Kelsey chided, apparently gaining some confidence in the proof that the legendary shield could, as the bard's pen had declared, "turn the fire of a dragon's breath."

Robert launched another blast, Kelsey just barely ducking behind the protective shield in time. Now the stone around the elf hissed and sputtered, that sulphuric smell permeated the room.

But when the fires ceased, Kelsey poked his head around the shield—and he was wearing a smile.

Simply surviving Robert's breath was insult enough, but the elf's taunts, and now his smile, sent the dragon into a rage beyond anything Gary had ever imagined.

"Oh, begorra," he heard Mickey whisper, and then came the scraping and pounding of the dragon's charge that tore the cavern floor in its wake.

Claws hammered down at Kelsey, a hit so fierce that Gary thought the elf surely dead. Somehow Kelsey held his ground, but then the terrible maw snapped down, cat-quick, to bite at him. Somehow again—it seemed impossible to Gary—Kelsey managed to dodge, even to smack Robert several times before the dragon got its massive horned head back out of range.

Claws rained destruction, back legs kicked, wings beat down mercilessly, and once, the dragon's tail snapped around with force enough to fell a thick-trunked oak. But Kelsey was ahead of nearly every attack, and those that did connect did no more than slow the elf's own frenzied offense. The slaps of Kelsey's sword sounded as a tap dance, rhythmical and constant, beating at every target Robert presented to him.

Dragon fire came roaring in again, but the shield repelled it, and Kelsey even managed to close in under the fiery cover and snap off three vicious strikes.

"That's impossible," Gary groaned, turning to Mickey. The leprechaun was too intent on the action to answer him, but Geno replied, tossing a hammer casually off the side of Gary's helmet.

"Shut your big mouth," the dwarf growled, his unexpected anger stunning Gary to silence.

Robert's frenzy did not relent—Gary came to fear that all the mountain would crumble under the dragon's pounding. But neither did Kelsey relent, snapping, slicing, poking, beating at the dragon from every angle, moving with such speed and precision that at times he seemed no more than a thin blur.

A claw sent him reeling backwards, a solid hit, and as he started forward once more, Robert's great maw fell over him. Gary nearly swooned as the dragon's head came up with Kelsey in his mouth.

Kelsey wasn't finished. Somehow, impossibly, the elf had wedged his shield between the dragon's jaws, and Robert's actions now actually worked against the dragon, for now Kelsey was within reach of the beast's only vulnerable area.

With his slender, wicked sword dancing less than an inch from the dragon's yellow, reptilian eye, Kelsey asked evenly, "Do ye yield?"

"I could breathe you to char!" the dragon hissed between its locked jaws.

"And ye'd lose yer eye," Kelsey proclaimed.

Robert made not a move, considering his options.

"I don't believe it," Gary breathed, his voice full of stunned elation. He just shook his head and stared blankly as the god-like dragon obediently lowered the elf to the floor and released him.

"Bring the ancient spear and be done with it!" the dragon roared, stamping his foreclaws, and several stones in the wide cavern did indeed split apart under the force of Robert's outrage.

"Unbelievable," Gary muttered again.

"Keep quiet, lad," Mickey implored him. "Say not a word and get yer part done as quickly as ye can."

Gary considered the leprechaun curiously, wondering why Mickey was so full of intensity and trepidation. Was that a bead of sweat on Mickey's forehead?

Why? Gary wondered, for the greatest trial had been passed—Kelsey had won. The elf had survived the wrath of Robert, had taken blows that would have toppled ancient trees and flattened mountains . . .

Gary abruptly halted his confused train of thought. "Ye'd lose yer eye?" he mumbled under his breath, imitating the accent that Kelsey had used when demanding Robert's surrender. Now he understood Geno's anger at his proclamation that Kelsey's feats were impossible.

Gary turned his attention to the scene before him. Robert had started away, shifting his great scaled body to the side, towards a wide and high tunnel running off of the main chamber. Kelsey stood in the same spot where Robert had released him, impassive, apparently basking in his victory.

Gary looked right through the illusionary elf.

"The first hit," Mickey whispered to him, seeing that he had finally figured out the game.

Gary quickly recalled the events of the battle, the first powerful sidelong swipe that Robert had launched Kelsey's way, then looked to the appropriate side. Crumpled beside a stalagmite mound lay Kelsey, curled in a ball and covered in blood. The elf was alive, Gary could see, and trying hard not to make any move or sound.

"You will need the shield," Geno remarked to Gary. With the illusionary scene dispelled to him, Gary noticed the shield lying where Kelsey had first placed it on the floor, beside the scars of dragon fire and the fast-cooling stone. He wondered how he might retrieve it without alerting Robert to the trick, but Mickey was already taking care of that part. The illusionary Kelsey walked over to the real shield and laid the illusionary shield atop it.

It was all very confusing to Gary—and he didn't understand why the dragon hadn't seen right through the leprechaun's trick—but he went over and picked up the shield and followed Geno and Robert into the side chamber.

He looked back as he exited the room, and watched Mickey's illusionary elf go and sit beside the real Kelsey at the stalagmite mound, the leprechaun going as well to tend to the real Kelsey's very real wounds.

GARY slumped even lower behind the shield when he heard the sharp intake of the dragon's breath. He felt like he had to go to the bathroom—feared that he would embarrass himself right then and there. But he could say nothing. The spear was laid out on a flat stone before him and he, as the prophecies dictated, held tight to its bottom half. Geno had tied the two ends of the shaft together with a leather thong and had sprinkled some flaky substance—Gary couldn't tell if it was metal scrapings or crushed gemstones—along the part to be rejoined. Now Geno stood far back, hammer in one heavy-gauntleted hand and bag of the same flaky substance in the other.

Gary reminded himself that he had not actually witnessed the shield deflecting the dragon's terrible breath, that what he had seen had been no more than one of Mickey's illusions. He peeked up over the rim of the shield, wanting to protest, but saw that he hadn't the time.

Then the flames came and Gary didn't know if he had wet his pants or not—and in that heat, they certainly would have dried in an instant anyway! Great gouts of white fire licked at Gary around the edges of his shield; his hand holding the magical spear warmed and then burned with pain. He held onto the weapon's shaft, though, for Geno had promised him some very unpleasant consequences if he didn't.

And then it was over, suddenly. Gary blinked the sting out of his eyes, almost fainting with relief that the shield had indeed turned aside the white-hot flames. On the flat stone before him, the magical spear glowed an angry orange in the dimly lit room. Immediately the dwarven craftsman fell over it, sprinkling flakes and pounding away, sprinkling and pounding. Geno muttered many arcane phrases that Gary couldn't begin to understand, but from the dwarf's ritualistic movements and reverent tone, Gary correctly assumed it to be some sort of smithy magic, a spell to strengthen the bonding beyond the might of simple metal.

The work went on for many minutes, Geno tapping and banging, chanting and sprinkling still more of the flaky substance on the still-hot metal shaft. Then the dwarf lifted the spear up and looked along the shaft, checking to be certain that it was perfectly straight.

He dropped it back to the stone, gave a few more taps, and lifted it for another inspection. Geno's smile was all the answer that Gary Leger needed. The dwarf backed away and slipped his hammer into a loop on his belt.

The glow dissipated; the spear seemed remarkably cool.

"So now you are in the legends once again, mighty Robert," Geno called to the dragon. "All the world will know that it was Robert, greatest of wyrmkind, who gave the fires to reforge the ancient spear!"

The dwarf's attempt to placate the fuming dragon seemed to have little effect.

"Get you gone from my mountain!" the beast roared.

Gary concurred with Geno's nodding head; they wouldn't have to be asked twice.

"Pick it up," Geno instructed Gary, indicating the spear. With one hand, Gary easily hoisted the long weapon. It seemed even lighter now than either of its previous parts, and even more balanced. If before, Gary had believed that he could hurl it a hundred yards, now he felt as though he could throw it two hundred.

The sentient spear did not communicate to Gary in any discernible words, but Gary could clearly feel its profound elation.

TWENTY-FOUR

Crows

TWOSCORE lava newt escorts walked in tight formation right behind the companions, their leveled spears guiding wounded Kelsey and his friends out of the lower tunnels. The dragon had warned them not to go anywhere near the castle on their way out.

"Or ever again!" Robert had roared, and it had seemed to Gary that he directed his warning particularly at Mickey McMickey. Had Robert guessed the trick? Gary wondered, but he dismissed the notion, thinking that the beast would never have let them out if it had.

Truly Gary was glad now to be out of sight of the awesome dragon, and had no intentions of ever coming anywhere near Robert's castle again. He hadn't yet shaken off his fears, though. Fully supporting Kelsey now, he kept looking back over his shoulder, fearing an imminent attack from the lava newt guards.

"Don't ye worry, lad," Mickey told him, noticing his uneasiness. "Robert would not dare to break his oath."

"Never trust a dragon," Geno added. "Unless you have beaten him in a challenge. Even wyrms have some sense of honor."

That's what it always seemed to come down to in this strange and magical world, Gary noted. Honor.

"He's no choice but to let us go," Mickey finished smugly. The leprechaun's gray eyes turned up in a profound smile of victory as he drew another long drag of his pipe.

Gary was glad to hear it, but his face, unlike the leprechaun's, reflected no hint of elation. Kelsey winced in agony with every passing step, and Gary thought the elf would surely faint away. One of Kelsey's arms was badly twisted and possibly broken—and a great tear ran along Kelsey's side, where dragon claws had ripped through armor and skin alike. Blood matted the elf's golden hair and caked on his delicate face, and only the luster in Kelsey's golden eyes, a profound look of satisfaction, showed that he was even conscious of what was happening around him.

Then they were outside—the new day had dawned—on the lower trails of the mountain's east side, far below the barracks of Robert's lava newt garrison. Half of their escorts remained to block the tunnel behind them; the other half took up defensive positions on the sloping road above.

"As if they fear we're heading back that way," Mickey scoffed, seeing the blocking line.

The leprechaun's words and tone struck Gary profoundly. They were free— even Gary realized it fully then. They were free of Robert, and Gary was free of Faerie, for he held the reforged spear. The terms of indenture had been met; Gary could soon go home.

Home.

The word sounded strange to Gary, walking along a towering mountain in a land so unlike his own. It seemed like many years since he had been in Lancashire, seemed almost as if that other world had been just a long dream, as if this land of Faerie was somehow more real.

More real than the plastics factory. More real than the tedium of standing beside the humming grinder, dropping in chunks of scrap plastic and dreaming of absurd adventures.

Gary bit back a chuckle at that notion. Absurd adventures? They didn't seem so absurd to Gary Leger anymore, especially not with an elf leaning heavily on his shoulder, with a leprechaun and a dwarf trotting along beside him.

Gary couldn't bite back his chuckle, despite Kelsey's wounds. He looked back up the mountain path, to the red-scaled lava newts standing solemn guard across the road.

"So tell me how," he bade Mickey as they put even more distance between themselves and the lava newts.

Mickey looked up at him to consider the vague question, staring as if he had no idea of what Gary was talking about.

"You said that illusions were of no use against dragons," Gary clarified, though he guessed correctly that Mickey already knew what was on his mind.

"I said that they weren't about to work well on the dragon," Mickey corrected. "As it is with dwarfs, lad. Not so good." He gave Gary a wink. "But I can always find a bit of use for them."

"It worked perfectly," Gary remarked, both his tone and his subsequent expression revealing clear suspicion. "Too perfectly."

"It was a fight," Mickey reminded him. "Suren Robert would have seen right through me tricks if he had the time to think on them!

"But he had a mighty foe before him, and he knew it," Mickey asserted. "Besides, me magic was at its strongest in there." Mickey stopped abruptly and turned his eyes back to the trail before them, as if he hadn't wanted to make that statement.

Gary didn't fully appreciate the leprechaun's slip of the tongue, though, too involved with his own recollections of the battle. "Then we cheated," he said at length. "Robert really won and was under no obligation to forge the spear or to even let us out of there."

Geno kicked him hard on the shin, a blow that nearly sent both Gary and Kelsey tumbling to the ground.

"Give me the elf, then!" the dwarf snorted at Gary. "And you walk back up there and surrender yourself to the dragon! Let your conscience be appeased while your body is being devoured."

Gary never took his glowering eyes off the dwarf as he reached down and rubbed his bruised shin.

"Yer reasoning is right, lad," Mickey put in. "But so's the dwarf. Ye cannot play fair with a beast like Robert—it's not a fair fight to begin with, ye know."

"The end justifies the means?" Gary replied.

Mickey thought over the strange phrase for a few moments, then nodded. "When playing with a dragon," he agreed. "Besides, lad, the real Kelsey had Robert beaten before he ever turned into the dragon. It was Robert who chose the swords for the challenge, and in that fight, Kelsey truly won."

Gary let it drop at that, glad for the reminder and glad that he could agree with Mickey's reasoning. For some reason, he had to feel that honor had been upheld in the challenge. Kelsey patted him on the shoulder then, a minor movement, but one that struck Gary profoundly. He turned to regard the wounded elf, and found, to his surprise, sincere approval in Kelsey's golden eyes.

They continued on down the mountain at as great a pace as they could set with Gary half carrying Kelsey. The castle was soon far behind them, to Gary's relief, but he couldn't help noticing that Mickey kept glancing back that way. It wasn't as though the leprechaun feared any imminent attack (again, to Gary's relief), but rather, Mickey's gaze reflected a longing, a heartache, as a young mother might glance over her shoulder after dropping her child off for the first day of school.

Gary tried to put it all together in private, knowing that Mickey would offer no explanations. He recalled the leprechaun's meeting with the pixie on their first night out of Dvergamal, and only then did he make note of Mickey's remark that his magic was at its strongest in Robert's lair. Truly it had been the finest illusion Gary had witnessed yet—the image of the fighting elf resembled Kelsey in every detail and moved perfectly to compensate for the give-and-take maneuvers of the battle.

But that did not explain to Gary why Robert had been so fooled. The only reason Mickey's illusions had once been able to trick Geno, back in the dwarf's cave when it appeared as though Kelsey had walked into the wall trap, was that Mickey had shown Geno what the dwarf had expected to see. Not so in Kelsey's fight against Robert. Most likely the dragon would have expected what had really happened, would have expected to see a broken Kelsey go flying away after the first claw strike. If Robert was truly an ancient and wise wyrm, a beast befitting the common and apparently accurate legends of dragonkind, he should have seen through the illusion, if not at first, then at least later on, in the lull before he had led Gary and Geno into the side chamber to reforge the spear.

Then why was Robert fooled? And why did Mickey keep looking back up at the castle?

No matter how hard Gary tried, the pieces of the puzzle would not add up.

The trail split in several directions as they neared the bottom of the obelisk-shaped mountain. Mickey took up the lead and headed north. "This way will get us back quicker to the crevice and the giant," the leprechaun explained.

"And to the Crahgs?" Geno asked dryly.

Mickey shook his head. "No need to go back that way," the sprite replied firmly, and his face and the dwarf's lit up at that welcomed declaration. Mickey hopped up into the air and kicked his curly-toed shoes together. "The quest is done, don't ye know?" he said, overly exuberant and looking mostly at Kelsey. "We can take our time in walking now and enjoy the fine weather!"

Even as Mickey landed, his joyous façade slipped and he cast a concerned look back up the trail. Gary understood then why the leprechaun had suddenly acted so full of cheer—for Kelsey's sake. And looking at the pained elf, Gary gave an approving nod to Mickey. Gary held the spear out before him, so that Kelsey might see it in all its reforged splendor. Kelsey's face did indeed brighten, and it seemed to Gary as if his elvish load lessened somewhat, as if some of the spring suddenly returned to Kelsey's step.

"And you'll go down in the legends," Gary remarked to Geno, vying to get the dwarf to join in the celebration, "as the dwarf who reforged the legendary spear."

He felt Geno's spittle splatter against the back of his leg and said no more. He thought again of the prospects of returning home, wondered if he would wake up in some white room with padded walls, or in his own bed, maybe, to learn that it had all been no more than a wistful dream.

His mind played the adventure, from Tir na n'Og to the Giant's Thumb, trying to hold on to the many sights he had seen, the wondrous smells, the fears and excitement. He should have reminded himself that he was a long way from home, a long way from Tir na n'Og even, and that the adventure had not yet ended.

Kelsey cried out in pain. Gary looked around the elf's slumping form to see a small hunk of moving rock, vaguely humanoid in shape, though less than half Gary's height, grabbing tightly at Kelsey's leg. Instinctively Gary released his hold on the elf, trying to use his leg to cushion Kelsey's inevitable fall, but more intent on readying his spear.

"Dwarf magic?" Gary cried out in disbelief. He jabbed the spear against the stone, wincing as it struck, for he feared that the rock might break it once again. Sparks flew as the metal tip connected, and Cedrick's spear slashed right through the stone, its magic blasting the curious little creature to a pile of rolling rubble.

"Dwarf magic?" Gary cried again, but when he looked to Geno, he knew how ridiculous his question, his accusation, must have sounded.

Several rock men surrounded the dwarf, clubbing and grabbing at his arms and legs. Geno's hammers smashed away, each swing sending large chips of his enemies flying.

"My sword!" Kelsey called weakly as more rocks suddenly animated along the sides of the trail and rushed in. Gary held the spear in both hands as he straddled the prone elf, knowing that Kelsey could not begin to defend himself.

"Mickey!" Gary yelled. He slashed and jabbed repeatedly and the air all around him became a shower of multicolored sparks.

"I cannot do a thing against them!" Mickey called back. Gary noticed the leprechaun, floating up in the air beneath his open umbrella, bending his curly-toed shoes under him to avoid the reaching grasp of still more of the creatures.

Metal rang on stone repeatedly, sparks filled the air, but the fearless creatures came on relentlessly, too many to beat back.

"Mickey!" Gary yelled again, fearing that Kelsey would soon be crunched.

A rock man slipped inside the wide swing of Gary's spear and bore down on the man and the elf. Gary had nowhere to run, nowhere to even back up enough to bring his spear to bear.

A single hammer stroke shattered the rock man into a hundred pieces.

Gary looked up from the pile of blasted stones to see Geno, wearing that wide one-tooth-missing, mischievous smile, wading through a sea of broken stones. Rock men closed in on the dwarf from both sides, and, "Bang! Bang!" the path around him was clear once more.

"They are just stones," Geno muttered, and to further display his superiority, he grabbed the limb of the closest creature and bit off its stubby rock fingers.

"What'd I tell ye about that one's meals, lad?" came Mickey's call from above, a sense of relief evident in the leprechaun's tone.

A hammer flew past Gary, connecting on a creature that had closed behind him.

"Keep them away from you," Geno instructed. "Play defensive and protect the elf." Geno smiled as another rock man came into range. He casually reached out and bashed it apart. "Just keep them back," he said to Gary again, "and let the dwarf do what a dwarf was born to do!"

Gary whipped his spear across in a wide arc, back and forth, slashing any of the rock men that strayed too near. Geno, true to his boastful promise, marched all about the perimeter of that area of sanctuary, seeming impervious to the creatures' stone-handed attacks and shattering every opponent with a single stroke. "You have to know where to hit them!" he said to Gary on one pass, tossing a playful wink. As if to accentuate his point, the dwarf absently launched a backhanded stroke that seemed to just nick another of the creatures.

It exploded and lay in a hundred pieces.

More of the area's rocks animated and fearlessly came in at the companions, but with Mickey up high guiding Geno's positioning, the creatures had no chance.

But then Gary felt the ground buck under his feet, as if the whole side of the mountain had shifted. He looked to Geno curiously for some answer, but the dwarf only shrugged his broad shoulders, having no more of an explanation than did Gary.

"Uh-oh," they heard Mickey mumble from above. The leprechaun stared numbly and pointed back along the trail. Gary and Geno, too, dropped open their mouths when they looked back, looked back at the huge slab of humanoid-shaped stone rising up, fifty feet away but still towering over the companions.

"Lead on!" Gary cried to Geno. He grabbed Kelsey roughly and slung the elf right over his shoulder as Geno rushed by, the dwarf, obviously as frightened as Gary, frantically clearing the path ahead of the smaller rock men.

The ground shook with the thunder of a gigantic footstep; Gary didn't have to look over his shoulder to know that the stone behemoth was close behind.

"Do you know where to hit that one? Gary cried to Geno.

"Even if I did, I could never reach the spot!" the dwarf roared back.

Another small rock man appeared in the path ahead of Geno's frantic rush; another rock man disappeared into a pile of broken stones.

"Only one thing stupider than blocking a dwarf's charge," Mickey explained to Gary, floating down near to Gary's shoulder.

"What's that?" Gary had to ask, realizing that Mickey would wait all day for the correct prompt. Another rock man rose before Geno, lifting its arms threateningly for the split second it took the dwarf to reduce it to a pile of rubble.

"Blocking a dwarf's retreat," Mickey answered dryly. Gary shook his head and looked over Kelsey's form to regard the leprechaun. He appreciated Mickey's humor at that dark time, but he noticed that Mickey, glancing back at the pursuing behemoth, did not wear a smile.

Geno continued to keep the path clear before them, cutting a wide swath along the trail, even smashing apart some boulders that showed no signs of animating. But even on a smooth and clear path, Gary, burdened by Kelsey, could not hope to outrun the stone giant.

"*Thou must not throw me!*" came an emphatic cry from the sentient spear, sensing Gary's intent.

Gary didn't bother to answer. When he came to a small climb in the trail—not too great an obstacle, but certainly one that would slow him more than it would slow the pursuing giant—he turned about and lifted the mighty spear in one hand.

"*I am the cause!*" Cedric's spear protested. "*I must be protected!*"

"You've got that backwards," Gary muttered. He aimed for the approaching giant's chest, then realized that the minuscule weapon, powerful though it was, would probably not even penetrate that thick slab deeply enough to affect the monster.

Gary lowered the angle and heaved. The balanced spear's flight was true and the magical tip buried deep in the stone giant's knee. Great cracks appeared around the vibrating shaft, encircling the whole of the giant's leg. The monster stopped its advance and swayed dangerously.

Gary turned and fled.

"You cannot . . . leave . . . the spear," Kelsey, on the verge of unconsciousness, implored him.

"You want to go and get it?" was Gary's immediate reply. He trotted more easily now, trying to keep Kelsey's ride less bumpy and thinking the giant left behind. But then there came a tremendous crash, followed a moment later by another. Gary looked back to see the giant once again in pursuit, hopping across great distances on its one good leg.

"Damn!" Gary spat, and he put his head down and ran on.

"*I warned thee,*" came a distant call in his mind, a reminder that now he had no weapon at all.

Gary was still looking more behind him than in front when he heard Geno cry out in surprise. He glanced ahead to see another gigantic form rushing over to them. At first Gary thought them doomed, thought that another animated stone giant had cut off their retreat. This second form moved right past the companions, though, lowering its broad shoulders and charging headlong into the pursuing giant.

"Tommy!"

Tommy was not nearly as large as the stone giant, and, of course, just a fraction of the animated monster's weight. But the bigger giant was unbalanced with its wounded leg and did not react quickly enough to brace itself against Tommy's powerful shoulder tackle.

The two behemoths tumbled down in an avalanche of flesh and stone, breaking apart the rocks all about them.

"Keep running!" came Geno's cry from in front, but Gary ignored the call. He gently laid Kelsey to the ground and headed back the other way.

"No, lad," Mickey called behind him.

"Oh, begorra," the leprechaun added as Geno, too, rushed by, going to the aid of his friends and spitting curses with every step.

The instant Gary got his hands around the shaft of Cedric's spear, he wondered how smart he had been in returning. The movements of the wrestling giants whipped the shaft every which way—Gary got it in the face once, and only his helmet prevented the blow from splitting his skull. To his own amazement, he did manage to pull the spear free, and he stumbled back a few steps, looking for a vital target.

Geno was already hard at work on the stone giant's shoulder, cracking apart one of the arms squeezing Tommy. Fortunately Tommy was on top of the larger giant; Tommy would have no doubt been crushed if the stone monstrosity had come down on top of him. Still, the giant's constricting arms worked hard on poor Tommy, who could not hope to draw breath under that brutal assault.

Gary danced and dodged, keeping clear of the flailing feet. He poked the spear in whenever he could, but knew that his halfhearted attacks were doing little damage.

Down the path, Mickey cried out, and Gary heard the twang of a bowstring. He looked up to see the leprechaun and the elf huddled under a virtual rain of black-winged crows. Kelsey lay on his back, swiping across with his longbow to keep the birds away and trying to notch another arrow amidst the chaos. Mickey crouched low next to the elf, his umbrella an impromptu shield above him.

"Run on!" the dwarf instructed Gary when the stone giant's arm finally broke free.

Gary rushed off, pausing to jab his spear once into the stone giant's other knee. A hammer spun past him as he bore down on the flock, taking down two birds in its flight.

By the time Gary got close enough to skewer one squawking bird, three more of Geno's hammers had crashed through, showering the area in black feathers.

Free from the immediate assault, Kelsey managed to fire off a few effective bow shots.

But the crows were not alone; more rocks animated and moved in on the group.

"Robert's word isn't so good," Gary grumbled.

Mickey started to reply, to correct Gary, then changed his mind. The leprechaun knew that only the dwarfs of Faerie and one other person, a certain witch, could animate stones so effectively, and Mickey understood the significance of crows flying near to Robert's mountain.

Gary grabbed Kelsey by the arm and got him to his feet as Geno intercepted the approaching stone men.

"Take the helmet," Gary offered, and before Kelsey could begin to protest, he plopped it over the elf's head and moved Kelsey along.

The chase was on once more, even more miserable now with crows pecking and scratching at Gary's face and eyes every step of the way. Mickey found a perch below Gary's shoulder, sheltered by Kelsey's leaning form.

How convenient for him, Gary thought, brushing away a nagging crow.

Something smaller and much swifter than a crow zipped past Gary's head. He looked around to see a falcon tear through the crow pack, emerging with one blackbird in its deadly clutches.

Another bird of prey rushed by, and then another.

"Falcons?" Gary whispered. It didn't make any sense. And when something didn't make any sense, Gary could be relatively certain that Mickey was involved.

"I've always been partial to hunting birds," the leprechaun remarked. His illusion proved quite effective in driving off the flock, and Geno soon had the situation of new rock men fully under control, his crunching hammers battering them to littler and littler pieces.

Even more good news came a moment later as Tommy lumbered down the path, finally free of the stone giant's stubborn grasp, and with no pursuit evident behind him. Limping, the giant still had no trouble catching up with the companions. He came up beside Gary and gently hoisted Kelsey into his great arms, cradling the wounded elf before him.

Gary clenched a fist in victory; all about them the enemy ranks dissipated and fell away altogether.

Mickey was not so exuberant. Nor was the leprechaun overly surprised when they turned a bend in the mountain trail and came face-to-face with a fuming Ceridwen.

TWENTY-FIVE
End of the Road

GARY heard a small, resigned sigh escape Mickey's lips as the leprechaun turned himself invisible. Gary honestly couldn't blame the leprechaun for his tactical retreat. Looking at Ceridwen, beautiful and terrible all at once in her black gossamer gown, and standing on a ledge against the mountain wall, high enough up so that she seemed to tower over even Tommy, Gary knew that they were doomed.

"Well, giant, what have you to say for your treachery?" the witch hissed evenly. Tommy blanched and trembled so violently that Gary thought the giant would surely fall right over and grovel on the path.

Kelsey pulled free of Tommy's weakened grasp and dropped to the ground, somehow finding the strength to get to his feet and move in at the witch. The elf pulled himself up straight and proud before the evil sorceress, drawing out his magical sword.

"This is none of yer affair!" he growled.

Ceridwen laughed so hard that tears streamed down her porcelain-white cheeks. She snapped her fingers and Kelsey vanished—or at least Mickey's illusion of Kelsey vanished. Gary saw the real elf then, on the ground and crawling doggedly, stubbornly, towards the witch.

Ceridwen paid him no heed. She snapped her fingers again and Mickey reappeared, off to the side of the trail now, sitting atop a flat boulder.

"It was worth the try," the leprechaun remarked, trying to appear unconcerned. He pulled out his pipe and tapped it on the stone.

Ceridwen seemed amused as she watched his movements.

"Ye cannot win, ye know," Mickey went on absently. "For all yer tricks and all yer traps, the spear is whole again. Even yerself cannot break it."

Ceridwen's smile faded, replaced by a glare so cold that it stopped Gary's heart in midbeat.

"That is of no matter," the raven-haired witch replied. "The spear is forged, but it will not be seen again in the wide realm of Faerie."

"Empty promises," Mickey answered, conjuring a tiny flame above his fingers. He took a long and easy draw on his pipe as he lit it. "The word will get out—ye know it will. Once the people of Faerie know that the spear is whole again, they'll play up against King Kinnemore. They'll force his hand and tell him to go and find the thing."

Ceridwen smiled confidently and shrugged. "And so the King will begin a search, and so will the finest knights of the land. But will they come to Ynis Gwydrin? And if they do, do you really believe that they will ever leave?" She looked down to regard Kelsey then, still stubbornly crawling towards her and muttering breathless curses with the little air his injured body could draw.

Mickey returned the witch's shrug, but stopped short of smiling. "But the word will be out," he said. "'The spear is whole!' they'll cry in the streets of Dilnamarra. 'The spear is whole!' they'll whisper in Connacht, through the halls of yer puppet King's own castle. And the Tylwyth Teg, Lady; let us not forget the fair folk of Tir na n'Og. Kelsey's quest is fulfilled. When his kin hear the word, and hear of yer interference, they're sure to unite against ye. They're a tolerant bunch, the Tylwyth Teg, but I'm not for getting them angered at me!"

Ceridwen laughed again, this time an evil cackle. "Then none shall return to deliver that word!" she retorted.

"Damn you!" cried Kelsey, defiantly tucking his feet under him and hurling himself the remaining distance to the witch. His sword flashed across Ceridwen's face, but the stroke didn't even turn Ceridwen's head to the side, had no more effect than to heighten the witch's mocking laughter. Bravely, stupidly, his rage beyond reason, Kelsey drove his sword in again, this time point-first.

Ceridwen caught the blade in her bare hand and held it before her, motionless.

"I have already told you, foolish elf," the witch explained. "Your weapons, even weapons forged by the magic of the Tylwyth Teg, cannot bring harm to me." She released her hold on Kelsey's sword suddenly and slapped the elf across the face with an easy backhand motion that launched Kelsey through the air. He flew a dozen feet, crashing down heavily against the mountain wall, where he crumpled and lay very still.

"Stonebubbles!" Geno roared. "How will you do against my weapons, filthy witch?" The dwarf banged his hammers together and drew back as if he meant to launch them.

A simple wave of Ceridwen's hand loosed a huge slab of rock right above Geno's head.

The dwarf immediately dropped his hammers and managed to get his hands up in time to catch the falling stone. But though he broke the slab's initial momentum, this hunk of rock was too large even for Geno to handle. He stood under it, his legs and arms trembling violently under the tremendous strain.

"How ironic that a dwarf of Dvergamal would die so!" the witch cackled. "A dwarf crushed by a stone! Such a fitting end!"

Gary looked to Geno, to Kelsey, not knowing where he should begin to help.

"Keep still, lad," Mickey whispered to him, coming back to his side and apparently guessing his intent to act. "We'll try to get her to accept a surrender."

Gary wanted to scream "No!" a thousand times in the leprechaun's face, a million times in Ceridwen's face. So many obstacles had been overcome—poor Kelsey should not die knowing that his life-quest had failed, after all. But Gary saw no other course, saw no way to harm the terrible witch.

"Ye must be desperate to come so near to Robert's mountain," Mickey reasoned, trying to make some headway in his discussion with the obstinate sorceress. "Even sending crows—yer calling card if ever ye had one. I'm not thinking that Robert likes having ye about."

"But you have fixed that for me already, haven't you, leprechaun?" Ceridwen spat back. "The spear is forged; thus, the dragon lost the challenge. A hundred years is it, before Robert might emerge from his castle?"

Mickey thought fast to get around the logic trap. "But his minions," the leprechaun started to reply.

Ceridwen's renewed laughter cut him short. "Lava newts?" she scoffed. "And what else, leprechaun? Do tell me. What other mighty minions has Robert the Ridiculous prepared to drive me off?"

"This isn't going to be easy," Mickey muttered to Gary.

"You have done so much for me," the witch went on, ignoring Mickey's remark. "Delivered the forged spear and banished Robert for a hundred years. A hundred years! The Crahgs will again be mine, decades before the dragon can even step out of his castle once more to challenge me."

"So let us go and we'll call it even," Gary remarked.

Ceridwen's smile disappeared in the blink of an eye. "Let you go?" she muttered incredulously.

"If we have done so well by you," Gary began.

"Silence!" the witch roared. "Anything you have done to aid me, you have done inadvertently. I have not forgotten your disobedience." She looked directly at Tommy as she said this and Tommy suddenly didn't seem so large to Gary.

"You were told to remain on Ynis Gwydrin," the witch fumed. "Yet I returned to find my guests gone!"

"Ye must admit that the lad was resourceful in finding a way through yer spell," Mickey put in, in the hopes that Ceridwen would think it better to keep Gary alive and at her side.

If she even heard the leprechaun's words, she made no indication of it. "Gone!" she growled again, her ire rising dangerously.

"And you, giant," she spat. "I took you in and gave you a home! This is how you repay me?" She waggled one finger and a small flame appeared atop it, dancing in the air, growing hotter and larger. "I will burn the skin from your bones, ungrateful beast," the witch promised. "And feed you to my goblins, more loyal by far."

What a pitiful thing Tommy One-Thumb now seemed. The giant who had casually tossed a mountain troll through the air, who had charged fearlessly into the grasp of a stone behemoth much larger than he, fell to his knees before the threats of the sorceress. He tried to speak out, but only undecipherable blabber came past his trembling lips.

Ceridwen snapped her fingers and a burst of flame appeared next to Tommy's head, singeing his hair. He slapped at it wildly, began to blubber and scream out his pleas.

"He hasn't hurt anyone," Gary breathed.

"Easy, lad," implored the leprechaun. "We're not wanting to share a similar fate. We'll go for the surrender."

A sudden thought came over the outraged man. He looked at Mickey, his lips curling into a wicked smile. "Who made the spear?"

Mickey shrugged, seeming confused.

"That's what I thought," Gary replied. There was more to Ceridwen's desires to have the spear than any fears she might hold for the feelings and heroic recollections of her pitiful and unwitting subjects.

"Wait!" Gary cried at Ceridwen, to Mickey's dismay. "You came to retrieve the spear, and it is mine to give." He held the spear out before him, ignoring its sudden stream of telepathic protests. "We overcame so many obstacles to re-forge this weapon, many of them inspired by you, no doubt. But we did it, and Kelsey, brave Kelsey, faced down the dragon—fairly. But for all its value, this piece of metal is not worth the lives of my friends."

"Give it to me!" Ceridwen roared, verily drooling at the sight of the magnificent weapon.

"*Yes, do,*" agreed the spear, suddenly satisfied.

Ceridwen's icy-blue eyes widened in surprise as Gary drew back the spear, his face contorted suddenly in open hatred. The witch waved her hand, sending a blast of fire rolling out from her fingers towards the threat.

"No, lad!" Mickey cried, trying to scramble away.

Gary's scream came from the pit of his stomach, emanated from every muscle and every nerve in his entire body. All of his anger, all of his frustration, strengthened his movements as he hurled the mighty weapon. The spear dove into the flames, just a few feet away from Gary by then, and disappeared behind the orange and smoke-gray ball.

The witch's fires blew away the instant before they engulfed both Gary and Mickey, and when the flames were gone, the companions looked again upon Ceridwen, the spear through her belly, pinning her to the mountain wall. Horrified, the witch grasped at the quivering shaft with hands that hadn't the strength to even close about it.

Vile blackness flowed out from the wound, spreading across the witch's gown and down her bare arms.

"I shall repay you!" she spat at Gary, a hollow threat as the blackness spread up her neck and over her face. Her mouth contorted in a silent scream, her hands still trembled over the vibrating shaft of black metal.

Then Ceridwen seemed no more than a shadow against the wall. Gary could see the back of the spear's tip, buried deeply in the stone.

"Would ye look at that?" Mickey gasped.

Ceridwen's final, agonized scream split the air, then there was only the mourn of the wind, and the spear, and the marked stone, covered still, covered forever, by the witch's shadow.

"How did ye know?" Mickey asked Gary.

Gary shrugged. "I did not," he answered honestly. "But Robert claimed that no fires wrought by mortal hands could soften the blade. If he spoke truly . . ."

"Ah, what a fine lad ye are," Mickey chuckled.

Gary looked down at the leprechaun, his green eyes catching Mickey's in a wistful gaze. "I did not know," he said again. "But I had to believe."

"If you are done with your congratulating over there . . . ," came a strained call from behind. The startled companions turned to see Geno, his bandy legs finally beginning to bend under the tremendous weight of the fallen slab.

Tommy got to the dwarf first and, with Gary and Geno's help, managed to angle the slab to the side, away from the dwarf, where they let it crash down to the path.

"Lad!" Mickey called from across the trail. They turned to see Kelsey, struggling to his feet with the leprechaun's diminutive support. Gary rushed over and hooked Kelsey's arm over his shoulder.

The elf was surely wounded and surely exhausted, but, looking at the luster in his golden eyes as he regarded the spear, hanging still in the bare stone, it was obvious that he would survive and heal well.

"Ding dong, the witch is dead?" Gary offered hopefully, bringing a smile to Kelsey's bloodied lips.

"Not dead, lad," Mickey corrected. "But she'll do a hundred years on Ynis Gwydrin before she finds her way back out again, and a better land it'll be with both Ceridwen and Robert out of the way!"

"THERE goes the last buckle for this leg," Mickey said to comfort Gary as the leprechaun helped the man strip out of the bulky armor. Dilnamarra was in sight; the companions had come to the end of their long road.

"Where is the damned elf?" Geno muttered, not happy at all about the unexpected delay. They had come into the region many hours before, but Kelsey,
seeing an uncommon number of king's soldiers milling about, had determined
that they would wait outside of the town, hidden by a large hedgerow, (it had to
be a large one, since Tommy was still with them) until he could determine what
was going on. Taking the guise of one of the many beggars of the pitiful region,
the elf had slipped out into the fading daylight.

"Another one," Mickey declared, loosening the buckle low on Gary's back. The
leprechaun noticed something curious then, and after a moment's consideration,
he quietly lifted an item from Gary's belt and slipped it under his own cloak.

"Damned elf," spat Geno, paying no heed to either Mickey or Gary. Geno
had actually been quite hospitable after the defeat of the witch, on the uneventful road home north around the dreaded Crahgs, down a narrow pass between
them and Dvergamal. But then Kelsey had informed the dwarf that he would
not be released straight to his mountain home, that he would have to accompany the group all the way to Dilnamarra in case there arose a question concerning the authenticity of the forging.

A movement to the side turned all of them about. They relaxed immediately, recognizing the slender form of Kelsey.

"King's guards," he confirmed. "All about the keep. It would seem that I
am an outlaw, as are you, Gary Leger, and you as well, leprechaun, if they ever
figure out that it was you posing as a babe in Gary's arms when we procured the
items."

"They gave us the armor freely," Gary protested.

"Aye," Mickey agreed. "But then me illusion on the King's edict went away
and Prince Geldion realized the truth."

Kelsey nodded his confirmation.

"How long, then?" Geno interrupted gruffly. "I've a hundred contracts to
fulfill before the first snows of winter!"

Kelsey honestly had no answer for the dwarf. "Baron Pwyll remains in
charge only of his keep," he explained. "The outlying lands are heavily guarded.
I do not know how we might get through to deliver the forged spear."

A moment of silence hung about them as they privately considered their
options.

"But if we did get the spear to Pwyll," Gary prompted, "then what?"

"Geldion'd not be a happy sort," Mickey replied.

"But likely there would be little that the Prince could do," reasoned Kelsey.
"With the spear in his possession and the armor and shield returned, Baron

Pwyll would prove that he was in the right in giving the items to me. The truth would free Pwyll of Geldion's evil grasp."

"Then let Geno deliver it," Gary said casually.

Geno glowered Gary's way.

"They're looking for a man, an elf, and a leprechaun, not a dwarf," Gary reasoned. "Disguise the items and let Geno walk them right into Baron Pwyll."

"It might work," Mickey muttered. "Geno leading a burdened mule, bearing pots"—he held up the helmet of Donigarten, suddenly appearing as a rather beat-up old cooking pot—"and other items less interesting to Geldion than a magical spear and a suit of mail."

"Mule?" Kelsey and Geno remarked together.

"Come here, would ye now?" Mickey asked Tommy. "And kneel down on all fours—there's a good giant."

Geno snickered. "This might be worth the trouble," he said. "And then I am free to return to my home?"

Kelsey looked around and then, seeing no problems, nodded.

"Tommy does not like this," the giant put in, finally figuring out his equine role in the deception.

"Aw, it'll be fine," Mickey assured him.

"That it will," Geno added, giving Tommy a look of sincere confidence. "I will watch out for you. And when we're done, you come along with me to Dvergamal. There are many holes in my mountains. I will find you a proper place for a giant to live—not too near to my people, you understand!"

Tommy's face brightened and he assumed his best mule posture, waiting for Mickey to work another of his tricks.

A few moments later the dwarf tradesman and his pack mule set off, passing through the many guards who indeed were not so concerned with the "mundane" items Geno carried.

"NEVER did I expect so much of you," Kelsey admitted when he, Mickey, and Gary came to the great oak tree of Tir na n'Og, the very spot where the elf had first met Gary Leger. Kelsey cast an amused look up the tree, to the lair of Leshiye.

Gary agreed fully with the elf's observations. He, too, recalled that first meeting, where Kelsey had stolen him away from his pleasure. It had been an auspicious beginning, to be sure, but now that the adventure had ended, neither would deny their friendship, publicly or privately.

"I am glad that your quest went so well," Gary replied. "And I hope that Ceridwen's fears concerning Cedric's spear prove well founded. The people of Dilnamarra could use a new attitude."

Kelsey nodded, patted Gary on the shoulder, and took his leave, disappearing into the darkness of the thick forest underbrush so quickly and so completely that Gary almost had to wonder if the elf had ever really been there.

"Are ye ready, lad?" Mickey asked. "The pixies'll be dancing in the blueberry patch; I can get ye home this very night."

Gary cast another longing gaze up Leshiye's tree. "Another hour?" he asked, half-serious.

"Don't ye be pushing yer luck," came Mickey's warning. "It's time for ye to get back to yer own place."

Gary shrugged and moved away from the tree. "Lead on, then," he said, but in his heart he wasn't so sure that he ever wanted to return home.

Gary said little on their trek back through Tir na n'Og to the blueberry patch. He wondered again what his return trip might be like. Would he simply awaken, in his own bed, perhaps? Or would he come out of a delusion to the startlement of those concerned people around him?

Truthfully Gary didn't believe either explanation; they seemed no less strained to him than to simply accept what had happened as reality.

But wasn't that exactly what an insane person might believe? Disturbing questions, questions of reality itself, nagged at Gary, but he found he had no time then to contemplate them. Blueberry bushes were all about him, and in sight, too, was the small ring of light within the joyful and mysterious dance of the tiny fairies.

He cast a final look to Dvergamal, where the moon was coming up behind the great and stony peaks. And then, on Mickey's nod, he stepped into the faerie ring.

As soon as Gary had melted away into the enchanted night, Mickey McMickey pulled a curious item out from under his cloak: a jeweled dagger, ancient and marvelously crafted, that Gary Leger must have inadvertently taken from Robert's castle.

The implications of the theft, inadvertent or not, were quite grave, but Mickey tried not to view things that way.

He wondered now how he might use this unfortunate twist to his advantage in his quest to retrieve his bartered pot of gold from the treasure hoard of the wicked wyrm.

Epilogue

GARY Leger groaned as he rolled over on the scratchy ground, prickly bushes picking at him from every angle. He managed to roll to a sitting position, smelling blueberries all around him, but it took him some time to figure out where he was. Images of sprites and elfs, dragons and bandy-legged dwarfs, danced all about his consciousness, just out of his reach.

"So it was just a dream," he remarked, trying to hold on to at least a part of the grand adventure. But like any dream, the images were fleeting at best, and entire sections were missing or out of place. He remembered the general details, though, something about a spear and a horrendous dragon. And wearing armor—Gary distinctly remembered the sensation of wearing the armor.

Gary looked down to his side, saw *The Hobbit* lying on the ground next to him, and knew what had inspired his evening adventure.

He realized then that he had missed supper; he worried then how many hours (days?) had passed. Gary blinked at that thought and looked around him, studying the landscape beneath the light of the rising moon. Yes, he was in the woods out back, not in Tir na n'Og.

"Tir na n'Og?" he mumbled curiously. How did he know that name?

Confused beyond any hopes of sorting it all out, Gary scooped up his book and struggled to his feet. He started down the path to the fire road, but changed direction and went across the blueberry patch instead, to the ridge overlooking . . .

Overlooking what?

Gary crept up, alternating his gaze from the widening landscape beneath him to the distant hills.

Hills, he thought, not mountains, and dotted with the lights of many houses.

Still, Gary held his breath as he came to the lip of the small hill, and was then sincerely relieved—and also, somehow sincerely disappointed.

Southeast Elementary School.

"Some dream," he mumbled to himself, sprinting back as fast as he dared to go in the dim light towards the fire road. More sights, familiar sights, greeted him as he rushed along: the cemetery fence; the houses at the end of his parents' street; and then his own Jeep, sitting under the streetlight in front of the hedgerow.

"Where the hell have you been?" his father asked him when he burst through the kitchen door. The remnants of supper sat on the stove and counter. "You'll have to reheat it."

"Reheat it?" Gary muttered curiously, an image of a spear flashing through his mind, and white flames licking at him around the edges of a fine shield.

"Yeah, it got cold. You'll have to heat it up again," his father said sarcastically.

"Hey, I cooked it once," his mother, playing solitaire at the dining room table, added sternly. "If you can't be in on time for . . ."

"You won't believe this," Gary interrupted. "I fell asleep down in the woods."

"Fell asleep?" his father asked with a snicker.

"You're working too hard," his mother piped in, suddenly the concerned hen once more. She shook her head and gritted her teeth. "I hate that place."

It all seemed so very commonplace to Gary, so very predictable—say the seventeen words, Mom. He hadn't been gone a very long time; he was amazed that he had encapsulated so wild an adventure in so short a nap.

He grabbed a quick bite and went up to bed, announcing that he needed the sleep, and also privately hoping to recapture some of that strange dream. Honestly Gary didn't know how he was going to drag himself out of bed the next morning, how he was going to go back to the mundane realities of life around him, back to the grind.

"Well," he told himself, slipping out of his clothes and falling onto his bed, "at least I'll have something new to think about while I'm loading those chunks into the grinder."

Almost as an afterthought, Gary took up *The Hobbit*, opening it to mark the spot where he had left off.

His eyes nearly popped from their sockets.

For Gary Leger looked upon not the expected typeset of a paperback, but upon the strange and flowing script of Mickey McMickey.

THE
DRAGON'S DAGGER

Prelude

KELSEY the elf ran his slender fingers through his shoulder-length, pure golden hair many times, his equally golden eyes unblinking as he stared at the empty pedestal in Dilnamarra Keep.

The empty pedestal!

Only a month before, Kelsey had returned the armor and reforged spear of Cedric Donigarten, Faerie's greatest hero, to this very spot. What pains the elf had gone through to repair that long-broken spear! The reforging had been Kelsey's life quest, the greatest trial for any member of Tylwyth Teg, the fair elven folk of the Forest Tir na n'Og. Kelsey still carried the wounds of his challenge against mighty Robert, the dreaded dragon, the only creature in all the land who could billow fire hot enough to bind the magical metal of that legendary weapon.

And now, with word just beginning to spread throughout the countryside that the spear was whole once more, the mighty weapon and the fabulous armor were simply gone.

Baron Pwyll entered his throne room through a door at the back of the hall, escorted by several worried-looking soldiers. Nearly a foot taller than Kelsey and easily twice the elf's weight, the big man, gray beard flying wild (Kelsey knew that the Baron had been pulling at it, as was his habit when he was upset), ambled to his seat and plopped down, seeming to deflate and meld with the cushions.

"Do you know anything?" he asked Kelsey, his normally booming voice subdued.

"I know that the items, the items which I placed in your care, are missing," Kelsey snapped back. A hint of anger flashed in Pwyll's brown eyes, his droopy eyelids rising up dangerously. He did not immediately reply, though, and that fact made Kelsey even more fearful that something dreadful had happened, or was about to happen.

"What is it?" the elf prompted, instinctively understanding that the Baron was withholding some important news.

"Geldion is on his way from Connacht," Pwyll replied, referring to the up-start Prince of Faerie, by Kelsey's estimation the most dangerous man in all the land. "With a score of soldiers, a knight included, at his side," Pwyll finished.

"Geldion could not have already heard that the items are missing," Kelsey reasoned.

"No," Pwyll agreed. "But he, and his father—long live the King"—Pwyll added quickly, and glanced around to see if any of his own men was wearing a suspicious expression—"have heard that the spear was reforged. It seems that Kinn . . . King Kinnemore has decreed that the treasure rooms of Connacht would serve better as a shrine for so valuable an artifact."

"Cedric Donigarten's own will bequeathed the items to Dilnamarra," Kelsey protested, against Pwyll's dismissing wave. "You have the documents, legally signed and sealed. Kinnemore cannot . . ."

"I do not fear the legal battle about the placement of the items," Pwyll interrupted. The Baron grabbed at his beard and tugged hard, leaving a kinky gray strand hanging far out to the side of his huge face. "King Kinnemore, even that wretched Geldion, would tread with care before removing the spear, or the armor. But do you not understand? I thought that they had already stolen it, and the fact that Geldion is only now on his way, fully announced, confuses the facts."

"A cover for the theft?" Kelsey reasoned.

"Do you believe Geldion to be that clever?" Baron Pwyll replied dryly.

Kelsey sent his graceful hands through his golden hair once more, turned his questioning gaze to the empty pedestal. If not Kinnemore, than who might have taken the items? the elf wondered. Robert had been defeated, banished by unyielding rules of challenge to remain in his castle for a hundred years. Similarly, the witch Ceridwen had been banished to her island, defeated by the reforged spear itself. No doubt, the conniving witch could still cause havoc, but Kelsey did not think that Ceridwen had had time yet to muster her forces—unless she was working through her puppet king in Connacht.

A clamor by the main door, several groans and the sound of someone spitting, turned Kelsey around. Five soldiers entered, bearing a short and stout character, tied—ankles and wrists, knees and elbows, and neck and waist—to two heavy wooden poles. The dwarf—for it was, of course, a dwarf, though he did not wear the beard typical of his folk—twisted stubbornly every step of the way, forcing his head to the side so that he could line up another man for a stream of gravelly spit.

None of the soldiers seemed overly pleased, and all of them carried more than a few hammer-sized dents in their metal armor.

"My Baron," one of them began, but he stopped abruptly as a wad of spit slapped against the side of his face. He turned and raised his fist threateningly at the dwarf, who smiled an impish smile and spat another stream into the man's eye.

"Cut him down!" the frustrated Baron cried.

"Yes, my Baron!" one of the soldiers eagerly responded, snapping his great sword from its sheath. He turned on the dwarf and brought the weapon up high, lining up the bound prisoner's exposed head, but suddenly Kelsey was between him and his target, the elf's slender sword at the soldier's throat.

"I believe that your Baron meant for you to free the dwarf," the elf explained. The soldier looked at Pwyll, a horrified expression on his face, then blushed and slid his weapon away.

"We cannot free him, my Baron," said the first soldier as he continued to wipe his face. "I fear for your safety."

"There are five armed soldiers around the damned dwarf!" Pwyll replied, tugging at his beard.

The soldier gave the dangerous prisoner a sidelong glance.

"And there were twenty in Braemar!" the dwarf bellowed. "So do let me down, I beg."

Pwyll's big face screwed up as he regarded his troops. He had indeed sent a score of soldiers to the town of Braemar in search of Geno Hammerthrower.

"The others will return to Dilnamarra after their wounds have healed enough to permit travel," the soldier admitted.

Pwyll looked to Kelsey, who turned about and promptly sliced the thongs holding Geno to the pole. Down crashed the dwarf, but he bounced back to his feet immediately and slapped a fist into his open palm.

"I was not among the score of men you battled in Braemar," Kelsey quickly and grimly reminded Geno. "You will cause no further ruckus in Dilnamarra Keep."

Geno held the elf's unyielding stare for a long while, then shrugged, pushed his straight brown hair back from his rough-hewn but strangely cherubic face, and smiled that mischievous grin once more. "Then give me back my hammers," he said.

Kelsey nodded to one of the soldiers, who immediately put his hand on a bandolier lined with a dozen heavy hammers. The man retracted the hand at once, though, and looked from smiling Geno to Baron Pwyll.

"Do it!" Kelsey demanded before the Baron could respond, and so great was the respect carried by the Tylwyth Teg that the soldier had the bandolier off his shoulder and over to Geno in an instant.

Geno pulled a hammer from the wide strap and sent it spinning up into the air. He casually draped the strap over one shoulder, then put his thick hand out at precisely the right moment to catch the descending hammer.

"My thanks, elf," the dwarf said. "But do not presume this capture to mean I owe you anything. You know the rules of indenture as well as I, and twenty against one doesn't make for a fair catch."

"You were not brought back for any indenture," Kelsey explained, and Geno, despite his taciturn façade, let out a profound sigh of relief. The dwarf was reputably the finest smithy in all the land of Faerie, and as such, was almost constantly fending off capture attempts from Barons or wealthy merchants, or simply upstart would-be heroes, all wanting him to craft the "finest weapon in the world."

"The armor and spear are missing," Baron Pwyll added rather sharply, leaning forward in his chair as though he had just placed an accusation at the dwarf's feet. The blustery man backed off on his imposing stance immediately, though, when Geno's scowl returned tenfold.

"Are you accusing me of taking them?" the dwarf asked bluntly.

"No, no," Kelsey quickly put in, fearing one of Geno's volatile explosions. It occurred to the elf for a fleeting instant that his gesture of trust to the dangerous dwarf by giving him back his hammer supply might not have been such a wise thing. "We are merely investigating the matter," he went on calmly. "We thought that you, as the smithy who reforged the spear, should be alerted."

"We are simply trying to solve a mystery here," Pwyll said calmly, wise enough to understand the prudence of following Kelsey's lead. "You most certainly are not suspected of any wrongdoing." The statement wasn't exactly true, but Pwyll thought it an important diplomatic move, one that might keep a hurled hammer off his head.

"Your men could have asked," Geno said to Pwyll.

"We did . . ." the spit-covered soldier started to respond, but Pwyll's upraised hand and Geno's sudden grip on his nearest hammer shut the man up.

"Also, rest assured that you will be richly compensated for your assistance in this most important matter," the blustery Baron went on, trying to sound official.

Geno looked around doubtfully at the rather shabby dressings of the room. It was no secret in Faerie that since Kinnemore had become King, the wealth of the independent Baronies, particularly those such as Dilnamarra who did not play as puppets to Connacht, had greatly diminished. "Are the Tylwyth Teg paying?" Geno asked Kelsey, and the elf nodded gravely.

Baron Pwyll winced at the subtle insult. "Where is the giant?" he asked, referring to Tommy One-Thumb, the giant who had reportedly accompanied Kelsey and Geno on their quest to reforge the spear.

"You think I'd be fool enough to walk a giant into Dilnamarra Keep?" Geno balked. "How'd you ever get to be a Baron?"

Kelsey faded out of the conversation at that point, falling back into private contemplations of the unsettling events. Despite the impending arrival of Prince Geldion, he still suspected that King Kinnemore, on orders from wicked Ceridwen, was somehow behind the theft. The dragon Robert's hand was not as long as Ceridwen's, after all, and who else might have precipitated . . .

Kelsey's musings suddenly hit an unexpected wall and shot off in a different direction altogether, a direction that indicated that this theft might be more mischief and less malice. Who else, indeed?

MICKEY McMickey shifted his tam-o'-shanter and rested back easily against a tree trunk at the edge of a glade in the beautiful forest of Tir na n'Og. The leprechaun soon resumed his twiddling with a dagger that Gary Leger, the man from the other world, had inadvertently taken from the lair of Robert. Because of this dagger, because the companions had broken their agreement to the rules of challenge, the dragon's vow of banishment would not hold up to scrutiny.

Mickey's thoughts drifted to his precious pot of gold, bartered to Robert before the leprechaun had ever entered the dragon's lair. How dearly he missed it, and how weak his magical powers had become with the gold lost!

"Not to worry," the usually cheerful fellow said to himself. He looked over his shoulder, to the gorgeous artifacts, the armor and spear of Cedric Donigarten. "This'll bring 'em running."

Smart Bombs and M&Ms

FISCAL month end. Fun time for the finance group at General Components Corporation, a high-tech, high-pressure supplier for the giants of the computer industry. Gary Leger put a hand behind his sore neck and stretched way back in his chair, the first time he had been more than a foot from his terminal screen in over two hours. He looked around at the other cubicles in the common office and saw that everyone else had already gone to afternoon break, then looked up at the clock and realized that they would be back any minute.

Gary let out a profound sigh. He wanted a Coke, could really use the caffeine, but it was already three-thirty, and Rick needed this field service summary report finished before the management meeting at five. Gary looked back to the computer screen, and to the pile of notes—revenue plans, revenue forecasts, and actual monthly figures—sitting beside the terminal. He had to input the data for three more offices, a hundred numbers for each over two pages, then hit the space bar and hope everything added up correctly on the "totals" page.

Gary hated the data entry part of it, wished that Rick would fish out a few bucks from the budget to get him an assistant just one day a month. He loved the totaling, though, and the inevitable investigations that would follow, tracking down missing revenues and delinquent credits. Gary chuckled softly as he thought of the many television shows he had seen depicting accountants as wormy, boring individuals. Gary, too, had believed the stereotype—it had seemed to fit—until, following the trail of bigger bucks, he had inadvertently stumbled into a position as an accountant. His first month-end closing, filled with the seemingly impossible task of making the numbers fit into seemingly impossible places, had changed Gary's perception, had thrown the image of the job as "boring" right out the office window.

"You look tired," came Rick's voice from behind.

"Almost done," Gary promised without even looking over his shoulder. He stretched again and pulled the next office sheet off the pile.

"Did you get a break?" Rick asked, coming over and dropping a hand on Gary's shoulder, bending low to peer at the progress on the computer screen.

"At lunch."

"Go get one," said Rick, taking the paper from Gary's hand. He pushed Gary from his seat and slid into the chair. "And take your time."

Gary stood for a moment, looking doubtful. He wasn't one to dole out his work, was a perfectionist who liked to watch over the whole procedure from beginning to end.

"I think I can handle it," Rick remarked dryly over one shoulder, and Gary winced at the notion that he was so damned predictable. When he thought about Rick's answer to his doubts, he felt even more foolish. Rick, after all, had been the one who created this spreadsheet.

"Get going if you want a break," Rick said quietly.

Gary nodded and was off, crossing by his associates as they were coming back from the break room. Their talk, predictably, was on the war, detailing the latest bombing runs over the Arab capital, and describing how the enemy was "hunkering down," as the popular phrase went.

Gary just smiled as he passed them, exchanged friendly shoulder-punches with Tom, the cost accountant, and made his way quickly to the break room. Rick had told him to take his time, and Gary knew that Rick, always concerned for his employees, had meant every word. But Gary knew, too, that the report was his responsibility, and he meant to get it done.

Someone had brought a television into the break room, turned always to CNN and the continuing war coverage. A group was around the screen when Gary entered—hell, he thought, a group was always around the screen—watching the latest briefing, this one by the French commanders of the U.N. forces. Gary tried to phase it all out as the reporters assaulted the commanders with their typically stupid questions, most asking when the ground assault would begin.

Of course, they'll tell you the exact time, Gary thought sarcastically. Never mind that the enemy command was also tuned to CNN's continuing coverage.

Gary lucked out: it only took five quarters to coax a seventy-five-cent Coke out of the battered vending machine. He moved to a table far to the side of the TV screen and pulled up a chair. He took a pair of hand-grips from one pocket and began to squeeze, nodded admiringly at the ripples in his muscular forearm. Gary had always been in good shape, always been an athlete, but ever since his unexpected trip to the land of Faerie, he took working out much more seriously. In the land of dragons and leprechauns, Gary Leger had worn the armor and carried the weapon of an ancient hero, had battled goblins and trolls, even a dragon and an evil witch. He expected that he would go back to that enchanted land one day, wanted to go back dearly, and was determined that if the situation ever arose, his body at least would be ready for the challenge.

Yes, Gary Leger would like to go back to Faerie, and he would like to take Diane with him. Gary smiled at the notion of him and Diane sprinting across the thick grass of the rolling, boulder-strewn fields, possibly with a host of drooling goblins on their heels. The goblins would get close, but they wouldn't get the pair, Gary believed, not with friends like noble Kelsey and tricky Mickey McMickey on Gary's side.

The image of Faerie waned, leaving Gary to his more tangible thoughts of Diane. He had been dating her for only three months, but he was pretty sure that this was the woman he would eventually marry. That thought scared Gary more than a little, simply because of the anticipated permanence of the arrangement in a world where nothing seemed permanent.

He loved her, though. He knew that in his heart, and he could only hope that things would work out in their own, meandering course.

A couple of MIS guys, computer-heads, infiltrated the table next to Gary, one asking if he could borrow a chair from Gary's table, since most of the other chairs in the room had been dragged near to the TV screen.

"Friggin' war," one of them remarked, catching Gary's attention. "We're only fighting it so we don't realize how bad the economy's getting. Wave the flag and drop it over the balance sheet."

"No kidding," agreed the other. "They're talking layoffs at the end of Q3 if the Sporand deal doesn't go through."

"Everybody's laying off," said the first guy.

Gary phased out of the bleak conversation. It was true enough. The Baby Boomers, the Yuppies, seemed to have hit a wall. Credit had finally caught up to cash flow, and Gary constantly heard the complaints—usually from spoiled adults whining that their payments on their brand-new thirty-thousand-dollar car were too steep.

In spite of the few with no reason to complain, there was a general pall over the land, and rightly so. So many people were homeless, so many others living in substandard conditions. The gloom went even deeper than that, Gary Leger, the man who had visited the magical land of Faerie, knew well. The material generation had fallen off the edge of a spiritual rift; Gary's world had become one where nothing valid existed unless you could hold it in your hand.

Even the flag—drape it over the balance sheet—had become caught up in the turmoil, Gary noted with more than a little anger. The President had called for an amendment to the Constitution outlawing flag burning, because, appar-

ently, that tangible symbol had become more important than the ideals it supposedly symbolized. What scared Gary even more was how many people agreed
with the shallow thought, how many people couldn't understand that putting
restrictions on a symbol of freedom lessened the symbol rather than protected it.

Gary shook the thought away, filed it in his certainly soon to be ulcerous
stomach along with a million other frustrations.

At least his personal situation was better. He had to believe that. He had
come out of the dirty plastics factory into a respectable job earning twice the
money and offering him a chance to use more talents than his muscles on a day-
to-day basis. He had a steady girlfriend whom he cared for deeply—whom he
loved, though he still had trouble admitting that to himself. So everything was
fine, was perfect, for Gary Leger.

A burst of laughter from the gathering turned Gary to the television just in
time to see a truck, in the gunsights of a low-flying jet, race off a bridge an instant before a smart bomb blew the bridge into tiny pieces. The technology was
indeed amazing, kind of like a Nintendo game.

That thought, too, bothered Gary Leger more than a little.

He got caught up in the images as the press briefing continued, a French officer pointing to the screen and talking of the importance of this next target, a
bunker. A tiny figure raced across the black-and-white image, entering the bunker
a split-second before the smart bomb did its deadly work, reducing the place
to rubble.

"Poor man," the French officer said to a chorus of groans, both from the reporters at the press briefing and from the gathering around the TV at General
Components.

"Poor man?" Gary whispered incredulously. It wasn't that Gary held no
pity for the obviously killed enemy soldier. He held plenty, for that man and for
everyone else who was suffering in that desert mess. It just seemed so absolutely
ridiculous to him that the French officer, the reporters, and the gathering
around the screen seemed so remorseful, even surprised, that a human being
had been killed.

Did they really think that this whole thing *was* a damned Nintendo game?

Gary scooped up his Coke and left the break room, shaking his head with
every step. He thought of his mother, and her newest favorite cliché, "What's
this world coming to?"

How very appropriate that sounded now to Gary Leger, full of frustrations
he didn't understand, searching for something spiritual that seemed so out of
reach and out of place.

NESTLED in a mountain valley at the northeastern end of the mighty Dvergamal Mountains, the gnomish settlement of Gondabuggan was a normally peaceful place, lined with square stone shops filled with the most marvelous, if usually useless, inventions. Half the town was underground in smoothed-out burrows, the other half in squat buildings, more than half of which served as libraries or places of study. Peaceful and inquisitive; those were the two words which the gnomes themselves both considered the highest of compliments.

The Gondabuggan gnomes were far from the protection of Faerie's official militia, though, and far even from the help of the reclusive dwarfs who lived within the mountains. They had survived for centuries out here in the wild lands, and though certainly not warlike, they were not a helpless group.

Huge metallic umbrellas were now cranked up from every building, popping wide their deflective sheets and covering the whole of the gnomish town under a curtain of shining metal. Beneath the veil, great engines began turning, drawing water through a score of wide pipes from the nearby river and sending it shooting up into the air.

The dragon roared past, his flaming breath turning to steam as it crossed the spray and hit the wetted sheets of the umbrellas. Robert the mighty was not dismayed. He banked in a wide turn, confident that he could continue his fires long after the river itself had been emptied.

One of the umbrellas near to the center of the small, square town detracted suddenly and as Robert veered for that apparent opening, he heard the *whoosh!* of three catapults. The dragon didn't understand; the gnomes in that area couldn't even see him, so what were they shooting for?

Almost immediately, the umbrella snapped back into place, completing the shield once more.

Robert figured out the catapult mystery as he crossed through the area above that shield, as he crossed through the tiny bits of stinging metal chips the catapults had flung straight up into the air. Flakes ricocheted off the dragon's scales, stung his eyes, and melted in the heated areas of his flaring nostrils.

"Curses on the gnomes!" Robert roared, and his deadly breath spewed forth again. Those areas of metal shielding that were not sufficiently wetted glowed fiercely, and all the valley on the northeastern corner of Dvergamal filled with a thick veil of steam.

Robert heard several umbrellas retract, heard the sound of many catapults firing, and felt the sting of hanging metal all the way as he soared across the expanse above the protected town. The great wyrm banked again, arcing high and wide for several minutes, and then turned in a stoop, just a black speck on the misty southern horizon, but flying fast.

"Pedal! Oh, pedal, pedal, pedal!" Mugwiggen the gnome implored his Physical Assault Defense Team. A hundred gnomes on stationary bikes pumped their little legs furiously, their breath popping out in rhythmic huffs and puffs from the thin line of their mouths under their fully bearded faces. Sweat rolled down a hundred high-browed, gnomish foreheads, down a hundred long and pointy gnomish noses, to drip in widening puddles at the base of the spinning wheels.

Mugwiggen peered into his "highlooker," a long upright tube, hooked horizontally on each end, that could be rotated in complete circles. At the opposite end of the horizontal eyepiece was an angled reflective sheet, catching the images from a similar sheet near the top of the tube, that first caught the images from the horizontal top-piece. This gnomish periscope also featured several slots wherein magnifying lenses could be inserted, but Mugwiggen needed no amplification now, not with the specter of the dragon fast growing on the horizon.

The gnome took a reading on the exact angle of his scope, then looked to a chart to determine which umbrella soaring Robert would likely hit.

"Fourteen D," the gnome barked to his assistant, a younger gnome whose beard barely reached his neck.

Wearing heavy gloves molded from the thick sap of the Pweth Pweth trees, the assistant lifted the end of the charged coil, connected by metal lines to resistors on the wheels of the hundred bikes, and moved in front of the appropriate slot in a switch box hooked to every umbrella in the city.

"Fourteen D!" Mugwiggen yelled into a tube, and his words echoed out of similar tubes in every corner of Gondabuggan, and warned those gnomes in section fourteen D (and those in thirteen D and fifteen D, as well), that they would be wise to get out of harm's way. Then the gnome went back to his scope, alternately eyeing charts that would allow him to predict the air speed of the soaring dragon, and the timing of the collision.

Robert swooped down over the southern edge of the compact town, narrowed his reptilian eyes to evil slits against the continuing sting of the flak. Like a great ballista bolt, the dragon did not swerve, dove unerringly for the targeted umbrella, which the gnomes had labeled "fourteen D."

"Threetwoone!" Mugwiggen cried rapidly, seeing that his calculations were a split-second slow. His assistant was quick on the draw, though, immediately plugging the end of the coil into the appropriate slot in the switch box.

Metal sheets folded upward as the dragon smashed in, encasing Robert. The mighty wyrm wasn't immediately concerned, knowing he could easily rip his way through the flimsy barrier, shred the metal to harmless slivers.

But confident Robert didn't see the arcing current shoot up the umbrella pole, though he certainly felt the jolt as the charge fanned out along the encasing metal sheets.

Those gnomes nearest to fourteen D were deafened, some permanently, by the dragon's ensuing roar. Loose rocks in the Dvergamal Mountain range a mile away trembled at the vibrations of the titanic sound.

A hundred sweating gnomes pedaled furiously, keeping the charge steady and strong, and thrashing Robert's nostrils filled with acrid smoke as his leathery wings began to smolder.

Another roar, a crash of metal sheeting, and the dragon burst free, was hurled free, spinning into the air, trailing lines of smoke from every tip of his reptilian body. Two hundred feet up, Robert righted himself, spun right back around and loosed his flaming fury on the breached section of Gondabuggan's umbrella shielding.

Many hoses had already been turned on the vulnerable area, and the steam was blinding, but the town wouldn't escape unscathed. Fires flared to life in several buildings; metal turned to liquid and rolled down the gnomish streets.

"Which one?" Mugwiggen's assistant asked him, holding the loose coil once more.

Mugwiggen shook his head in frustration. "I cannot see for the steam!" the gnome cried in dismay, and he thought that his precious town was surely doomed.

"Free fire!" came the gnomish Mayor's command over the calling tubes. Immediately there came the sound of an umbrella snapping shut, followed by the *whoosh!* of a catapult. A loud *thonk!* thrummed over the network of open horns as a ballista sent a bolt the size of a giant's spear arcing into the air.

But the gnomes were shooting blindly, Mugwiggen knew, with hardly a chance of hitting the fast-flying wyrm. He flipped a few balls on the abacus he always kept by his side and shook his flaxen-haired and flaxen-bearded head at the long, long odds he had just determined.

Robert, though, drifting hundreds of feet above the steam-covered town, couldn't see any better than the gnomes. The great dragon's muscles continued to twitch involuntarily from the electrical jolt; his wings continued to trail dark smoke behind him. He was exhausted, and hurt far worse than he had anticipated from the surprisingly resourceful (even for resourceful gnomes!) defenses.

More flak filled the air about him and several huge spears whipped through the steam, arcing high into the clear blue mountain sky, one spear nearly clipping the dragon's long, trailing tail as it rocketed past.

Robert had seen enough for this day. He angled his wings and swooped away, seeking a perch many miles to the south, confident that when he returned, his wounds would be fully healed, but the gnomish defenses would remain depleted.

"I will feast yet on the flesh of puny gnomes," the dragon snarled, his drool sizzling as it dribbled past the multitude of daggerlike fangs in the great wyrm's maw. "And on man flesh and dwarf flesh and elf flesh, as well! Oh, fool, Kelsenellenelvial Gil-Ravadry! Oh, fool to take the dagger from Robert's lair, to banish wicked Ceridwen while Robert flies free!"

Despite the unexpected setback, the wyrm let out a roar of victory and beat his smoking wings, soaring like the wind to the protective peaks in the south.

On a high plateau, a flat-tipped uprighted finger of rock in the greater peaks four miles to the southwest of Gondabuggan, a handful of gnomes put down their spyglasses and breathed a sincere sigh of relief, a sigh only a bit tainted by the lines of darker smoke rising from the distant city to mix in with the veil of white steam.

"It would seem as if we have held the wyrm back," said Gerbil Hamsmacker, a three-foot-tall, pot-bellied gnome with an ample gray beard, tinged with orange, and sparkling, inquisitive blue eyes. "Heeyah hoorah for Gondabuggan!"

"Heeyah hoorah!" the other gnomes cried on cue, and the group gathered in a circle, all with one hand extended so that their knuckles were all together like a central hub, and giving the thumbs-up signal.

The cheer ended as abruptly as it had begun, with the gnomes turning away from each other and going back to the business at hand.

"Held him back?" came a call from the top of the next plateau, fifty feet west and thirty down from the highest group. The two gnomes down there returned the thumbs-up signal, gave a hearty "Heeyah!" and rushed to the back edge of their platform, calling down to the next group, farther to the west and farther down from them. And so the victory signal was sent to the next group and to the fifth, and final, group, some two hundred feet west and one hundred feet down from the original watchers at the top plateau.

Certainly these five flat-topped and roughly evenly spaced and evenly descending pillars of stone seemed an unusual formation in the wild mountains—until one understood that the gnomes, with their incredible machines and explosives, had played more than a little hand in creating them. Gerbil had needed the pillars for his latest invention, and so the piece, the Mountain Mes-

senger, now stood, a long and hollow tube running from finger to finger, supported by metal brackets at each plateau. It resembled a gigantic Alpine horn,
though it was not flared on the end, but instead of issuing booming notes, this
contraption spat out packages.

In Gerbil's original proposal to the Gondabuggan Invention Approval
Committee, the Mountain Messenger had been designed as a long-range delivery service for parcels to the mostly human towns of Drochit and Braemar on
the western side of the rugged Dvergamal Mountains. In truth, though, the
Mountain Messenger, like almost every gnomish invention, had been built just
to see if it could work. The first trials had not been promising, with dummy
loads lost in the mountains and never retrieved, and with one load even clipping the top of the town chapel in Drochit. Constant monitoring and painstak-
ing calculations, fine-tuning the explosive charges along the length of the M&M
(as the express had come to be called) and the amount of Earth-pull reversal solution coating the delivery packages, had actually made the contraption quite
accurate, crosswinds permitting. At the present time, the gnomes could skid
one of their delivery balls down the side of a sloping field north of Drochit,
some forty miles across the mountains to the west, eight out of ten tries.

Never before, though, had one of those three-foot-diameter delivery balls
been packed with a living creature, let alone a gnome.

"I do so envy you!" young Budaboo, a dimple-faced female gnome with
quite a statuesque figure in spite of her three-foot height, said to Gerbil as the
older gnome continued to check his packing on the lower hemisphere of the
split-open metal ball. "To be the first M&M'onaut!"

"I built it, after all," Gerbil said humbly.

"But you might even be squashed like a fly in one of Yammer's Splat-o-
Mallets!" the younger gnome squeaked excitedly, hopping up and down so that
her ample chest bounced like the landing delivery balls. "Your name would then
be forever etched into the *Plaque of Proud and Dead Inventors* in the University!"

"Indeed," Gerbil said solemnly, and he managed a weak smile as he remembered when he, too, as a younger gnome, had thought that distinction to be the
ultimate of gnomish goals.

"Oh, how I would love the honor of being squashed," Budaboo continued.

Gerbil glanced over one stocky shoulder to regard the excited youngster.
Gerbil easily guessed where pestering and manipulative Budaboo's flattery was
heading. She was an ambitious one, like most young gnomes, and blessed with
an intelligence uncommon even among the exceptionally intelligent race. "You
cannot go," he said bluntly.

Budaboo, thoroughly deflated, slumped her rounded shoulders and limped away to check on the cranking progress of the huge crossbow, the initial launching mechanism.

When he was finally convinced that he had his traveling gear, including a quadricycle, properly packed, Gerbil took out his spyglass and gave one last glance at Gondabuggan. The steam and smoke had cleared and the gnome could see the buckled umbrella, and another one with several metal sheets melted off. At least one of the stone buildings beneath the opening had been flattened, its wooden supports charred, but as far as the distant gnome could see, there appeared to be no casualties. He couldn't be sure, of course, and even if his hopes proved true, Gerbil suspected that merciless Robert would soon return.

He shook his head, called to his companions, and curled into the last open area of the ball's lower hemisphere, securing the flat, sappy ends of a breathing tube around his lips.

Led by Budaboo, the other gnomes efficiently lined up the other half of the ball and slowly lowered it into place—not an easy feat since the ball had two outer layers, a hard shell for handling the explosions and the impact, and a rotating inner shell that would soften the spin and the jolts for contents. Of the intricate details and calculations needed for the Mountain Messenger, the delivery balls themselves had proven the most difficult for Gerbil, and had required the assistance of the entire staff of GAPLA, the Gondabuggan Application of Physical Laws Academy.

Using a sealed tube with twin earpieces and a hollowed interior, Budaboo listened carefully for all six of the inner hinges to click. That done, the young female set the timer that would release the hinges, giving it an extra three minutes, just to be sure that the ball would have stopped bouncing and rolling before it popped open.

Other gnomes opened a small hole and inserted a hose through both layers of the ball's shell. On cue, two of the gnomes simultaneously opened valves in joining hoses, while a third pumped away on a connected bike. The materials mixed together and rushed into the ball, becoming a fast-coagulating foam that would further secure everything within the capsule, and contained as well the needed potion for keeping the ball aloft.

Then the gnomes gathered together flat-ended levers and rolled the ball up a slope and into place right in front of the cranked crossbow's heavy line. A leather pouch, connected to that line, was wrapped halfway around the ball and the signals began, the duo of gnomes on each of the successive four plateaus scrambling to light torches and insert them into hanging arms on either side of the tube.

"Heavy load," one of the gnomes on the top plateau remarked. "Gerbil has put on some weight."

"The charges have been adjusted accordingly," Budaboo assured him, and she looked to the trigger man.

"Stand clear!" the gunner called through a horn, and the gnomes on the lower plateaus scrambled for trap doors built into their platforms and disappeared from sight.

Budaboo took out her spyglass and examined the lines of torches, four on each side, to ensure that the gusting wind had not blown any out. If only one side of the twin explosives anywhere along the length of the M&M fired, Gerbil's ball would pick up an unwelcome rotation that would curve it wildly to soar far wide of the intended mark, probably to smash into a mountain wall.

"As you will," Budaboo said to the trigger man, seeing that everything was in place. "Lucky Gerbil," she whispered under her breath, wishing that she might have been the first M&M'onaut.

The trigger man heaved a lever and the giant crossbow snapped, rifling the delivery ball down the tube. Bells attached to the tube near to the first plateau tinkled, and the levers holding the torches dropped, flames on each side hitting the tightly packed charges at precisely the moment Gerbil's ball zipped past. Before the sound of the explosions had even begun to ebb, the other six charges went off in rapid succession and with a humongous *thwoosh!* the delivery ball soared out of the M&M and flew out of sight on its trip across Dvergamal.

"Forty miles out and three down to a bouncing stop along the field north of Drochit," one of the gnomes on the top plateau remarked.

"Unless a crosswind catches him and slams him against a stony mountainside," added another.

"Lucky Gerbil," muttered Budaboo, and she could only hope that Gondabuggan would need another messenger when Robert returned.

TWO

With Her Face Against the Windshield

THERE came a measure of freedom for Gary Leger that late August eve, tooling home from work in his Mustang, the rag-top down and the wind snapping his straight black hair back and forth across the sides of his face. Rick had his report and the month was closed, and though the next week promised the hectic time of fine-tuning hundreds of numbers, twenty trips to the copier a day, and several dozen phone calls from District Office Managers, ranging from curious to irate, Gary didn't have to think about that now.

He had left the office a half-hour later than usual and much of the afternoon traffic was far ahead of him, leaving Route 2 west out of Concord clear enough for him to ease the reins on the powerful Mustang. He put his head back, pumped the volume up on the stereo, and cruised down the fast lane at an easy seventy-five, the 5.0 liter eight cylinder hardly working at all. Gary liked the drive home from work when the traffic wasn't too tight. Route 2 was wooded on both sides and wide open to the horizon, where the sun was dipping low, turning the lines of clouds a myriad of colors. Many times on this daily commute, Gary was able to daydream, and inevitably, those dreams took him back five years, to the journey he had taken to the magical land of Faerie.

He remembered Mickey—who could ever forget Mickey?—and Kelsey, and the chase through Ceridwen's castle and the battle with mighty Robert the dragon. He remembered running scared through the wood called Cowtangle, chased by a horde of goblins and feeling more alive than he had ever felt in this "real" world.

Everybody wants to rule the world, the radio blared, an old Tears for Fears song and one of Gary's all-time favorites. He started to sing along, gave a quick glance at his instruments, and noticed flashing headlights in his rearview mirror. A closer look showed him a red Toyota so close to his ass-end that he couldn't see the thing's front bumper!

Gary immediately looked to the slow lane, instinctively reacting to the flickering signal for him to let the car behind him pass. He noticed that the lane was absolutely clear—why the hell didn't the car behind him just go around on the right?—and noticed, too, that he was pushing eighty.

"Jesus," he whispered, and he took a closer look in the rearview mirror, caught by the image of the young woman in the shiny Toyota, her face up close to the windshield as she issued a stream of curses Gary's way, and every now and then flipped him the finger. Her impatient headlights blinked on and off, her mouth flapped incessantly.

"Jesus," Gary muttered again, and he put the Mustang up to eighty-five. The Toyota paced him, couldn't have been more than a single car length off his rear bumper. Normally Gary, hardly ever in a real hurry, would have just pulled over and let the Toyota fly past.

A horn sounded to accompany the incessant headlights. The Toyota inched even closer, as though the woman meant to simply push Gary out of her way.

Gary backed off the accelerator, let the Mustang coast down to seventy-five, to seventy.

The lips against the windshield of the Toyota flapped more frantically.

Sixty.

Predictably, the Toyota swerved right, into the slow lane, and started by.

"Everybody wants to rule the world," Gary sang along, and as the Toyota's front bumper came halfway up the Mustang's side, he dropped the Mustang into third and gave the accelerator a slight tap. The eager engine roared in response and the car leaped ahead, easily pacing the Toyota.

Now he could hear the crabby woman, swearing at him at the top of her lungs.

Up went the volume on Gary's radio, up went the Mustang's speed, as Gary paced her at eighty-five, side by side.

"You son of a bitch!" she hollered.

Gary turned and offered a cat-got-the-canary smile, then eased the Mustang back into fourth as the speedometer needle flickered past ninety.

The Toyota backed off, and Gary did, too, keeping side by side with her, keeping her in the slow lane, where he figured a nut like that belonged. Curses and a flipping middle finger flew from the Toyota's open driver's side window.

"Everybody wants to rule the ROAD," Gary sang to her, altering the last word and nodding ahead, indicating that they were fast coming up on a perfectly maintained old Apsen—and that could only mean a more conservative driver—cruising down the highway at a perfect fifty-five.

Gary tucked the Toyota neatly in behind the Aspen and held pace for another half-mile, until a line of faster-moving cars came up on his bumper. Understanding that she had been had, the woman in the Toyota slammed her hands hard against her steering wheel several times in frustration and began flicking her headlights, as if the contented Aspen driver had anywhere to go to get out of her way.

"You son of a bitch!" she screamed again at Gary, and he blew a kiss her way, kicked the Mustang into third and blasted off, smiling as he looked back in his mirror, watching car after car zip by the frazzled driver in her Toyota and the contented driver of the Aspen.

Some pleasures in life just couldn't be anticipated.

Two hours later, Gary's Mustang was sitting quietly in the driveway of his parents' home in Lancashire, and Gary was sitting quietly in his bedroom unwinding from the long day and from the ride home. His radio played quietly in the background; outside the window, a mockingbird was kicking up its typical ruckus, probably complaining that the sun was going down and it hadn't found the opportunity to chase any cats that particular day.

Gary moved across the room to the stereo cabinet, opened the top drawer and removed his most precious possession, a worn copy of J.R.R. Tolkien's *The Hobbit*. Gary ran his fingers slowly across the cover, feeling the illustration, feeling the magic of the book. He opened past the credits pages, the introduction by Peter S. Beagle, and the table of contents. Nothing unusual about these, but when Gary turned the next page, he found not the expected, standard typesetting, but a flowing script of arcane runes that he could not begin to identify. Mickey had done it, had waved his chubby hand over the book and changed the typesetting to a language that the leprechaun could understand.

Gary heard a knock on the door, looked out his window to see Diane's Jeep (Gary's old Jeep), parked on the street, in front of the bushes lining the front yard. He dropped the book back in the drawer and slammed it shut just as Diane cracked open the door.

"You in there?"

"Come on in," Gary replied, hand still holding the drawer shut. He watched Diane's every move as she crossed the room to give him a little kiss, watched her dirty-blond hair bouncing carelessly about her shoulders, her wistful green eyes, so like his own, and that mischievous smile she always flashed when she first saw him, that I-got-you-Gary-Leger smile.

And it was true.

"What'cha doing?"

Gary shrugged. "Just hanging out, listening to some music." He poked his head under the bottom of the open window, putting his mouth near to the screen, and called loudly, "Whenever that stupid mockingbird shuts up long enough so that I can hear the music!"

"You want to go get an ice cream?" Diane asked when he turned back to her. Again came that mischievous smile, telling Gary that she had more on her mind than ice cream.

It seemed so perfectly natural to Gary Leger, the way things were supposed to be for a guy in his early twenties. He had a decent job paying more money than he needed, the security of home, and a great girlfriend. He had his health (he worked out every day), his minor glories on the softball field, and a car that could trap jackasses in the slow lane on the highway.

So why wasn't he, happy?

He was contented, not frazzled like the woman in the Toyota, or like so many of his coworkers who had families to support in a struggling economy, who had to keep looking over their shoulders to see if they still had a job. But Gary couldn't honestly say that he was happy, certainly not thrilled with the everyday tasks and pleasures that life offered to him.

The answer, Gary knew beyond doubt, lay in that cabinet drawer, in the flowing script of a leprechaun he wanted to speak with again, in the memories of a world he wanted to see again.

Gary tapped the drawer and shrugged. He and Diane went for their ice cream.

HIGH and far, the M&M ball flew, through low-hanging clouds, through a "V" of very surprised geese, and past the high doors of the holes of mountain trolls, the not-too-smart creatures scratching their scraggly hair and staring dumbfoundedly as the missile fast disappeared from sight.

Tucked in tight and surrounded by pressing foam, Gerbil couldn't see out of the delivery ball. If he could, the gnome might have died of fright as he neared the end of his descent, came soaring up on the lip of the field north of Drochit. The load was indeed heavy—too heavy—and the ball angled in a bit low, diving for the rocky ridge bordering the top of the field.

Good luck alone saved Gerbil, for the ball struck the turf between two stones, narrowly missing each, and skittered through, spinning into the air again, then landing in a roll down the descending slope of the long field. The ball had two shells, separated by independent bearings designed to keep the inner area somewhat stable.

No gnomish technology could greatly soften this bouncing and tumbling ride, though, and Gerbil bit his own lips many times, despite the tight-fitting mouthpiece, as he blabbered out a hundred different equations, trying to figure his chances for survival.

Gerbil heard the splat, and he was yanked to a sudden stop and turned upside-down as the ball bogged down in a muddy puddle.

"Oh, I hope, I hope, that I do not sink!" the gnome mumbled around the edges of his mouthpiece. The next few minutes, waiting for the timers to release the locks, seemed like an hour to the trapped (and increasingly claustrophobic) gnome. As soon as he heard the telltale clicks, Gerbil heaved and straightened with his legs, popping the ball in half, only to tumble over backwards and splat rump-first into the mud.

He was up in an instant, fumbling with the many compartments of the half-submerged ball, trying to salvage all the pieces of the contraption he had brought along. Again, luck was with him, for just a few moments later, he saw a group of Drochit villagers riding down the road on a wagon, coming to retrieve the gnomish delivery.

"Didn't know ye was sending anything," one farmer, the oldest man of the group of six, said when he noticed Gerbil.

"Hey, how'd you get here?" another man asked.

"He flied in the ball!" a third reasoned.

Poor Gerbil had to answer a hundred inane questions concerning his trip over the next few minutes, all the while coaxing the men to help him in his salvage operations. Soon the dry ground near to the puddle was covered with metal tubing, springs, gears, and a box of tools, and Gerbil had to slap curious hands away repeatedly and firmly scold the inquisitive humans.

"Robert the dragon is loose and in a fury!" the flustered gnome said at last. Gerbil had meant to keep that news private until he could meet with Drochit's leaders, but that meeting seemed longer away indeed if these simple men did not leave his equipment alone and let him get on with his assembling.

Six faces blanched, six mouths fell open.

"You," Gerbil said to the oldest, and apparently most intelligent, of the group. "Hand me items as I call for them—promptly, for we have not a moment to lose!"

The farmers were more orderly then, and Gerbil's work progressed excellently, with all the parts fitting neatly together. There came one moment of terror for the gnome, though, until he reached into the bulging pocket of a young man and took out his missing sprocket.

"Thought it'd be good for hitting birds," the young farmer apologized, drawing a slap on the back of his head from the oldest of the group.

"What is it?" Gerbil heard the question fifty times as the contraption neared completion. He figured that it would be easier to show this group than to try to explain, so he waited until he was done, then climbed into the back-leaning seat, tooted the small horn on the four-wheeled thing's steering bars, and began pumping his legs.

For a few moments, he did not move. One wheel had snagged on a half-buried rock and was spinning in the mud. Just as the farmers, scratching their heads like not-too-intelligent mountain trolls, moved near to figure out what the gnome might be trying to do, the wheel cleared the obstruction with a jerk and Gerbil rolled off slowly across the thick grass.

"Well, I'll be a pretty goblin," one man said.

"You wouldn't be pretty if ye was a goblin," answered another.

The first slapped him on the back of the head, and they would have started an all-out fight right then and there, except that Gerbil then turned onto the road, little legs pumping furiously, and the quadricycle sped away.

"Well, I'll be a pretty goblin," they both said together, and the whole group ran off for their wagon. They turned the cart about and shook the reins, spurring the horse into a gallop. But the burdened beast was no match for precise gnomish gearing and well-oiled axles, and Gerbil continued to outdistance them all the way to Drochit.

THREE

Mischievous Twinkle

KELSEY stood on a low hill, east of Dilnamarra Keep, watching the sun go down behind the square, squat tower that centered the simple village. The clouds beyond had turned orange and pink with the sunset, and all the mud of the town was lost in a rosy hue.

"You just do not understand," the elf said to Geno, who sat on a stone with his arms crossed over his sturdy chest, pointedly looking away from the beautiful scene.

Kelsey turned about to face the dwarf squarely. "Geldion holds Pwyll solely responsible for the missing armor. Connacht has found its excuse to hang the troublesome Baron."

"Why would I care, you dumb elf?" Geno snorted, and he spat on the ground. "I never did any business with Pwyll, or with any in Dilnamarra. I've got no customers there, so I plan to go and watch and enjoy the hanging!"

Kelsey's golden eyes narrowed, but he bit back his angry retort, knowing that gruff Geno was simply baiting him for a fight. "If Baron Pwyll is hung," the elf explained, "then Geldion will appoint an acting Baron, a man, no doubt, who will nod his head stupidly at every edict passed on from Connacht."

"Aren't all humans stupid?" Geno asked in all seriousness.

"Not as stupid as you are acting."

Geno's gaze dropped to the many hammers on his belt. He wondered how many he could put spinning into the air before Kelsey closed on him.

"Stupid, indeed, if you do not understand the implications of losing an ally such as Pwyll," Kelsey added, reading Geno's expression and promptly qualifying the statement. Kelsey needed no fights with Geno, not now with so much apparently at stake. "Only a few of Faerie's human landowners remain independent of Connacht," Kelsey explained. "Duncan Drochit and Badenoch of Brae-mar are two, but they took to Pwyll for support. King Kinnemore dearly desires to bring Dilnamarra into his fold, craves an outpost so near to Tir na n'Og, that he might keep an eye on the Tylwyth Teg."

"Sounds like an elfish problem to me," Geno remarked.

"Not so," Kelsey quickly replied. "If Pwyll is hung and Dilnamarra taken, then Kinnemore can look east, to Braemar and Drochit, and farther east, to the other two goodly races who have ever been a thorn in the outlaw King's side."

Geno snorted derisively. "That weaselly King would never have the belly for a fight in Dvergamal," the dwarf reasoned, waving his hands as if to brush the absurd notion away.

"But Prince Geldion would," Kelsey said gravely. "And if not Geldion, then certainly the witch Ceridwen, whose hand moves the lips and limbs of Kinnemore."

Geno stopped his waving hand, and his smug and gap-toothed smile melted away.

"Even if war did not come to the dwarfs and the gnomes, the trade would surely suffer," Kelsey went on, casually turning back to the sunset as though his proclamations were foregone conclusions. "Perhaps, after Pwyll is hung, you will get the opportunity to clear up your pile of overdue orders, good smithy."

Geno chewed on his lower lip for a while, but had no practical response. He could bluster that he didn't care for the fate of Faerie's bothersome humans, but the men were by far the most populous of the goodly races, far outnumbering the Tylwyth Teg elfs of Tir na n'Og, the Buldrefolk dwarfs of Dvergamal, and the gnomes of Gondabuggan combined. And while the populations of the elfs, dwarfs, and gnomes had held steady for centuries untold, the humans seemed to breed like bunnies in an unhunted meadow, with new villages dotting the countryside every year—new villages needing metal tools, armor, and weapons.

"You have an idea of where to find the armor?" Geno stated as much as asked.

"I have an idea of where to start looking," Kelsey corrected. "Are you coming with me, or will you return to the mountains?'

"Damned elf," the trapped Geno muttered under his breath, and Kelsey smiled, taking the grumbling to mean that he had hooked the tough dwarf into his quest once again.

Kelsey set a course straight north, and when towering trees came into view a short while later, it wasn't hard for Geno to figure out where the elf was heading.

"No, no," Geno stuttered, setting his boots firmly in the turf, shaking his head and his hands as he regarded the majestic forest. "If you plan to walk into Tir na n'Og, elf, you walk alone."

"I need your help," Kelsey reminded him. "As do your people."

"But why the forest?" Geno asked gruffly, if a bit plaintively. "If the witch took the armor, then it would more likely be headed for Ynis Gwydrin, the other way."

Kelsey's eyes narrowed as he listened, getting the distinct impression that Geno would prefer a trip to Ynis Gwydrin, Ceridwen's dread island, over a walk through the elven forest.

"If Kinnemore took the armor," Geno went on, ignoring the look, "then it would be headed for Connacht, again the other way. Who would be stupid enough to steal something so important to the Tylwyth Teg, then drop it in Tir na n'Og, right under their flower-sniffing noses?"

"Who indeed?" Kelsey mused, and his wry smile sent a myriad of questions through Geno's mind.

"Did you take the damned stuff?" Geno balked, and it seemed to Kelsey as though the dwarf was ready to start heaving a line of warhammers.

Kelsey shook his head, his mane of golden hair bouncing wildly about his shoulders. "Not I," he explained. "Whatever my reasons, I would never act so rashly when so much is at stake."

Geno mulled over the words for a few moments, knowing that Kelsey had put a clue or two in his answer.

"McMickey!" the dwarf cried suddenly, and Kelsey's nod confirmed the guess. "But what would the leprechaun want with armor that is five times his size? What would he want with a spear he could hardly lift off the ground?"

"Those are exactly the questions I plan to ask him, once we find him," Kelsey paused, looking from the now not-so-distant wood to Geno. "In Tir na n'Og," Kelsey finished, and he started off again, motioning for the dwarf to follow.

"Damned sprite," Geno bitched. "I'll pay that one back in hammers for putting me through this."

"Perhaps you will find, after walking the smooth paths of the wondrous forest, that you owe the leprechaun some thanks, Geno Hammerthrower," Kelsey remarked rather sharply. He really didn't expect a dwarf to understand or appreciate the elven wood, but he was beginning to find Geno's grumbling about the place more than a little annoying. "Few of the Buldrefolk have ever seen the wood, and none in centuries. Perhaps your fear of it . . ."

"Shut your mouth and walk on fast," Geno growled.

Kelsey said no more, realizing that advice to be the best he would get out of the surly dwarf.

The sheer vibrancy of Tir na n'Og's primal colors sent Kelsey's spirit soaring, and sent Geno's eyes spinning, as they made their way along the forest paths. It was early summer, and Tir na n'Og was alive, bristling with the sounds of chattering birds and humming bees, the thumping of a rabbit, the splash of a beaver, and the continuing song of a dozen dancing brooks. To Kelsey, to all the Tylwyth Teg, this was home, this was Faerie at its most precious, its most natural and correct state. But to Geno, who lived his life in rocky caves in the rugged Dvergamal range, Tir na n'Og seemed foreign and unwelcoming. In his dwarfish homeland, Geno's ears were filled with the rhythmic sound of hammers ringing on heated metal, and with the unending roar of the waterfalls at the Firth of Buldre. Tir na n'Og's more subtle, but many times more varied, noises kept the dwarf off-balance and on his guard, his gnarly fingers clutching tightly to the handle of a hammer and his blue eyes darting to and fro, searching the impossible tangles to try to discern what creatures might be about.

Birds squawked in the boughs above them, dogging their every step with telltale shrieks.

"They are announcing our presence to my people," Kelsey explained to the nervous dwarf. "The birds are Tir na n'Og's sentries."

The elf had thought that the explanation would put Geno more at ease, but, if anything, the dwarf seemed even more agitated. Every few steps, he would skid to a stop, hop around, looking up, and yell, "Shut your beak!" which only agitated the birds even more. Kelsey was glad that the dwarf was behind him, and could not see his smile, as the chatter multiplied in their wake.

Wider indeed did the elf's smile grow when they came through a small lea, lined by huge pines, and the birdsong reached a new crescendo.

"I told you to shut your beaks!" unnerved Geno roared, but then the dwarf saw through the illusion, saw that the birds were not really birds at all, but were Tylwyth Teg, scores of them, grim-faced and with bows drawn as they watched from the branches.

"Oh," Geno offered, and he said not another word for the next several hours.

After they passed the meadow, Kelsey stopped many times and whistled up trees, waiting for the whistling reply, then starting off once more, often in a different direction. Geno figured that the elf was getting information about the leprechaun in some strange code, but he didn't ask about it, just followed in Kelsey's wake and hoped that the whole trip through the miserable forest would soon be at its end.

It was late afternoon when Kelsey crouched in a bush and motioned for Geno to come up beside him. The elf pointed across a small clearing to a huge tree, and to the leprechaun resting easily against the trunk, twirling a jeweled dagger atop one finger. His hair and beard were brown, fast going to gray, his smiling eyes shining the color of steel in the afternoon sun. His overcoat, too, was gray, and his breeches green. He absently kept the dagger spinning, its tip on the tip of his finger, while he filled a long-stemmed pipe with his other hand and popped it into his mouth. And all the while, the hard heels of Mickey's shiny black, curly-toed shoes tap-tapped a frolicking rhythm on a thick root of the gigantic oak.

Using hand signals and facial gestures, Kelsey communicated to Geno that he should wait for the elf to get into position, then charge straight ahead at Mickey. Knowing how tricky fleeing leprechauns could be, and wanting nothing more than to get out of the forest, Geno readily agreed, though he was more than a little unsettled when Kelsey slipped away, fast disappearing into the brush, leaving him alone.

Just a moment later, though it seemed an interminable period to Geno, the elf poked a hand up from the tangle to the side and back of Mickey. "Damned sprite!" Geno roared again, bursting from the brush, a hammer held high so that he could throw it at the ground in front of the leprechaun's feet if Mickey took flight.

"Ah, there ye are, me friend dwarf," Mickey said easily, not even upset or surprised enough to drop the spinning dagger off his finger. "Suren it took ye long enough. And yerself, too, Kelsey," Mickey said without turning around, just an instant before Kelsey's hand grabbed him by the collar.

Kelsey and Geno exchanged incredulous looks and Kelsey let go, though Geno kept his hammer ready. The elf looked closer at the sprite, wondering if he was merely an illusion, fearing that the real Mickey McMickey was standing on the edge of the clearing, or up in the oak, laughing at them as they stood there confused. None in all of Faerie, not even Robert or Ceridwen, could see through an illusion as well as the Tylwyth Teg, though, and as far as Kelsey could tell, this was indeed Mickey sitting before him.

"You expected us?" Kelsey asked, unsure of himself.

"I called ye, didn't I?" Mickey replied with a huff.

"Then it was you who took the armor and spear," Geno growled.

Mickey glanced over one shoulder, his eyes pointing the way to the leaf-covered items, sitting neatly against a tree at the clearing's edge.

Kelsey grabbed the leprechaun by the collar again and hoisted him to his feet, the jeweled dagger falling to the ground. "Do you realize what you have done?" the elf demanded.

"I have brought ye both out here, as I needed," Mickey replied easily.

"Geldion has come to Dilnamarra," Kelsey growled, roughly letting go of the sprite. "Connacht holds Baron Pwyll responsible for the theft, and thus, he will be hung at noontime tomorrow. You should look farther down the corridors behind the doors you open before you act."

"And yerself should look east, Kelsenellenelvial Gil-Ravadry!" Mickey roared back, and his uncharacteristic tone and use of Kelsey's formal name (which Mickey had never seemed able to properly pronounce before) gave Kelsey pause. He watched curiously as Mickey retrieved the dagger, holding it up for both Kelsey and Geno to see, and wearing an expression which showed that the dagger should explain everything.

To both the others, the weapon seemed out of place in the leprechaun's hand, first because leprechauns rarely carried weapons—and on the few occasions they might, it was usually a slingshot of shillelagh—and second because the man-sized weapon seemed so unwieldy, practically a short sword, to the diminutive sprite.

"Look east, Kelsenellenenen . . . Kelsey," Mickey said again, "to where Robert may have already taken wing."

"The dragon was banished to his castle for a hundred years," Kelsey started to argue, but all the while he stared at the dagger, and began to understand. "Where did you get that?"

"Gary Leger," Mickey explained.

"Stonebubbles," Geno spat, the very worst of dwarfish curses.

"Not the lad's fault," Mickey explained. "He taked it from the tower, not the treasure room, and taked it for fighting, not for stealin'."

"But the theft releases Robert from his banishment," Kelsey reasoned. "And with Ceridwen banished and posing no deterrent to Robert . . ."

"The wyrm might well be already out and flying," Mickey finished. "And so did I bring ye all together, that we might put the wyrm back in his hole." All the while, Mickey was thinking not of Robert, but of his precious pot of gold, bartered to the dragon in exchange for his life before the friends had ever entered Robert's castle. Mickey didn't think it wise to tell the others that little detail, though, preferring to take the altruistic route this time, knowing that it would more likely appeal to the honorable Kelsey.

"If the dragon has discovered the missing dagger, then he will not likely be easy to put back in his hole," Kelsey reasoned, mimicking Mickey's words derisively.

"Oh, ye should better learn the terms of banishment before ye go insulting me," Mickey replied. "If we get the dagger back to the Giant's Thumb afore the change o' the season, then Robert'll be obliged to return." It was a plausible lie, and one that Mickey hoped would get him near to his pot of gold once more.

Kelsey's fair face screwed up incredulously. He had lived for centuries among the Tylwyth Teg, his people, among the most knowledgeable of races where ancient codes were concerned, and he had never heard of such a rule.

"'Tis true," Mickey went on, puffing on the pipe to hide his smirk. Leprechauns were the best liars in all the world, but the Tylwyth Teg were the best at seeing through those lies.

"I have never heard of this rule," Kelsey answered.

"If Robert hasn't found the lost dagger and we get it back, then no harm's done," Mickey replied. "And if he has found it, even if he's taken wing, then he'll be bound to return."

"And if you are wrong?"

Mickey shrugged. "Ye got a better plan? Ye meaning to go off and fight the wyrm?"

"Stonebubbles," Geno spat again.

Kelsey didn't immediately answer, caught in Mickey's web. He certainly did not wish to fight Robert, if that could in any way be avoided.

"And so I bringed ye together," Mickey went on. "It's our own fault that Robert's about, and our own job to put him back where he rightly belongs."

"You could have just asked," Geno grumbled, and he, too, seemed subdued, caught in Mickey's sticky web.

"I needed to get ye all together," Mickey argued. "And I didn't even know where yerself had gotten off to. I figured to let Pwyll do me hunting for me, and it seems like he catched ye good."

Geno grumbled and lowered his eyes, preferring to keep his memories of the wild fight in Braemar's Snoozing Sprite tavern private.

"At what cost?" Kelsey demanded. "Your games have put Baron Pwyll in jeopardy."

Mickey chewed on the end of his long-stemmed pipe for a few moments, thinking it through. "Then we'll just have to take the good and fat Baron along with us," he decided, his big-toothed and pearly smile beaming once more.

Mickey's obvious confidence set Kelsey back on his heels and ended that debate—for the time. "And what of the armor?" Kelsey demanded, determined to find some problem with Mickey's simple reasoning.

"Oh, I'll be filling it soon enough," the leprechaun replied, his gray eyes twinkling mischievously. "Don't ye worry."

FOUR

Click Against the Window

DIANE lay across Gary's bed and Gary sat on the floor, both of them tired as midnight approached. Fleetwood Mac's *Tusk* played softly in the room, and candles burned low while Stevie Nicks rolled through the haunting lyrics of *Storms*.

> *Every night that goes between,*
> *I feel a little less*

She was singing to Gary, about Gary, the young man felt, singing the sad truth that Gary was indeed beginning to feel a little less with every passing day away from the enchanted land of Faerie. Gary remembered it all so vividly, remembered Mickey and Kelsey, and surly Geno. Remembered the vibrant colors of Tir na n'Og and the mud-filled streets of Dilnamarra. Gary thought of Faerie every night as he was drifting off to steep, usually while this same CD cooed softly at the edges of his consciousness.

"They're hitting Baghdad again!" came a call from downstairs, Gary's father watching the coverage on the late news.

Diane shook her head in disgust. She was one of the few people Gary knew who openly expressed her disdain for the war. You could throw every logical argument at Diane for fighting the war, from oil reserves to the need to defeat terrorism, and she'd just smile and say, "When historians look back on this, they'll see that it could have been avoided, just like every other war." No argument could shake Diane from her convictions.

A tough lady, and that's what Gary loved most about her.

"They're creating their own Robert," Gary mused aloud, thinking of how the media, probably with government's full support, had made the leader of the enemy country out to be the worst criminal since Adolf Hitler. There were no dragons in Gary's world, no real ones, anyway, so it seemed that, from time to time, people had this need to create one. Gary Leger had met a dragon, a real dragon, and his fear of ever meeting a real one again far outweighed his all-too-human need for the excitement.

"What?" Diane asked. "Who's Robert?"

Gary thought long and hard about an answer to that simple response. Many times he had considered telling Diane about his trip to Faerie, about showing her the book and trusting in her to believe in him. "Nothing," he said at length. "Just an evil king I read about somewhere."

The answer satisfied weary Diane, who was already drifting off to sleep. She didn't make it a habit of falling asleep in Gary's room, but the door was open and his parents didn't mind, and the quiet music was so inviting . . .

Something snapped against the window, jolting Diane from her sleep. The candles were out now, the digital clock reading 2:30. The room was perfectly quiet, and dark, except for the dim light of the streetlight coming in through the edges of the front window's shade. As her eyes adjusted, Diane could make out Gary's silhouette, propped against the bed in the same position he had been in when they were awake.

Puk!

"Gary," Diane whispered. She reached out and jostled his shoulder a little, and he responded by shaking his head and looking back to the bed.

"Huh?" he replied dreamily.

Puk!

"The window," Diane said. "Something's clicking against the window!"

"Huh?" Gary rubbed his bleary eyes and looked to the window, just in time to hear yet another click. "It's probably just a squirrel on the roof," Gary announced rather loudly as a yawn intermingled with the words. He pulled himself up and moved across the floor, trying to appear bold. He moved the shade aside and looked out, but the front yard and the street seemed empty.

"There's nothing out there," he said firmly, turning back into the room.

Puk!

Diane reached for the light as Gary pulled up the shade, lifting the bottom half of the window as soon as the weak springs of the old shade had moved it out of the way. "Don't turn the light on!" he told her, knowing that he wouldn't be able to see outside if she did. With nothing revealed, he put the screen up, too, and leaned out, his hands resting on the windowsill as he scanned the front and side yard.

"There's nothing out here . . ." he started to protest, but he stopped in mid-sentence, the words caught in his throat as he looked down to regard several tiny arrows protruding from the wooden sill.

"No way," the young man breathed. Gary's mind rushed in a hundred different directions at once. Could it be true? Had the fairies come back for him? He knew instinctively that this was a signal, that a sprite was summoning him, probably to go down to the woods out back, to the same spot from where he had once been taken to the enchanted realm.

"What is it?" Diane demanded, coming to within a few feet behind Gary.

It, Gary thought, is time for some revelations. He could tell her now, he mused, could make her believe him with evidence that her stubborn and rational side could not dispute.

"Come here," Gary said, motioning for Diane to join him. He pointed out the little darts and Diane bent low to the sill, shaking her head.

"Some kind of pellet?" she asked.

"Arrows," Gary corrected.

Diane looked at him blankly, then peered low to better regard the darts. "Who could shoot an arrow that small?" she asked incredulously, but then she nodded as if she understood. "Oh, from a blowgun?" she asked, remembering the stories Gary had told her about his blowgun fights at the office.

"No," Gary replied cryptically, trying to build the suspense so that his answer, when he gave it in full, would not be too overwhelming.

"From one of those—what do you call them?—crossbows?" Diane reasoned.

"Nope," Gary replied, working hard to keep the mounting excitement out of his voice. "From a longbow."

Diane looked back to the tiny dart, her face twisted in confusion. "Couldn't be too long a bow," she said with a smirk.

Gary thought of going to his stereo cabinet and showing Diane the leprechaun-transformed version of *The Hobbit*, of showing her the flowing script and blurting out everything that had happened to him.

Take it slow, he reminded himself, thinking of his own doubts even after the sprites had abducted him, even after his first full day in the land of Faerie. Gary had lived the adventure, and yet it had taken him a long time to believe that it had actually occurred—even after it was over and he found himself waking in the woods out back, only the still-transformed book had proven to him that the whole thing hadn't been a dream.

But he had to make Diane believe it, he told himself. It was important to him, vital to him, that someone else, especially Diane, believe his tale and maybe share another adventure with him. He took a deep breath, turned on the room's light, and retrieved the book from the stereo cabinet handing it over to Diane.

"Yeah," she prompted, not understanding.

"Open it."

Diane's eyes widened as she considered the flowing runes on the strange pages, not at all what she would expect, of course, from a printed book. She looked to Gary and shook her head, totally confused.

I took that to a professor at the college," Gary explained. "Dr. Keough, who knows Irish history better than anyone else around here. It's Gaelic, as far as he could tell, but a form of the language he had never seen before. He couldn't decide if it was some hybrid of the language, or some pure form."

"You've got Tolkien in Gaelic?" Diane asked breathlessly. "This must be a collector's edition, and must be worth a fortune."

"It's not a collector's edition," Gary replied. "But it's probably worth more than a fortune."

"What are you talking about?"

"Look at the beginning," Gary explained. He went to his book shelf and took out the second book in the series, opening it to the credits page. "Same publisher, same edition, even the same printing," Gary explained, showing Diane the identical information in both books.

She continued scrutinizing the pages, looking for some clue, and Gary wondered if it was time to spring the truth on her. He trusted her, and knew that she wouldn't ridicule him (once she realized that he was serious) even if she didn't believe him. But Gary simply couldn't figure out where to begin. Wild ideas came into his thoughts every time he tried to think of an opening sentence. He imagined his name spread across the headlines of tabloid newspapers:

LANCASHIRE MAN ABDUCTED
BY FAIRIES
GARY LEGER:
I WAS IMPREGNATED BY A LEPRECHAUN

Gary laughed in spite of his dilemma, drawing Diane's attention away from the book.

"What's going on?" she demanded, the perfect cue, but again Gary couldn't find the words to respond.

"I can't tell you," he admitted. He looked back to the open window. "But I think I can show you."

They rushed through the house, out the front door, and Gary led the way down the street, towards the black line of trees, the beginning of the small wood.

"If you wanted to make out, couldn't we have gone for a ride?" Diane asked him, resisting the urgent pull of his hand and not liking the look of those dark and ominous trees.

"This is better than making out," Gary replied excitedly, not taking the time to choose his words more carefully.

Diane tugged her hand free and skidded to a stop on the road. When Gary turned back to her, she was standing with her arms crossed over her chest, one foot tapping on the tar, and her head tilted to the side. The dim light of the distant streetlights did nothing to diminish the appearance of her scowl.

"What?" Gary asked blankly.

"Better than making out?" Diane replied, emphasizing every syllable.

"No, no," Gary stammered. "You don't understand, but come on, and you will!"

"Better than making out?" Diane asked again, but caught up in Gary's over-boiling enthusiasm, she accepted his hand once again and followed him down the street and into the woods.

It was pitch black in there, but Gary knew his way, had grown up playing in these woods. They moved down the dirt end of his parents' street, turned onto a fire road, and soon moved through the blueberry bushes, past the wide break atop the high ground overlooking the area that had been cleared for an elementary school.

The view there was beautiful, with the shining dots of stars dotting the sky, and Diane slowed, her eyes drinking it in.

This was the spot where Gary had encountered the fairy ring, but not where he had first encountered the sprite. He allowed Diane a few moments of the grand view, while he snooped around, looked for the telltale lights of dancing fairies.

"Come on," he said at length, taking Diane's hand once more. "Down there." He started along the path once more, heading for where it dipped down the side of a thickly wooded vale.

Diane resisted, slapped at a mosquito that had stung her on the neck. "What's going on?" she asked again. "What does this have to do with those arrows, and that book?"

"I can't explain it," Gary replied. "You wouldn't believe . . . you wouldn't understand it. Not yet. But if you'll just come along, you'll see it for yourself."

"I always pick the nuts," Diane muttered under her breath, and she took up Gary's hand and followed him down the dirt path.

They came to a mossy banking—Diane had to take Gary's word that it was a mossy banking, for she couldn't see a thing. He plopped down, and pulled her hand, patting the ground to indicate that she should sit behind him.

The minutes passed uneventfully, quietly, except for the rising hum of hungry mosquitos gathering about them, smelling human food.

"Well?" Diane prompted.

"Sssh!" Gary replied.

"I'm getting eaten alive," she protested.

"Ssssh."

And so they sat in silence, save for the annoying buzz and the occasional slaps. Their eyes adjusted enough to the dark so that they could at least make out each other's black silhouette. Diane nuzzled into Gary's shoulder and he instinctively put his arm around her.

"We should have taken the car," she whispered.

"Sssh." Gary's tone grew more agitated, more impatient, aptly reflecting the frustration building within him.

The minutes became an hour, a chill breeze blew by, and Diane nuzzled closer. A twist of her head put her lips against Gary's neck, and she gave him a long kiss, then moved her head up so that her lips brushed lightly against his ear.

"Do you want some ice cream?" she asked teasingly.

Gary sighed and pulled away, causing Diane to straighten.

"Do you want them to watch us?" Gary asked sharply.

Diane leaned back from him.

"Well?" Gary asked.

"Who?"

"Them!" Gary snapped back, pointing to the empty darkness. He shook his head and closed his eyes. When he had seen the arrows, his hopes had soared. But now . . .

Gary desperately wanted it to be true, wanted the sprites to come back for him, to take him—and Diane, too—into Faerie for some new grand adventure. To get him out of the world of month-ends and highway games.

Diane looked confused, even a little scared. "Who?" she demanded again.

"The sprites," Gary answered softly and bluntly.

Diane was silent for a long moment. "Sprites?" she asked, and her voice had dropped at least an octave.

"Fairies!" Gary snarled at her, snarled at the obvious doubt in her tone and at his own mounting doubts.

"What the hell are you talking about?" Diane replied. "And why is it that I seem to keep asking you the same questions over and over without getting any real answers?"

"Because I can't explain it!" Gary cried in frustration.

"Try."

"That book," Gary began, after taking a deep breath to clear his thoughts and steady his nerves. "It wasn't printed the way you saw it. It was normal, perfectly normal typesetting."

"Then how did it change?" The obvious doubt in her tone stung the young man.

"A leprechaun waved his hand."

"Cut it out," replied Diane.

"I'm not kidding," Gary said. "That's why I brought you down here. You don't believe me, you can't believe me. Hell, I didn't believe myself—until I saw that book."

Diane started to ask a question, but stopped and held her arms up high to the sides in surrender.

"You'll have to see it," Gary explained. "The words are too impossible."

To Diane's credit, she didn't reply, didn't tell Gary that he was out of his mind, and didn't rise to leave. She took Gary's hand and moved him back beside her.

"Just give me this night," he asked her. "Then, maybe, I'll be able to explain it all."

Diane pulled him closer, put her head back on his shoulder. Her sigh was resigned, but she held her place and Gary knew that she would trust in him, despite the mosquitos, despite the fact that, by all appearances, the young man was out of his mind.

A gentle singing awakened Gary some time later, some time not far before the dawn.

"Diane," he whispered, nudging the sleeping woman. She didn't move.

The fairy song drifted on the breeze, too soft for Gary to make out the individual words, though he doubted that he would understand the arcane language anyway.

"Diane." He gave her a harder nudge, but still she didn't move.

"Come on," Gary prompted as loudly as he dared, and he rubbed his hand across Diane's back, then stopped abruptly as he felt the tiny dart sticking from her shoulder.

"Oh, no," he groaned, and Diane's next snore came as an appropriate reply. The fairies had put her to sleep.

Gary rose into a crouch, saw the flicker of tiny lights, like fireflies, atop the ridge, back near to the blueberry bushes. He half-walked, half-crawled up the slope, the lights and the song growing more intense with every passing foot. And then he saw them, a ring of dancing fairies, like tiny elfish dolls barely a foot tall. They twirled and leaped, spun graceful little circles, while singing in their squeaky yet melodic voices. This was the gateway to the enchanted land.

"Get in," came a chirping voice, the words running so fast that it took Gary a long moment to sort them out. He looked down to see a small sprite standing beside him.

"You came for me?" Gary stated as much as asked.

"Get in!"

"What took you so long?" Gary demanded, wishing that they had arrived hours before. The sprite replied with an incredulous look, and only then did Gary realize that the few hundred yards back to his parents' house must have seemed like miles to tiny sprite legs.

Gary looked back down the trail, to where Diane was sleeping soundly. He needed her to witness this, to come with him to Faerie.

"Get in!" The squeaky voice sounded more insistent with each demand.

"Not without her," Gary replied, looking from the vale to the sprite. The sprite was holding something, Gary noticed, though he couldn't quite make it out in the darkness. His mind told him what his eyes could not, but too late, for then he felt the sting of an arrow against his calf.

"Dammit," he groaned, feeling for the dart and then tearing it free. A few moments later, his vision went double, and through blurry eyes he saw two rings of dancing fairies.

"Dammit," he said again, and for some reason, he was down on his knees. "Diane?"

"Just you!" the now-unseen sprite answered emphatically.

"Dammit!" But despite the protest, Gary was crawling, moving slowly and inevitably for the fairy ring. There he collapsed, his strength drained by the sleeping poison, his legs too weak to support him.

Gary Leger wouldn't need his legs for this next portion of his journey.

FIVE

The Rescue

HE knew as soon as he opened his eyes on a glorious dawn that Diane was no longer beside him. He knew by the vivid colors, almost too rich for his eyes, that he had come again to the enchanted realm of Faerie, and he was not surprised at all a moment later to see Mickey McMickey, Kelsey, and Geno, staring down at him as he lay on a patch of thick grass, surrounded by blueberry bushes.

Still groggy from the pixie poison, Gary stretched and yawned and forced himself to sit up.

"No time for sleeping, lad," Mickey said to him. "Baron Pwyll's to be hung at noon, and we've to get ye in the armor and get to Dilnamarra in a hurry."

Gary's stare took on a blank appearance as he tried to orient himself to his new surroundings and tried to digest the sudden rush of news. The Baron . . . the armor . . . Dilnamarra . . .

Geno grabbed him by the shoulder, and with strength far beyond what his four-foot-tall body should have possessed, easily hoisted, flung, Gary to his feet.

"Comes from eating rocks?" a shaken Gary asked Mickey, remembering what the leprechaun had told him of dwarfish power.

"Now ye're catching on," Mickey said with a wide grin. "There's a good lad."

"My welcome, Gary Leger," Kelsey added solemnly, and from what Gary knew of Kelsey's aloof demeanor, that seemed like the warmest greeting of all.

Gary took a moment to look all around, to bathe in Faerie's preternatural colors and in the continual song that seemed to fill the ear, just below the level of conscious hearing. Music had been an important part of Gary's life in his own world, and the feelings bestowed by the best of the songs that he heard came close, but did not match, the subliminal and unending magical notes that filled Faerie's clear air.

Mickey tugged at daydreaming Gary's belt, pointing out that Kelsey and Geno had already started away.

When they arrived at the great oak tree and retrieved the armor, Gary was suddenly relieved that Diane had not come with him. Up this tree lived Leshiye, the wood nymph, a gorgeous and ultimately seductive creature with whom Gary had shared a most pleasurable encounter on his last visit to Faerie. Inevitably, Gary's eyes now drifted up the wide-spread branches, and he put a hand to one ear, wondering if he might catch a hint of Leshiye's enchanting and enticing song.

Kelsey tapped Gary on the shoulder, and when the young man turned about to regard the elf, he looked into the most uncompromising glare he had ever seen. It was Kelsey who had climbed this very tree to pull Gary from Leshiye's tender, and inevitably deadly, clutches. The elf had been angry then, as dangerous as Gary had ever seen him, and Kelsey's glare now came as a clear warning to Faerie's visitor that he should concentrate on the business at hand and leave any sought-after pleasures for later.

"Why not give back the armor, instead of putting that one in it?" Geno asked suddenly, drawing the attention of the other three. "Geldion would let Pwyll go and I could get back to my home."

"But then Geldion would take the artifacts back to Connacht," Mickey reasoned. In truth, the dwarf's plan seemed simple, but Mickey couldn't let it come to pass, not if he wanted to retrieve his pot of gold. Worried that pragmatic Geno might spoil everything, Mickey found some unexpected support from Kelsey.

"We shall need the armor and spear if it comes to battle with Robert," the elf explained.

Geno snorted. "Let Geldion and Pwyll raise an army to battle the dragon," he said.

Mickey chewed his lip as the situation seemed to hang on a fine wire.

"No," Kelsey said flatly, and Mickey tried hard to keep his relieved sigh quiet. "Robert is our responsibility, since it was our actions that loosed him on the land. It seems a simple thing to return the item to the dragon's lair and force him to honor the terms of banishment."

"The dragon's out?" Gary asked incredulously.

"Just a small issue," Mickey replied, straightening his tam-o'-shanter.

Gary looked to Mickey and shrugged, hopelessly confused, but the leprechaun put a finger to pursed lips, calling for silent patience.

"Your responsibility, elf!" Geno balked, poking a stubby finger Kelsey's way. "The quest was yours, never mine, and you bear the responsibility of the theft."

"What?" Gary mouthed silently to Mickey, though he thought that he was beginning to catch on. The word "theft" led Gary to believe that Mickey had taken something from Robert, something that had broken the dragon's indenture. The notion that the friends had somehow loosed a dragon on the land began to weigh heavily on the young man's shoulders, began to make him think that going right back to the forest behind his mother's house might not be such a disappointment.

"Our responsibility," Kelsey promptly corrected. "And we, together, shall see it through, shall put the wyrm back in his hole, and perhaps right many other wrongs in the land along the way."

Mickey was smiling easily then, realizing that he had indeed appealed to Kelsey's overdeveloped sense of honor.

"Pretty words, elf," Geno said grimly. "Let us hear them again in the face of an angry dragon." Despite his grumbling, though, the dwarf was the first to move for a metal plate.

Gary felt the balance of the magnificent armor as Geno and the others went about the task of strapping it on. On his initial visit to Faerie, when he had first donned the armor, it had felt bulky and he had felt clumsy in it. Gary had spent the last five years strengthening his muscles, though, preparing himself for this return, and now, as the armor fell into place, his body remembered. When the last piece of metal plating was strapped securely into its place, Gary felt no more encumbered than if he had been wearing a set of heavy clothes and a long leather coat.

Gary lifted the huge and ornate helm and tucked it under one arm. This was the only piece that didn't fit well—Cedric's head must have been huge indeed—and Gary saw no reason to put it on just yet. Then he went for the spear, pausing a long moment to study it, to bask in the view of its splendor. It was long, taller than Gary, and forged of black metal, with a wide tip that flared out back at the top of the handle and turned around on both sides into secondary points, making the whole appear almost like a distorted trident. It looked as if it would weigh a hundred pounds, but so balanced was it, and so heavily magicked, that Gary could easily hurl it fifty feet.

"*Well met again, young sprout,*" came a call in Gary's mind, a telepathic greeting from the sentient spear. Gary let a reply drift from his thoughts, and then, almost as if they had never been apart, he and the weapon were communicating continuously, subconsciously, each becoming extensions of the other. It was in this telepathic joining that Gary Leger had learned to fight, that Gary Leger had come to see the land of Faerie as one of Faerie might, and make his battle decisions quickly and correctly when the situation demanded. The spear had given to Gary a different point of reference, and the confidence to act on his newfound instincts. When Ceridwen had caught them on the mountain outside Robert's castle, when all seemed lost, Gary had listened to those instincts and had hurled the spear into the witch's belly, saving them all and banishing Ceridwen to her island home.

"Lead on," Gary said to Kelsey as he took up the magnificent spear. The elf shook his head, put his slender fingers to his lips, and blew a shrill whistle, and a moment later, three horses and a pony burst into the clearing by the oak, flipping their heads about and snorting (Gary almost expected to see fire puffing from the nostrils of the mighty steeds). All four were pure white, and bedecked in an array of tinkling golden bells that rang out in perfect harmony as the beasts jostled about. Rich satiny purple blankets peeked out from under their smooth and delicate saddles.

"A bit noisy, don't ye think?" Mickey asked Kelsey.

"The bells ring only when they are commanded to ring," Kelsey replied. "No mount walks as quietly as a steed of Tir na n'Og, and no mount runs as fast."

"Not likely," Geno grumbled, eyeing the pony with disdain.

Kelsey and Mickey regarded the dwarf for a long while, not understanding what he was talking about, until the pony pawed near to Geno and the gruff and fearless dwarf verily leaped away, his hand snapping down to grab at a hammer.

"He's afraid of horses," Mickey chuckled, but his smile wrapped tight against his long-stemmed pipe when Geno turned his glare Mickey's way.

"Dilnamarra is many miles away," Kelsey said to the dwarf. "We have no time to walk. You have ridden before," the elf reasoned, for horseback was the primary means of travel in Faerie.

"Ye rode the giant when I made him look like a mule," Mickey added.

"I rode the cart the giant pulled," Geno promptly corrected.

"I don't know how to ride," Gary cut in, looking apologetically to his friends. The young man thought himself incredibly stupid. He had spent five years in his own world preparing himself in case he ever got back to Faerie, and he had never even thought to take a riding lesson!

"Horses aren't so common in my world," he tried to explain.

"And when ye got here the last time, ye didn't know how to fight, either," Mickey reminded him. "Ye learned, Gary Leger, and so ye'll learn again. Besides, don't ye worry, I'll be up in yer saddle beside ye."

Gary looked doubtfully to the horse that had padded near to him, but shrugged and nodded Mickey's way. He started for the saddle, plopped the cumbersome helmet on his head, and put his foot up to the stirrup.

"From the left side," Kelsey corrected.

"Uh-oh," Mickey muttered under his breath.

With a single fluid motion, Kelsey was up in his seat, taking the reins of the riderless horse beside him as well. Gary had to straggle a bit more—the leggings of the armor didn't quite spread wide enough for an easy mount—but he managed to get into place, and Mickey floated up in front of him, taking a comfortable seat between Gary and the horse's muscled neck.

"The lad can do it," Mickey said to Geno. "Are ye not as brave?"

Geno grabbed the pony's bridle and pulled the beast's face right up to his own, nose to nose. The dwarf started to speak several times, but seemed as though he had no idea of what to say to a pony. "Behave!" he barked at last, sounding ridiculous, but when he turned his unrelenting scowl about to regard his friends, they all three quickly bit back their chuckles.

When the dwarf finally settled on the pony's back, Kelsey nodded to the others and clicked his teeth, and the mounts leaped away, hooves pounding as they thundered through the thick brush, bells ringing gaily, though it seemed to the stunned Gary Leger that not a leaf was shaking in their wake.

The wild run through Tir na n'Og was among the most exciting things Gary had ever experienced. The mounts seemed out of control, running of their own free will. Once his mount headed straight for the trunk of a wide elm, head down in a full gallop. Gary screamed and covered his eyes with his arm. Mickey laughed, and the horse veered slightly at the last moment, passing within inches of the elm. Gary fumbled to straighten the helmet, then looked back and saw that Geno's pony, following closely, had taken the same route, and the dwarf, who apparently had tried to jump off, was now struggling to right himself in his saddle, complaining all the while.

"Keep low in the saddle," Kelsey warned from the side, seeing the man upright, and Gary bent as far over as he could. Still, he felt more than one low-hanging branch brush across his shoulders, and the long spear cut a swath in the foliage along the tight side.

Gary heard the singing of running water somewhere up ahead. A moment later, his helmet spun around on his head and he felt as if he was flying, and then he heard the sound of the water fading fast behind him.

"Unbelievable," he muttered, straightening the helm.

"That's the fun of it," Mickey quickly replied, still sitting easily in the crook between Gary and the horse's neck. "Say, lad, ye didn't happen to bring me another book, now, did ye?"

Gary smiled and shook his head. He wished that he had brought several books, the rest of Tolkien's series, at least, so that he might hear Mickey's comments as the leprechaun read them—read them as if they were factual historical books. Gary smiled again as he realized that they just might be, from the perspective of Faerie's folks.

The party charged out of Tir na n'Og just a few minutes later, thundering across the hedge-lined fields, causing the many sheep and hairy "heeland coos," as Mickey called the highland cows, to pause and look up to regard their passing.

It all seemed a wondrous blur to Gary, the miles rolling under him as surely as if he had been flying down Route 2 after work back home. But even with the rag-top down, the sensations in the Mustang could not come close to equaling the thrill of riding this near-wild steed, a beast that Gary might coax, but certainly could not control.

Some time later they came in sight of Dilnamarra, the single stone tower that served as Baron Pwyll's keep poking above the rolling plain and the low wooden shops and cottages. On Kelsey's command, the magical bells stopped ringing, and the elf slowed, bringing them in at an easy and quieter pace.

A crowd had gathered at the muddy crossroads in the center of the small village, gathered around the gallows, to which a trembling and blubbering Pwyll was now being dragged.

Kelsey led the others down around a low hill, where they left the horses and crept up on foot, pausing to watch from a hedgerow a hundred feet down the north road from the gathering, with the squat tower directly across the gallows from them.

"We've come not a moment too soon," Mickey remarked. "But how're we to get in there and get away?"

"If we had walked, our concerns would soon be at their end," Geno grumbled, drawing angry stares from both Kelsey and Mickey.

"There are a lot of soldiers down there," Gary remarked.

"Aye," Mickey added, "and most o' them wearing the colors of Connacht." He tapped Gary's hand, clutching tightly to the magnificent spear. "We're for needing tricks, not weapons," he said, and Gary nodded and eased his grip.

"What tricks do you have, leprechaun?" Geno asked gruffly. "The fat one will be hanging by his neck in a ten-count." It was true enough; even as they crouched and tried to figure out a plan, Prince Geldion was reading from an unrolled parchment while a contingent of his men prodded and kicked the reluctant Pwyll up the stairs.

"Will the crowd help us?" Gary asked eagerly, picturing some grand revolt with himself at the lead, dressed as Cedric Donigarten, the most famous hero of Faerie.

"Not likely," Mickey answered, bursting Gary's daydreams. "They're commonfolk, and not likely to find the courage to go against Connacht, even if yerself's wearing the armor of their hero of old."

"You must get in close to the Baron," Kelsey said suddenly to Geno, stringing his bow as he spoke. "My arrows have cut ropes before."

Geno laughed at him.

"Geldion and the others will believe that Pwyll is hanging," Kelsey, undaunted, said to the dwarf. Kelsey turned to Mickey with a questioning stare, and the leprechaun understood what role the elf meant for him to play.

Mickey looked back doubtfully to the gallows, where a soldier was putting the hangman's noose around Pwyll's neck. If he had his pot of gold, his source of magical energies, Mickey could have woven an illusion that would have curious onlookers staring at the hanging man for a week. But he didn't have that precious pot, and without it, the leprechaun wasn't sure that his magical imagery would be precise enough to fool half the people around the gallows.

"I see no better way," he answered, though, and he rubbed his plump little hands together and began weaving the words of a spell.

Geno continued to smirk doubtfully and shake his head.

I will go if you're afraid," Gary offered, and he shifted away as the dwarf's disbelieving and threatening scowl fell over him. With a growl, Geno was up and running, cutting from bush to bush, then darting behind a water trough just a few feet behind the back ring of onlookers. There, Geno spat in his hands and tamped down his powerful legs like a hunting cat, preparing to rush out at the exact moment.

Gary shot a mischievous wink Mickey's way. "A little motivation for the dwarf," he explained.

"It's good to have ye back, lad," the leprechaun replied with a chuckle.

Gary went out next from the hedgerow, slipping closer to the crowd, spear in hand. He heard Kelsey whistle softly and looked back to see the horses walking in behind the elf and Mickey. Then Gary turned his attention fully to the scene ahead, inching up as close as he could get to the anxious crowd. He noted the thickness of the rope and began to doubt Kelsey's plan, began to doubt that any arrow, no matter how perfect the shot, could cut that hemp cleanly. He heard Geldion complete the damning proclamation, labeling Pwyll as a thief and a traitor to the throne.

"And we hang traitors!" the Prince cried out, a pointed reminder to everyone in attendance. "Executioner!"

A whine escaped doomed Pwyll's thick lips; the executioner's hand went to the long lever at the side of the gallows platform. It all happened at once, suddenly, with Geno hopping the trough and plowing through the onlookers, cutting a wide wake with his broad shoulders, an arrow splitting the air above him as the trap door dropped open, and Gary finding himself instinctively heaving the great spear behind the arrow in its flight.

Kelsey's arrow hit the rope squarely, cutting an edge. Still the hemp held, and Pwyll's neck would surely have snapped, had not Gary's spear completed the task, its wide head easily shaving the rope in half as it flew past.

The crowd roared, a unified groan.

Baron Pwyll felt the sudden, sharp jerk, felt as if his head was about to be ripped off, and then he was falling, turning horizontally, and looking up to see himself hanging by the neck!

"I am dead!" he cried, and he was surprised to hear the sound of his own voice. He slammed against the ground, but was back up again, seeming to float in the air as he continued to stare blankly at his own corpse.

"You should be," Geno agreed, grunting under the tremendous weight as he whisked the Baron away.

Poor confused Pwyll didn't know what to think, caught halfway between what his senses were telling him and what his mind, what Mickey's illusions, were telling him.

From the far side of the crowd, Gary blinked, for he hadn't witnessed any of it. Horror and revulsion welled up inside him as he stared at the hanging and twitching Baron. But then Gary noticed Geno, his arms full of a second Pwyll, rushing out the back side of the gallows, and Gary remembered Mickey.

He looked through the illusion then, saw the severed rope, the dwarf running off, and his spear angled out of the ground twenty feet to the other side of the gallows. No one else was moving, though, caught up in the illusion, and Geldion hadn't called for any to block the fleeing dwarf's path.

A rumble of confusion and a cry of alarm began its inevitable roll through the crowd. Up on the platform, Geldion and his soldiers glanced all around, trying to see what the commotion was about, for to their eyes, Pwyll was hanging securely right below them.

Gary nearly jumped out of his armor when he felt something tap his shoulder. He turned to see his mount, down on its front knees, tossing its head anxiously. Gary hadn't even put his leg all the way over the beast's back before it took flight, flying around the side of the gathering.

More and more people were beginning to recognize the deception, beginning to point this way and that, mostly to the northeast. Prince Geldion looked down through the trap door and screamed in shock.

"Cedric Donigarten is come!" one villager cried, spying the armored rider.

"Woe to Connacht!" cried another.

"Kill him!" Geldion yelled,, stuttering over the words, spittle streaming from his thin lips. "We have been deceived! Oh, devil-spawned magic!"

"The game's over," Gary whispered, bending low and urging his steed on. He saw Geno link up with Kelsey and Mickey, the leprechaun up behind Kelsey. The dwarf heaved Pwyll up on the spare horse, then rushed to his pony.

A crossbow quarrel clicked off the shoulder-plating of Gary's armor. The road before Gary seemed clear, though, except that one soldier had rushed out of the keep's open door. The man had gone to the spear and was now tearing it from the ground.

"Dammit," Gary growled, and his steed seemed to read his thoughts, veering straight for the man. Gary thought he would have to run the man down, trample him flat, then wheel about and retrieve the spear on the second pass.

"*Hurry, young sprout!*" he heard in his mind, and he watched in thrilled amazement as a flashing jolt of energy coursed through the spear handle, hurling the soldier to the ground a dozen feet away and sending the weapon flying high into the air.

Gary caught the free-flying weapon in midstride, heard the sitting soldier cry out in terror as the horse bore down at him. But the beast of Tir na n'Og was intelligent indeed and not evil, and it lifted its legs and easily cleared the ducking man, landing solidly far beyond him and thundering about in a tight turn to get away from the occupied keep and catch up to the fleeing companions.

Gary held on for all his life, nearly went flying free as the horse wheeled. He heard a whistle in the air as another quarrel flew past.

"Mounts! Mounts!" one soldier was yelling above the din of the frenzied villagers, the angry shouts of Prince Geldion, and the sudden blare of horns.

Another quarrel zipped past and Gary bent as low as he could go, trying to present a small target. He saw the cloud of dust ahead as his sweating steed approached his companions, heard the tumult behind him fast fading.

He came up between Geno's pony and the horse bearing Pwyll, and nearly laughed aloud, despite the danger, when he saw that the Baron still had the noose and length of rope around his neck. Three long strides brought Gary beyond those two, up beside Kelsey and Mickey.

"The illusion did not hold!" the elf was claiming to the leprechaun.

"Didn't say it would," Mickey replied casually, puffing on his long-stemmed pipe—which Gary thought an amazing feat, given that they were in full gallop. He noted that there seemed to be an underlying tension behind the leprechaun's carefree façade, and thought it curious, as did Kelsey, that Mickey, who had created illusions to fool a dragon for many minutes, had not been able to trick the crowd for any length of time.

"They're coming!" Geno called from behind. Kelsey pulled up his horse and the others followed the lead, turning about to regard the now-distant keep. They saw the dust beginning to rise on the road back to the north and could hear the distant dull rumble of many hooves.

"How come every time we leave that place, there's a Prince chasing us?" Gary asked.

"Oh, my," groaned the thoroughly flustered Baron Pwyll. He growled repeatedly, getting all tangled up as he tried to get the noose off his neck. "Now I am in serious trouble."

Gary blinked in amazement; Geno snorted.

"More trouble than hanging?" Mickey asked, equally incredulous.

"Fear not," Kelsey assured them all, turning his mount back to the open road to the south. "No horse can match the pace of the mounts of Tir na n'Og!"

The elf handed Mickey over to Gary and kicked his steed away. Geno's pony flew past, with Pwyll's horse coming right behind.

"Ready for a run, lad?" Mickey asked, settling into his seat in front of Gary.

"Do I have a choice?" Gary replied, smiling.

Mickey glanced around the man, to the north and the approaching cavalry. "No," he said easily, puffing the pipe once more as Gary loosed his grip on the reins and the powerful steed of Tir na n'Og charged off.

SIX

A Sense of Strength

TWO score of villagers, peat farmers mostly, gathered on the western road out of Drochit to watch the curious gnome's departure. Gerbil had brought grave news to the Duncan Drochit, Lord of the town, word that mighty Robert the dragon had taken wing again, that darkness would soon descend over all the land. In return, the gnome had been given some news of his own, information about the reforging of Cedric's spear and the subsequent theft of the artifacts.

It didn't take a clever gnome to suspect that the two unusual events might be related (especially since Robert had reportedly been the one to supply the breath for reforging the spear), and so, with Duncan Drochit's promise that Braemar would be alerted, Gerbil had struck out west instead of south, for Dilnamarra and the riddle that might shed some light on the appearance of the dreaded wyrm.

The quadricycle gained speed steadily, despite the mud left over from an early morning rain and the load of supplies Gerbil had strapped into a basket behind his seat. Less than a hundred yards out of town, he had to stop and wait, though, as a shepherd herded his flock across the road, an all-too-common scene that would be repeated four times over the next few hours, with poor anxious Gerbil making sporadic headway to the west. Then he cleared the immediate farming areas near to the village, came into the more wild region between Drochit and Dilnamarra, and made more steady progress.

"I must figure a way to smooth out this road," the easily distracted inventor said to himself, his little legs pumping tirelessly as he bumped and slid along the uneven cart path. And so Gerbil filled the hours with thoughts of extending the Mountain Messenger, or of developing a better road system through the land, or, perhaps, of possible improvements to the quadricycle, such as stronger bump absorbers and a gear ratio designed for mud.

THE pursuit lagged behind, but was not given up, as the five companions continued their run down the south road. Soon they came to a crossroads, with four high poles stuck into the ground, one at each corner, and with torn corpses, barely recognizable as men, hanging by the neck from each of these.

This very spot had burned an indelible image into Gary Leger's memory, perhaps the worst memory he had of the land of Faerie. He remembered these very poles, and, he realized a moment later, remembered these very same men hanging by their necks!

They were more bloated now, pecked by the vultures, and one was so badly decomposed that it seemed as if he would soon break loose from the rope. But they were the same, Gary believed, to his horror and his confusion. He reared up his mount in the center of the intersection, staring unblinkingly at the garish sight.

"How long has it been?" he asked Mickey.

"They leave 'em until they fall of their own accord," the leprechaun answered grimly.

"No," Gary corrected. "I mean, how long has it been since I've been gone from Faerie?"

"Oh," Mickey answered. He began silently counting and looked to Kelsey. "Near to a month."

"One moon cycle," Kelsey agreed.

"Why, lad, how much time has passed in yer own world?" Mickey asked.

"Five years," Gary replied breathlessly.

"I thought that you looked older," Geno remarked dryly. "And older are we all getting, sitting here in the middle of this wonderful smell."

"With Prince Geldion coming fast behind!" the fearful Pwyll added, wiping the sweat from his blotchy face.

"Right ye are," said Mickey. "Off we go, then."

"The road to Connacht is surely blocked," Kelsey said. "So we go east, to Drochit and Braemar."

"Right ye are," Mickey said again, and he, too, now looked back to the north, growing fearful that Geldion would soon be upon them. "Off we go, then."

Kelsey wheeled his mount to the left, to the east, and started off a stride, but stopped abruptly as Gary Leger said, in a determined voice, "No!"

"No?" Geno echoed incredulously.

"I came through here once before," Gary explained. "And we let these men hang, fearful that cutting them down would tell Geldion that Kelsey of the Tylwyth Teg had passed through this spot." Gary looked directly at the elf. "For who but the Tylwyth Teg would dare to cut down lawfully convicted criminals?"

"We have not the time," Mickey interjected, guessing where Gary's speech was headed. The leprechaun, too, looked to Kelsey for support, but realized that Gary had cunningly struck a solid appeal to the elf's sense of honor.

Mickey was not surprised to see the elf dismounting, a determined and grim sparkle in his golden eyes.

"We'll make the time," Gary Leger replied to Mickey, throwing his leg over the saddle and sliding down to the ground. "I'm not passing through here and leaving these poor men to hang, not when, by your own words, they did nothing wrong."

"You cannot cut them down!" Baron Pwyll verily shrieked. "That is a crime against Connacht punishable by . . ."

"Hanging?" Gary finished for him, in an unshaking voice. "Well, if I am caught and hung, then I hope someone will do for me what I am about to do for these men."

Noble Kelsey was nodding his complete agreement through it all.

"We have half an hour's lead, elf," the pragmatic Geno said. "No time for digging graves."

"Not even shallow ones?" Kelsey asked, pleaded, and Geno shrugged and hopped off the pony, motioning for Pwyll to come and help him. The Baron seemed hesitant and made no move to dismount, until the dwarf walked over and spoke to him privately—a line of deadly serious threats, no doubt.

Kelsey shimmied up the poles and worked the ropes, while Gary used the butt end of the long spear to gently guide the rotting bodies down. By the time they had the four men cut down and planted in the shallow graves, the cloud of rising dust had reappeared just a few minutes behind them on the road to the north.

"Time for flying," Mickey, the first to spot the dust, remarked. The others were back in their saddles in a moment, Pwyll moaning and looking back in sheer terror, and Kelsey leading the charge to the east.

"Ye've grown a bit in yer five years, lad," Mickey remarked when Gary was back up behind him. The leprechaun gave a squeeze on Gary's rock-hard forearm. "In body and in spirit, so it'd seem."

"*Well done, young sprout,*" Cedric's spear telepathically added.

Gary accepted both compliments in silent agreement. The fact that he had grown in strength was obvious, and increasingly obvious, too, was his new-found strength of character and confidence. The last time he was in Faerie, Gary hadn't been able to understand the motivations of Kelsey, so noble and so aloof. Kelsey's life was one dedicated slavishly to principles, to intangibles, something not quite foreign, but certainly not familiar, to the young man raised in a world of material possessions, a world that he himself had come to think of as spiritually bereft.

Gary could accept those faults in his own world, the real world, could play games on Route 2 with stressed-out drivers, could smile at the jokes about the latest enemy, the latest "created Robert," and had no choice but to accept the "progress" that was inevitably eating away at the woods out back and at the quality of life in general all about him.

But not in Faerie. The wrongs here were more black and white, more definitive, tainting an air that was too pure to be clouded with smoke. Bringing up the rear as the party charged down the eastern road, clutching tightly to that most mighty spear of legend with an evil prince and his soldiers only a few minutes, behind, Gary Leger felt a sense of euphoria, a sense of righteousness.

A sense of strength.

"HE will be trouble again!" the raven-haired witch snarled as she stared into her crystal ball, stared at the tiny images of Gary Leger and Kelsey and the others taking flight to the east, past the crossroads.

"Trouble for Lady?" Geek the spindly armed goblin asked, trying to sound incredulous. "Who could be trouble for most mightiest Lady?"

"Dear Geek," Ceridwen purred at him, turning slowly about on the satiny covers of the pillowy-soft bed, a disarming smile on her face. Her hand whipped across, catching Geek on the side of the head and launching him several feet before he crumpled against an ornately carved night table, to fall whimpering on the floor. The goblin quickly scrambled back to the foot of the bed when Alice, Ceridwen's pet lion, leaped up from her bed on the opposite wall, startled by the noise.

"You stupid goblin," the witch growled, looking from Geek to her always-hungry pet. Geek whimpered, understanding what she was thinking, and crawled under the bed. "Trouble like he was trouble for me before!" Ceridwen continued, talking more to herself than to the hidden and cowering goblin. The witch's belly ached with remembered pain as she thought of that fateful day on the mountain outside Robert's castle. She had them, the whole group, at her mercy, until that wretched Gary Leger had thrown the cruel spear.

Ceridwen's wounds had not been mortal, of course. In Faerie, the witch could not truly be killed. But Gary's action had defeated Ceridwen, had banished her to Ynis Gwydrin, her island home, for a hundred years.

The Lady Ceridwen was not a patient witch.

She looked back to her crystal ball, still focused on the crossroads. More horsemen charged into the scene, paused to study the tracks, then veered east, as Prince Geldion continued the pursuit.

Ceridwen's lips curled up in an evil smile. "Geldion," she purred, and then she waved her hand quickly across the ball, dispelling the image to smoky nothingness.

"Geek!" she called, snapping her fingers. A crackle sounded, along with a flash of sparking light under the bed, and Geek rolled out rubbing his smoldering posterior. "Go and fetch Akk Akk," Ceridwen instructed, referring to the leader of the giant monkey-bats that lived in the tunnels far below Ynis Gwydrin.

Geek cringed. He didn't like dealing with Akk Akk, or any of the unpredictable and stupid (even by goblin standards) monkey-bats. Twice before, when he was delivering similar messages from Ceridwen, Akk Akk had tried to nibble on flat-faced Geek's large and pointy ears.

Ceridwen dropped an angry glare on the goblin, then, and Geek realized that sitting in the middle of the witch's private chambers was not a good place to be when deliberating whether or not to obey one of her unbending commands. Ceridwen's icy-blue eyes flashed dangerously and she snapped her fingers again, and Geek cried out, hopped to his feet, and ran off, skipping about wildly and patting at the igniting sparks crackling across his butt.

As soon as he was gone, the witch ordered her bedroom door to swing closed. "Let us see who will win this time, dear Alice," she said to her pet, now in the form of an ordinary housecat, circling about and kneading at the pillows in its soft bed. "Let us see if Gary Leger and his pitiful friends can escape when I am guiding the pursuit."

Ceridwen's smile grew wider than it had for a month. There were ways to break banishments, the witch knew. Robert had found one, and was out and flying, and, with Gary Leger back in the land of Faerie, so, too, might she.

The witch's eyes flashed again. A second wave of her deceivingly delicate hand and a soft chant brought a new image into focus in the crystal ball, that of the throne room in Castle Connacht, where King Kinnemore, Ceridwen's perfect stooge, sat waiting.

KELSEY led the way down the wide road into the thick forest of Cowtangle. A short way in, the elf paused to get his bearings, then nodded and moved his mount to the side of the road, to a narrower path barely visible behind some thick brush. Kelsey dismounted and motioned for his friends to pass by, then took a wide branch and brushed the narrow trail and the main road clear of tracks.

"This should put Geldion back a while," the elf explained, coming past Gary and Mickey.

"Even if Geldion goes straight through," Gary said grimly, "he'll stay on the east road. Can we afford to have him riding directly ahead of us all the way to the mountains?"

"We will not stay on the road," Kelsey replied, nodding to show that he agreed with Gary's surprising show of reasoning. "We shall parallel it to the east, come to the mountains south of Braemar."

"Where I take my leave," Geno put in.

Gary started to reply to the dwarf, but Mickey tapped him on the wrist and whispered that it wasn't worth the argument.

"There, we will skirt the mountains south, and then east," Kelsey continued, "following our original course through the Crahgs and to the Giant's Thumb."

"If the wild hairy haggis doesn't get you all first," Geno put in with a wicked smile, a smile that turned into a belly laugh when the dwarf noticed how pale Baron Pwyll's face had become.

The dwarf was still roaring when Kelsey took up the lead and started off again down the narrow trail. A short while later, they heard Geldion's contingent gallop by on the main road, and they were relieved.

But it was short-lived, for a notion came into Prince Geldion's mind, an insight sent by a spying hawk serving a witch in an island castle more than a hundred miles away. Soon the companions on the narrow trail heard the unmistakable clip-clopping of horse hooves on the path behind them.

"How'd he know?" Mickey asked incredulously.

"Good fortune," Kelsey replied grimly, before any of the others could utter any more ominous possibilities. The trail forked a short distance ahead and Kelsey veered from the main easterly course, turning southeast.

"Where are we going?" Gary asked Mickey quietly, as the path continued to turn, and soon had them heading right back to the west.

"Kelsey knows the wood better than any," was all that Mickey would reply, though his grave tone sent alarms off in Gary's head. "Keep yer faith." Gary had to be satisfied with that, though he suspected that the leprechaun knew more about their course than he was letting on.

And indeed Mickey did. The leprechaun knew that the path they were riding would take them to the southwestern corner of the small wood, a place of steamy fens and bottomless bogs, and horrid monsters that appreciated having their dinners delivered.

SEVEN

Ghosts in the Wood

WHAT had gone from a gallop down a wide road to a trot down a narrow path soon became a plod along a barely discernible and winding way around steamy wet bogs. The annoying buzz of gnats and mosquitoes replaced the chatter of birds, and low-hanging fog stole the crystal blue from the sky.

"The land of fantasies," Gary Leger remarked quietly, and even his whisper seemed to come back at him ominously.

"And of nightmares," Baron Pwyll put in, sweat covering his thick-skinned face and his eyes wide and darting from side to side as though he expected some horrid monster to spring out and throttle him at any moment.

"Not so bad," Mickey said to keep Gary calm. "She's a quiet place really, even if she's looking like a home for the spooks."

The three of them hardly noticed that Kelsey and Geno, up in front, had stopped their march, with Kelsey turning his mount sideways along the narrow path so that he could look all about. The elf sat shaking his head, golden eyes squinting and lips pursed as though he had just taken a big bite out of a grapefruit.

"What is it?" Mickey prompted.

"I did not believe that Geldion would follow us in here," Kelsey admitted. "Even the mounts of Tir na n'Og have difficulty navigating the treacherous bogs. The Prince is likely to lose more than a few men."

Gary looked all around, confused. "How do you know that he's following us?" he asked, for he had noticed nothing that would indicate pursuit.

Kelsey put a finger to his lips, and all the companions went perfectly silent for a few moments. At first, Gary heard nothing but the endless din of insects, and the occasional nicker from one of the mounts, but then came the unmistakable, though distant, clip-clop of horses plodding through the soft ground.

"I'd lay ye a good-odds bet that our Geldion's got eyes guiding his way,"

Mickey remarked to Kelsey, and the elf didn't have to ask whom the leprechaun was referring to.

Kelsey clicked softly to his mount and tugged the reins to right the stallion on the path. The elf had hoped to skirt the bogs and come back into the forest proper before nightfall. But now, though the sun was fast sinking in the western sky, he turned deeper into the swamp.

"Damned elf ears," Mickey said softly to Gary. "If he hadn't gone and heard Geldion's horses, we'd be away from this place afore the night."

"She's not so bad," Gary said, echoing the leprechaun's earlier remarks.

"Ye just keep believing that, lad," Mickey replied, and Gary didn't miss the honest look of trepidation that crossed the leprechaun's face as he lit up his long-stemmed pipe once more.

The moon was up soon after the sun went down, and the swamp did not become so dark. The ground-hugging mist glistened, seemed to have a light of its own, starkly outlining the reaching branches of dead trees, and swirling to create images that had names only in the imaginations of frightened witnesses.

Kelsey was glad for the glow, for he could continue to walk his mount along, but Gary found himself wishing for blackness. Mickey pretended to be asleep, but Gary often saw him peeking out through a half-closed eye from under his tam-o'-shanter. Even Geno seemed fearful, clutching a hammer so tightly that his knuckles had whitened around it, and poor Pwyll fell into several fits of trembling and whimpering, and would have broken down altogether had not the dwarf promptly stepped his pony back to the Baron and whispered in his ear—probably threats, Gary realized.

The young stranger to Faerie couldn't blame the Baron, though, couldn't fault the man for his weakness in this place that looked "like a home for the spooks," as Mickey had put it. Bats were out in force, squeaking and squealing as they darted all about, easily getting their fill of insects. The sucking noises of the horses' hooves pulling free of the grabbing mud came to sound like a heartbeat to Gary, or like the gurgling spittle of a rasping ghoul.

He peered closely into the fog at his side when they passed one fen, watching the edge of an angled log half floating in the stagnant water. Another branch was sticking straight up, just a few inches above the pool, its twigs resembling the dried fingers of a long-dead corpse.

Just your imagination, Gary stubbornly and repeatedly told himself, but that thought held little weight when the supposed "twigs" clenched suddenly into an upraised fist.

"Oh, no," he muttered.

"What is it, lad?" Mickey asked, the leprechaun's gray eyes popping open wide.

Gary sat perfectly still, holding tight to the bridle of his nervous and unmoving horse.

The arm began to rise up out of the pool.

"What is it?" Mickey asked again, more frantically.

Gary's reply came as a series of deep breaths, a futile attempt by the young man to steady his nerves.

"Oh, Kelsey," the leprechaun quietly sung out, seeing no real answer forthcoming.

Nervous Baron Pwyll looked back to discern the problem with the trailing mount, looking from Gary's frozen stare to the pool. The fat man immediately spotted the arm, and then the top of a head, with matted, blotchy hair surrounding many open sores. Pwyll meant to cry out, "Ghost!" but his stuttered cry came out as simply "GAAA!"

The Baron was nearly jerked from his saddle then, as Kelsey rode back, grabbed the bridle from Pwyll's hands and bolted away. Geno acted equally resourceful, skipping his pony past Pwyll's mount (and growing more than a bit frightened as his pony's hooves splashed into foot-deep water), and similarly grabbing at the bridle on Gary's horse.

Gary never saw the face of the ghoulish creature rising from the bog, but he pictured it a hundred different ways, none of them overly pleasant. The group raced off as fast as Kelsey could lead them, and when the commotion had died away, they were all startled once more, this time by the calls of pursuit not far behind them. Kelsey veered into a brush tangle and pulled up there to get his bearings, the others coming in right behind, all of them eager to remain in a tight group.

"They're even following us at night," Mickey whispered to Kelsey. "Who do ye know that'd come through the fens without being chased through the fens?"

"We're being chased through, and I don't want to be here," Gary put in sarcastically.

"The witch," Geno reasoned, to Pwyll's accompanying groan.

"Our pursuit is being guided," Kelsey admitted. "Surely. Perhaps by Ceridwen, but in any case, I do not believe that we will leave them behind."

"We'll leave them behind," Geno promised grimly, pulling out a hammer and slapping it across his open palm.

"Prince Geldion rides with at least a score of men," Pwyll argued.

"Twenty more ghosts for this haunted swamp," the dwarf solidly replied. Geno tossed the hammer up into the air, then caught it perfectly in his gnarly hand.

"More than a score, I'd be guessing," muttered Mickey, poking his chin out to the side, not behind, where the others were generally looking. A line of torches, two dozen at least, was evident through the fog and the trees, moving slowly and parallel to the path the companions had been riding.

"Flanking us," Geno remarked, his surprise obvious.

"And many more behind, would be me own guess," Mickey said. Kelsey ran his slender fingers through his thick and long golden hair, then put a questioning stare on Mickey as he reached for his long bow.

"I can slow 'em perhaps," the leprechaun replied. "But I'm not likely to be stopping 'em." He closed his eyes then, and began chanting and waggling his fingers in the air before him, in the direction of the flanking soldiers.

A second grouping of torches appeared, farther down the trail from the line of riders.

"There they are!" came a cry, followed by a unified roar and the instant rumble of charging hoofbeats. The torches intersected and became a scramble of lights through the fog. Horses whinnied, complaining of being pulled up so short, and there came several wet thuds, as though mount and rider had gone down.

"Will-o'-the-wisps!" came one cry above the general tumult.

"Not really," Mickey said to his friends, taking another long draw on his pipe. "It's just lookin' that way. A bit o' pixie lights, actually."

The flanking line was soon in wild retreat, most riding, but some men running, and with less than half the torches burning that the companions had previously noted. One rider came splashing through the bogs directly for the brush that held the companions, though he obviously couldn't see them. His cry sounded remarkably like Pwyll's stuttered attempt at "Ghost!" and he was looking too much over his shoulder for such a pace in so treacherous an area.

His horse hit some deeper water and rolled over headlong, pitching the soldier through the air. He slammed heavily into a dead tree and plopped down into the water, springing right back to his feet and running on, trying to wipe the blood and muck out of his eyes.

"They're as scared as we are," Gary reasoned, an idea coming to him along with a smile.

"As you are," Geno, gruffly corrected.

"Even better," Gary replied.

"What are ye thinking, lad?" Mickey asked, but the leprechaun would have to wait for his answer, for the fleeing cavalry apparently had linked up with Geldion's main force, and there came the sound of many riders approaching quickly from behind.

"Be off," Kelsey instructed, and his companions didn't have to be asked twice.

Gary Leger had an idea. "When I was a kid, we always threw scary parties on Halloween," he said to Mickey as they tromped along at the back of the line.

"Allhallows Eve?" the leprechaun asked.

Gary nodded. "Everyone was afraid," he explained with a wry smile, "except for the kids doing the haunting."

Mickey took a long draw on the pipe and rolled his eyes as he considered Gary's point. His smile soon outshone Gary's.

"I told you to get the damned bugs out!" Geno grumbled at Pwyll as the fat Baron slipped a hollowed log over the dwarf's arm. Pwyll immediately retracted the limb and brushed aside a few bugs, then slipped it back over the dwarf's outstretched arm.

"Quietly!" Kelsey demanded, his voice muffled because his shirt was pulled up high over his head and buttoned tight.

"Can you see?" Gary asked the elf.

"Well enough," Kelsey answered.

"Well enough to ride?"

The "headless" elf pulled open a space between two buttons and glowered at Gary. "Just point me at the horse," he growled, his frustration only heightening at the sight of Gary's smirk.

"This will work," Gary said to calm him.

Kelsey nodded, making the whole top part of his tightly pinned torso bob crazily. Despite his frustration—frustration born of fear—the elf approved of Gary's plan and thought it the best way for the companions to escape Geldion without an all-out battle. Gary helped him get to his horse, then, and helped him get up, and soon Kelsey seemed to settle into the saddle.

"Perfect!" Baron Pwyll proclaimed, popping a stubby piece of rotting wood over Geno's head and lining it with brush.

"There ye go, lad," Mickey said, bobbing over to join Gary. The leprechaun cradled a curved piece of bark, a makeshift bowl, filled with some type of golden glistening mud. "Stand still and put yer arms out wide."

"What is it?" Gary asked.

"Something to give ye a ghostly glow," Mickey assured him. The leprechaun rubbed some of the mud on the hip-plate of Gary's armor and indeed, that section of the mail suit took on an eerie golden glow.

"Our enemies approach," Kelsey announced. He kicked his horse away, taking a side route so that he might flank Geldion's force. Pwyll took the reins of the other two horses and the pony and started away, turning back once to remind Geno to "Look like a tree!"

"Geno'll hold this spot," Mickey said to Gary. "And Kelsey will hit 'em on the right. There's a ford across the bog to the left, a place Geldion might know."

"Lead on," the glowing warrior bade the leprechaun.

Soon after, the area was quiet, except for the shuffling feet of Geno the tree as the dwarf tried to get into a better position. The toes of his hard boots stuck out from under the trunk he wore from shoetops to armpits, and his stubby finger couldn't even reach the end of the logs Pwyll had slipped over his arms. Even worse, Geno could hardly see at all, peeking out from under his treelike helmet, through strands of thick brush, and he feared that he might trip and fall, and lie like a helpless turtle on his back until (hopefully) one of the others came back for him.

"Stupid plan," the dwarf muttered, and then he went silent, hearing a group of soldiers moving along the path.

KELSEY took many a stinging hit from low-hanging branches as his horse trotted through the thick brush. He held his seat easily, though, his strong legs wrapped tightly around his mount's back while he clutched his longbow, an arrow notched and ready.

"Find me a wide and safe run," he whispered to his horse when the torches of Geldion's flanking line came into sight. Gary had told Kelsey—and Kelsey thought it good advice—that his only chance was to make quick, fleeting passes at the soldiers, never to give the enemy a good view of him.

A few moments later, Kelsey's mount waited patiently behind a copse of trees, with a clear run before it and Geldion's soldiers coming along a paralleling course barely twenty feet to the side.

Kelsey held his horse back until the very last instant, then burst from the copse, groaning loudly, as Gary had instructed.

"There's one of . . ." a soldier cried, but his sentence got cut short, turned into an indecipherable gurgle, when an arrow drove into his hip.

The flanking line took up a cry of attack and swung about to charge out and intercept the fast-flying specter. Kelsey thought that the game was up. He fired a steady stream of arrows into the air, having no idea of how many, if any, might hit the mark, and kept his limited vision focused straight ahead, trying to discern an escape route once the wide run ended.

Soldiers crashed their mounts through the blocking brush, a solid line of horsemen at first, but gradually dissipating until those few who suddenly found themselves out in front looked back curiously, then looked ahead to see what had stopped their eager comrades.

"Hey, he ain't got no head!" one man cried—one man and then many.

Kelsey heard the call and smiled under his high-pulled shirt. He dropped the bow across his lap, and in a powerful motion drew out his enchanted long sword, its rune-etched blade glowing a fierce blue that accurately reflected the elf's inner fires. Kelsey pulled hard on the reins, reared the stallion and then swung him about.

"Ring!" he commanded the bells, and a thousand tinkling chimes accompanied his return charge.

"He ain't got no head!" another man cried.

"Give me back my head!" Kelsey answered in a mournful, crooning voice, again as Gary Leger had instructed him.

One of the front soldiers, the captain of this contingent, sitting right in Kelsey's path, chewed on his lip and rubbed his fingers anxiously, desperately, along the hilt of his sword. He heard some of his forces breaking rank altogether, and didn't know which way to go.

"Give me back my head!" Kelsey growled ominously once more.

"If any's got it, then give the damned thing back!" another soldier, farther down the fast-disintegrating line, cried out desperately.

"Hey," the captain realized suddenly, straightening in his saddle. "If he ain't got no head, then how's he talking?" Thinking that he had uncovered the ruse, the captain turned smugly to one side and then the other.

Only to find that he was sitting out there all alone.

"I ain't got your damned head!" the captain shrieked at the closing horseman, and he threw his sword Kelsey's way, wheeled his horse about and galloped away, screaming, as were his deserting soldiers, of "headless horsemen in the bog!"

"THEY were here," one of the lead scouts said to his companion, studying the area where the five friends had split up. "And none too long ago." The man bent low to study the fog-enshrouded ground beneath one small tree, his companion right at his back, waiting for news.

Something hard conked the standing man on the back of the head.

"Who?" he stuttered, spinning about.

"What're you about?" the crouching scout asked him, looking back over his stooped shoulder.

"Something hit me on the head," the other man explained.

"This place is scary enough without your imagining things," the scout scolded. "Now, be alert."

The other man shrugged and adjusted his cap, looking back to his searching friend.

Something hard conked him on the back of the head again, harder this time.

"Ouch," he said, stumbling into the crouching scout and grabbing at the back of his noggin.

"What?" the exasperated scout began.

"Something hit me on the back of the head," the man protested, and the fact that his cap was five feet out in front of the two of them added credence to the claim.

The scout pulled a small axe from his belt, motioned for the other man to go around one side of the small tree, while he went around the other.

They hopped in unison around the trunk, coming to a standstill facing each other above one of the tree's two low-hanging branches.

"Nothing here," the scout said dryly.

"I'm telling you," the other man began, but he stopped as the tree suddenly began to shake, its two limbs bobbing, its twiggy clump of branches rustling.

"What in the name of a hairy haggis?" the scout asked, scratching his forehead.

Geno brought his arm, his limb, straight back, clunking the scout on the nose, then shot it forward with all his strength, catching the unfortunate other man under the chin and launching him into the air. He landed in the muck on the seat of his pants, gasping and scrambling to get away.

The tree spun about to face the scout squarely, but the man was not so intimidated. He wiped the blood off his upper lip and regarded it angrily. "Damned haunted tree!" he roared and his hatchet rushed in, splitting the bark and coming to a sudden stop close enough to Geno's face so that the dwarf could stick out his tongue and lick the weapon's razor-sharp edge.

Geno turned quickly, one way and then the other, back and forth, his straightened limbs battering the scout's arms and shoulders. The man let go of his axe and tried to run, but got clipped and fell to the ground. Geno, trying to follow, tripped over the scout's feet, and he, too, came tumbling down.

The tree-dwarf flattened the scout under him, burying the man in the soft muck.

"Now what?" the dwarf muttered under his breath, helplessly prone with the frantic man trying to scramble out from under him. Geno began to shake wildly again, twisting so that his still-widespread arms continued to batter at the man. He added a haunting groan to heighten the effect.

But then Geno was cursing his encumbering suit as the scout wriggled free, knowing that it would take him a long time to get to his feet, knowing that the man had him helpless.

The scout didn't know it, though, for he had seen more than enough. As soon as he came up, spitting mud, he took off in full flight behind his already departing companion.

He never looked back—and soon after, he retired as a scout and took up basket weaving.

THE five soldiers approached the ford, and the ghostly limned and impressive figure in the metal plate-mail armor, with due caution, their weapons drawn and the five of them repeatedly looking to each other for support.

"Standing and waiting for us to come and get you?" one of them said as they neared the man.

"I am the ghost of Cedric Donigarten!" Gary Leger growled at them, standing resolute, the wondrous spear planted firmly in the ground before him.

Two of the soldiers backed away, two started to follow, but the fifth, a dirty-faced man with the green cap of a forest tracker, laughed aloud. "Oh, are ye, then?" he asked between chuckles. "Then ye wouldn't happen to be that Gary Leger lad from Bretaigne, beyond Cancarron Mountains? Ye know who I mean, the one who fits so well in old Donigarten's armor?"

"Trouble, lad," Mickey whispered, perched out of sight on a low branch right behind the young man.

Mickey had recognized the speaker, and now so too did Gary, as one of Prince Geldion's personal escorts, one of the men who had been in attendance when Gary had gone with Kelsey and Mickey to originally retrieve the armor from Baron Pwyll, before they had ever set out to reforge the legendary spear. Gary feared that Mickey's estimate was correct, that the game was suddenly over, but some of the whispers behind the confident soldier gave him hope.

"No man, you fool," one of the retreating men remarked. "See how he's glowing."

"Moon-mud," the sly man replied. "He's a man in a suit of metal, is all he is, and no more a ghost than meself. Don't ye know at least Cedric's spear, if not the armor?"

"I am the ghost of Cedric Donigarten!" Gary growled again. "I am invincible!"

"Let's see," the sly man retorted, and he came forward a few steps, two of his comrades tentatively at his sides.

Gary Leger tore the spear from the ground and held it out sidelong in front of him. "NONE SHALL PASS!" he declared in a booming voice, and the two flanking men stopped, causing their sly companion to pause and stare at them incredulously.

"Oh, that's good, lad," Mickey whispered from behind.

"Monty Python and the Holy Grail," Gary whispered over his shoulder. "When he hits me, make my arm fall off."

Mickey started to question that last remark, but the men were advancing again, swords ready. The sly man came suddenly, in a wild flurry, and Gary worked the spear all around, parrying the measured swordthrusts. The soldier quickly grew frustrated, and came ahead with a straightforward thrust.

Gary hopped aside and slapped down with the spearhead, likewise forcing the swordtip to dip. He put his opposite foot forward and turned his body beside his lunging opponent, coming near to the man and smacking him on the side of the head with the long handle of the spear.

"I am invincible!" Gary declared again, hands on hips, as the soldier retreated a few steps to shake the dizziness from his vision.

"Five of us can take . . ." the soldier cried, looking around, only to find that the two men at the back of his group were long gone. "Three of us can take him!" the man corrected. "Together, I say, or face the wrath of Prince Geldion!"

The other two looked doubtfully at each other. The indomitable forest tracker slapped the sword from one man's hand. "I'll not be asking again," the cruel and sly man said evenly.

They came at Gary together, and only through his symbiosis with the magnificent weapon, the lessons the spear had subconsciously taught him, was Gary able to dance about, twirling the spear, and fend off the initial attacks. Fortunately, his enemies' attacks were not well coordinated, though they certainly kept Gary back on his heels. He whipped the spear side to side, brought it up suddenly to stop an overhead chop, then whipped it to his left, knocking aside a darting sword.

Gary didn't know how long he could keep it up. He knocked away the sword to his left again, then the one to his right, and when he brought the spear back in line to halt the sly man's straightforward thrust, he saw an opening.

He could have driven his speartip right through the man's chest, and with that man—who was obviously the leader—dead, the other two would likely have turned and fled. But Gary had to face the consequences before he made the move, had to come to terms with killing another human being.

His hesitation cost him the opening, and nearly the fight, as the man on his left came in stubbornly again, the sword just missing as the spearshaft deflected it aside.

The man jumped back and whooped with delight, and the sly man turned and punched him victoriously on the shoulder.

Gary didn't have a clue of what they were so excited about—until he looked down to see his armored arm lying at his feet.

"Right," Gary cried, trying to defeat his own shock and remember the script. He lifted the mighty spear in one hand, the one remaining hand that appeared to his opponents to be intact. "Have at it!"

The three soldiers screwed up their faces and looked to each other, then back to the stubborn knight.

"Come along then," Gary growled at them, lifting the spear in his right hand and leveling it in front of him.

"Yield," the sly man replied and he sarcastically added, "ye one-armed ghost."

"'Tis but a scratch," Gary insisted. "And though the blood may SPURT from my shoulder, it will soon heal," he added putting a heavy emphasis on the missing visual effect. On cue, a gusher of blood spurted from Gary's shoulder, splashing to the ground.

"I've had worse," Gary said calmly to the disbelieving men.

"AAAAH!"

The tracker found himself suddenly all alone, and even he did not seem so keen for the fight. Gary waved the spear again, and the man advanced a step, but then looked back to Gary's feet, his eyeballs nearly falling free of their sockets, and promptly turned and ran away.

Gary's stomach did a flip-flop when he, too, looked down, to see his severed limb grabbing at his ankle and trying to crawl back up in place.

"Enough, enough," he whispered harshly, gagging in tune with the leprechaun's merry chuckling.

"Oh, a fine plan it was, lad," Mickey congratulated, coming from his hiding place, and privately patting himself on the back for being able to pull off the somewhat simple illusion. "Our tricks'll put Geldion and his men on their heels for sure."

"If the others had similar success, we should get far away," Gary agreed, breathing easier now that the image of his own severed arm was no more.

"Now," Mickey began in all seriousness. "I'm knowing about the holy grail and where the thing is hidden, but tell me who or what this Monty Python fellow might be."

EIGHT
Gerbil's Ride

MICKEY and Gary found Geno lying half-buried in the soft ground, spitting curses and spitting muck, with Baron Pwyll standing helplessly over him. It took some effort—the dwarf seemed to weigh as much as an equal volume of lead—but by freeing up Geno's arms from their encumbering logs and using those logs as levers, Gary and Pwyll finally managed to stand the grumpy tree-dwarf upright.

"Stupid plan," Geno growled, smashing wildly at his bark trappings until he had split the log in half. He came out of the suit and scraped the mud from his body, flicked a few confused insects from his arms and shoulders, and ate a few more that looked too tasty to resist. Even the meal did little to improve the dwarf's mood.

"Stupid plan," he said again. On impulse, before Gary could react, the dwarf reached up and slugged Gary in the shoulder, launching him sidelong to land in the muck.

"It worked!" the startled young man protested, louder than he should have. All four went quiet immediately, fearing the consequences of Gary's cry, but when they stopped making so much noise, they heard the general commotion Gary's plan had caused. Screams and shrieks cut through the night fog, calls of ghosts, of headless horsemen, and of the trees themselves turning against the force. Further confirmation of the success came a few moments later, when Kelsey rode up, his head free of the high-laced tunic and a smile wide upon his fair face.

"They are in complete disarray," the elf remarked.

"Stupid plan," Geno said again, under his beetle-tainted breath.

"The Prince was not swayed by the claims of his returning men," Kelsey explained. "He blamed it on demon magics, and said that we would surely hang for our evil tricks."

"Then some of them are still coming," Mickey reasoned.

Kelsey's smile widened as he shook his head. "For all of Prince Geldion's determination, even he was taken aback by a trick that was not of our doing."

The elf paused, inviting a guess, and Mickey's grin came to equal Kelsey's as he caught on. "Geldion passed the swamp with the ghoul," the leprechaun reasoned.

Kelsey laughed aloud. "It seems that Prince Geldion called it an illusion, a magic trick. He even walked up to it as it crawled out of the muck to prove to his men that it was only an image and nothing substantial. The Prince wears a scar on his cheek for his foolishness."

It was all very welcome news, but Gary only half listened as Kelsey went on to explain that the Connacht soldiers had backtracked out of the swamp and would be far from the trail when they exited Cowtangle. Gary thought of the monster, the undead ghoul, they had seen crawling out of the muck, a monster that was, apparently, very real indeed. Now that the tricks were over and the immediate threat had been put off, the hairs on the back of Gary Leger's neck began to tingle. What the hell were they so happy about? he thought. They were in the middle of a haunted swamp, complete with ghouls, on a dark night.

Gary's heart did not slow any when he saw a stilted, leaning form coming slowly through the glowing mist.

"Where are the horses?" he asked, loudly enough to interrupt the continuing conversation.

"I tethered them a short distance ahead," Baron Pwyll explained. "Couldn't have them wandering about in this evil place."

"We should get to them," Gary offered, and he nodded ahead to guide the curious gazes of the others. A rare gust of the wind cleared the mist temporarily, and Gary's mouth dropped open wide. He saw the creature, a badly decomposed body of a long-dead man, skin hanging in loose flaps, one eye fallen back into its head, and, to his horror, Gary Leger recognized the corpse.

"Dad," he mouthed, hardly able to spit the word.

"We weren't for staying anyway," he heard Mickey say, and a moment later, Kelsey grabbed him by the shoulder and tugged at him. Gary resisted, or, at least, his planted feet made no move to help the movement. Kelsey called for help and Geno came over, wrapped his muscular arms around Gary's legs, and hoisted the man clear of the ground. They soon outdistanced the night creature, leaving it behind in a swirl of fog, but that awful image hung heavy in Gary's mind, stealing any words from his impossibly dry mouth, long after they had retrieved the mounts, long after they had picked their way along the muddy paths, long after they had exited the swamp and then the wood altogether.

Sitting in the nook between Gary and the horse's neck, Mickey soon recognized the true source of his friend's distress. "Ye knew the ghost," the leprechaun stated, understanding the tricks of night creatures quite well.

Gary just nodded, couldn't even manage a verbal response, his words caught fast by the image of his father as a corpse.

"They'll do that to ye," Mickey explained, seeing clearly what had happened and trying to put Gary at ease. "Them spirits're smart, lad. They look into yer head and see what'll most get at ye."

Gary nodded and Mickey fell silent, knowing that he could do no more for his friend. The words did comfort Gary a bit, but that image remained, powerful and horrible. A large part of Gary wanted to be done with this adventure at once, wanted to go back to the other world, the real world, to ensure that his dear father was all right.

They rode hard and fast over the course of the next day, and started out early the day after that, the Tir na n'Og mounts running easily in the low brush not too far from the side of the eastern road. Kelsey had determined that they would go into the small farming and mining community of Braemar, unless Geldion beat them to the place, and learn if the dragon had been spotted out from his mountain home.

With his sharp eyes, the elf, in the lead, spotted a disturbance farther up the road, a commotion he feared might involve the Prince. He veered his mount farther to the side, putting some distance between himself and the road, and bidding the others to follow.

"Something up ahead?" Mickey asked, shielding his eyes with one hand and peering to the east, below the late morning sun.

There came a distant shriek in answer.

"Damned Prince," Geno muttered.

"Or someone in trouble," Gary offered. He looked to Kelsey, almost begging permission to ride out and see what was about.

"It is not our affair," the elf said coolly, but Gary saw Kelsey unintentionally cringe when another cry cut the air.

"Of course it is," Gary said, and he gave a tug on the bridle and sent his mount leaping beyond Kelsey. A whistle and single word from the elf stopped the mount so abruptly that Gary nearly fell from his saddle, and Mickey did topple, popping open an umbrella that came from somewhere, somehow, and floated to the grass, a not-happy expression splayed across his cherubic face.

"You feel no responsibility to check this out?" Gary asked bluntly, turning back in his saddle as soon as he was sure that Mickey was all right.

Kelsey didn't immediately reply—which caught Gary somewhat off guard. "I fear to proceed," Kelsey explained calmly. "There is too much at stake for us to risk an encounter with Prince Geldion."

"Well, you won't have to proceed, elf," Geno offered, pointing past Gary to the road up ahead. "Looks like the fight is coming to us."

It was true enough. Gary turned back the other way to see a cloud of dust rising from the road, and stringing out in their direction. Above it fluttered a group of strange and ugly creatures, appearing as vicious monkeys, dark-furred, with too-wide eyes and red mouths lined by long fangs. They flew about on leathery bat wings, twelve feet across, and even from this distance, Gary could make out the hooked claws extending from their back feet.

The road was up higher than the companions, and from this angle, they could not discern what the monstrous group was pursuing. Gary figured it to be a horseman, though he hadn't yet heard the pounding of hooves, for whatever or whoever it might be was moving with great speed.

"That looks more like Ceridwen's doing than Prince Geldion's," Mickey said, aiming his remark at Kelsey.

"They may be one and the same," the elf retorted, but it was obvious from Kelsey's hurried tone, and from the fact that he had already strung his bow, that the noble elf would not abandon whoever it was that was in peril on the road.

"Surely you're not thinking of attacking those monstrous things!" Baron Pwyll said to him, blanching as he spoke.

"Find a rock to crawl under," Geno said, juggling three spinning hammers as he walked his pony beyond the fat man's mount.

Gary liked what he was hearing, liked the fact that his companions, even surly Geno, seemed concerned with something beyond their specific business. How many times in his own world had he heard about people turning their heads and looking away when someone else was in trouble?

"Let me down, lad," Mickey said unexpectedly. Gary's ensuing stare was filled with disappointment, even disbelief.

"I'll only hinder yer fighting," Mickey explained. "I'll be doing what I can, don't ye doubt, but ever have I been better at fighting from a distance."

A sudden popping sound turned their attention back to the approaching fight. A burst of spinning missiles—they reminded Gary of the blades used on a circular saw—shot up into the air, cutting a myriad of angles that many of the monkey-monsters could not avoid. Two got their wings clipped; a third caught a missile squarely in the face, and dropped from sight.

"It's a gnome," Geno, who had gone up to the edge of the road, called back, and that fact inspired the dwarf to kick his pony into a roaring charge. Gary angled his horse right up to the road and thundered behind, easily catching up to the dwarf's pony, while Kelsey ran full out along the side of the road, holding fast to his mount with his legs, and fast to his drawn bow with his hands.

He had ridden with leprechauns and fought against twelve-foot-tall trolls and mighty dragons, but Gary could hardly believe the sight that greeted him. It was a gnome, as Geno had declared, a creature somewhat resembling the stocky dwarf, but slighter of build and with a face not so carved of granite. The gnome sat low in a contraption that resembled two bicycles lashed side by side, a steering wheel and two panels full of levers encircling him. He pulled one, and Gary saw a coil at the side of the left front wheel unwind suddenly, hurling another handful of circular missiles up into the air.

One monkey-monster, swooping low in an attack pass, caught the whole bunch in its face, wings, and belly, and was torn apart and thrown aside. But a score or more monkeys remained, synchronizing their dives at the frightened gnome.

The monsters never even realized that the gnome had found some unlooked-for allies until an arrow cut the air and drove hard into the side of one monkey. A second arrow followed in quick order, and a third after that, both scoring hits. The monsters sang out with their shrieking voices, looking first to the side, the flying elf, and then ahead, to the fine knight and his long spear and to the dwarf, hammer cocked back over his head, charging side by side down the road.

A few squeals from the largest of the monster band put the monkeys in order immediately, one small group breaking off in pursuit of the elf, another group, including the leader, remaining to dive at the gnome, and the largest band rushing straight ahead at the approaching riders.

"Keep a tight hold!" Geno yelled at Gary. "They'll try to pull you from your saddle!" The dwarf hurled out his first hammer then, but the closest approaching monkey was agile enough to swerve aside. Geno, too, swerved, purposely splitting apart from Gary and going down to the side of the road opposite Kelsey in hopes of confusing the monsters. They were not stupid beasts, though, and while a few turned to follow the dwarf, the bulk kept their focus ahead, zooming for Gary.

He brought the great spear up before him, resisted the urge to hurl it into the face of the closest monster. Keep your nerve, he thought, and told himself to trust in his armor and in his mount, and to follow the warrior training Donigarten's spear had given to him.

Still, Gary Leger thought he was surely doomed as the group of more than ten of the winged monsters closed on him. They were larger than Gary had thought from a distance, fifty to eighty pounds apiece, surprisingly agile and swift, and with long and pointy white teeth, and hooked claws that certainly could, as Geno had warned, pull Gary from the saddle. Gary remembered the time when, as a kid, he had cornered a raccoon under his best friend's front porch. He'd put on some work gloves and thought to climb under the porch and catch the critter, a cute little raccoon like the kind he had seen on TV. When that wild animal reared up on its hind legs and bared its formidable teeth, young Gary Leger had been smart enough to turn tail and scramble out.

So how come I'm not that smart now? he wondered, and then the time for wondering was over as he and the monkeys made their first pass. Ducking low, Gary poked ahead with the spear, nicking the lead monkey as it spun completely around in midair to avoid the strike.

Riding past, Gary tried to bring the weapon back in line ahead of him, but he was into the gauntlet too fast. He took a hit on the shoulder, a wing buffeted him, spinning his helmet about so that he could not see, and his horse grunted as a claw opened a deep scratch along its muscled neck.

Still, the pass was not nearly as bad as Gary had thought it would be; he took less than half the hits he had expected. He managed to right himself in the saddle, managed to right his helm, and looked back to find that many of the monkeys had swerved to either side of him and were now hovering some distance down the road, looking curiously Gary's way.

And no wonder, for riding right beside Gary, one on either side, were two exact replicas of the man, complete with spear and armor.

So surprised was Gary that he nearly charged on blindly right into the approaching gnome contraption. He found his wits, and realized the company to be Mickey's handiwork, in time to begin his turn to the side of the road.

THE six monkeys that went for Kelsey were met by a seemingly solid line of arrows, coming out so rapidly from the fast-riding elf that his hands were no more than a blur. The terrain was rough on the side of the road, though, and Kelsey bounced about, many of his shots going wide and wild.

He scored three hits, two on the same beast that took that monkey down altogether. The other five came stubbornly on, though, even the one sporting an arrow shaft from its shoulder. They shrieked eagerly above the clapping pounding of their bat wings, and were almost upon Kelsey, wicked claws extended as they angled down for a swooping pass.

Kelsey's horse cut so sharp a turn, right back towards the monkeys, that the elf was forced to grab on, hands and legs, just to keep in the saddle. Surprised, too, were the monkeys, and the horse dipped its head low, and Kelsey fell flat across its back as they passed right under the beasts, who were still too high to attempt any raking attacks.

Kelsey straightened immediately and reared up his mount, readying his bow as he turned about and getting off several more shots before the monsters were able to reverse direction and come at him again in any coordinated fashion.

THE four monkeys that went after the smallest of the new foes were surprised indeed when a barrage of flying hammers—it seemed like there were at least twenty of the missiles—came out suddenly as they closed the final few yards. Metal slapped hard against leathery wings, crunched monkey bones, and took all the front teeth, top and bottom, from one hooting maw.

Geno's pony came around, following the dwarf's call for a charge. Smiling that mischievous, gap-toothed smile, Geno took the bridle firmly in one hand and stood up on the pony's wide back, his stubby legs cocked for a spring.

The closest monkey had just recovered from the hammer attack when its eyes widened once more in surprise, this time as the hammer-thrower, and not a hammer, soared its way.

Geno hit the monster squarely, wrapping his powerful smithy arms about it and hugging as tightly as he could. The monkey clawed and bit, and beat its wings furiously, but even if those wings had not been entangled by the dwarf's ironlike grasp, they would not have supported Geno's solid weight. Down came the two, Geno twisting so that the beast was below him.

The monkey stopped thrashing, stopped breathing, when they hit. Geno bounced off the flattened thing and hopped about. Just in time, for a second foe was in full flying charge, swooping for the fallen dwarf.

"Catch!" Geno politely roared, whipping a hammer the monkey's way. The sharp crack as the weapon bounced off the creature's skull sounded like a gunshot, and the aimed plummet became a dead drop.

A third flying beast, following the charge, wisely turned aside, though the fourth of the group continued on. This one was walking, however, not flying, with one wing tucked tight against its back and the other, shattered in the initial hammer barrage, dragging on the ground beside it.

Geno's mischievous smile did not diminish. He flipped his hammer repeatedly into the air, catching it with the same hand, while his other hand beckoned the monsters to come and play.

A monkey dove for the low-riding gnome—Gary thought that the little man, who already showed a line of blood across his high-browed forehead, was surely doomed. A tug on a lever and a metallic umbrella sprang up, angled above and to the side, and the monkey-monster bounced harmlessly aside.

A second monkey, coming the other way, was closer, though, and Gary saw the gnome frantically reach for another, similar lever, probably designed to complete the umbrella covering. The gnome pulled, and there came a clicking sound, but nothing happened—nothing except that the gnome's face drained of blood as he looked at the swooping menace.

Purely on instinct, Gary let fly the spear. It skewered the diving monkey and carried it away, launching it far over the back of the speeding quadricycle.

Gary's horse thundered past the gnome a split-second later, Gary just catching the thumbs-up sign as he galloped past. Back up over the bluff and onto the road, his steed charged, and Gary bent low to the side, reaching down in an effort to retrieve the spear, lying with its dead quarry along the top of the bluff on the opposite side. He saw that it was just beyond his fingertips as he came near, and so he reached lower.

Too low.

The world become a spinning blur, filled with solid bumps and ringing armor, over the next few horrible seconds. When Gary finally stopped his tumbling fall, he found himself sitting against the base of the bluff. He heard his horse nickering, calling, from the road up above and behind him, and he instinctively struggled to stand, though he hardly remembered the fight in that confusing moment, and hardly remembered that there remained many monsters yet to battle.

He got almost halfway up before the ground seemed to writhe to life, to leap at him and swallow him.

GENO'S muscled legs twitched, launching him ahead suddenly, and he barreled into the walking monkey. They wrapped arms and went into a roll, each biting hard into the other's neck. Geno's maw was not as strong as the beast's, but his neck was as hard as granite, and he did not fare badly.

He looked up over the monkey's shoulder and saw its companion rushing in. Smiling, his mouth full of monkey flesh, the dwarf waited until the unsuspecting monkey was almost upon him, then jerked his arm free and met the charge with a flying hammer.

The monkey tumbled to the ground, stunned but not dead, and the dwarf used that free arm to promptly pull it into the pile.

They rolled about, all three thrashing wildly, the monkeys clawing and bit-ing and Geno punching, kicking, head-butting and biting, and doing whatever else seemed to work. Blood, dwarven and monkey, mixed with dirt, caking all three in grime.

Geno, grabbed a tuft of hair on the back of one monkey's head and pulled the thing perpendicular across his chest as he rolled once more. Yanking as they came over, Geno managed to plant the facedown monkey's forehead firmly against the ground. With a growl, the dwarf forced the pile to continue to roll and the monkey screamed out in agony, its head bending over backwards and its neckbone snapping apart.

With surprising strength, the beast jerked free of the dwarf's iron grip and went into a series of wild convulsions. It was out of the fight, though, twitching on the ground and fast dying.

That left Geno one on one, and he looked down to see that the remaining monkey had used the distraction to its seeming advantage, its strong maw clamped tightly around Geno's bleeding forearm. The dwarf grunted and flexed his muscles, and his right arm, his smithy-hammer arm, tightened and bulged, forcing the monkey's mouth wider.

Wider, too, went the disbelieving beast's eyes.

"You think that hurts?" Geno asked it incredulously. He looked to the gnawing monkey, then to the hand of his free and cocked arm. "That doesn't hurt," he explained, and he extended his pinky finger and his index finger. "Now this hurts!"

Geno's free arm shot about, his fingers diving into the monkey's eyes, driv-ing the beast off his forearm. Geno's arm recoiled immediately, his hand balling into a fist, and he punched the creature square in the face.

The monkey seemed to bounce to its feet, but stood there dazed, offering no defense as the dwarf stalked in and slammed it again. It bounced, but still stood, and then Geno's forehead splattered its nose all over its face and it flew away.

It never hit the ground, though, as a strong dwarven hand caught it by the throat and held it up.

Geno looked to his bloodied arm, wondered if the wound might slow his smithing business for a while.

"You shouldn't have done that," he explained to the semiconscious beast, and his powerful hand began to twist.

IN the span of six seconds, and a like number of zipping arrows, five monkeys had become two.

Kelsey dropped his bow and drew out his sword, kicking his mount into a charge to meet headlong the next stubborn attack. The monkeys came at him together, one to pass on either side of his mount.

Kelsey veered to the side at the last moment, trying to put them both on his right, but the monkeys were just as quick, and turned accordingly. Undaunted, the elf lifted his sword up and over to the left, angling for that beast. Predictably, the frightened thing opened its wings for drag and fell back, and Kelsey's blade whipped across to the right, deflecting a diving claw and severing half the monkey's foot.

Kelsey knew instinctively that the one to the left was diving for him, had him vulnerable, so he continued to the right, falling all the way over the side of the horse. The monkey's hooked claws caught nothing but air.

Kelsey did not fall from his seat, as had Gary. The Tylwyth Teg were said to be the finest riders in all of Faerie, and Kelsey did not diminish that reputation in the least. Right under his steed's belly, between the pumping legs, he rolled, tugging himself back up the other side, and tugging tight to the bridle, rearing his mount. He had won the first pass, but the monkeys were coming back the other way for the second.

Kelsey kicked his mount into a charge, happy to oblige. Again, the monkeys tried to flank him, one on either side, and this time, Kelsey went right through the gauntlet, his sword snapping left, right, and left again, so quickly that he took only a minor nick on his forearm.

He was better prepared, his cunning warrior mind working fast, as he brought the mount around for the third pass, this time turning before the monkeys had even come about.

Down the middle, Kelsey started again, but then he lifted one leg over his horse's back, standing at the side of the charging beast, using the horse's body as a shield between him and the monkey on the right. Again, Kelsey perfectly anticipated his opponents' reactions. The monkey on the left swerved wide, having no desire to face the elf head-on, and the one to the right cut in for the horse, thinking the elf concerned with its companion.

Kelsey started left, then jumped back across his horse's back, sword leading in a straightforward thrust. The weapon suddenly weighed an extra fifty pounds, exploding through the monkey's chest, but Kelsey managed to hold on to it, taking the skewered monkey along for the ride. He heard a shriek close behind, and knew that the monkey which had fled the pass had come around quickly. Lying sidelong across his running horse's back, his sword stuck fast in a dead enemy, Kelsey was not in an enviable position.

With few options, the elf heaved the dead monkey out behind him. It slipped free of the blade, right into its flying companion's path, and the charging monkey had to kick off from the body, its momentum stolen by the ploy. By the time the living monkey recovered, recovered, too, was Kelsey. He turned his horse about once more and began yet another charge. Alone, the monkey wanted no part of the elf, and its wings beat furiously, tying to get it out of harm's way.

Kelsey's sword slashed its wing, and its flight became an awkward flutter. It swooped and rose, turned sideways and rolled right over in midair, finally fluttering down to the ground. The frightened monkey ran on, but it was no match for the speed of Kelsey's powerful mount. The horse ran it down, monkey bones crackling under the pounding hooves.

The monkey lay in the dirt and dust, its backbone shattered, and watched helplessly, dying, as Kelsey turned his steed once more.

But Kelsey had no time to finish the unfortunate beast. He looked back to the road, saw Gary's horse trotting, suddenly without a rider, and saw the gnome on his curious contraption rolling fast into a snapping and slashing tangle of nearly a dozen monsters.

And Kelsey's bow lay on the ground many yards away.

GARY had saved Gerbil, but the gnome realized that the reprieve would not last for long. A handful of monkeys still pursued him, and several others, the band that had rushed past Gary Leger, were now coming at him from the other direction.

"Drat'n'doggonit, drat'n'doggonit!" the gnome cried, his little legs pumping the pedals furiously, and his hand working the jammed umbrella lever.

"Not to be pretty," Mickey McMickey, watching from some distance away, muttered. It appeared as a strange game of "chicken," with Gerbil leading one band of monkeys at top speed one way, and a larger band flying fast the other.

Monkeys shrieked, Gerbil screamed, and at the last instant before the collision the gnome grabbed the steering bar in both hands, jerked it sharply one way and then back the other, sending the quadricycle into a spin, its skidding wheels shooting a swirling cloud of dust into the air.

Gerbil yanked yet another lever as the groups came crashing together, this one dropping his seat flat, getting him down as low as he could go between the contraption's high wheels.

Monkeys smashed together, smashed into the quadricycle, and slammed against poor Gerbil. The whole of the group seemed to hang motionless—a communal stun, it seemed—and then the quadricycle rolled slowly out the side of the group. The monkeys, beginning to recover, had the gnome helpless.

Nets flew up from the road, flying in at the throng. Monkeys shrieked and scrambled and would have battered each other into complete chaos, but Mickey, his powers at a low ebb, couldn't hold the illusion and the nets dissipated.

More real were the arrows that suddenly flew in, and the hammers that came spinning from the other side. The gnome was helpless, unconscious actually, but not so helpless was the grim-faced elf, rushing in on his shining white steed, or the running dwarf, laughing wildly, his little legs rolling under him, his arms heaving hammer after hammer.

One of Geno's hammers and one of Kelsey's arrows got the large leader of the group at the same time, blasting its breath from its lungs and then turning that burst of breath into a whistling gurgle through a neat hole in its neck.

Those monkeys that could still fly did so, and seven of the nine got away, the other two falling prey to Kelsey's bow. The three living monkeys on the ground joined together in a unified defense against the charging dwarf . . . and were summarily buried where they stood.

NINE

Braemar

THE huge red-bearded man walked slowly down the rocky mountain trail, great sword resting easily over one shoulder. Below him, nestled beneath the veil of rising mist in the secluded mountain dell, lay the quiet town of Gondabuggan.

Robert's hand clenched tightly about his swordhilt. He hated being in the confining human form, wanted to be out soaring on the high winds, feeling the freedom and feeling the strength of dragonkind.

But Robert had lived many centuries and was as wise as he was strong. He suspected that the resourceful gnomes had sent word of his coming, figured that the tough dwarfs in the mountains and the puny humans across the towering range were well into their preparations to battle him. Even with the euphoric knowledge that the witch, Ceridwen, his principal rival, had been banished to her island, Robert would not forget due caution.

If he were to rule the land, he would have to do it one village at a time, and Gondabuggan had the misfortune of being the closest settlement to the wyrm's lair.

Though he was in human form, Robert retained the keen senses of dragonkind, and he sniffed the gnomish sentries, and a different scent that he had not expected, long before they suspected that he was anywhere about. He moved to a rocky outcropping, some fifty feet from the gnomes, and perked up his ears, hearing their every word.

"Kinnemore's army is on the field, by one report," said a dwarfish voice.

"It is truly amazing," replied an excited gnome. "Truly amazing!"

"Of course the meddlesome king is involved!" the dwarf replied. "The spear and armor of Donigarten have been stolen, by the elf who defeated Robert (with the help of Geno Hammerthrower, of course) and the hero of Bretaigne. Kinnemore is nervous, and all the land is in chaos."

"Truly amazing," the gnome said again. "To think that Gerbil Hamsmacker simply flew through the mountains! Truly amazing!"

"Oh, he will go down in gnomish records," another gnome agreed, clapping pudgy hands together.

The exasperated dwarf groaned. "The artifacts and the king's army are more important!" he tried to explain.

"Yes," agreed a booming, resonant voice as a huge and muscled red-haired, red-bearded man stepped into view. "Do tell me about the artifacts and the king's army."

An hour later, Robert was a dragon again, gliding easily on the warm updrafts rising from the cliffs on the eastern edge of Dvergamal, waiting for his meal of two gnomes and a dwarf to settle—dwarfs had always been so indigestible! The news of events in the west had saved Gondabuggan, for the time being, for Robert now understood that there was more about all of this than his being free and Ceridwen's being banished.

Robert knew as well as any that Kinnemore was Ceridwen's puppet, and that, guided by the witch, the king would certainly cause him trouble. And there were heroes in the land now, for the first time in centuries, for the first time since the days of Cedric Donigarten. Dragons, whose power was as much a fact of intimidation as actual strength, did not like heroes.

Gondabuggan would have to wait.

GERBIL opened bleary eyes to see the sculpted features of a golden-haired, golden-eyed elf looking back at him. A leprechaun sat on the front right wheel of Gerbil's quadricycle, puffing on a long-stemmed pipe and saying, "Hmmm," repeatedly as he studied the gnome.

Gerbil quickly straightened himself in his seat, tried to put on his best greet-the-visitors face.

"Gerbil Hamsmacker of Gondabuggan at your service," he said as politely as could be, and indeed, Gerbil meant every word to this troupe that had rescued him from certain doom. "I pray that none of your most helpful party was too badly injured."

"The laddie, there, got a few lumps, is all," Mickey answered, motioning to Gary, who was kneeling in the road while Geno and Baron Pwyll tried to hammer a fair-sized dent out of one shoulder plate.

"The armor," Gerbil breathed under his breath, his gnomish eyes, typically blue, shining brightly and his head bobbing as if it all suddenly made sense to him. "Oh, I do say that I thought Sir Cedric himself had come a'bobbing to my rescue! Of course, of course, I do know better than that. Humans do not live so long, and Cedric . . ."

"Of course," Mickey replied. "But I'm agreeing that the lad has come to wear the armor well."

"Yes, yes," Gerbil said excitedly. "That is why I came west, you know, because the word is spread that the armor and spear were missing . . . stolen, actually."

"What concern would that be to a gnome of Gondabuggan?" Kelsey asked gravely.

"None and lots," Gerbil answered. "You see, Robert the Wretched was the one who reforged the spear."

Kelsey and Mickey looked to each other and seemed not to understand the connection, at least not as far as Gondabuggan was concerned.

"Well, the missing spear and armor might offer some clues as to why Robert has come out on wing, so to speak," Gerbil explained at length. "The two events were too closely related . . ."

"What do you know of the dragon?" Kelsey interrupted, his voice stern. Kelsey knew, as did most of Faerie's folks, that a gnome could ramble for hours if not properly guided through a discussion, and from what Gerbil had just referred to, Kelsey wasn't certain that he had hours to spare.

"What do I know?" Gerbil balked. "Indeed, what do I? Of course, that depends mostly on the subject matter. Take explosives, for instance . . ."

"About the dragon," Kelsey clarified.

"He was over Gondabuggan, that is what I know!" Gerbil said. "Just . . ." He paused and lifted his plump gnome hand, counting on the fingers so that he could be precise. "Just fifty-one hours ago."

"What do ye mean by he 'was over' Gondabuggan?" Mickey asked. "Did he attack the town, then?"

Gerbil nodded rapidly. "With fire and talon!" he replied. "Of course, that is what one must expect from a dragon, unless the dragon is one of the lake variety. Then the expected attack mode . . ."

"Ye're sure?"

"I am, if the dragon treatise is correct," Gerbil replied.

"Not about water dragons!" Mickey retorted. "Ye're sure that Robert flew over yer town, just fifty-one hours ago?"

"I watched it with my own two eyes, of course," replied Gerbil. He nodded a greeting as the other three walked over to stand beside Kelsey. "Oh, he came down in a tirade, breathing and kicking," the gnome went on, and his level of excitement seemed to rise accordingly with the rising audience. "We held him at bay, but I would guess that Robert is not yet finished with Gondabuggan! Oh, woe to my kin!"

Some of the others began to whisper; Pwyll's remarks were filled with forlorn, but Kelsey steeled his gaze, seemed to find something not quite right with Gerbil's dire tale.

"You were in Gondabuggan for Robert's attack just two days ago?" the elf asked. As soon as Kelsey put it so plainly, Mickey went silent, understanding the elf's quite reasonable doubts.

Gerbil counted quickly on his fingers again. "Fifty-one hours," he replied with a nod.

"You have come a long way in fifty-one hours, good gnome," Kelsey remarked. "Even though the weather has been fine and your . . ." He looked to the weird contraption.

"Quadricycle," Gerbil explained.

"And your quadricycle is swift," Kelsey went on, "Gnome Pass is many days from Drochit, and Drochit is still a day's ride from here."

"Oh, I could not take the quadricycle through the mountains, of course," Gerbil retaliated. "Too many rocks and trails too narrow, after all! Oh, no, I did not ride. I flew."

"On Robert's back, then?" Mickey asked sarcastically.

"On the Mountain Messenger," Gerbil replied without missing a beat. "It is a long descending tube, packed at precise points . . ."

"I know of yer M&M," Mickey assured the gnome. "Are ye telling me that ye climbed into one o' them balls and got shot across the mountains?"

"Landed in the field north of Drochit," Gerbil replied with a proud smile. "Of course, if I had been splattered, then I would have had my name etched into the *Plaque of Proud and Dead Inventors.*" The gnome gave a long sigh. "Better to live at this time, though," he conceded. "With the dragon about, after all."

Gary, confused and intrigued, couldn't take any more of the rambling. "What are you talking about?" he demanded.

"It's a big cannon," Mickey answered before the gnome could get into a lengthy explanation. Mickey was more familiar with Gary's world than any of the others, having often snatched people from that place, and he knew how best to put the M&M in terms that Gary Leger would understand.

"And he climbed in a hollow ball and got blasted across the mountains?" Gary asked incredulously.

"Something like that," Mickey replied. He turned back to the gnome, wanting to hear more of Robert, but Gary wouldn't be so easily satisfied.

"How far?" he asked.

"The distance has never actually been measured," Gerbil was happy to explain. "My calculations approximate it at forty miles, give or take seven hundred feet."

Gary leaned back to consider this. He knew of battleships in his own world that could throw two-ton projectiles more than twenty miles, but, as he found the proper perspective, the prospect of hurling a ball with a living gnome inside twice that distance—and have the gnome crawl out alive—seemed absolutely ridiculous. He tuned back in as Gerbil was describing Robert's attack on Gondabuggan, how the gnomes put up a wall of water, and metallic umbrellas to fend off the attack.

"Impossible," Gary cut in as soon as the gnome paused to take a breath.

"No, really," Gerbil came right back. "Umbrellas of properly folded plates, just like this." He reached for the handle to his smaller versions of similar umbrellas on the quadricycle.

"Not the umbrellas," Gary explained. "There's no way you can hurl a ball that far."

"No way?" Gerbil cried, throwing his hands up in absolute disgust.

"Never be saying 'no way' to a gnome, lad," Mickey whispered to Gary. "Puts them all in a tizzy."

And indeed, Gerbil Hamsmacker was in a tizzy. If Gary Leger had called the gnome's mother a thousand dirty names, or had called the race of gnomes thick-headed, it would not have upset the proud M&M inventor any more than this. Gerbil blustered and threw his hands this way and that. He rambled off a series of calculations, followed by a series of curses at the thick-headed, dim-witted, slow-to-learn, never-to-understand humans.

"I just don't believe that you can launch a projectile that far," Gary began, wanting to explain that the speed and the impact would surely kill any passengers. "How high up was the cannon? That ball would have to travel at . . ."

"Two hundred and seventy-two miles per hour," Gerbil proudly interjected. He looked sidelong at Kelsey. "Two-seventy-three and you clip the overhang at Buck-toothed Ogre Pass."

Geno tugged at Kelsey's tunic. I saw one hit that overhang once," he said. "At night, and the sparks were far-to-see!"

Kelsey nodded, not doubting the tales, but Gary shook his head, finding it impossible, even amidst this land of impossibilities, to believe a word of it.

"But the landing," he started to protest, hardly able to find the words to properly express his whirling thoughts.

"Of course the target area was the descending slope of a field," Gerbil cut in. "Peat mostly, and cow droppings. The trick, you see, is for the valves to release the precise amount of Earth-pull reversal solution at precisely the moment to slow the flight and soften the landing."

"Earth-pull reversal solution?" Gary had to ask.

"Flying potion," Mickey quickly explained.

"I don't believe it."

"Ye don't believe in leprechauns either, lad," Mickey remarked. "Remember?"

Gary stuttered over a few responses, then turned back to Gerbil, armed with more questions.

"He'll have an answer for anything ye ask," Mickey said before Gary could get on a roll. "He's a gnome, after all."

Gary's determined look faded to resignation. "Precise amounts at precise moments?" he asked the gnome.

"Precisely!" Gerbil proudly cried, his cherubic face beaming as only the face of a gnome who had been praised for an invention could beam.

Gary Leger let it go at that, just sat back and listened as the intriguing little gnome finished his tale. Then Gerbil stood up straight in his seat, looking all around as though he wasn't sure of where to go, or of where he had been.

"What were those nasty things?" he asked.

"Some witch-mixed monsters, by me guess," Mickey replied, and he looked gravely at Kelsey as he spoke. Had Ceridwen extended her evil hand once more? they both wondered, and both, inevitably, knew the answer.

"I do not believe this to be a chance meeting," Kelsey added, speaking to Gerbil. "You may find the road to Dilnamarra difficult, at best."

"Well, I am not so sure, not at all, that I have to go there anymore, though I would like to speak with the fat puppet, Baron Pwyll, to see what I might learn of the theft," Gerbil answered, but then he looked at Gary, obviously in possession of the supposedly stolen items, and gulped loudly.

"Then speak with him," Mickey offered with a mischievous grin, "for to be sure, the fat puppet's but a few feet away."

"At your service," Pwyll remarked dryly, and Gerbil gulped again. But Pwyll took no real offense, and the overdue introductions were not strained at all. Kelsey was already figuring that they might have to go to Gondabuggan, and in that case, Gerbil would prove a great help. Leprechauns got along well with gnomes, as did dwarfs, and even Geno put on a genuinely warm expression as he clasped the gnome's little hand.

In the end, it was decided by all that Gerbil would remain with the group, backtracking to the east. The gnome spent a long while milling over the proposition, looking east and west repeatedly as though he wasn't sure of how he should proceed, but when Mickey reminded him of the airborne attack, he nodded his agreement and turned the quadricycle about.

The group of six came to a ridge above Braemar, a small village of two dozen mostly single-chambered stone houses, late the next afternoon. There was no keep here, as there was in Dilnamarra, just a large central building, two stories high—which Mickey called the "spoke-lock," the hub—surrounded by a cluster of town houses, including a blacksmith and other craftsmen, a trader, a supplier, and, of course, the infamous Snoozing Sprite tavern, wherein Geno had been captured by Baron Pwyll's men. Beyond the central cluster of town rolled rock-lined fields of grazing sheep and highland cows, dotted here and there by the customary squat stone houses with their thick thatched roofs.

"We're sure to make a stir if we walk right in," Mickey reasoned. "Especially if Geldion's got men down there."

Kelsey looked around, in full agreement with the leprechaun. He didn't know how to weigh the potential reaction of Braemar to the disturbing news. Badenoch, the village's leader, was one of the few independent Barons in Faerie, often showing more support for Pwyll than for the emissaries of Connacht. But certainly, this unusual troupe would attract much attention. Geno could go in relatively safely, as dwarfs were not uncommon to Braemar, and though Geno might be recognized, he could easily concoct a story of escape from Pwyll's humbling soldiers. Gerbil had already been to the sister town of Drochit, twenty miles to the north, and gnomes often visited Braemar, as well. The Tylwyth Teg were not common this far from Tir na n'Og, not in these days of King Kinnemore's reign, but Kelsey, too, could probably go into Braemar without too much difficulty.

Both humans would be more than welcome in the friendly town, except that if Pwyll was recognized, the word of his passing would spread throughout the countryside. And the armor, more fabulous than anything in all the land, would keep a crowd milling around Gary for every step. Few knights rode the fields in this dark time, and even the wealthiest of those who did had no metal plating to match the craftsmanship of Donigarten's legendary suit. Word of the theft had come this far north, according to Gerbil, and with it, undoubtedly, word that King Kinnemore wanted the armor retrieved. Who knew what friends of the throne, and independent bounty hunters perhaps, might be about, ready to seize the opportunity to get into Kinnemore's good graces and abundant treasures?

Mickey would have the most difficulty of all in going into Braemar, though. Braemar was primarily a human settlement, and few men would look upon a leprechaun and not make chase, seeking the famed pot of gold. Mickey rarely ventured into any town, and never without using a clever disguise. Kelsey couldn't be certain, but it seemed to him that the leprechaun's illusions were not carrying the same strength as in the past.

"I doubt that Geldion has come this far," Kelsey said at length. "And I wish to learn more of Robert's movements. Perhaps the dragon has been seen on this side of the mountain, and if not, we will need supplies to properly cross Dvergamal."

Mickey nodded, but was not in agreement—not with the elf's planned course, at least. Kelsey was talking about chasing the wyrm, but Mickey wanted only to get back to the Giant's Thumb, Robert's castle, and get back his precious pot of gold.

"Send in a couple, then," Mickey offered. "Dwarf and gnome, and even . . ." Mickey put his stare on Pwyll, but shook his head suddenly and looked to Gary instead. ". . . Gary Leger, as well," the leprechaun finished. "But leave the spear and armor here," Mickey said to Gary. "Ye'll not likely be needing them in the peaceable town."

Few eyes turned with anything more than passing curiosity when the three companions wandered down the dirt streets of Braemar an hour later, Geno at the lead with Gary and Gerbil right behind. Many people were about, rushing mostly, and several approached the strangers with "Have you heard of the dragon?" or "Good gnome, does Gondabuggan survive?"

Gary would have liked to stop and question these villagers in more depth—that was why they were in town, after all—but Geno gruffly excused himself from any budding conversation (usually with a stream of spittle heading the villager's way), and pulled the others along, moving with purpose towards the large central structure, the spoke-lock. Gary thought that the dwarf meant to go and find Lord Badenoch, Braemar's leader, and so he did not argue, but Geno went right past the main house, into a long and low building. Gary couldn't make out the runes on the sign outside the place's wide door, but the accompanying painting, that of a small pixie curled up peacefully amidst a patch of white clover, confirmed to him that this was the Snoozing Sprite tavern.

The place was bustling, mostly with villagers, men and women, having their supper and talking of the dragon, and of the missing armor.

"Where should we sit?" Gary asked, but he realized when he looked down to his sides that he was talking to himself. Gerbil had scooted off to the side, to talk to a tall and lean barkeep, and Geno was making his way through the crowd, spreading stumbling people in his wake, towards a far table where sat three other dwarfs. Gary started to follow, but remembered what he had learned of dwarven manners—mostly that the four would probably pick him up and heave him away if he interrupted them—and so he went to find his own table instead.

He wound up along the far wall, well past the bar, at a round table built for four, and still covered with the bowls and spoons of the previous occupants. Gary looked around, saw no one objecting to his choice, and slipped into a chair, defensively putting his back against the wall. He leaned this way and that, trying to keep an eye on his friends among the crowd.

Geno was still with the dwarfs, apparently they were friends, and Gary had to wonder if perhaps the dwarf's part in this adventure had just come to an end. Geno was ever the reluctant companion; if he had found some allies and was inclined to be done with the group, not Kelsey's sword nor Mickey's tricks would get him away.

Across the way from Geno, Gerbil was sitting atop the bar, chatting easily with the barkeep, and with a crowd of curious men who had gathered around the gnome. They were seeking information about the dragon, Gary figured, and Gerbil was undoubtedly trying to find out what more, if anything, had happened to his town.

"That's me dad," came a sweet voice at Gary's side.

Acting as though he had been caught Tom-peeping, Gary straightened suddenly in his chair—too suddenly, for he overbalanced and nearly toppled to the floor. Standing beside him, tray in hand, was a young lass of not more than twenty years, with shining red hair and a fresh complexion that no makeup could ever improve. Her eyes sparkled innocent, childlike, and Gary got the distinct feeling that she had grown up in a field of wildflowers, smiling at the simple pleasure of the warming sun.

"Sorry to startle ye," she offered, catching hold of Gary's shoulder and helping him to regain his balance. That done, the lass started to load the used bowls onto her tray. "Me name's Constance, and that's me dad talking to yer little gnome friend."

"Oh," Gary replied, trying to digest it all. He extended his hand, pulled it back in to wipe the grime of the road off it, then held it out again. "Pleased to meet you, Constance," he offered lamely with a strained, still-embarrassed smile.

"I've not seen ye before in Braemar," Constance noted. "Are ye passing through, or have ye come to find a hiding place from the dragon?"

"What do you know of the dragon?" Gary asked, trying futilely to hide his anxiety. "Has he been seen near to here?"

"Some say they've seen him, but I think they're just trying to make themselves more important than they are," Constance replied with a mischievous wink—a wink that sent a shiver along Gary's spine. This was a beautiful girl, and though she was polite and proper, there remained something untamed about her, something that could melt a man's willpower.

"The only trusted word we've heared came from Drochit," Constance went on. "A gnome was there, so 'tis said, with word that Robert had attacked Gondabuggan. Last we heared, the gnome went west, to Dilnamarra, to speak with fat Pwyll and find out what had happened to Donigarten's suit. The two're related, so 'tis said."

Gary nodded and pretended that it was all news to him.

"Anyway, it is exciting, isn't it?" Constance asked, and her smile nearly knocked Gary off his chair as he nodded his agreement. "And who might ye be?"

It took Gary a moment to even realize that he had been asked a question. "Gary Leger," he replied without thinking.

"A strange name," Constance remarked offhandedly, and her delicate face screwed up as though she was trying to place the name.

"From Bretaigne, beyond Cancarron Mountains," Gary quickly added, using the alias that Mickey had concocted for him on his last trip through Faerie.

"Ah," Constance mewed. "Ye're the one who came to Dilnamarra for the armor!"

Gary suddenly realized his error, knew that it was not good for him to be connected in any way with the events in Dilnamarra—not with Prince Geldion hot on their trail.

"No," he said, trying vainly to sound calm, and trying vainly to weave a believable lie. "That was a different man, a cousin, I believe, though if he was, he was not one I've ever met."

Constance's doubting expression showed him how ridiculous he sounded. "Oh," was all that she replied.

"Yeah, not one that I ever met," Gary said, and he glanced around to Geno and Gerbil again, wanting nothing more than to crawl out of that place.

"What might I be getting ye?" Constance asked unexpectedly, her smile genuine, and enticing once more.

Too many stutters escaped Gary's mouth.

"The leek soup's hot and warming," Constance suggested.

"Good enough," Gary replied, and Constance turned away. Gary realized that he might have a problem, though, so he grabbed frantically at her elbow.

"I'm sorry," he said suddenly, letting go as Constance abruptly spun about to face him, and realizing that he probably shouldn't have done that. The girl, though, seemed to take no offense. "I mean . . . I have no money," Gary quickly explained.

"Oh." Constance seemed truly perplexed. "Ye're traveling with not a pence?"

"My friends . . ." Gary started to reply, but he wasn't sure what he might say about those two, so he didn't continue.

"Go and see then," Constance offered. "And if they got nothing for ye, then let me talk to me dad. He's got something needing done around here, don't ye fret. I've not ever seen him turn one away without a proper meal in his belly!" Constance spun and kicked away, a young foal in an open field, and Gary slumped back in his chair, thoroughly charmed.

His smile did not last, though. Not when he noticed that another group had taken an apparent interest in him. Four men, wearing the clothing of villagers, but with long dirks at their sides, were looking his way, their stubbly faces grimly set. They stopped Constance as she walked past, and asked her some questions, all the while looking back at Gary as he sat there, feeling very conspicuous.

Constance went by them without incident and they talked among themselves for a few moments, as though everything was perfectly natural. Every now and then, though, one of them would look Gary's way, locking stares with the stranger.

Gary felt the tension mounting as the minutes slipped past, felt all alone and dangerously out of place in a suddenly unwelcoming town. He tried to figure out what his next move should be, and only realized then that he did not have the sentient spear and the armor.

"Hurry up, Geno," he muttered under his breath, hoping that if it came to sudden blows, the dwarf and his tough companions would rush to his aid. But to Gary's shock, when he looked to the table, Geno and the others were not to be found. Gary groaned quietly; he could only believe that the dwarf had quit him and the whole adventure, had left him vulnerable.

All four of the men were staring at him intently then, and his instincts told him to jump up and run for his life. The men whispered among themselves, started towards him.

A hand clasped on Gary's shoulder, and he would have fallen to the floor had not the dwarf grabbed a tight hold and hoisted him to his feet.

"Come on," Geno said, and Gary really didn't have much choice but to follow, bending low in the unyielding grip, as the dwarf stormed away, for a side door that Gerbil was holding open leading to the wing of private rooms.

"HERE come some," Mickey remarked, and Kelsey and Baron Pwyll came up to the crest of the bluff, lying in the grass beside the leprechaun.

Mickey pointed to the road, but it was obvious what he was talking about as six horsemen approached the town, some sporting longbows over their shoulders and others with sheathed swords at their hips.

"We must expect that the people of the surrounding areas will flock to the town, prepared for battle," Kelsey reasoned, trying to figure out what significance, if any, this group indicated. "Lord Badenoch may have put out a call to arms."

Mickey nodded hopefully, but Baron Pwyll was not convinced. "In that case, he could not expect this group," the large man whispered. "There, the one in the lead." He pointed to a large square-shouldered man with a bushy black beard, riding a tall roan stallion. The man carried no bow, but had an immense broadsword strapped to his back, its pommel rising up high behind him, higher than his head.

"Ye know him?" Mickey asked.

"That's Redarm," Pwyll explained. "Named for a wound he got in a sword fight, a wound that would have defeated a lesser man. He's one of Geldion's lackeys, by all that I've heard." The Baron shook his head. "No, this group would not have come to Badenoch's call."

Mickey and Kelsey exchanged serious glances, both then instinctively looking to the unoccupied armor lying in the brush behind them at the base of
the bluff.

TEN

Midnight Ride

"WAKE up." The whisper, accompanied by a repeated tapping on his shoulder,
sounded harsh, urgent, in Gary's ear. The young man was well settled into a
wonderful dream, of a walk through beautiful Tir na n'Og with Diane beside
him, of bringing some of his other friends to Faerie and letting them see this
different side of Gary Leger, this heroic side.

"Wake up!" This time the call was accentuated by a finger snapping against
Gary's cheek. He opened his eyes, saw that it was Gerbil standing in the dim
light beside him. The gnome appeared anxious, but Gary couldn't figure out
what might be wrong. The room was perfectly quiet, and the night outside the
open window was dark, no moon this night, and still.

Gary stretched his shoulders; the room had only one bed, claimed by Geno
(though Gary couldn't figure out why, since the dwarf had flipped it over so that
he could sleep across the hard slats), and Gary had fallen asleep sitting on the
floor with his back against a wall. His accompanying yawn was too loud for
poor Gerbil's sensibilities, and the gnome slapped a hand across Gary's open
mouth.

Gary pushed him away. "What?" he demanded in a soft, but firm, whisper.

Gerbil looked nervously to the door. "We have been discovered, it just very
well might be," the gnome replied. Gary sat up straighter and rubbed the sleep
from his eyes as Gerbil climbed up on a chair and dared to light a single candle
sitting in a tray on the room's small desk. Only then, in the quiet light, did Gary
realize that Geno was no longer in the room.

They heard a commotion in the hall, a scuffling noise followed by several
bumps, and looked to each other curiously. Gerbil hopped down from the chair
and padded over to the door, glancing back at Gary, and then taking a tentative
hold on the high knob.

The door burst open; poor Gerbil came right off the floor, hanging onto the
knob with his little feet kicking as he and the door swung about.

"The window!" Geno cried, rushing into the room. The dwarf skidded to a stop and spun about, hammer swiping low. Gary winced at the resounding crack as the weapon connected on the kneecap of the man pursuing the dwarf. He howled and pitched headlong, grabbing at his crushed joint.

"Window!" Geno cried again, and he grabbed Gerbil's freely waving hand and pulled the gnome from his doorknob perch. Gerbil's other hand immediately tugged a bottle from his belt. He brought it up to his mouth, bit off the end, and splashed its contents all over himself.

"Get me there!" he bade the dwarf, and Geno was already thinking along those very lines. With a single, powerful arm, the dwarf twirled the seventy-pound gnome about his head once and then again, and hurled Gerbil across the room.

Gary blinked in disbelief at the gnome's flight. Gerbil started fast, but soon lost momentum and seemed as though he would crash to the floor. He continued to float, though, turning several perfect somersaults and winding up in a straight-armed, slow-motion dive that slipped him through the open window without a scratch against the wooden frame.

Geno turned back to the hall, facing four more dirk-wielding opponents— the same four men Gary had seen earlier in the tavern.

"Window!" the dwarf shouted to Gary. Gary looked that way, then looked back to Geno curiously, surprised by the dwarf's uncharacteristic altruism. Geno was under no debt to protect Gary, or even to accompany them at all on this journey. And yet, here he was, fighting furiously, telling Gary to run off while he held the enemy at bay.

Gary began to understand, then, the urgency of it all, the apparently desperate situation that Faerie had been placed in with the return of the dreaded dragon. But he would not run away from the dwarf, he decided. For perhaps the first time in his life (no, the second, he realized, counting his first trip to Faerie), Gary Leger felt as though he was part of something bigger than himself, something more important than his own life. He would go to Geno's side, use fists if need be against the daggers.

"Waiting . . . the window."

The silent call came into Gary's mind, a voice he recognized clearly. How it had gotten there, he didn't know, but the spear of Cedric Donigarten was leaning above the rosebushes under his room's window, waiting for him to retrieve it.

Geno cut a wide swath in front of him with his heavy-headed hammer, but came nowhere near to hitting the three agile men who had fanned out before him. Daggers thrust in behind the flying weapon, but the dwarf reversed his grip quickly and started with a reverse backhanded cut that forced the men to hop back once more.

This time, though, Geno did not hold onto the hammer. It spun from his grasp, slamming one man in the chest and knocking his breath from his lungs. He staggered backwards, slamming into the door and then tripped to the floor, dazed.

A companion, seeing the dwarf's weapon fly, snarled and thrust ahead more forcefully, but quicker than he anticipated, Geno pulled another hammer from his belt and snapped it across, slamming the man's fingers.

The dagger, stained with the blood of the dwarf, fell to the floor. Geno had only been scratched, but when the newest of the wounded men fell away, the dwarf found the fourth of the party waiting for him, daggers in each of his hands, cocked back over his head.

Geno went into a frenzy, started to charge, but got hit by the other man standing near to him. The dwarf blocked one of the daggers, but the other dug into his thigh. He shot a death-promising glance towards the thrower, only to see that the man had two more daggers up and ready.

Geno fell to the side, threw his hammer up before him, and somehow managed to escape the deadly throws. He was vulnerable, though, off-balance and with the remaining uninjured man, the man who had gotten back up from the floor near to the door, and the man with the broken fingers, coming back in at him.

The huge black tip of an enormous spear slashed the air between the combatants, forcing the three men to fall back. In stepped Gary Leger, grim-faced, whipping his powerful weapon about furiously, using its length so that the men, with their much shorter weapons, could not get anywhere near him or Geno.

"Window!" the young hero cried to his dwarfish companion.

A fifth man staggered through the crowd unexpectedly; Gary had to pull back on his cut to avoid disemboweling him. It didn't matter anyway, for the man looked at Gary plaintively, then fell to the floor, an elfish arrow protruding from his back, just under the shoulder blade, and through, Gary realized, the back of the dying man's heart.

Gary's stomach did a flip-flop, but he determinedly swallowed the bile and continued his defensive frenzy.

Geno patted him on the hip and was off and running, pounding across the room while issuing a long scream, then leaping headlong out the window and into the night.

Gary heard Pwyll shriek from outside and figured that the dwarfish missile hadn't missed the fat Baron by far.

"Up!" The sentient spear's warning came in time for Gary to snap the tip upward and knock aside a flying dagger. Instinctively, Gary came back the other way, covering his exposed flank, and he grimaced in anger as his spear cut deeply into an opportunistic enemy's side. Down the man went, screaming in agony, and Gary yelled, too, if only to block out the man's cries.

"No!" Gary growled as he noticed again the man Kelsey had shot, now lying perfectly still in the unmistakable quiet of death. Gary's denial was useless, helpless, and realizing that, the young man buried his own frailties under a curtain of sheer rage.

Now the spear came flashing across with renewed fury, Gary driving the remaining men backwards. He stopped a cut in midswing and gave a short thrust that forced the closest of the group to suck in his gut and hop up onto his toes, falling backwards a moment later and tangling with his companions.

Gary turned and ran for the window. He smiled in spite of his revulsion, conjuring an image common to old Errol Flynn movies. As he came towards the window, Gary dipped the tip of his spear, thinking to fancifully pole-vault his swashbuckling way outside.

His calculations weren't quite correct, though, for the enchanted spear's tip sliced right through the flooring, shifting Gary's angle and stealing his momentum. He came up in the air, up even with the vertical shaft, then went nowhere but down, to one knee on the floor just beyond the stuck weapon.

He saw his enemies regrouping back by the door, and they saw him, and quickly came to understand his dilemma.

Gary pulled hard on the spear, bending the metal shaft his way, but making no progress in freeing it. He thought of fleeing, of diving out the window, but he couldn't leave the spear behind—not to these men, who were obviously working for Prince Geldion.

But still, what choice did Gary have? Three of the cruel men charged at him, verily drooling at the thought of such an easy kill, and a fourth hopped on his one good leg behind the pack. Gary tugged hard until the very last moment, then cried out and let go.

The bent shaft sprang back the other way with tremendous force. The nearest enemy lifted a forearm in front of himself defensively, then howled as his bone snapped apart, jagged edges of it cutting out through the skin right before his disbelieving eyes. He flew away, into a companion, and both of them tumbled backwards, tripping up the man with the shattered kneecap.

Gary could hardly believe his luck, went desperately for the spear as the remaining man came in around the quivering weapon. Gary almost reached his spear, but then he fell back, thinking that he had been punched in the side.

Wide did Gary Leger's eyes go when he looked down to see not a fist, but a dagger, above his hip, to see his blood gushing out through torn skin.

I've been stabbed! The thought rocketed through Gary's mind, horrified him and confused him, for he honestly still felt as if he had only been punched; the pain was dull and not too intense. Still, the image was more than Gary could rationally take, and he didn't think of his actions, didn't hear the primal cry of sheer survival instincts escape his lips.

His opponent was well balanced, crouching with the bloodied dagger held ready. He got the weapon up to block Gary's furious left hook, but Gary didn't even wince as his hand and arm scraped across the blade, continuing on to slam the man in the face. A right cross followed, coming in under the surprised man's rolled shoulder, finding an open path to the man's chin.

The next left hook met no resistance at all until it smashed the man's cheek, whipped his head across the other way.

This was pure street-fighting, not delicate boxing, and wild Gary didn't look, didn't aim, as he continued to swing, left and right, left and right. His own yelling prevented him from hearing the solid smacks, or the cracking bones in knuckles and cheeks alike.

The man fell away, but Gary kept swinging, four more punches flying freely through the empty air before he even realized that he had knocked his opponent down. He regained his composure then, and saw the man on the floor, trying to crawl, trying to get up, apparently trying to remember where and who he was. He managed to get to his hands and knees, and Gary started to kick at him, but he rolled over to his side of his own accord, lay still and groaned.

Gary put a hand to his side, wincing as he brought it up and regarded the generous amount of blood. It had all happened in mere seconds—the other three in the pile hadn't even sorted themselves out yet. Gary dove for the spear, grabbed its shaft in both his aching hands, and heaved with all his might.

The back-and-forth action of the weapon had loosened the floor's hold on it, and it came out more easily than Gary anticipated. Spear in hand, he stumbled backwards, pitched head over heels in a backward somersault out the open window, his toes smashing glass and snapping the bottom wood on the window frame, and fell heavily into the thorny rosebush.

"Dammit!" he groaned and he looked up from his natural prison to see an enemy come to the window—and then go flying away with a hammer tucked neatly into his face.

"About time ye're getting here, lad," Gary heard Mickey say. He tried to turn his head about to regard the leprechaun, but a thorny strand tugging painfully against his neck changed his mind.

Baron Pwyll and Gerbil were at his side in an instant, pulling him free, while Geno lined up the window with another readied hammer.

"Hurry, then," Mickey implored them. "We're to meet Kelsey down the south road, and the elf's not in any mood for us being late!" Behind the leprechaun, the two horses and the pony whinnied nervously, but did not scatter. One of the horses, Gary's, had a large sack strapped over its back, bulging with the metal plates of Donigarten's armor.

They finally got Gary untangled—Geno heaved another hammer into the room to turn away the two men stubbornly continuing the pursuit—and went for the horses. Pwyll hoisted Gerbil, who didn't seem thrilled at the prospect of riding so tall a beast, up to his mount, but before the little gnome had even swung his leg over, he pointed down the road and whispered, "Trouble, oh, yes."

"Oh, yes," Gary echoed when he looked that way. Half a dozen riders lined the road a short distance from the tavern, regarding the friends and seeming almost amused by it all. One of the men wore full metal plating, like the armor of Donigarten, and carried a long lance tipped by a pennant bearing the standard of the lion and the clover, the emblem of Connacht. On his back was strapped a huge sword, one that Mickey and Baron Pwyll had seen before.

"Yield or be killed!" the knight declared.

"Five on six," Geno muttered mischievously. "Even up, if the damned elf would get here."

"I'm thinking that Kelsey's got his hands full of fighting already," said Mickey.

"Oh, well," replied the dwarf without the slightest hesitation. "Then Kelsey will miss all the fun."

"Not so quick," Mickey whispered back, sitting easily in his place in front of Gary's saddle. "I'm knowing that knight, and knowing that he didn't have the armor when he rode into town, not so long ago."

"So?" Geno's question reflected no doubts and no fears.

"He's got friends in town," Mickey reasoned. "More than we've seen, don't ye doubt."

"Archers in the hedge," Gary whispered, nodding to his right, and even as he spoke, they heard several voices from men congregating in the room behind them.

Baron Pwyll groaned.

"You got anything to trick them?" Gary asked Mickey.

The leprechaun shrugged. "Me magic's not so good," he answered honestly. "And the knight'd see through it, if none o' the others would."

It seemed to Gary as if they had few options other than the demanded surrender. But to do so would surely doom Baron Pwyll, and in looking at the precious spear he carried, Gary realized that the cost might be much higher than that.

"Yield or feel the tip of my lance!" the knight bellowed. "I have no time and no patience for your delay!"

Gary recalled all that he could about chivalry and codes of behavior, knew that this man was driven by a sense of honor, warped though it might be. Gary's smile widened; what his friends needed was a distraction. He hoisted Mickey from the horse and set him down on the ground.

"Get up with Geno," he explained quietly. "You'll know when to ride."

"What're ye thinking?" Mickey demanded, sounding not too pleased.

Gary was already climbing up to his seat, and paying the leprechaun little heed.

"My friends will yield," Gary called to the knight.

"When gnomes fly," Geno growled, but Gerbil threw him a reminding smirk to defeat that protest.

"If you can defeat me in a challenge of honor," Gary finished. He couldn't see the knight's face for the faceplate, but he imagined a wide smile curling up under that metal.

"My dear Gary Leger of Bretaigne," the knight began, chuckling with every word and slowly lifting the grilled faceplate up onto his head.

"These guys don't miss a thing," Gary, surprised at being so easily recognized, whispered to Mickey.

"You have been blinded by your pride," the knight continued. "For have you forgotten that you wear no armor?" His comrades broke into laughter—too loudly, Gary noted, and that told him just how much they respected this knight. One of the men, though, trotted his horse up beside the knight and whispered something in his ear that the armored man apparently did not like.

"I remember!" the knight roared, and he slapped the man away.

"They want him alive," Gary heard Mickey remark to Geno. The leprechaun continued to whisper to the dwarf, but Gary could only make out the name "Ceridwen" in the ensuing moments.

"What's the knight's name?" Gary mumbled over his shoulder.

Mickey directed Gary's gaze to Baron Pwyll.

"I don't know his proper name," the Baron said. "But he is called by Redarm."

"Have I forgotten?" Gary balked incredulously to the knight. He held the spear of Cedric Donigarten up high. "Good Redarm, have you forgotten that my spear will cut through your feeble armor more easily than your lance will pierce my skin?"

"*My thanks, young sprout,*" came a call in Gary's head.

The laughter down the road stopped abruptly.

"Don't mention it," Gary whispered to the sentient weapon.

"Laddie," Mickey warned.

"Are these horses as fast as Kelsey says?" Gary asked.

"Faster," answered the leprechaun.

"Then get ready to prove it," Gary whispered. "These guys, the archers, too, and especially Redarm, are going to be more interested in the joust than in you."

"Laddie," Mickey said again as the dwarf verily tossed the leprechaun atop the pony. Both Geno and Mickey understood what Gary Leger had in mind.

"Laddie," Mickey muttered again, not so sure that he liked the decision.

"Have a good ride to the netherworld," Geno said evenly to Gary, cutting Mickey's concerns short. "Though I hate to lose the spear."

"Hey, Geno," Gary replied, smiling as wickedly as was the dwarf. "Suck pond water."

"Thanks," the dwarf answered. "I have, many a time. Nothing like it after a hot day at the forge."

Gary unstrapped the sack of armor and handed it over to Pwyll, who nearly fell from his horse as he tried to secure it. "By the way," Gary asked the dwarf, needing to know before he went for his apparently suicidal ride, "how did you throw the gnome so far?"

Gerbil started to answer, "Earth-pull reversal . . ."

"Never mind." Gary cut him off, holding his hand up high and shaking his head.

"I am waiting, Gary Leger of Bretaigne!" growled Redarm, seeming larger and more ominous as his huge horse plodded out away from the other.

"We're all to die," muttered Pwyll.

Gary ignored the gloomy Baron and trotted his mount out from the group. He looked to Redarm, to the road and fields around the man, and knew that his was a desperate choice. Perhaps Baron Pwyll was correct, at least as far as Gary was concerned, but even so, the young man would not despair. He felt again like something larger than himself, like a part of a bigger whole, and if he died allowing his friends to escape, then so be it. Gary paused as he fully contemplated those thoughts; never once in his own world had he felt this way.

Gary lowered the mighty spear.

"If I win, then my friends are allowed to ride free," Gary declared.

"As you wish," Redarm replied exuberantly, and Gary knew that cocky knight didn't mean a word of it—not that Redarm expected Gary to win anyway.

It was, perhaps, the hardest thing that Gary Leger had ever done, something that went against his very instinct for survival. But he gritted his teeth and kicked his horse into motion, commanding the bells to "Ring!" and charging off down the road. The thunder of hooves doubled as Redarm similarly charged, that long and deadly lance dipped unerringly Gary's way.

Gary moved to the left side of the road, opposite the archers, held the spear across his body with his left hand, and clutched the bridle tightly with his right. Only with the bouncing of the charge did the young man realize how severe the wound in his side might be, and his battered knuckles ached so badly that he feared he would simply drop his weapon. He squinted against the sudden sharp pains, kept his focus straight ahead.

"*Oh, valiant sprout!*" came the spear's cry in his head, a cry that showed the spear to be thrilled to be in a joust once more.

"Oh, shut up," frightened Gary growled back through a grimace, working as hard as he could to hold his balance while keeping the spear out in some semblance of an attack posture.

The combatants closed, weapons leveled (though Gary's spear had begun to dip), elfish bells ringing and horses snorting for the exertion. In Gary charged, grim-faced, roaring in rage and pain.

And then he veered, at the last moment, away from the knight, turned his horse to the side of the road and charged off into the darkness.

"*Young sprout!*" came a cry of telepathic protest.

"Shut up!" Gary yelled back.

It took Redarm several moments to understand what had just happened in the pass. "Treachery!" he roared, in the direction of the diminishing sound of elfish bells. "Coward! Kill him! Kill them all!" The infuriated knight looked back towards the tavern wall, to the dissipating illusion of a horse and a pony where Gary's friends had been.

The surprised archers put a few wild shots the way Gary had fled, then came out of the bushes, scratching their heads.

The wind in Gary's face, the wind of freedom, almost erased the continuing pain in his side. He had outsmarted the enemies, used their strict adherence to codes against them, knowing that they would believe that he would not avoid a challenge of honor. But Gary would not confuse honor with stupidity. He had no armor on, hadn't even a shield to turn aside Redarm's deadly lance.

He heard one arrow cut the air not so far away, but was more concerned with the sound of hooves as his enemies took up the chase. He bent low in the saddle, told the bells to stop ringing, and trusted in his steed.

Kelsey had not lied; the sound of pursuit fast faded behind Gary as he flew on across the rolling fields. He heard the distant ringing of similar elfish bells and took it to be a signal from his friends. His mount apparently thought so, too, for the horse veered and snorted and took control of the ride from Gary. A few moments later, Gary saw a dark line up ahead, a stone wall probably. Whether he held doubts or not did not seem to matter to the horse, for the beast picked up its pace and did not turn to the side.

Equestrian jumping looked so easy on television. And indeed, the mount of Tir na n'Og easily flew over the low wall, clearing it on the far side by more than a dozen feet.

They had to land, though, and Gary Leger immediately gained tenfold respect for the straight-backed riders he had watched in equestrian competitions. He jerked forward, almost flying over, as the horse's forelegs slammed down, then went straight down, though of course he could not go straight down, when the horse came fully to the field.

His breath long gone, Gary thought that he should reach up and feel his throat to see just how high his testicles had bounced.

He was still leaning when he caught up to the others, Kelsey included, his horse trotting in beside Baron Pwyll's mount.

"Well done!" shouted the sincerely relieved Baron, and he clapped Gary hard on the shoulder. The dazed and wounded Gary would have fallen right off the other side of his horse, except that Geno was there to catch him and toss him roughly the other way.

The others watched in confusion as Gary struggled to gain an unsteady seat on his mount. "I think I need some help," the young man explained, and this time he did fall, between his horse and Pwyll's, the blood running freely from the knife cut in his side.

ELEVEN

Spirituality's End

"WHY did you bring him?" The voice was distant to Gary, but he recognized it as Kelsey's, and the elf did not sound happy.

"I telled ye before," Mickey replied. "It's bigger than yer spear and yer armor, bigger than Robert himself."

"Enough of your cryptic babble," Kelsey demanded.

"He did get us out of there," offered another voice, Baron Pwyll's.

"He dishonored himself, and us!" Kelsey snarled back.

Gary had been trying to convince his sleepy eyes to open, trying to shift his prone, weary body so that he could get up and join in the conversation. But now he knew what his friends were talking about, who his friends were talking about, and he was not so eager to join in.

"Ye couldn't expect the lad to fight it through," Mickey reasoned. "He didn't even have on the armor!"

"He challenged the man," Kelsey declared, and his words sounded with the finality of a nail being driven into Gary Leger's coffin. "Honorably."

"He fooled the man," Mickey corrected. "Fittingly. Besides, ye're the only one o' the group who's angry with the lad. Even Geno, who'd fight yerself to a draw, feels he owes the lad his thanks."

"Dwarfs don't mix honor and stupidity," came another voice, Geno's voice, from a different direction. "That's an elfish trait, and one for humans, though you cannot trust any human, even on his word."

Gary blinked his eyes open. He was lying flat on his back, sunk deep in a thick bed of soft clover and looking up at the most spectacular display of twinkling stars he had ever seen. To his left, he saw the horses, and saw Geno and Gerbil ride up on the gnome's quadri-contraption. Across the other way sat Gary's remaining companions, circling a pile of glowing embers, Baron Pwyll eagerly digging the remaining food out of a small bowl.

"Is he alive?" Geno asked with his customary gruffness as he and the gnome crossed by Gary's feet.

"Oh, sure," Mickey answered. "His wound's not too bad, and the salve should fix it clean."

Gary instinctively dragged his hand to his side, felt a poultice there, and realized that the sharp pain had become no more than a distant and dull ache.

"Did you note any signs of pursuit?" Kelsey asked.

"Plenty of signs," Geno replied with a chuckle. "But all going in the wrong directions. Geldion's bunch lost the trail altogether when Mickey made the horse bells sound back to the north."

Gary had seen and heard enough of the leprechaun's tricks to understand what had occurred. Redarm and his minions were probably twenty miles away by now, chasing illusionary bells through dark fields.

"And we can keep goin' to the south," the leprechaun reasoned.

"East," Kelsey bluntly corrected. There came a long pause, as all of the others waited for Kelsey to explain. Gary wanted to hear it, too.

"We shall cross Dvergamal," the elf decided. "The dragon was last seen near to Gondabuggan. Perhaps he will still be about, or perhaps some of your folk"— Gary knew that Kelsey was speaking to Geno—"have seen him crossing the mountains."

"Oh, yes, yes, a fine plan," Gerbil interjected, above the stuttered protests of Baron Pwyll. "If Robert is still about my town, then won't he be surprised—oh, his dragon eyes will pop wide!—when a whole new group of heroes arrives to battle him!"

"If the wyrm is still about your town, then your town is no more a town," Geno put in, and from his tone, it didn't seem to Gary that the dwarf was particularly fond of Kelsey's plan.

"Have you a better idea?" Kelsey demanded, apparently thinking the same thing.

"I have an idea that chasing a dragon, a dragon that can fly," the dwarf emphasized, "across mountains, will get us nothing more than tired. Besides, whoever said that the plan was to catch up to the damned wyrm?"

"We have not the time to go all the way to Robert's lair," Kelsey reasoned, his voice firm and even.

"And you won't catch a flying wyrm crawling along mountain trails!" Geno said again.

"He's right," Mickey interjected. "We won't be catching Robert by going where the dragon's last been seen. We'll find charred trees and charred bones, to be sure."

Gerbil groaned.

"But not a sight o' the fast-flying wyrm," Mickey finished.

Gary chanced a look to the group, saw Kelsey, obviously agitated, jump up to his feet and stalk a few steps away.

"More than that," Geno said roughly, "the dragon is nowhere near to Gondabuggan anymore."

"What do you know?" Kelsey demanded, spinning about.

"The Buldrefolk have seen him," Geno answered. "In a foul mood, soaring across the peaks of Dvergamal. Robert is out and flying free with Ceridwen banished to her island for the first time in centuries. He has a lot to see, elf, and a lot to conquer. Did he destroy the gnome town? Will he go for the Crahgs next, try to find some allies out of the pile of monsters lurking in there? Or might he go straight for Connacht, to burn the castle and the King? Robert knows as well as we that Kinnemore is Ceridwen's puppet. With the witch banished, if he can bring down the throne, then what might stop him?"

How true rang every one of Geno's suppositions, and how hopeless the desperate task seemed then to Kelsey. His scowl became a look of dread and resignation, and he turned back away, staring out into the empty night.

"We'll catch him," Mickey said to him. "But not by going where he's been— by going where he's sure to be."

Kelsey turned about once more, his eyes, shining golden even in the dim light of the embers, narrowed with an expression that seemed to Gary half anger and half intrigue.

"Oh, we'll go east, like ye said," Mickey went on, lighting his long-stemmed pipe. "But not 'til we get south around the mountains."

"To Giant's Thumb," Kelsey said.

Pwyll groaned again, and Geno's stream of spittle sizzled as it hit the embers.

"Dragons don't like thieves walking into their empty lairs to their backs," Mickey said with a conniving smile. "Robert'll come rushing back as fast as his flapping wings'll fly him when he senses that we're there. And when he sees what we bringed back to his hoard, then he's bound to stay put for a hundred years."

"What you brought back," Geno corrected.

"You have decided not to accompany us?" Kelsey asked.

"I never decided to accompany you!" the dwarf corrected. "I came east because east is my home, to get away from that stupid Prince Geldion and from yourself!" He poked a stubby finger Pwyll's way. "Don't you think that I've forgotten who put me in this trouble in the first place!"

The fearful Baron blanched.

"Ah, a load o' bluster," Mickey said, and Gary half expected Geno to leap up and spring across the embers to throttle the leprechaun. The dwarf did some mighty glowering, but kept his seat.

"Ye're here because ye got put in the middle of it, that much is true," Mickey continued. "But ye've stayed because ye know ye have to stay. Like our friend gnome, there. He'd like nothing more than to get back to Gondabuggan and his own, but he won't go, not if our best plans don't take him there."

"True enough, I figure. I figure," Gerbil replied, stroking his gray beard, shining more orange in the firelight than Gary had noticed before. "I figure?"

Geno sent another stream of spittle sizzling against the embers, but he did not openly dispute the wise leprechaun's reasoning. The dwarf knew more than the others, though, knew that Prince Geldion and his small band were but a tiny fraction of the resistance stemming from Connacht. Geno's companions in the Snoozing Sprite had told him that the King's army was on the march, northeast across the fields, drawing a line between Connacht and Braemar.

"South and east it is, then," Kelsey agreed. "To the Giant's Thumb, to lure the wyrm and to trap the wyrm."

A series of clucking noises issued forth from Baron Pwyll's twisting mouth, obvious protests against the seemingly suicidal course.

"You can stay here and wait for Geldion," Geno offered, punching the Baron in the arm. The dwarf spat again and rolled over, propping a rock for a pillow. "Too fat and slow anyway."

Gary shook his head, tried to lift his arms to clasp hands behind his neck, but found that he could only lift his right arm, his bound left side being too sore for the maneuver. He grimaced and tucked his left arm against his side, hoping that it would heal before he found himself in another battle.

That thought led Gary's gaze down between his feet, to the pile of armor and the long black spear, resting easily against it. Gary propped himself up on his elbows—gingerly—and reached his toe down to tap against the weapon.

A blue spark erupted from the butt end of the spear, singeing Gary's toe and coursing through his body, sending his thick black hair into a momentary standstill atop his head.

"Hey!" he exclaimed

"Coward!"

The message stole all the surprise from Gary's body, stole his strength and just about everything else, as well. He stared blankly at the mighty weapon, confused and distressed.

"I'm not a coward," he replied, quietly aloud, but with the protest screaming in his thoughts.

He waited, but the spear did not dignify the declaration with a response.

"Problems?" Mickey asked, skipping over to sit in the clover beside the young man. Gary looked to the spear.

"Damned thing zapped me," he explained.

"Coward!"

"I am not a coward!" Gary growled.

"Ah," muttered Mickey. "The proud spear's not liking yer choice to run from Redarm."

"I didn't run from Redarm!" Gary snapped back, more angrily than he had intended. "I mean . . . I just . . . we were trying to get away."

Mickey stopped him with a low whistle and a knowing wave of his little hand. "I know what ye were doing, lad, and you did well, by me own guess," the leprechaun explained. 'The spear's a proud one, that's all, and not liking missing any fight, needed or not."

"*Coward!*"

Gary growled at the spear; images of heaving it over a bottomless ravine in Dvergamal came into his thoughts. The spear responded by imparting telepathic images of Gary going over the edge, and of the spear plunging down behind, chasing him, point first, all the way down the sheer cliffs.

And then the connection was broken, simply gone. Gary looked around curiously, suspecting, but not certain of, what had occurred. Had the spear rejected him? Would it refuse his grasp in the morning, and forever after?

"How stubborn can a weapon be?" the young man asked Mickey.

"Less bending than the metal they're forged with," the leprechaun replied.

"Then we might be in trouble."

Mickey nodded and took a long draw on his pipe, then blew a large smoke ring that drifted the length of Gary's body and settled around the tip of the mighty spear.

"Have it your own way," Gary remarked to the spear, and he lay back down in the clover, head in his hand and looked again to the wondrous nighttime sky of Faerie. Hundreds of stars peeked back at him, pulled at his heart. He wanted to fly up there suddenly, to soar out into the universe and play in the heavens.

"'Tis a beauty," Mickey agreed, seeing the obvious pleasure splayed across Gary's suddenly serene features.

"Better than anything I've ever seen in my own world," Gary agreed.

"The same sky," Mickey replied.

Gary shook his head. "No!" he said emphatically, and then he took a moment to figure out where that firm denial had come from. "It's different," he said at length. "My world is too full of cities, maybe, and streetlights."

"They burn all the night?"

"All the night," Gary answered. "And dull the sky. And the air's probably too dirty for the stars to match this." Gary chuckled resignedly, helplessly. It was true enough, true and sad, but there was even something more profound that made Gary believe that even without the night lights and the dirty air, the stars of his own world would not shine so brightly.

"It's different," he said again. "We have a different way of looking at stars, at all things." Yes, that was it, Gary decided. Not just the actual image of the night sky, but the perspective, was very different.

"We have science and scientists, solving all the mysteries," he explained to a doubtful-looking Mickey. "Sometimes I think that's the whole problem." Another pitiful chuckle escaped Gary's lips. He considered the demise of religion in his world, when the mysteries of faith became not so mysterious. He thought of the Shroud of Turin, long believed to be the actual cloth covering the body of Jesus. Only a few days ago, Gary had watched a show on PBS where scientists had dated the cloth of the shroud to sometime around a thousand years *after* the death of Christ.

It was an inevitable clash, science and religion, and one that Gary was just now beginning to understand that his people had not properly resolved or accounted for. Religions hung on to outdated myths, and science ruthlessly battered at them with seemingly indisputable logic.

"Explaining everything," Gary said again, and again, he laughed, this time loudly enough to attract the attention of Kelsey and Pwyll, sitting by the glowing embers. "Do you know what it feels like to be mortal, Mickey?"

"What're ye talking about?" the leprechaun replied sincerely, honestly trying to understand this thing that was so obviously distressing his friend.

"Mortal," Gary reiterated. "You see, when you take the mysteries away, so too goes the spirituality, the belief in something beyond this physical life."

"That's a stupid way to live."

Gary chuckled yet again and could not disagree. But neither could he escape, he knew. He was a product of his world, a product of an era where science ruled supreme, where no balance between physical truths and spiritual needs had been struck. "It's . . ." Gary searched for the word. ". . . despairing. When the physical world becomes explained to a level where there is no room . . ." Gary let the thought drift away and simply shook his head.

"Ye think yer scientists got all the answers, then?" Mickey asked.

Maybe not for this trip of mine, Gary thought. Whatever the hell this placed called Faerie might actually be.

"There is no magic in my world," Gary answered solemnly.

"Oh, there ye're wrong," the leprechaun replied, taking the pipe from his mouth and poking Gary in the shoulder with its long stem. "There ye're wrong. The magic's there, I tell ye—yer people have just lost their way to seein' it!"

"No magic," Gary said again, with finality, and he looked away from Mickey and stared back up at the incredible night canopy.

"Can yer so-smart scientists tell ye then why yer heart leaps up at the sight o' stars?" the leprechaun asked smugly, and he snapped his little fingers right in front of Gary's nose.

"Thought not!" Mickey continued in the face of Gary's incredulous stare. "Yer science won't be telling ye that, not for a long while. It's a magic common to all the folk—never could a man or a sprite or even a dwarf look up at the stars and not feel the tug o' magic."

Gary wasn't sure that he bought Mickey's description of it all, but the leprechaun's words were, somehow, comforting. The man from the other world stole a line from a song, then, again from that haunting *Tusk* album, a quiet song by the group's other woman singer. "Oh what a wonderful night to be," he half sang, half chanted. "Stars must be my friends to shine on me."

"Ah, the bard McVie," Mickey said with obvious pleasure.

Gary's forthcoming reply stuck in his throat. The bard McVie! How the hell could Mickey . . .

Gary shook his head and let out a cry that startled Mickey and sent Kelsey leaping to his feet. Seeing that nothing was askew, no enemies nearby, the elf threw a threatening glare Gary and Mickey's way and slowly eased himself back down.

"What?" Mickey started to ask, but Gary cut him short with a wave of his hand.

"Never mind," was all that he cared to say at that time.

"As ye wish, lad," Mickey answered, hopping to his feet. "Get yerself some rest, then. We've a long road in the morn."

Gary continued to look at the stars for a long time, thinking hard. The bard McVie? The last time Gary was in Faerie, when he had brought *The Hobbit* along with him, Mickey had hinted that the author of that book, J.R.R. Tolkien, had probably crossed into Faerie, as Gary had done, and that the books that Gary considered so fantastical might be the true adventures of that remarkable man, or adventures told to him by another visitor to Faerie, or by one of Faerie's folk.

Now the leprechaun had inadvertently expanded upon that possibility. Could it be that many of the artists, the sculptors and the painters, the musicians penning haunting songs, the writers of fantastical works, had actually crossed into this realm, had found the magic and brought a little piece of it back with them to share with a world that so badly needed it? Might the artists of Gary's world be people who could find the magic beneath the dulling cover, who could see the stars despite the city lights?

It was a comforting thought, one that led weary and wounded Gary Leger into a deep and much-needed sleep.

TWELVE
Arrayed for War

MICKEY'S salve worked wonderfully, and most of the pain was gone from Gary's side when he awakened the next morning, despite the fact that moisture hung thick in the air, grayed by a solid curtain of heavy clouds. There remained some uncomfortable pulling in the scar tissue when Gary stood up and stretched, and a soreness when Geno and Baron Pwyll began strapping on the armor, but it was nothing too bad.

Gary spent most of the minutes looking over to the spear, lying prone on the grassy field. There had been no mental contact, at least none that Gary could consciously sense, since he had awakened. It seemed to him that the spear was brooding—he got the feeling, too, that it didn't like the fact that he was donning its complementary armor—and he feared that he might have to find himself another weapon.

Even more worrisome to Gary was the fact that Kelsey, who also had labeled him a coward, was giving him the proverbial cold shoulder. The elf looked his way several times while the armor was being put on, always locked gazes with Gary for just an instant, and then his golden eyes would narrow and he would brusquely turn away.

Not that Gary was overly thrilled with Kelsey at that time, either. He kept seeing images of the man stumbling into the room at the Snoozing Sprite, an elfish arrow dug into his back. Gary understood the necessity of fighting, understood the grim consequences of not winning, but it seemed to him as though Kelsey could have achieved the same margin of victory by shooting the man in the leg instead, or in the shoulder, perhaps. Gary knew well how marvelous a shot the elf was with that deadly bow; if the arrow was sticking through the man's heart, it was only because that was exactly where Kelsey had meant it to be.

The armor was on, then, and Gary worked his arms about in circles, stretching this way and that to try to better the fit. Kelsey walked by him, on his way to the horses, again throwing an angry, dangerous glare Gary's way.

"Did you have to kill them?" Gary asked reflexively, grabbing at something, some accusation, with which to shoot back at the judgmental elf.

"Of what do you speak?" Kelsey replied to him seeming honestly confused.

Mickey and Gerbil, over by the gnome's quadricycle, and Pwyll and Geno, already readying their mounts, paused and looked Gary's way.

"The men back at the inn," Gary pressed, trying to ignore the elf's cavalier attitude about it all and the continuing concerned stares of his other companions. "You shot to kill."

"Perhaps we should have stopped to reason with them," Kelsey said sarcastically, coming up to stand right before Gary.

"You didn't have to kill them," Gary said sternly.

"They came at us," Kelsey pointedly reminded him, and the elf snorted derisively and turned away, as though he felt that the conversation wasn't worth continuing.

"I am not a coward!" Gary growled at his back. Gary never considered his next move, never took a moment to think things through. He slammed his hands against Kelsey's back and shoved as hard as he could.

Kelsey flew several feet, diving headlong. He was agile enough to tuck his shoulder, and wise enough not to fight against the undeniable momentum, and he rolled right back to his feet, spinning as he went so that he came up facing Gary. In the blink of an eye, Kelsey's sword came out and he rushed Gary's way, launching a swing.

Gary hardly flinched, reminding himself that Kelsey would not kill him. He instructively brought his arm up to block, caught the sword on his forearm as it whipped to a stop barely inches from his neck. The two stared unblinkingly for several moments. Gary realized a throbbing ache in his arm, believed that he might be bleeding under the armor, but he did not relent his hold, even growled and pushed the weapon farther from him.

"I am not a coward," he said again.

"But are you a fool?" Kelsey asked dangerously and Gary heard Mickey suck in air and hold his breath.

Gary didn't blink, didn't flinch at all, just held the pose, and the weapon, as the long seconds slipped past.

"You fled," Kelsey remarked at length.

"Wasn't it Kelsey who led the flight from Geldion in Dilnamarra?" Gary replied coyly.

"I made no challenge of honor!" the elf snarled, snapping his sword away and slipping it into its scabbard so quickly that Gary could hardly follow the movement.

"To hell with your challenge," Gary replied without hesitation. "I had to get my friends out of there. Their lives were worth more to me than any false conceptions of honor. Brand me a coward if you choose, Kelsenellenenen . . . whatever the hell your name is, but you know better."

Kelsey's visage softened somewhat for just a moment. The elf seemed to realize his slip, though, and his scowl returned as he turned away to go to his horse.

Gary only then realized that he was trembling—with anger and not with fear.

"*I am waiting, young sprout,*" came a call in his head, slightly reluctant perhaps, but Gary realized then that his bold words had deflected more than Kelsey's outrage. He went over and roughly grabbed up the spear, and, under the continuing gazes of his surprised friends, walked steadily to his horse. He hoisted Mickey up first, then moved to put his foot in the stirrup.

The white steed shied away and Gary understood that it was smart enough to react to Kelsey's emotions.

"Tell the stupid horse to behave," Gary demanded of the elf. Kelsey scowled at him and said nothing, but the horse did not shy away when Gary took hold of it a second time.

At Geno's insistence, they rode out at a leisurely pace. Kelsey didn't offer much argument against that, since he wanted to learn much more about what Robert had been up to before they ever got near the Giant's Thumb. They kept mostly to the south, skating the towering rocky peaks of Dvergamal, and only occasionally skipping away from the mountains' protective shadow to ride up to lonely groupings of farmhouses and see what they might learn.

For the most part, the group remained quiet, each caught in his own private swirl of worries and contemplations. Gerbil did not even know if Gondabuggan had survived, Baron Pwyll felt that he surely would not, and Kelsey's fair features were clouded by the weight of tremendous responsibility. Geno kept looking every which way, as though he expected the dragon, or something else, to spring out at him at any moment, and in watching the dwarf, Gary recognized that Geno's insistence that they ride more slowly had nothing to do with a sore backside.

For Gary Leger, the enormity of the situation around him, the incredible danger, far beyond anything he had ever experienced in his own world, kept his mind more than occupied. Again there was that strange sense of calm accompanying it all, though, that feeling that he was part of something bigger, the feeling that his actions, whatever the personal cost, held a profound effect on something more important than his own mortality.

More important than his own mortality!

But it was true; Gary knew that to be truly how he felt. He wondered how many people of his world had ever experienced this sensation. He thought of the war raging back home, of the fanatical, suicidal people facing off against the

United States-led coalition. Were they really so altruistic, so believing in their
religion, that they were not afraid of death itself?

The thought sent a shudder along Gary's spine. He feared people so fanatical. But also, Gary envied them, for their purpose in life, however Gary might
judge the merits of their religion and loyalties, was larger than his own, was
larger than the next fifty or sixty years, or however long he had left to live.

An inevitable smile cut through the trepidation, and Gary glanced around
at his five companions. He saw Gerbil sitting low, casually pumping the wondrous quadricycle, and felt sympathy for the gnome, and prayed that Gerbil's
fears for his homeland would not come to pass. He noticed Geno, glancing
about again, and knew that the dwarf was up to something. He felt for Kelsey,
so noble and proud, and inadvertently the cause of this terrible strife.

Gary's gaze lingered long on Mickey. The leprechaun sat before him on his
horse, resting easily against the beast's high-held neck and holding his pipe
(though it was not lit) between his teeth. Gary had seen this same faraway look
in Mickey's gray eyes before, a sadness and a longing.

"What are you thinking?" he eventually asked the sprite.

"Of long ago," Mickey answered quietly. "When all the goodly races were as
one. Maybe there's not enough true evil in the world today, lad."

Gary thought the comment odd, especially considering the company Mickey
was now keeping: two men, an elf, a dwarf, and a gnome, all riding side by side
towards a common goal.

"It would seem as if they're united again," Gary remarked.

Mickey shrugged and made no comment.

"Why did you bring me here?" Gary asked bluntly, and for the first time in
the talk, the leprechaun looked directly at the young man. "I need to know,"
Gary explained.

Mickey's huge smile erupted. "I needed a body to carry around that armor,"
the leprechaun remarked coyly. "Couldn't be leaving it in a bush, and wouldn't
want to sack it and lift it over me shoulder!"

"No," Gary said seriously, somberly. "It's more than that."

"Well, ye've fought the dragon once already . . ."

"And more than Robert," Gary interrupted. "I might help against the dragon,
but not enough to make it worth your while to pluck me from my own world."

"Ye don't want to be here?" Mickey asked evenly.

"I didn't say that," Gary quickly replied, refusing to let the tricky leprechaun
deflect the conversation.

Mickey let out a deep sigh and clasped his hands behind his hairy head, the tip of his tam-o'-shanter dipping low over his sparkling gray eyes. He looked away from Gary and off into empty air. Gary waited patiently, understanding that the leprechaun had something to say, was just trying to weigh every word carefully.

"Ye know it's more than the dragon," Mickey began. He motioned for Gary to slow the horse, to put some ground between them and the others. "Ye knew last time ye came here that bad things been brewing between Connacht and Dilnamarra."

Gary nodded, remembering the confrontation between Baron Pwyll and Prince Geldion when they had first gone for the armor, a time that seemed like several years before to Gary (and from his perspective, it was!).

"And so goes Dilnamarra, so goes Braemar," Mickey went on. "And Drochit as well, and a dozen other hamlets that have so far resisted King Kinnemore's greedy hands."

"Kinnemore is Ceridwen's puppet," Gary remarked. He had heard this much before.

Mickey nodded. "Aye, and with the witch stuck to her island, and Robert flying free, she's been forced to play out her hand, to take the aces outa her sleeves," the leprechaun explained, in language that he knew Gary would fully comprehend. "That's why Ceridwen went for the armor, and went for Pwyll when the armor could not be found. And she'll be going for more before all's ended, lad, and so'll greedy Robert."

Gary sat back in his saddle. He had suspected those very things, of course, both from Robert's reported raids and the actions of stubborn Prince Geldion. But to hear Mickey put it so plainly nearly overwhelmed the young man. There was a tug-of-war going on here, between Ceridwen with her puppet king and the dragon, and all the commonfolk of Faerie, and the dwarfs and gnomes and Tylwyth Teg, and even the leprechauns, were caught squarely in the middle of it.

"That's why Geno's coming along," Mickey remarked, easily understanding the train of Gary's thoughts. "And Gerbil, too, though the little one hasn't figured it all out yet. Yerself played a part in bringing it to this point, lad, and so there might be things that only yerself can do. I thinked it proper and right that ye should get to help in finishing the tale."

Gary wasn't so sure that he liked where this particular tale might be headed, for his own sake and for the sake of Faerie's goodly folk, but he nodded his appreciation to Mickey, for he did indeed want, and need, to be an active participant in the writing of the tale.

———

THE armored captain fidgeted impatiently atop his armored warhorse, look-ing to his lightly clothed servant and the great black bird perched upon the man's upheld arm. With a squawk to cut the morning air, the crow lifted off and flew away furiously, swiftly becoming a black speck among the ominous gray of the heavy sky.

"What did the damned bird say?" the captain demanded, obviously not thrilled in dealing with supernatural creatures. By the edicts of his own dear King, magic had been declared demonic and outlawed, and here they were, the army of Connacht, talking to birds!

"We must not be straight for Braemar," the servant informed the captain. "The outlaw Pwyll and his renegade band, along with the stolen artifacts, are making south along the mountain line. We need veer to the east and intercept them. King Kinnemore has declared that they must not make the Crahgs."

The large and straight-backed captain scowled. The outlaw Pwyll, he thought, and the notion didn't sit well with him. He and many of his soldiers had gone to Connacht from Dilnamarra, and they had never known Baron Pwyll, for all his bluster and love of comfort, to be anything short of generous.

But Kinnemore was King, this lowly captain's King, and to this man's sensi-bilities, that placed Kinnemore just one rung on the hierarchical ladder below God himself.

"What of Prince Geldion?" the captain asked.

"The Prince and his force are riding west of the outlaws," the servant ex-plained. "We will join on the field."

The captain nodded and motioned for his sergeants to get the force mov-ing once more. He didn't like dealing with supernatural creatures on a supersti-tious level, but in all practicality the information being passed between the crows was proving invaluable to the mission, and thus, to the King.

"FRIENDS of yours?" Gerbil asked Geno when the party had broken for a midday meal. The gnome motioned across the camp, beyond the tethered horses and the parked quadricycle, to the foothills, where a group of dwarfs fully ar-rayed for battle were marching in a single line along a narrow trail, just under the low-riding layer of thick gray clouds. Gary and Pwyll turned in unison with Geno to regard the dwarfs, noticed Kelsey crouching behind a stone, bow in hand. Mickey was nowhere to be seen, but Gary knew the leprechaun well enough to realize that he had certainly spotted the dwarfish marchers.

"Better go to them," Geno remarked dryly. "Before the elf gets himself clob-bered." He jumped up and brushed the biscuit crumbs off him, then spotted a large one that had fallen to the ground and greedily scooped it up, along with a good measure of dirt, and stuffed it into his mouth.

It struck Gary as more than a little curious that Geno did not seem the least bit surprised by the appearance of the dwarfs.

"Put the puny bow away!" they heard Geno rumble at Kelsey, and he kicked a stone the prone elf's way as he ambled past. He and the dwarfs exchanged signals of greeting, and then they all disappeared over a ridge.

Kelsey came back to the group, then, obviously fearful, and Mickey came in right behind him.

"What is it?" the leprechaun asked as soon as he saw the elf's darting eyes.

"We may have just lost Geno's aid," Kelsey replied.

"Or worse." The way he kept glancing about revealed to Gary, and to fearful Pwyll, that Kelsey almost expected the dwarfish band to attack. In an instant, the Baron's eyes went this way and that, more anxiously than Kelsey's.

"The dwarfs're not our enemies," Mickey offered calmly to Kelsey, and to nervous Pwyll. "Ye'll know that soon, me friend. The dwarfs're not our enemies, and Geno's not for leaving."

"What do you know?" Kelsey demanded.

Mickey nodded to the ridge, to where Geno had just reappeared, stomping his way back to the campsite. Kelsey nodded, too, calmed by the sight, and Pwyll let out a profound sigh of relief. Gary tossed the man a curious glance, and wondered, and not for the first time, how Pwyll had ever become a Baron.

"They are out searching for the dragon?" Kelsey reasoned hopefully.

"Dwarfs are too smart to go out looking for dragons," Geno grumbled back.

"What about you?" Gary remarked, seeing the obvious fault in Geno's logic. Hadn't Geno, after all, already accompanied them once to Robert's lair?

"Shut your mouth!" came the predictable response.

Gary did.

"Then why?" Kelsey asked, and it seemed to Gary as if the elf already knew, had known all along.

"I learned it in Braemar," Geno replied. "From friends at the Snoozing Sprite."

"Learned what?" piped in Gerbil, stroking his orange-and-white beard and appearing more openly anxious than he had previously let on.

"Oh, it is King Kinnemore!" Baron Pwyll, knowledgeable in the politics of the land, wailed. He threw up his hands and verily danced in circles, crying that they were all doomed.

Geno nodded grimly. "A force rides from the southwest," he confirmed. "Five hundred strong by some reports, larger than that by others."

Gary could understand that, knew how badly Ceridwen, and thus the King in Connacht, wanted to get her hands on the armor and spear of Cedric Donigarten. "Why are the dwarfs out?" he had to ask, somewhat confused by where Geno's folk fit into all of this. "Do they care that much for us? For him?" Gary added, pointing to Baron Pwyll.

"They care that little for Ceridwen's king puppet," Geno corrected.

Gary looked to Mickey, who only shrugged and nodded, seeming not surprised in the least by the sudden turn of events. More than ever, Gary Leger understood why Mickey had brought him back to Faerie, and though he was terribly afraid, more than ever did Gary Leger appreciate the leprechaun's choice.

He had helped to bring things to this point, for better or for worse, as Mickey had said. He felt duty-bound now to finish the tale.

For better or for worse.

"Lord Duncan Drochit and Badenoch of Braemar should be told," Kelsey reasoned. "If so huge a force is coming this way, then they'll likely not stop at catching Baron Pwyll and retrieving the artifacts."

Baron Pwyll let out another of his increasingly annoying whines.

Geno nodded grimly to Kelsey and pointed back to the north, where a cloud of dust was just beginning to climb into the midday air.

"The King has come!" Pwyll cried out. "Oh, woe . . ."

"Shut your mouth," Geno barked at him.

"Badenoch and Drochit," Kelsey reasoned. "With the combined militia of the two towns."

"Still not a third of what Connacht has sent," Geno replied grimly "Riding plowhorses and carrying wood axes and hay forks."

Gay looked at his own armor, his own mighty weapon, and could well imagine what those poorly outfitted common farmers might soon meet in the field.

Baron Pwyll continued to wail; a shudder ran along Gary Leger's spine.

THIRTEEN

Hold Yer Breath, Lad

THE companions caught up with the ragtag militia of Drochit and Braemar a few hours later, on the high edge of a field looking down across the rolling hills to the west and south. Despite Geno's assurances concerning what his dwarfish kinfolk had told him, Kelsey kept the companions outside the ring of farmer-soldiers, unsure of where the lines of alliances had been drawn. By all reports and all previous actions, Duncan Drochit and Lord Badenoch would seem to be friends, but in these confusing and dangerous times, and with so much hanging on the success of their quest, the friends had to exercise all caution.

The sentries within the camp, too, seemed unsure, eyeing the riders with some concern and clutching tightly to their pitchforks and axes. Finally, a contingent of dwarfs came marching out of the rocky foothills, and Geno, Kelsey, and Gerbil fell into step beside them, going with them to meet the militia leaders.

"They'll have no trouble," Mickey assured Gary and Baron Pwyll, whose fate seemed to hang so precariously in the balance. "We're all looking for the same thing, to stop the dragon and Connacht."

"Unless Badenoch and Drochit think it safer to hand me over to Prince Geldion," Baron Pwyll said gloomily, but there was a trace of accepting resignation in the large man's tone that Gary had not noticed before.

"They won't hand you over," Gary said firmly, to comfort the troubled man.

"Ye should have more the faith in yer friends," Mickey added. "How many times have both Badenoch and Drochit looked to yerself with support, mostly in matters concerning the witch-backed throne?"

Pwyll nodded, but the grim expression did not leave his round face. "Perhaps we would all be better off if I just surrender to Prince Geldion when he arrives," the Baron said with unexpected altruism.

"Better for all?" Mickey quipped. "Not so much better for yerself, unless ye're fancying hemp collars."

Pwyll shrugged, but his mounting determination did not seem to ebb. It appeared to Gary as though the man was fighting an inner battle, conscience against cowardice, mustering his courage and looking beyond his own needs, even his own survival. Pwyll was formulating his own secret agenda, Gary knew, one that might well send him running to Geldion.

"Besides," Mickey quickly put in, apparently beginning to understand things the same way as Gary, "Geldion's not really looking for yerself."

Both men cocked curious eyebrows Mickey's way. "For the spear and armor?" Gary asked.

"That's a part of it, by me guess," Mickey replied, eyeing Gary directly and grimly. "But he's wanting yerself, lad, and that we cannot let him get."

Gary was about to ask what in hell Prince Geldion might want with him, but he thought things through silently instead, remembered from where the King, and thus the Prince, was being directed. Beautiful, raven-haired Ceridwen was the power behind Faerie's throne, and Gary was the one who had put a spear through the witch's belly, had banished her to her island home for a hundred years.

It was not a comforting notion, and hung heavily in Gary's thoughts for the rest of that day, even after a group of men rode out from the encampment and bade the three companions to come in.

Baron Pwyll was immediately summoned to join the conference with Kelsey, Badenoch, and Drochit. Seeming more assured than before, the big man squared his shoulders and walked with a confident stride.

"He was thinking of surrendering to Geldion," Gary remarked to Mickey, though he realized that the leprechaun had already figured that much out.

"That one'll surprise ye," Mickey replied. "Pwyll, above all the other lords, has held out against Kinnemore. Just the fact that Geldion's taking the trouble to come out after him shows Pwyll's strength."

Gary nodded, but had a hard time reconciling what he knew about the fat Baron—particularly how Pwyll seemed to spend more time trembling than anything else—against the obvious respect the man commanded from friends and enemies alike. The guards standing on opposite sides of the command tent, wherein Kelsey was meeting with the two lords, beamed happily at the sight of Pwyll, as though their salvation was at hand, and straightened their posture as he passed between them.

Gary sighed, and figured that Pwyll must have been something more spectacular when he was a younger man. He looked to Mickey again, and found the leprechaun walking away, towards a small cook-fire where Gerbil, Geno, and a few other dwarfs were gathered.

"What's the matter with the little one?" Gary heard Mickey ask as he rushed to catch up with the sprite. One look at Gerbil, head down and a pained expression upon his normally cheery expression, told Gary where that question had come from.

"Word has spread of casualties from the dragon attack on Gondabuggan," Geno informed them. The beardless dwarf gave a surprisingly sympathetic look Gerbil's way, then piped in heartily, "The gnomes beat him off, though! Sent Robert fleeing to the mountains to lick grievous wounds." Geno reached over and gave Gerbil a swat on the back, but the gnome did not visibly react.

"But not without cost," another dwarf, one with a blue beard tucked into a wide, jeweled belt with a golden buckle, added. "An entire section of the town was destroyed and a fair number of gnomes killed. And it is said that Robert came back, but did not go into the town."

"A gnome patrol is missing in the foothills," Geno added. "Along with one of my own kin."

Pangs of guilt turned Gary's stomach. He had been part of the group that had gone to Robert's lair, an act that had apparently coaxed the dragon out. And Gary had been the one to banish Ceridwen, a good thing by one way of thinking, but the act that had upset the balance, had given Robert the Wretched the confidence to fly free so far from his mountain home.

Gary had found that he liked Gerbil, and if Gerbil was typical of his race, as Mickey had said, then the loss to Gondabuggan was surely a loss to all the world.

"They're going to send us around the fighting, if there is to be any fighting," Geno remarked, pointedly changing the subject. "If Geldion blocks the way, then we are to go around while Badenoch and Drochit hold him at bay."

Mickey nodded, apparently in agreement, but something discordant tugged hard at Gary's sensibilities.

"We all want the same thing," the young man replied angrily. "How can we think about battling the Prince with the dragon soaring about? Why don't we all just band together against the dragon, then worry about our personal feuds?"

There came no immediate response, the simple logic of Gary's words seeming to steal the words from Geno and Mickey and all the others. At first, Gary took this to mean that he might be on to something, but he soon came to realize that he simply did not understand the depth of the budding feud between Connacht and the outlying baronies.

"Who's going on to the dragon?" Mickey asked Geno.

"Same as before," the dwarf replied. "Though we might bring a few of my kinfolk along, and Pwyll might be asked to stay behind."

"He'd hate that," Gary remarked sarcastically.

"And the little one," Geno went on, patting Gerbil again. "His path is his own to choose. He might want to get back to Gondabuggan and help with the repairs."

"No," Gerbil said resolutely, lifting his head so that the others could see the determination in his inquisitive eyes. "No, no! I go to sting the dragon's home, I do, just as he attacked my own! Be afraid, wretched wyrm!" the gnome proclaimed loudly. "Oh, do, if you are half as smart as the legends say. You have never had an angry gnome in your nest, I would guess, and when you do, you will not be so happy a wyrm!"

Gary was just coming to terms with Geno's unexpectedly sympathetic posture when Gerbil launched his uncharacteristic tirade. He stared at the suddenly fierce gnome incredulously, then to Geno and the other dwarfs, lifting their mugs in a toast Gerbil's way.

"Slow to anger, but fierce as a badger when they do," Mickey whispered to Gary, referring to Gerbil and the race of gnomes in general. Gary did not argue; standing there, one foot up on a log, his head tilted back proudly, Gerbil seemed almost four feet tall.

GENO was the only dwarf accompanying Kelsey, Gary, Mickey, and Gerbil as they walked their mounts (and Gerbil pumped his quadricycle) to a ridge above and to the side of the field where the opposing forces would meet. Kelsey and Geno moved behind a brush line overlooking the field, while Gary, with Mickey tucked in front of him, stayed back, and Gerbil found a level and out-of-the-way place to park his rolling contraption. With all that was happening, politically and militarily, the village leaders had decided that speed and stealth would be absolutely necessary if the small group was to have any chance of getting through to the Giant's Thumb to replace the stolen dagger. Thus, Badenoch, Drochit, Pwyll, and Kervin of the dwarfs had determined that the other dwarfs would not accompany the band, that the responsibility fell upon the shoulders of those who had taken the dagger, and upon Gerbil, who insisted that he be allowed to go along. Surly Geno, hoping for a little dwarfish companionship on the hard road, hadn't stopped grumbling since.

Neither would Baron Pwyll accompany the friends, for Lords Badenoch and Drochit had begged the man to remain with them (right before Pwyll had begun to beg to be allowed to remain with them), to lend support and wisdom as they tried to fend off Connacht's encroachments from one side, and Robert's impending appearance from the other. That left one Tir na n'Og horse free, Gary noted. He was about to ask about that, wondering if they should perhaps take the mount along as an extra, when he got his answer. Up padded the proud horse, bearing a short but stout and heavily muscled man with an impossibly thick black beard and tanned arms the size of Gary's thighs. He wore a sleeveless jerkin and simple breeches (that were too small for him), and carried an immense hammer over one shoulder. His skin was darkly tanned and seemed darker still, with patches of soot ground in against the brown flesh. His beard and thick-cropped hair were matted with the dirt and sweat of hard labors.

"Well met," Kelsey called to him, apparently expecting the ally. Geno and Mickey greeted the man as well, though Gerbil seemed too consumed by his private thoughts to even recognize that another had joined them.

The huge man started for the ridge, then noticed Gary and gave a fierce tug that promptly wheeled his horse about, aiming it straight for the armored man.

"Cedric," he said, extending a calloused hand Gary's way and flashing a huge, broken-toothed smile.

"Cedric?" Gary echoed.

"Cedric the smithy," the man replied. "Best shoer in the world."

"Gary Leger," Gary replied, and he was nearly pulled from his saddle when the man grabbed his extended hand and pumped it vigorously.

"An honor, spearwielder," the man growled, and Gary was surprised by the obvious admiration in his tone. The smithy let go—Gary unconsciously wiped his now-grimy hand on his side—and jerked his horse about roughly. He nodded once more to Gary before padding up towards the crest of the ridge to join Kelsey and Geno.

"They're to meet in the field," Cedric explained loudly, and then Gary could make out no more as the powerful smithy moved in close to the others.

"Cedric?" Gary asked Mickey

"All the smithys—the human smithys—are named Cedric," the leprechaun explained. "In honor of Donigarten. Ye couldn't find an ally more loyal, lad. Ye're carrying the spear and wearing the suit of the man's idol. That's why he was given the extra horse. Cedric'll die for ye, die for the spearwielder, smiling all the while if he thinks he's helped yer noble cause."

It sounded crazy to Gary Leger, and he wasn't so sure that he liked having a man so willing to die for him. He started to mention that fact to Mickey, but changed his mind, suddenly realizing those thoughts as condescending. Who was he to determine another man's motivations? If Cedric the smithy would die smiling for the noble cause, then Cedric was a noble man, and Gary was the fool if he confused that sense of honor with foolishness.

"A good thing to have him along," Mickey remarked, and Gary nodded sincerely.

They saw Kelsey's arm jerk out suddenly, pointing to the field below, and Mickey bade Gary to walk the horse over so that they might see the arrival of Geldion.

The Prince came in from the southeast, the soldiers of Connacht arrayed behind him in the even lines of a well-trained army. Geldion rode out from the ranks on a black horse, flanked by three soldiers on either side. Redarm was not among this guard, Gary noted, and nowhere to be seen among the front ranks of Connacht soldiers, though what that might mean the young man could not discern.

Gary focused his attention on the Prince instead. Geldion looked far from regal, looked almost haggard, actually, his skin too browned from the long road and pulled tight to his bones. He wore his worn brown traveling cloak, tied only at the neck, and a suit of armor that had seen many, many encounters. Jeweled scabbards at his side held sword and dagger, though, and Mickey assured Gary that Geldion was well versed in the use of both weapons.

In response to Geldion's bold approach, Badenoch and Duncan Drochit trotted their mounts out from their ragtag force, Kervin the dwarfish leader running along beside them.

"Well met, Prince Geldion," the friends heard Badenoch call. The wind was behind the Lord, blowing in the faces of the hiding companions, and they heard the words clearly, "Glad are we that Connacht came to us in our time of need," Badenoch went on, "for mighty Robert has taken wing and threatens all the land!"

Geldion rocked back in his saddle; he seemed a bit surprised to Gary.

"Will you and your forces ride to Braemar beside us?" Badenoch continued, his tone anything but hostile.

"Is Geldion to become an ally?" Gary whispered to Mickey. For a moment, the young man thought that his earlier words might prove true, that these supposed enemies would band together against a common foe more powerful than either of them separately.

"Badenoch uses diplomacy to force Geldion to move first," Kelsey explained grimly, and Gary was somewhat surprised, and certainly pleased, that the elf was apparently talking to him again. "The lords feign friendship so that Geldion will have no excuse to attack."

Prince Geldion sat atop his mount, eyeing the lords suspiciously. His father had told him of the conspiracy, had even hinted that outlawed magic was being used to bring the lesser towns into line against Connacht. The thought did not sit well with the Prince of Faerie. Geldion was an extension of Kinnemore's throne, the most loyal of sons, but a part of him had been thrilled, and not so angry, when the ancient spear of Faerie's greatest hero had been reforged. His father, though, had been purely outraged, a fact that bothered and confused Geldion more than a little.

That confusion would not deter him from executing the duties Kinnemore had given to him. Not at all. Geldion would not let this Gary Leger of Bretaigne steal the repaired spear away, even if he had to kill the man personally!

"We may ride to Braemar," he replied in his shrill voice. "But not for any defense against Robert. The dragon is only one of our concerns, and not the most immediate one."

"Surely the dragon . . ." Badenoch began, but the always impatient Prince cut him short.

"I demand the return of the outlaw, Pwyll, and the stolen artifacts!" Geldion explained. "And there is a young man, a Gary Leger from Bretaigne, a spy from beyond Cancarron Mountains, who desires to bring the precious items back to his homeland."

"Now, that'd be a trick," Mickey remarked quietly, seeming not at all surprised by the lie.

"Where the hell is this Bretaigne place?" Gary asked him.

"Beyond Cancarron Mountains," came the predictable answer, which told Gary, who had no idea of where the Cancarron Mountains might be, absolutely nothing.

"Are you so certain of his intent?" Badenoch asked. "Was it not Gary Leger who accompanied Kelsenellenelvial Gil-Ravadry . . ."

"Well said!" Mickey exclaimed, and he winked at Gary. "He got that damned name right." The leprechaun's smirk drew a glare from Kelsey.

". . . to Robert's lair to reforge the spear?" Gary heard as Badenoch continued. "Was it not Gary Leger who banished evil Ceridwen to her island fortress?"

"All by himself," Geno muttered sarcastically.

"*Well done, young sprout,*" came the telepathic call in Gary's head.

Badenoch's last comment forced a visible wince from the haggard Prince, a wince that none of the friends on the not-too-distant ridge, and none of the three leaders facing Geldion, missed.

"Reforging the spear increased its value to Bretaigne," Geldion argued. "As for any fights with Ceridwen, they were merely incidental, and not looked for by any of the traitors."

"True enough, except for the 'traitors' part," Mickey put in dryly.

"Connacht seems eager to brand traitors," Badenoch replied.

"Hold yer breath, lad," Mickey remarked at hearing the firm response, and even Geno gulped in some air.

Geldion verily shook from boiling rage, his anger fueled by confusion. This was not how the kingdom was supposed to respond! His father was King, after all, the rightful King. How dare these lessers speak ill of Connacht! "You seem eager to place yourself among that list!" he snapped at Badenoch. "I demand the return of the traitors, and of the stolen artifacts!"

Cool Badenoch, sitting tall on his proud stallion, his neatly cropped salt-and-pepper hair blown across his face from the breeze off the mountains, slowly glanced around from one side to the other, then looked directly at the opposing Prince.

"We do not have them," he answered calmly.

Geldion wheeled his black horse about, jostling a couple of his escorts, and galloped back to the Connacht line.

"Hold yer breath, lad," Mickey said again.

"The bells must not ring," Kelsey said to the others, turning his mount away from the bushes and walking the horse down to the side of the ridge. Geno and Cedric followed immediately, and Gerbil pumped his quadricycle into position right beside the group.

Gary waited a moment longer, though, sensing that the storm was about to break and unable to tear his gaze from the field.

Geldion took a position in the center of the front rank. He stared across the field, his features grimly set, his right arm upraised. Badenoch, Drochit, and Kervin had not returned to their force; they sat far out from the lines, talking easily, and this seemed to upset Geldion all the more. Gary could hardly believe their courage, and understood that their apparent indifference to the coming storm was merely to give the unmistakable appearance to all witnesses, even the Connacht soldiers, that it was Geldion and the throne, and not the eastern villages, who precipitated this battle.

Whatever the appearance, Prince Geldion would not be deterred. He moved as if he meant to call out again to the opposing leaders, probably to speak the accusation one final time, but the first word came out as a growl and Geldion just snapped his arm down to his side.

Gary nearly jumped out of his seat, so surprised was he by the sudden thunder, the shaking of the ground beneath him, and the roar of a unified battle-cry, as five hundred horses and five hundred soldiers charged to battle.

Prince Geldion sat very still in his saddle, letting his soldiers flow out around him in their wild charge across the field. "So be it," Geldion muttered grimly. "So be it."

The three leaders in the field were not surprised in the least, though. They wheeled about and started off, Kervin accepting Drochit's extended hand and half climbing to the side of the horse, flying with all speed for their own ranks.

FOURTEEN

A Mind of Its Own

"RIDE on!" Kelsey commanded, starting down the side of the ridge behind the smithy Cedric, leading the group to flank the impending battle on the western side.

Geno, alone among the companions, seemed hesitant, looking back to his left, back where his dwarfish comrades stood to face the overwhelming odds. His torment was obvious, and not unexpected to Kelsey, and the elf quickly reversed direction, sidestepping his mount around the rolling quadricycle and slapping Gary's pony on the rump as it trotted by. A few words to Geno, reminding the dwarf of the importance of the mission, brought Geno along, though many times did the beardless dwarf look back over his left shoulder.

The field was lost from sight almost immediately as the companions went low in a gully. They heard the continuing thunder of pounding hooves, the cries of battle, the wails of the wounded and dying, but it seemed not nearly as intense as Gary had expected.

"Our allies are in flight back to the foothills," Mickey explained to him, seeing his quizzical look. "That was the plan all along, to bait Geldion in and keep him running the opposite way from us."

Gary looked back, using one hand to adjust the too-big helmet with his head as he turned. He heard shouts of frustration from Geldion's hungry force, confirmation of the leprechaun's claims, and was glad. The whole thought of the battle—especially with a greater common enemy, the dragon, free to terrorize the land—made bile rise in Gary's throat.

Cedric was still leading the way, driving his horse hard along the gully, then into a perpendicular trail running straight west and even lower from the battlefield. They went around a hillock, turning back to the south, now with a wall of grass between them and Geldion's force, the cries and thunderous hooves fast fading into the background.

It seemed not enough distance to the eager smithy, and he kicked his big boots against his mount's flank, spurring the horse full out as they rounded yet another bend, this one wrapping right behind the battlefield, back to the east.

"What ho, with ease good smithy!" Kelsey warned. "We have put them behind us."

Gary understood where Kelsey's words were leading. The elf knew that Geldion's main force could not catch them, but he feared—and rightly so, Gary believed—that scouting parties, or groups held back to flank the enemy, had been deployed in the region.

Around the bend went reckless Cedric, and his horse whinnied immediately and skidded to a stop in the soft turf. All the others broke stride as Cedric's horse backpedaled, the smithy yanking hard on the reins, trying not to fall backwards off the mount.

Cedric reappeared fully from around the bend, a stunned expression on his bushy-bearded face and an arrow sticking from his chest.

Kelsey, in full charge, fitted an arrow and ducked low, his mount galloping with all speed around the back of the wounded Cedric, using the smithy as a shield. As soon as he came clear on the other side, the elf let fly his arrow, then dropped the bow across his saddle horn and drew out his gleaming sword.

Geno, ever hungry for battle, charged right behind, and Gary followed. Gerbil skidded the quadricycle to a stop and pulled open a compartment to the side of his seat, removing a long metal pole, a crank, and two iron balls secured to either end of a four-foot length of hemp.

Cedric was still up on the horse when Gary caught up to him, the smithy's mouth still wide with surprise, and his hands tight around the reins. Hardly thinking of the movement, Gary lifted Mickey across to the man's horse, yelled for the leprechaun to help him, and kicked his mount away, following Kelsey and Geno.

Eight Connacht soldiers had been positioned in the gully, looking for potential flanking maneuvers from this very direction. That number was now seven, with one man slumped low in his saddle, face against his horse's mane, and an elfish arrow sticking diagonally into his collar.

But the scouts, still twenty yards away and with bows in hand, had not been taken by surprise. A line of crimson appeared on Kelsey's neck as an arrow narrowly missed its deadly mark. Another bolt would have hit the elf squarely, except that Kelsey fell to the side and threw up his sword, luckily tipping the missile wide. Those same two bowmen were the closest foes for the elf, and he roared in, hoping to get to them before they were fully prepared for close melee.

The hiss of metal on metal split the air as broadswords slipped free of their scabbards. One of the soldiers foolishly kicked his mount ahead, relinquishing the two-on-one advantage for the first attack routines.

Kelsey's sword, blue-glowing with magical fires, slashed across as the horses came side by side, and the broadsword intercepted it and forced it wide.

Quicker than the soldier believed possible, Kelsey let go the sword, flipped his hand around and caught its hilt with an upside-down grasp. He jabbed it back, daggerlike, into the man's knee.

The soldier howled, his horse reared, and Kelsey, already going to the side, turned his mount further and called into its ear. The intelligent beast readily complied, lifting its haunches from the ground and kicking out with both hooves, blasting the wounded soldier from his saddle.

Kelsey continued the turn, came around a full circle, moving behind the now-riderless horse to bide some time as the second soldier bore down on him, broadsword slashing through the air.

GARY worked hard to catch up with Geno. The gully was not wide—just a few horses could fit side by side, and with Kelsey already in tight against the enemy, Gary knew that poor Geno would take the brunt of the remaining bow attacks.

One arrow went wide, at least one other hit the charging dwarf with a popping thud. But Geno hardly seemed to flinch, bent low over the side of his pony, a hammer cocked and ready.

It wasn't until he felt the smack against his chestplate that Gary Leger realized his error in focusing his attention on the fate of his diminutive friend. It took him many moments to get past the shock of being hit so that he could even realize that the arrow had splintered harmlessly against his fabulous armor, its stone tip barely scratching the marvelous suit. Still, the shock had broken Gary's momentum, had sent Geno rushing far out ahead of him.

Gary looked up ahead and prodded his horse forward, but then reared his mount as another archer drew a bead on him and let fly.

ONE soldier, the only knight among the group, lowered a long lance and charged out for the approaching dwarf. Geno straightened as though he meant to come across on the pass as if in joust. But the dwarf on his pony was barely half the height of the armored man on the tall black stallion. Geno had come to Gary's defense when the young man had tricked Redarm, and now the dwarf proved that he, too, would not confuse stupidity with honor. The knight came thundering on, thinking to skewer the apparently helpless dwarf and charge past to the next rider. Before he ever got close, though, Geno's arm whipped out, one, two, and three, and a line of hammers twirled in low, clipping the front legs of the knight's horse.

The beast stumbled with the first hit, began to pitch with the second, and the third only ensured that it was going down head first. The surprised knight did not react nearly quickly enough as the tip of his long lance dipped and then caught into the ground. The weapon's butt end slammed hard into the man's armpit, and he pitched forward in a fumbling pole-vault. He nearly went up vertically before the lance snapped, dropping him hard to the ground, where he lay, dazed and weighted by the heavy armor, and unable to crawl or even roll out of harm's way.

Geno tightened his muscular legs around the pony's sides and forced the mount to veer sharply, hooves slamming atop metal plating, driving the wounded knight deeper into the soft turf.

Another arrow hit the dwarf then, in the left shoulder, but Geno only growled and snapped his legs around the other way, making a tight turn towards the archer.

THE arrow tore a gash in his horse's ear, continued on to deflect off Gary's armored side, stinging him though it could not penetrate the enchanted metal.

The man was already reaching for another bolt, and now eyeing Gary's horse dangerously.

Gary knew that he couldn't give the archer that next shot, that the man would likely kill his mount and leave him sprawling helplessly in the grass. He had just seen Geno's maneuver, and the thought of being crunched under fifteen hundred pounds of horse and rider didn't seem overly appealing.

Gary cocked the mighty spear over his shoulder and brought his arm forward as if to throw.

"Do not!" screamed a voice in his head, and to his amazement his fingers would not loosen from the black shaft.

Gary's horse bolted away, apparently of its own accord, charging straight for the archer. Instinctively, Gary leveled the spear at his hip, while desperately clinging to the reins of the out-of-control beast.

The archer's face paled. He fumbled with his arrow, then seemed to realize that he could not possibly ready the bow and fire in time. He threw the bow aside and grabbed at his swordhilt.

Gary knew that he had the man dead.

Dead!

Gary Leger was about to kill a human being. His conscience screamed at him, his heart missed many beats, but his horse, nostrils flaring and head down in full charge, did not sway an inch.

At the last moment, Gary flipped the balanced spear around in his hand.

He nearly toppled off the side of his galloping mount for the effort, and clicked himself painfully in the shoulder with the mightily enchanted speartip. Somehow he managed to get the butt end of the spear out in front, though, and it cracked off his terrified opponent's raised forearm, blasted through as Gary's mount rushed by, and smacked full force into the man's chest, knocking him flat out on his back across his horse's rump.

Gary heard him groan as be rushed past, was grateful for the sound, though he winced as he heard the man drop heavily to the ground.

Gary's horse swung about sharply, unexpectedly, and Gary lurched in the saddle, rolling far to the side.

"Slow down!" he called helplessly to the horse. He focused ahead just in time to see another archer, arrow nocked and eyes set on Gary, pull back on his bowstring.

The horse jostled over an uneven patch of ground, and Gary's poor-fitting helmet dropped down over his eyes.

"Oh, God!" he cried, thinking that he was about to die. Something slammed his forehead, dented his helm, and he saw little stars explode behind his eyelids.

"Oh, God!" he said again, but he realized that he was still alive, still on his horse. He grabbed blindly across the mount's back and pulled himself as upright as he could, and spotted the archer under the top edge of his fallen helm, fast moving off to the side.

Gary realized that he couldn't go by the man, couldn't give him any more clear shots. He fell over the other way, tugging hard on the reins. The horse apparently had the same idea, and turned more easily, and at a sharper angle, than Gary expected.

And at a sharper angle than the archer had expected, Gary realized as he brought his forearm up to bat the troublesome helm so that the slit somewhat aligned with his eyes.

"Oh, God!" Gary cried a third time, just as his horse rammed full force into the archer's.

It wasn't pretty, it wasn't graceful, but somehow it proved effective as the enemy soldier and horse toppled sideways, the horse crushing the man's leg as they slammed down to the ground. Gary's agile mount quickstepped, bucked and hopped, among the tangle, and came out beyond, Gary still holding the reins and still holding the spear, though his helmet had flown completely around on his head.

"*You do not fight to kill,*" the spear remarked—accused?—in Gary's mind.

Thinking that the weapon was belittling him, Gary started to respond with a stream of silent curses.

"*That is good, young sprout,*" the spear went on, ignoring the ranting man. "*You value life, even the lives of your enemies.*"

Gary had no more time to pay attention to the telepathic barrage. More enemies remained, and he couldn't see them!

"*But I'll not let you get killed,*" the sentient spear imparted. "*Not yet.*"

The thought seemed curious to Gary, and he was too muddled and afraid to put two and two together when, an instant later, his mount cut a nasty turn (and again, Gary had to hold on for his life) and leaped away, running full out. Gary tried to get a hand free so that he could at least figure out where he was going. Not that he was sure he wanted to see ahead, for he feared that he would find another knight with a lowered lance, patiently waiting to skewer him.

Just as he let go the reins with one hand, his horse leaped high and long, coming down with a jolt that forced Gary to grab on with both hands again. Grab on and tighten his legs about the steed's sides, lying low in the saddle all the while.

It took Gary another long moment to discern that the sounds of battle were fast fading behind him, that he was running free and far away from enemies and friends alike.

His first thoughts went to Ceridwen, the troublesome and dangerous witch. Had she taken control of the horse? Was she reeling Gary Leger in to her like an angler with a hooked fish?

"Help me!" Gary cried, his shout ringing inside the helmet and inside his own ears. He yanked on the reins with all his strength, but the horse pulled back, kept its head low and flew on across the rolling fields.

KELSEY and the swordsman continued their fight across the back of the riderless horse, the agile elf easily parrying the lunging attacks of the angry fighter. The elf would have liked to play this out longer, to take no chances against an opponent he could obviously defeat, but he heard Geno's arrow-inspired grunts and saw Gary Leger bolting about wildly, dangerously.

The fighter gave a straight thrust across the horse's back, his sword diving for Kelsey's thigh.

Confident in his mount, Kelsey let go the reins altogether and caught the man's wrist, shifting himself about and tugging hard, drawing the overbalanced man right across the riderless horse's back. The elf's sword was free, and his opponent was trapped and helpless.

Surprisingly, to Kelsey, an image of Gary Leger came into his thoughts. The tip of Kelsey's blade was just an inch from the helpless, terrified man's exposed forehead when Kelsey turned it aside, sent it snapping into the man's biceps instead so that he cried out in pain and lost his grip on his own sword.

Kelsey let go the wrist and grabbed the man by the hair, tugging him fiercely, pulling his face down towards the ground. His sword came in again, this time hilt-first, slamming the man on the base of his neck. The soldier struggled no more, went limp under Kelsey's grasp and slowly slid over the back of the riderless horse and fell to the ground.

Kelsey took care not to trample the unconscious man, sidestepped his mount around the back of the riderless horse, and looked for his companions.

He saw Geno, two arrows already sticking from the dwarf, charging the two remaining opponents, both archers, sitting composed, side by side, bows drawn and ready.

"Now you die, dwarf!" one of them cried, as much in fear as in anger.

A horn blast to the side—not the winding horn a knight might carry, but a curious beeping sound—turned all eyes.

Gerbil's quadricycle rushed and bounced along the steep slope of the gully's side. One of the gnome's arms worked frantically on the contraption's steering bar, while the other pumped wildly on a crank, turning a high pole tipped by spinning bolas. Gerbil tried to watch the rough path ahead, while eyeing a sighting device attached to the pole.

"Oh, yes!" the gnome cried, letting go the crank and flicking a trigger. The bolas flew free, spinning fiercely, looping about the nearest archer. The hemp wound fast, iron balls cracking the unfortunate man about the shoulders and pitching him sidelong into his similarly surprised companion.

"Oh, yes, yes!" Gerbil shouted in victory, but he should have paid attention to his own precarious perch instead. The front left wheel of the quadricycle slammed against a rock and bounced up high, taking the whole side of the gnome's vehicle off the ground.

Gerbil's victory shout turned to a shriek as he tried to hold the quadricycle steady on two wheels. He lost the valiant fight when his right front wheel plopped into a ditch and got yanked sidelong. Poor Gerbil and his contraption pitched head over heels, crunched down in the soft turf, and slid to a stop at the base of the gully's slope.

Geno wasn't watching the gnome, more concerned with the tangle of enemy archers before him. The one who had been hit with the bolas went down hard between the horses, one shoulder obviously broken, wailing loudly and trying to keep his own horse from stepping on him. The other archer was still in the saddle, though, righting himself and trying to ready his bow. Sheer terror covered his face when he looked up to see the charging dwarf, face contorted in rage and a hammer high above his head.

The archer fell backwards, fell away from the chopping hammer, as Geno's pony slammed in. Geno leaped right from his mount, dove forward into the leaning man and forced them both off the back side of the archer's horse. The man twisted about so that he did not land flat on his back and tried to break his fall with outstretched arms. One wrist exploded with a tremendous crack, and the surprising weight of the short but compact dwarf drove the man facedown into the turf.

Geno grabbed a handful of hair and jerked the man's head back, then face-slammed him into the soft grass. Seeing a better target, the dwarf yanked him back again, shifted the angle slightly, and rammed him into a half-buried rock.

The man's ensuing scream came out as a blood-filled gurgle. His nose and cheek shattered, but that only seemed to urge the ferocious dwarf on. Geno slammed him again, then hooked an arm under the man's shoulder and tugged so fiercely that he dislocated the arm. A dwarfish knee crunched the half-turned man's stomach, rolling him right over to his back, his arm garishly wrapped behind him.

Geno was up to his feet in an instant, deadly hammer ready to do its grim work.

"Do not finish him," Kelsey advised, trotting his mount over. Both elf and dwarf looked around to see that, amazingly, not a single opponent had been killed, though the man whom Geno had trampled with the pony was grievously wounded.

"Go to the gnome," Kelsey ordered. The elf turned about to see Mickey steering Cedric's horse forward. The huge smithy sat very straight in the saddle, caked with sweat, his dark eyes unblinking.

"Whatever ye're to do, do it fast," Mickey advised, and he looked to poor Cedric, then back to Kelsey, shaking his head.

The man on the ground flopped about, jostling Geno, and the dwarf's hammer came up in an instant.

"Geno," Kelsey said slowly.

"Bah, good enough for you!" the dwarf yelled at his wounded victim, and he followed the growl with a stream of spittle, then stomped off to extract the fallen gnome.

Kelsey looked around, was somewhat relieved to see that no other enemies were in the area. But neither was Gary Leger.

"Where'd the lad run off to?" Mickey asked.

Kelsey shook his head, having no answers.

"There's suren to be other enemies about," Mickey remarked.

Again, Kelsey had no answer for the leprechaun. He, too, was concerned for Gary, and he was concerned for himself and the others as well, for Cedric seemed to be hovering near death, and Gerbil and his gnomish contraption had gone down hard.

FIFTEEN
In the Name of Honor

GARY finally righted his helm enough so that he could see, but with the dizzying blur of the broken landscape rolling beneath, he almost wished he hadn't. Stifling a scream, the young man who wished he had taken some riding lessons tucked the magical spear tightly under his arm and held on for all his life. His horse leaped across shallow ravines, zigzagged through boulder-strewn fields, and splashed across several small streams. Gary sensed that enemy soldiers were about, even saw one group, resting under a widespread tree at the base of a hillock, eating a meal. One of them noticed Gary as well, pointed and called out.

But Gary was a white blur, a trick of the eyes, gone from sight before the other soldiers even reacted to the cry.

Still, the young man knew that he was vulnerable, and if the clopping of hooves, the rattle of armor plates, and the occasional snort from the fiery horse weren't enough, the elfish bells began to ring!

I didn't command them to do that! Gary thought, trying to sort out what in the world was happening to him. He hadn't thought about the bells at all, actually, and yet they were ringing. He couldn't control the horse, couldn't control the bells, and that led him to the inevitable conclusion that someone else had taken command of everything around him.

Gary Leger had met the witch Ceridwen on his last journey through Faerie; he figured that he knew who that someone else might be.

He had to jump off. As terrifying as that thought seemed, Gary believed that he had no practical choice. It had to be Ceridwen, after all, and Gary figured that anything would be better than meeting her again. Jumping was easier thought than done, though, for the armor prevented Gary from making a clean leap, and the ground, turf-soft in some places but boulder-hard in others, promised to smash him apart.

"You have to do it," he whispered grimly to himself, and he forced himself to make the first move, to bring the spear out from his side so that he could toss it away from him as he went.

Gary's arm jerked, but he found, to his disbelief and his horror, that his fingers would not let go.

"*Do not throw me away, young sprout!*" came the mental command.

Gary's thoughts rushed back in a jumbled blur, too fast for him to clearly spell out to the sentient spear what he believed was happening. He took a deep breath, forced himself to slow down at last, and pointedly imparted, *I did not command the elfish bells to ring!*

"*I did,*" came the surprisingly calm response.

Gary nearly fell out of the saddle; under his helm, his mouth drooped open. What the hell was going on?

The horse bounded around another bend, leaped a low hedgerow, and padded to a quick stop, and Gary Leger had his answers.

"*Restore my honor!*" the spear commanded.

Gary was as surprised as the three men facing him across the way—two Connacht soldiers centered by the knight, Redarm.

THE surprisingly resilient quadricycle rolled away, Gerbil taking care to avoid the groaning forms of the fallen Connacht soldiers. Carefully, too, went Kelsey on his horse, leading the horse bearing Mickey and Cedric. The leprechaun had done his best in binding the wounded smithy, and Kelsey had helped as well, the elf, like all the Tylwyth Teg, being greatly versed in the healing arts. Gerbil had even added a potion and healing salve, from yet another compartment in his amazing vehicle. They had not been able to dig the arrowhead out of Cedric's chest, though, and despite the warm blankets they wrapped about the man, cold sweat continued to stream down his face.

"We won't catch Gary Leger tugging him along," Geno grumbled to Kelsey.

Kelsey had no rebuttal, except to ask, "Would you prefer that we leave the man behind?"

Geno thought that one over for a long while, even nodded a few times.

"Stonebubbles!" he cursed at last, and he walked his pony out ahead of the slow-moving elf, taking the point position.

Mickey took a deep draw on his long-stemmed pipe, feeling more helpless than he had ever before. The continued absence of his pot of gold, his source of magical energy, had depleted the leprechaun to the point where he practically hadn't been able to help out at all in the last fight. He called upon what little magical energy he had remaining now, though, imparting to the grievously wounded smithy images of a spreading chestnut tree, a hot forge, and glowing metal. Better for Cedric to rest easily with the thoughts that would most comfort him, Mickey figured, and he watched the man's muscled chest, expecting that each shallow breath would be Cedric's last.

HIS face alone could frighten the heartiest of men. Redarm sat atop his great stallion, the hinged faceplate of his plated armor up high on his head. Despite his obvious delight at seeing Gary, his expression was grim, his skin ruddy and scarred in a dozen places. He wore a thick black moustache that covered both his lips when his mouth was closed, and his similarly thick eyebrows converged above the bridge of his oft-broken, crooked nose. Even from twenty yards, Gary could tell that Redarm's eyes were dark, black actually, and bloodshot. Angry eyes, Gary thought. always angry.

The man forced a smile, a curiously evil sight. "Geldion relegated me to the back lines," he said, a coarse chuckle accompanying his gravelly voice, "in punishment for my obvious eagerness to kill you! And here, by the fates, do you come to play."

Not so fateful, Gary thought grimly.

"*Restore my honor,*" the spear commanded.

Eat shit.

The sentient spear had no response to that, seemed somewhat confused to Gary, and that gave him some pleasure—muted pleasure, of course, since the young man believed with all his heart that he was about to die.

"By Prince Geldion's word, this man from Bretaigne is to be taken alive," the soldier to Redarm's right reminded the knight, placing his hand over Redarm's wrist as the knight reached for the hilt of his sword.

"Geldion did say that," Redarm agreed calmly, and the soldier removed his hand. Redarm had the sword out in the blink of an eye and slashed across, smashing the cruel blade downward into the side of the man's neck, nearly decapitating him. The soldier sat very still in his saddle, his expression frozen.

Then, as though the residual energy of the tremendous hit had rolled down to his feet and come storming back up, he seemed to leap out of his saddle, falling dead to the grass.

The now-riderless horse nickered and pawed the ground in helpless protest.

Redarm swung about the other way, but the remaining soldier had already kicked his horse into a run, fleeing with all speed.

Gary looked on dumbfoundedly, felt his stomach churning and his pulse pounding in his temples. He had seen battle in Faerie, had even seen men cut down, but never so ruthlessly and never by another man.

"Now it is as it should be," the scarred knight said to Gary. Without even wiping away the blood, Redarm replaced his sword in its scabbard and took up his lance.

"Have you made your peace with whatever god you serve?" the knight asked politely, and before Gary could stutter an answer, Redarm dropped his faceplate, set his lion-and-clover-emblazoned shield, and dipped his lance atop its concave-cut corner.

What the hell do I do now? Gary asked the spear.

"Restore my honor!"

"Will you say something else!" Gary cried out, and Redarm straightened in his saddle, lifting his faceplate once more.

"What else is to be said?" the knight asked confusedly. "Prepare to die, Gary Leger of Bretaigne, impostor of Cedric Donigarten!" Down came the faceplate, down dipped the lance.

"Son of a bitch," Gary groaned.

"You say the most curious of things," remarked the sentient spear.

"Eat shit," Gary told it again.

"Indeed," replied the spear, and Gary could sense that it was not happy. *"We will talk of that comment again, young sprout."*

At that moment Gary Leger didn't think that he would get the chance to talk of anything ever again. He looked around, wondering where he might run, but remembered that the spear, and not he, was in control of his horse. He groaned again, realizing that he didn't even have a shield, and dipped the speartip Redarm's way.

"No shield," Gary whispered to himself, thinking that he might bring that up to the knight, might at least get Redarm to relinquish the unfair advantage, might get the honorable knight to throw his own shield aside.

Gary never got the chance to mention it, though, for his horse kicked away suddenly, and Redarm's did likewise, and the thunder of hooves and the jingling of elfish bells filled the air.

It seemed to Gary a macabre game of chicken, a game of nerves as much as skill. He saw Redarm's approach, saw mostly the deadly tip of the knight's lance, lined perfectly with his breastplate. Gary tried to shift about, tried even to turn his horse more to the side, for the two mounts seemed as though they would collide head-on.

All that Gary could do was hold on, though, and hold tight to the spear, bracing it against his hip. With only a few strides to go, Gary understood another disadvantage of jousting with a spear, however strongly magicked.

Redarm's lance was at least three feet longer.

PRINCE Geldion's force continued the pursuit long after the eastern militia had cleared the field. Duncan Drochit, Badenoch, and the dwarf Kervin had urged their forces on as fast as Geldion had urged his—the other way. The three leaders had no intention of battling Connacht's well-armed and well-trained army on an open field and had never planned to do so. They had come out to meet Geldion only to keep him from their towns, and to keep him distracted while the small party slipped around.

Now they rode and ran with all speed, back into the foothills of rugged Dvergamal. Stragglers who could not keep up, or those who inadvertently turned down the wrong narrow trails and wound up blocked from further retreat, were mercilessly cut down.

Kervin's dwarfs offered the only real resistance to the Connacht army. They had secretly dug trenches, carefully replacing the top turf so that Geldion's riders would not see the traps. They had rigged small rockslides in the lower hills, both to hinder and crush pursuing enemies and to block off some of the trails used by their fleeing allies. Half the dwarfish force, ten sturdy warriors, had crouched among a rocky outcropping at the lip of the wide field, and when Geldion's lead riders came rushing past, intent on those men in full flight, out they came, battleaxes and warhammers chopping, a hearty song on their lips. They died, all ten, in bloody heaps, but not until they had taken down four times their own number in enemy soldiers.

And so the tumult died away on the wide field, the thunder of hooves, the flying mud, and shouts of battle and agony, rolling away to be swallowed up in the diminishing echoes of rugged Dvergamal. The field bore the scars, quick though the charge passed, with lines of broken, churned turf, and with its northeastern corner bloodied by more than three score casualties.

———

THE instant of impact, when the tip of Redarm's lance poked hard against Gary's chestplate, seemed to move in slow motion for the terrified young man. He felt the hard jab against his breast, saw the lance bend, its tip sliding to the side, to find a niche in the crease of his armor at the front of his shoulder.

Gary felt himself being pushed back, knew that his mount would not slow, and could not break momentum or turn away fast enough to save him. On came relentless Redarm, driving hard, roaring in victory.

The lance bowed and snapped, and suddenly the magical spear was the longer weapon. Its tip flared with energy as it battered Redarm's ornate shield, turning it around on the man's arm. Any lesser weapon would have been deflected, but Donigarten's spear was the mightiest in all the land, and was angry now, determined to win back its honor.

Gary felt the magic throb up his arm, telepathically compelling him to keep the weapon level and keep his course straight, the horses passing barely six inches apart. Gary flinched, knowing that he would surely be hit again by the remaining portion of the lance. But again, it all happened in the span of an eyeblink, and Gary had no time to formulate any logical arguments against the sentient spear's demands.

He watched through the slit in his helm, his green eyes widening in blank horror, as the spear fought through the blocking shield and dove for Redarm's chestplate. Metal armor curled up beneath its killing touch, tore apart and rolled inward as the spear bit at the knight's flesh hungrily, ate into the man's broad chest.

Gary felt the crunch as the remaining portion of Redarm's lance slammed him in the belly, but there was no strength behind the blow, no strength left at all in his opponent.

The spear continued its plunge, through the man's lung and spine, bloodied tip driving out his back.

The horses passed and both men, connected by the spear, were jerked about to face each other. Gary felt as though his arm would be pulled from its socket, but he held on stubbornly, and was promptly yanked half out of his saddle, lying sidelong across his mount's bouncing rump. He hooked his free arm under the front of his saddle, watched as his helmet fell bouncing to the ground.

Redarm, too, fell back, and tumbled off his horse altogether. Gary could not support the sudden weight and had not the strength to tear the imbedded spear from the dead man. He let go and tried to right himself instead, figured to turn his horse about and somehow retrieve the bloodied weapon. And all the while, black wings of guilt flapped around Gary's ears, told him what he had just done, made him look at the fallen, broken knight.

Redarm lay on his side in a widening pool of blood, the spearshaft protruding from one end, its tip sticking out the other. He was not moving, would never move again, Gary knew.

Gary winced in pain as he started to shift his weight closer to the center of his now-trotting mount. Both his shoulder and belly had been hit hard and he knew without looking that blue-black bruises were already widening in those areas. He could only hope that he was not bleeding under the armor.

When he had found his balance, he caught the bridle again and slowed the horse even more. For the first time since the pass with Redarm, Gary managed to look ahead of him to look where he was going.

Two twelve-foot-tall giants, their legs as thick as the trunks of old oaks, their chest broad and strong, stood side by side, a few feet apart, holding a thick net between them and grinning stupidly through pointed and jagged greenish-yellow teeth.

Gary knew them, had seen mountain trolls on his last journey through Faerie. He gave a yell, tried hard to turn his mount aside, but the surprisingly quick monsters shifted with him, and both he and his horse plunged headlong into the net.

The powerful trolls were moved backwards no more than a single step by the impact, and they quickly wrapped their captured prey so tightly that Gary's terrified horse could not even continue to kick and thrash.

Gary thought that he would surely be crushed in that pile. He strained to get his face out to the side so that he could at least try to draw breath.

"Horsie for supper," a third troll remarked happily, coming over to join its companions. He poked a huge and dirty finger into Gary's face. "But none fer you!" he laughed. "No food fer you all the way!"

"All the way?" Gary whispered. This had not been a random stroke of bad luck, he knew then. Someone else, not Prince Geldion or even King Kinnemore, had guided these monsters, and Gary, already fearful of a certain witch, had little trouble in figuring out who it might be.

He took some small comfort when the band started away, realizing that the trolls had been too stupid to even go over and retrieve the magical spear.

Small comfort.

SIXTEEN

The Deal

AN enormous smacking of lips bade Gary to awaken. Before he ever opened his eyes, he realized that he was no longer netted beside his horse, no longer in crushing quarters. He found that his arms were bound tightly together behind him, though, the edges of the metal armor digging painful creases into his shoulder blades.

"'Orsie's a good supper," he heard a resonant troll voice declare.

"Arg, but me'd like a bit o' man-meat," said another, and Gary's eyes popped wide and he let out a tremendous shout when the troll reached over, caught an exposed piece of skin between two huge fingers and twisted so brutally that Gary soon after felt warm blood oozing from the spot, just above his hip.

There were five of the monsters, giant and appearing human, except that their ears were far too small, and their eyes and noses too large, and their skin was the color of granite, as was their long and dirty, tangled hair.

"That waked the little feller up!" roared another of the group, and when he laughed, a thousand elfish bells that he had draped around his body began to jingle.

Gary winced and looked away, understanding what had happened to his courageous mount. The tinkling bells did not seem so gay to him anymore, mixed in with the smacking sounds of trolls devouring the beautiful horse.

It went on for many minutes, trolls slobbering and talking to each other in their typically unpleasant way. Every once in a while the same one of them near Gary would beg for just a bite of man-meat, and Gary seemed to always wind up getting sorely pinched at least once. The other trolls were adamant against that, though, and after a few occasions, seemed to tolerate their too-hungry companion less and less. At one point, the troll gave Gary a pinch, but was hauled away by another, lifted to his feet, then punched right in the eye. He tumbled back, hitting the ground hard just a foot away from prone Gary's head. He leaped up immediately, surprisingly fast given his half-ton bulk. Gary looked at the deep depression the thing had left in the ground and nearly fainted away, imagining what his head might have looked like if the troll had fallen atop him.

"Yer turn to carry!" one of the trolls growled, picking his teeth with a horse bone.

"Arg, he can't carry!" protested another, the fattest of the group, with black eyes and a tongue that didn't quite seem to fit inside his mouth. "'E'll eat the man, and then the witch'll eat us!"

"Troll-bunny pie," another remarked, nodding stupidly.

Gary did not miss the obvious reference to Ceridwen.

"Then you carry 'im!" snarled the tooth-picker. The fat troll protested more, but the tooth-picker whipped the horse bone out of his mouth, then set on him, punching and biting. Two others joined in, the fifth staying back so that he wouldn't damage his precious elfish bells, and soon the fat troll relented.

"You wiggle and I'll squeeze ye good!" the behemoth promised as he easily lifted Gary with one hand and tucked him under his round, though still rock-hard, arm.

The strength of the thing horrified Gary. He had fought trolls before, a couple of times, on his first visit to Faerie, but he was still surprised at how solid these monsters were. He felt as though he had been lifted by the steel shovel of a backhoe and tucked tight against the side of a brick wall. He was facing forward, at least, and the wind felt good in his face as the trolls ran off with long strides that could match the pace of a race horse.

Gary settled into a bouncing rhythm as the minutes became an hour. His shoulders ached with his arms bound so tightly behind his back, but he knew that if he complained, the trolls would probably just rip his arms off so he wouldn't have to worry about them anymore.

"Caught by trolls on your way to see the evil witch," Gary whispered sarcastically under his breath. "You've done good."

A huge hand came across in front of his face, the nail of the troll's middle finger held tight against its thumb.

"Arg, stop the spellcastin'!" the creature demanded, and it snapped the finger into Gary's forehead. Gary's head jerked back, his vision blurred, and he felt as if he had been kicked by a horse. He lay limp in the troll's grasp for a long while, watching the pretty stars that had suddenly come up, though night was still far away.

GENO was not gentle as he pushed the magical spear the rest of the way through the dead Redarm.

"There," Mickey, obviously upset, spat at Kelsey. "Did the lad get his honor back in yer own stupid way o' seein' things?"

Holding the empty helmet, Kelsey nodded gravely. "Gary Leger has done well," the elf admitted. "On almost every occasion."

"Damned good spear," Geno proclaimed, examining the incredible wound, with Redarm's metal armor folded into his chest around the gaping hole.

Mickey looked from the spear to Kelsey, and took an impatient draw on his pipe. He knew that Kelsey, in his typically understated way, had given Gary about as great a compliment as anyone could expect from one of the haughty Tylwyth Teg, but it didn't seem enough to the leprechaun at that grim time. Mickey had brought Gary back to Faerie, was leading a quest through dangerous lands by holding to a lie. The leprechaun felt responsible now, one of the few burdens the carefree Mickey hadn't been able to simply let roll off his rounded shoulders.

"Well, he won the fight," Geno said, hands on hips as he regarded the ground around Redarm. The other soldier, the one Redarm had cut down with his sword, lay in a pool of blood to the side, his horse and Redarm's grazing easily on the grassy field in the distance. "So where in the name of a stupid gnome did he go?"

Gerbil glared at the dwarf.

"Just a saying," Geno grumbled. "No such thing."

"Indeed," replied the gnome. "And can we conclude that this other unfortunate soldier was killed by the knight?"

Geno drew out Redarm's bloodied sword. "Seems that way."

"Thus did the knight and the soldier come at odds," reasoned the gnome, determined to prove Geno's insulting "saying" far from the truth. "Might we conclude that the disagreement came from the sight of Gary Leger?"

"Redarm wanted him dead," Mickey put in. "But the others had orders to take him alive."

"Others?" Geno and Kelsey said together, that thought sparking new lines of reasoning. The two of them went into a search immediately, certain that other clues would not be far away.

They found their answer not far to the south of the dead men, in the form of the huge tracks of bare-footed monsters right where the tracks of Gary's horse abruptly ended.

"Trolls," Kelsey announced grimly, looking to the south as he spoke, for he understood the potential implications.

"What?" Geno asked in surprise.

"Trolls," Kelsey said again, turning to regard the dwarf. Only then Kelsey realized that Geno hadn't been addressing him at all. The dwarf stood unblinking, staring at the spear he held in his hands. He looked over to Kelsey and Mickey a moment later, a stupefied look on his normally unshakable features.

"Damned spear just told me that they're taking him to the witch," the dwarf announced. He beamed a helpless smile a moment later. "Been good to know you, Gary Leger!"

The spear responded to that unfaithful farewell by jolting Geno with a burst of electrical energy. The dwarf growled, his straight, sandy brown hair standing up on end, one eye twitching uncontrollably. He spun the spear about in his hands, and planted it deep into the ground, then prudently hopped away. "Damned spear."

"We've got to go and get the lad," Mickey said to Kelsey, recognizing that the elf was truly torn. In truth, Mickey, too, did not like the prospects. Trolls could move with incredible speed, and would not tire for many days. They already had a head start, and even without it, would get to Ynis Gwydrin, Ceridwen's enchanted island, long before the companions.

Kelsey sighed and looked around. The mounts from Tir na n'Og were certainly up for the run, and Gerbil had done well to keep pace in that curious contraption of his, but what of Cedric?

The smithy had managed to ease his way down from the horse, but leaned heavily against it. Sweat covered his face; his breath came in shallow, forced gasps. He seemed incoherent, staring away into empty air, but he apparently understood more than the others realized, for he announced, "I am dying," and bade them to leave him there.

Mickey and Kelsey believed the man's claim, but even so, neither of them could simply leave the brave smithy behind.

"Geno and I will go for Gary," the elf decided. He looked to Mickey. "You and the gnome can get him to cover." He indicated Cedric, looking that way as he spoke, and was surprised to see the man walking away from the supporting horse.

"No!" Cedric declared in a voice that amazingly did not quiver. He strode, defiant of his garish wounds, over to the spear and, somewhere finding the strength, roughly tore it from the ground. The huge man's eyes glistened as he held the magnificent weapon before him, seeming to draw strength from simply holding the artifact that was so dear to one of his trade. Cedric nodded and smiled, as though he was holding a private conversation with the sentient weapon. This was the spear of his namesake, an item most holy to smithies all across the land of Faerie, and never before had Cedric of Braemar been so serene.

"Can he ride hard?" Kelsey asked Mickey.

The leprechaun shrugged, not even chancing a guess about what was going on, about where this grievously wounded man had found the sudden burst of strength.

"I understand," Cedric said to the spear. He came out of his private conversation then, and looked to the friends and nodded. Then, to their surprise and horror, the altruistic smithy turned the spear suddenly and plunged its tip into his breast, smiling with supreme contentment.

He held the pose for a long, horrible moment; then his legs buckled under him and he went down in a heap.

"Oh, oh, oh!" a stunned Gerbil uttered repeatedly, a stubby gnome finger poking out from the low seat of the quadricycle to the spectacle of the dead man. "Oh, oh, oh!"

"I'm not getting that out!" Geno roared in rage, pointing to the again-imbedded spear. The gruff dwarf turned and walked away, spitting curses about "stupid peoples!"

"Oh, you should have a plaque for that," the gnome offered in all sincerity.

"Indeed," Mickey muttered, and took another long draw off his pipe.

THEY were in the mountains, and the daylight was fast disappearing. This was not Dvergamal, Gary knew, for these peaks were not quite as tall and rugged as in the dwarfish homeland. The trolls were carrying him through the region called Penllyn, whose heart was Ynis Gwydrin, the isle of glass.

Ceridwen's isle.

Act fast, Gary told himself. He stretched and yawned loudly, gaining the attention of the troll carrying him.

"How long have we been running?" he asked, trying to sound calm, even relaxed.

The troll's other hand came around again, middle finger tight against the thumb, and Gary thought he was about to take another nap.

"'Ere, shut yer mouth," the monster growled, and it shook its free hand dangerously, but did not snap Gary in the head again.

Gary knew that he had to speak directly, had to say something that would immediately attract the dim-witted troll's attention—else the stupid thing might knock him cold before it ever realized that he had something important to say. He squirmed a bit so that he could look around, tried to find something that might lead the conversation forward. He found himself thinking of *The Hobbit*, and of Bilbo's encounter with similar trolls, and of how those adventurers got out of their rather sticky predicament. He heard the elfish bells ringing gaily, draped about one of the monsters.

"Why does he get the magical bells?" Gary asked suddenly, without even thinking.

The troll carrying him slowed noticeably. Its hand, finger cocked, started around towards Gary, but it held back, apparently intrigued.

"Magical?" it asked as quietly as a troll could, which meant that Gary was not quite deafened.

"Of course," Gary replied. "The bells make a horse run swifter, make the wearer stronger."

"Stronger?"

"Of course," Gary whispered, his eyes flashing excitedly. "Stronger" was the perfect buzz-word for any troll, the word that brought drool to the bully's lips. Gary knew from the troll's tone that he had started something important here. "The troll wearing the bells . . ."

"Petey," Gary's bearer interrupted.

"Petey," Gary continued, "will soon grow much stronger. As he absorbs the magical energy of the elfish bells, he will likely become the strongest troll in all the world."

There came a long pause as the troll considered the news. "Hey, Petey," he called a moment later. "I wants to wear the bells."

The ringing stopped as Petey stopped, looking around to consider his garment. "They're mine, they is," he snarled. "I tooked 'em, and I'm keepin' 'em."

"Gimme the bells!" Gary liked the urgency of the troll's tone as the monster stepped towards stubborn Petey. He would have liked it even more if his troll had thought to put him down first.

"Go pick a goblin's nose!" Petey yelled back.

The troll reacted the only way trolls ever react—with violence. The monster wasn't close enough to punch Petey in the eye, so he hurled something instead, the only thing he had in his hands at the time.

Gary's cry ended with a guttural grunt as he connected on Petey's blocking forearm and was roughly deflected off to the side. He spun down to the rocky ground, dazed and battered, his thoughts screaming all the while that he had to get up and get away.

Predictably, the troll fight soon became a general row, with all five of the monsters rolling and, clawing, biting each other and landing some incredibly heavy punches. One rolled Gary's way, nearly rolled over him, and that surely would have been the end of him!

"Get away!" he whispered under his breath, and he, too, rolled, over the side of a rock into a short drop. Then, when he found his breath again, he began to crawl on his knees, stumbling and tumbling across the broken landscape. He managed to get up to his feet, but soon tripped back to the ground.

He took some comfort in the continuing thunder of the troll battle. But that ended soon enough when one of the monsters, Petey, Gary believed, yelled out above the din, "Hey, where'd he go to?"

"Oh, damn," Gary muttered, and he forced himself up again, running with all the speed he could manage, hoping he wouldn't fall blindly into a deep ravine in the fading light. He bounced off rocks, clipped his shoulders and head on low-hanging branches as he disappeared into one copse, and finally tripped facedown over the roots of a scraggly bush. Dazed, he rolled to his side, looking for some place to crawl into and hide.

He saw the giant, smelly foot of a troll instead, and a moment later felt as though he was flying. He stopped his ascent even with, and looking into, a bruised troll face, contorted with frothing rage.

"'Ere, don't kill him!" one of the monsters ordered from the side, and Gary was glad to hear those words, for he thought that this troll certainly meant to kill him.

"Yeah, the witch says that we don't kill him!" another troll emphatically agreed.

"Little sneakster's gonna run again!" the troll holding Gary declared.

"Bite 'is feets off," another offered, and the troll holding Gary smiled wickedly and turned him upside-down. An instant later, Gary felt the pressure of troll jaws against the sides of his sneakers.

"Ceridwen wouldn't like that!" he squeaked frantically. He felt the pressure ease, but not relinquish, and knew that he had to concoct some story, some excuse to save his feet, at once.

"I'm already bruised and cut," Gary stuttered. "Ceridwen won't like that, but these wounds will heal. If you bite my feet off, though, they won't grow back!"

"What's that got to do with it?" Petey demanded.

"Yeah, yous's just a prisoner," added another.

Gary laughed—it wasn't an easy thing to do in his predicament. "Just a prisoner?" he asked incredulously. "Don't you know why Ceridwen wants me?"

"Duh?" came the common response as the trolls, having no idea of what the man was babbling about, looked around at each other.

Gary considered the best way to put this. He had no idea of what horrid trolls understood of love and sexuality. They seemed to be carved out of stone, not born, and he had never seen a female troll, after all.

"Ceridwen thinks I'm cute," he announced. "She wants me as a husband."

"Duh?" Gary went up into the air, coming to a stop hanging upside-down right in front of the troll's confused face.

"I don't think the witch—whom I've seen turn trolls into bunnies," he added quickly, "would like a husband with no feet."

The troll looked to its companions and shrugged heavily, Gary bobbing three feet with the movement. A moment later, he was tucked under the troll's arm, every limb still intact, and the group headed off.

Gary thought of *The Hobbit* again, but came to the conclusion that he was not quite as sneaky as the wizard in that tale, and so he kept his mouth shut, all the way to the crystalline lake.

Geek and some other goblins were waiting for them there. They tied Gary down in a rowboat, then finished their business with the trolls.

Despite his grim situation, Gary Leger twisted about to stare with admiration at the castle that came into sight as they neared the distant island. Its walls were of glass, sparkling wondrously in the first light of twinkling stars. It was beautiful and icy, a palace fitting for Ceridwen, Gary decided as he remembered the witch, so alluring and so dangerous.

Beautiful and icy.

GARY had been in this room before. He had battled a demon here, which had caused many of the scorch marks that marred the otherwise beautiful decor. The doors had been repaired, as had Ceridwen's canopy bed, and the large leather-bound book—the book that had distorted time itself—was no longer out in plain view on the carved desk.

Gary continued his scan of the witch's bedroom, pointedly keeping his gaze away from the wall to the right of the door. There sat Alice, Ceridwen's pet. She appeared as a normal house cat now, but Gary had seen her in more ominous trappings. When he and his friends had escaped Ceridwen's castle, Alice had taken on the form of a lioness and attacked them. Gary had skewered the cat with the magical spear, a vicious fight that the young man remembered all too well.

Alice apparently remembered it also, and recognized Gary. From the moment Geek had escorted him into the bedroom, Alice had eyed him like he was a field mouse come to play. Geek had quickly departed, leaving Gary feeling oh, so vulnerable.

He was almost relieved when the door opened—almost, until he saw Ceridwen enter the room, her posture typically perfect, seemingly taller and more ominous than Gary remembered her. She verily floated across the way, Geek the goblin cowering in her wake, her icy-blue eyes locked into Gary's gaze.

Gary had met a few women at least with black hair and blue eyes, a somewhat unusual combination, in his own world, but that mixture paled when measured against this standard. Ceridwen's eyes burned with an intensity Gary could hardly believe, an intelligence that transcended her human trappings. The luster of her thick and long hair showed every other color within its general blackness, like a raven's wing shining in the sunlight.

She sat on the bed next to Gary, and he unconsciously brought his suddenly sweaty palms in close to his sides. Ceridwen had made romantic overtures towards him before. Only her evil reputation, and the fact that Gary knew she was looking for no more than a conquest, had given him the strength to keep the witch at arm's length.

He could resist her now, he knew, for all the previous reasons and for the fact that he had a marvelous friend waiting for him should he manage to get out of Faerie alive. Still, he couldn't deny the powerful allure of the witch.

"Again, you have done well, Gary Leger," the witch said, and Gary was surprised by her tone, seeming almost subdued.

Gary nodded but did not reply, fearful that anything he might say would give the witch too much information. Ceridwen looked down at him, nodded in the face of his nod, as though his silence, too, had proven revealing.

Gary wanted to crawl under the bed; he knew that he was outmatched here.

Ceridwen motioned to a mirror on the wall. She waved her hand and spoke a word and the glassy surface clouded, and then reformed into an image of the field on the southeastern edge of Dvergamal. Geldion was there, in the midst of Connacht's encamped army, along with several dead dwarfs and dead farmers, butchered in the field as they tried to flee. Several human prisoners sat in a heavily guarded area, looking thoroughly miserable, their expressions hopeless. Gary remembered the high poles at the crossroads, and could easily guess what Geldion had in mind for them.

"You may talk freely, Gary Leger," the witch explained. "I know all that I need to know." Ceridwen waved her hand again and the image in the mirror disappeared.

Gary tried not to show his revulsion for the brutal scene. He couldn't help but think how much like his own world Faerie could sometimes be. But why had Ceridwen chosen to show him that particular view? he wondered.

He looked over to her, sitting perfectly straight, eyeing him closely and licking her red lips in anticipation. Then Gary understood. The gruesome battle scene had overwhelmed him, mainly because he had played such a large part in bringing it about. He was indeed one of the authors of this tale, as Mickey had said, and Ceridwen wanted to show him the flip side to the adventure and the glory, the harsh price of victory. Inevitably, Gary's shoulders began to slump, but he straightened immediately, reminded himself that to show such weakness now could only help this alluring enemy sitting beside him.

"Do you know why I have brought you?" the witch asked calmly.

"The spear and armor," Gary replied indignantly, and his eyes narrowed, for he did not possess the spear. Fortune had aided him in getting one up on Ceridwen.

Ceridwen chuckled softly. "I could have had that and left you dead on the field," she reminded the young man. "And did you not think it odd that my trolls took you and did not bother to retrieved the spear?"

Gary fought hard to hide his surprise. Ceridwen knew about that! Suddenly none of this was making any sense to him. He believed that the witch must be bluffing, at least in part. She had not ordered the trolls to specifically bring her the spear, and so it had been left, but Gary could not believe, for whatever reason Ceridwen needed him, that the witch would not want the precious spear, possibly the only weapon in all of Faerie that could even hurt her, in her clutches.

So that might have been part of it, but if not for the artifacts, then why had Ceridwen taken such trouble to get him alive? Only one thought came to Gary, and it was not a pleasant one: revenge.

"You do not know our ways," Ceridwen said, rising from the bed and moving over to Alice, who was curled up in a purring ball. Gary tensed, fearing that the witch was about to send the vicious feline his way.

"You understand the general principles of the land," Ceridwen continued, absently draping a hand over the furry ball. "That much you proved in your first fight—in your flight—from the knight Redarm. It is the particulars that you need a lesson in, Gary Leger." Ceridwen rose again and turned suddenly on Gary, her blue eyes flashing with the first indication of eagerness Gary had seen.

"The particulars," she said again.

Gary had no answer for her, didn't even have a clue about what she was talking about.

"You were the one who banished me," the witch said. Gary's mind whirled in several different directions, most of them holding terrible implications. Might it be that Ceridwen could reverse the banishment by killing him?

The witch calmed again, apparently realizing the young man's distress. "Let me explain it differently," she offered. "Robert is free upon the land, more free than in centuries, since I do not stand to oppose him."

"The two evils kept each other in check," Gary remarked, and then he thought his choice of words incredibly stupid. Still, Ceridwen seemed to take no offense at being referred to as an "evil."

She nodded, as if to say touché, and went on. "In your victory, you and your pitiful friends have inadvertently plunged the world into dire trouble," she said. She waved at the mirror and an image of Gondabuggan came into view, many parts of the town still smoldering from Robert's initial attack. Ceridwen didn't let the image hang for long, though, and Gary saw through the propaganda, sensed that the gnomes had gotten off fairly well.

"This will be but the beginning," the witch proclaimed. "Robert will fly unhindered from one end of Faerie to the other, his breath burning a swath of destruction. And when he is fully convinced that his day has come, he will bring out his lizard soldiers."

Gary shuddered, remembering all too well Robert's strange and dangerous troops, the lava newts.

"Farewell, then, to Braemar," Ceridwen remarked. "And to Drochit and Dilnamarra, and all the towns and hamlets within the dragon's long reach."

"We'll stop that," Gary declared, and he caught himself one step shy of revealing the whole plan to the witch.

"No," Ceridwen replied. "Nor will I, banished as I am on my island. In a hundred years I will come out to find all the land under Robert's shadow."

"What are you getting at?" Gary demanded, his anger pushing aside all fears. If killing him would have released Ceridwen, then the witch would have already done so. This elaborate explanation, apparently trying to convince Gary that no scenario could be as bleak as having Robert flying free in Faerie, told Gary much about what was going on, told him that Ceridwen needed his willing assistance.

"Faerie does not have a hundred years," the witch snarled back at him, but she quickly put her dangerous frown away, taking on an innocuous appearance once more.

"You want me to release you," Gary replied, finally catching on. "I banished you, so by your rules, the particulars of which I do not know," he had to add, "I am the only one who can release you from that banishment."

Ceridwen did not answer, did not have to, for the firm set of her sculpted features told Gary that he had hit the mark.

"Not a chance," the young man said smugly.

"Consider the consequences," Ceridwen replied, her voice deathly calm. "For Faerie, and for yourself."

The threat certainly made an impression on Gary Leger, altruistic though he wanted to be. Ceridwen could hurt him; he could boast all he wanted to and pretend to hold the upper hand in this meeting, but he couldn't forget for one moment that Ceridwen could utterly destroy him with a clap of her deceivingly delicate hands.

"There is one evil upon the land, and you advise me to loose another to counter it?" Gary asked incredulously, trying to put this conversation back into the hypothetical.

"I advise you to consider the consequences," Ceridwen said again. "For Faerie, for yourself, and for your pitiful friends!" With that, the witch cried out at her mirror. Again an image formed, this time of the passes in Penllyn near the lake.

Gary saw his companions—four at least, for Baron Pwyll and Cedric the smithy were not with them—moving slowly along the trail, Kelsey carrying the magical spear and Gary's lost helmet.

Ceridwen muttered under her breath and the scene shifted, scanning the rocky ridges in the companions' wake, where lurked many, many trolls.

"Two score of them," Ceridwen remarked. "Awaiting my word to descend upon your friends and destroy them."

Gary forced himself to sit up straight. "How do I know that you're telling me, showing me, the truth?" he asked, though the obvious quiver in his voice proved that he believed what he was seeing. "I'm sure that your mirror could show me whatever you wanted it to."

Ceridwen didn't justify the remark with an answer. "You are the one who can end my exile," she said coldly. "You alone, Gary Leger. Consider the weight that has been placed upon your shoulders." Ceridwen looked to the mirror, showing again the four companions moving slowly along the winding trail. "A pity that friends so loyal should perish." She looked to Geek and started to say something, but Gary, his nerves at their end, cut her short.

"We can deal," he said.

"Deal?"

"You let me go, and my friends," Gary explained. "Guarantee us safe passage out of Penllyn." Gary paused, to study Ceridwen's reaction as well as to carefully weigh the confusing thoughts that were rushing through his head. What should he do? The answer was obvious, as far as he and his friends were concerned, but what would truly be the best course for Faerie? Would the land be better off if Ceridwen were allowed to come forth and help put Robert back in his hole?

"I'll reduce the terms of your banishment to one year," Gary finished, as good a compromise as he could think of on such short notice.

Ceridwen laughed at him. "A year?" she balked. "In a year, Robert's hold on the land will be nearly absolute."

"Unless my friends and I can stop him," Gary was quick to put in.

"And if you cannot?" Ceridwen asked simply, revealing Gary's dilemma.

Gary didn't know how to respond. He thought of Mickey's words when the leprechaun had explained why he had retrieved Gary. "There might be things that only yerself can do," Mickey had said, and that made perfect sense to Gary now, though it did little to show him which choice was the proper one.

"Two weeks," Ceridwen snapped, seeing nothing forthcoming.

"Six months," Gary shot back, instinctively bargaining for every advantage. "Not so long a time to one such as Ceridwen."

"Three months," the witch replied. I will be free before the onset of winter, that I might find my wintry allies to battle against Robert."

Gary thought long and hard, his eyes never leaving the dangerous situation revealed in Ceridwen's mirror.

"My friends and I run free?" he asked.

"For whatever good that will do," Ceridwen agreed.

Gary felt as though he was forgetting something—until he thought of the previous image in the magical mirror. "And you retract the army of Connacht," he said. "And let those prisoners go free."

Ceridwen acted surprised. "I?"

"Get off it, witch," Gary snarled. "Everyone, even a newcomer to Faerie, knows that you pull Kinnemore's strings. Badenoch, Drochit, their men—all their men—and the dwarfs can return to their homes unhindered, while Geldion and the army go back to Connacht, where they belong."

Now it was Ceridwen's turn to carefully consider the deal. She was not an impatient witch, and three months certainly was not a long time. "King Kinnemore's army will be recalled to Connacht," she agreed.

"Three months," Gary said grimly, and he was surprised to hear the words, surprised that he and Ceridwen had come so quickly to a deal. Surprised that it was, suddenly, over. "On condition that I have your word that you will no longer interfere with my progress," he quickly added, wanting everything to be exactly spelled out.

"Interfere?" Ceridwen asked, feigning surprise. "I?" Gary scowled and Ceridwen cackled like a crow. "Agreed," she said quickly, before anything more could be tagged on.

Gary nodded, hoping that he hadn't forgotten anything else, hoping that he had made the best deal he could—for himself, and for the land.

"But why would I interfere, my dear Gary Leger?" the witch asked a moment later, her tone sincerely incredulous.

Gary thought that somewhat surprising question over, but had no answer, even had no answer as to why Ceridwen would ask it.

"I will go so far as to tell you something, my unwilling associate," the obviously thrilled witch purred on. "Robert knows of your return, and of the missing armor and spear. The dragon is onto your little game, Gary Leger, and if you think that Connacht and Prince Geldion are the worst of your troubles, then think again!"

Gary's face was twisted in confusion—both at the news and at why Ceridwen would offer it to him.

"Do you not understand?" Ceridwen innocently asked him. "I hope that you and your friends are successful. That way, when I walk free in three months, Robert will not be there to oppose me.

"But you cannot change your mind and not go after Robert, now, can you?" the witch teased. "He will lay waste to all the land."

Gary chewed on his lips, wondering how badly he had fared in this meeting. He had followed his heart, and had, indeed, put a secondary plan of action into effect should he and his friends fail in recapturing Robert, a plan that could save many lives across the land. But at what cost? Gary had to ask himself. He didn't know the particulars, as Ceridwen had said, and he had been forced by a desperate situation to make a quick decision that he was not fully prepared to make.

He looked to the mirror, to his friends, and realized that others, and not he, would suffer the consequences if he had chosen badly.

SEVENTEEN

Cackling Crow

"THERE'S trolls all about us," Mickey said softly.

"Well, why don't they just come out and play?" Geno growled, slapping a hammer across his open palm. He looked towards a pile of rocks two dozen yards away, suspecting that several trolls were concealed behind it, and let out an angry snarl.

Kelsey's hand was on his shoulder in an instant, bidding him to calm down. The elf, above all the rest of them, understood just how many trolls were circling about them, and the last thing he wanted was a fight.

"We may have to leave," he whispered to Mickey.

"What about the lad?"

Kelsey shrugged helplessly, and Mickey couldn't really argue. He knew that the others wanted to rescue Gary as much as he, but the young man had obviously already been taken to Ynis Gwydrin, and with these trolls looming all about, they would have a hard enough time even getting close enough to see the surrounding lake.

Kelsey glanced around, scanning their options. Geno and Gerbil sat atop the rugged pony (the gnome's quadricycle wasn't much good in rough mountain terrain), while Kelsey and Mickey shared Kelsey's steed. The riderless horse, Cedric's, was tied behind, the magical spear and helm strapped upon it, waiting for Gary.

Kelsey looked back to Mickey and shook his head grimly. He wasn't one to quit easily, but this trek seemed foolhardy. Even if they could get to the lake, how would they get out to the island? And even if they got out to the island, how might they deal with Ceridwen?

But all the logic in the world couldn't overrule the fact that one of their companions, a trusted friend, was in dire trouble.

"We cannot leave him to her," Mickey said firmly, grabbing the elf's wrist. Kelsey looked to Geno and Gerbil, and both responded with a nod ahead, to the path that would take them to the lake, and Kelsey nodded, too, thinking then that if they died in their foolhardy attempt, then so be it.

Kelsey just turned his attention to the path ahead when out stepped a surprising, and welcome, sight. "Troll!" Geno screamed, hoisting his hammer as if to throw.

Gary Leger looked back over his shoulder. "Where?" he asked innocently.

"Laddie!" Mickey cried.

"What in the name of a smart goblin are you doing here?" Geno demanded, lowering the deadly hammer. I thought you were a damned troll!"

"Trolls are taller," Gary replied sourly. He caught some movement to the side out of the corner of his eye, "Like those over there," he growled and picked up a stone. "Get out of here!" he cried, pegging the missile into the tumble of boulders. "Before Ceridwen turns you all into bunnies and puts you into a pie!"

The stone skipped off several boulders, might have hit a troll or two (for the sound wouldn't be much different from that of a stone hitting boulders), and a group of the monsters skittered away, boulders rolling about in their blundering wake.

Mickey and Kelsey exchanged incredulous looks. "What've ye been doing, lad?" the leprechaun asked slowly, cautiously.

"Arguing, mostly," Gary replied, moving up to the riderless horse and seeming in no mood to talk about anything. Indeed, the young man was deeply troubled by his meeting with the witch, terribly afraid that he had acted wrongly in reducing Ceridwen's sentence. He put one foot in the stirrup and started to hoist himself up, then changed his mind, realizing that someone was missing.

"Where's Cedric?" he asked anxiously, privately guessing the answer.

"He died happy," Mickey replied solemnly.

"Son of a bitch," Gary muttered, burying his face into the side of the saddle. He died happy, the young man thought. That meant he died thinking that he was helping Gary, the spearwielder.

Gary was surprised a moment later to feel the cold tip of Kelsey's sword pressed tightly against his shoulder blade, in a crease in the armor. He understood the elf's doubts and fears, and knew enough not to make any sudden moves.

"How did you come out?" Kelsey asked evenly, positioning his horse so that Gary was cut off to the right.

"Ceridwen sent me out," Gary answered.

Kelsey poked him. "Do not play me for a fool," he warned. Geno walked the pony around to the side, blocking off any escape to the left, as well. Gary could not see Kelsey, but he could see the dwarf and gnome, and while Gerbil seemed almost as confused and shocked as was Gary, there was little compromise in the sturdy dwarf's stern expression.

"Ceridwen let me go," Gary declared, his voice firm and confident. "She wants me to slay Robert."

"That makes sense," Mickey offered, but Kelsey kept the swordtip in tight against Gary's back.

"You're hurting me," Gary remarked.

"I will kill you," Kelsey replied in all seriousness, "if I find that you are not who you appear to be."

"How did you chase off the trolls?" Geno asked, and the question seemed more like an accusation.

"I didn't," Gary snapped back.

"Then who?" the elf demanded, prodding him again.

"They were working for Ceridwen," Gary explained. "Before she ever sent me out of her castle, she sent word to the trolls that we were not to be harmed, or bothered at all." Gary snapped his fingers as an idea popped into his head.

"The spear," he started to explain, reaching across the saddle. What he had intended was to take the weapon, reestablish a telepathic bond, and let it inform the others that he was indeed who he claimed to be.

What he got instead was the smack of an elfish sword off the side of his head, and a flying tackle from an outraged dwarf. The next thing he knew, he was sitting on the ground facing Kelsey's horse, his arms wrenched up high behind his head by the snarling dwarf.

"Should I break them off?" Geno asked in all seriousness, and it seemed to Gary as if the powerful dwarf wasn't waiting for an answer.

Kelsey slid down from his seat and put his sword to Gary's throat. "Who are you?"

"Someone who wants to go home," Gary said to Mickey. He tugged hard against Geno's grasp, but the dwarf's viselike hands did not loosen. "Someone who's feeling unappreciated."

"Enough of the cryptic answers!" Kelsey demanded.

"I'm Gary Leger, you stupid elf!" Gary shouted. "Ceridwen let me off of her island because I dealt fairly with her, and she told her trolls to leave us alone because that was part of the deal!"

Geno let go, stood staring blankly at Kelsey.

"Deal?" Kelsey asked.

Gary ran his hand through his thick black hair and sighed deeply several times. He didn't want to admit what had happened on Ynis Gwydrin, but he didn't see any other way to gain back the trust of his friends—friends he dearly needed now, perhaps more than ever.

"Ceridwen will walk free in three months," he admitted.

"Stupid . . ." Geno stammered. He spun and punched the horse, and it snorted and leaped away. "Stupid! You really are a coward! You'd just do anything to save your worthless bones!"

Kelsey's forlorn, disappointed stare hurt more than the dwarf's tirade. The elf's swordtip dipped slowly to the ground.

"Oh, shut up," Gary said to Geno, though he never blinked in the face of that elfish stare.

The dwarf was upon him in an instant, curled fist only inches from Gary's face.

"I didn't do it to save my life," Gary said firmly. "Ceridwen wasn't going to kill me, anyway." He didn't know if that last statement was true or not, but it sounded good, and Gary needed something that sounded good at that moment. "I did it to save the four of you," he said.

"What are you saying?" Kelsey asked.

"She showed me your progress," Gary explained. "In a . . . magic mirror, or something."

"A scrying device," Mickey helped, more versed in the ways of witches than the man from the other world.

"Whatever," Gary said. "I saw you, and saw the trolls." Gary eyed Geno directly. "Dozens of trolls."

"We would have willingly died," Kelsey boasted. "Rather than . . ."

"Rather than what?" Gary snapped at him. "If you had died, and I was captured, and Kinnemore's army was on the field, and Robert was flying free . . ."

"The lady paints a glum picture," Mickey offered.

"Any worse a picture than having that witch out and about?" Geno asked.

"Oh, yes," Gerbil piped in unexpectedly. All eyes turned on him, and the gnome sank low in the saddle. "I mean, she was out before, after all, and things didn't look so very bad. Not like now, I mean."

"True enough," remarked Mickey.

"I had to make a choice," Gary said resignedly. "I don't know if it was the best one—maybe I should have let her out right away so that she could go against the dragon and save us the trouble." He shrugged and ran his fingers through his black hair once more. "I did the best I could."

Kelsey took hold of Gary's hand and hoisted him to his feet. "It was a difficult choice," the elf admitted. "You said that Ceridwen would let us out of the mountains?"

Gary nodded. "I made her agree that she would not hinder us in any way in our quest to put Robert back in his hole."

"Why would she want to?" Mickey asked in all seriousness.

"Exactly," Gary agreed. "But I also made her agree to send Geldion and his troops back to Connacht. I figured that would give Pwyll and the others some time to regroup, maybe put up some defenses."

Kelsey was nodding approvingly, and Gary relaxed somewhat. "'I did the best I could," he said again.

"You did well," Kelsey replied.

"Just fine, lad," agreed the leprechaun.

"But what are we to do next?" Geno put in. "If we put the wyrm back in his hole, then the witch runs free."

Gary didn't miss the curious way Mickey's face seemed to pale.

"The dragon must be stopped!" Kelsey and Gerbil said together, and they both looked at each other, surprised.

"Owe me a Coke," Gary said for both of them, though neither of them knew what the hell he was talking about, or what the hell a "Coke" might be.

"Never mind," was all that Gary offered in reply to their curious stares, and he turned to his new mount.

Any levity that Gary had managed to forge, any relaxation that had come over him in learning that his friends approved of his desperate choice on Ynis Gwydrin, was washed away the moment the young man laid eyes on that riderless horse.

Cedric had died happy.

For the spearwielder.

Gary gritted his teeth and pulled himself up into the saddle, roughly taking the reins and turning the horse the other way on the trail. "Let's get the hell out of here," he said angrily, and he started the steed at a swift trot and then a gallop, playing his own anger out in the strong movements of the willing horse.

THEY came out of Penllyn later that afternoon, the sun fast disappearing behind the mountains. As Ceridwen had promised, no trolls, or any other monsters, blocked their way or hindered them in any manner at all.

They retrieved Gerbil's quadricycle, stuffed under a bush for safekeeping. The gnome immediately opened yet another of the thing's seemingly endless compartments, pulling out a pile of badly folded parchments.

"Maps," he explained to the curious onlookers. "The most up-to-date and detailed in all the land. I know that I have one in here, oh, yes I must, showing the trails between Penllyn and the Giant's Thumb."

Kelsey nodded in deference to the gnome, knowing that Gerbil needed to feel helpful, needed to believe that he was doing something to take revenge on Robert for what Robert had done to his village. In truth, Kelsey already knew the route they would take—the very same route he, Gary, Mickey, Geno, and the giant Tommy One-Thumb had taken on their first trip to the dragon's lair.

Kelsey waited patiently for the gnome to sort through the pile, though, and Mickey took that opportunity to leave Kelsey's saddle and go up to his customary position in front of Gary Leger.

"We will ride out a few miles from the shadow of Penllyn," Kelsey explained, as they regrouped and prepared to start away once more. Gerbil nodded eagerly and fumbled with the pile of parchments, narrowing down the possibilities. The light was fast fading, and none of the companions wanted to remain near to the witch's mountains after dark, but again, Kelsey waited patiently for the gnome.

"Then we set a short camp," he explained. "In the morn, we ride northeast until we reach the Crahgs, then cross them as best as we can."

"Not so best," came a cackling reply. The companions all looked to each other for a moment, until they realized that the source of the response had not been any of them.

"There," Gary said a moment later, pointing to a large crow sitting on the low branch of a lone tree not far from the bushes where they had stashed the quadricycle.

Instinctively, Geno's arm came up, a hammer at the ready, and Kelsey, his glare unrelenting, went for his bow.

"Don't shoot it!" Gary growled at both of them. "The bird seems to know something."

"Spy of Ceridwen," the dwarf remarked, for it was no secret among the peoples of Faerie that the talking crows were in alliance with the witch. Rumors had it that Ceridwen bought the birds' alliance by enchanting them with the gift of speech.

"And no friend to us," Kelsey added grimly, fitting the arrow to his bowstring.

"But an ally of our quest," Gary remarked.

"Crahgs are blocked," the crow cackled, and the actual sight of a talking bird gave even the stern elf pause. "Wolves and haggis, dragon friends."

"That'd make sense," Mickey agreed, looking to Kelsey to lower his bow. "Robert's sealin' off the eastland for his own uses."

"Or he's looking for us and thinking that we'll go through the Crahgs," Gary added. Three grim faces turned on him (four when Gerbil took a moment from his mapwatching to look up and figure out that something was amiss), none of his friends appreciating him speaking out that little possibility.

"Robert has more to think about than this bunch," Geno put in derisively, wanting to fully dismiss Gary's thought. The dwarf threw a smirk Gerbil's way, and the gnome responded in kind, but then went right back to his tangle of maps.

"And that crow is working for the witch," Kelsey added, lifting the bow once more. "For no better reason than to deter us, than to keep us confused until Ceridwen might come forth."

"Robert knows about us," Gary said immediately, before either Kelsey or the dwarf could take any rash action. Again, the grim gazes descended over the young man.

"Ceridwen told me," Gary explained. "The dragon knows about the armor and the spear, and knows that I've returned."

Geno looked hopelessly to Kelsey, as if to say, "Now what?" but the elf seemed to have no answer.

"Even if that's true," Mickey put in hopefully, "he'd not expect us to go walking of our own free will back to his stronghold."

"Unless he thought we had something which could put him back in his hole," Gary remarked.

Kelsey looked questioningly to Mickey.

"It's a little-known detail of honorable challenging," the leprechaun said smugly, striking flint to steel to drop sparks into his long-stemmed pipe. "Robert'll never guess the truth." Mickey wasn't nearly as confident as he appeared. The last thing the leprechaun wanted, either out here or in the caverns beneath the Giant's Thumb, was an encounter with Robert. Mickey wanted his pot of gold back, nothing more, but his original lie seemed to have taken on monumental proportions suddenly, with so many side-players and kingdom-wide intrigue.

Kelsey looked to the northeast, as though he was spying out the distant Craghs. He looked back to the smug crow, sitting confidently on the branch.

"Do you believe the bird?" the elf asked Gary suddenly.

Gary nodded. "I don't think that Ceridwen would have any reason to lie," he replied. "It's like she said, our victory over Robert will only make things easier for her."

"I'm starting to hate this," Geno remarked, impatiently slapping his hammer across his open palm. His pony nickered and started to rear, but the powerful dwarf tightened his legs around the beast and it went still.

"Your point is well made," Kelsey said. "And the Crahgs will offer us little cover from the flying dragon." Kelsey turned his gaze more directly east, south of the distant hills.

"What're ye thinking?" Mickey asked him grimly, guessing exactly what Kelsey had in mind.

"There is a wood near here," the elf replied. "Dark and tangled. It might provide us cover for the next portion of our journey."

"There!" shouted the gnome, poking a finger so forcefully into the map that he drove it right through the parchment. He retracted the digit and looked at the map, scratching his head curiously. "Readwood?" he asked.

"Dreadwood," Geno corrected, the dwarf's gravelly voice grave. "You poked out the first rune."

From Mickey's intake of breath, Gary could tell that this Dreadwood was not a nice place.

"I see no choice," Kelsey said to the leprechaun. "Not if the crow speaks truthfully about the Crahgs."

"Wolves and newts," the bird cackled.

"Shut your beak!" Geno roared, and he hurled his hammer the bird's way. The heavy weapon smacked the branch near the bird and ricocheted away, the crow taking wing into the dark air, shrieking in protest all the while.

"Shut your beak!" the dwarf roared again. "If I wanted to hit you . . ." Geno let it go at that, just spat up into the darkness after the long-gone bird.

"How bad is this Dreadwood?" Gary asked Mickey privately when the commotion died away.

Mickey shrugged, seeming nonchalant about the whole thing. "We'll get through, lad," he answered. "Don't ye fret."

Gary took faith in that, believed in his friends and in himself. "And once we get the dragon put away," he reasoned, a new idea popping into his head, "I'll make a deal with him."

"Full of deals that don't even concern you," Geno grumbled, crashing around in the brush to find his hammer.

"What are you thinking?" Kelsey asked, pointedly ignoring the dwarf, and his visage unexpectedly stern.

"I reduce Robert's time of banishment," Gary answered, smiling widely. "To three months, as I did with Ceridwen. Then they both come out together and neither of them has any advantage." Gary thought his idea perfectly logical, and he wasn't prepared for the heightening intensity of Kelsey's glower. From that unyielding stare, Gary almost believed that the elf would trot his horse over and strike him down.

"Ye're forgetting something, lad," Mickey whispered.

"What?" Gary asked, to the leprechaun and the elf. Kelsey let his stare linger a few moments longer, then turned his mount away.

"What?" Gary asked again, this time straight to Mickey.

"It was not yerself that challenged the wyrm," Mickey reminded him, and Gary's breath hissed as he sucked it in through his gritted teeth. He hadn't even thought of that, hadn't even realized that he might be overstepping his bounds and insulting his proud friend.

"Kelsey," he said, as apologetically as he could. "I didn't mean . . ."

"It does not matter," Kelsey replied, turning his mount back around.

"Of course, you are the one who can reduce the dragon's banishment," Gary offered. "You're the only one who holds any right to deal with Robert. I just got carried away."

"You just might," Geno remarked dryly, and Gary glared at him, thinking that the dwarf might be enjoying this awkward situation just a bit too much.

"It does not matter," Kelsey declared again, his melodic voice firm. "We must worry first about putting the dragon back in his hole. Then we will decide which is the best course for the good of the land."

Gary agreed with the elf's choice of priorities, as did the others, but Mickey's thinking was following a slightly different course. Mickey understood the dragon better than any of them, and he knew that if Ceridwen's claims were correct, if Robert was on to them, then they could expect to meet him long before they ever got near his castle. Mickey understood, too, that Robert the Wretched had long kept spies in the dark forest of Dreadwood, and that those thick boughs might not provide as much cover as Kelsey hoped. Robert was going to have to be tricked—not an easy task—and the cost might be high.

But leprechauns were the best in the world at deception. In truth, Mickey was deceiving his own companions even now. And so Mickey tuned out of the conversation altogether, began to plot as only a leprechaun can plot.

Whatever the cost, he meant to get back his pot of gold.

EIGHTEEN
Dreadwood

EVEN the hardy mounts of Tir na n'Og nickered and whinnied and flipped their heads side to side, shying away as the group approached the dark and tangled forest. Dreadwood started abruptly, a thick clump of trees in the middle of the plain between the mountains of Penllyn on the south and the rolling Crahgs on the north. Kelsey took them near to the Crahgs, the narrowest expanse of the forest, but still the wood seemed dark and wide to Gary Leger.

He had spent many days of his youth in the woods, even after sunset, with no fears beyond the very real possibilities of mosquito bites or of inadvertently stepping on a bees' nest. Now, though, as his horse approached the tangle, a feeling of dread rose up within Gary, a feeling that there was more evil within this place than biting bugs.

Already he knew that whoever had named this forest had named it right.

It didn't seem possible to Gary that they would even find a path through the forest. The twisted trees seemed a solid wall, gnarled and writhing, a living barrier that would not permit visitors.

Kelsey held up his hand for the others to stop, and sat atop his horse, eyeing the wood suspiciously. He motioned to the side, and the whole troupe shifted.

"There is a road," Mickey remarked to Gary, and to Gerbil, who seemed nervous about the possibility of getting his quadricycle through. "The trees just aren't wanting to show it to us."

Again Kelsey motioned, back the other way, and the group followed accordingly. They reversed direction again, several more times, Kelsey studying the trees, looking for hints of the path.

"None better at spotting illusions than the Tylwyth Teg," Mickey said quietly, trying to keep his less informed friends patient and comfortable.

Finally, Kelsey sat up straight on his mount and sighed deeply. He gave a look Mickey's way that seemed to say that he was pretty sure of the path, but also that it was only a guess. He reached down to the back of the saddle and drew an arrow out of his quiver, examining the fletchings. Apparently not finding something he needed, he shook his head and replaced it, drawing out another.

After a similar examination, Kelsey put his mouth against this arrow's tip, whispering to it as though it could hear. He then produced a length of cord, fine and silvery as a spider's web, from his saddlebags, and threaded it through a tiny hole near to the arrow's fletchings. Then Kelsey fitted the arrow to his bow and lifted it towards the forest, closing his golden eyes.

Again he whispered—some sort of an enchantment, it seemed to Gary—and he moved the bow slowly, first to the right, then back to the left. Seemingly at random, the elf let fly, and the arrow cut through the air, making for a huge elm. It didn't hit the tree, though, and Gary had to blink, thinking his vision had deceived him.

The fine cord continued to unwind for some time, Kelsey holding its other end and nodding Mickey's way. At last, it went slack and the elf slipped down from his saddle and took it up, walking his mount as he collected the cord.

"What just happened?" Gary had to ask.

"Arrows o' the Tylwyth Teg have a way of finding their way around the trees," Mickey explained with a sly wink. "They'll not hit a living thing if telled not to by their makers."

They were near the forest by then, near the living, seemingly impenetrable wall, when Gary, to his surprise, noticed a break in the trees, wide enough even for Gerbil's quadricycle to pass through. Why hadn't he seen that from the field? he wondered, and he shrugged his amazement away, reasoning that Kelsey's arrow magic had countered the forest's own magic.

No matter how many times he returned, or how long he stayed, Gary Leger knew that he would ever remain a stranger to the land of Faerie.

Kelsey disappeared into the dark forest, the shadows swallowing him as soon as he crossed the threshold. Right behind the elf, Geno's pony shied away, but the dwarf grunted angrily and with a single powerful tug put the beast back in line and kept it moving.

Gerbil went next, his quadricycle bumping up one way and then the other as he passed over the nearest tree roots, and Gary came last, eyes determinedly straight ahead. It seemed to the young man as if he had walked into the night. Rationally, he knew that he was no more than a few feet from the entrance, the sky outside sunny and clear, but when he looked back, he saw a distinct hole of only dim light, as though the sun itself feared to peek into Dreadwood.

"Easy," Mickey coaxed, to the horse and to Gary. "Easy."

"Some light, leprechaun," Kelsey called back as he retrieved his arrow, sticking at an angle from the forest path, and climbed into his saddle. Mickey gave a grunting response—it sounded more like a groan to Gary—and began a long chant, which seemed strange to Gary, since on his last visit to Faerie he had seen the leprechaun merely snap his fingers to produce globes of glowing light.

Finally, Mickey did snap his fingers and a tiny ball, barely a candle's flicker, appeared atop them, hovering in the air and weaving wildly back and forth as though it would soon go out.

Then it diminished even more and Mickey shrugged helplessly. "Me magic's not so good against the weight of Dreadwood," he explained.

Kelsey, who had just put an arrow through the trees' illusion, eyed the leprechaun suspiciously, and Gary understood the elf's obvious doubts. Something was wrong with Mickey, with Mickey's magic at least, for the leprechaun's bag of tricks had been far less helpful this time around than on Gary's first trip through the enchanted land. Gary remembered his first encounter with the sprite, when Mickey had tricked him repeatedly, when Mickey had him plucking giant mushrooms out of the ground, commanding them to take him to their pot of gold. Most of all, Gary remembered Mickey's cocky swagger, the leprechaun's sincere belief that tricking a human, or a monster, was a matter of course and nothing to get overly concerned about.

Where had the leprechaun's confidence, and his magic, gone to? Gary wondered, and his look Mickey's way reflected his confusion.

Mickey only shrugged and brought the brim of his tam-o'-shanter low over his eyes, as deep an explanation as Gary or any of the others was going to get. The little faerie light winked out altogether a moment later, and with the dim portal fast fading behind them the friends soon found themselves fully engulfed by the gloom.

In truth, the road inside the forest was flat and clear, and wide enough so that Gary could walk his horse beside the gnome's rolling contraption. Gary's eyes soon adjusted to the darkness, and he found that it was not so bad. Some sunlight did make its way through the leafy boughs, diminishing as it wove down to Gary's level, but enough so that he could distinguish general shapes around him, could see Kelsey and Geno, leading the way on their mounts. On the road beside him, Gerbil was at work again, fumbling with some items too small for Gary to make out, and absently pumping his little legs, his quadricycle easily pacing the horses. Gary realized that, though he and Gerbil had been traveling companions for several days now, he hadn't really gotten to know the gnome. He noticed Mickey, resting easily against his horse's neck, hat still low, long-stemmed pipe in his mouth, and little legs crossed at the knee, and realized that he wasn't going to find much company there.

"What are you making?" Gary asked the gnome.

"Light," came the polite, if short, answer.

Gary nodded, but then screwed up his face. "You're making light?" he asked. "You mean, you're going to light a torch?"

"Torches are for dwarfs and elfs, and the human folk," Gerbil replied, again pointedly not elaborating. "Even for goblins, I suppose."

Gary considered the condescending tone for a few moments. "How do gnomes make light?" he politely asked.

"Potions."

Now Gary was intrigued, but he understood that the typically talkative gnome obviously didn't want to be bothered at that moment. He continued to walk his horse even with the quadricycle, watching Gerbil's every move. Soon the gnome had a pole erected in the front section of the contraption, its top a tube, rotating end around end in tune with the turning of the pedals. Gerbil had a funnel between his working knees, its narrow end connected to the bottom of the tube, and in his hands he held two beakers.

"Potions?" Gary asked.

"Ssssh!" the gnome hissed.

"Ye take a chance on blowin' yerself up if ye distract a workin' gnome," Mickey quietly added, and Gary went silent, having no doubts of Mickey's claims and having no desire to blow himself up. He watched curiously as Gerbil poured specific amounts of each potion into the funnel. A moment later, a glow came from the turning tube atop the pole, intensifying with each rotation.

Kelsey and Geno both looked back curiously, and neither seemed pleased.

"Ye're makin' yerself into a target," Mickey remarked to the gnome.

"I cannot work in the dark, of course!" the flustered gnome shot back. A bit
more of the contents of one beaker went into the funnel, and the light brightened accordingly.

"Suit yerself," was Mickey's casual reply.

Gary sat mystified. He had seen rings that used chemical reaction to produce light, but he hardly expected to find such a process utilized in this enchanted place. He was about to question Gerbil, and to congratulate him for
his fine light, but then a tree branch reached down suddenly and plucked
the gnome from his seat, lifting him up, kicking and squealing, into the dark
boughs.

Gary tried to call out, but found his voice stuck in his throat. He lunged
over to grab at Gerbil as the gnome shot by, was overbalanced to the side when
another branch swung down the other way, bashing him in the shoulder and
sending him flying from the saddle to crash halfway over the side of the quadricycle. Gary turned back in time to see the same branch, a foot thick, slam
straight down on the back of his horse, narrowly missing the purposely falling
leprechaun. Gary heard a tremendous cracking sound as the poor horse's legs
buckled, and the beast went right down to the ground.

A hammer spun through the air, whacking off of the low branch, but doing
no real damage. It was soon followed by a flying dwarf as Geno, leaped from his
mount, wrapping his powerful arms about the limb of the attacking tree. With
a growl, the dwarf bit hard into the branch, tearing off a large piece of bark.

Kelsey was already up the boughs, scampering along writhing branches to
get near to the caught Gerbil. Smaller branches whipped at the elf as he passed
and his sword flashed, often dropping pieces of tree free to the ground.

"*Get up!*" came the call in Gary's thoughts, and he was already on his way.
He fumbled to get his helmet straightened, then searched out the spear and
hoisted it in eager hands.

But where to hit a tree?

Geno spat out another hunk of branch above him; Kelsey had reached Gerbil and was hacking mightily at the entrapping branch, but hadn't yet begun to
free the gnome.

Gary roared and went for the trunk, driving the spear straight ahead, its tip
plunging through the hard wood. The tree went into a shaking frenzy, and poor
Gerbil whined in pain.

Gary turned and readied the spear for a throw, thinking to sink it into the
branch holding the gnome, thinking that Gerbil would surely be squashed before too much longer. Another branch swung about first, though, slamming

Gary's armored back and launching him through the air, where he landed, again, half across the quadricycle.

"Are ye all right, lad?" asked Mickey, sitting low in the contraption's seat.

"I've been better," Gary replied, forcing himself back up to his knees. He heard a crack above him and had to shift aside as Geno and his branch came tumbling down, the wild dwarf having bitten clear through the limb.

"Not half bad!" Geno proclaimed, quickly biting off another chunk. And off he ran, leaping straight into the trunk, throwing a hug about it and chomping away with dwarfish ferocity.

The branch hit Gary again, but not so hard, since the tree then seemed to focus on the dangerous dwarf. An instant later, back to his knees yet again, Gary understood the effectiveness of the dwarf's tactics, for the tree could not easily get at Geno when he was in so close.

And Gary was glad for Geno's efforts, because, for the moment at least, he had been left alone. He immediately looked above him, to the squirming gnome and the battling elf, and knew that he had to react.

Don't miss, he thought, to which the spear gave an indignant reply, as though it had been insulted.

"I'm talking to myself!" Gary explained gruffly, and he let fly.

The spear cracked into the branch just a foot away from the gnome, nearly splitting the limb down the middle. Another great tug from Kelsey pulled the gasping Gerbil free, and then the elf and the gnome simply hung on as the branch cracked apart, dropping the spear straight back to the ground and sending its passengers on a wild swing that ended in a free-fall into a thick bush far to the side of the path.

Gary grabbed up the spear, nearly chuckled aloud when he regarded the dwarf, seeming a wild cross between a famished beaver and a lumberjack. Then he fell flat to the ground in terror and shock when all the thick canopy above him erupted suddenly in flames.

Horses whinnied and fled, wood crackled and burst apart. At first, Gary thought that Mickey had pulled off a clever illusion, but when he took a moment to think about it, it made no practical sense. How do you visually fool a tree?

Besides, Gary realized as flaming brands began to fall all about him, as the air began to burn his lungs and sting his eyes, this was no trick.

He knew he had to run. He got up as high as he could and felt a tug on his arm that put him over the side of the quadricycle for the third time.

Mickey sat low in the seat, looking horrified and helpless. "Suren it's the dragon!" he called out, beckoning Gary to get in beside him.

A tree not so far away exploded from the heat; Gary heard a horse shriek in agony and knew that the thing had been engulfed. He couldn't see Geno, or Kelsey and Gerbil, had no idea at that confusing moment if the others were dead or running. And every second that slipped past put Gary's own escape into deeper jeopardy.

He scrambled in beside Mickey and found, to his relief, that the clever gnomes had put a notched and sliding adjusting bar on the seat (though even sliding it all the way back did not allow Gary to straighten his legs). Gary gave a scream as a branch fell into his face, and batted the thing away, then kicked hard with one foot, hoping just to start the quadricycle moving on such rough and uneven ground. To Gary's amazement, the contraption leaped away. He didn't know whether incredible gearing, or magical potions, enhanced the ride, but merely a few pumps later, he was flying free of the fiery zone, rushing down the wide path.

"Ride on!" the leprechaun commanded when Gary slowed and looked back to find his friends.

"We can't leave them!" Gary retorted, surprised by Mickey's callous attitude.

"Go!" came a call from back down the trail. Gary looked to see Kelsey emerging from the blazing region, waving him away.

"The dragon is on to us," Mickey explained. "Our only chance is to separate and lead him in two different directions at once."

As if on cue, Gary heard a whoosh of air from the canopy over his head, looked up to see a huge shadow cross above him.

"Ride on, for all our lives, lad!" Mickey implored him, and Gary put his head down and pedaled with all his strength, sending the quadricycle careening down the winding road as fast as any Tir na n'Og horse could run.

He was more than a mile away before he even realized that Kelsey—the Kelsey who had told him to go—had not a bit of soot on his fair elven face.

SOOT-COVERED, his golden hair singed, and the gnome tucked unconscious under his arm, Kelsey crawled out the side of the bush, looking back helplessly and wondering if any of his friends or any of the precious mounts had survived. Gerbil groaned repeatedly, at least, and the elf knew that he was still alive.

As was Geno, Kelsey learned a moment later when he heard the dwarf grumbling and growling and smacking his hammer off any nearby tree. Following the sounds, Kelsey was soon beside the dwarf.

"Where are the others?" he asked.

"Stonebubbles!" was all that Geno would reply.

"I thought that you had surely perished," Kelsey remarked.

Geno snorted. "I work at a dwarfish anvil, elf," he explained. "It would take more than a bit of dragon fire to burn through this hide!"

"But what of the leprechaun and Gary Leger?" Kelsey asked, and gruff Geno could only shrug and curse, "Stonebubbles!" once more.

The three kept low (and, with Kelsey's begging, Geno kept quiet) for the next half-hour as Robert continued to pass overhead, every now and then setting another section of the forest ablaze. Finally, the dragon seemed to tire of the game and swooped away, and Kelsey led his companions off. They found the pony, at least, wandering terrified to the south of the disaster, and then, when they hit the road, found the unmistakable tracks of the quadricycle, dug deeper than usual, as though the contraption was carrying more than the normal weight.

"They escaped," Kelsey proclaimed, deciding, as much on hope as on what his tracking skill was telling him, that both his friends must have been aboard. The elf's initial excitement ebbed as the three followed the tracks and came to realize that their companions were long gone.

"How fast does that thing go?" Geno asked Gerbil, the dwarf obviously angered that Mickey and Gary had apparently run off.

"How fast?" Gerbil echoed, scratching at his soot-covered beard. "Well, indeed, with the added weight . . . I put it at two hundred and fifty pounds . . . but then, of course, Gary Leger is much stronger than the average gnome . . ."

"How fast?" the dwarf growled.

"We cannot catch them on foot," Gerbil quickly replied. "Or even with the single pony."

Geno kicked a nearby tree and swung about to face Kelsey—then looked back over his shoulder to make sure that this particular tree wouldn't kick back. He looked back to the elf, then back to the tree right away, eyeing it suspiciously. Finally, convinced that this one was quiet, like a tree should be, Geno focused on the elf, and was surprised to see Kelsey taking a parchment from the trunk of a nearby tree. Geno thought it more than curious that none of them had spotted that note before.

"From the leprechaun," Kelsey said, and that alone explained many things. Kelsey read on and nodded, then held the parchment out for the others to see.

Under control. Meet you at Braemar.

"Braemar?" Geno roared. "Why Braemar? I thought we were going to Giant's Thumb, to put the damned wyrm back in its damned hole."

"But now the dragon is out," Gerbil reasoned.

"The dragon was always out!" Geno growled. "On to Giant's Thumb, I say, and let's get this business finished!"

"You forget that we do not have the stolen dagger," Kelsey interjected. "If Mickey has returned to Braemar, then so must we."

Geno wiped some soot off his unbearded face and shook his head helplessly. To all of them, it seemed as though they had been defeated, been turned around at the first sign of trouble. "Damned stupid sprite," the dwarf muttered. "What did he go and turn around for?"

Kelsey nodded, but his thoughts were heading in a different direction. Why indeed would Mickey turn back at this time? They were as close to Giant's Thumb as to Braemar, and would likely face Robert again whichever way they turned. Kelsey chuckled, understanding it all, understanding that Mickey had turned them around as a decoy, to hopefully turn Robert around as well.

"What is it?" Geno demanded.

Kelsey shook his head. "I am only glad that we are all still alive," he lied, and he waited for Geno to look away before he turned his gaze back to the east, where he now knew that the leprechaun and Gary Leger were in full flight.

NINETEEN

Pot o' Gold

"KEEP it rollin' straight," Mickey assured Gary, the leprechaun standing in front of the quadricycle's steering bar and peering intently ahead. Gary looked at the leprechaun's back incredulously, for all he saw ahead of them was a wall of thick trees blocking the exit from Dreadwood.

"And keep it fast," Mickey remarked, with absolute confidence.

Gary didn't disagree with that second request. Many times over the last two hours, sentient trees had reached down to grab at them, and only their great pace had gotten them through. But now, Gary didn't see how they could go on. He closed his eyes, as Mickey had previously suggested, and trusted the leprechaun to guide him past the forest's illusions. He sensed the wooden wall coming up fast, though, and had to look, nearly screaming aloud when he saw that the wall of trees loomed just a dozen feet away.

Instinctively, Gary threw up his arms in front of his face, locking the steering bar with his knees. He thought a crash unavoidable, but suddenly a break appeared as the road bent around one wide elm. In the split-second it took the rambling quadricycle to rush past, that break widened, and then it was as though someone had switched on a powerful light as the gnomish contraption burst out of the tangled wood.

Lathered in sweat from his run, Gary let the quadricycle roll to a stop. He looked back to the forest, simply amazed that they had gotten through. Lines of black smoke continued to rise in the west, a reminder that though they were out, they were far from safe.

"What are we going to do?" Gary whispered harshly, as though he expected the dragon to descend on them at any moment.

Mickey peered up into the sky in all directions, then settled a firm and un-blinking gaze on the young man. "We're going to get to Giant's Thumb," he an-nounced. "And finish our business."

"How far is it?" Gary asked.

"How fast and long can ye pump this thing?"

Gary had no honest answer. He was tired from his wild rush, but again, whether it was the incredible gearing or some hidden magic, the quadricycle had outperformed his wildest expectations, had taken him farther and faster, and with far more ease, than the most expensive racing bikes of his own world ever could. "What about the dragon?" he asked suddenly, looking back to the smoke, remembering that most of the land between here and their destination was open and barren.

Mickey shrugged and seemed to Gary, for perhaps the very first time, very much afraid.

"We can go back through the forest," Gary offered. "Maybe we'll find Kelsey and the others."

"No!" The leprechaun's tone was cutting-edge sharp, and an angry light flared in the normally cheerful sprite's gray eyes. "We're on to the mountain," he declared. "To finish our business. Now, if ye've got the wind and the strength left in ye, get this thing running fast."

"What about the dragon?" Gary asked again, more firmly.

"Robert's tired," Mickey reasoned. "He's been flying a long way, by me guess, else he'd not have let us out o' Dreadwood alive. That's the weakness o' dragons, lad. They're all fire and muscle and killing claws, but it takes a mighty effort to move that mountain body about, and they do get tired."

"He'll be rested long before we get to Giant's Thumb," Gary replied omi-nously.

"Aye." Mickey nodded. "But will he know that we're well on our way? Kelsey and Geno'll have a trick or two to keep Robert busy back here, don't ye doubt, but if ye plan on sitting here talking, their efforts will go for nothing."

Gary took a deep breath, adjusted himself as well as he could in the low and tight quarters, and started to pump his legs. He stopped abruptly, though, and snapped his fingers, then began unstrapping the metal leggings of his armor and the bulkier plates along the rest of the suit.

"I don't think this will help much if we meet up with Robert," he explained.

Mickey nodded gravely.

Barely fifteen minutes later, the quadricycle kicked up a trail of road dust in its wake.

KELSEY nodded to the north, to a high perch on the nearest Crahg, where sat Robert, his great leathery wings wrapped about his gigantic torso and his reptilian eyes closed to evil slits.

The three companions were still under the thick cover of Dreadwood, still back near the eastern entrance of the wood.

Kelsey took an arrow from his quiver and fitted it to his bow. He nodded to Geno and Gerbil, as if asking their opinion, but he knew in truth that they could not disagree with this action. Gary and Mickey were out of the forest, headed for Robert's lair by Kelsey's reckoning, and that gave Kelsey, Geno, and Gerbil the unenviable job of keeping Robert's eyes away from the east, of keeping Robert's eyes focused on them.

"Find some cover," Geno whispered to Gerbil, and he pushed the gnome off, then scampered in a different direction. Kelsey gave them a good start, then lifted his bow the dragon's way and drew back on the bowstring. He knew that he couldn't really hurt the beast, not from this distance and probably not even from a point-blank position, but he could certainly get Robert's attention. The trick, Kelsey reminded himself, was to be far, far from this spot before the arrow ever clicked against Robert's thick armor.

He fired and never watched the projectile, running with all speed in a direction different from the ones taken by Geno and Gerbil. A moment later, the ground rumbled under the thunder of a dragon roar, and then a shadow crossed over that section of Dreadwood and all the trees went up in a line of furious fire.

Robert made several passes, but, as Mickey had said, the dragon was weary and could not sustain the assault. He dropped into one group of trees and thrashed them into kindling, then lifted away to another perch near the eastern end of the wood and sat back, watching, waiting.

"Your cover will not last!" Robert's roar promised. "I will burn away all the trees and then where will you hide, puny enemies?"

Gerbil, in a deep hole under the roots of a great oak, Geno, comfortably flattened under a boulder, and Kelsey, farthest from the sight of destruction, heard the dragon's reasonable claims and each of them, even the sturdy dwarf, wished at that time that he was back in his homeland, many miles from Dreadwood.

THE miles rolled out behind them, Gary pedaling relentlessly that morning of the first day out of Dreadwood. For an hour, the bumpy horizon of the Crahgs remained north of them, but it soon gave way to flatter plains.

Mickey's spirits soared that day, with no sign of the dragon apparent and the Giant's Thumb fast approaching. The leprechaun could feel his magical energies returning as he drew ever nearer his precious pot of gold. "Keep it straight and keep it fast," he would often say to Gary, always careful to temper his boiling excitement, always remembering that Gary Leger didn't know the whole truth of the matter.

Gary seemed not so happy. He was glad, of course, that Robert was nowhere to be seen, but his thoughts were behind him, not ahead, back to the tangled wood where he had left his three companions, where black lines of smoke were still rising into the sky. Even if they succeeded in putting Robert back in his hole, Gary would consider it a hollow victory indeed if Kelsey, or Geno, or Gerbil had perished in the process.

Still, barely hours later, after a short midmorning rest, Gary could not deny his own excitement when they came around the southern edge of the ruined forest and saw the great solitary obelisk that was the Giant's Thumb protruding from the dragon-ravaged plain.

On Mickey's orders, Gary veered to the north and came in by the dry lake bed of Loch Tullamore, up to the lip of the valley before the mountain, sheltered by the few living trees east of the Crahgs.

"Now where?" Gary asked, realizing their dilemma as he began strapping on his armor once more. He saved the helmet for last, and wound up simply strapping the bulky thing to his back, realizing that he could not possibly climb with it bouncing about his head. With that thought, Gary looked up again to the towering obelisk, to the castle walls that seemed to grow right from the stone, several hundred feet above the vale.

The last time they had come to the mountain, they had gone in through a cave above the red waters of a steamy pool, hidden around a rocky outcropping

not so far away. But Gary and his friends had a giant with them on that occasion, a giant who was able to carry them across the deep water to the cave entrance. Even if they could now get to that entrance, which Gary doubted, the
tunnels would only take them so high. And again, it had been the work of Gary
and Mickey's companions, and not of either of these two, that had allowed
them to scale the rest of the way and get over the walls.

"Leave the gnome's contraption here," Mickey explained. "There's a wide
and easy road around the other side of the mountain that's fit for walking."

There was indeed an easy way up, Gary knew, but he knew, too, that the
road the leprechaun spoke of led right between rows of barracks, right through
the heart of Robert's army, lizardlike humanoids called lava newts, as tall and
strong as a man, that would swarm the intruders at first sight.

"Don't ye worry," Mickey casually remarked into Gary's doubting expression. "I'm feeling me magic today. We'll get through the stupid lizards." Mickey
gave a cocky chuckle, which seemed odd to Gary, considering the leprechaun's
almost pitiful use of magic thus far on the adventure.

The young man only shrugged and followed, though, when Mickey started
away, for he had no better ideas and he didn't want to remain anywhere near
this dangerous place a moment longer than necessary.

It took them more than an hour to make their careful way around the south
of the mountain to the long sloping road up the eastern side. Many times, Gary
thought he saw movement on the high walls, lava newt soldiers, probably, halfheartedly manning their positions.

To Gary's amazement, Mickey faded into invisibility. Gary realized then
that this was the first time the leprechaun had done that on this adventure. The
last time through the land, Mickey had faded away every time danger loomed
near, but this time, even when Gary had faced the soldiers in the haunted
swamp, Mickey had taken to a more ordinary form of hiding.

Now the leprechaun was gone, though, and he floated up to a comfortable
perch on Gary's shoulder, seeming more like the old, at-ease Mickey, seeming
confident that he could get them out of whatever trouble came their way. Gary
saw a spark in the empty air and knew that the leprechaun had lit his long-
stemmed pipe.

"Now ye walk right up the path, lad," Mickey explained. "Big, proud steps,
like the kind that Robert'd take. With yer sword over yer shoulder."

Gary was beginning to catch on to what the leprechaun had in mind. He
smiled in spite of his trepidation and reached for his helm, then changed his
mind, remembering that Robert had not worn one. "Trust in the illusion," Gary

whispered to himself, and he hoisted his spear in one hand, bringing it towards his shoulder.

"Not that shoulder!" Mickey snapped at him. "Ye trying to skewer me through?"

Gary quickly brought the spear around to the other side, thinking how hard it was to ignore such a blatantly illogical thing as an invisible leprechaun. Gary could feel Mickey atop his shoulder—if he stopped and thought about it—but he couldn't see the leprechaun there.

"You're making me look like the returning Robert," Gary reasoned.

"Already have," Mickey replied. "Be a good lad and run yer fingers through yer red beard."

Gary looked down, looked for the illusion, then brought his hand tentatively through the image. He could almost feel the thick and tangled hair. His cheeks itched, he realized. His cheeks itched! Gary half believed that Mickey had magically grown a beard for him.

Gary smiled again and chuckled nervously. He could hardly believe that he was about to openly walk through Robert's army, and so he tried not to think about it, just took a huge breath and strode off forcefully, up the inclining path.

"Proud and stern," Mickey told him. "Don't ye talk to any o' them, and don't ye let any o' them talk to yerself!"

Gary glanced over at the invisible sprite—and noticed a line of white smoke drift lazily into the air, coming from, seemingly, nowhere.

"The pipe, Mickey, the pipe," he whispered. "The smoke is showing."

"So it is," came the reply a moment later, but the line of white smoke continued.

"Put it out," Gary ordered.

"Ye can hardly see it," Mickey argued. "Besides, shouldn't there be some smoke beside a dragon? Go on, then."

Gary grumbled, but decided not to argue the point. He was, after all, depending on Mickey more than Mickey was depending on him.

Rows of wooden buildings lined the trail higher up and Gary, and Mickey's illusion, got the fist test before they even reached the area. Two ugly lizards, humanoid lizards with red scales and reptilian eyes, rushed down to greet him, their eager tongues flicking repulsively from between yellow-stained fangs. Each had a shield strapped about its arm, a loincloth about its slender waist, and a short sword on one hip. Other than that, the lizard soldiers were naked, though their scaly skin seemed a solid armor.

They garbled something in a hissing language which Gary could not understand. He growled from deep in his throat and pushed them aside, striding by and not bothering to look back.

"Well done," came Mickey's whisper.

Gary barely heard the sprite. He expected the two lizard soldiers to rush up from behind and cut him down at any moment. *Are you ready?* he asked telepathically of the spear.

Gary felt his hands tingling with the unspoken response and knew that the weapon was more than ready, was eager, to begin the bloodletting.

Having more to lose than did the spear, Gary hoped it wouldn't come to that.

And it didn't. Lava newts approached, and fell away at sight of Gary's uncompromising scowl. The great doors on this end of the castle swung wide before Gary ever got near them, and he passed between the portals without even a look to the soldiers. The road before him was cobblestoned now, continuing on this level inside the castle's outer wall, overlooking the steep cliff, and forking to Gary's right, up an incline to another set of doors that would lead him into the inner, and upper, bailey.

"Which way?" Gary whispered to Mickey, for he still wasn't sure where they had to go, and what this item was that they had to put back.

"Get to the great hall," the leprechaun replied.

Gary thought it over for a moment, then headed to the right. Again the doors swung wide at his approach, lizard soldiers scrambling to keep out of scowling Robert's way. Inside the inner wall, Gary immediately turned right again, and headed for the oaken door of a long and low structure facing him from the nearest corner.

"Hey," Gary quietly mouthed. "What happens if Robert is already back here? And will you put out that freaking pipe?"

"Don't ye worry," said Mickey in as calm a tone as he could muster. "Lava newts can't count to two."

Gary nodded and started to say, "Good," then realized the absurdity of the leprechaun's reply.

They had no trouble entering the building, coming into a narrow but short corridor. The wall to the right was solid and bare stone, but the one to the left was thickly curtained. More guards appeared at a break to the left, but Gary waved them away forcefully and they fled from sight.

Gary turned the corner, to the left beyond the curtain, and sighed profoundly when he saw that the dragon was not at home. Still, many soldiers watched his every move intently, and the young man believed that the battle-hungry spear might soon get its fight.

"*Byuchke hecce,*" came a telepathic call.

"What?" Gary inadvertently spoke loudly, and several lava newt heads turned on him, though whether they were suspicious or simply awaiting commands, the young man could not know. How does one discern the meaning of a lizard's expression? Gary wondered with a shrug.

"*Byuchke hecce,*" the spear implored him more forcefully. "*Tell them, Byuchke hecce!*"

Gary had no idea what the sentient thing was talking about, but, like during the successful walk up the path, the young man felt it better to trust in his more knowledgeable companions. "Byuchke hecce," he called to the soldiers.

They regarded him with curiosity, almost disbelief.

"Say it like ye mean it," Mickey whispered.

"*!*" the spear agreed.

"Byuchke hecce!" Gary roared, and the lizard soldiers looked at each other and then ran from the room.

"What did I tell them?" Gary asked when he was sure that they were far out of hearing distance.

"Ye said ye were hungry," Mickey explained, and he popped back to visibility, his cherubic features turned up in an approving grin.

"*Hungry for lizard meat,*" the spear added.

"Though how ye thought to say a thing like that, I'm not for knowing," Mickey went on uninterrupted, for he, of course, had not been a part of the telepathic communication between Gary and the spear.

Gary hoisted the spear off his shoulder, held it before Mickey and shrugged, the leprechaun nodding accordingly. Mickey led on, then, to the great hearth at the opposite end of the room. Gary shuddered at the sight of Robert's immense sword, resting in its customary place against the wall beside the hearth. At first, he thought that the sword indicated the dragon to be at home, but then he realized that if Robert had "taken wing" as everybody had said, he probably wouldn't have brought the weapon with him. Still, whether the dragon was home or not, Gary found the sight of that monstrous sword, taller than Gary and with a blade nearly six inches across at its base, completely unnerving. He had seen Robert, in human form, wielding the weapon and could not bear to imagine having that incredible sword swung his way.

The nimble leprechaun fumbled about the hearth's brickwork, easily locating the mechanism to the secret door within the fireplace. To Gary's surprise, the eager sprite then led the way in, rushing into the tunnels, and pulling Gary along en route to the dragon's treasure room. They came to many twists and turns, many forking intersections, but Mickey never slowed, as though he knew this place intimately, or, Gary suddenly came to think, as though something was leading the leprechaun on.

All in all, Mickey's behavior struck Gary as strangely out of sorts. The leprechaun verily leaped in joy as they burst through a curtained portal, coming into a chamber piled with gold and gems, armor and weapons, and other treasures too great for Gary to comprehend. He stared in blank amazement as Mickey rushed past it all, ignoring the gem and jewel baubles, some bigger than the leprechaun's chubby hand, and scrambled up the pile, kicking a shower of gold in his wake.

"Oh, I know ye're here!" Mickey chirped, and those simple words told Gary more than anything the leprechaun had said since he had brought Gary back to the land of Faerie.

Gary had suspected it all along, and now he knew for sure that Mickey had a secret agenda, that the leprechaun's claims that all this was "bigger" than Robert had another element in them, an element that Mickey was telling no one.

Gary followed Mickey's trail up the pile, trying not to be overwhelmed by the wealth splayed before him. He crested the hoard just in time to see Mickey wrapping his little arms about . . .

"Your pot of gold!" Gary cried.

"And isn't it fabulous?" the leprechaun squeaked back, and then Mickey suddenly seemed nervous to Gary, like a kid caught with his hand in the proverbial cookie jar.

"I'm not normally bringing it forth," Mickey stammered, as unsure with words as Gary had ever seen him. "I'm just thinking that it'll be a good thing to have on hand should Robert come walking in."

"I'm just thinking that the pot was here all along," Gary replied evenly. Gary thought back to his last journey through Faerie, to all the clues that might now lead him to believe that Mickey had arranged a secret deal with Robert, a deal that included the leprechaun's fabled pot of gold. Gary had seen Mickey making arrangements with a sprite on the road, soon after the leprechaun had learned that Kelsey would take him along all the way to the Giant's Thumb. And Mickey had used illusions to fool the dragon in these very caves, something that, by the reputation of dragons, should not have happened. When Gary had asked Mickey about it, the leprechaun had claimed that he only showed Robert what Robert thought to be the obvious truth, and that Robert had been too busy fighting with Kelsey to look carefully at the trick. Mickey had even gone so far as to say, "Besides, me magic was at its strongest in there."

Those words echoed in Gary Leger's mind, and now he understood them as a slip of the tongue, as a vague, probably unintentional reference to the fact that Mickey had secretly bartered his pot of gold to the dragon.

So many things came clearer and clearer to Gary Leger, and most of them did not shed a positive light on the leprechaun. Gary thought of Cedric, who had died, and of so many others who had suffered. And for what? the young man now wondered.

He looked on incredulously as Mickey lifted the pot from the floor and folded it! Then folded it again, and a third time, as though it was no more than a piece of paper! Soon, it was all but gone, and Mickey prudently tucked it into a deep pocket, then turned, beaming, at Gary.

His smile went away in the face of Gary's scowl.

"Was it?" Gary asked sternly.

"Was what?"

"Was the pot here all along?" Gary asked, speaking each word with perfect clarity.

"Why, laddie . . ."

"Was it?" Gary's yell set Mickey back on his heels.

"Not all along," Mickey replied, and Gary could see that the leprechaun was squirming.

"All along since we last left the dragon's lair?" Gary clarified and qualified, understanding Mickey's semantic games.

"Well, laddie, what are ye getting at?" the leprechaun asked innocently.

"What am I getting at?" Gary echoed softly, shaking his head and chuckling. "You said we were coming here to return something, to put the wyrm back in his hole."

"Aye," Mickey agreed, leading Gary on.

"You took the pot."

"It's me own pot."

"You gave it to Robert."

"I done what I had to do," Mickey argued, and admitted. "But I'm not to let the wyrm keep me pot. Suren I'm a leprechaun, lad, and suren I'm to die without me pot in hand!"

"That's not what I'm talking about!" Gary roared. "You said we were coming to put the wyrm back in his hole, but we never were. We were coming so that you could get back your precious pot of gold!"

"How do ye know we're not here to do both?" Mickey asked coyly, flashing his cherubic smile.

"Because you're taking the stupid pot!" Gary screamed. "And even if we put back whatever it is we came to put back, it won't work, because you're taking something else!"

"Good point," Mickey agreed casually.

Gary wanted to pull his hair out—no, he decided, he wanted to pull Mickey's hair out! He roared again at the futility of it all, at Cedric's death and at the loss of those killed on the field southwest of Dvergamal. He remembered that he had bargained to let the witch loose on the land again, had freed Ceridwen because he believed that this trip to the Giant's Thumb was of the utmost importance.

Mickey did not continue his innocent act. His scowl soon matched Gary's and he pulled a jeweled dagger out of another of the seemingly endless supply of pockets in his gray jacket and threw it at Gary's feet.

"What . . ." Gary started to ask, looking down at the weapon, at first thinking that Mickey had actually thrown the dagger at him. Then the truth hit Gary, though, like the slap of a wet towel in his face. Gary knew this dagger, had seen it in this very castle, had taken it from this very castle!

"Don't ye get thinking that ye're any better!" Mickey yelled at him. "There it is, lad. There's the item that was stolen from Robert's lair. There's the missing piece that let the wyrm fly free."

Gary found his breathing hard to come by. The souls of a hundred dead fluttered about his shoulders, threatening to bend them low under their burdening weight. He, Gary Leger, had taken the dagger!

He had freed the wyrm!

"I didn't know," he breathed. "I didn't mean . . ."

"Of course ye did not," Mickey agreed, his tone honestly sympathetic. "It was a mistake that not a one could blame ye for."

"But if we put the dagger back, then Robert is bound?" Gary asked as much as stated.

Mickey slowly shook his head.

"Then it's true," Gary snapped, his rolling emotions putting him back on the offensive again. "We came here for no more than your pot of gold."

"Aye," Mickey admitted. "And that's not as small a thing as ye're making it to be."

"People died," Gary snarled.

"And more will," Mickey answered grimly. "I did not do this just for meself, lad," he went on, his tone grim and rock-steady. "I came for me pot, lied to ye all to get ye to help me, but it's for the better of us all. Yerself and Kelsey, the gnomes and the folk o' Braemar, have got a dragon to fight, and the fighting'll be easier now that I've got me pot. Ye seen it yerself, seen how little I helped ye in the swamp and on the road. And ye seen how much more I helped when we neared me pot. We walked right through Robert's army, and walk through 'em again we will, without a one of them thinking anything's outa place!"

Gary could not deny the leprechaun's reasoning, and he found that his initial anger was fast fading.

"Ye'll need me in the trials ahead," Mickey added. "And now I'm ready to be there to help ye out."

"What about the dragon?" Gary asked. "I could go back to Ynis Gwydrin and let Ceridwen out now. We could just let her and Robert go back to their own fighting."

Mickey thought it over for a minute, then shook his head once more. "Even the witch'd not stop Robert until all the eastland was in flames," he reasoned. "With Dilnamarra already under Kinnemore's evil grasp, Ceridwen'd like to see Braemar and Drochit burned. She'd like to have Robert get the pesty gnomes and the mighty Buldrefolk out of her way. No, lad, Robert's got to be fought, and got to be fought soon—sooner than the witch'd have a mind to do it."

Gary sighed and nodded and looked around. "But not here," he said. "We won't fight the dragon in the middle of his stronghold."

"Then we're to be fast flying," Mickey reasoned. "Dragons know their treasure better than a babe knows its mother, and Robert's sure to soon figure out that we're poking around his own."

Gary had no objections to Mickey's suggestion. "We should take something to lead the wyrm on," he reasoned, looking eagerly at the glittering mound.

Mickey tapped the pocket wherein he had dropped the pot. "We already have, lad," he muttered grimly. "We already have."

Gary didn't disagree, but then a thought came to him, a perfectly conniving thought.

Before the sun had set that same day, Mickey and Gary were back in the quadricycle, zooming across the barren lands west of the Giant's Thumb. On one side of Gary rested the spear of Cedric Donigarten—on the other, Robert's huge sword.

TWENTY
Broken Trees and Burning Homes

WEARING again the mantle of a large, red-bearded man, Robert stalked into the ruined edge of Dreadwood, casually batting aside blackened, still-smoldering trees with mighty arms that suffered no pain from the heat. He grabbed one large log up in his hand and heaved it away, smiling with evil pleasure as it smashed against another standing tree, its ember-filled inner core exploding into a shower of sparks.

"Are you in here, little elf?" the dragon-turned-man bellowed, crunching through the hot area without the slightest regard for the minor fires.

No fire could ever harm Robert the Wretched.

"Do come out and play, Kelsenellenelvial Gil-Ravadry!" the dragon called. "Else I will have to burn down the rest of the forest."

There came no reply, not even the chirp of a bird in the ruined area. Robert's eyes narrowed, and he scanned the immediate region carefully, looking for some sign. He had hit the woods a third time, again with all his strength and fiery fury, and he had figured that Kelsey and his friends, including that puny impostor Gary Leger from Bretaigne, were probably already dead. Thinking about it now, though, with no sign of charred corpses anywhere about, the dragon believed that he might have erred in attacking so openly and in such a straightforward manner. Robert had let his fury get in the way of good sense, and now he was tired—too tired to spread dragon wings and search out the countryside, too tired to summon his killing breath anymore and lay waste to the rest of the forest.

He wasn't worried, though. Even in this human form, Robert knew that he was more than a match for the elf and his friends, was confident that they had nothing which could truly harm one as powerful as he.

The dragon continued his search for more than an hour, finally stumbling upon the tracks of a horse, and beside them the light bootprints of an elf, running northwest, back out of the woods the same way Kelsey and his friends had entered.

"So a few escaped," the dragon mused, thinking that they would not escape for long. Robert followed the trail right towards the edge of Dreadwood, saw that it continued on in the same direction, cutting a line across the rolling fields to the southern tip of Dvergamal. The dragon nodded; he had turned Kelsenellenelvial and his friends around, at least, and it seemed as though their numbers had been diminished.

Robert briefly considered a quick pursuit, but the sun hung low in the sky before him, and he was tired. He might spend the entire night searching, without luck, and then the morning would leave him more weary.

"Running home," the dragon said, and his wicked smile returned tenfold, for Robert knew where "home" might be.

"HOW long can you keep that up, elf?" Geno asked, and the dwarf seemed more amused than concerned, watching Kelsey half running, half flying along the side of the fast-trotting pony. Behind the dwarf, Gerbil, bouncing wildly and wishing for his quadricycle, moaned in sympathy.

"We will continue long past the sunset," the elf informed Geno. "And I will run as long as I must."

"Do you believe that the dragon will be following us?" Gerbil asked nervously, glancing back to the southeast. "They are reportedly stubborn, after all, but this one seems to have his nose pointed in many different directions all at once, if you know what I mean."

"Robert will be out in the morn, if not before," Kelsey replied. "We can only hope that he finds our trail and not that of our companions."

"Now there's something to hope for," Geno put in sarcastically, and just for the fun of it, the dwarf let the pony's bridle out a bit more, picked up the pace so that Kelsey, holding a rope attached to the mount's neck, was more flying than running.

Their camp was restless and nervous that night, with Kelsey pacing all the while, and Gerbil too nervous to even close his eyes. Geno, though, was soon snoring loudly, something that disturbed both the elf and the gnome more than a little. Having no luck either waking the dwarf or turning Geno's body over, Kelsey wound up splitting a small stick and pinching it over the dwarf's nose.

The three were moving again before any hint of dawn found the eastern horizon, with Kelsey constantly glancing back over his shoulder, as though he expected the dragon to swoop upon them at any time. This, of course, unnerved poor Gerbil more than a little, and the gnome finally just wrapped his arms as tightly as possible around the dwarf's waist and buried his face in Geno's back.

Dawn did little to brighten anyone's mood, for the three felt vulnerable indeed trotting across rolling and, for the most part, open hills under the light of day.

"Is that the witch's crow?" Geno asked a short while later. Kelsey turned his eyes back to the trail ahead to see the large black bird standing calmly on the grass, and to see the dwarf lifting a hammer for a throw, Geno's icy-blue eyes sparkling eagerly.

"Hold," Kelsey bade him, drawing a disappointed, even angry, look. "We do not know what news the bird brings."

"What lies it brings, you mean," Geno corrected, but he did bring his hammer back down, slowing the pony so that they might stop and speak with the bird.

"Dragon, dragon," the crow cackled. "Get away!"

"We did," Geno answered dryly.

"It could be that the bird means that the dragon is coming and that we should NOW get away," Gerbil intervened.

"Dragon, dragon, get away!" the crow cried and it flew off, cutting a fast track for a small but thick copse of trees not too far to the south.

"I don't see any dragon," Geno huffed, looking back behind them.

"By the time you saw Robert, Robert would see you," Kelsey warned. "And then it would be too late."

"Dragons are bigger than dwarfs," Geno argued.

"But they see better than eagles," Kelsey shot back. He was already heading for the south, tugging the rope so that the pony turned to follow.

From the shadows of the trees, they watched Robert's passage. The dragon came by incredibly low, barely twenty feet off the ground, his nostrils snuffling and his eyes as often turned down as ahead. The beating of his wings crackled and rolled like thunder, and the wind of his wake shivered the trees of the copse, though they were fully fifty yards away.

"He's hunting," Geno remarked.

"Us," Gerbil added, and Kelsey nodded grimly. Both the dwarf and the gnome took some consolation in the fact that Robert had zipped by, and was already long out of sight, but Kelsey's expression remained grave.

Geno looked around to the boughs of the trees. "I hope that crow is still about," the dwarf admitted. "When that dragon does not find us on the road ahead, he'll be sure to turn around."

Kelsey shook his head and began, to Geno and Gerbil's dismay, to lead the pony back out of the trees. "Robert will not be back," the elf assured them. "Not for some time."

Kelsey winced at his own words, though the claim seemed to brighten the moods of his two companions. They were safe enough for the time being, Kelsey sincerely believed, but he also believed that he knew the price of that security.

Like Kelsey, Robert was heading for Braemar.

THE dragon sensed that the trail had gone cold, understood that the elf and his friends had probably turned aside and let him pass. He thought to turn about and hunt the group down, but other instincts argued against that move. Robert's hunger was up; his course had him speeding straight for Braemar.

He beat his wings more fiercely, climbed into the air, then stooped low again, gaining momentum, gaining speed. He forgot his weariness in those minutes, his dragon-hunger urging him on, urging him to begin the destruction.

Robert whipped past the fast low foothills of Dvergamal, cut in behind the closest mountain peaks so that the helpless folk of the village would have less warning. The sky about the mountains was heavy with dark clouds, but as far as the dragon could tell, it had not yet rained.

The thatched roofs and wooden planks of the houses would still be dry.

Soon Robert saw the chimney smoke rising to meet the overcast, drifting lazily into the air above Braemar, and an anxious growl escaped the dragon's maw as he thought of how much thicker that smoke would soon become.

The lone bell in Braemar's small chapel began to ring; Robert's keen ears caught the cries of the distant villagers, rousing the town, calling out the approach of the dreaded wyrm.

The dragon cut a sharp turn around a jutting wall of stone, leveled out with the town in sight, and began his swooping descent.

Arrows zipped out at him, bouncing harmlessly from his armored body. Robert's snarl came again, for these were simple farm folk and miners, and not the clever gnomes of Gondabuggan. No metallic shields would come up to stop the dragon this time; no catapults would send stinging flak into the air to hinder Robert's passage.

Barely thirty feet up, he swooped over the edge of the town, loosing his fiery breath in a line that sent one, and then another, and then another, thatched roof up in flames. The dragon began his turn before he even passed beyond the cluster of houses, his great tail snapping about to clip the second floor of the spokelock, collapsing one corner of the building.

Below him, the people were in a frenzy, rushing about with bows and spears, others running with buckets of water to fight the fires.

"Useless!" the proud dragon bellowed as the missiles continued to bounce away. Useless, too, were those battling the fires, their buckets a pitiful sight against the flames leaping high, so high, into the air. Already one of the houses was gutted, the fires dying low simply because their incredible intensity had consumed the thatch and wood fuel.

It took the huge wyrm a long while to bank enough to make a second pass, and this time, Braemar's defense proved more organized. Robert came in over a different section of town, from the west, finding no resistance as his breath consumed yet another farmhouse. As Robert passed the central area, his tail taking another swipe at the two-story structure, he met a wall of arrows and spears, fired nearly point-blank. Again, the dragon's sturdy armor deflected the brunt, but one missile nicked Robert's eye.

His roar split stones a mile away, deafened those near him, as he banked suddenly up into the air, then dropped to his haunches upon the ground.

A second volley shot out at him from behind a long and low building, the Snoozing Sprite tavern. More than one arrow knifed into the dragon's mouth, and stuck there painfully, until Robert's breath came forth, disintegrating the missiles and lighting the corner of the building. Despite the unexpected pain, the evil dragon hissed with pleasure when he heard the screams of several archers, when one man, engulfed in flames, came rolling out from behind the Snoozing Sprite.

Robert's continuing hiss was cut short, though, as a score of hardy villagers, accompanied by Kervin and his rugged dwarfs, charged out from another hiding spot, axes, hammers, swords and spears, even pitchforks and grass scythes, going to vicious work on the sitting dragon.

Robert snapped his tail about, launching a handful of enemies away. A lasso hooked about his foreclaw, and when the dragon instinctively jerked against it, he found that the thick rope was secured to a huge oak tree.

A dwarfish hammer smashed the dragon's ankle. Robert lifted his foot and squashed the troublesome dwarf into the dirt.

But the sheer fury of the villagers' response had surprised the wyrm. While Robert crushed the poor dwarf, a dozen other weapons smashed hard into his armor plating. One great axe cut a slice through the lower portion of the dragon's leathery wing. Robert buffeted with the wing, sending the axe-man flying away.

The dragon's breath melted another man to his bones; Robert's tail whipped again, and three dwarfs flew through the air.

From the other end of the burning tavern came yet another volley of arrows, the whole group concentrating on the area of the dragon's face. Robert's rage multiplied; his thrashing sent more men and dwarfs spinning away. And then he set his wings to beating, leaped off the ground, forgetting about his hooked foreclaw.

The rope jerked him around, and he stumbled, crashing headlong into a stone house, smashing the place to tiny bits of rubble. Up leaped the outraged dragon, issuing another stone-splitting roar. He spun and tugged, and the great oak tore from the ground. Stubborn villagers came at him once more. Another volley of arrows sent stinging darts into his reptilian eyes.

Robert leaped into the air, his wings pounding furiously.

The ground ripped wide open as the tree was pulled along, its roots tearing free until Robert, tiring, turned his maw about and breathed again, disintegrating the thick rope.

A group of men fled screaming, and the shadow of the dragon covered them, Robert swooping low and snapping up more than one of them to his great maw.

All of Braemar would have been leveled and burned, every person in the town would surely have perished, except that the wyrm was tired. The defense had been stronger than Robert had anticipated, and since his last true rest, he had burned half a forest and had flown a hundred miles.

He gave another roar, its tone triumphant, and soared away to find a mountain perch, confident that when he had rested, he would return and finish the town.

Good fortune was on the side of the village that day, for soon after the dragon attack, the low clouds opened up and sent heavy rains to quench the dragon fires, and to soak the remaining thatch and wood.

"Rain is no friend to a dragon," one villager remarked hopefully, but the encouraging words rang shallow in light of the destruction and the dead.

From the empty window of another building, the glass blown out by the sheer thunderous force of the dragon's passage, Badenoch of Braemar and Baron Pwyll looked on helplessly.

TWENTY-ONE
Sobering Return

"THE axle's bent," Gary explained, crawling out from underneath the quadricycle and sitting up on the dry ground south of the Ruined Forest. He looked back to the east, to the thick tree root sticking like a speed bump from the ground, the jolt that had caused the problem.

Mickey nodded and said, "Hmmm," though the leprechaun had no idea what Gary was talking about. "Well, can ye fix it, then?" he asked.

Gary sighed deeply and looked to the angled front wheel, and his expression was not hopeful.

"Ye got to fix it, lad," Mickey implored. "Or to be sure that Robert's going to find us sitting here in the open."

Gary reached over to take the spear of Cedric Donigarten, then slid back under the front end of the gnomish contraption and angled the spearshaft above the bent axle. He found rocks and placed them around the front wheels to keep the axle from turning as he applied pressure, then slid a large, flat rock under the back end of the spear to make sure that it didn't simply slide downward when he pulled the other end up.

"*Young sprout,*" came a not-too-happy call in his head.

Gary ignored the spear, kept at his work.

"*Young sprout.*" This time the call was accompanied by a tingling feeling in the metallic shaft, a clear warning that the spear might soon blast Gary's hands away.

We have to fix this, Gary telepathically replied.

"*I am a weapon forged to battle dragons and fell unlawful kings,*" the spear answered. "*I am the tool of the warrior, not the tradesman. I am the instrument with which . . .*"

All things in place, Gary put the top end of the spear over his shoulder and heaved upward with all his strength, pressing the spear between the bent axle and the front bumper of the gnomish vehicle. He felt the too-proud spear's anger, felt an energy charge beginning to build within the sentient weapon's shaft. But Gary growled in anger and pushed harder, pushed until a blue flash erupted from the spear.

And then he was sitting on the ground again, his hair dancing on its ends.

"Are ye all right?"

Gary nodded quickly to Mickey, then rolled to his hands and knees to inspect the axle. It still wasn't perfectly straight, but Gary's efforts had bent it back enough so that he believed the thing would drive.

"*I am not pleased, young sprout.*"

"Oh, shut up," Gary said aloud, and he grabbed up the spear. Again he felt the charge building, and he instinctively started to drop the weapon to the ground. He stopped, though, with a determined growl. "You do it, and I'll leave you here on the plain," he promised. "Let the dragon find you and put you in his lair as a trophy, and see how much fighting you'll find there!"

The spear did not respond, but the tingling in its metallic shaft ceased.

Their progress was limited over the next few hours. The quadricycle bumped and bounced, and Gary kept it to as easy and level a course as he could find. The contraption wasn't built to handle this much weight, he realized, and with the axle already weakened, Gary feared that any hole or bump could buckle it once again.

They made it to Dreadwood, though, as twilight descended over the land, and even though the forest had seemed an evil place to Gary, he was horrified to view it now. Tangled boughs had been replaced by charred, skeletal limbs, and all the northern section of the forest glowed with residual heat. Orange embers appeared as mischievous eyes in logs lying prone, as though a hundred little goblins had climbed inside the fallen wood, daring Gary and Mickey to walk past.

"Now what?" Gary asked the leprechaun.

"Now we're going through," Mickey replied sternly, as though the answer should have been obvious.

Gary understood and accepted his companion's sudden anger. In looking at the devastation, Mickey could not help but worry about their friends, worry that Kelsey and Geno and Gerbil had not escaped the dragon fires. Blowing a deep breath, Gary set the quadricycle into motion, veering this way and that along the path to avoid fallen branches. Several time he had to get out of the seat altogether, to remove debris, and always, those orange ember eyes watched him, their glow intensifying as the night deepened.

"We'll camp on the other side of the forest," Gary decided after two hours of inching along. His hands were blackened from soot, his whole body was lathered in sweat under the armor from the residual heat, and he felt as though his lungs would simply explode.

"No, lad," Mickey replied grimly, "we'll keep going right through the night."

Gary looked at the sprite curiously. It seemed as if Mickey's euphoria at finding his pot had fully worn away, to be replaced by a level of despair that surprised Gary.

"I've a feeling that there's worse trouble brewing," Mickey explained. "We've a hundred miles to go to get to Braemar, and I'm wanting to be there before tomorrow turns to the next day."

Gary nearly laughed aloud. "I can't even see the path ahead," he complained.

Mickey spoke a quick rhyme and snapped his fingers, and a ball of light appeared, hovering a few feet in front of the quadricycle. "It'll stay out in front of us," the leprechaun explained.

"I'm getting tired, Mickey," Gary said bluntly. "I'm not a pack horse, and we've gone a long way already."

"No, ye're not getting tired," the leprechaun replied.

Gary scoffed at him.

"Ye're not getting tired," Mickey said again, his tone compelling. "Slip deeper into the seat, lad. Let yer body become a part of the gnomish contraption."

Gary eyed the leprechaun closely, but somehow, Mickey's words seemed to make sense to him. Without even thinking of the movement, he did indeed slip deeper into his seat.

"There's a good lad," Mickey, said, and now his voice seemed incredibly soothing to Gary. "Ye can even close yer eyes." Mickey shifted so that he was sitting right on Gary's lap, and eased Gary's hands away from the quadricycle's steering bar.

"There's a good lad," Mickey said again, nodding approvingly at Gary's deep and steady breathing. "Just keep yer legs turning, turning easy."

Gary was soon fast asleep, caught in the throes of the leprechaun's hypnotic magic. His legs continued to pedal, though, and would throughout the night, as Mickey subconsciously compelled him, every so often whispering magical, coaxing words into his ear.

Many times that night, Mickey looked back anxiously to Gary. There was a very real danger in doing this to the young man, Mickey knew, a danger that the exertion would explode Gary's heart, or tire him to the point where he would never recover. Mickey had to take the chance, though, for he, unlike Gary, had heard the dragon's call from the north, from above the Crahgs. Robert had sensed his missing sword, Mickey believed, and when the wyrm came back out of Giant's Thumb, probably the very next morning, his mood would not be bright.

"Smooth and easy," the leprechaun gently prodded. "Smooth and easy." Mickey looked to the slightly flip-flopping wheel of the quadricycle and could only hope that the thing wouldn't fall apart before they got to Braemar.

WEARING grim faces, Kelsey, walking, and Geno and Gerbil atop the pony, made their slow way around the last barrier of stone before the sheltered vale of Braemar on the morning of the next day. They saw the lines of black smoke rising out of the valley, and could guess easily enough where Robert had flown off to. Half expecting to find all of Braemar razed, Kelsey paused a long while before mustering the courage to step around the bend and get his first view of the village.

Many of the structures remained intact, but many others had been destroyed. Stone skeletons of farmhouses, their ends pyramiding to a point, but not a piece of thatch left atop them, dotted the landscape. The spoke-lock was a one-story building now, with the top level flattened to kindling, cracked boards protruding from the edges of the still-standing first level, and the roads and even a huge tree had been ripped and torn by the angry dragon.

The normally stoic Geno let out an unexpected wail, spotting two cairns piled high on hills beside the town.

"Are those the normal burial mounds of your people?" Kelsey asked reverently, recognizing the source of his companion's distress. "Are dwarfs buried under those piled stones?"

"Look closer, elf," Geno replied gruffly.

"The dwarfs are not buried *beneath* the stones," Gerbil, who knew the ways of the Buldrefolk better than the elf, explained, emphasizing the word "beneath."

"Look closer," Geno said again.

Kelsey stared at the distant mounds and discovered, to his amazement, that bodies of dead dwarfs had been stacked together with the stones, holding up their places in the piles as solidly as the boulders.

"Two mounds," Gerbil added, his tone unintentionally impassive. "Which means, by all dwarfish records, that at least six dwarfs were killed."

Geno grunted.

"The Buldrefolk will, of course, put no more than five of their fallen kin in a single cairn," the gnome went on, speaking like a professor in some classroom far removed from so brutal a scene as Braemar after the dragon. "There is a belief among the dwarfs that . . ."

Kelsey held up his hand to gently stop the gnome. He knew that Gerbil wasn't intentionally being callous, but Geno, sitting dangerously close to the rambling gnome, seemed on the verge of an explosion, gripping the pony's bridle so tightly that Kelsey wondered if the leather thong would simply fall in half, squeezed apart by the dwarf's iron grasp. If Gerbil kept on going, Kelsey realized, the gnome might find that a dwarfish boot was nearly as strong a delivery system as his Mountain Messenger.

"Oh," Gerbil said simply, and apologetically, as he regarded the dwarf seated right before him, seeming to realize only then that his dissertation on dwarfish burial methods might have been somewhat out of place.

"Let's get down to the town," Geno offered, brushing off his moment of weakness. "It looks like it could have been worse. I see a few of the buildings still standing, and the Snoozing Sprite's up, if a bit blackened."

Kelsey nodded, and he held more than a little admiration for Geno at that moment. He had seen the dwarf's pain—perhaps the first time the elf had witnessed any emotion other than anger from one of the Buldrefolk—and had seen the dwarf sublimate that pain because Geno knew that they had no time for grief, not with Gary and Mickey wandering who-knew-where and with Robert still flying about, probably even then preparing to hit the village once again.

Braemar was bustling that morning, people rushing about, bringing supplies to various shelters, changing dressings on the nasty wounds, mostly burns, of the injured, and formulating defense plans should the dragon return. Braemar proper, like the actual town area of most of the outlying villages, was a small place, a cluster of just a few structures, with most of the people associated with the town living as far as several miles away. It seemed as if the majority of those farmers and miners had come in now, though, to help with the effort. These were admirable people, even to one of the Tylwyth Teg, who generally looked down their noses at humans.

Many sentries had been set, high on the slopes overlooking the town, and Kelsey's party was spotted and reported long before the three companions got anywhere near the village. No one rode out to meet them or to hinder them, though (Kelsey figured that no one would have the time), and few gave them more than a passing glance as they plodded along the street, muddy from the soaking rain and the firefighting efforts, into Braemar's central square.

Batteries of archers roamed the streets, pointing out angles of possible dragon descent and seeking out the best locations from which to strike back in the event of the wyrm's return.

One woman, three children in tow, cried out for her husband, trying futilely to get past the men blocking her entrance to her still-smoldering home. All three of the companions, even Geno, sent their hearts out to the apparent widow, and all three were truly relieved to see, unexpectedly, the supposedly missing man running down the street from the other direction, crying out for his beloved wife and children.

They were just turning their attention back to the road ahead when a familiar, plump face appeared from around a corner. Soot-covered, and lathered in sweat, Baron Pwyll seemed far less regal, seemed sobered, actually, as he walked solemnly out to greet his returning friends.

"You did not make the Giant's Thumb," the Baron reasoned.

"Have Mickey and Gary Leger returned?" Kelsey asked.

Baron Pwyll shook his head.

"Then they are still on their way," Kelsey said hopefully.

"They have the quadricycle," Gerbil interjected, smiling as widely as he could manage, given the grim scene all about him. "They have probably been there and are near to back again!"

Pwyll blew a deep breath, tried to turn up the edges of his mouth, but the smile would not come. "Perhaps that is why the dragon has not returned," he reasoned. "Robert flew in hard and fast, and was gone just as quickly. We spent a long night, expecting the darkness to be shattered by flaming dragon breath. But he did not come back."

"It is a hopeful sign," Kelsey agreed.

"How many dwarfs?" Geno said abruptly, and after a moment to digest the blunt question, Pwyll understood that Geno wanted to know how many of his people had perished.

"Seven," he answered.

"Kervin?"

Pwyll turned about and motioned to the Snoozing Sprite.

"Best place to be after a dragon attack," Geno agreed, and he handed the bridle to Gerbil behind him and slid down off the pony, cutting a beeline for the still-standing tavern.

"Even if the dragon does not return, there is much to do," Pwyll prompted the others, and Gerbil, too, slid down from the mount.

Kelsey removed his belongings from the pony's back and handed the reins over to Pwyll, bidding the Baron to find out where the pony would be of the most help to the People of Braemar. The simple gesture overwhelmed the Baron, for he knew how protective the Tylwyth Teg normally were of their precious steeds.

"Together we will not lose," Pwyll said finally, right before he led the pony away.

Kelsey nodded, his fair features stern and determined. He was glad to see the normally quivering Pwyll apparently rising to the occasion, but his hopes were tempered by the grim reality. Robert was flying free, and even if Mickey and Gary somehow managed to replace the dagger and put the wyrm back in his hole (which Kelsey had never actually believed to be the fact of the matter), and escape with their lives, there was still the matter of King Kinnemore's gathered army, a new puppet ruler coming to power in Dilnamarra, so near Kelsey's forest home, and a witch coming out of her banishment in three short months.

At that moment, the future of Faerie seemed as bleak to Kelsey as the blackened kindling that had once been Braemar's spoke-lock.

A cry from down the lane turned the elf about, to see the frantic woman and her children locked in a communal hug with the man they had thought dead.

"Then again," Kelsey said aloud, his suddenly hopeful tone drawing a curious glance from Gerbil, "one never knows what might happen."

THE quadricycle limped into Braemar soon after sunset that same day. Mickey steered it into the village square just outside the ruined spoke-lock, where it bogged down in the mud. A crowd of onlookers gathered about, keeping a respectful distance, but pointing Mickey's way and talking anxiously among themselves. Mickey had been far-sighted enough to enact an illusion before he and Gary ever got close to the village, one that made him appear as a normal human boy and not a leprechaun. Greedy human hands seeking the fabled pot of gold would surely have engulfed him, even after the dragon attack, if the leprechaun had gone in undisguised.

"Easy now, laddie," the leprechaun whispered to Gary, who was sitting back with his eyes closed, his body, except for his pumping legs, limp with exhaustion. The semiconscious man kept on pedaling, apparently oblivious to the leprechaun's calls, or to the fact that the quadricycle's back wheels were spinning uselessly in the mud.

"Stop and rest," Mickey quietly implored Gary. Then came a great bump as the contraption's front axle snapped in half, dropping the whole front end of the thing into the mud.

"Oh," Mickey muttered, and he was certainly glad that the contraption had waited until now to fall apart.

Gary remained oblivious to it all, his legs turning the pedals, the rest of his body thoroughly drained to support the hypnotic effort, and his mind too shut down to even dream. He lay in blackness, unaware of anything at all, even the fact that he could very well, and very soon, work himself to death.

"Oh, my dear," came a wail, and Gerbil Hamsmacker bolted out of the crowd and rushed to his ruined contraption. "Oh, what have you done?" the gnome asked accusingly. He looked at Mickey curiously for a moment, at first not recognizing the sprite-turned-boy. "Oh, what have you done?" he said at length, finally figuring out the deception.

"I put three hundred miles on the damned thing in three days," Mickey replied. "Ye built it good, gnome, good enough to get ye on any plaque, by me own opinion."

The high praise calmed Gerbil down considerably. He fell flat to the mud before the contraption, trying to assess the damage, then nearly got run over as the continually turning back wheels caught some solid ground under the muddy trenches and lurched the contraption forward.

"Do make him stop that," Gerbil calmly said to Mickey, and once more, the leprechaun whispered into Gary's ear for the man to stop pedaling.

And once more, Mickey was ignored.

"What is wrong with him?" Kelsey asked curtly, coming over with Geno to join his companions. Both elf and dwarf crinkled their expressions when they regarded Mickey, but understood the matter soon enough. "And where have you been?" Kelsey went on.

"Hello to yerself, too," Mickey replied dryly.

Kelsey nodded and dipped a quick bow, as much of an apology as he would ever give. "You have much to tell us, I would assume," he remarked.

"Aye," said Mickey. "But first ye two help me to get Gary Leger out o' the seat, afore the lad pedals himself to death."

Geno offered a callous remark that Gary seemed near that point already. The dwarf stepped over, grabbed Gary's metal shoulderplate in one hand, and heaved the man from his seat, allowing him to fall unceremoniously into the mud. Mickey held his breath, and was relieved that Geno never looked into the low seat, never seemed to notice the stolen sword.

Gary lay facedown—it seemed as though he could not even breathe—but made no attempts to turn about. And still, his legs kept pumping.

Kelsey, Geno, and Gerbil, and many of those gathered about, looked to Mickey suspiciously, awaiting an explanation.

"Had to get to the dragon's lair," Mickey explained with a dismissive shrug. "And back fast. I'll put a spell o' resting on the laddie and he'll be all right after the night."

"You have been to the lair, then?" Kelsey asked anxiously, hoping that this ordeal with Robert was at its end. "And you replaced the stolen dagger?"

"Aye," Mickey replied. "Aye, to both." It wasn't quite true; once the pot of gold had been recovered, Mickey had forgotten all about the dagger, and had it still, in a deep pocket of his gray jacket.

"Then Robert is banished once more," Kelsey reasoned, "and the folk of Braemar can begin to plan for troubles from another direction."

"That'd be dangerous thinking," Mickey put in. All three of the leprechaun's companions eyed him curiously. "I seen the dragon, fast flying to the east," Mickey went on. "Whether he's to stay put in his hole or not, I cannot be saying. But I wouldn't take it as fact, nor should ye all, until we're knowing for sure."

"You said that the replaced dagger would . . ." Kelsey began.

"I said an obscure rule in an old book," Mickey pointedly argued, for of course, the leprechaun knew that the wyrm had not been put back in his hole, knew all along that replacing the dagger would have no effect at all on Robert.

Only then did Kelsey, leaning forward on the gnomish contraption as though he needed the support, notice Robert's huge sword, lying in the seat where Gary had been sitting. Mickey watched the elf's face contort weirdly, knew that Kelsey was now, as Gary had done in the dragon's lair, putting the pieces together and figuring out the entire deception. Even if the dagger had been put back, the presence of the sword, a weapon that Kelsey knew all too well, would have defeated the whole purpose for the trip to Robert's lair.

To the leprechaun's relief, Kelsey did not mention the logical problem then and there, just offered a knowing smirk Mickey's way. "We will get him into a warm cot," Kelsey said, looking to Gary. "Be ready for a long night," he said to Mickey. "There is much to be done before the dawn."

"And much to be done after the dawn," Mickey added under his breath. "Unless I'm missing me guess."

TWENTY-TWO

Bait

THE rains came heavy the next day, a soaking downpour under thick black clouds that stretched from horizon to horizon. Never before had the people of Braemar so welcomed such gloom.

"The wyrm'll not come forth in this," Mickey remarked to his four companions when the group gathered in the remaining, unburned area of the Snoozing Sprite for breakfast.

"But how long will the rains last?" Kelsey was quick to put in, and to Gary, it seemed as if the elf was on the verge of a tirade. Every time Kelsey had looked upon Mickey the previous night, and this morn, his eyes had been filled with hatred, and every word he spoke in response to the leprechaun was edged with venom.

Kelsey's obvious rage seemed to roll off Mickey's rounded shoulders. The leprechaun had his precious pot of gold back; nothing in all the world bothered Mickey anymore.

"The defense will be stronger the next time Robert arrives," Kelsey promised the others, looking individually to each of them, with the notable exception of Mickey. "Gerbil will aid in the construction of a catapult this day, and with Geno . . ."

"Save your breath, elf," the dwarf interrupted. "Me and my kin are out of

Braemar this day. With the dragon still about, we've got our own homes to worry about."

Kelsey started to reply, but stopped short and gave a resigned nod. He couldn't rightly judge the dwarf's decision, for the Firth of Buldre, the dwarfish homeland, was not so far from Braemar, certainly less distance than a flying dragon could cover in just a few hours.

"That might be a good place for all of us to make our stand," Gary interjected, remembering the dwarfish place, remembering the towering waterfalls and the continuous spray, and the thick-walled rocky caves that Geno and his kin called home.

All eyes turned to the young man—three of Gary's companions seemed intrigued.

The exception, Geno, was quick to respond. "You're not bringing a bunch of human farmers to the Firth," he snorted.

"You'd let them die?" Gary answered sharply.

"Yes." The answer was plain and comfortably spoken, and Gary eased back in his chair, his pending arguments deflated by Geno's callousness. The dwarf only gave the man a gap-toothed grin, further evidence that he was perfectly content.

"I think that the lad's onto something," Mickey said.

"No," Geno replied evenly, his clear blue eyes sparkling and his grin replaced by a determined scowl.

"Not to the Firth," Mickey went on. "Ye couldn't rightly be bringing human folk in such numbers to that place." Mickey was talking more to Gary than to Geno now, filling in the details that Geno hadn't bothered to add. "Never again would the dwarfs find peace, and if human greed is more than legend . . ."

"And it is," Geno added, and even Gerbil was nodding.

". . . then ye'd be sure to be starting a war, if everything else sorted out," Mickey explained. He looked to Geno hopefully, his dimples evident and all his face turned up in a hopeful grin. "But there be other waterfalls and other deep caves in wide Dvergamal where the folk o' Braemar might hide."

"And what of the folk of Drochit?" the dwarf asked, hints of sarcasm growing with every passing word. "And the hamlet of Lisdoonvarna, to the north and west? And Dilnamarra? Are you thinking to put the whole of Faerie's humans in mountain holes, leprechaun?"

"I'm thinking to steal us some time," Mickey replied curtly. "For, as Kelsey said, the rains won't be lasting too long."

Baron Pwyll came in then, looking thoroughly exhausted and perfectly hopeless. He grabbed a stool and brought it near the companions' table, then paused, as if awaiting permission to sit down. Kelsey shifted his own seat and motioned for the Baron to join them.

Pwyll's account of the progress in the town was bleak indeed, and the Baron informed them that Robert had been seen again, flying from the east to a roost in the mountains north of Braemar. "As soon as the rains end," the Baron reasoned grimly, meaning that there was no doubt but that the angry dragon would return.

Geno sent a stream of thick spittle splattering to the floor. "Round them up, then," he growled, at Mickey and at Kelsey. "I'll find you a hole—little good it will do you when Robert comes a-calling!"

The dwarf's last grim statement was true enough, they all knew, but the simple fact that Geno had made the concession at all brought smiles to the faces of both the elf and the leprechaun. Gary, too, gained some hope, and some faith in his stocky companion. For all the dwarf's gruffness, Gary liked Geno, and the dwarf's refusal to open his home to people in such dire need had disheartened the young man profoundly.

Kelsey quickly explained their plan to Baron Pwyll.

"We will be ready to leave before nightfall," the Baron promised hopefully, and he rushed out of the tavern soon after, to speak with Badenoch and make the necessary arrangements.

"It's a short-term fix," Mickey offered after a short period of silence. "And not to last the length o' time we're needing."

"I should have let Ceridwen out," Gary said.

"Ceridwen wouldn't be helping us any," Mickey answered.

They all sat quietly for a few minutes, pondering their predicament. Again, Mickey was the first to speak. "Ye'll not be taking the sword along for the walk," he said to Gary. "Suren it's a torch on a dark night to Robert's eyes, and if ye bringed it in the caves, the dragon'd find the folk soon enough."

Gary narrowed his eyes and ran his hand through his matted, straight black hair, digesting the information. "How is it a torch on a dark night?" he asked.

"I told ye before," Mickey replied. "Dragons know their treasures, and I'd put that sword's value above any other treasures that Robert holds—to Robert, anyway. He can smell the damned thing a hundred miles away, I tell ye."

"Then why did you bring it?" Geno growled at the leprechaun.

In response, Mickey looked to Gary, laying the blame where it surely belonged.

"I knew that we'd have to fight the dragon, sooner or later," Gary replied with some confidence, for he was beginning to formulate a crazy and desperate plan. "I figured that the sword would be the bait we needed to get Robert on our own terms.

"Are you sure that Robert will come for this?" he asked Mickey.

"Like a babe to its mother," the leprechaun replied.

"We have to count on that," Gary said evenly.

"I can use me magic to set the sword a-singing," Mickey said, but it was obvious that the leprechaun wasn't thrilled with his own idea. And who could blame him? Not many would willingly call an outraged wyrm, especially one as powerful and wicked as Robert.

Gary didn't quite understand what the leprechaun was talking about, but he figured that Mickey meant that he could somehow enhance the sword's signals to its hunting master. He had to let it go at that, at least for the time being, for the plan was flooding his thoughts then, and he had to speak it out loud so that he and his friends might help him sort through it.

Geno scoffed and Kelsey shook his head, his lips tight with obvious doubts. Mickey listened impassively, seeming more polite than interested, and only Gerbil, the gnome inventor who understood the possibilities of precise measurements, leaned forward in his chair, certainly intrigued.

Gary fought off all interruption attempts by Kelsey, and especially the doubting dwarf, attempts that came less and less as he stubbornly went through the mechanics of his plan.

"Oh, begorra," the leprechaun sighed when Gary had at last finished speaking. Mickey looked around to the others, Gerbil smiling widely, Geno eyeing Gary doubtfully, and Kelsey sitting back in his chair, his slender arms crossed over his chest and his magnificent golden orbs staring blankly off into space.

Apparently sensing the leprechaun's gaze, the elf turned to eye Mickey directly and offered a shrug.

"Might be that we've got nothing better," Mickey admitted, turning to Gary.

Not so long afterwards, Kelsey and Gerbil, atop the pony, charged out of Braemar, running fast to the north. Normally it would take four days of hard riding to make the trip from Braemar to Gondabuggan, but Kelsey had promised his friends that he would make it within two, despite the deepening mud.

Mickey, Gary, Geno, and Pwyll watched him go, the fat Baron shaking his head doubtfully, not fully understanding what the unpredictable and dangerous friends were up to. To Pwyll's thinking, splitting the forces in such dark times was not a wise move.

"And now where are you three off to?" he demanded, for it was obvious that the remaining companions were packed for the road.

"Kelsey said two days," Gary said to Mickey, both of them ignoring the Baron. "So in two days, you'll use your magic to start the sword singing."

"It'll hum a merry tune," Mickey assured him.

"I had thought that you would be helping me to make the move," Pwyll firmly interrupted. "The people of Braemar . . ."

The folk'll get out on their own, don't ye doubt," Mickey interrupted, his tone casual. "And Geno's kin'll point them right." The leprechaun paused then, and scratched at his brown-and-gray beard, eyeing Pwyll all the while.

"What?" the anxious Baron demanded.

"Ye know, lad," Mickey said coyly to Gary. "I'm thinking that yer plan's to work—of course, it has to work, or nothing else is worth talking about. But I'm thinking beyond that plan o' yers, lad, thinking to what gains we might be making for the trouble that's sure to come even if old Robert is dead and gone."

The leprechaun's mischievous gaze then descended over Pwyll, with Gary and Geno gradually understanding and following the lead.

"What?" the Baron demanded again, looking from one hungry gaze to the other and wondering if he should, perhaps, turn tail and run off to find Badenoch.

"How are ye at mountain hiking?" Mickey asked.

IT rained for the remainder of that day, and all night as well. The soggy companions, trekking gingerly but determinedly along slippery mountain trails, found the sky brightening the next morn, a sign that brought mixed emotions.

"Suren the wyrm's rested by now," Mickey reasoned, looking back ominously along the trails towards distant Braemar. Then the leprechaun looked up to the gray sky, the overcast fast thinning. "We've another few hours of rain, and then Robert'll be hitting the town all in a fury."

Baron Pwyll groaned, a common sound to the companions. Pwyll had argued to his last breath with Badenoch that he should remain with the townspeople, and not go running off on some wild adventure into the mountains. But Mickey and Gary had gotten to Badenoch first, and the leader of Braemar would hear nothing of "holding back the valiant Baron of Dilnamarra." Still, even with none listening to his whining arguments, it took a dwarfish hand tugging Pwyll by the ear to get his feet moving on the first part of the trip, the trail from Braemar into the foothills. To Pwyll's credit, after that he had kept the pace fairly well, but now, in the uncomfortably humid and warm air as the sun tried to bake its way through the stubborn clouds, the overweight man was sweating profusely, huffing and puffing with every step.

"At least the people won't be there when the dragon arrives," Gary added hopefully.

"Aye, but the wyrm'll fast figure the truth of it," Mickey said. "Then Robert'll go a-hunting. Even with all the rain, the dragon will sniff them out for sure."

Gary cupped a hand over his eyes to diminish the glare as he stared up into the thinning overcast. "A few hours?" he asked.

"If you care as much for the folk of Braemar as you make out, then you'll get your legs walking faster!" Geno, who had spoken very little since they had set out the day before, said unexpectedly, poking a stubby finger into Pwyll's ample behind. "I can get us to the spot in a few hours," the dwarf explained to Mickey and Gary, "but not if this one's meaning to stop every twenty steps for a rest!"

Mickey started to respond, words of comfort to Pwyll, it seemed, but Gary cut him short. "Go on, then," the young man said to Geno. "The Baron will keep up—or he will be left behind."

"Left behind?" Pwyll cried out. "In these perfectly awful mountains?" The Baron sucked in his breath immediately, realizing that it was not so wise a thing to insult Dvergamal in the presence of a dwarf.

"How would you like to take a perfectly awful flight?" Geno grumbled.

"Left behind," Gary said more forcefully, drawing a surprised "Oo" from Mickey. "I value the lives of the more than two hundred fleeing Braemar over the safety of a single man, even a Baron." Unblinking, uncompromising, Gary looked over to Geno and said, "Go."

The dwarf's stout legs churned powerfully, sending Geno rolling along at a great pace. They had been traveling a narrow path around the girth of a wide mountain, but now Geno led them straight up its side, then into a ravine, and up a wall across the way, this one almost sheer. They had no ropes, but Geno led the way, speaking to the stones and then jabbing his granite-hard hand straight into the rock wall, leaving a ladder of hand- and footholds for his companions to utilize. Despite the bulky armor, and the weight of Mickey, Gary went on tirelessly, hand over hand, reminding himself every few feet not to look down. Baron Pwyll came far behind, had managed to climb just a few rungs before he eased himself back down and announced that he simply could not go on.

"Carrying fat Barons will surely slow me down!" Geno growled, regarding the man, now a hundred feet below them.

"Leave him," Gary said firmly. "His chances here will be no worse than his chances beside us!" Mickey started to protest, but Gary's last statement, so terribly true, locked the leprechaun's words fast in his throat.

Geno yelled down directions to Pwyll, told him to follow the raving to the north, then fork to the east, where he would find a rocky vale below the intended pass. The Baron called up some typical complaints, but the friends, nearing the top of the climb, weren't listening. Just over the lip, Geno led them into a tight and dark cave, and Mickey put up a ball of faerie light as he and Gary followed the dwarf in.

Geno looked back at the sprite, scowling, and Mickey remembered how Geno felt about lights of any kind in his dark caverns.

"We can't be running along in the dark," the leprechaun reasoned, and the dwarf snorted and led on, and both Gary and Mickey were surely relieved.

They exited the tunnel more than an hour later, coming to a high and flat rock that afforded them a panoramic view of the region south and east. The sun was beaming by then, the overcast fully burned away.

Lines of gray smoke drifted lazily into the air far to the southeast, painfully visible though the companions were more than twenty miles from Braemar.

"Alas for the Snoozing Sprite," remarked Geno, honestly wounded.

"Ye can't get a log wet enough to resist dragon fire," Mickey added grimly.

Even as they watched, another stream of smoke came up, rising to mesh with the unnatural cloud hanging over the ruined town. All three winced, Mickey shaking his head and Geno squeezing a rock that he held in his hand into little pieces. Gary, though, after his initial shock, found some welcome information in the newest column, for the smoke told him beyond doubt that Robert was still over the town.

"How far are we from the pass?" he asked Geno.

"An hour's walk," the dwarf replied.

"Half an hour's run," Gary corrected. He turned a wistful grin on Mickey.

"Lad, what're ye smiling about?" the leprechaun wanted to know.

"Set the sword to singing," Gary replied. "Let's pull Robert away before he can find the villagers' trail."

"We don't even know that Kelsey and the gnome have got to Gondabuggan," Mickey argued. "We can't go calling the dragon until we know!"

Gary understood the logic, understood that to call the dragon now would be gambling the lives of Braemar's folk against the entire success of his plan, against the potential for a complete disaster. But Gary wouldn't sit by and watch any more of Faerie's fine people be slaughtered. This was his plan, he trusted in Kelsey, and he was in a gambling mood.

"Do it," he said.

Mickey looked to Geno for some answers, but the dwarf just looked away. From the beginning, Geno had made it clear that he was their guide and nothing more, that he would be long gone into deep caverns at first sight of the wyrm.

Mickey let out a heaving breath, then reached down Gary's back to touch the hilt of the huge sword. He uttered an enchantment over the blade and tapped his finger atop the hilt.

"We'd best be running," Mickey said to Gary.

"Will the dragon hear it?" Gary asked.

"Already has," the sprite answered grimly.

Gary turned back to say some word of encouragement to Geno, and saw that the dwarf was off and running along the trail.

They came to the spot some time later with no sign of the dragon yet evident. Gary considered the layout of the place carefully, trying to fathom how he could choreograph this delicate situation. Geno showed him the marks he was looking for, deep scratches and scorches along the wall of stone. A wry smile crossed Gary's face when he noticed that this spot was conveniently located above a flat area that would serve as a perch, even for a beast as large as Robert. Gary pointed this out to the dwarf, then handed over the sword.

Taking the weapon, Geno scrambled up some stones and onto the intended perch. He moved under great hanging slabs of stone, resembling the enormous front teeth of some gigantic monster, but if the dwarf cared that tons of rock were hanging precariously above his head, he did not show it. Holding the sword out before him (he couldn't even reach the crosspiece to the hilt with its tip poking against the stone), Geno closed his eyes and began to chant quietly, a grumbling, grating sound, as though he was talking to the mountain itself.

And he was. A moment later, the dwarf gently pushed the weapon down, the stone simply parting around the blade as it sunk deeper and deeper. When Geno had finished, only the hilt and a couple of inches of steel showed above the flat area.

Mickey, meanwhile, had not been idle. Peering to the north and east, the leprechaun pulled out his umbrella and floated high into the air. He extended the fingers of his free hand and uttered a fast chant. Sparks erupted from Mickey's fingertips, drawing green and red lines in the air. He kept up the display for several seconds, then fell quiet, feeling incredibly vulnerable hanging in midair, with a flying dragon almost surely on the way.

"Come on, then," Mickey whispered to himself, peering towards distant Gondabuggan, and then all around anxiously.

A silver flash showed in the far distance, once and then again.

Mickey's smile took in his prominent ears. He snapped his umbrella shut and dropped like a stone, to be caught by a surprised Gary Leger.

"Kelsey got there, laddie!" the sprite cried. He grabbed Gary's ears and pulled him close, giving him a kiss on the cheek. "Oh, he got there!"

The mirth was stolen a split second later, by a roar that only a dragon—only a tricked and robbed dragon—could make.

"Time to go," proclaimed the dwarf, and, true to his word, Geno hopped down from the small plateau, rushed up to an opposite mountain wall and called to the stone. What had seemed just a small crack widened suddenly, and the dwarf, with a look back to Gary and Mickey, prudently stepped in.

"If you get killed," he offered hopefully to Gary, and he paused, as if fumbling to think of something positive to say. "Well, stonebubbles, then you'll get killed!" Geno bellowed, and he was gone and the stone snapped shut behind him.

"Loyal bunch, them dwarfs," Mickey said dryly. "But Geno would let us in, lad, if ye've changed yer mind."

That was among the most tempting offers Gary Leger had ever heard—and it only got more tempting when another roar, a closer roar, echoed off the mountain walls.

Gary shook his head resolutely. "We've got to do this," he said, reminding himself privately that he was part of something bigger, that there was a point to this that transcended his own mortality.

Another roar sounded, seeming to come from just beyond the next ridge.

Gary Leger set Mickey down on the ground and took up his spear. He hadn't come this far to turn and run at the moment of truth.

TWENTY-THREE
Precisely Overpacked

ROBERT cut around jutting rocks, flying low and fast through rugged Dvergamal. The dragon sensed the magic of his missing sword, as though the weapon was crying out to him, crying out against the thieves who had dared to steal it away. Robert knew these thieves, had smelled their too-familiar scent when he had returned to his lair. If that scent wasn't enough of a clue, the missing pot of gold certainly was.

Now he would find the miserable leprechaun and his companions, find them and melt them away with all his fiery fury.

He came up over one low peak, then dropped fast into a ravine. He thought he saw some movement below—a large man scrambling—but he whisked away overhead, compelled by the calling sword.

Then Robert saw it, held aloft proudly by the man, Gary Leger from Bretaigne, with that miserable rat Mickey McMickey sitting on the ground beside him, counting the pieces of gold in his retrieved pot.

How dare they! the dragon fumed. Standing tall and proud on an exposed ledge, so open, so vulnerable to Robert's wrath. Their impudence drove the dragon on with all speed. He swooped high and issued a tremendous roar, then stooped powerfully and loosed his killing breath.

To Robert's horror, both his sword and the pot of gold melted beside the thieves. The dragon started to bellow out a denial, and only then realized that he had been lured by a simple leprechaun illusion. Robert blinked his reptilian eyes, looking closer, as his dive brought him beyond the area, and there was only the empty high ridge, scorched by his fires, some of the stone bubbling still.

"I know you are near!" the dragon bellowed. "I will tear down the mountain," he promised.

For Gary Leger, looking up at the not-so-distant wyrm, seeing the unbridled fury and the bubbling stone, Robert's last words did not sound like any idle threat.

According to the plan, Gary had to call out, and Mickey, invisible in a deep nook behind him, prodded him to do so. Gary rationally reminded himself that he must, that Robert's fiery display had surely been seen across the miles and the plan had already been set fully into motion. But at that time, mere logic seemed a useless tool for Gary Leger in his battle against the plain horror of the dragon.

"Here," he started to say, but his voice cracked and he had to stop and clear his throat.

Robert banked sharply and rose straight up, breaking his momentum, his long neck snapping about so that he could look in the direction of Gary's meek call.

"Over here," Gary called again, more firmly. He stepped out from around a boulder, coming into a flat stone clearing just below the plateau that held the dragon's dwarfish-stuck sword.

Robert came in slowly, making an easy pass, eyes narrowed that he might better study the young thief. He noticed his sword, then, and issued a long and low growl.

"What tricks have you left, young thief?" he asked from on high.

"The deception was necessary," Gary replied, trying to hide his relief that the dragon had actually paused long enough to speak with him.

Wind buffeted Gary as Robert did as close to a hover as a massive dragon could.

"Of course, mighty Robert could fly past and burn us away," Gary went on, speaking quickly and glancing somewhat nervously to the northeast. "But that would ruin what you came to retrieve."

"What you stole!" Robert corrected.

"That, too, was necessary," Gary quickly continued, before the dragon's ire could gain momentum once more. "Stole, yes, but not to keep. You may have your sword back, mighty Robert." He held his hand out towards the embedded weapon and, to his relief, the dragon plopped down behind it, eyeing it curiously, suspiciously.

"It was I who took the dagger," Gary explained, his hand dramatically banging against his chest. His tone changed, deepened, as he recited the words, as though he was some actor in a grand Shakespearean production. "The dagger that allowed you to escape the terms of banishment."

"Again, a theft!" Robert interrupted, his drool sizzling from the edges of his dagger-lined maw.

"Again, necessary!" Gary shouted back, pointing an accusing finger the wyrm's way. "How else might I have lured Robert from his lair? How else might I have found the challenge that I deserve and demand?"

Robert's great head moved back, a clear signal that the dragon was somewhat confused.

"Did you think that I had come all the way from Bretaigne simply to play lackey to an overly proud elf?" Gary asked incredulously. "Of course I did not! It was my desire to see the spear reforged," he admitted, holding the magnificent weapon aloft. "But it was my greater desire to view mighty Robert, the legendary wyrm, whose reputation has come to all lands."

Gary sighed deeply, and snuck another glance to the northeast. What is taking so long? he wondered.

"I have defeated every knight in my land in honorable combat," Gary went on. "I have defeated the dragon of Angor."

"Where is Angor?" Robert demanded.

"It is an island," Gary replied quickly, trying not to get caught in his sticky web of lies.

"I know of all dragons," Robert sneered. "Yet I know not of any island called Angor!"

"A small dragon, he was," Gary stuttered. "Certainly of no measure against Robert the Wretch . . . Robert the Righteous."

The dragon chuckled, a curiously evil sound, at the apparent slip of the tongue. Old Robert knew well enough what the peoples of the land called him.

"I am Gary Lager of Bretaigne," Gary cried suddenly, proudly. "And I make my challenge against Robert honorably. Will you fight with me, mighty dragon? And will you withhold your killing breath?"

"Withhold my breath?" the dragon echoed incredulously, and Gary thought that the game was up, thought that Robert would fry him then and there.

"Unless you are afraid," Gary stammered. Again, he looked nervously to the east. "I have brought your sword, and the spear which I took from Dilnamarra. I had thought . . ."

"Behold Robert!" the dragon bellowed, and Gary's ears hurt from the volume. "He who killed a hundred men on the pass at Muckworst. He who cowed the painted savages of the Five Sisters, and who brought the humanoid newts under his protective wing. He who . . ."

The dragon's list of accomplishments—mostly horrible accomplishments—went on for many minutes. Gary was glad for the delay, but wondered what in the world was taking so long.

"Easy, lad," Mickey whispered from his hiding place behind Gary, sensing the man's distress. "These things take time."

Robert stopped suddenly, bellowed again—it seemed as if he was in some pain. And then, before Gary's incredulous stare, the dragon began to transform. He rolled his great wings in close to his sides, where they melded with his red-gold scales. His long neck contracted, as did his tail, and all his great dragon form hunched down and began to shrink.

The marks on the wall behind him became visible to Gary, and the young man nearly fainted.

Then Robert, the great red-bearded human, grasped the huge pommel of his stuck sword. Corded muscles flexed and tugged, and the stone itself groaned in protest.

Robert let go and rubbed his hands together, then grasped the hilt and tugged again, with all this strength. Amazingly, the stone held fast; the sword would not come free.

"What trick is this?" the dragon growled at Gary.

Gary shrugged helplessly, as surprised as Robert. "I did not think the simple dwarfish magic would prove the stronger," he said, slyly putting his emphasis on the word "simple."

Robert's eyes flared dangerously. "Stronger?" the dragon echoed. "Let us see who is the stronger!"

Gary was glad for Robert's roars in the ensuing moments, as the wyrm reverted to his gigantic dragon form, for they covered the man's heaving, relieved breaths.

"They better hurry," Gary managed to remark privately to the hiding leprechaun.

There came no reply, and Gary was surprised only for the instant it took him to realize that the leprechaun, having lost faith in the plan, had slipped away for safer parts.

When Gary turned back to the higher plateau, he was facing the mighty dragon again, Robert the Wretched in all his evil splendor.

"Let us see who is the stronger!" Robert roared again. "I will melt the stone away, and then hack you down, foolish Gary Leger of Bretaigne."

Gary nervously clutched tightly to his spear, and the dragon, noting the movement, actually laughed at him.

"Would you like an open throw?" Robert invited, arcing his wings back and sticking his massive, armored chest out towards Gary.

"Throw, then, feeble human!" the wyrm invited. "A clear shot, but one that will do you no good. Do you believe that your puny weapon, though it be the most powerful in all the land, could bring harm to Robert?"

The dragon laughed again, his rumbling shaking the mountain stones, and Gary had no response, could find no words at all in the face of his terrible predicament.

"Shield your eyes from my breath," the dragon warned. "And make peace with whatever god . . ."

A hissing, whistling sound stopped Robert short. "What?" he demanded, turning his gaze, as Gary had turned his, to the northeast.

The M&M Delivery Ball, its cannon precisely overpacked to heave it at two hundred and seventy-three miles per hour, soared into Buck-toothed Ogre Pass, caught the dragon at the base of his left wing, smashing his seemingly impenetrable scales to little pieces. The wyrm's evil face twisted in sheer disbelief in the split-second he remained on the ledge before the force of the blow sent him tumbling, serpentine neck over tail, into the canyon west of Gary's position. The very ground shook under Gary's feet, and the sound of the falling wyrm outdid any thunder the young man had ever heard.

Stones dropped down behind the falling monster, Robert's weight bringing about a small avalanche. But these mountains of Dvergamal were old and solid, and the upheaval died away to dusty stillness in a few moments.

"Oh, ye got him, lad!" Mickey cried, becoming visible and leaping out from his nook. A crack on the stone wall opposite the target plateau split wide, and out hopped Geno, shaking his head in disbelief, his gap-toothed smile, the look of a mischievous little boy, as wide as Gary had ever seen it.

"Bah, I knowed ye wouldn't be going too far!" Mickey roared at the dwarf.

Geno laughed aloud—the first time Gary had actually heard the dwarf do that—and, to Gary's surprise, it came out as the laughter of a little boy, not the grating and grumbling sound the young man would have expected.

"Suren the world's a brighter place!" Mickey squealed, hopping a little dance all about the high pass.

A roar from below stopped the leprechaun's quick-steps and erased Geno's smile.

Gary rushed the ledge and looked down. There flopped Robert, sorely wounded, with one wing wrapped all the way around his back and a huge garish wound running the length of his side. He thrashed and kicked among the boulder-strewn debris of his fall, tangled along a row of low mounds. The sheer violence of the dragon's actions split the stones apart, but caused more injuries from the flying debris to mighty Robert.

"We've got to finish him," Gary said to his companions, who had come up beside him.

Both Geno, and Mickey stared at the young man in disbelief. "You want to go down there?" the dwarf scoffed. Geno's face crinkled suddenly. "Oh," he said as if he had just remembered something. "The fat Baron's somewhere down there."

"Show me the path," Gary insisted, and Geno willingly obliged, pointing out a narrow trail leading down the canyon's side.

Gary spun to go, and bumped into a hovering dragon scale.

"Take it, lad," Mickey said grimly. "If ye're meaning to go. Take it and use it as a shield. Robert's hurt, but he's got his breath left, don't ye doubt."

Gary grabbed the thing out of the air, found it to be nearly as large as he, and wondered how in the world he was supposed to carry it along. He found it surprisingly light, though, and looking at Mickey, he understood that the sprite was still concentrating, still using his magic to partially levitate the thing.

Gary found a handhold along a crack on the back side of the scale, and, with a deep breath to steady himself and a silent reminder that they would never find a better chance to end this, he started off down the path.

"*Oh, valiant young sprout!*" came the expected call from the bloodthirsty spear.

"Oh, shut up," Gary mumbled back, feeling more stupid than brave and wanting nothing more than to wake up in the woods out back of his parents' home next to Diane.

Robert spotted him coming when he was halfway down the exposed trail. The wounded wyrm stopped its thrashing, its reptilian eyes narrowing to evil slits.

"Here it comes," Mickey whispered to Geno, and the leprechaun quickly ended his levitation of the scale and instead enacted an illusion to make Gary's position appear a few yards to the side.

Gary dropped the suddenly too-heavy scale-shield atop his foot, cried out in pain and fear, and fell back against the mountain wall behind the thing. Then he screamed in sheer terror as Robert's breath, the dragon not fooled by the leprechaun's illusion, completely surrounded him, licking at him from around the heavy scale.

Rock melted away; the hair on Gary's arm holding the shield disappeared, his skin turning bright red. He thought he was surely dying, then realized that he was falling, for the ledge beneath him had been burned to dripping liquid.

He crashed down among the stones, slamming hard, feeling as though he had broken every bone in his body, his lungs aching as though they would soon explode. His helmet flopped around so that he could not see, and he didn't want to see, expecting the dragon's great maw to fall over him, snapping him in half. He thought of the shield that had saved his life, but it was far gone, nowhere near the stunned man.

Gary lay dazed for a few moments, moments that passed too slowly, and then he realized that the dragon was crying out in pain. Gary slowly lifted his head and turned up the bottom of his backward helm. He saw Robert, thrashing again as a steady stream of hammers twirled through the air and banged against his unprotected, grievously wounded side.

The dragon's head came around to face the ledge, to face Geno and Mickey, and Robert hissed sharply, sucking in the air, fueling his inner fires.

A wall of protest rose within Gary Leger an outrage that stole his pain. He felt the spear lying beside him and grabbed it up, clambering to his feet and throwing aside his troublesome helm.

"No!" he cried, running as fast as he could go in the bulky armor. He went up the side of a mound and leaped ahead, spear extended as he flew for the dragon's throat.

The distracted Robert saw him coming at the last moment and tried to spin about as he loosed his fires. Gary was in under the line of the blaze, though, and then the huge tip of his powerful weapon was into the dragon's neck, caught fast under the creature's maw.

Gary felt the waves of energy running the length of the hungry weapon, coursing through its metal and into the roaring dragon. Robert thrashed about, sending Gary on a wild ride, back and forth. Up went the dragon's long neck, lifting Gary high into the air.

"Hang on!" the spear implored him, perhaps the most ridiculous request Gary had ever heard. Hang on? What the hell else was he supposed to do?

Then Gary felt a tingling rising from the bottom of his feet, like the pins and needles he might experience if he sat with his leg curled under him for too long. This tingling continued to spread, though, rising throughout his body, then leaving him altogether and, he somehow understood, climbing through the spear.

Robert screeched in pain, and Gary, to his own horror, came to realize what the sentient weapon had done. The spear was sucking out his very life force, converting it to energy and blasting it into the wyrm. And to Gary's further amazement, the ploy seemed to have had some effect. Down went the serpentine neck, bowed under the tremendous assault.

Gary felt his grip weakening, and suddenly he was flying free, crashing again against the rocky ground. It took him some time to reorient himself to his surroundings, some time to remember even that he was in big trouble.

When he finally looked back, he saw not a dragon, but a huge, red-bearded man, one arm hanging limply at his side, blood dripping from an open wound in his neck. Throaty growls erupted from Robert's bloody mouth as the beast stalked over and hoisted the fallen spear. Blue energy arced into Robert again, smoke rising from his hand and forearm.

On the ledge, Geno whipped his last hammer.

Robert only growled at the spear's impertinence, turned Gary's way, and lifted the weapon for a throw.

"Flee, young sprout!" came the call, and Gary understood that the sentient weapon could not match the dragon's willpower or sheer strength, and could not help him. Gary knew in that instant that he was doomed.

Robert's arm shot forward; the dwarf's hammer clipped his hand and the spear, and the throw went wild.

Robert looked incredulously to the ledge, then back to Gary. He gave an evil snarl and held aloft his working arm, clenching his hand so that his cordlike muscles bulged to superhuman proportions.

Gary nearly fainted. Robert would simply walk over and throttle him! Would just reach down and crush his skull as though it was some empty eggshell! Despair told Gary to lie back and close his eyes, get it over with as quickly as possible, but Gary, thinking once more of the fleeing folk of Braemar, of the carnage the dragon would soon cause, reacted explosively instead. He scrambled forward on all fours, got up to his feet just long enough to roll over one mound, then cut quickly to the side.

Robert did not hesitate, charging right for him.

With a wild leap, diving straight out, Gary got his fingers around the spear-shaft. He spun and came up to a sitting position, and the dragon-turned-man skidded to a stop barely inches from the waving weapon's tip.

Robert's surprise showed clearly on his face, an instant of hesitation, a slight and short-lived opening.

Gary lurched forward, tucked one foot under him, and pushed ahead with all his strength. The spear's tip slipped more than an inch into Robert's massive chest before the red-bearded man could clamp his hand onto its shaft, abruptly stopping its progress.

Robert and Gary stood facing each other, gruesomely joined by the metallic shaft, staring defiantly into each other's eyes.

Robert looked down to his newest wound. When he looked back, he was smiling evilly once more. "I will grind your bones," he promised.

Gary felt another tingle sweep through him, a pulse of energy that the spear had sent to blast the dragon's hand from the metallic shaft. Jolted and surprised once more, Robert reached back for the weapon immediately, but was too late to stop Gary's brutal surge.

"To make your bread?" the young man spat sarcastically, driving the enchanted spear through the dragon's heart.

Robert's breath went in, his chest heaving one final time. He grabbed up the stuck spear and yanked it free from Gary's grasp, stumbling back several steps.

"Well done," Robert offered, his tone full of surprise and admiration. He held in place for a long while, trembling, the shaft protruding from his muscled chest and quivering gruesomely, its end fast gaining with the wyrm's lifeblood.

And then the dragon who had terrorized the land of Faerie for centuries fell down and died.

Epilogue

"YOUNG *sprout.*" Gary heard the call in his mind, distantly, as though he himself was far removed from his own consciousness. It came again, and then a third time, leading him like a beacon back to the world of the living.

A myriad of pleasant aromas greeted him, and a thousand sounds, birds and animals mostly, and a quieter, more solemn humming that Gary knew somehow to be the song of the Tylwyth Teg.

Gary opened his eyes to the glory of Tir na n'Og. The sun was fast sinking in the west, but that did little to dull the vivid and beautiful colors of the magical forest. Mickey was beside Gary, and Kelsey, as well, along with the pony that had carried Kelsey and Gerbil to Gondabuggan, the valiant steed that had nearly given its life for the exhaustion. Like Gary, the pony was on the mend—who wouldn't be in the splendor of Tir na n'Og?

"Welcome back," Mickey said as Gary propped himself up on his elbows. He found that he was out of the armor, back in his clothes alone—and these had been sewn in several places to repair the tears and (Gary nearly fainted away again when he thought of this) dagger holes. The armor lay piled not far to the side, with the spear a short distance beyond it, leaning against a birch tree on the edge of the blueberry patch.

"How'd we get here?" Gary asked.

"We walked," Kelsey replied. "At least, some of us walked."

"Tommy carried ye, lad," Mickey added.

Tommy? It took Gary a moment to recognize the name, and then he glanced all around anxiously, dearly wanting to see his giant friend once more. "Where is he?"

"Not about," Mickey explained. "He and Geno went back to the east to prepare for the coming o' the witch."

Gary winced, and everything that had transpired over the last few days rushed back into his thoughts.

"Robert is dead?" he asked.

"*Of course,*" answered the cocky spear, from its perch against the birch tree.

"Aye," Mickey answered. "Ye sticked that one good."

"Does that mean that he's banished for a hundred years?" Gary wondered.

"Robert is no witch," Kelsey answered. "The dragon is simply dead."

"Aye, and a good thing for all the land," Mickey remarked. "We taked his horns, lad, and a few o' his teeth."

Gary's face twisted with confusion. The last he had seen, Robert was a man, and no horned monstrosity.

"Of course the wyrm went back to being a wyrm when he died," Mickey explained, understanding Gary's confusion. "His human form was magic, and no more."

"Then where are the horns?" Gary asked. "And what happened to Baron Pwyll?" he added, suddenly remembering that the man had been somewhere about the vale wherein Robert the Wretched had met his doom.

"The two go together," Mickey replied with a chuckle. "We gave the horns to Pwyll, for 'twas he who slew the wyrm."

"Pwyll?" Gary balked. "I killed . . ."

"Pwyll killed the wyrm," Kelsey interjected. "For the good of Faerie."

Gary started to protest again, but stopped, digesting Kelsey's last statement. Baron Pwyll had been branded an outlaw by the throne, and Dilnamarra, by all accounts a strategic position, had been given over to a puppet ruler. But if Pwyll could be manufactured into some hero, some dragonslayer . . .

Gary nodded. "For the good of Faerie," he agreed.

"We knowed ye wouldn't mind, lad," Mickey said cheerily. "Pwyll will return the missing spear and armor, and return as a hero."

The words led Gary's gaze back to the pile of metal. He could see that the magnificent armor was battered. One of the arm pieces lay in plain sight, its metal torn. Gary looked down to his own forearm and saw a similar scar. He realized that to be the broken place in the dragon scale shield, a crack that Robert's fiery breath had apparently slipped through.

"Don't ye fear for the armor," Mickey remarked. "The Tylwyth Teg'll clean it up good, and any dent it's got, it rightly earned."

"Cedric Donigarten would be truly pleased," Kelsey agreed.

"It will look better if I'm in it when Pwyll brings it back to Dilnamarra," Gary reasoned.

"Aye, ye might be right," Mickey replied. "But that cannot be, since ye're leaving now." Mickey glanced to the other side of the blueberry patch, where a group of fairies had gathered and were now forming into their dancing ring.

Not so long ago, particularly at the moment he was forced to face the dragon, Gary would have welcomed those words. Now, though, his emotions were truly mixed. How could he leave, he wondered, with Ceridwen about to come forth, especially since he had been the one to release her?

"No way," Gary remarked firmly. "This isn't over and I'm not leaving."

"But ye are, lad," Mickey replied. "The witch'll be free in the next season, but she'll find a different world awaiting her. The folk're rallying around the Baron, both here and in the east, and, don't ye doubt, Connacht will find a fight on their hands that Kinnemore and Ceridwen never expected."

"I should be here," Gary reasoned. Looking for some support, he sent his thoughts to the sentient spear, reminding the weapon that he was the rightful spearwielder and that it was the only weapon in all the land which could truly harm the witch. To Gary's dismay, no reply came forth, and he could sense that the spear had broken off contact, even the continual subconscious contact, altogether.

"Ye go back to yer own place," Mickey said. "Who's knowing how long our next war will run? Ye've a life, don't ye forget, a life beyond the realm of Faerie."

For a moment, Gary couldn't decide if he wanted to remember that life or not. He was playing a monumental role here, in this land. He was the dragon-slayer; he was making a difference. What could he do in his own world to possibly make any difference?

But the line of reasoning inevitably led Gary to remember Diane, and his family. He made a difference to them.

In the end, it wasn't his choice anyway. Kelsey helped him to his feet and led him over to the dancing fairies.

"Go on, then," Mickey said, and it seemed to Gary as if the falsely cheery sprite was on the verge of tears.

"This is not finished," Gary said determinedly. "I should be here."

"Ye never know what the wind will blow," Mickey answered with a smirk. "Now get yerself in the ring, lad, and go back where the fates determined ye belong."

Gary stepped in and sat down. He looked back to his friends and saw that Mickey had popped his long-stemmed pipe into his mouth. The fairy song compelled Gary to lie down, then, and close his eyes, and he fell asleep with that peaceful vision still in mind.

WHEN Gary woke up, he found that he had left the realm of Faerie, but not the soreness of his exploits, behind. He was in the woods out back of his parents' house again, up in the blueberry patch, with the sky in the east growing lighter shades of blue.

"Diane," he breathed, and he rushed over the edge of the vale, heading for the mossy banking. To his utter relief, he found Diane sleeping still, groaning and stretching and about to awaken with the approaching dawn. Gary skittered down the hill and fell into place beside her, closing his eyes and pretending to be asleep.

Diane woke with a start, and looked all around, her face crinkling disgustedly. "Hey!" she said, and she punched Gary hard in the shoulder, then put her hand up to cover her nose. "I can put up with morning breath, but . . . did you get sprayed by a skunk or something?"

Gary opened his eyes and regarded her curiously, then took the moment to sniff at his armpit. He nearly fell over backwards. "No, just breathed on by a dragon," he replied with a chuckle.

Diane punched him again. "You must have been dreaming and kicking," she reasoned.

You run around for a week in heavy armor, under a summer sun and through soaking rains, Gary thought privately, and let's see how wonderful you smell! To Diane, he simply offhandedly replied, "Maybe."

Diane waved a hand in front of her face. She stopped short, though, her eyes locked on Gary's hip.

"What?" he asked, and when he looked down, he got his answer. Across the side of his cotton shirt was a long stitch line.

"What happened to that?" Diane asked.

"It's an old shirt," Gary stammered, trying to tuck it in quickly and put the stitch line out of sight. Diane grabbed it from him and tugged hard, pulling the shirt all the way out and revealing, to her horror, the scar of a deep wound, a knife wound.

"What happened?" she demanded again.

"An old cut," Gary replied, though he, too, was obviously horrified to see the wicked scar.

"No, it's not!" Diane growled. "And don't you lie to me!"

"Do you think that you would believe the truth?" Gary replied evenly, his green eyes locking an unblinking stare into Diane's similar orbs.

She understood, then, remembered all that they had talked about, remembered the flowing script in *The Hobbit* and the tiny arrows on the windowsill. Gary had gone back!

"Don't ask," he said to her before her lips could form the obvious string of questions. "I don't believe it myself." Gary rolled to get up, and felt a lump in his pants pocket. He shifted and reached down, and produced a tooth, an incisor several inches long. He held it up, both his and Diane's expressions full of disbelief.

"Lion?" she asked, her eyes wide.

Gary shook his head slowly and corrected her.

"Dragon."

Dragonslayer's Return

To Susan Allison,
my editor, my friend,
with all my thanks for letting me write this tale,
so very dear to me, and with the sincere hope
that we will work together again

Prelude

THE October wind bit hard, tossing leaves, yellow and brown and red, into a swirling vortex and sweeping them past the man standing solemnly at the top of the hill, near to the road and the spiked green fence that marked the boundary of the cemetery. Cars buzzed along Lancaster Street just beyond that fence, the bustle of the living so near to the quiet cemetery. White flakes danced in the air, an early-season flurry. Just a few flakes, and fewer still ever seemed to reach the ground, carried along on the wind's continual ride.

Gary Leger, head bowed, hardly noticed any of it, the snow, the wind, or the cars. His black hair, longer now than usual for lack of attention, whipped about into his stubbly face, but that, too, he didn't notice. The *feel* of the day, that classic New England autumn melancholy, was in Gary, but the details were lost—lost in the overwhelming power of the simple words on the flat white stone set in the ground:

Pvt. Anthony Leger

Dec. 23, 1919–June 6, 1992

World War II Veteran

That was it. That was all. Gary's dad had spent seventy-two years, five months, and fifteen days alive on this Earth, and that was it.

That was all.

Gary consciously tried to conjure memories of the man. He remembered the cribbage games, remembered the great blizzard of '78, when his dad, the stubborn mailman, was out at five in the morning, trying to shovel his car out of the driveway.

Gary snorted, a sad chuckle at best, at that recollection. The weatherman had forecasted a few inches, and Gary had awakened with the hopes that school would be canceled. Yeah, right. Gary peeked through the side of his shade, and saw that it had indeed snowed. Perspectives were all askew that February morning fifteen years before, though, and when Gary looked down to the driveway beneath his window, trying to gauge how much snow had fallen, all he saw was a black circle a few inches in diameter. He thought it was the driveway, thought his car, his precious '69 Cougar with the 302 Boss and the mag wheels, had been stolen.

Gary ran downstairs in just his underwear, screaming, "My car!" over and over.

The car was still there, the embarrassed young man soon learned, standing practically naked in front of his mother and older sister; the black spot he had seen was not the driveway, but the vinyl roof of his car!

And there was his father, stubborn Dad, at the end of the driveway, plunging the shovel upward—up above his shoulders!—into a snowdrift, trying to get his car out so that he could get to work. Never mind that the city snowplows hadn't even been able to climb up the Florence Street hill; never mind that the snowdrift went on and on, down the street and even down the main road.

Gary could see it all so clearly, could even see the cemetery, across the street and across their neighbor's yard. Even in that memory, Gary could see the statue marking his father's family grave, the virgin with her arms upraised to the gray sky.

Just like now. Just like forever. The plaque that marked his father's grave was a few feet behind that same statue, and Gary's eyes wandered to the virgin's back, followed its lines and upraised arms into the sky, full of dark clouds and white clouds, rushing along on the westerly breeze. Gary's chuckle was gone, replaced by a single tear that washed from his green eye and gently rolled down his cheek.

Diane, leaning on the car twenty feet away, noted the glisten of that tear and silently bit her bottom lip. Her eyes, green like Gary's, moistened in sympathy. She was helpless. Totally helpless. Anthony had been gone four months and in that short time, Diane had watched her husband age more than in the seven years they had been together.

But that was the thing with death, the helplessness. And as much as Diane felt it in looking at wounded Gary, Gary felt it ten times more in looking down at the simple words on the simple stone in the wind-strewn cemetery.

Gary had always been a dreamer. If a bully pushed him around at school, he would fantasize that he was a martial arts master, and in his mind he would clobber the kid. Whatever cards the real world had dealt to him, he could change his hand through his imagination. Until now, looking down at the grass covering his father.

There were no "conquering hero" daydreams for this reality.

Gary took a deep breath and looked back to the stone marker. He didn't come to the cemetery very often; he didn't see the point. He carried his father's memory with him every minute of every day—that was his homage to the man he had so loved.

Until June 6, things had been going well for Gary Leger. He and Diane had been married for almost two years, and they were starting to talk about children. Both were building careers, following the paths that society said was proper. They had lived with Gary's parents for a short while after their wedding, saving for an apartment, and had only been out on their own for a few months.

And then Anthony had died.

His time had come. That was the proper cliche for it, the most fitting description of all. Anthony had always been the most responsible of men; Anthony would dig at that towering snowdrift because by doing so, he was making progress towards fulfilling his responsibilities. That was Anthony's way. Thus, when Gary, the baby of the family, youngest of seven, had moved out of the house, Anthony's responsibilities had come to their end. His children were out and on their own; his daughters and his sons had made their own lives. The time had come for Anthony to sit back and relax, and pass the time in quiet retirement.

Anthony didn't know how to do that.

So Anthony's time had come. And though he felt none of the I-wish-I-had-told-him-while-he-was-alive guilt, for his relationship with his dad had been truly wonderful, Gary couldn't help thinking, in the back of his mind, that if he had stayed at home, Anthony would have stayed responsible. Anthony would have stayed alive.

Gary felt that weight this chill and windy autumn day. But more than that, he felt pure and unblemished grief. He missed his dad, missed having him down at third base, coaching softball, missed watching TV, sharing grumbling sessions at the always bleak daily news.

As that summer had began to wane, Diane had talked about children again, but her words seemed ultimately empty to Gary Leger. He wasn't ready yet for that prospect, for the prospect of having children that his dad would never see.

All the world was black to him.

All the world, except one sliver of hope, one memory that could not be dulled by any tragedy.

When the grief threatened to engulf him, overwhelm him and drop him listless to the leaf-covered ground, Gary Leger turned his thoughts to the mystical land of Faerie, the land of leprechauns and elfs, of a dragon he had slain and an evil witch who would soon be free—or perhaps already was free, bending the land's independent people under her iron-fisted rule.

Gary had been there twice, the first time unexpectedly, of course, and the second time after five years of wishing he could go back. Five years in this world had been just a few weeks in Faerie, for time between the lands did not flow at the same rate.

For a fleeting instant, Gary entertained a notion of somehow getting back to Faerie, of using the time discrepancy to come back to a living Anthony. If there was some way he could get back on the night Anthony's heart had stopped, some way he could be beside his father, so that he might call the emergency medics . . .

Gary dismissed the wild plan before it could even fully formulate, though, for he understood that the time discrepancy did not involve any backward time travel. Anthony was gone, and there was not a thing in all the world that Gary could do about it.

Still, the young man wanted to get back to Faerie. He wanted to get back to Mickey McMickey the leprechaun, and Kelsey the elf, and Geno Hammerthrower, surly Geno, the dwarf who never seemed to run out of fresh spittle. Gary had wanted to go back, off and on, in the four years since his last adventure, and that desire had become continuous since the moment he saw his dad lying on the hospital gurney, since the moment he realized that there was nothing he could do.

Maybe his desire to return was merely a desire to escape, Gary fully realized.

Maybe Gary didn't care.

ONE

Crumbling Bridges

THE three unlikely companions—leprechaun, elf, and dwarf—crouched behind a vine-covered fence, watching the ranks of soldiers gathering to the south. Five thousand men were in the field, by their estimate, with hundreds more coming in every day. Infantry and cavalry, and all with helms and shields and bristling weapons.

"Kinnemore's to march again," said Mickey McMickey, the leprechaun, twirling his tam-o'-shanter absently on one finger. Only two feet tall, Mickey didn't need to crouch at all behind the brush, and with his magical pot of gold safely in hand (or in pocket), the tricky sprite hardly gave a care for the clumsy chase any of the human soldiers might give him.

"Suren it's all getting tired," Mickey lamented. He reached into his overcoat, gray like his mischievous eyes, and produced a long-stemmed pipe, which magically lit as he moved it towards his waiting mouth. He used the pipe's end to brush away straggly hairs of his brown beard, for he hadn't found the time to trim the thing in more than three weeks.

"Stupid Gary Leger," remarked the sturdy and grumpy Geno Hammerthrower, kicking at the brush—and inadvertently snapping one of the fence's cross-poles. The dwarf was the finest smithy in all the land, a fact that had landed him on this seemingly unending adventure in the first place. He had accompanied Kelsey the elf's party to the dragon's lair to reforge the ancient spear of Cedric Donigarten, but only because Kelsey had captured him, and in Faerie the rules of indenture were unbending. Despite those rules, and the potential loss of reputation, if Geno had known then the ramifications of the elf's quest, from freeing the dragon to beginning yet another war, he wouldn't have gone along at all. "Stupid Gary Leger," the dwarf grumped again. "He had to go and let the witch out of her hole."

"Ceridwen's not free yet," Kelsey, tallest of the group—nearly as tall as a man—corrected. Geno had to squint as he regarded the crouching elf, the morning sun blinding him as if reflected off Kelsey's lustrous and long golden hair. The elf's eyes, too, shone golden, dots of sunlight in an undeniably handsome and angular face.

"But she's soon to be free," Geno argued—too loudly, he realized when both his companions turned nervous expressions upon him. "And so she is setting the events in motion. Ceridwen will have Dilnamarra, and likely Braemar and Drochit as well, in her grasp before she ever steps off her stupid island!"

Kelsey started to reply, but paused and stared hard and long at the dwarf. Unlike most others of his mountain race, Geno wore no beard, and with a missing tooth and the clearest of blue eyes, the dwarf resembled a mischievous youngster when he smiled—albeit a mischievous child bodybuilder! Kelsey was going to make some determined statement about how they would fight together and drive Kinnemore, Ceridwen's puppet King, and his army back into Connacht, but the elf couldn't find the words. Geno was likely right, he knew. They had killed Robert the dragon, the offsetting evil to Ceridwen, and with Robert out of the way, the witch would waste little time in bringing all of Faerie under her darkness.

At least, all of Faerie's human folk. Kelsey's jaw did firm up when he thought of Tir na n'Og, his sylvan forest home. Ceridwen would not conquer Tir na n'Og!

Nor would she likely get into the great Dvergamal Mountains after Geno's sturdy folk. The dwarfish Buldrefolk were more than settlers in the mountains. They were a part of Dvergamal, in perfect harmony with the mighty range, and the very mountains worked to the call of the Buldrefolk. If Ceridwen's army went after the dwarfs, their losses would surely be staggering.

And so Faerie would be as it had once been, Kelsey had come to believe. All the humans would fall under the darkness, while the dwarfs and elfs, the Buldrefolk of Dvergamal and the Tylwyth Teg of Tir na n'Og, fought their stubborn and unending resistance. After quietly reminding himself of the expected future, the elf's visage softened as he continued to stare Geno's way. They would be allies, like it or not (and neither the dwarfs nor the elfs would like it much, Kelsey knew!).

A horn blew in the distant field, turning the three companions back to the south. A force of riders, fully armored knights, charged down onto the field on armored warhorses, led by a lean man in a worn and weathered gray cloak.

"Prince Geldion," Mickey remarked sourly. "Now I've not a doubt. They'll start for Dilnamarra all too soon, perhaps this very day. We should be going, then," he said to Kelsey. "To warn fat Baron Pwyll so that he might at least be ready to properly greet his guests."

Kelsey nodded gravely. It was their responsibility to warn Baron Pwyll, for whatever good that might do. Pwyll could not muster one-tenth the force of Connacht, and this army was superbly trained and equipped. By all measures of military logic, the Connacht army could easily overrun Dilnamarra, probably in a matter of a few hours. Kelsey's allies had one thing going for them, though, a lie that had been fostered in rugged Dvergamal. After the defeat of the dragon, Gary Leger had returned to his own world, and so the companions had given credit for the kill to Baron Pwyll. It was a calculated and purposeful untruth, designed to heighten Pwyll's status as a leader among the resistance to Connacht.

Apparently the lie had worked, for the people of Dilnamarra had flocked about their heroic Baron, promising fealty unto death. Connacht's army was larger, better trained, and better armed, but the King's soldiers would not fight with the heart and ferocity of Baron Pwyll's people, would not hold the sincere conviction that their cause was just. Still, Kelsey knew that Dilnamarra could not win out; the elf only hoped that they might wound Connacht's army enough so that the elves of Tir na n'Og could hold the line on their precious forest borders.

"And what of you?" Kelsey asked Geno, for the dwarf had made it clear that he would soon depart when this scouting mission was completed.

"I will go back with you as far as the east road, then I'm off to Braemar," Geno answered, referring to the fair-sized town to the north and east, under the shadows of mighty Dvergamal. "Gerbil and some of his gnomish kin are waiting for me there. We'll tell the folk of Braemar, and go on to Drochit, then into the mountains, me to my kin at the Firth of Buldre and Gerbil to his in Gondabuggan."

"And all the land will know of Ceridwen's coming," Kelsey put in.

"For what good it will do all the land," Mickey added dryly.

"Stupid Gary Leger," said Geno.

"Are ye really to blame him?" Mickey had to ask. Geno had always remained gruff (one couldn't really expect anything else from a dwarf), but over the course of their two adventures, it seemed to Mickey that the dwarf had taken a liking to Gary Leger.

Geno thought over the question for a moment, then simply answered, "He let her out."

"He did as he thought best," Kelsey put in sternly, rising to Gary's defense. "The dragon was free on the wing, if you remember, and so Gary thought it best to shorten Ceridwen's banishment—a banishment that Gary Leger alone had imposed upon her by defeating her," he pointedly added, staring hard Geno's way. "I'll not begrudge him his decision."

Geno nodded, and his anger seemed to melt away. "And it was Gary Leger who killed the dragon," the dwarf admitted. "As was best for the land."

Kelsey nodded, and the issue seemed settled. But was it best for the land? the elf silently wondered. Kelsey certainly didn't blame Gary for the unfolding events, but were the results of Gary's choices truly the better?

Kelsey looked back to the field and the swelling ranks of Ceridwen's mighty hand, an evil hand hidden behind the guise of Faerie's rightful King. Would it have been better to fight valiantly against the obvious awfulness of Robert the dragon, or to lose against the insidious encroachment of that wretched witch?

Given the elf's bleak predictions for Faerie's immediate future, the question seemed moot.

GARY'S first steps off the end of Florence Street were tentative, steeped in very real fears. He had grown up here; looking back over his shoulder, he could see the bushes in front of his mother's house (just his mother's house, now) only a hundred or so yards and five small house lots away.

The paved section of Florence Street was longer now. Another house had been tagged on the end of the road, encroaching into Gary's precious woods. He took a deep breath and looked away from this newest intruder, then stubbornly moved down the dirt fire road.

Just past the end of the back yard of that new house, Gary turned left, along a second fire road, one that soon became a narrow and overgrown path.

A fence blocked his way; unseen dogs began to bark.

Somewhere in the trees up above, a squirrel hopped along its nervous way, and the lone creature seemed to Gary the last remnant of what had been, and what would never be again.

He grabbed hard against the unyielding chain links of the fence, squeezing futilely until his fingers ached. He thought of climbing over, but those dogs seemed quite near. The prospect of getting caught on the wrong side of a six-foot fence with angry dogs nipping at his heels was not so appealing, so he gave the fence one last shake and moved back out to the main fire road, turned left and walked deeper into the woods.

Hardly twenty steps farther and Gary stopped again, staring blankly to the open fields on his right, beyond the chain-link fence of the cemetery.

Open fields!

This fence had been here long before Gary, but the area inside it, these farthest reaches of the cemetery, had been thickly wooded with pine and maple, and full of brush as tall as a ten-year-old. Now it was just a field, a huge open field, fast filling with grave markers. It seemed a foreign place to Gary; it took him a long time to sort out the previous boundaries of the cleared regions. He finally spotted the field where he and his friends had played football and baseball, a flat rectangular space, once free of graves and lined by trees.

Now it was lined by narrow roads and open fields, and rows of stone markers stood silent and solemn within its sacred boundaries. Of course, Gary had seen this change from the cemetery's other end, the higher ground up near the road, where the older family graves were located.

Where his father was buried.

He had seen how the cemetery had grown from that distant perspective, but he hadn't realized the impact. Not until now, standing in the woods out back. Now Gary understood what had been lost to the dead. He looked at the playing field of his youth, and saw the marker of his future.

Breathing hard, Gary pushed deeper into the woods, and could soon see the back of the auto body shop on the street that marked the eastern end of the trees. Somewhat surprised, Gary looked back to the west, towards Florence Street. He could see the light-shingled roof of the new house! And he could see the auto body shop! And across the open cemetery, across the silent graves, he could see the tops of the cars moving along the main road.

Where had his precious woods out back gone? Where were the thick and dark trees of Gary Leger's childhood eye? He remembered the first time he had walked all the way through these woods, from Florence Street to the auto body shop. How proud he had been to have braved that wilderness trek!

But now. If he and Diane had kids, Gary wouldn't even bother taking them here.

He cut left again, off the fire road and into the uncleared woods, determined to get away from this openness, determined to put all signs of the civilized world behind him. Up a hill, he encountered that stubborn chain-link fence again, but at least this time, no dogs were barking.

Over the fence Gary went, and across the brush, growling in defiance, ready to pound any dog that stood to block him. He was in the back lot of the state-run swimming pool, another unwanted encroachment, but at least this section of land hadn't been cleared. Beyond this stretch, Gary came into the blueberry patch, and he breathed a sincere sigh of relief to see that this magical place still existed, though with the trees thinned by the season, he could see yet another new house to the west, on the end of the street running perpendicular off the end of Florence Street. That road, too, had been extended—quite far, apparently. Now Gary understood where the dogs were kept chained, and predictably, they took to barking again.

Gary rubbed a hand over his face and moved across the blueberry patch, to the top of the mossy banking that settled in what was still the deepest section of the diminishing wood. Here, he had first met the sprite sent by Mickey McMickey, the pixie who had led him to the dancing fairy ring that had sent him into the magical land.

He moved down the steep side, out of sight of anything but trees, and re-moved his small pack, propping it against the mossy banking as a pillow.

He stayed for hours, long after the sun had gone down and the autumn night chilled his bones. He called softly, and often, for Mickey, pleading with the leprechaun to come and take him from this place.

No sprites appeared, though, and Gary knew that none would. The magic was gone from here, lost like the playing field of his youth, dead under the markers of chain-link fences and cement foundations.

TWO

Say It Loud and Say It Often

PRINCE Geldion stomped across the muddy field, cursing the rain, cursing the wind, cursing the night, and cursing the impending war. Head down and thoroughly consumed by his anger, the volatile Prince walked right into one guard, who started to protest until he recognized the perpetrator. Then the common soldier stood straight and silent, eyes wide and not even daring to blink or breathe!

Geldion's dark eyes bored into the frightened man, the Prince's well-earned reputation for ferocity making the look more ominous indeed. Geldion said not a word—didn't have to—just let his imposing stare linger over his shoulder as he sloshed away.

He wished a star would come out, or the moon. Anything but these clouds. Geldion hated riding in the mud, where with every stride his horse took he felt as if they would slip sideways and pitch over. And this coming ride would be forced, he knew, driven by his father's insatiable desire to put Dilnamarra under Connacht's widening thumb.

Dilnamarra, and all of Faerie. Kinnemore had always been ambitious and protective of his realm, but now those feelings had reached new heights. Geldion wasn't sure what had changed, beyond the reforging of Cedric Donigarten's spear and the slaying of the dragon. So Robert was gone, but when was the last time anyone had seen the wyrm out of his distant mountain hole anyway? And so the spear was whole, but who might wield it, and even if such a hero might be found, what grudge would he hold against Connacht? To Geldion's think-ing, the politics remained the same. Kinnemore was still King and as far as the

Prince knew, the people of all the communities still swore fealty to him. True, the army of Connacht, led by Geldion, had skirmished with the folk of Braemar and Drochit, but that had been an excusable faux pas, an indiscretion born on dragon wings as Robert the Wretched had terrorized the land. Diplomacy would certainly calm the realm and put all back in line.

That didn't seem good enough for King Kinnemore.

No, not Kinnemore, Geldion decided, and a hiss escaped his lips as he continued on his trek around the muddy perimeter of his encampment. Not his father, because his father made no independent decisions concerning the kingdom. Not anymore. This impending war was driven not from Connacht, but from Ynis Gwydrin, the Isle of Glass, the home of Ceridwen the witch.

"A place yous ne'er been," a raspy voice remarked, and the Prince skidded to a stop, went down into a crouch, and peered all around, his hand on the hilt of his belted dirk. A moment later, with nothing in sight, he straightened. A puzzled expression crossed Geldion's face as he came to realize that whoever, or whatever, had spoken to him had apparently read his mind.

Or had it been merely the drifting words of a distant, unrelated conversation?

"Nay, I was spaking to yous, Princes Geldion," the voice replied, and Geldion whipped out his dirk and fell back into the crouch once more.

"Above yous," croaked the voice. Geldion looked up to watch the descent of a bat-winged monkey, its torso nearly as large as his own and with a wingspan twice his height. The creature landed quietly in the mud before the Prince and stood at ease, showing no fear of or respect at all for Geldion's waving dirk.

"Who are you, and where are you from?" Geldion demanded.

The monkey bat smiled, showing a wicked row of sharpened fangs. "Where?" it echoed incredulously, as though the answer should have been obvious.

"Ynis Gwydrin," Geldion reasoned. He saw some movement to the side and behind the monkey bat, his soldiers rushing to the scene. As the creature chuckled its confirmation that it was indeed a messenger of Ceridwen, the Prince held up his free hand to keep the soldiers at bay.

"Come from Ceridwen for Geldion," the monkey bat rasped. "The Lady would see Geldion."

"I am to ride . . ." the Prince started to ask.

"To fly," the monkey bat interrupted and corrected. "To fly with me." It held out its clawed hands towards the Prince, inviting him into an embrace.

An involuntary shudder coursed along Geldion's spine, and he eyed the creature skeptically, not replacing his weapon on his belt. His mind soared down several possibilities, not the least of which was warning him that Ceridwen, sensing his doubts and his anger at his father, might be vying to get him out of the way. He didn't replace the dirk on his belt; he'd not walk into such a trap.

But the witch had apparently expected his resistance. There came a sudden flurry from above, and a second monkey bat dropped down atop the Prince's shoulders, clawed feet and hands catching a tight hold on Geldion's traveling cloak. Geldion was off the ground before he could react, and with the cloak bundling about his shoulders, his overhead chop with the dirk did little damage.

Soldiers cried out and charged; the first monkey bat leaped away, pounding wings quickly taking it above the reach of the soldiers' long pikes and swords.

Geldion continued to struggle, freed up one arm and half turned to get into a striking posture.

"Would yous fall?" came a question from the darkness, from the first monkey bat, Geldion realized.

Those sobering words forced the Prince to look down and consider his position. He was already fully thirty feet from the ground and climbing rapidly. He could stick his captor, but a wound on this monkey bat would result in a drop that was not appealing.

"The Lady would see Geldion," the first monkey bat said again, and off they soared, through the driving rain and wind. There were more than two of the creatures, the Prince soon learned; there were more than twenty.

Ceridwen was never one to take chances.

Half the army was roused by that time, torches sputtering to life against the rain all across the muddy field. Hosts of archers bent their great yew bows skyward. But the night was dark and their efforts futile. Word went immediately to Kinnemore, but the King, apparently not surprised by Ceridwen's visitors, brushed away his soldiers' concerns and bade them go back to their watch and their sleep.

PRINCE Geldion saw little from his high perch in the dark sky. Every so often, the winged caravan would pass over a hamlet nestled in the rolling fields east of Connacht, and the lights from windows would remind the abducted man of just how high he was.

Then the monkey bats fast descended, touching down on the wet grass, where they were met by a second group. Again the Prince was scooped up, and off the fresher couriers flew. There came a second exchange, and then a third, and not so long after that, with the sky still dark in the throes of night, Geldion saw great looming shadows all about him.

They had come to Penllyn, the mountainous region surrounding Loch

Gwydrin, the Lake of Glass. Geldion had never been here before—few had—but he knew many tales of the place. Everyone in Faerie had heard tales of the witch's home.

The sun was just peeking over the eastern rim, in their faces, as the troupe flapped through a pass between two towering peaks and came in sight of the still waters of the famed mountain lake.

Slanted rays touched upon its surface, turning the waters fiery golden. Geldion watched unblinking as the light grew and the scene unfolded. Ynis Gwydrin, the isle, came into sight, and then, the witch's castle, a crystalline palace of soaring spires that caught the morning light in a dazzling display of a million multi-colored reflections.

Despite his general surliness, and his more pointed anger at being abducted, the helpless Prince could not hide his awe at the magnificent sight. No tales could do Ynis Gwydrin justice; no paintings, no sculptures, could capture the magic of this place and this crystalline castle.

Geldion took a deep breath to compose himself, and to whisper a reminder that the magic of Ynis Gwydrin was surely tainted by danger. This was Ceridwen's island, Ceridwen's castle, and a single wrong word would ensure that he never left the place alive—at least, not as a human. Ceridwen had a reputation for turning people into barnyard animals.

With that disquieting thought in mind, Geldion stepped down onto the isle, on a stone path through the sand that led to the crystalline castle's towering front doors. The monkey bats herded him towards the door, and he offered no resistance. (Where did they think he might run?) At the portal, he was met by a group of goblins, ugly hunched creatures with sloping foreheads and overgrown canines curling grotesquely over saliva-wetted lips that seemed too stretched for their mouths. Their skin was a disgusting yellow-green in color and they smelled like raw meat that had been too long in the sun.

"Geek," one spindly-limbed goblin explained, poking a gnarly finger into its small chest. The goblin reached out to take Geldion's arm, but the Prince promptly slapped the dirty hand away.

"I can offer no resistance on Ynis Gwydrin," Geldion explained. "If you mean to lead me to Ceridwen, then lead on. Else move away, on threat of your life!"

Geek sputtered and shook his ugly head, muttering something uncomplimentary about "peoples." He mentioned the name of Ceridwen, his "Lady," as Geldion had expected, and motioned for the Prince and the goblin guards to follow.

Inside the castle, they moved swiftly along mirrored corridors, and Geldion soon lost all sense of direction. He didn't much care, though, for he had no expectations of escape. He was in the lair of mighty Ceridwen, the sorceress, and in here, he knew well, he could only leave when Ceridwen allowed him to leave.

Geek stopped at a large wooden door and tentatively clicked the knocker a couple of times.

Geldion understood the goblin's nervousness. The guards shuffled uneasily behind him, and he got the distinct feeling that they did not want to be in this place.

The door swung in, apparently of its own accord, and suddenly Geek and Geldion were standing alone in the corridor, for the other goblins had taken full flight back the way they had come.

A warm glow emanated from beyond the opened door, the tinge of an inviting, blazing fire. From the corridor, Geldion could see only a portion of the room. A pair of overstuffed chairs were set on the end of a thick bearskin rug, and rich tapestries hung on the far wall. One Geldion recognized as a scene of the court in Connacht, though the work was old and Geldion did not know any of the men and women depicted.

Geek nervously motioned for Geldion to lead the way. If the Prince held any doubts that Ceridwen was in there, they were gone now, considering the goblin's truly fearful expression. Geldion took a deep breath, trying to fully comprehend what was at hand. He had never actually met the witch, though he had spoken several times to the talking crows that were Ceridwen's messengers. His father certainly had sat with Ceridwen, on many occasions, but Kinnemore rarely spoke to anyone of the meetings.

Now Geldion was to meet her, face to face. He looked down at his muddy traveling clothes, realized that in the confusion of the dragon-on-wing and the skirmishes with the eastern towns, he hadn't bathed in several weeks.

Geek made a whining sound and motioned again, more forcefully, for the Prince to go in. Without further delay, proud Geldion obliged, stepping boldly into the room (though he winced a bit when Geek pulled the door closed behind him).

At the head of the bearskin rug was a small divan and next to it a tall woman, taller than Geldion, wearing a white gown that clung to her many curves like some second skin.

There she stood, the legendary sorceress, undeniably beautiful, unearthly beautiful, her hair the color of a raven's wing and her eyes the richest blue. A simple look from those penetrating orbs sent icy chills along Geldion's spine. He wanted to lash out at the witch and fall on his knees and worship her all at the same time. Kinnemore had revealed little about the woman after his meetings with Ceridwen, and suddenly Geldion understood why.

No words could truly communicate the imposing specter of Ceridwen, no words could accurately re-create the aura surrounding this beautiful and awful creature.

"My greetings, Prince Geldion," she said in the sweetest of voices. "It strikes me as odd that we have not met before."

"Lady Ceridwen," Geldion replied with a curt bow.

"Please, do sit down," the witch purred, and she moved to the front of the divan, her shapely legs appearing through a slit in the gown. She sat and stretched languidly to the side, tucking her feet up inside one of the divan's arms and resting her arm over the other.

Geldion never took his eyes off her (couldn't take his eyes off her) as he slid into an overstuffed chair.

"Did you enjoy the journey?" Ceridwen asked.

Geldion looked at her curiously, for a moment having no clue as to what she might be talking about. With a start, he suddenly recalled the monkey bats, and the extraordinary trip that had brought him to Ynis Gwydrin.

"I prefer to ride," he stammered, feeling positively stupid. "Of course, your . . ." He paused, searching for a word to describe the monkey bats. "Your creatures," he said finally, "were faster than any horse."

"I needed to see you this day," Ceridwen explained.

"Had one of your crows called, I would have come," the Prince started to reply.

"This day," Ceridwen said again, forcefully, coming forward in the divan, blue eyes flashing dangerously. Geldion squirmed and clenched the arms of his seat, and hoped that the witch had not noticed the tremor that ran along his backbone. Geldion had fought a dozen battles, had led his army into combat without hesitation against powerful foes, including giant mountain trolls. But he was scared now, more so than ever before.

"And of course, I cannot yet go out from my island," Ceridwen went on calmly, and to the Prince's profound relief, she rested back in the divan. "Else I would have come to you. That would have been easier."

Geldion nodded, again feeling small and stupid. Ceridwen seemed to sense his discomfort, and she smiled, but did not say anything for a long while.

Increasingly uncomfortable, Geldion cleared his throat several times. Why wasn't she talking? he wondered. She had been the one, after all, to convene this meeting. So why wasn't she talking?

A few more minutes slipped by, the witch relaxing comfortably, stretching her porcelain legs (and revealing more of them with every move), while her blue eyes scrutinized the Prince's every nervous shift.

"Why am I here?" Geldion finally blurred.

"Because I wished to speak with you," Ceridwen replied, and she went silent again.

"Then speak!" Geldion cried out another long minute later, and he regretted the outburst as soon as it had come forth, thinking that Ceridwen would probably strike him down with a snap of her fingers. And sitting in that room, Geldion held no doubts that, she was indeed powerful enough and wicked enough to do it!

But Ceridwen did not strike out at him. She merely laughed, heartily, and tossed her long mane of impossibly thick black hair back from her face.

Geldion had a sudden urge to fall on the floor and grovel before her, and the mischievous way she looked at him made him think that she recognized and understood—indeed, that she had purposely inspired—that urge. That realization gave the Prince the courage to withstand the mental assault, though his grip on the arms of his chair grew so tight that his knuckles whitened for lack of blood.

Ceridwen nodded a moment later, as if in approval that Geldion was still stubbornly in his seat.

"The army is gathered?" she asked unexpectedly, shattering the silence.

Geldion stammered, then nodded his head. "Ready to march to Dilnamarra," he replied.

Ceridwen nodded. "Why?" she asked.

Geldion looked at her curiously. Wasn't she the one behind all these plans of conquest? he wondered. "To put down any potential uprising," he answered. "The people are uneasy, speaking of old heroes and dragonslayers. King Kinnemore fears . . ."

Ceridwen cut him off with an upraised hand. "And where are you to go from Dilnamarra?" she prompted.

Geldion shrugged. "To Braemar, I would guess," he said. "And then to Drochit. If the three main villages can be put in line, then all the land . . ."

"And you will fight all the way?" Ceridwen again interrupted. "Your wake will be messy indeed, flooded with the blood of your enemies."

Geldion stroked his stubbly chin with his hand, not quite understanding.

"You do not approve of the plan for conquest," Ceridwen stated more than asked.

Geldion's eyes widened, and he worked hard to keep his breathing steady, wondering why, if Ceridwen knew his thoughts, she had not simply ordered her monkey bats to drop him to his death.

"Speak your thoughts without fear," the calculating witch prompted after a moment of silence, Geldion showing no inclination to respond to what he perceived as an accusation.

"Baron Pwyll slew Robert, so 'tis said," Geldion explained. "Or at least, he was among the group who slew the dragon. I do despise the fat man, but in the eyes of Dilnamarra's peasants, he is a hero. I do not like the prospects of killing a hero."

"Good," Ceridwen purred.

"What game do you play?" the frustrated Prince, growing bolder by the moment, asked bluntly.

Ceridwen sat up straight, and Geldion nearly lost his breath in surprise. The sorceress seemed suddenly tired of the whole affair. "The army goes to Dilnamarra," she said firmly. "But not for conquest."

"Then why?" Geldion was neither disappointed nor hopeful, just perplexed. He managed to sit back again and regain a bit of his calm.

"You go on the pretense of a ceremony for a hero," Ceridwen said. "Baron Pwyll cannot refuse."

Geldion scratched at his face yet another time, beginning to catch on.

"To let the people view the true hero of the day," Ceridwen continued.

"The true hero," Geldion echoed. "And not Baron Pwyll."

"To let them see King Kinnemore of Connacht," Ceridwen agreed, smiling widely. "The warrior who slew Robert."

Geldion's face crinkled with disbelief and Ceridwen laughed at him. Geldion only shook his head back and forth in reply, hardly believing what the witch was proposing.

"Of course they know the truth," Ceridwen declared. "But Pwyll, that cowardly Baron, will not disagree. He will proclaim your father as the dragonslayer, for all to hear."

Geldion was still shaking his head doubtfully.

"Kinnemore killed the dragon," Ceridwen insisted. "Pwyll will say so with the prospect of war on his doorstep. King Kinnemore will become the hero, and our army will already be in place in Dilnamarra. What then, will poor Baron Pwyll do?" the witch cackled.

"What indeed?" said Geldion, and he did not seem so happy.

"From Dilnamarra, we announce the treachery of Drochit and Braemar," Ceridwen went on, and Geldion was nodding before she even finished the thought, completely expecting it. "Dilnamarra will thus be forced into an unintentional alliance, and when we march to the east, Baron Pwyll will ride between you and your father at the head of the army."

Geldion was still nodding, but he was far from convinced. The plan seemed perfectly simple and devious, and if it worked, it would bring all the land under Kinnemore's thumb in a short time and with minimal fighting. Perfectly simple and perfectly devious, but Geldion noted one serious hitch that the supremely confident Ceridwen might have overlooked. The Prince suspected that there might be more to this fat Baron Pwyll, and to the people of the land, than Ceridwen believed. By all accounts, Pwyll had faced a true and huge and terrible dragon, and not only had survived, but had walked out victorious. And Pwyll had been present on those eastern fields, beside Lord Badenoch of Braemar and Duncan Drochit, when the armies had skirmished.

Ceridwen took no note of Geldion's sour expression. Her eyes held a faraway, glassy look, as though she was basking in anticipated conquests. She would be free soon, Geldion knew, and Robert would no longer oppose her. All the land would be Kinnemore's, and Kinnemore was Ceridwen's.

The witch snapped her fingers and the door swung open—and Geek, who had obviously been kneeling against the wood, trying to eavesdrop, stumbled into the room.

"Show the good Prince the way out," the witch purred, showing no concern for her overly curious attendant. "He has much to do."

Geldion remained silent for the rest of the time he was in the crystalline castle, and offered no resistance or no complaint when the monkey bats grabbed him up in their clawed hands and feet and set off from Ynis Gwydrin.

But Geldion was fuming, angry with Ceridwen and her malicious and dangerous plans, and, for some reason that he did not understand, Geldion was angry with his father. He had been anxious for the war, more than willing to take on the upstart Barons and put things aright. His father was the rightful King, and woe to those who did not profess undying fealty to the rightful King!

Suddenly, though, it seemed to Geldion that a righteous war had become a web of intrigue.

THREE

A Sense of History

"I told you we should have come here later in the summer," Diane complained halfheartedly. She brushed back her dirty blonde hair—which was shorter now, for she had gotten into one of her I-need-a-change moods and cropped it tight about her ears, leaving the front longer than the sides and back, as was the fashion—and blew a raindrop off the end of her nose.

"It'll be raining in the summer, too," Gary assured her. "This is England. It always rains in England."

Diane could hardly disagree. They had been in London for three days and had actually seen the sun on several different occasions. The brightness had been fleeting, though. Always another dark cloud rolled in from one horizon or the other, pelting them with a cold spring rain.

What made it worse was that Gary insisted that they always be outside. Diane could think of a hundred places to visit in London, most of them indoors, but Gary was too restless for such orderly sightseeing. He wanted to walk London's streets, and walk they did—to the palace, to the tower, to Big Ben and Parliament and Westminster Abbey. But even in Westminster Abbey, where one could spend an entire day just reading the tomb markers of the famous dead, Gary had been restless. They had spent no more than an hour inside, rushing over Charles Darwin's floor stone, sliding past the great ornate caskets of the kings and queens, of Elizabeth and Mary, ironically buried side by side, romping through Poet's Corner, where lay Geoffrey Chaucer and the Brontës, and a score of other writers whose works Diane and Gary had grown up with and come to love.

Diane could have spent the entire day and the day after that just sitting in Poet's Corner, thinking of those books and those writers, feeling their ghosts hovering about her and taking comfort in the perpetuity of the human condition.

So why were they outside and walking along the wet streets again? she wondered. And in a completely different section of London? Diane sighed and looked about, watched a black cab zip past at about fifty miles an hour on the wrong side of the street. To her right was a large brownstone building, another of London's many museums, she figured—not that she'd get to spend any time *inside* one!

Gary plodded along a few steps ahead of her, and Diane had the distinct impression (and not for the first time!) that he hardly noticed that she was even there. More than once in the last three days, Diane had wondered why Gary had asked her to come along, and why he had picked London for their yearly vacation. The thought of taking separate trips, something the young woman would never have dreamed of before, was beginning to sound appealing.

"What is it?" she asked, somewhat impatiently, when she caught up to Gary. He was standing in the middle of the uneven sidewalk, staring down at a small crater in the stone.

Gary pointed to the mark.

"So?"

"It's not new," Gary remarked. He bent down and ran his fingers around the smoothed edges of the hole. "This happened a long time ago."

"So?" Now Diane's tone showed that she was clearly growing flustered. "It's a hole in the sidewalk, Gary. It's a stupid hole in a stupid sidewalk, a hole that's filling up with rainwater."

Gary looked up at her, and the pained expression on his face, as though she had just insulted him profoundly, stole some of the drenched woman's ire.

"What do you think made this?" he asked.

"What do you think?" she echoed, not really in the mood for such games.

"A V-1 rocket?" Gary asked more than stated. A wistful smile came over his face. "It was, you know," he added: "Or some other German bomb from World War II."

"Am I supposed to feel guilty?" Diane asked sarcastically, wondering if Gary was snidely referring to her German heritage.

"No," he assured her, standing once more, "but do you feel . . ." He stopped and flapped his hands in frustration, as if he was trying to physically pull the needed word from his mouth.

"Feel what?" she asked impatiently.

"The history," Gary blurted. "The sense of history."

Diane sighed. "You don't know what made that hole," she reminded him, though she did not doubt Gary's claim of the German bombing and had, in truth, thought the same thing when she first saw the crater. "It could have been a car accident, or an IRA bomb from just a few years ago."

Gary was shaking his head.

"Besides," Diane went on stubbornly, "if you want a sense of history, then why did you rush us out of Westminster Abbey? You can't get more historical than that! Every king and queen from Britain's history, and the people who wrote their stories are buried in there. But here we are, out in the stupid rain, standing over a bomb hole in the sidewalk."

"That's different," Gary insisted, and he took a deep breath to clear his mind of the clutter. Diane did not seem convinced. "The history in there was our history," Gary explained deliberately. "Human history, purposely designed for us to go and see."

"Well then what's this?" Diane asked incredulously, pointing down at the crater. "Human history."

"It's not the same."

"Of course it's the same!"

"No!" Gary insisted. "It's . . . this wasn't put here on purpose, for us to look at it. This was an unintentional side effect of a historical event. No after-the-fact markers, just a moment in time, caught and preserved. It's like finding a dinosaur footprint out in the woods. That's different from going to a museum and seeing reconstructed bones."

"Okay," Diane readily conceded, still having no idea of the point of it all.

"That's why we're in London," Gary went on.

"I thought we were here on vacation," Diane quickly interjected, and though her words obviously stung Gary, he stubbornly pushed forward with his argument.

"That's why we're in England," he finished. "They've got more history here—without trying—than we can find back home."

"The United States was in World War II," Diane sarcastically reminded him.

Gary sighed and ran his hand over his cheek and chin. "But if we had any craters from German bombs, we would have filled them in," he lamented. "Like the Arizona Memorial at Pearl Harbor. We'd have built a bunch of new stuff around the site, explaining what happened in great detail, probably complete with movies you could watch for a quarter, instead of just letting the history speak for itself."

"I really don't know what you're talking about," Diane sighed. "And I'm really getting tired of walking in cold rain." She gave the crater a derisive look. "And you really don't know what made that," she added.

Gary had no retort; he just shrugged and started away, Diane loyally following. They soon found more craters—in the sidewalk and on the stone wall surrounding the large building—and then they spotted a small, unremarkable plaque set in the wall. It named this building as the Victoria and Albert Museum, and confirmed Gary's suspicions about the craters' origins, proclaiming that they were indeed a result of the German blitz.

The proclamation came as only a very small victory for Gary, though, for Diane still didn't understand the point of it all and didn't look too happy. He understood and sympathized with her disappointment. This was supposed to be their vacation—their one vacation of the year!—and he was dragging her around in the rain, searching for sensations that she didn't understand.

Gary, of course, had not come to England to see the typical sights. He had come in search of something more elusive, in search of one of those diminishing bridges Mickey McMickey had spoken of, a link between his world and the world of Faerie. This would be the place, he had figured. Somewhere in the British Isles.

Somewhere. But England, even London, wasn't quite as small as Gary Leger had figured. With that innate superiority so typical of third- and fourth-generation Americans, Gary had thought England and all the isles a small and rural place, a place he could thoroughly search in the two weeks he had off work.

There was nothing small or rural about London.

Three of those fourteen days were gone now, and all Gary had found was a small sense of history beside a chip in the sidewalk on a rainy London street. He was beginning to privately admit that London was too metropolitan, perhaps all of England was too metropolitan. Earlier that day, he had inquired of some Brits about the possibility of visiting Nottingham, remembering the "Robin Hood" movies and thinking Nottingham the pure English hamlet.

But the Brits assured Gary that Nottingham was not as he pictured it. It was a rough, blue-collar town, and according to those who knew, the remnants of Sherwood Forest amounted to about three trees. That notion stung Gary, reminded him of what had happened to his own precious woods in a land three thousand miles away.

It was true, as Mickey had lamented; the bridges from the real world to Faerie were fast disappearing.

The next morning, Gary announced that they would leave London, would take Britrail to Edinburgh, four hundred miles to the north. To her credit (and partly because she wanted to see Edinburgh), Diane went along without complaint. She understood that something was deeply troubling her husband, and figured that the loss of her vacation was a small price to pay if allowing him his strange quest would bring him some measure of comfort. They weren't so far away from the first anniversary of Anthony's death, and Diane realized that Gary had hardly begun to recover from that loss.

Four hundred miles in four hours, and the two walked out of the Edinburgh train station for their first glimpse of Scotland. Since they were carrying all their luggage, Gary agreed to take a cab.

"So where ye goin'?" the cabby asked, more casually than any of the stuffy gents in the London black cabs had ever been.

Gary and Diane stared blankly at each other; they hadn't booked a room.

"Ah, ye've got no hotel," the cabby reasoned, and Gary looked at him hard, thinking how much his accent resembled Mickey's.

"Well, it's a wet time and there aren't too many visitors," the cabby went on. "We might be able to get ye something near to the castle."

"That'll be great," Diane quickly replied, before Gary could offer some other off-the-wall suggestion, and off they went.

A short while later they turned onto a wide boulevard, lined on the left by hotels, restaurants, and other shops that showed this to be a tourist section. A long park was on the right, down a grassy slope that put the widest part of the many blooming trees in the park at about eye level with the street.

"Castle o' the Rock," the cabby announced, looking to the right across the park.

Gary shifted low in his seat to get a better view past Diane and out the window. At first, he couldn't tell what the cabby was talking about, for all he saw through the tangle of trees was the park, and an occasional glimpse of the base of a hill across the way.

"Wow," Diane breathed when the trees thinned, and when Gary considered her, he realized that he should be looking up, not straight out. He leaned farther over her lap and turned his eyes skyward, up, up the hill that suddenly loomed more as a mountain. Up, up, hundreds of feet, to the walls of a castle that seemed to be growing right out of the top of the pillarlike mountain.

Gary couldn't find his breath.

"Stop the cab!" he finally blurted.

"What's that now?" the cabby asked.

"Stop the cab!" Gary cried again, crawling over Diane and grabbing at the door handle.

The cabby skidded over, and before the car had even come to a full stop, Gary was out of it, stumbling forward to the edge of the park.

Diane rushed to join him and took his trembling arm as he continued to stare upward, transfixed by the specter of Edinburgh Castle. Gary had seen this place before, this mountain and this castle. He had seen it in a different world, in a magical place called Faerie.

There the mountain was known as the Giant's Thumb, and this castle, Edinburgh Castle, was the home of a dragon named Robert.

A wyrm that Gary Leger had killed.

"YOUR father . . ." the soldier began, but Geldion waved a hand to silence the man. Though he had only been back on the field for a few minutes, the Prince had been told already—a half dozen times, at least—that his father was looking for him. And the last soldier, a friend of Geldion's, had added that King Kinnemore was not in good humor this day.

Neither was the exhausted Geldion, flustered from his uncomfortable flights to and from Ynis Gwydrin and even more so from his encounter with devious Ceridwen. The witch had made Geldion feel small, and Prince Geldion, forever fighting for respect in his father's cold eyes, did not like that feeling. The guards standing to either side of Kinnemore's tent apparently recognized the volatile Prince's foul mood, for they stepped far to the side, one of them taking the tent flap with him, offering Geldion an opening large enough for several men to walk abreast.

"Where have you been?" the scowling, always scowling, King Kinnemore asked before his son had even entered the tent. "I have an army sitting dead on a field." Kinnemore stood behind a smallish oaken desk, making him seem even taller and more imposing. Few men in Faerie reached the height of six feet, but King Kinnemore was closer to seven. His frame was lean, and yet he was broad-shouldered, and obviously physically powerful. He had seen fifty years, at least, but was possessed of the energy of a twenty-year-old. A nervous energy that kept him constantly moving, wringing his hands or stroking his perfectly maintained and regal goatee. His gray eyes, too, never stopped, darting back and forth, taking in all the scene as though he expected an assassin behind every piece of furniture.

"Ceridwen summoned me," Geldion remarked casually, and Kinnemore's continuing tirade came out as undecipherable babble. He finally slammed a fist down on the table, its sharp bang giving him a moment of pause (and opening a crack in the wood) that he might regain his always tentative edge of control.

"You above any should know that we must jump to the witch's call," Geldion finished, and there was a measure of sarcasm in his voice. He couldn't resist goading his father just a bit more. Geldion rarely pushed the King, knowing that he, like any other fool who opposed Kinnemore, would likely wind up with his head on a chopping block, but every now and then, he could not resist the opportunity to offer up a slight tweak.

His father, eyes set in the midst of widening crow's feet, jaw so tight that Geldion could hear the man's teeth grinding, looked very old to the Prince at that moment. Old and angry. Always angry. Geldion could not remember the last time he had seen Kinnemore smile, except for that wicked smile he flashed whenever he ordered an execution, or whenever he talked of conquest. Had he always been like this, always so filled with hatred and blood lust? Geldion couldn't be sure—all his clear memories fell in line with Kinnemore's present behavior.

But the Prince sensed that something had indeed changed. Perhaps it was only wishful fantasies, and not true memories, but Geldion seemed to recall a time of peace and happiness, a time of innocence when talk was not always on war, and play was preferred above battle.

A low growl escaped the King's lips, a guttural, animal-like growl. How could anyone be so horribly and perpetually angry? Geldion wondered.

"What did she want?" Kinnemore demanded.

The Prince shrugged. "Only to speak of Dilnamarra," he replied. "Of how we will use Baron Pwyll to anoint you as the slayer of Robert."

A sweep of Kinnemore's arm sent the small desk sliding out of the way, and the King advanced.

"If you are plotting with her against me . . ." Kinnemore threatened, moving very close to his son, his long finger poking the air barely an inch from Geldion's nose. Geldion was more than a foot shorter than his imposing father, a fact that was painfully evident to the Prince at that moment.

Still, Geldion didn't bother to justify the threat with a denial. He could be rightfully accused of many less than honorable things in his life, but never once had he entertained a treacherous thought concerning King Kinnemore. Geldion's loyalty wasn't questioned in the least by any who knew him. By all his actions, he was the King's man, to the death.

He didn't blink; neither did Kinnemore, but the King did eventually back off a step and lower his hand.

"What else did Ceridwen have to offer?" he asked.

"Nothing of any consequence," Geldion replied. "We force Dilnamarra into an alliance, and march east. Little has changed."

Kinnemore closed his eyes and slowly nodded his head, digesting it all. "When Braemar and Drochit are conquered, I want Baron Pwyll executed," he said, calmly and coldly.

"Baron Pwyll will be an ally," Geldion reminded him.

"An unintentional ally, in an alliance he will surely despise," Kinnemore reasoned. "And he will know the truth of the dragon slaying. That makes him dangerous." The King flashed that wicked smile suddenly as a new thought came to him. "No," he said, "not after the conquest. Baron Pwyll must die on the road to Braemar."

"Ceridwen will not approve."

"Ceridwen will still be imprisoned upon her isle," Kinnemore retorted immediately, and then Geldion understood his father's reasoning. By the time Drochit and Braemar fell, Ceridwen would likely be free, and then, unless the witch was in agreement with the double-dealing, Kinnemore would have more trouble striking out against Pwyll. But Ceridwen could do little to prevent the treachery while on her island.

Geldion smirked, marveling at the misconceptions the people of Faerie held concerning his father. Most of the commoners believed that Kinnemore was no more than Ceridwen's puppet, but Geldion knew better. Ceridwen might indeed be the power behind the throne, but that throne held a power all its own, a savage strength that scared Geldion more than the witch ever could.

"And what will that bode for the alliance?" the Prince asked as forcefully as he could.

"You will do it," Kinnemore went on, so entranced by his line of thought that he seemed not even to hear Geldion's protest. "You will make it appear as an assassination by one of the eastern towns. Or if you are not wise enough to follow that course, you will make it appear as though the fat Baron had an accident, or that his poor health simply overcame him."

Geldion said nothing, but his scowling expression revealed his sentiments well enough. He wondered of his own fate, should the truth come out. Would his father stand behind him if he was named as Baron Pwyll's executioner? Or would King Kinnemore wash his hands of Geldion's blood, brand him an outlaw and execute him?

Kinnemore just kept smiling, then, suddenly, snapped his hand down to grab Geldion by the front of his tunic. With horrifying strength, the older man easily lifted Geldion into the air.

Purely by reflex, the Prince put a hand to his belted dirk. His fingers remained on the hilt for only a moment, though, for even in defense of his own life, Geldion knew that he could not muster the nerve to strike out against his father.

"Get my troops moving," King Kinnemore growled. "You let Duncan Drochit and that wretched Lord Badenach escape once. I'll not tolerate another failure from you."

Geldion felt the man's savage power keenly at that moment. Felt it in his father's hot, stinking breath, the breath of a carnivore after a bloody kill.

He left Kinnemore's tent obviously shaken and walked across the field, trying to summon those distant, fleeting memories of his younger years, when Kinnemore had not been so angry.

FOUR

The Hero

THE meager forces of County Dilnamarra, some two hundred men and boys, and a fair number of women as well, stood quietly about the perimeter of Dilnamarra village and watched helplessly as the flood that was the Connacht militia, rank after rank, flowed across the rolling fields towards their village. The Dilnamarrans would be no real match for the trained and well-armed soldiers of the southern city, but they were ready to fight and to die, in defense of their homes and their heroic Baron.

Still, more than one sigh of relief was heard when a small contingent rode out from the swollen Connacht ranks under two flags, one the lion and the clover symbol of Connacht, the other a scythe in a blue field, Dilnamarra's own standard. The horsemen trotted their mounts into the town unopposed, stopping and dismounting by the main doors of the square and squat keep that anchored the village proper.

Rumors ran along the Dilnamarran ranks that it was Prince Geldion himself who had ridden in, and there was quiet hope that the fight might be avoided—especially when the stone building's iron-bound door was opened and the Prince and his men admitted.

For the little boy (who was really a leprechaun in disguise) sitting atop one of the unremarkable houses, news of the Prince's arrival did not bring optimism. Mickey had dealt with Geldion before, had been chased halfway across Faerie by the man and his soldiers twice in the last few weeks. In Mickey's estimation, Geldion's apparently peaceful foray into Dilnamarra did not bode well.

In Mickey's estimation, nothing concerning Prince Geldion boded well.

BARON Pwyll met the Prince and his entourage in the main audience room of the keep's first floor. The fat Baron rested back easily in his chair, trying to appear composed, as the always cocky Geldion briskly strode in.

"Good Baron," the Prince said in greeting, and he jumped a bit when the heavy door slammed closed behind him. There was only one window in the room, barely more than a tiny crack, and two of the four torches set in the sconces at the room's corners weren't burning—and the two that were aflame were burning low.

Geldion glanced around knowingly, guessing correctly that Pwyll had ar-

ranged for the darkness. In the dim light, the obviously nervous Baron's true
feelings might be better disguised, as would any of Pwyll's henchmen, lying in
wait in case of trouble. Geldion did not doubt for an instant that at least one
loaded crossbow was trained upon him at this very moment.

"Back in Dilnamarra so soon, Prince Geldion?" Baron Pwyll asked sarcastically. He was playing with one of the long and straggly hairs on his bristling
beard, pulling it straight and twisting it so that it would stand out at an odd angle.

"And I was not expected?" Geldion slyly replied. "Really, good Baron, you
should set better spies out on the road. Our approach was more than a little
conspicuous."

"Why would we care to set out spies?" Pwyll asked, matching sly question
for sly question, trying to get Geldion to play his hand out first. He had not
missed the Prince's reference to the sheer size of Connacht's army, though he
did well to hide his fears.

"I am not alone," the Prince said gravely and bluntly.

"Ah, yes," Baron Pwyll began, straightening his large form in his seat. "Yes,
you have brought your army. Really, my good Prince, was that such a wise thing
to do? The dragon is dead, the land is again at peace—and long live the dragonslayer!" he added, simply for the sake of his guards standing tall behind him
and for the other secret allies, men hiding behind the room's many tapestries.
As far as the soldiers of Dilnamarra knew, their own Baron had taken on mighty
Robert and had won out; at this dangerous time, Pwyll thought it a good thing
to remind his soldiers of the reasons for their loyalty.

"But considering the unfortunate incident on the eastern fields," the Baron
went on, trying to turn the situation back on Geldion, "parading around the
land with your army on your heels might be considered tacky, at the very least."

Pwyll thought he had the Prince at a disadvantage with the reminder of the
unnecessary skirmish, a battle facilitated by Geldion. He expected an explosion
from the volatile Prince, a tipping of the man's true intentions. He expected it
and hoped for it, for Pwyll was not unprepared. If he could wring the truth
from Geldion in here, then he and his men would simply not honor any pretense of truce. Geldion would be taken prisoner and ransomed to force the
army back to Connacht.

So Pwyll hoped, but Geldion's next statement caught him off guard.

"The dragon is dead," Geldion echoed, and he bowed low. "But that is the
very reason that brings us to Dilnamarra."

"Do tell," said an intrigued Pwyll.

"Robert is dead," Geldion reiterated with a grand sweep of his arm. "And we of Connacht are indeed 'parading,' as you so eloquently described it. We have come for celebration, in honor of the dragonslayer. Faerie has few too many heroes in this time, wouldn't you agree?" As he spoke, Geldion looked over to the fabulous armor and reforged spear of Cedric Donigarten, in place on its rightful pedestal in Dilnamarra Keep. The fabulous and shining shield rested in front of the suit, facing Geldion, and it seemed to the Prince as if its embossed standard—the mighty griffon, a legendary beast, half eagle, half lion—was watching him suspiciously.

Pwyll didn't miss the look, and he narrowed his eyes at the clear reminder of Geldion's treachery. Geldion, by the edict of his father the King, had tried to prevent the quest to reforge the spear. When that had failed and the spear was whole once more, the Prince had come back to Dilnamarra and had tried to forcefully remove the artifacts. That, too, had failed, for the items had been stolen away by Mickey McMickey before Geldion had ever gotten near to them. Was that the point of all this once more? Pwyll wondered. Was Geldion back in Dilnamarra, at the head of an army this time, in yet another attempt to remove the artifacts?

"And so we have a new hero, that we might place on a pedestal, that we might sing his praises," Geldion began again, excitedly. He looked back to Pwyll, stealing the Baron's private contemplations.

Pwyll didn't know how to react. Why was Geldion and the throne in Connacht ready to give him any praise? He was among Kinnemore's most hated rivals, and certainly, with his newfound mantle of dragonslayer (whether that mantle had been truly earned or not), Pwyll had become among the largest threats to Kinnemore's apparent quest for absolute rule.

There was another possibility, one that Baron Pwyll's considerable vanity would not let him ignore. Perhaps his fame had become too great for Connacht to openly oppose him. His name was being loudly praised in all the hamlets and all the villages of Faerie. By the actions and manipulations of Gary Leger and Mickey McMickey, and several others, he, Baron Pwyll of Dilnamarra, had been elevated to the status of hero. Did King Kinnemore need him? he dared to wonder. Did the smug ruler of Connacht fear that all the people of the kingdom would rise behind their newest hero and threaten Kinnemore's rule?

The thought intrigued Pwyll more than a little, and, try as he might, he could not hide that intrigue from his expression.

Geldion fully expected it, and did not miss the superior look.

"We may ride in, then?" the Prince asked. "To pay honor to one to whom honor is due?"

Pwyll, in spite of his vanity and his hopes, remained more than a little suspicious. But he was on the spot. How could he rightfully refuse such a gracious request?

"Ride in," he agreed. "We will do what we might to make your stay comfortable, but I fear that we have not the lodgings . . ."

Geldion stopped him with an upraised hand. "Your generosity is more than we ever expected," he said. "But the King's army will be back on the road this very day. We have been too long from Connacht."

Pwyll wouldn't disagree with that last statement. He nodded, and Geldion bowed.

I will arrange the ranks about the platform in the village square," the Prince said, "and return with a fitting escort for the heroic Baron of Dilnamarra."

Again Pwyll nodded, and Geldion was gone. The soldiers behind Pwyll bristled and whispered hopefully at the unexpected turn—one even reached down to pat Pwyll's broad shoulder. But Pwyll did not acknowledge their relief. He sat on his throne, fiddling with his wild beard, trying to peel away the layers of possible treachery and figure out exactly what Prince Geldion truly had in mind.

The significance of the appointed site, of that platform in the square, didn't bode well, either. It had been erected a few weeks before by Geldion's men as a gallows for Pwyll, and only the last-minute heroics of Kelsey and Gary Leger had freed Pwyll from the noose.

But that was before the skirmish on the eastern field, before the slaying of Robert. Might it be that Connacht would try a new approach to their rule, a softer, more insidious touch? Might it be that Connacht would indeed pay Pwyll the honors due him, trying to wean him into their fold with coercion instead of force?

Baron Pwyll, like his men behind him, wanted to believe that, wanted to believe that Faerie might know an end to the warfare, and that diplomacy might again be the rule of the day. For the man who had spent many years battling Kinnemore's iron-fisted and merciless rule, that was a difficult thought to swallow.

"WHAT is Geldion about?" Kelsey asked Mickey a short while later. The elf, Mickey, and Geno were holed up in a barn, a quarter-mile north of Dilnamarra proper. Geno had meant to go straight on to the east, to Braemar and Drochit, but Mickey had convinced him that he should stay around a bit longer. If the Connacht army meant to roll over Dilnamarra, then why had they hesitated? Certainly Baron Pwyll's ragtag militia would offer them little resistance.

Mickey looked out the barn's south window, to the squat keep in the distance, and shrugged.

"You did not overhear?" Kelsey questioned.

"I'm not for certain what I heared," Mickey replied. "Prince Geldion went in to speak with Pwyll, and so he did. I seen it meself from the keep's small window. It's what I heared that's got me wondering. By the Prince's own words, the army's come to honor the dragonslayer."

"King Kinnemore has come a hundred miles to honor Baron Pwyll?" Geno asked skeptically, and Kelsey's expression showed that he, too, doubted that possibility.

"That's not what I said," Mickey replied after a moment of thought. Geno's incredulous question had sparked another line of reasoning in the leprechaun, made him recall all that Geldion had said to Pwyll, and more pointedly, what Geldion had not said.

"By all accounts, Baron Pwyll killed Robert," Geno argued, but Mickey was hardly listening.

"Ye know," the leprechaun remarked, more to Kelsey than to Geno, "not once did the Prince mention that his father had come along for the ride."

Geno, of the rugged and secluded Dvergamal Mountains and not well schooled in the etiquette of humans, didn't seem to understand any significance to that point, but Kelsey's golden eyes narrowed suspiciously.

"Aye," Mickey agreed.

"Enough of this banter!" Geno protested. "I'm for the eastern road, to tell Drochit and Braemar to prepare for war, and then to my own home, far away from foolish humans and their foolish games."

"Don't ye be going just yet," Mickey warned. "By me thinking, things aren't all they seem in Dilnamarra. The day might grow brighter yet."

"Or darker," Kelsey added, and Mickey conceded the grim point with a nod.

THEY came into Dilnamarra to a chorus of blowing trumpets and the hoofbeats of two hundred horses. Prince Geldion rode at their lead, the proud army of Connacht. No longer did he wear his stained traveling cloak, but was rather outfitted in the proper regalia for such a ceremony. Long purple robes flowed back from his shoulders, and a gold lace shoulder belt crossed his thin chest. Even so, he wore no sword, only that famous dirk, tucked into his belt, not far from reach.

"And still there's no showing o' Kinnemore," Mickey remarked suspiciously. He, Kelsey, and Geno had moved closer to the village, to a hedgerow not far from the square (despite Geno's constant grumbling that he was getting more than a little tired of hiding behind hedgerows and fences).

Kelsey shook his head and had no practical response to the leprechaun's claims. Normally the King led his forces. It could be that Kinnemore feared a potential assassin, but that didn't sit well with Kelsey's understanding of the fierce King. Kinnemore was Ceridwen's puppet—all in Faerie knew that—but despite that fact, he was not known as a cowardly man.

The brigade formed into neat semicircular ranks about the perimeter of the platform that centered the square, while Geldion and a group of armored knights again went to the keep. They were admitted without incident, to find Baron Pwyll and a handful of his closest advisors waiting for them inside.

The Prince put a disdainful look on the fat Baron. Pwyll was wearing his finest robes, but even these were old and threadbare, reflective of the difficult times that had befallen all of the baronies in the last dozen years of Kinnemore's reign. The Baron held himself well, though. He seemed neither intimidated nor exuberant, had settled into a confident calm.

Geldion's expression changed when his gaze went from the threadbare clothes to the Baron's resolute features. The Prince's doubts about Ceridwen's plans came rushing back.

"I am ready," Pwyll announced.

"Are you?" Geldion asked slyly. He nodded to his knights, and as one they brought out their great swords and shifted about, each moving within striking distance of one of Pwyll's associates.

"What treachery is this?" Pwyll demanded. "What murder?"

"Fool," Geldion said to him. "There need be no spilling of blood. Not a man of Dilnamarra need die."

Pwyll raised a hand to keep his men from reacting, then to stroke at his bristling beard. He changed his mind before his fingers touched the woolly hair, not wanting Geldion to recognize his growing nervousness.

"We will march out of here as planned," Geldion explained. "To the square, between the thousands of my army. There, you will announce the dragonslayer."

"King Kinnemore," Baron Pwyll reasoned.

Geldion nodded. "My father awaits your call," he said, and he stepped back and to the side, turning to the door and sweeping his arm for Pwyll to lead.

"I should not be surprised by your treachery," Baron Pwyll retaliated. "We have come to expect nothing less from the throne of Connacht. But do you really expect the people to believe . . ."

"They will believe what they are told," Geldion interrupted. "A man at the wrong end of a sword will believe anything, I assure you." As he spoke, he looked around to the grim faces of Pwyll's helpless advisors.

Baron Pwyll, too, glanced about at the fuming men. They had no practical chance against the armed and armored knights—even the two crossbowmen whom Pwyll had strategically placed behind tapestries in the room could do little to prevent a wholesale slaughter by Geldion's men.

The Baron motioned again for his men to be at ease, then stepped forward, moving past the Prince. Geldion's hand came up to block him.

"I warn you only once," the Prince said. "If you fail in this, the price will be your life, and the lives of all in Dilnamarra."

Pwyll pushed past. When he exited the keep, he had no intentions of failing the task. What harm was there in granting King Kinnemore the honors for slaying Robert? he figured. Surely the cost would not approach the massacre Geldion had promised.

Pwyll and Geldion moved out through the parting ranks, Geldion's knights close behind. Pwyll's men drifted apart and scattered into the crowd.

"I'm not liking the fat Baron's look," Mickey remarked when Pwyll, Geldion, and three of the knights emerged above the crowd, climbing the steps of the platform.

Geno grumbled something and sent a stream of spittle into the hedgerow.

The group shifted about on the platform, with Geldion finally maneuvering Pwyll forward. Pwyll glared at him, but the stern Prince, always loyal, did not relent, did not back down an inch.

Baron Pwyll surveyed his audience, saw how vulnerable his people were with two hundred cavalry in the town and thousands of soldiers camped just outside Dilnamarra's southern borders.

"Good people of Dilnamarra," the Baron began loudly. Then he paused again, for a long moment, looking out over the crowd, looking to the hedgerow wherein hid Mickey and the others, the same hedgerow that they had used to get near to the action on that day when Pwyll was to be hung.

Hung by the edict of an outlaw King, the same King that Pwyll was about to announce as the hero of all the land. How could he do that? Baron Pwyll wondered now. How could he play along with Kinnemore's continuing treachery, especially with the knowledge that wicked Ceridwen, the puppetmaster, would soon be free of her island?

The Baron sighed deeply and continued his scan of his audience, looked at the dirty faces of the men and women and children, all the people who had been as his children, trusting in him as their leader, looking to him for guidance through the difficult years. Geldion had more trained soldiers in and about the town than all the people of County Dilnamarra combined. Images of carnage worse than anything he had ever seen before rushed through Pywll's mind.

"Go on," Geldion whispered, nudging the Baron with his elbow, a movement that sharp-eyed Mickey and Kelsey did not miss.

"It was not I who slew the dragon," Pwyll began. Immediately there arose from the gathered folk of Dilnamarra a crestfallen groan and whispers of disbelief.

"So there ye have it," Mickey remarked. "With Pwyll and Dilnamarra in their fold, nothing will stop Ceridwen and Kinnemore."

"Time to go east," Geno growled, and he spat again and turned from the hedgerow. But Kelsey, who knew Pwyll better than anyone, perhaps, saw something then, something in the look of the fat man. He grabbed Geno by the shoulder, roughly turned him about, and bade him to wait a few moments longer.

Baron Pwyll had reached the most crucial test of all his life. Just as he was about to announce Kinnemore—and he saw the King then, out of the corner of his eye, bedecked for the ceremony and sitting astride a white charger at the back of the cavalry ranks—he came to consider the full implication of his words. He came to understand that by so proclaiming Kinnemore, he would be pledging fealty to the King, he would be surrendering Dilnamarra without a fight.

What would that imply for the people of Drochit and Braemar, and all the other villages? What would that bode for the Tylwyth Teg in their forest home not so far from Dilnamarra Keep? These were Pwyll's allies, friends to the Baron and to his people.

"In truth, the dragonslayer was . . ." Pwyll saw the smug look come over the advancing King, a superior look, an expression of conquest.

". . . Gary Leger of Bretaigne!" Pwyll cried out. Geldion turned on him, shocked and outraged. "And Kelsenellenelvial Gil-Ravadry of Tir na n'Og, and famed Geno Hammerthrower of Dvergamal, and Gerbil Hamsmacker, a most inventive gnome of Gondabuggan!"

Pwyll's body jerked suddenly as a crossbow quarrel entered his chest.

"And a leprechaun," he gasped. "My friend Mickey. Beware, people of Dilnamarra!" Pwyll cried. "They will kill you with weapons if they cannot snare you with lies!"

Geldion grabbed him roughly, and only that held Pwyll upright on his buckling legs.

"Do not hear the hissing lies of a serpent King!" Pwyll roared with all the strength he had remaining. "These I have named are the heroes. These are the ones who will lead you from the darkness!"

Pwyll groaned in agony as one of the knights came over near to the Prince and plunged a sword into the Baron's back.

"My friend Mickey," Pwyll said, his voice no more than a breathless whisper, and he slumped to his knees, where the darkness of death found him.

"Where did that come from?" a stunned and obviously appreciative Geno wanted to know.

"From Baron Pwyll of Dilnamarra," Kelsey declared firmly.

"Me friend," added Mickey, and there was a tear in the leprechaun's eye, though he knew that he had just witnessed Baron Pwyll's finest moment.

Geno nodded and without another word ran off, knowing that the road east would surely soon be blocked.

All about the platform erupted into a sudden frenzy. The people of Dilnamarra could not hope to win out, but their rage consumed them, and they pulled many soldiers down.

Through it all, Geldion stood on the platform, holding fast to the dead Baron. He felt a twinge of sympathy for this man who had so bravely died, felt as though his father, and that wicked Ceridwen, had underestimated Pwyll all along.

King Kinnemore and his bodyguards pushed through the throng to the platform, the King rushing up to stand by his son. Geldion glared at him as he approached, and Kinnemore had no words to deny the Prince's anger.

Kinnemore tried to call for calm, but the riot was on and out of control. Flustered, Kinnemore turned to Geldion, and smacked his son hard, trying to wipe that I-told-you-so look from Geldion's face.

Geldion started to blurt out a retort; then his eyes went wide as a long arrow knocked into Kinnemore's breastplate.

"Ye just had to put yer thoughts in," Mickey said to Kelsey, the elf's great bow still humming from the incredible shot.

"I thought the voice of the Tylwyth Teg should be heard at this time," Kelsey said easily.

Mickey looked back to the platform, to King Kinnemore, still standing, looking with surprise upon the quivering shaft.

"I think he got yer point," Mickey snickered.

To their amazement, to the amazement of Geldion and all the others who had noticed the arrow, Kinnemore calmly reached down and snapped the shaft. He took a moment to study its design, then casually tossed it aside. "Find the elf and kill him," he calmly ordered some of his nearby men, pointing in the general direction of the hedgerow.

"He's a tough one," Mickey remarked, his voice full of sincere awe. "And we should be leaving."

Kelsey didn't disagree with either point. He scooped Mickey up to his shoulder and ran off to the north, towards Tir na n'Og, where he knew that his fellow Tylwyth Teg would be waiting to turn back any pursuit.

As soon as the initial shock of the riot faded, the skilled army of Connacht systematically overran the village. Dilnamarra was secured that very night, with more than half the populace slain or imprisoned.

Refugees, more children than adults, came to the southern borders of the thick forest Tir na n'Og all that night, where the normally reclusive Tylwyth Teg mercifully allowed them entry.

"Ceridwen might get her kingdom," Mickey remarked, standing by Kelsey's side and looking south from the tree line. "But by the words o' Baron Pwyll, suren she's to fight for every inch o' ground!"

Kelsey said nothing, just watched solemnly as another group of young boys and girls ran across the last moonlit field to the forest's dark border, pursued by a host of soldiers. A hail of arrows from unseen archers high in the boughs turned the soldiers about, and the youngsters made it in to safety.

The war for Faerie had begun.

FIVE

A Call on the Wind

THE tour guide was full of good cheer, all in all a remarkably entertaining old Scottish gent, complete with a button-top cap and a plaid kilt. Even Gary, not thrilled that he had to tag along with a group of tourists, couldn't hide his chuckles at the man's continuing stream of humor as they moved past the outer walls towards the castle proper.

"Pay no attention to these doors," the guide ordered in his thick brogue as they passed between two massive open portals, iron-bound wooden doors with an iron portcullis hanging overhead, each of its imposing pegs as thick as Diane's arm.

"They're not old," the Scotsman went on. "They were made when I was a boy, just two hundred years ago!"

The wide-eyed people of the tour group were so intrigued by the sight of the portals, and of the castle that lay beyond them, that it took every one of them many long seconds to even figure out the joke.

And Gary, transfixed as he stared at the lower courtyard of the castle, of Robert's castle, missed it altogether.

Diane, laughing, looked to him, but her mirth was quickly washed away by his firm-set features, that same determined and wide-eyed look that had led them to England, then to Scotland, in the first place.

"Two hundred years ago," she echoed, grabbing Gary's strong arm.

"What?" he asked, turning to regard her.

Diane let it drop, with only one final sigh of surrender. She took Gary's arm in tow and halfheartedly followed the group around the lower courtyard, its stone wall overlooking the city of Edinburgh. Antique cannons, preserved museum pieces showing the twilight of the years of castles, sat at regular intervals along the walls. The guide was speaking of them, but Gary didn't bother to listen. He thought it curious that cannons lined the castle wall, yet it was the cannon that made the castle an obsolete defense. More than curious, though, Gary thought it terribly wrong to see cannons in this place. There had been no cannons in Robert's castle, of course, no guns at all. Gary preferred things that way.

"They don't belong," he whispered.

"The cannons?" Diane asked.

Gary looked at her curiously. He hadn't been speaking to her, hadn't been speaking to anyone. "The cannons don't belong—especially that one," he said, pointing to the farthest edge of the curving wall, to a modern Howitzer standing silent vigil in a roped-off area that indicated it was not for show, and certainly not a piece for children to climb upon.

"I think it's neat," Diane argued. "You can see how this castle evolved through the ages. They've got a chapel up there that's from the fifth century! You can see how this place was built, and expanded, and modernized to adapt to the changes in the world around it." She was growing noticeably excited, reveling in the fun of it all—until she looked again at Gary, and that determined smirk of his.

"What?" she asked sternly.

"I'd like to show you this place before the cannons," he said. "When the only sentries were lava newts and . . ."

"Are you going to start that again?" asked a flustered Diane. She turned away, and noticed that the tour group was ascending a flight of exposed stairs up to the higher level, the inner bailey.

"Are you coming?"

"I can tell you everything that's up there," Gary boasted, following her lead. "Except for the newer changes."

"You're starting to get on my nerves."

"You've been saying that for a week," Gary pointed out.

Diane spun about, halfway up the stairs, and glared down at him. He fully realized that his obsession was ruining her vacation, but he simply could not let go of it. Gary needed to get back to Faerie, but if the Howitzer was any indication, those tentative bridges between the worlds were crumbling faster than he had expected.

Still, he realized that it wasn't fair for him to play out his frustrations on poor Diane, and he apologized sincerely.

By the time they got to the courtyard atop the stairs, the tour group was moving through a door to a tall tower.

"We'll go there later," Gary explained as he grabbed Diane's hand and rushed off diagonally across the courtyard, to an open door at the far end of a long and lower building.

Diane went along without complaint, sensing the urgency in her husband. They rushed through the door, into a dimly lit short corridor. Just a few steps in, they turned to the left, into a massive hall.

This was the place where Gary had first met Robert. It seemed very much the same, with spears and other weapons arranged on the walls, empty suits of armor standing guard in pretty much the same positions as Robert's lava newt sentries had been.

"This is it," Gary breathed.

"Come on, Gary," Diane said quietly. "Tell me what's going on."

He could tell by her tones that his cryptic words and actions had gone beyond simple annoyance. He was beginning to frighten her.

"This was Robert's hall," he explained. "Just like this. It looks the same—it feels the same. Even the gigantic interlocking beams of the ceiling."

Diane looked up along with Gary to that fabulous ceiling—more wondrous still when the two took a moment to realize how high it actually was, and thus, the true width of those supporting beams.

"Incredible," Diane mouthed.

"And I've seen it before," Gary assured her. She looked to him as he turned away, moving out from the wall.

Diane didn't reply, just followed Gary as he crossed the great hall, turning with every step to take in the view and the feel of the place. Suddenly he stopped, as if his gaze had fallen on a new and brighter treasure. Diane followed the line of that stare to an immense sword, leaning from a pedestal base against the far wall.

"Robert's?" she asked, following the logic.

Gary tentatively moved up to it. Without even bothering to look around, he grabbed the weapon's massive hilt in his two hands and tilted it against his chest.

"Mickey," he called. "You have to hear me now, Mickey." By Gary's reasoning, this sword had to be deeply connected with Faerie. It had to be.

"You're not supposed to touch it," Diane whispered, glancing about nervously, expecting a host of police to run up and arrest them on the spot for disturbing a national treasure.

"Mickey," Gary called again, loudly, defiantly.

"Robert," a voice corrected, and for an instant Gary thought he had made an otherworldly connection. Then a hand crossed in front of him and gently eased the sword back to its original place. "The sword of Robert," the guard explained.

Gary's mind swirled at the possibilities that name evoked. He realized that he was still in his own world, but in that case, how could this modern-day man know of Robert?

"Robert the Bruce," the guard clarified, pointing to a plaque on the wall. "And ye should'no' be touchin' it."

Gary fell back, nodding, and Diane caught his arm in her own. Robert the Bruce was one of Scotland's legendary heroes, a man of Gary's world and certainly no dragon in Faerie. Still, Gary was sure there was some connection between this sword and the sword Robert the dragon had used when in his human form, the same sword that Gary had stolen to lead the dragon into a trap.

And it was connected to Faerie; Gary had felt that keenly when he touched it. But he had heard no answer to his call to the leprechaun, and whatever magic had been in this place was gone now, stolen by the mere appearance of the guard.

Gary and Diane didn't finish that castle tour.

"WHAT do you hear?" an observant raven-haired elf asked Mickey, seeing the leprechaun's faraway look.

Mickey glanced over at Kelsey, who was sitting across the campfire, talking with some friends and smoothing the buffs from the edge of his crafted sword.

As if he had felt that gaze, Kelsey stopped his talk and his work, and stared hard at Mickey.

"It was not a thing," the leprechaun answered the elf standing beside him, though he was still looking across the fire to Kelsey. "Just a song on the wind, is all. A bird or a nymph." The other elf seemed satisfied with that, and he took no notice as Mickey walked away from the fire and into the thick brush. Kelsey caught up to the leprechaun twenty yards away, the elf's stern golden-eyed expression demanding a better explanation.

"Not a thing," Mickey said and started to walk by. Kelsey grabbed the leprechaun's shoulder and held him in place.

"What're ye doing now?" Mickey asked, pulling free.

"It was no bird, nor Leshiye the nymph," Kelsey said. "What did your clever ears hear?"

"I told ye it was nothing," Mickey replied.

"And I asked you again," Kelsey retorted and again grabbed a firm hold on the elusive sprite's shoulder.

Mickey started to argue once more, but stopped, figuring the better of it. They were in besieged Tir na n'Og, Kelsey's precious home, with Kinnemore's army forcefully knocking on the door. Kelsey would grab at any hope, at any hint, and he would not be dismissed by avoiding answers.

"It was the lad," Mickey admitted. "I heared a call from the lad."

Kelsey nodded. This time, the call must have been closer, for the leprechaun was visibly disturbed.

"Gary Leger wants to return," Kelsey reasoned.

"Only because he doesn't know," Mickey quickly added, shaking his head. "We were all thinking that things'd be better with Robert gone and Pwyll named as hero. Ye seen it yerself—when the lad left, he left with a smile."

The leprechaun paused and closed his eyes, and it seemed to Kelsey that he was hearing that distant call once more.

"No, Gary Leger," Mickey whispered. "Ye're not wanting to come here. Not now."

Kelsey let go of Mickey, and let the leprechaun walk off alone into the dark forest night. He didn't dismiss what Mickey had revealed, though, and he wasn't so sure that Mickey's answer to that call was correct.

Kelsey and a handful of stealthy elfish companions left Tir na n'Og later that night, after the moon had set. The quiet elfish band had little trouble slipping through the Connacht lines and making its way to Dilnamarra Keep.

GARY leaned his head against the window of the tour bus, watching the countless sheep as the rolling fields of the Scottish Highlands drifted by. He had planned to stay in Edinburgh, so he could return to the castle and to the sword as often as possible, seeking that tentative link to Mickey.

Diane had other ideas. As soon as they had returned to their hotel, she had secretly booked a three-day bus tour of Scotland. Gary, of course, had resisted, but Diane, so patient with him all these weeks, had heard enough. He was going with her, she said, or he would be alone for the rest of the vacation. She hadn't said anything more outright, but Gary believed that if he didn't go on this tour, he might find himself alone longer than that.

Diane sat in the seat next to him, very close to him, chatting with a Brazilian couple across the aisle. Music played over the bus's intercom, pipers and accordions, mostly happy and upbeat, but every so often a mournful tune.

They were the perfect tourists, riding along the winding roads in the majestic and melancholy Scottish scenery. All Gary saw were the sheep.

His mood brightened, to Diane's sincere relief, as the day wound on and the bus approached their first stop, Inverness. Gary was thinking of Faerie again, of Loch Devenshere, nestled in the Crahgs, where he had seen a sea monster. Perhaps Loch Ness would show him the bridge.

They didn't get to the legendary loch until the next day, and Gary was in for a disappointment. He saw a monster, a plaster replica of Nessie, sitting in a small pond (a large puddle) next to the Drumnadrochit Monster Exhibit, but despite the dark waters of the cold loch across the highway, and the stunning view of the mountains across the long lake, there was little magic here, little sensation that Mickey would hear his call.

"Two more days," he said as the bus rolled west, towards the next stop, the Isle of Skye.

"Then we're going to Brighton," Diane announced.

"Brighton?"

"South coast of England, near Sussex," she explained. "It will take us about six hours from Edinburgh. We'll go right from the bus drop to the train station."

Gary's first instinct was to protest. He had gone along with the bus tour, but planned to spend some time back in Edinburgh after the three days. He bit back his retort now, though, seeing no compromise in Diane's green eyes.

When he spent a moment to consider that determined look, Gary found that he couldn't really blame Diane. She had been wonderful about his obsession with Faerie over the years, listening to him without complaint or ridicule as he repeated his wild stories at least a hundred times. Before this trip, Diane had allowed him his many nights sitting in the woods out in back of his mother's house, had even gone and sat by his side on several occasions.

And Diane really didn't believe in Faerie, he knew. How could she? How could anyone who had not gone there? Diane had compromised—even the first half of their vacation. Now it was Gary's turn to compromise.

"Brighton," he agreed, and he settled back in his seat and tried very hard to enjoy the highland scenery.

SIX

Isle of Skye

HIGH in the boughs of a pine tree, Mickey awoke from a restful sleep to the twang of bows and the screams of men later that night. Truly the leprechaun was bothered by what was going on in the woods all about him, and by the turmoil that had become general in Faerie, but he meant to stay out of the battle. He had gone on the quest to fix the spear, had recovered his precious pot of gold, had helped to put the dragon down, and had even done a bit of spying for Baron Pwyll and the others resisting King Kinnemore, but now Mickey was back in Tir na n'Og, the forest he called home, and by his sensibilities, all of this had become someone else's problem.

He rested back on the pliable pine branch, pulled the front of his tam-o'-shanter down over his eyes, and dreamed of running barefoot through a field of four-leafed clover.

Then Mickey heard someone cry out for Kelsey, and the image of the clover field disappeared in the blink of a mischievous gray eye. "O begorra," Mickey muttered, realizing that he could not dismiss it all, not with friends as loyal as Kelsey in danger down below. He popped open an umbrella that conveniently came to his hand, used the pine branch like a spring board and leaped out into the night air, floating down gently to the forest floor.

On the ground, the leprechaun tried to figure out from which direction the noise of the fighting was coming, but there were apparently several separate battles raging all at once.

Mickey tapped his umbrella (now appearing as a small and carved walking stick) atop a mushroom. "Good toadstool," he asked of the fungi, "might ye know where Kelsey the elf's hiding?"

Mickey listened for the answer, and got one (because leprechauns can do those kinds of things), then he politely thanked the mushroom and moved to a crack at the base of the pine in which he had been sleeping. He politely asked the tree for permission to enter, then did, magically traveling along the root system from tree to tree (because leprechauns can do those kinds of things) until he stepped out of a crack in a wide elm near to the fighting.

To Mickey's surprise, he saw not an elf in the small clearing ahead of him, but a human, a Connacht soldier, clutching tightly to a sword and glancing nervously about, as though he had gotten separated from his fellows.

How the man's eyes widened when he turned about and saw a leprechaun standing before him! It seemed as if some craziness came over the soldier then, and all fear flew away, his eyes bulging and his face brightening with a smile. He tossed his weapon aside and dove down at the leprechaun, thinking his fortune found and all the life's prayers answered. The soldier came up a moment later, clutching his prize, eyes darting this way and that in case any saw.

Then he peeked at the catch—and found that he was holding a dirty mushroom. He took off his helmet and scratched at his head.

"Ye got to be quicker than that," he heard, and he spun about to see the leprechaun leaning easily against a tree.

Cautiously, still holding tight to the mushroom, the soldier approached. "How'd you do that?" he asked.

Then he blinked, seeing that the leprechaun on the ground was really a mushroom. He looked back to his catch, still a mushroom, and scratched his head again.

"Behind ye," Mickey said.

The soldier spun about, and saw the leprechaun once again. The man's hungry grin lasted only the moment it took him to realize that the sprite was sitting atop the shoulder of a very angry elfish warrior.

"Have ye met me friend Kelsey?" said the leprechaun's voice, and though this newest illusionary image of Mickey disappeared, the very real Kelsey remained.

The soldier threw the mushroom at Kelsey, and the elf promptly batted it aside and advanced—pausing and wincing only when he heard the slapped "mushroom" groan.

The soldier looked all about for his weapon, spotted it on the ground and dove for it. But Kelsey's foot stamped upon his fingers as they closed about the swordhilt, and Kelsey's deadly sword came down, stopping with its keen edge against the side of the soldier's neck.

"Don't ye kill him," the disheveled Mickey, who was not a mushroom anymore, said to Kelsey. "It's not really his fight."

The soldier turned his head to nod his full agreement with the plea for mercy, but when the man looked upon the stern elf, he fainted away, thinking his life at its end.

Kelsey growled and lifted his sword as if to strike.

"By me own eyes," Mickey moaned from the side. "And here I be, thinking the Tylwyth Teg're the good folk."

Kelsey winced and let the sword slowly come back to rest against the man's neck. The elf narrowed his golden eyes as he regarded the smug Mickey.

"Candella is dead," Kelsey said, referring to a female elf, a good friend to Kelsey, and more than a mere acquaintance to Mickey.

Mickey shook his head slowly, helplessly. "And what o' yerself?" he asked, pointing to Kelsey's arm, the elf's white sleeve darkened with fresh blood.

Kelsey looked down at the wound. "A crossbow," he explained. "Just before you appeared."

Mickey glanced about. They were fully a hundred yards inside the border of Tir na n'Og, and it suddenly struck him as odd to see a soldier so deep in the wood. "Is he the only one left alive?" the leprechaun asked, realizing that many other soldiers must have accompanied this one for him to get so far in.

"The only one of two score," Kelsey answered grimly.

Something seemed very wrong to Mickey, very out of place. "They tried to get in, then," the leprechaun reasoned. "But why would soldiers, human soldiers who do'no' see so well in the dark, try to get into Tir na n'Og under the light o' the moon? Why would they come in at night to fight the elfs that do see well in the dark?"

"They were pursuing us," Kelsey explained. Mickey shrugged and seemed not to understand.

"On penalty of their deaths, were we to escape," Kelsey went on. "Since King Kinnemore prizes the armor and spear of Cedric Donigarten above all other treasures in his realm."

"Ye stole the spear and the armor?" Mickey gawked.

Kelsey nodded gravely.

"Then Candella died for the sake o' the spear and armor?" Mickey asked incredulously.

Kelsey didn't flinch.

"But ye got none to wear it or wield it," the leprechaun reasoned. "Ye all got yerselfs shot at and chased for the sake of a treasure that's only for show!"

The leprechaun continued his tirade for a few moments longer, until he realized that Kelsey wasn't blinking, wasn't even listening to the arguments. Mickey stopped with a loud huff and stood trembling, hands on hips, one holding the umbrella-turned-walking-stick.

"Well?" the leprechaun demanded.

"You said that Gary Leger wanted to get back," Kelsey answered, as though that should explain everything.

It took Mickey a long moment to digest this unexpected turn. In their two adventures side by side, Kelsey had come to trust in Gary, and even to like the man, but Mickey could hardly believe that any member of the haughty Tylwyth Teg would risk his or her life for the sake of any human!

"But I didn't say I'd bring him in," Mickey reasoned.

Kelsey didn't flinch.

GARY stood transfixed at the end of a bay, staring across the dark waters of the North Atlantic to the westering sun, its slanted rays skimming the waters about the many pillarlike rocks that stood like gigantic sentinels, silent and proud testaments to ancient times, to times before men and science had dominated the world. The wind was constant and strong, straight off the water, blowing the salty mist into Gary's face. Its bite was fierce and chill, but Gary didn't care, couldn't pull himself away from this place.

A hundred yards out in the bay lay a rock island, triangular and imposing. How many ancient mariners had tried to sail in past that rock? Gary wondered. How many had braved the winds and the cold waters to come to this shore, and how many more had died out there, their feeble boats splintered against the timeless rocks?

It seemed likely to Gary that more had perished than had successfully navigated this stretch. There was a power here far greater than the wood of boats, one that transcended even the human spirit. A preternatural power, a sheer strength that had not been tamed by the encroachment of civilization.

Standing near that bay, in Duntulme, on the northern rim of the Isle of Skye, Gary Leger felt at once insignificant and important. He was a little player in a great universe, a tiny drop of dye on the great tapestry of nature. But he was indeed part of that tapestry, part of that majesty. He couldn't tame these waters and these pillars, but he could share in their glory.

That was the most important lesson Gary had learned in the land of Faerie. That is what the Buldrefolk living amongst the mighty peaks of Dvergamal, and the Tylwyth Teg, so at home in the forest Tir na n'Og, had shown to him.

"It's incredible," Diane whispered, standing beside him, her arm in his. In full agreement, Gary put his hand over her forearm and led on, picking his way across the sharp rocks and wet sand.

The land climbed steeply along the left side of the bay, coming to a high point where the somewhat sheltered water widened into the North Atlantic. On that pinnacle stood the ruins of a small castle, an ancient outpost. Diane resisted as Gary made his way along the curving beach, to the narrow trail that topped the edge of the cliff face.

"Most of the others are going up there tomorrow," she explained, for the trail seemed treacherous in the fast-dying light. She noticed, too, that Gary had his small pack with him, and she worried that if he got up on that cliff, it might be a long time before she could coax him back down.

"That's why we're going up there today," Gary replied calmly, and moved on.

Despite her very real fears, Diane didn't argue. The sight was spectacular, to say the least, and her heart was pulling at her to go up to that pinnacle, that lost outpost, almost as much as Gary's was pulling at him. She pictured what the sunset might look like from the high vantage point, realized that she would glimpse an eternal scene, the same view as that of the men who had once manned that outpost. As was her habit on this trip, Diane carried two cameras with her: her reliable old Pentax 35mm and a Polaroid. All along this trip, whenever Diane spotted what looked like a reasonable shot, she'd click one off with the Polaroid. As that picture developed before her eyes, she would get a better idea of the effect of the lighting and the scenery, and then she'd go to work with the Pentax, often clicking off two rolls at a stretch.

The worst part of the climb was the ever-present sheep manure on the trail, slimy and slippery. A rope had been strung to the right side of the path, offering some protection from a drop into the bay, and a sturdier fence (though it was broken in many places) had been erected on the left, portioning off a sheep field. Diane had always thought that sheep were cute little beasties, but when they came towards her now, on that narrow and slippery trail, she was more than a little nervous.

Gary would have been nervous, too, if he had been paying any attention to the sheep. His eyes were squarely focused, transfixed, on the ruins up above. He felt the energy of this place more keenly with every step, felt the tingles of magic building in the air about him.

The wind increased tenfold when the pair crested the hill, and they could both understand what had so battered the walls of this ancient bastion. Men had come to this place and built their stone fortress, and had probably thought themselves invulnerable up on that cliff, behind thick stone walls and surrounded by the treacherous and rocky waters.

Gary couldn't imagine that any enemy humans had conquered this fortress, or destroyed its walls, that any hostile ships (the longships of Vikings, perhaps?)

had put up on the beach. But the fortress had been defeated. It had been taken down by the incessant and undeniable power of nature. Like the men who had manned it, the constructed castle had been taken down and turned to crumbling dust, a temporary bastion in an eternal universe.

Gary found a high perch on a fallen slab. He looked to the low sun, then spread his arms high and wide above him to catch as much of the wind as he possibly could, to feed off its strength.

Diane milled about behind him, clicking away with her Pentax. So entranced was she, so alive at that moment, that the normally sensible woman crawled out through a hole in the wall to a precarious perch on the very edge of the northern cliff, simply to get a good angle on a shot. Then, when she came back within the boundaries of the fortress, she braved a trek into a small and dark tunnel, though a plaque on the stone warned against entry.

Gary noticed some flickers of light, and turned to the side curiously as Diane emerged from the other end of the tunnel, her camera flash in hand and her smile from ear to ear.

"You're not supposed to go down there," he remarked.

Diane's smile was infectious, made Gary picture her as a little girl with her hand in the proverbial cookie jar. He was glad that she was so entranced by this place, because he had already made up his mind that the sun would be long gone before he made his way back down to the bay and the inn.

It got cold after sunset and the two huddled together behind a fallen slab of rock.

"It will probably rain," Diane remarked, a reasonable guess in this perpetually gloomy land. There were stars shining up above them, but both had been on the isles long enough to realize that could change in the matter of a few minutes.

They talked and they cuddled; they kissed and they cuddled some more. Gary spoke of his adventures in Faerie, and Diane listened, and under that enchanting sky in that enchanting place, she could almost hear the song of the fairies and the rhythmic ringing of the Buldrefolk hammers.

Gary realized that Diane's patience with his wild stories was a precious gift. In all the years since his first trip, Diane had been the only one he had told. Even his father had not known.

"Were there any unicorns?" Diane asked him at one point, a question that she often asked him during his recountings.

Gary shook his head. "None that I saw," he replied. "But I wouldn't bet against it."

"I'd love to see a unicorn," said Diane. "Ever since I was a little gir . . ." She stopped abruptly and Gary turned to her, hardly able to make out her features in the dark night.

"What?" he prompted.

There came no reply.

"Diane?" he asked, nudging her a bit. She rolled with the push and let out a profound snore.

Gary laughed, thinking it cute how quickly she had fallen off to sleep.

Too quickly, Gary suddenly realized. How could she possibly be talking one instant and snoring the next?

Gary went on the alert, rolling up into a crouch. "Where are you?" he asked into the quiet night.

He fully expected what came next, but still found that he could hardly draw his breath. A tiny sprite, no more than a foot tall, stepped up onto the rock slab, small bow in hand.

The same bow the creature had used to shoot Diane, Gary knew, remembering well the sleeping poison of the sprites.

"Mickey wants me back?" Gary reasoned.

The sprite gave him a smirk and half turned on the slab, leading Gary's gaze to a small clearing just beyond the back edge of the ruins. A glow came up, a ring of soft lights, accompanied by a sweet melody, tiny voices singing arcane words that Gary did not understand.

With a disarming smile on his face, Gary lifted his small pack and started to rise. His hand reached into the pack and shot out suddenly, and the sprite, quick as it was, could not avoid the wide-spreading reach of the hurled net. The creature thrashed and scrambled, but Gary was on it, quick as a cat. He grabbed it up in one hand, cried out as it drove a tiny dagger into his palm, then closed his other hand over its head.

"All I want is for you to take her along with me," he explained to the suddenly calm sprite. "Just take her to Faerie. You can do that."

The creature uttered some response, its high-pitched voice moving too fast for Gary to decipher any words.

Gary closed his hand a bit tighter over the sprite's head. "Tell them to dance around her," he said, suddenly grim. "Or I'll squish your little head." It was an idle threat, of course; Gary would never harm one of Faerie's fairies. But the sprite, engulfed by a pair of hands that were each nearly half the size of its entire body, was in no position to take any chances. Again came its squeaking voice, and a moment later, the fairy ring broke apart, the soft lights flickering away into the darkness.

Gary didn't know if he had been deceived, and he clutched the sprite a bit tighter, fearing that it too would fade away into the night. He breathed easier when the lights and the song reappeared, encircling Diane with their magic. Gary let go of the sprite and removed the net and quickly joined his wife in the ring. He winced when a not-unexpected little arrow stung him in the butt—but he figured he had earned that.

Gary didn't fall asleep immediately, though, felt no tingling poison coursing through his veins. He looked back to the sprite, on the slab still, bow in hand and glaring wickedly his way, and he realized that the arrow had not been poison-tipped, had not been fired for any better reason than payback. Gary started to say, "Touché," but stopped and fought hard to hold his balance as all the world blurred around him, blurred and began to spin, slowly and smoothly, like the soft lights of the fairy ring.

And then they were on a ridge in Tir na n'Og, under a beautiful starry sky and with a very confused Mickey McMickey staring open-mouthed at the sleeping Diane.

Gary tossed a mischievous wink and a smile at the leprechaun's unusually stern expression, but Mickey just shook his head slowly, back and forth.

SEVEN

Into the Fire

THEY charged in fiercely, every man carrying a sword, axe, or spear and a blazing torch. By Prince Geldion's assessment, the thick edge of Tir na n'Og was akin to a castle wall, and the assault on the elfish stronghold was on in full.

Bows hummed in retaliation from every bough. A deadly rain of arrows cut deep into the Connacht ranks, leaving men sprawled and screaming. But many were Geldion's soldiers, and whether out of loyalty to the crown or simple fear of Geldion, their line would not waver. Their voices raised in a singular battle cry, they reached the forest's edge and hurled their torches, hundreds of torches, into the thick underbrush.

Flames, the forest's bane, sprouted in a dozen places, two dozen, and through all the openings between the fires, the Connacht soldiers flowed into the wood, hacking at the trees themselves for lack of any apparent elfish targets.

Kelsey, commanding the guard, looked down from his high perch in a tall elm and knew immediately that the perimeter had been overwhelmed. He heard a rumble of thunder overhead and took hope, for the elfish wizards had gone to work, using their magic to try to counteract the fires.

"Down!" the elf-lord called to his ranks, a cry echoed from tree to tree. The elfs had miles of forest behind them and could easily escape the clumsy humans in the darkness. But Kelsey had no intention of running, not yet. If the Tylwyth Teg allowed Connacht any foothold into Tir na n'Og, their greatest advantage, the open fields surrounding the forest, would be lost.

Kelsey verily ran down his tree, bow ready in his hands. He spotted the black silhouettes of three men in front of the nearest fire, and fired as he stepped lightly down to the ground, dropping one of the soldiers in his tracks. Out came Kelsey's magical sword, gleaming with elfish magic in the flickering light.

He was hard-pressed almost immediately as the two trained soldiers rushed to meet him. One snapped off a series of cuts with his sword, and Kelsey parried each one, while the other jabbed ahead with a long spear, keeping the elf on his heels, preventing him from launching any counterattacks.

Though the fires reflecting in the golden eyes truly revealed his inner rage, the elf suddenly wondered if he could win out—especially when he saw two more soldiers rushing in from the side.

He heard a bow from somewhere behind him, once and then again, and both the newcomers skidded down, one dead, the other curled in a ball, clutching at his bleeding belly. Kelsey took heart in the unexpected help, while his attackers eased up cautiously, as if they expected the next shots to be aimed at them.

The cat-and-mouse game went back and forth for several minutes. Kelsey working a defensive dance and every so often snapping off a thrust of his own. Always that long spear kept Kelsey's strikes measured, though, the tip of his marvelous sword whipping across short of its mark as the elf was continually forced back on his heels.

And no more bows sounded from the trees. The fighting was all about them by then, the ring of steel on steel, graceful elfish blades smacking against the heavier and thicker weapons of the burly humans. Melodic elfish songs joined in the chorus of the Connacht battle cries, and Kelsey took heart again. This was his home, the elfish home, beautiful Tir na n'Og.

A bolt of lightning split the dark sky, followed by a sudden downpour, rain pelting the fires of the invaders.

"You cannot win!" Kelsey screamed at the two men he was fighting. "Not here!" His sword darted ahead, three times in rapid succession. He slashed it out to his right, knocking aside a halfhearted counter by the human swordsman, then brought it back hard and down to his left, catching the shaft of the thrusting spear, bringing its tip down to the ground and cutting right through its thick wood.

The spearman cried out and threw his hands up in front of his face, thinking the elf's ensuing backhand aimed at him. But Kelsey's sword cut short of that mark, whipping back to his right to knock aside the swordsman's next thrust. Kelsey stepped ahead and jabbed, quicker than the swordsman could react, and the man grasped at his punctured breast and stumbled to the ground.

The spearman had turned to flee by the time Kelsey came back the other way, but he wasn't fast enough to get out of range of Kelsey's deadly sword. The thrust started for the man's back and would have easily slipped right through his meager armor and into his lung. But Kelsey thought of Mickey then, and their earlier encounter with the pitiful human. He remembered Gary Leger, his friend. Candella had given her life in retrieving Donigarten's armor and spear, for the sake of Gary Leger, and ultimately, for the sake of all of Faerie.

The adventures of the last few weeks had taught haughty Kelsenellenelvial Gil-Ravadry many lessons; had, in many ways, allowed the elf to rise above his xenophobic kin. He was Tylwyth Teg, and certainly proud of that, but the world was a wide place, big enough to share with the other goodly races.

His sword caught up to the fleeing human, but dipped low, taking the soldier in the back of the hamstring. The man fell to the ground, crying in agony, but very much alive.

That was why the defenders of Tir na n'Og were better than their attackers, Kelsey told himself. That measure of mercy was why the goodly folk of Faerie would, in the end, win out over the evil that darkened Faerie's clear skies.

On ran the elfish warrior, leaping burning brands, the fires already lower, and many of them sputtering from the drenching rain. Kelsey boldly rushed in wherever he saw battle, his ferocity and deft swordplay quickly turning the tide in the favor of his kinfolk. And then he ran on to the next battle, sweeping those elfs in his wake, spearheading an undeniable force. With every skirmish Kelsey joined, more elfs came into his fold and more of the Connacht army was turned away. Soon the whole line of elfish warriors was moving as a singular unit through the darkness, silent as death on the soaked leaves.

By contrast, the Connacht assault was scattered, the small groups of soldiers wandering disoriented. They heard the cries of the wounded, and more and more of those cries were human and not elfish. Any of the soldiers who found the edge of the forest ran off across the fields, seeking to regroup with Geldion's rear lines halfway to Dilnamarra, or merely to flee altogether, wanting no part of Tir na n'Og and its staunch defenders. Other groups wandered aimlessly in the forest, lost without their fires to guide them, until Kelsey and his warriors fell upon them.

Several of the Tylwyth Teg died that night, most in the first furious moments of battle. Many more humans died, and many more than that were taken captive. Kelsey took note of how readily many of the humans surrendered their weapons. It seemed to him as if their heart was not in this fight. In contrast, not a member of the Tylwyth Teg would surrender, no matter the odds, nor would their likely allies, the tough Buldrefolk of Dvergamal, Geno's folk. Kelsey had once seen Geno fighting wildly in the midst of a dozen huge trolls, outnumbered and with no chance of winning. But fighting on anyway, with no thought of surrender.

This, too, was the strength of the outnumbered opposition to King Kinnemore. Their strength, and the Connacht army's weakness.

"YE should'no' have brought her," Mickey remarked, and his words were accentuated by the distant sounds of the raging battle. They were in Tir na n'Og, Gary knew, just by the smell of the place. He looked around, his eyes adjusting to the darkness. They were in a small empty gully edged by dirt and moss walls, and both sides capped by tangles of birch. The night sky weighed low with thick clouds, and the heavy rain sent rivulets of water streaming down the gully's side.

"It's not a good time in Faerie, lad," the leprechaun remarked.

"Unlike the other two times I've been here," Gary replied sarcastically. He skipped up to a high bluff and peered into the distant blackness, trying to catch a glimpse of the action. "Geldion?" he asked.

"Who else?" Mickey replied.

"Ceridwen is free, then," Gary reasoned.

"Not yet," answered the leprechaun. "She's another couple o' weeks to go, but she's sent her calling card, first to Dilnamarra, and now to Tir na n'Og."

Gary paused to consider that for a moment, always amazed at the different rates at which time passed between the worlds. He had been on two adventures in Faerie, each lasting weeks, and yet, on both occasions, he had awakened back in his own world barely hours later than when he had left. This time, years had passed in his own world, while only weeks had gone by in Faerie. Mickey had explained it as depending upon which way the sprites were turning in their dancing ring when they opened the portal between the worlds. Gary could only hope they had danced correctly again—else he and Diane might well miss the turn of the century!

With that thought tucked behind him, Gary considered the leprechaun's words. "First to Dilnamarra," Mickey had said, but what did that bode for Gary's friends in the muddy hamlet?

"Baron Pwyll . . ." he started to inquire, but he stopped when he turned to look upon Mickey, the leprechaun slowly shaking his head, his cherubic features more grim than Gary had ever seen them.

"No," Gary breathed in denial.

"He died a hero, lad," was the best that Mickey could offer. "He could've saved his skin by giving praise to King Kinnemore, but he knew what that praise—and Dilnamarra's unintentional alliance with the Connacht army—might mean for the folk o' the other towns."

"Where's Geno?" Gary asked immediately, fearing that he had lost more than one friend in his absence. "And Gerbil?"

"The dwarf's halfway to Braemar by now, would be me guess," Mickey answered easily, glad that he could deliver some good news, as well. "And there, the gnome's waiting for him, so he said."

Gary breathed easier. Down in the gully, Diane groaned and shifted, wakened by the stream of chilly water rushing past her prone form.

"I'll be expecting a proper introduction," Mickey announced.

Gary nodded. He had every intention of letting Diane get well acquainted with Mickey. By the sound of that battle, the war was not so far away, and Gary couldn't afford to have Diane wandering about in a state of denial. She would have to be "convinced" that Faerie was very real in a short time.

An agonized cry split the night. Gary looked down upon Diane and wondered if he had been wise to bring her to this place.

DESPITE Mickey's claims to the contrary, Geno Hammerthrower was far from all right, and a lot farther from Braemar than the leprechaun believed. The dwarf had camped in Cowtangle Wood, a small forest along the eastern road, two days before, after making fine progress out from Dilnamarra.

A short nap was all the sturdy dwarf allowed himself, rising long before the dawn and running off. More than once, Geno slammed face-first into trees in the dark wood, but the impact hurt the trees more than the dwarf. He cleared the eastern edge of Cowtangle with the breaking dawn, but skidded to a quick stop after climbing over the first rise in the rolling fields.

There sat Connacht soldiers, twenty at least, their speartips gleaming in the morning light, their horses blowing steam into the brisk air with every snort.

Geno paused for a split second, trying to decide whether he should turn

back, or walk on calmly, feigning ignorance of the events in Dilnamarra. He had
just dismissed the latter course, and was turning back to the wood, when one of
the soldiers spotted him and cried out.

"Stonebubbles!" the dwarf grumbled, perhaps the very worst of dwarfish
curses. The thunder of hooves sounded behind him, one soldier called out for
him to halt, and Geno suspected that this was no chance encounter.

He figured that he had a chance if he could get within the protective thick
boughs of Cowtangle. If he could keep the soldiers scattered, their horses moving slowly through the heavy underbrush, he could outmaneuver them and hit
at them individually.

That plan was lost almost immediately, though, when the dwarf saw riders
flanking him, outdistancing him back to the tree line. Geno veered for a hillock
instead, and got to the high ground at the same time as a rider, coming up the
back side.

The soldier lowered his speartip as he closed on the dwarf, but a second
later, he was rolling over backwards in his saddle, knocked unconscious by a
spinning hammer. He tumbled heavily to the ground, and Geno tried to catch
hold of his horse. But the beast was too tall for the dwarf, and for all his frantic
efforts to leap onto the nervous beast, all Geno got was a horseshoe-shaped
bruise on the side of his chest.

"Stonebubbles!" the dwarf growled again, planting himself firmly in the
center of the high ground, looking around at the tightening ring of soldiers.

"You cannot escape, Geno Hammerthrower," one man asserted, and the
dwarf growled again at the sound of his name, at the confirmation that he had
been expected all along. He cursed Kelsey and Mickey for convincing him to
follow them back to Dilnamarra before turning east; cursed Kinnemore and
Geldion, those two upstart pretenders who knew nothing about ruling and
nothing about the land; cursed Ceridwen, and Gary Leger for ever letting the
witch out of her hole; cursed Robert for forcing all of this; cursed Gerbil for not
going along on the scouting mission to the fields near Connacht; cursed everything and everyone, except for his Buldrefolk kin and the stones they lived among.

Geno was not in a good mood, as the next soldier who tried to scale the hill
found out. The rider came up slowly, talking calmly, explaining to the dwarf
that it would be better for all if he simply surrendered and went along with
them back to Dilnamarra, "where all would be explained."

Geno's first hammer spun between the ears of the ducking horse, and
caught the man full on the chest. Before he could even try to draw his breath
again, Geno's next shot nailed him square in the faceplate of his great helm,

bending the metal against the man's nose and crossing his eyes. If he had been a wise man, the soldier would have fallen over, but he grasped the bridle tightly and stubbornly held his seat.

Geno's third hammer got him in the head again, and all the world was suddenly spinning.

Geno cursed himself for being so foolish as to throw three hammers at one target. With four on the ground, he only had six remaining. Six for twenty enemies.

The dwarf just sighed as the charge came on. He spun a complete circuit, launching hammers at equal intervals so that all sides of the hillock got one. Three of four shots took down riders; the fourth knocked a horse so silly that it began turning tight circles, hopping up and down, despite its frantic rider's tugs and cries.

The ring closed about Geno, but only a few riders could get up the hillock at one time. Holding his last remaining hammers, one in each hand, the dwarf looked for the area of most confusion and boldly charged, his muscled arms pumping away at rider and horse alike. He couldn't reach up high enough to strike at any vital areas, but found that a hammer smash on a kneecap more often than not drained an enemy's desire for the fight. One horse, confused as its rider lurched in agony, turned sideways to the dwarf, banging into him. Geno growled and grabbed, and heaved with all his strength, turning the beast right over on the uneven ground.

Geno saw his break and meant to charge ahead, meant to leap right over the fallen man and beast and plunge through the surprised second ranks, using their confusion to give him a head start back towards the wood.

He couldn't ignore the speartip jabbing through the back of his shoulder as a soldier caught him from the other side.

Geno spun wildly, hammers chopping. One got hooked under the tip of the bloody, waving spear, the other slapped against the shaft.

"Hah!" Geno roared in victory. "No dwarf made that child's weapon!" In Geno leaped, smacking the broken shaft free of the man's grasp. The soldier threw his arm out to block, and Geno's hammers snapped upon the outstretched hand, one on either side.

How the soldier howled!

Geno crashed into the side of the horse, but bounced away, hearing another enemy approaching from behind. He turned his shoulders down as he hit the ground, falling into a roll at the approaching horse's feet.

The horse kicked and skipped, but Geno had the leverage. Ignoring the punishing hooves, the dwarf pressed onward, barreling under the steed, bringing it to a halt so abruptly that the rider pitched over the horse's head, crashing face down to the ground.

Up came Geno, spitting dirt and laughing wildly. A rider dove upon him and wrapped him in a bear hug, but Geno grabbed the man's thumbs, turned them outward, and simply fell to his knees, using his tremendous weight (it was said in Faerie that a dwarf weighed as much as an equal volume of lead) as a weapon. The man's hand bones broke apart and Geno was free, scooping up his hammers once more and darting back the other way, again into the area of most confusion.

A spear prodded towards him; he snapped off a hammer throw, caught the spear just below its tip and tugged, bringing the rider forward, bringing the man's face right in line with the spinning hammer.

Geno caught the hammer on the rebound, and paused, staring curiously for a moment, for the man's helmet had turned right about on his shoulders and Geno wondered if his head had turned with it. With a shrug, the dwarf hopped about.

And caught a flying spear right in the belly.

"Now that hurt," Geno admitted. One hammer fell from the dwarf's hand, and he clutched at the spear's shaft.

Using that moment of distraction, the nearest rider charged right for Geno, trampling the dwarf under his mount's pounding hooves.

Another man dismounted and cautiously approached. "He's out," the soldier announced, reaching down to see if the battered dwarf was still alive.

Geno bit that reaching hand, bit it and held on like a bulldog, growling and crunching even after a handful of soldiers fell over him, punching and kicking, battering him with their spearshafts and shields.

The beating went on for many minutes, and finally Geno fell limp. But even then, it took the Connacht soldiers a long time to extract their comrade's hand from the vise-grip that was the dwarf's mouth.

DIANE yawned deeply and stretched, her eyes still closed and the thick slumber of sprite's poison still dulling the edge of her consciousness. She groaned and rolled over onto her belly, and finally managed to crack open one eye.

It took some time for the image to solidify in her thoughts, for her to appreciate that she was staring at the strangest, curly-toed little pair of shoes she had ever seen. She rubbed both her eyes and forced them open, then locked her gaze on those shoes and scanned upward.

"Mickey?" she asked, her voice cracking with the effort. This was a leprechaun in front of her—this, had to be a leprechaun in front of her!—and she was no longer in Duntulme.

"Ah, good lad," Mickey replied, looking up the side of the muddy gully to Gary. "I see that ye've told her about me."

Diane shrieked and rolled away. She scrambled up to her knees, would have risen altogether and run off, had not Gary caught up to her and stopped her with an embrace.

"So good to know ye're speaking highly o' me," Mickey remarked dryly.

"She's just scared," Gary tried to explain, and he leaned his weight onto Diane, trying to hold the trembling woman steady. "This is all so different to her, so . . ."

"I'm knowing that better than yerself, lad," Mickey assured him. "I've seen more than a few of ye first awaken in Faerie. And, by yer stories, it seems she's already knowing it's no dream."

Diane pulled away, but the effort cost her her balance and she fell on her rump against the soft banking, skidding down in the loose mud and winding up seated squarely before Mickey. "This can't be happening," she whispered.

"Did you think that I was lying?" Gary asked her sharply.

Diane looked to regard him, was embarrassed that her reactions had wounded him. "I thought . . ." She searched for a way to complete the answer. "I believed that you believed," she stammered, "but that didn't mean that I believed!"

Gary's jaw dropped open as he tried to decipher that one.

"She'd be one to talk a gnome into a corner," Mickey put in, and he tossed a wink Diane's way, thinking that she needed a friend at that moment.

"I mean, this can't happen," Diane blubbered on. "Those stories . . . your adventures . . . they couldn't have been real. I mean . . . oh, hell, I don't know what I mean." She put her head in her hands, staring down at the ground.

"I know what ye mean," Mickey said reassuringly.

"Oh, shut up," Gary said to the leprechaun.

"And let yerself take care of it?" Mickey was quick to respond. "Rest yerself easy, lad, but it's not seeming to me that ye're taking much care of it."

Gary started to retort, but stopped, mouth open and one finger pointing accusingly Mickey's way. In thinking about it for that instant, though, Gary realized he had nothing to accuse Mickey of.

"Is it so bad that the lad's stories were true?" Mickey asked Diane in all seriousness. The leprechaun waved his hand and a rainbow-colored flower, each of its soft petals a different hue, appeared in Diane's hand. She looked at it incredulously, sniffed its delicate aroma, then turned a questioning gaze upon Mickey.

"Is it?" Mickey asked again. "Wasn't there just a bit o' ye that wanted to go where the lad said he'd gone?"

"More than just a bit," Diane admitted. "But that . . ."

"But that's all ye need," Mickey interrupted. "And so ye've found yer way. Be happy with that, and happy with this. Tir na n'Og's a beautiful place, I tell ye, though ye could've picked a better time to come."

Diane sat staring, from Gary to Mickey, and back to Gary again. She looked to her cameras, the Pentax in its case at her side and the Polaroid bouncing in front of her, and then turned her gaze back to Mickey again.

"Here then, what'd ye bring?" the observant Mickey asked.

Diane's green eyes narrowed.

"Not now," Gary said to her. She turned to him, her expression revealing her surprise.

"Not now," Gary said again. "You'll have plenty of time for your pictures later."

"Pitchers?" Mickey asked, not understanding.

"Pic-tures," Gary clarified. "A bit of magic from our world."

"Oh, that I'd dearly love to see," said Mickey, to which Diane snickered and Gary emphatically reiterated, "Not now!"

Both Diane and Mickey turned a sour look upon Gary.

The man snapped his fingers. "But I did bring you these," he explained, pulling off his small book bag and fumbling with the tie. He produced a boxed set of four books, *The Hobbit* (but not the copy that Mickey had changed) and *The Lord of the Rings* trilogy.

"The rest of the story," Gary explained to the beaming leprechaun. "For you to keep."

Mickey waved his little hand, and the boxed set rose into the air from Gary's hand and floated gently across the empty space to Mickey's waiting fingers. Obviously thrilled, Mickey waggled those fingers, and the boxed set seemed smaller suddenly, then smaller still, then no more than the size of a postage stamp.

"I'll be keepin' this safe," Mickey remarked, tossing another wink Diane's way, and he tucked the shrunken treasure into one of his gray waistcoat's many pockets.

Diane found that she was laboring to find her breath again. It wasn't only the leprechaun's telekinesis that astounded her, but the way Mickey had accepted the books. Diane remembered keenly that time Gary had shown her his special copy of *The Hobbit*, the book that he claimed had been altered by a leprechaun's magic. According to Gary, Mickey McMickey had cast a spell over the book so that its type had transformed into the flowing Gaelic-looking script that now adorned its pages. It was the most solid evidence that Gary had ever shown to Diane concerning his journeys to this magical land, and the one piece that she had always found difficult to rationalize in her logical doubting of Gary's tales.

Now that book, and the others in the series, seemed a link to reality for the young woman. Everything fit together too perfectly to be denied. She was in Faerie, in this land that Gary had told her about for all these years. She was sitting before a leprechaun!

She broke out in laughter, wild laughter, and both Gary and Mickey looked at her with more than a little concern, fearing that the shock of it all had driven her to hysteria.

Diane was flustered, overwhelmed, but she was not hysterical, and she gulped down her laughter, sobered in the blink of an eye, when a beautiful, golden-haired and golden-eyed creature, too delicate to be a man, walked into the sandy gully from the trees behind Gary.

Gary turned, and a smile widened on his face to see Kelsey once again.

"Well met, Gary Leger," the elf greeted, walking over to clasp arms with the man. "You are needed now, perhaps more than ever before."

Gary nodded, and Kelsey's remark took on a suddenly greater significance when the man noticed the blood staining the elf's boots, as though Kelsey had been standing in a deep puddle of the crimson liquid.

Diane came up to Gary's side, staring blankly as she studied the elf from head to toe.

"This is Kelsey," Gary explained.

"Kelsenellenelvial Gil-Ravadry," Diane quickly corrected, remembering the proper name Gary had given to his elfish companion.

Kelsey did not blink at the surprise correction, but gave a slight approving nod—Diane could not have said anything else to make a better first impression.

Watching the three, hearing Kelsey's greeting, Mickey was beginning to believe that maybe the elf had been right in insisting that Gary be brought back to Faerie. After Pwyll's startling defiance, and subsequent demise, the people of the land might be looking for a hero—a living hero—to lead the struggle, and it just so happened that this would-be hero fit perfectly into the armor of the legendary Cedric Donigarten.

Mickey didn't know where Diane might fit in, but considering the way she had just handled (indeed, the way she had charmed) the stern elf, she seemed resourceful enough.

"Oh, begorra," the leprechaun muttered, and a snap of his fingers brought his long-stemmed pipe floating from a pocket to his mouth, lighting as it went.

EIGHT

An Oath to Sir Cedric

THE overcast dawn came quietly, with no more fighting along Tir na n'Og's southern border. Many men had been slain the previous night, and only a few elfs, but with Connacht's overwhelming odds, the Tylwyth Teg could hardly claim a victory.

Mickey spent the early morning with Diane, talking to her in great detail about the events of the last few weeks, and particularly about Gary's role in those events. While they were chatting, Gary and Kelsey wandered off. At first Diane was nervous about being left by Gary in this strange world, but Mickey's charming manner soon put her at ease.

She began to think about leprechauns, about the stories in her own world. Images of rainbows and pots of gold came to mind, and she fixed an intent stare upon Mickey, hardly hearing his words.

Mickey understood that look, had seen it from humans for years and years. He said nothing, figuring that she'd just have to learn for herself, and confident that if the woman came after him, he could easily evade her.

To Diane's credit, her expression gradually softened and she relaxed back, the moment of greedy weakness passed. Mickey didn't miss the point, and he silently applauded the young woman.

Gary and Kelsey returned soon after, bearing heavy bundles and Gary holding the most incredible spear Diane had ever seen. She got up to her feet and moved near to him, running her hands over the flat part of the magnificent weapon's wide head.

"This is for you," Kelsey explained, putting down his bundle and turning it over so that a coat of fine, interlocking links of chain rolled out onto the grass.

Gary overturned his bundle as well, and the bulky plates of Donigarten's armor spilled onto the ground.

Diane was staring open-mouthed at the fabulous armor—of course Gary had described it to her in great detail, but seeing it was something altogether different!—when Kelsey approached her, the chain mail coat in hand.

"Put this on," he bade her. "Tir na n'Og has ever been a safe place for those whom the Tylwyth Teg name as a friend, but in these dark times, we cannot be sure."

While Kelsey turned to help Gary in strapping on the bulky pants, Diane slipped the metal jacket over her head. It was surprisingly light, no more encumbering than a winter coat, and though it was a bit tight about her chest and shoulders, the fit was acceptable.

"Suits ye well," Mickey remarked, and he gave a wink as Diane looked over to him.

Kelsey came over just long enough to offer Diane a belt and scabbard, holding a slender sword. The woman eyed it suspiciously, nervously.

"Take it," Kelsey instructed.

"Just in case," Mickey added, seeing the woman's dilemma.

Diane did as she was told. She handled the sword tentatively, strapping on the belt and eyeing Gary all the while. For the first time, she began to understand that they might be given specific assignments by the leaders of the elfish resistance, that they might be separated. And with a sword strapped around her waist, Diane could hardly ignore the possibility that she might see battle.

Gary had most of the armor on by then, and he returned Diane's stare, almost apologetically. Gary knew how Diane felt about violence, knew that she thought of war as an incredibly stupid exercise in futility. Whenever he had tried to tell her of the battles he had seen in Faerie, she had only half listened, waiting for him to get past the violence and back to the story.

"You will be shown to a guard position," Kelsey explained to Diane. "We have many prisoners, and can spare few of our warriors to watch over them."

Diane didn't stop looking at Gary, and didn't blink.

"Gary Leger will accompany me," Kelsey went on, understanding her questioning look. "His presence will bolster the defense of the forest and bring fear to our enemies."

Diane's look quickly turned sour, and Gary flinched. Diane was wondering why he was apparently being given a more important role than she, he knew.

I wear the armor of Cedric Donigarten," he said, as though that should explain it all.

"So I'll sit back here while you go off to fight," Diane retorted. "Like a good little wife."

Gary flinched again, suddenly more afraid of the next time Diane got him alone than any horrors he might encounter on the battle lines.

"Be reasonable," he said. "You've got no idea of how to fight with a sword."

"What about you?"

"I have the spear," Gary replied. "It talks to me, and has told me how to fight. I explained all of that to you a long time ago."

"Then let me use it," Diane stubbornly replied, though she knew that to be impossible, and didn't really want the blasted thing anyway.

Young sprout! came the sentient spear's telepathic scream of protest in Gary's mind.

"I think it's a chauvinist," Gary explained with a helpless shrug.

"SHE is strong-willed," Kelsey remarked after he, Gary, and Mickey had left Diane with the other guards, the three heading back to the south, where the fighting had renewed. The rain, too, had begun again, a heavy drenching downpour. Kelsey understood the implications of the storm; elfish wizards were in control of the weather over Tir na n'Og, and they were using the rain to douse fires set by Kinnemore's men. Given the strength of this storm, Kelsey figured that the assault on Tir na n'Og must be on in full.

"Lucky me," Gary answered, but his sarcasm was apparently lost on Kelsey.

"Indeed," the elf said sincerely.

Gary regarded Kelsey for a moment, then chuckled softly. Of course the Tylwyth Teg valued the role of the elfish females, he realized, and precisely because there was no defined "role" for elfish females. They fought alongside the males, led and followed. They went out on life-quests, as serious as the one Kelsey had undertaken to reforge Donigarten's spear. In fact, that very morning Gary had learned that the King of the Tylwyth Teg was not a "King" at all, but a Queen, an elfish female who had ascended to the rather informal seat of power in Tir na n'Og through her leadership and battle prowess in a war a century before.

And it struck Gary, too, how complete a person Kelsey was. The elf could be the fiercest of warriors (Gary had seen that side) or the quietest of poets. Kelsey seemed equally at ease to Gary with a sword in hand or a flower. Gary nearly laughed aloud at the notion, thinking that the elf, without even trying, would surely fit into the "political correctness" of his own world. Within the society of the Tylwyth Teg, there were none of the preconceived notions, the barriers, sharply defining gender roles, and yet, their existence was certainly more primitive and harsh than Gary's society.

He'd have to spend more time thinking about that issue, he decided. It seemed to Gary that Kelsey held the answer to the frustrations of feminists and the confusion of men in his own world.

But he'd have to think about it later, a cry of pain from somewhere not too far ahead pointedly reminded him. The business now at hand was battle.

Kelsey went down into a crouch and signaled for Gary to hold steady. In an instant Kelsey was gone, disappearing into the heavy brush without a whisper of sound. Gary tensed, went down to one knee, then breathed easier as Mickey appeared atop his shoulder.

Mickey, whose senses were by far the keener, nodded ahead a moment later, signaling Kelsey's return.

Again, Kelsey came through the brush without a whisper of sound. He looked to Gary, nodded, and held up six fingers, then motioned for the man to flank to the left.

Gary eased up and moved slowly and deliberately, though he felt awkward and noisy indeed compared to the graceful forest dance of Kelsey. He stopped when he felt the burden on his shoulder lighten, and a panicked look came over him at the thought that Mickey wouldn't be by his side.

"Easy lad, I'll be about," Mickey promised from a low branch just behind him.

Gary adjusted his great helm, which was far too loose-fitting, and moved on through the thicket, coming to the edge of a small and shady clearing beneath the thick boughs of a wide elm.

Patience, young sprout, came the spear's call in his head, and Gary agreed with the assessment and crouched low in the brush, waiting.

There came a groan from not so far away.

Patience, the spear reminded him once more, sensing Gary's desire to rush off and investigate. A few moments later, Kelsey came running through the brush, to the edge of the clearing to Gary's right. A leaning log marked that border, about waist high, but hardly a barrier to the nimble elf. Bloodied sword in hand, Kelsey dove headlong over the log, touched the ground with his free hand and ducked his head so that he rolled right over and right back to his feet. He crossed the clearing with a few graceful strides, lifted his arm and leaped up, catching the elm's lowest branch. He was gone in the blink of Gary Leger's astonished eye, rolling up around the limb and disappearing into the cover of the trees' thick boughs.

"There's only one!" came a cry, a human voice, not so far behind.

"Flank to the right!" called another.

Gary watched as three men came to the log. They slowly crossed the barrier, two crawling under, readied crossbows in hand, and the third scrambling over. These were trained soldiers, Gary realized, from the way they complemented and covered one another's movements. They entered the clearing cautiously, looking all about, particularly to the sheltering elm. The fully armored crossbowmen kept the lead, holding close to the brush and easing around to their left, towards Gary. The third man, wearing only a leather jerkin and holding no weapons that Gary could see, took up the rear, quietly directing.

The man looked to the right more than once, and Gary figured that his companions would soon be coming around the clearing, probably entering from the other side.

Gary wrung his hands nervously over the metal shaft of the great spear. His stomach was in knots; he felt like he had to go to the bathroom.

Easy, young sprout.

So nervous was he that Gary almost replied to the spear's reassurance out loud! He didn't know where Kelsey had gone off to, didn't know what Kelsey expected him to do. The soldiers were close to him then; he could leap out and likely take one of them down.

He wondered how good Donigarten's armor might be against a crossbow fired point-blank.

Gary's relief at seeing Kelsey's return lasted only the moment it took him to realize that the elf had just walked out from around the elm's trunk, right into the open! He opened his mouth and almost called out, then fell back and winced as the crossbows fired and Kelsey fell.

Now! the sentient spear implored him, and purely on instinct, Gary leaped from the brush, right before the two armored soldiers. He slashed the spear straight across in front of him, taking the blocking crossbow from the hands of the nearest man, crunching the crosspiece on the bow of the second man.

Back across came the slicing spear, and Gary blindly thrust straight ahead. The soldier almost dodged, but got hit on the shoulder. A normal weapon would have done little damage, would have merely deflected off the metal plating of the man's armor to ride high to the side. But Donigarten's hungry spear bit hard and the soldier's armor melted away, the spear's wicked tip diving deep into the man's shoulder. He fell to the ground, clutching the wound, writhing in pain.

Overbalanced to the right, Gary stopped his momentum and jabbed straight back with the butt end of the spear. He was aiming for the second soldier's belly, but the spear came in a bit low.

The new angle proved even more effective, though, and the soldier groaned and lurched, his eyes crossed with pain.

Gary retracted and whipped the butt end straight up, slamming the man under the chin, under the faceplate of his helm. He straightened and staggered back a step, but not out of range of the long weapon as Gary butt-ended him again, squarely in the faceplate.

Down he went, flat on his back, his feet skidding out from under him on the slippery grass.

Gary came up straight, spinning to his right to face the third man squarely. He screamed out and tried frantically and futilely to dodge the sliver of metal spinning his way.

The man's shot was near perfect, the dagger coming point in at Gary's face-plate. Its tip sliced through the slits in the great helm and gashed the side of Gary's nose and his cheek. He screamed again and fell away, and purely out of fear, purely on a survival reflex, he hurled the spear.

The man in the leather jerkin, another dagger in hand, threw his arms out defensively in front of him.

The soaring spear crossed between them, though, and blasted right through the pitiful leather defense, right through the man's chest and back. He flew backwards, staggering many steps until he slammed against the log, where the spear tip bit again, through the dead wood, holding the dead man upright against it.

Gary, on the ground, one eye closed because of blood, the other teary, didn't see the hit. He was looking the other way, to the tree and beyond, where the missing two soldiers had entered the clearing and were looking over the fallen body of the elf, prodding the corpse with their swords.

At that moment, the real Kelsey dropped down from the boughs, right between them.

Gary didn't understand—until the image of the fallen elf dissipated into nothingness and Gary remembered that Mickey was not far away and that the leprechaun was especially proficient at crafting illusions of Kelsey.

The soldiers were not caught unawares. Kelsey's sword darted straight ahead, but was turned aside. It came streaking right back in, at a lower angle, but was slapped downward by a perfect parry.

Left, right and left again, Kelsey snapped his sword, now on the defensive and blocking the press of the two soldiers. Back to the right came the elf's fine weapon, steel rang out against steel, and Kelsey thrust straight ahead, aiming low. The soldier recovered quickly enough to parry, his sword again coming down atop Kelsey's, driving the elf's blade harmlessly low.

Kelsey expected the block and went with it, moving his sword down and to the right, towards the tip of the blocking sword. Kelsey stepped right, as well, just out of the reach of the other soldier's lunge. A subtle twist of the wrist brought Kelsey's sword around the soldier's, and the elf promptly stepped ahead.

The soldier snapped his angled sword upward, trying to throw Kelsey's weapon high and wide. The elf's forward thrust was too quick, though, and Kelsey's fine sword cut into the man's breastplate, drawing a deep red line up his chest and forcing him to fall back.

The other soldier came in furiously and Kelsey just managed to free up his blade and snap it across, deflecting his enemy's prodding sword when it was barely an inch from his side. Kelsey spun on his heel and launched a weak two-strike combination that had no chance of hitting. The maneuver bought him enough time to square up, though, putting his parries in line as the outraged soldier came forward once more.

The wounded soldier stubbornly stepped ahead, and worse, Kelsey heard the heavy footsteps of another enemy approaching from behind him. He plot-ted an evasive maneuver, a ducking spin that would allow him to swipe at the legs of the man coming in from the back and roll away from all three attackers.

But then the healthy fighter pressing the elf stepped back suddenly and dropped his weapon to the ground. He fell to his knees, swearing fealty to the memory of Sir Cedric Donigarten!

Kelsey batted away the weak swing of the wounded man, and looked back over his shoulder to see Gary Leger, weaponless and with blood running out from un-der his great helm. Obviously dizzy, Gary staggered stubbornly to join his friend.

"And what of you?" the quick-thinking Kelsey demanded, spinning back and thrusting his sword viciously at the wounded man. He batted the weak at-tempt at a parry aside and stood firm, his swordtip a foot from the man's wounded breast.

The soldier looked to his kneeling comrade, to the other two on the ground behind Gary and to the man standing limp, impaled against the log.

"Donigarten," he said quietly.

"On your word of honor!" Kelsey snarled, lunging ahead, closing the dis-tance between swordtip and breast. "Swear fealty."

"To Donigarten," the man said again and dropped his sword to the dirt. "An oath to Sir Cedric."

Kelsey eased his sword away, his golden eyes continuing their unrelenting stare at the man. Finally, convinced that this one would cause no more mischief, Kelsey turned a sidelong glance at Gary.

"I'm all right," Gary assured him, lifting his arm to keep the concerned elf at bay.

Kelsey nodded and looked beyond him. "We have five prisoners," he ex-plained. "For I injured but did not kill the man back in the woods."

Gary didn't have to look back to the log for the grim reminder that his spear throw had apparently claimed the only kill.

Mickey appeared then, atop the low branch just above them.

"A fine deception," Kelsey congratulated. "But temporary. My enemies would have been held longer off their guard if the illusion had held."

"I do what I can," Mickey replied, somewhat sourly.

"I have come to expect more of you," said Kelsey.

"And so ye got it," the leprechaun explained. "I was not so far away, turning aside another dozen o' the enemy. Suren the forest's thick with Kinnemore's army! And ye got four prisoners, not five, for the others found the man in the woods and took him off with them."

"Where are they now?" Kelsey demanded.

"Chasing yerself," Mickey explained. "Back the other way. Don't ye worry, I telled a fair amount o' yer kinfolk they'd be coming."

Kelsey nodded, Gary swayed, and the elf stepped over and offered him a supporting arm. He helped Gary sit down against the elm's thick trunk and gently removed the helm. The wound was superficial, though bloody and obviously painful. Kelsey reached into a pouch for some healing herbs, but Gary stopped him.

"They need you more," Gary explained, indicating the Connacht soldiers. The one healthy man was trying to tend the other three.

Kelsey agreed with the observation and left Gary with a clean cloth and a vial of clear water. He started to clean the wound, and nearly swooned from the sharp pricks of pain. Mickey walked up next to him and took the cloth.

"Nasty nick, but not so deep," the leprechaun assured him. Despite Mickey's comforting words, Gary noted a good measure of tension in Mickey's voice. He studied Mickey closely, with the usually perceptive leprechaun too involved to even notice.

"Are there that many enemies in the forest?" Gary asked, thinking that to be the cause of Mickey's distress.

"What's that?" Mickey asked, startled by the unexpected question. "Oh, no, lad, not too many for Kelsey's kin to fight off."

"Then what is it?" Gary demanded.

"There's some fires burning," Mickey answered.

"In this rain?" Gary could hardly believe it; the ground was near to flooding, and the tree branches sagged low under the pounding and unrelenting downpour.

"Our enemies got their means," was all that Mickey would say, and he went back to his work.

A group of Tylwyth Teg entered the clearing a few minutes later, a handful of human prisoners in tow. They immediately went to help Kelsey with the wounded, and to speak with the elf-lord, and by their grim expressions Gary realized that they had learned what Mickey had learned. The young man pulled himself up from the ground and walked over to join them. By the time he got there, Kelsey too wore a grave look.

Gary was about to ask for an explanation when he got his answer. A flaming ball of pitch soared through the gray sky, slamming the high top of a tree not so far away. Despite the rain, the burning pitch clung to the tree's branches.

"Catapults," one of the elfs explained. "Across the field and out of bowshot, and with ranks of soldiers dug in between them and the forest."

"They'll not take Tir na n'Og," Kelsey added. "But surely they mean to despoil it."

The targeted tree exploded as the pitch burned its way to the sap core. Flames shot high into the air, defying the rain.

NINE

The Oldest Trick in the Book

THE determined group was in agreement that the Tylwyth Teg had to get to the catapults—what else might these creatures of Tir na n'Og think with their beautiful forest being despoiled right before their eyes? Kelsey and two of the other older elfs spoke of gathering as many warriors as they could spare to launch a full-out attack through the Connacht lines.

They were desperate, and, by Gary's estimation, so was their plan. How many elfs would die for the sake of stopping those catapults? And if the cost to the Tylwyth Teg was high, what would stop Kinnemore from simply constructing new ones? Gary told Kelsey and the others just that, and though, to their credit, none of them responded with the "Have you got a better idea?" cliche, resourceful Gary did indeed have a better plan.

"Our targets are the catapults," he explained. "And only the catapults. There's no reason to fight Kinnemore's men all the way to them."

"We have no time to flank the long lines," Kelsey interjected. Despite the fact that Kelsey was the sole elf voicing any doubts, he alone among the gathering was listening intently to Gary's ideas. The young man from Real-earth had proved his worth and his ability to improvise several times over the last two adventures. Gary Leger was the one who had devised the plan that allowed them to escape from imprisonment on Ceridwen's isle; Gary Leger was the one who had figured out a way to beat the dreaded dragon.

"No need to go around," Gary calmly and confidently explained.

"You mean to walk right through the enemy?" another elf, a noble-looking, black-haired creature by the name of TinTamarra, asked skeptically. Thinking he had solved Gary's puzzle, TinTamarra turned a suspicious eye, a green eye that seemed to burn with inner fires, on Mickey. "The leprechaun is good with tricks, but he cannot fool so large a concentration of men, not when they are lined in battle trenches, expecting danger."

"Mickey's role will be minor," Gary assured the elf. "But those two"—he pointed to two of the men who had sworn fealty to the memory of Cedric Donigarten—"will perform the deception."

Every elf in the clearing wore a sour expression—every elf except for Kelsey, who was beginning to catch on.

"Prisoners?" he asked, and Gary nodded, understanding that Kelsey was not referring to the captured Connacht soldiers.

"Caught by the men," Gary answered. "Caught by those two soldiers and by the wearer of Donigarten's armor."

"Kinnemore, or at least Prince Geldion, knows your allegiance to Kelsenellenelvial," TinTamarra put in.

Gary was shaking his head before the dark-haired elf even finished. "The Prince knows only that I accompanied Kelsenellenellenell . . . Kelsey on the quest to reforge the spear and in the matter of defeating Robert. If Kinnemore is as close to Ceridwen as everybody says, then he likely knows that it was I who banished her to her island, but also that it was I who released her from her bondage. Even more, by the King's own words, it was said that I came along only to steal the armor and spear and make for Bretaigne, for my own purposes and without the blessings of the Tylwyth Teg. They don't know my true allegiance, and I would bet that they'll be thrilled to learn, and eager to believe, that I have come to join their cause."

It sounded somewhat reasonable, but more than a little dangerous, and most of the elfs were shaking their heads as they whispered among themselves.

"Perhaps it would be best if you remained behind," Kelsey offered at length to Gary. "I, and two or three of my kin will go, along with the two Connacht soldiers. If we get through to the catapults, they'll not fire again against Tir na n'Og."

"I'm thinking it's a bit more believable if ye take the lad," Mickey interjected, drawing the attention of all in the field. "It'll take more than a trick to
make Kinnemore's men—who've battled the Tylwyth Teg these last few days
and heared tales of elfish warriors all their lives—believe that the two o' them
catched any of ye. But if Gary Leger's along, and the men say he helped, it'll look
more believable. He's wearing Donigarten's armor, after all, and has been
named as the one who beat the dragon."

Kelsey stared hard at Gary, trying to determine which was the better reasoning.

"It's my plan," Gary said with a smile, and Kelsey appreciated that loyalty,
appreciated that Gary would be so willing, even eager, to undertake such a dangerous venture for the sake of Tir na n'Og.

"He goes," Kelsey announced, and there were a few grumbles, but no elf
spoke openly against the trusted elf-lord.

Just a few minutes later, Gary, Kelsey, Mickey, two other elfs including Tin-
Tamarra, and the two soldiers left the field. On Mickey's suggestion that it
would add credibility both to the illusion and to Gary's stature, and reasoning
that it would allow them to travel more easily, Kelsey called one of the magnificent white-coated Tir na n'Og horses for Gary.

Magnificent indeed did the wear of Donigarten's armor look, sitting tall
upon that steed! And, of course, with the mount, Gary could more than keep up
with the others.

Another benefit of Mickey's plan, one that the leprechaun didn't bother to
mention, was that he too, cuddled in his customary nook at the base of the
steed's neck, might enjoy the comfort of a ride.

They left Tir na n'Og in a line, Gary at the head, the four "captured" Tylwyth Teg behind him, and the two armed soldiers behind them. Gary appreciated how great a leap of faith Kelsey, and particularly the other two elfs, were
making at this point, to allow armed Connacht soldiers at their backs. Their
trust was a wonderful thing, Gary decided, and he was confident that they
would not be betrayed.

The group was surrounded immediately when they neared the Connacht
line. Mickey's illusion at this point was a simple one, the leprechaun merely
masking the fact that Kelsey and the other two elfs carried weapons and were
not nearly as wounded as they appeared.

"What is this about?" the field commander of the Connacht forces demanded, bypassing Gary and speaking to one of the traitorous soldiers. More

than once he looked suspiciously at Gary Leger; by all previous accounts, the stranger from Bretaigne was no friend to Kinnemore's throne.

"It is about prisoners," Gary answered boldly. He swung his mount about and walked it right before the field commander, demanding an audience.

The man eyed him dangerously. "I was speaking to . . ." he began, but Gary, sitting tall on the shining white stallion, looking magnificent indeed in his un-rivaled armor and holding the legendary spear, cut him short.

"You will address me!" Gary growled. "It was I who saved your pitiful sol-diers, and I who captured the three Tylwyth Teg."

"And left a dozen more lyin' dead in the woods," one of the traitorous sol-diers unexpectedly replied. In truth, the man had not spoken at all; the words had been thrown by an invisible Mickey McMickey, still nestled comfortably in the crook between Gary's saddle and his mount's strong neck.

The field commander continued to eye Gary suspiciously, unblinking. "It is rumored that you are allied with Tir na n'Og," he remarked and looked to his bristling soldiers, standing ready a short distance away.

"Would you prefer that I was?" Gary asked. "You impertinent insect! How many weeks will you lie here in the mud, while those wretched Tylwyth Teg dance free under the stars? Have you no desire for order?"

The man seemed truly perplexed, as Gary had hoped, but if he was con-vinced then of Gary's friendship, he did not show it.

"Stand your men aside and let us pass," Gary demanded.

The field commander straightened and narrowed his eyes. "Prisoners are to be kept in a barn to the east, not behind the line to the south," he said.

"These prisoners are not to be 'kept' at all!" Gary roared back. Mickey crin-kled his brow at that one, though, of course, nobody saw the movement. Kelsey too seemed concerned, for Gary was obviously improvising, trying to wriggle around the soldier's unexpected declaration. Next to Kelsey, TinTamarra closed his hand tightly about the hilt of his masked sword, ready for trouble.

"I have a surprise for the defenders of the forest," Gary went on, and he put so wicked a glare over Kelsey and the other elfs that they, for an instant, honestly wondered if he was betraying them. "Let us see how the elfish morale holds up when the living, screaming missiles crash in!"

The field commander swayed, overwhelmed by the unexpected announce-ment, and several of his soldiers began whispering and smiling at the devilish plan.

"By whose order?" the obviously shaken field commander asked.

"By my order!" Gary yelled at him. "By order of the dragonslayer, of the knight who defeated Redarm on the field of honor, and who now plans to take that fool's place by Prince Geldion's side.

"Bring them!" Gary instructed the two traitors, and he walked his steed forward, and, to his ultimate relief, the Connacht ranks parted.

"You may tell Prince Geldion that I await his presence at the catapults," Gary boldly called to the field commander. "Tell him to hurry, before I change my mindset and my loyalty!"

Kelsey and the other elfs could hardly believe how easily Gary had played on the man's fears. The other two looked to Kelsey for some explanation, and the elf-lord smiled and nodded, convinced again of this one's resourcefulness. Truly, the bluff had been perfect, as had the lie about launching living elfs from the catapults.

"Ye got a set on ye, not to doubt," Mickey praised when the group of seven moved beyond the ranks, not a word of dispute filtering from the soldiers they had left behind.

"A set?" Gary asked, not understanding.

"A set to make a heeland bull cry for envy!" Mickey laughed.

Gary chuckled and did not reply, not even to tell Mickey that, in truth, he had nearly wet his pants.

They came in sight of the catapult batteries a short while later, two of the war engines sitting low behind a ridge, each manned by a crew of half a dozen soldiers. Even as the companions watched, mesmerized by the workings, the closest catapult fired, the flaming pitch ball soaring high into the air towards Tir na n'Og.

On the second catapult, the men strained at a heavy crank, bending down the great beam.

"Hold!" Gary cried to them, kicking his mount out ahead of the others. "Hold and clear that basket!"

Twelve curious expressions turned on the armored man, the man from Bretaigne, they thought.

Gary walked his shining white steed down at a slow and comfortable pace, formulating his lies as he went. He meant to keep up the façade that they would launch the elfish prisoners into Tir na n'Og, to break the morale of the Tylwyth Teg. If the deception worked, Gary and his friends would be within the enemy ranks before the soldiers ever suspected anything amiss. If the deception worked, the fight might be relatively painless, the catapults quickly taken out of action.

Kelsey and the other proud elfs, watching the first pitch ball soar towards their precious forest home, watching the second catapult readied for another strike, had no more patience for deception and intricate plans. Gary was halfway to the enemy then, with more than one of the Connacht soldiers holding a weapon, when a volley of arrows raced in.

Gary's eyes widened in surprise. He heard the charge of Kelsey and the two other elfs (and of the two men, as well) coming behind him, and searched for some way to calm things back down, to put the situation back under control.

It had already gone past that, the young man realized. Two of the Connacht men lay in pools of blood, and the fight was on.

Gary kicked his steed into a run just as Kelsey came up even with him. Lifting his great bow, Kelsey skidded to a stop, and Gary charged on, screaming wildly. His scream changed in timbre as he saw one of the Connacht soldiers raise a loaded crossbow his way. But Kelsey saw the man, too, and the elf's arrow took him down before he could fire the crossbow.

The soldiers scattered before Gary's pounding charge. Another went down, an arrow in his side, and then a fifth, catching an arrow in the back as he scrambled to get over the bulk of the catapult.

Gary's mind raced frantically as he tried to pick out a target, looking from one fleeing group to another. A quick turn of his horse would have put him in line with one nearby man, would have allowed him to easily run the man down.

Gary missed the opportunity, and truly had little heart for killing these pitiful soldiers. He realized his best target a moment later, when he heard again the ominous clicking sound of the catapult bending to ready.

"Use all of your magic!" Gary cried aloud.

Throw well, young sprout! came the sentient spear's telepathic reply, the weapon reading Gary's thoughts and in complete agreement with the plan.

Gary lifted the spear in one hand as he came around the front of the closest catapult. He had to shift suddenly, though, when a form leaped out at him from the wooden base of the great war machine. The man crashed against Gary squarely, and Gary tightened his legs about his horse's flanks, just barely managing to hold his seat. One of the reins slipped from his grasp, and Mickey came visible holding tightly to it, hanging from the side of the horse's neck, his curly-toed shoes kicking frantically in the air. Gary let go the reins altogether, forced to hook his arm under the shoulder of his thrashing adversary.

The soldier's arm whipped across, his small axe slamming hard into Gary's chest. Cedric's armor turned the brunt of the blow and Gary heaved the man across his lap, laying him out straight over the saddle. They fumbled and struggled, and Gary freed up his arm just as the stubborn man started to rise, trying to pivot and bring his axe to bear once more.

Gary's metal-plated sleeve slammed hard against the back of the soldier's head, and he fell limp across the saddle. Gary grabbed him by the seat of his breeches and heaved him all the way over, then took up the reins again, and the spear, and turned his attention back to the catapult.

The great beading beam was only a few yards away by then, and Gary had no time to consider the implications of his actions, no time to consider that he would then be weaponless in the midst of armed enemies. He ignored Mickey's continuing cries for help for the moment, and hurled the spear. Its enchanted tip flashed like a lightning stroke as it hit, and then bit deeply into the neck of the bent beam. Energy surged from the powerful weapon, and cracks widened along the side of the beam.

The crew manning the weapon had no way of understanding the extent of the spear's damage, though, and they fired the catapult. The beam broke apart under the sudden jolt, the flaming ball lifting straight into the air, perhaps a dozen feet, then falling right back down, squarely into the framework of the disabled war machine.

Gary grabbed hard at the reins, reached desperately for Mickey, and swung his mount sharply to the side, smiling in grim satisfaction. That smile melted into horror as one man, covered with flames from the splattering pitch, ran screaming out from the other side of the catapult.

As he passed behind the bulky machine, Gary's horrified expression became one of fear. He pulled Mickey in close to him and tugged hard on the reins, and the Tir na n'Og steed responded by rearing onto its back legs at the same instant that the two crossbowmen fired. The evasive movement saved Gary's life, and Mickey's, but the horse, intercepting both bolts, was not so fortunate. The beast came back down to all four hooves, then continued down, headlong, throwing its riders straight to the ground.

Gary's breath blew away as he hit and started to roll, and that momentum was abruptly halted as his horse came all the way over, slamming against his twisted back. A blinding flash of pain exploded along the side of the man's neck and down the side of his back. The horse rolled right off him an instant later, lying dead on its side on the ground before him.

Only Gary's right arm came to his mental call that he had to get up and get out of there. He propped himself out of the muddy grass on his elbow and looked back to his left—to see his shoulder far out of place, far to the back of where it should have been. Waves of pain rolled out of that shoulder, washed over the fallen young man, and left him bathed in thick sweat. He stared incredulously at his twisted limb for many seconds, then looked beyond it, to Mickey, sitting on the grass and straightening his tam-o'-shanter.

A moment later, Gary felt the curious tickle of grass sticking through the slits in his helmet as he lay facedown on the field.

All six of the men on the first catapult, and one of the second crew, were downed by arrows before Kelsey and his kin got near the machine. Those losses, plus the man Gary had beaten and thrown from his saddle and the one who had died covered in fiery pitch, left only three soldiers remaining.

Three soldiers against three Tylwyth Teg.

Kelsey intercepted one, a large man wielding a two-headed axe, right beside Gary, the man apparently of a mind to finish Gary off. He swiped his axe across at Kelsey instead, but the elf nimbly jumped back out of range, the heavy weapon cutting the air an inch from Kelsey's sucked-in belly. Kelsey came forward a quick step, then retreated again as the axe came across in a furious backhand cut.

The action repeated, across and back, again, and then a third time, and with each swing, the growling soldier advanced a step, forcing Kelsey back. The man thought that he had the elf in trouble, thought he could back Kelsey all the way to the other catapult, where he would catch the elf, where he would cut the skinny elf in half.

But his swings were inevitably slowing, his arms fast tiring under the weight of the heavy weapon. Kelsey acted the part of a troubled adversary, feigning fear, even looking back nervously over his shoulder more than once. He had the man's measure, though, and only allowed the façade to continue because each swing slowed a bit more, ensured his victory a bit more.

"They're coming behind us!" one of the traitors who had accompanied Kelsey's band cried from the platform of the still-intact catapult. Kelsey heard chopping begin, the two men going to work on the machine.

The axe swiped across in front of the elf again, the growling man stubbornly coming on. But Kelsey had no more time for the game. The man reversed his grip, beginning the backhand, but suddenly the fierce elf was in his face, and the elf's fine sword was through his belly.

Kelsey caught the weakening swing of the axe in his free hand, eased the weapon, and then its wielder, to the ground. Looking ahead, he saw TinTamarra take down a second soldier, near the burning catapult, and saw the third elf chasing the remaining enemy away.

But suddenly there came from behind Kelsey a ticking sound, almost like the pounding of a hailstorm, and he spun to see a shower of arrows descend over the intact catapult. One of the men got hit a dozen times, stumbled off and staggered a few steps and fell to the ground dead at Kelsey's feet. The other, after taking a grazing hit in one shoulder, used the great beam as a barrier and continued his chopping.

Kelsey looked back the other way, trying to formulate some plan for retreat. Could he get to Gary Leger? he wondered. Was Gary Leger even still alive? And where had Mickey gone off to?

Kelsey's whirling mind was stopped in place as he turned, as he focused on his kin who had run off in pursuit of the last enemy. The elf floundered on the field, squirming and turning. His body jerked as another arrow plowed into him, and then again.

He continued to squirm, continued to take wicked hits.

Kelsey looked beyond him, up to the crest of the rolling hill, where sat a line of Connacht cavalry.

A hand signal from the man in the middle—Kelsey recognized him as Prince Geldion—and the archers lowered their bows. Behind Kelsey, the wounded man stumbled down from the catapult.

"I am sorry," he began, for the catapult still appeared operational.

Kelsey cut the man short with a curt wave of his hand. There was no need for any apologies; both this man and his dead companion had proven themselves worthy, despite the failure.

A second figure, a giant of a man, rode up beside Geldion, and the horsemen began a slow and steady walk down the hillock, the Connacht ring closing tight about the companions.

Thirty yards away. Twenty.

"What tricks have you, leprechaun?" Kelsey whispered to Mickey, the sprite still sitting on the grass near the groaning Gary Leger.

"Even if I made it look like we'd escaped, we'd not get this one far," Mickey replied. "I'm thinkin' that ye're catched."

Kelsey did not miss Mickey's choice of words, did not miss the fact that the leprechaun had said that Kelsey and the others, but not the leprechaun, were apparently soon to be captured. The elf-lord was not surprised as Mickey faded away into nothingness.

A commotion started almost immediately to Kelsey's right, the Connacht horsemen jostling, one even swiping with his sword. The elf understood that Mickey was involved, probably making it appear as though Kelsey's band was trying to get out that way.

Kelsey looked to TinTamarra; was this the time for them to try to make their break?

The tall man seated next to Geldion raised his arm and called for calm.

"Hold tight your ranks!" Geldion called on cue. "This group is known for trickery. Hold tight your ranks, and do not let what you see deceive you!"

The tall man was King Kinnemore, Kelsey now realized, though he hadn't seen the man up so close in many years, and did not remember him as being quite so large, and did not remember his face as being so . . . feral was the only word Kelsey could think of to describe Kinnemore's snarling features. Even viewing him on the platform in Dilnamarra, Kelsey hadn't realized quite how imposing a figure Kinnemore truly was. He towered over Geldion as the two made their way down, looked cleanly over his son's head as easily as if it had been a young boy sitting next to him.

Kinnemore closed his eyes as he did this, and then began turning his face deliberately from side to side. Kelsey's eyes widened with curiosity as he realized that the man was sniffing the air like some animal!

The King's eyes widened soon after, and a smile broke out on his stern face. "There is a leprechaun about!" he declared.

"Now how might he be knowing that?" the invisible Mickey, now perched on the base of the catapult behind Kelsey, quietly asked.

The Connacht ring tightened even more, the King and Geldion sitting no more than a dozen yards from Kelsey and TinTamarra, the two defensively flanking the fallen Gary Leger. Geldion smiled and whispered to his father when he came to recognize the elf-lord, long an adversary.

"I have lost one of my catapults," King Kinnemore announced a moment later. "In exchange for an elf-lord, another of the Tylwyth Teg, the stolen artifacts, and the pretender from Bretaigne. I'd call it a favorable trade. What say you, Kelsenellenelvial Gil-Ravadry?"

Kelsey held fast to his sword. He thought of grabbing for his bow, of trying to put another arrow into Kinnemore, or perhaps one into that wretched son of his. He had to admit that he wouldn't get near to readying the weapon, though. At least a dozen crossbows were trained upon him, and a dozen on TinTamarra and on the human traitor, as well.

"What say you?" Kinnemore demanded again. "Do you yield?"

Kelsey looked to his elfish kin and nodded, and both of them dropped their bloodstained swords to the grass.

The soldiers rolled in about them. "A thousand gold pieces to the man who captures that leprechaun!" King Kinnemore asserted, and every soldier who was not assigned a specific task began a wild search of the area.

The surviving raiders were bound by their wrists and ankles, Kelsey, Tin-Tamarra, and Gary Leger together (though Gary was still far from cohesive). On Kinnemore's orders, the traitor was taken in a different direction, to the one working catapult.

"You sang a fine lie to walk through my ranks," the King explained to Kelsey, his face just an inch from the elf's and his smelly breath hot on Kelsey's face. "I do thank you for the idea."

Kelsey wasn't sure what the evil King was talking about, until Kinnemore ordered the catapult readied and the traitor placed in the basket.

A cry from the side stole everyone's attention a moment later, and a soldier ran in, holding a frantically kicking Mickey McMickey. "I got him! I got him!" the man shrieked, moving to stand before his King.

Kinnemore grabbed the kicking leprechaun from the soldier's hands. Again came the curious sniffing. "Smells like a mushroom to me!" Kinnemore roared, and he squeezed with all his considerable strength.

"Oh, begorra," the real Mickey, still invisible and still by the catapult, muttered under his breath. Kings were supposed to be better at seeing through illusions, but this guy was uncanny.

Another soldier came running in, making a similar proclamation and holding a similarly kicking leprechaun. And then a third man cried out from across the way, and a fourth near the ruined catapult. Before King Kinnemore could sort it all out, a dozen men were standing before him, each holding a likeness of a very animated Mickey.

Prince Geldion couldn't bite back his chuckle—and Kinnemore promptly slapped him across the face, so hard that he tumbled to the ground. He sat there for a long while, staring unblinkingly at his surprising father.

"Send him flying to Tir na n'Og!" the embarrassed King roared at his soldiers manning the working catapult. "Show the Tylwyth Teg, and our own ranks, how King Kinnemore deals with those who oppose him!"

The poor man in the basket began a pitiful whining.

"Easy, lad," came a whisper from the invisible leprechaun who had secretly crawled in next to him.

Kelsey and TinTamarra, many of the Connacht soldiers, and even Prince Geldion gave a unified groan as the beam creaked into place and then launched with a great *whoosh* of air. The man's horrified scream diminished quickly as he flew away through the rain.

High over Tir na n'Og, arching down, the man felt a sudden drag, a sudden slowing, and Mickey, holding tight both to him and to an umbrella, came visible at his side.

"Easy, lad," the leprechaun said again. "I got ye."

Below Mickey's magical umbrella, they floated down slowly into the thick canopy of Tir na n'Og. By the time they got to the ground, they were both scratched and bruised in many places.

But far better off, in Mickey's estimation, than Kelsey, TinTamarra, and Gary Leger.

TEN

Witch for a Day

THE dreary weather seemed fitting indeed to poor Diane as she sat on the wet grass of a small, cleared hillock in Tir na n'Og, not far from the continuing battle.

"We should be getting ye back to the prisoners," Mickey, sitting beside her and honestly sympathetic, remarked. "Even though most o' the prisoners seem to have a heart to be joining our side instead of fighting with Kinnemore, and even them that don't join with us aren't showing much spirit for keeping their fighting for th'other side."

The leprechaun blew a ring of blue smoke out of his gigantic pipe. It floated up into the air, then descended over Diane, encircling her like some magical necklace. Mickey blinked his eyes alternately and the ring shifted hue, moving right through the rainbow spectrum of colors. "'Course, that might be soon to be changing," the leprechaun finished glumly.

Diane understood Mickey's reasoning. Many Connacht soldiers had sworn fealty to Tir na n'Og, or more particularly to the hero wearing the armor of Cedric Donigarten. But now that hero was gone, taken captive, perhaps even killed, and the armor was in Kinnemore's hands.

Diane sniffled back a wave of emotion. "I want to go home," she whispered. "If Gary's dead, then I want to go home."

Mickey had explained to her the ramifications of death in Faerie. If Gary or Diane died here, then dead they would be, in both worlds. If Kinnemore had killed Gary, and Mickey and Diane could not retrieve his body, then he would, as far as people in the other world were concerned, simply vanish.

Diane wondered how she might explain that one to her mother-in-law.

Even if they found the body, returned to the ruined castle on the hill in Dun-tulme, how was she going to get back to the United States and explain sword wounds?

"He's not dead yet, lassie," Mickey remarked.

Diane turned sharply on the sprite. "How do you know?"

"Kinnemore'll make a show of it," Mickey reasoned. "Gary Leger was hurt-ing, but not too bad, when I left him. If Kinnemore means to finish the job, he'll do it in grand style, an open hanging in Dilnamarra—or might be that he'll take Gary all the way back to Connacht, where a hundred times the number might watch. He was always one for crowd-pleasin'."

Diane thought it over for a moment. "If you get me beside him, can you just beam us out?" she asked.

"Can I what?" Mickey responded, eyeing her curiously.

Despite the awful predicament, Diane gave a small snort. With the accent, Mickey did sound a bit like Scotty. "Can you send us away?" she explained. "Back to our own world?"

Mickey took a deep draw on his pipe and nodded his understanding. "Only through a bridge," he replied. "And suren there's few o' them left. And truth be telled, I cannot do it. That's pixie work." Mickey studied Diane's crestfallen look for a moment, then his voice took on an angry and frustrated edge. "I told ye ye'd not want to be here," he accused. "Not now, not at this time!"

Diane looked away, but she did not blame Mickey.

"I'm not thinking that Kinnemore'll kill Gary and Kelsey at all," Mickey went on, trying to offer some comfort at least. "Ceridwen's coming free soon, and the witch'd not be pleased to learn that her puppet King stealed such plea-sure from her."

Diane started to respond, but stopped short, her mind working furiously down a new avenue of thought. "Is Kinnemore afraid of Ceridwen?" she asked.

"Ye'd be afraid o' her, too, if ye knowed her," Mickey was quick to respond.

"How often does he speak with her?"

Mickey shrugged, having no way to know the answer.

"And you told me that Gary was the only one who could shorten her ban-ishment," Diane rolled on, taking no further notice of Mickey's responses. "And he did shorten it, when the dragon was alive and loose. So he could shorten it again, right?"

"Lassie, we're in enough trouble now," Mickey said dryly.

But Diane's smile did not diminish; the weight had been lifted from her shoulders. She felt suddenly like she was in the middle of a delicious novel and, for the first time, like she might have some control over the pen.

THEY crouched at the corner of a small building, the sunlight fast fading behind them. Getting into Dilnamarra had not been much of a problem, as Diane's plan had worked wonders on the badly informed common soldiers of Kinnemore's army.

"There's Kinnemore," Mickey whispered, indicating the area before the door of the town's squat keep. "With Prince Geldion beside him."

"I thought you said that Gary was brought to Faerie in the first place because he was big enough to fit Donigarten's armor," Diane whispered. "Kinnemore's got to be a foot taller than him!"

"Aye," Mickey replied. "And bigger than I'm remembering him. But he's too big for the armor—and ye think we'd have had a chance o' persuading him to go, anyway?"

Diane nodded. King Kinnemore seemed indeed an aberration. Diane, at five-foot-eight, was taller than any man she had met in Faerie, except for the giant King.

The two remained in place for some time, watching Kinnemore and Geldion, and the King did not seem very pleased with his son!

Diane, carrying all of her otherworldly equipment with her, glanced back to the westering sun, then took out a small meter. Nodding happily, she brought her Polaroid around from her side and lifted it towards the King.

"Here now, what're ye up to?" Mickey wanted to know. "We can't go starting a fight in the middle o' Dilnamarra."

"No fight," Diane promised and clicked off the picture. The exposed film ejected and she took it away. "You'll see."

Geldion stormed away from the meeting and leaped atop his horse, thundering out of town, his father's scowl on his back and his own scowl set on the road before him. Then Kinnemore spun about, knocking one of the guardsmen to the ground, and entered the keep.

"Come along," Mickey instructed, wanting to get this over with quickly, before the King had the time to relax and sort things out (and, possible, to make some sort of contact with Ceridwen!).

The leprechaun, who looked like a spindly-armed goblin, skittered out, and Diane began to follow. She took one quick look at the developing photo, meaning to tuck it into a pocket.

"Hel-lo," she said in surprise. She looked to Mickey, who was too far ahead, and decided this newest "development" would have to wait. She tucked the picture safely away and rushed to catch up.

If Diane had any doubts about the power of Mickey's latest illusion, they vanished the moment the two guards standing beside the iron-bound door to Dilnamarra Keep noticed the pair coming. They bristled about and readied their weapons at the sight of Mickey, in goblin guise, and how they blanched, falling all over themselves in a feeble attempt to come to rigid attention, when they noticed Diane!

Mickey walked right up to them boldly, daring them. Neither dared to look down at the little goblin; neither dared to move his eyes at all, or even to breathe.

"Whereses is Kinnemore?" Mickey rasped in his best goblin imitation. "The Lady wantses to see Kinnemore!"

"The King is inside the keep," one of the guards was quick to answer. "I will announce—"

"Stop!" Diane said, and the man nearly fainted. "Where is Prince Geldion?"

The guards looked nervously at each other. "He went to the prisoners," the first answered. "Then he was off to the battlefield to direct the next attack."

"Ah, yes, the prisoners," Diane remarked, trying to hide her overwhelming relief that Gary and Kelsey were apparently still alive. "You have caught that wretched Gary Leger, and an elf-lord of Tir na n'Og. Pray tell me, where has Geldion put those two?"

"In a secluded barn," the guard promptly answered. "West of Dilnamarra, beside an abandoned farmhouse. They . . ."

"I'm for knowin' the . . ." Mickey interrupted, and he caught himself, and his unwelcome change of accent quickly and looked to the guards to make sure they had not caught the slip. "Geek knowses the place, lady," he corrected. "Geek knowses the place!"

Diane stood as if in deep thought. "Come along, Geek," she said at length, her tone wicked with thick sarcasm. "We will visit with Kinnemore later—for now, let us go and tell Gary Leger how fine it is to see him again!"

"And you!" she snapped at the pale guards. "Say nothing to Kinnemore of my coming. Ceridwen needs no announcement." She rose up, tall and terrible, completely amazed at the power granted her by this disguise. "If your King has even a hint that I have been here," she warned, "you will live out your pitiful lives as barnyard animals!"

She held her hand up and out towards the men, drawing their attention, and then with a *pop* there came a blinding flash, followed by clouds of leprechaun smoke, and when it cleared, Mickey and Diane were gone, leaving the bewildered and terrified guards to their uncomfortable watch.

"Fine trick, lassie," Mickey remarked as he and Diane skittered across the field west of Dilnamarra. "How'd ye do it?"

Diane held up the flash for her Pentax. Mickey eyed it curiously, his keen ears picking up the faint whining sound as the batteries brought the flash back to the ready.

"Fine trick," the leprechaun said again, and he let it go at that, having no time, with the barn prison now in sight, to search out the details. "Are ye ready?"

Diane nodded. "We go in hard and furious," she said, paraphrasing the leprechaun's earlier plans. "Intimidation is our ally."

"Aye," Mickey agreed. "And a bit o' luck wouldn't hurt."

Diane looked at the sprite's grim expression.

"I'm hoping Prince Geldion's not about," Mickey explained. "I've seen a lot o' that one, and he's seen a lot o' me, and suren he'll be harder to fool!"

Diane skidded to a stop, as though she had just realized the potential implications of failure. "Should we wait?" she asked nervously.

Mickey nodded ahead, to the dilapidated wooden barn and the many Connacht guards standing about it. "Yer Gary's in there," he grimly reminded her, and Diane said no more.

THE door to the keep swung open and King Kinnemore rushed out, his expression curious. He looked from one guard to the other (and both silently agreed that they were not having the best of days!), then began sniffing the air.

"Who has been about?" Kinnemore demanded in his most commanding voice.

One of the guards cleared his throat; his knees went weak.

"No one, my King!" the other guard quickly put in, fearing the prospect of viewing the world through a pig's eyes. "Er, just some beggars—there are so many beggars in this filthy . . ."

"Silence!" Kinnemore demanded, and he sniffed the air again, his face crinkling as though he had smelled something utterly foul.

"Be on your best guard," he said to his men, as he continued to glance all about. "I smell leprechaun, and that can only mean trouble."

Now the two guards were in a terrible dilemma. They looked to each other, exchanging unspoken fears about their previous encounter. If that was a leprechaun's trick, then they had played into their enemy's hands. But if they told

Kinnemore of the incident and that last visitor was truly Ceridwen, then the consequences would be horrid.

"Look alert!" Kinnemore roared, not understanding the silent exchange. He pushed between the men and back into his keep, slamming the door behind him.

"What are we to do?" one of the guards asked his companion.

The other guard hushed him, but had no answers. He didn't want to betray his King, but he didn't think he would look so good sporting a curly little tail.

There came the sound of a galloping horse, and a moment later Prince Geldion came charging through Dilnamarra, heading for the keep.

"That witch didn't say nothing about telling Geldion, now did she?" the first guard said slyly.

His companion smiled broadly, with sincere relief, thinking they had just been let off the hook.

WALKING up the dirt path to the barn, by the stone skeletal remains of the farmhouse, the pair met a small horse-drawn cart coming the other way. A dirty soldier drove the cart, one of his shoulders heavily wrapped in soiled and bloody bandages. The man widened his eyes in shock at facing the illusionary Lady Ceridwen, and he coaxed his horse to a near stop and pulled far to the side.

"Geek, see what he is carrying," Diane instructed, and Mickey rushed over and climbed the side of the cart.

"Ooo, Lady!" the leprechaun exclaimed in perfect goblin voice. "He's gotses the armor and spear! And an elfs's armor, too!"

"Turn that cart around," Diane said without hesitation.

"But the King has ordered the armor to Dilnamarra Keep," the poor soldier weakly protested. He started to go on with the explanation, but his next words, with help from a ventriloquist leprechaun's trick, came out sounding like the croak of a bullfrog. Predictably, the man's eyes widened in shock.

"A frog, Lady?" Mickey happily squeaked. "Can Geek eatses the frog?"

"Patience, dear Geek," Diane replied coolly. "Let us see if this one is ready to obey." She hadn't even finished talking before the cart swung about on the road and rushed off the other way, back for the barn.

"Well done," Mickey congratulated. "Just a bit more o' the tricks, and we'll all run free."

Diane nodded determinedly, but in truth, she was actually enjoying this charade. She, and not Mickey, led the rest of the way to the barn, passing among the dozen or so bewildered soldiers with a confidence that defeated any forthcoming words of protest before they were ever uttered. She stalked right up to the man holding a spear across his chest as he blocked the barn door, and, with a simple swish of her head, sent him dancing aside.

He turned on her as she started to enter, but the camera flash fired in his face and he shrieked and stumbled backwards, tripping over his own feet and falling to the ground.

"Leave us," Diane ordered the two men inside the barn, and she did well to keep her voice firm and steady at the sight of Gary, Kelsey, and TinTamarra, obviously beaten. They stood in a line, their arms chained above them, their feet barely touching the floor. One of Gary's arms was cocked at a curious angle as it went up above his head, held fast by the chains, and was paining him greatly.

Diane's gaze never left her love, and she jumped when the barn door banged hard behind her, swung wide by the fleeing men. A bit of leprechaun magic brought the door swinging closed.

"So you're free," Gary Leger growled defiantly at Diane, which confused her for just an instant. "Give me back the spear, witch, and I'll put you back in your hold!"

Kelsey, standing beside Gary, eyed Ceridwen and Geek curiously for a moment, then, to Gary's confusion, both he and his elfish companion began to laugh.

"Aye, none can see through tricks better'n the Tylwyth Teg," Mickey remarked, using his own voice.

Gary's eyes widened.

"Dear Geek," Diane said. "Do go out and have the good soldiers bring the equipment into the barn."

Gary, figuring it all out then, tried to laugh, but the attempt brought waves of stinging pain shooting through his shoulder. Diane was beside him immediately.

"Dislocated," she said after a quick inspection.

"Get away," Gary whispered, and Diane moved back just as the door opened again and Mickey entered, accompanied by three soldiers bearing piles of equipment.

"They broughtses the dwarfs's things, too," the illusionary goblin explained.

"The dwarf?" both Gary and Kelsey mouthed silently.

Diane was trying to figure out how she might convince the guards to leave the keys for the shackles as well, without making them too suspicious, but to her surprise, Mickey forcefully dismissed the men, practically chasing them out of the barn.

She met the leprechaun just inside the door. "We need to get the keys," she started to explain, but Mickey smiled wide, put a hand into a deep pocket, and produced a ring of keys.

Diane was back at Gary's side in a moment, carefully freeing him and helping him to a sitting position. She hugged him tightly, taking care not to press the dislocated shoulder.

"Get to Kelsey!" Mickey sharply reminded her. "We've not the time."

Diane fumbled with the ring, finally finding the right key, and Kelsey, too, was free. He rushed for the pile and quickly began donning his fine armor, while Diane went to the still-chained TinTamarra.

"Hurry," Mickey prodded her, but there were a score of keys on the chain and she fumbled about.

The leprechaun's declaration that they had little time rang painfully true then, as the barn door swung open.

"Out a bit early, aren't you, Ceridwen?" Prince Geldion remarked.

ELEVEN
Every Desperate Chance

THE slender man looked ominous indeed, silhouetted in the barn door, his soldiers at his back and his worn traveling cloak billowing in the stiff breeze.

Gary forced himself to his feet, Diane holding him by his good arm until he regained his balance. Kelsey dropped his armor—he had no chance of donning it—but held fast to his fine sword, its tip gleaming furiously in the slanted rays of light coming through the open barn door.

"You will drop that weapon," Prince Geldion said to him matter-of-factly.

Kelsey didn't flinch.

"Kill the chained elf," the Prince calmly ordered, and the two soldiers closest to him, both holding crossbows, stepped up to the threshold and took aim at TinTamarra.

Gary, Kelsey, and Diane all cried out denials at the same time, but it was Mickey's voice, his magical voice, raised in an illusion outside the barn, that saved the chained elf. Several soldiers cried out warnings of the ambush, and the crossbowmen, seeing a host of fierce elves coming at them down the dirt road, instinctively loosed their bolts in that direction.

Mickey couldn't witness the flights of the quarrels from inside the barn, of course, and so his illusionary force did not properly react, tipping the Prince and his men off to the truth of the matter.

"A leprechaun trick!" Geldion yelled above the general commotion. "My father said that a leprechaun was not long ago outside the keep. He said he smelled the foul thing!"

"I'm meaning to ask him how it is that he keeps doing that," Mickey replied, coming visible (and looking like a leprechaun again) and perched on a beam above where Gary had been shackled.

Before Geldion or his crossbowmen could react to the appearance of the sprite, Mickey waved his hand, and Cedric's mighty spear lifted from the pile near Kelsey and floated across the room, to Gary Leger's waiting grasp. Gary held the thing tentatively in his good hand, his other shoulder throbbing with pain.

Well met, young sprout! the spear emphatically greeted him.

"If you say so," Gary replied, a deep sense of hopelessness evident in his voice.

Geldion was fuming by this point. "Take them!" he cried. "Take them all, and if any die in the event, then so be it!"

The soldiers bristled about, but did not immediately advance. Some glanced to the side again, to the continuing, and unnerving, illusion of an elf host. Others looked to Mickey, their expressions revealing both greed and trepidation, and still others looked to Kelsey, and mostly to Gary, the spearwielder, supposedly the dragonslayer. He had been captured out on the field near the catapults, and had been taken easily, but on that occasion, Geldion and Kinnemore had more than ten times this number of soldiers surrounding him.

"Aye!" Mickey yelled unexpectedly, and unexpected, too, was his apparent agreement with Geldion's call. "Take them, as the foul Prince has spoken! Kill the wielder of Donigarten's own, he who slew Robert and saved yer precious town, and any other town in all the land. Take him now, this hero who's come from far off to show us the way!"

Whispers erupted among the soldiers; Geldion called again for a charge and drew out his dirk, and the men did come on—at least, most of them came on. There was some commotion near the back of the ranks, and before any Connacht men got near to Kelsey or Gary, the sound of steel against steel rang out, along with a call for "Sir Cedric!"

"That's me noble soldier," Mickey whispered, and the sprite faded away again to invisibility, honestly wondering how many tricks he had left. Diane's disguise went away as well, then, the leprechaun trying to conserve his magical energies—energies he had already depleted considerably.

Kelsey ran to the side, around a ladder and under the barn's loft. The closest two soldiers came fast in close pursuit. Kelsey dashed around a hay bale, turning to ambush the men, but they did not follow the course, stopping instead and rolling the bale aside.

As soon as the obstacle was out of the way, Kelsey charged ahead, right into the two, his sword slashing and hacking mightily as he tried to score a quick kill.

He got near one man's face, and struck the other's shield hard enough to break one of its straps and leave it hanging awkwardly on the man's arm. But he drew no blood in that initial flurry and the trained soldiers, well armored in thick leather jacks that were sewn with interlocking metallic rings, moved a few steps apart, measuring their strikes.

DIANE rushed back to TinTamarra, still hanging limply from the shackles. She fumbled frantically with the key ring, going through several keys before finding the one that fit. She got it in place, but before she could turn it, she yelped in pain and moved away, the key still hanging in the elf's shackle, as a swordtip pinched her side.

Two soldiers stalked her, and she fell back against the wall, stumbled along it. The chained elf lifted his feet from the floor and kicked one of the men hard in the thigh. The soldier grimaced and turned, slapping the still-kicking legs aside with the flat of his sword. "Get the woman!" he told his companion, and he moved in on TinTamarra, punching hard with the hilt of his sword repeatedly.

Mickey exerted some magical energy then, trying to telekinetically push the key all the way in and turn it. To the leprechaun's dismay, though, the soldier coincidentally reached up and pulled the key free of the shackle, throwing it to the hay-strewn ground.

NOT far away, Gary's only thought was to get back to Diane's side, to protect his love. But he too found two men facing him, circling him, feigning thrusts and swipes, one with a sword, the other with a club.

Gary jabbed with the sentient spear, waved it across in front of him frantically to keep the men at bay. As balanced as it was, however, the nine-foot-long weapon was unwieldy when used in one hand, and Gary spent a long time recovering from the momentum of each swing. Soon both the soldiers were smiling, then even laughing openly at Gary's feeble attempts to fend.

Across came the sword, and one of the men, instead of his typical retreat, stepped ahead, inside the slashing tip, dropped his own weapon, and caught the spearshaft in both hands.

"Here now, mighty dragonslayer," he taunted. "What are you to do now?"

The end had come, so Gary thought, as the other man lifted his club and advanced, while the man holding the spear gave a great tug. Gary held on stubbornly, though he didn't know what good that would do.

"What are you to do now?" the man chided a second time.

Cedric's spear answered for Gary.

Gary felt the telltale tingles an instant before the spear's magical energy gathered along the shaft and blasted into the man. His hair stood on end, and off he flew, across the barn, to crash into a fork and scythe and wheelbarrow. He came up on his elbows, staring incredulously, his hair still flying wildly and his whole body trembling from the jolt. Then his eyes crossed and he fell back to the ground, out of the fight.

The soldier's companion watched the flight in disbelief, but Gary wasted no time. As soon as the spearshaft was free of the man's grasp, Gary whipped it across, tucking it tight against his side for support. The powerful weapon easily cut through the remaining soldier's armor, gashing his side, and the man cried out in pain and fell back. He ran a hand over his wound, then stared at the blood in his palm.

"Son of a Bretaigne pig!" he roared at Gary. "You're to die for that one!" On he came fiercely, his club banging away at the blocking spear. Gary fought hard to keep the long weapon up between him and the man, not doubting the threat in the least, but each clubbing blow sent a shock wave of pain coursing up his side, and he feared that he would surely pass out.

DIANE was in trouble, Gary was in trouble, and Kelsey was fighting two against one without any armor. Even worse, the fighting had ended back at the door, leaving two men dead, but Geldion remained, his dirk dripping blood and four more soldiers ready at his side.

And Mickey could do nothing to help any of those situations, for Tin-Tamarra was in truly desperate straights. The chained elf was helpless, and the soldier meant to kill him—that much the leprechaun knew for certain.

"Here now, laddie," Mickey called from his perch, and he came back into view. "When ye're done with him, ye think ye might take a try for me pot o' gold?"

The bait didn't work quite as the leprechaun had expected, for, though the man pushed away from the battered elf and lunged for him, he did so with his long sword leading. Mickey was nearly skewered. He skittered back along the beam as the soldier pressed onward, up on his tiptoes and poking eagerly. Stubbornly, the man leaped up and grabbed the beam with his free hand, determined to skewer the leprechaun, or to chase the troublesome sprite away.

How his hungry expression changed when the open shackles, shackles that had been used to hold Gary Leger, seemed to come to life, grabbing at his wrists, locking fast about his wrists!

The soldier fell from the beam to a hanging position (for he was not as tall as Gary). He held fast to his sword, but the weapon would do him little good with his hands so tightly bound.

"WHERE are ye to run, pretty lass?" the pursuing soldier asked Diane, and it took all her courage to steel her emotions against the implications of his lewd tone. More ominous did he seem, for his face was dirty, his beard several days old, and judging from the abundance of dried blood on his tunic, he had seen quite a bit of fighting at the front lines.

She continued her slide along the barn's back wall, hoping to get under the loft, where she might dart around some of the hay piled in there and get to Kelsey's side.

That plan disappeared in an instant, though, first as Diane bumped into something hard protruding from the wall, breaking her momentum, and a moment later when she heard one of the newcomers to the fray call out to her pursuer.

"I've got her this way!" the second soldier declared.

The pursuing soldier stopped and held his arms out wide, spinning the heavy club in one hand. "You got nowhere to run," he chided. "So come along easy."

Diane glanced over her shoulder and saw the second man coming out from under the loft, smiling as wickedly as her pursuer. She glanced farther over her shoulder, to see what had stopped her retreat, to see what inanimate object had so deceived her.

A small windlass was set into the wall, running a rope to a pulley over the loft, and to a bale of hay, suspended near the loft's edge. Diane needed luck, couldn't stop to measure the angle or the timing. She grabbed at the windlass crank and pulled free its pin.

"What?" her closest pursuer asked as the rope spun out. The suspended hay bale dropped five feet to bonk the man's oblivious reinforcement on his thick head.

The man went down under the bale.

KELSEY worked magnificently, his sword darting so quickly from side to side and straight ahead that neither of the soldiers he faced scored as much as a nick on his unarmored body. But the few hits that Kelsey managed were not significant, his thrusts pulled short for fear of a counter, and the solid armor of his opponents absorbing most of what was left.

The elf went on undaunted, too angry at Geldion and Connacht to let the odds dismay him, too angry at Ceridwen and at the despoiling of Tir na n'Og to think of anything but his fury.

His sword banged hard off a shield, whipped back across to intercept a thrust from the other man, then snapped back again, this time slipping past the shield to deflect off the first man's shoulder.

Back the sword came again, and Kelsey stepped ahead, prodding and poking. The soldier worked desperately to counter, his sword flicking back and forth as he stumbled into a short retreat, but Kelsey would have had him cleanly had not his companion recovered from the stinging nick in time to come ahead and force the elf to relent.

Kelsey narrowed his golden eyes, his frustration finally beginning to build. These two were practiced swordsmen, and had fought side by side before, and Kelsey realized that he had little chance of scoring a fast kill.

The three were near to the loft's ladder then, Kelsey still forcing back his adversaries. For a moment, the elf thought himself tiring, thought that his vision was blurring. Then he understood. He held his smile and his hopes, and pressed the attack.

The soldier nearest the ladder reached for it, thinking to make use of its offered support and defensive advantages. His eyes deceived him, though, and he grabbed only air.

He lurched sidelong, through Mickey's illusionary ladder, to bang into the real one, a foot farther to the side.

On came Kelsey, before the man or his startled companion could recover. Wisely, the off-balance soldier twisted so that he would fall all the way around the ladder, farther from the elf's wicked reach, but Kelsey's move at him ended short anyway; it was only a feint.

The second man, sliding across to block the elf from his companion, widened his eyes in shock as Kelsey pulled up short and cut sharply to the side. The soldier got his sword up for a block, but Kelsey's blade was too swift, sliding past the parry to jab deeply into the soldier's belly. Kelsey did not have to fear a counter by the other man this time; there was nothing to stop his deadly progress.

Nothing but his expanding conscience.

The soldier fell away, grasping his wounded belly. He went to the floor, writhing, but very much alive, and totally confused as to why the fierce elf had pulled up short, had not finished him with a simple twist of the wrist, a simple change in the angle of the penetrating blade. In any case, the man was out of the fight.

DIANE spun back, but her pursuer was upon her, his club right over his head and coming to bear. Again the woman's reaction was purely instinctual, a simple movement she had learned in basic self-defense classes her work office had offered a year before. She brought her open hands up in front of her and stepped ahead and to the side, pivoting on one foot and turning her upper body as she went. Predictably, her attacker shifted the angle of his descending club, but Diane's nearest hand was too close for the weapon to strike effectively. She caught it right above the man's hands and continued her turning retreat, absorbing the energy of the blow and putting the man off balance.

At the same time, Diane tugged fiercely at the club and stomped hard on the man's instep.

"You witch!" he protested through a groan. He was stumbling forward, and let go of the club with one hand, trying to grab onto something for support.

Diane reversed her tug into a hard shove, and the butt end of the club smacked the soldier in the face, crunching his nose.

"You witch!" he shouted again, sputtering with warm blood.

Diane pivoted back in to face him squarely, only a few inches away, and up came her knee.

And up the groaning man went on his tiptoes, his eyes crossing.

"You witch," he tried to say again, but suddenly he had no breath for the words.

Diane yanked the club free of his grasp and stepped back, thinking to hit him. But there was no need. His nose broken, his breath nowhere to be found, the soldier fell hard against the wall and to the ground, curling into a fetal position.

"Ooo lassie, well done!" Mickey, finished with his latest trick, congratulated her.

Diane looked at the leprechaun in disbelief. She looked to the club, as though it might offer some answers. Then she looked back to the crumpled soldier and shrugged, embarrassed and apologetic, and sincerely amazed at the effectiveness of her self-defense tactics. The situation was pressing, and far from won, but Diane made a mental note then and there that if she got out of Faerie alive, she would enroll in more martial arts classes.

GARY winced repeatedly as the soldier's club slammed hard against his spear, jolts of energy coursing along the vibrating shaft. He hardly thought he could hold out against this single adversary, yet when he looked past the man, he saw two others steadily advancing, their swords already bloody from their fight with the traitors at the barn door.

Gary had no time to even think about those two, though, as his current opponent kept up the pressure. A few more parries, a few more stinging hits, and a distracted Gary wondered where the man's reinforcements might be. Why hadn't they come in yet to strike at him?

He glanced over the soldier's shoulder once again—and saw, to his disbelief, that the two others were battling each other!

Gary thought about it only long enough to come to the conclusion that Mickey was somehow involved. His relief did not last long, however, for his spear was slammed on the side, and wavered across his body. He instinctively reached for it with his other hand, and the sudden throbs of agony from his wounded shoulder nearly overwhelmed him.

Gary somehow managed to put the mighty spear back in line before his opponent, who was justifiably wary of the weapon, dared to advance. But Gary was still wobbly when the next hit came, and then the next, both clubbing straight down atop the spearshaft.

Gary hardly even realized that he was no longer holding the weapon. More from exhaustion and agony than from any set plan, Gary tumbled backwards and to the floor, his good hand coming to rest on the very end of the fallen spear's shaft.

Gary understood then his doom, realized that the soldier was fast advancing. He clutched the spear but, holding it so near to the back end, had no hope that he could even lift it.

Now, young sprout! the spear cried in his head.

A blast of energy came out from the sentient spear's tip, scorching the ground and blasting the tip upward. At the same moment, Gary pulled with all his strength, and to his amazement (for he had not seen the energy release), its huge tip rose up from the ground.

To the amazement of the approaching soldier, as well. The man caught the flying tip in the hip, the spear's hungry head biting hard through the meager padding of his armor, through his flesh and bone. He toppled to the side, screaming, taking the embedded spear from Gary's weakened grasp.

Gary was on the verge of unconsciousness, but he heard those pitiful screams, and surely they tore at his heart.

Diane heard them too, and was equally horrified. She wanted to run over to Gary, then, to offer support and to get some, but she had her own problems. The man she had clobbered with the bale was crawling out, more angry than hurt.

Fuming with unfocused rage, mad at all the violent world, Diane charged and leaped atop the rising man, bearing him to the ground. She whacked him with the club across the shoulder blades and told him to lie still, and when he did not, she whacked him again.

She hoped he would fall unconscious; she feared she would have to kill him.

KELSEY would have finished the remaining man at the ladder quickly, but then Prince Geldion was at the soldier's side and it was two against one once more.

The elf fell back in despair and went to the defensive, fending off the sword attacks and Geldion's surprisingly adept strikes with his long and nasty dirk. Even worse, Kelsey noticed that the other man, the one he had wounded in the belly, was starting to rise, and the elf wondered if his mercy had been misguided.

"He had me!" the wounded man cried breathlessly. "Liam, he had me. I tell ye!"

The man fighting beside Geldion eyed his wounded companion curiously, then turned his confused gaze upon Kelsey.

"Too many have died for an unlawful King!" the elf growled, seizing the moment and the possibility for further dissention in Geldion's shaky ranks. Kelsey had already seen enough evidence that the Connacht army's heart was not in this conquest to guess what his adversary might be thinking.

Geldion apparently understood the sentiments, too. "Fight on!" the Prince roared. "For the glory of King and country!"

"He had me dead, Liam!" the wounded man, staggering for the door, said again.

Liam looked to Geldion, his expression truly horrified. The Prince snarled in response and lashed out with his dirk—for Liam and not for Kelsey!

But Liam was quick enough to sidestep, and he ran off, grabbing his wounded friend and shuffling for the barn door.

Geldion threw a hundred empty threats at his retreating back.

"Now it is as it should be," Kelsey said grimly, stepping aside to momentarily break the melee. "You and I shall decide this, Prince Geldion, a course you began those weeks ago when you unlawfully tried to prevent my quest."

"Kinnemore is law!" Geldion spat. "And the Tylwyth Teg are outlaws all!" On came the bold Prince, his dirk slashing.

Kelsey hardly understood the tactic; with his longer yet equally wieldy weapon, he could easily defeat any of Geldion's thrusts.

But Geldion was not out of tricks. His dirk shot forward, and as Kelsey's sword moved to intercept, the Prince uttered an arcane phrase and the dirk elongated, its blade thickening, but holding still its razor edge. The angle of Kelsey's parrying sword was all wrong as the blade elongated, and the magical weapon slipped past the defense.

Kelsey threw his hips out behind him scampering with quick steps to be out of the Prince's surprising reach. He only took a small hit on the thigh, but his troubles came from behind, where Geldion's last soldier stood ready, club in hand. The soldier had left the barn when the Prince had joined the fight with Kelsey, and had subsequently crawled back in through a side window, behind the hay at Kelsey's back.

His club connected solidly on Kelsey's lower back, and the elf straightened, his arms falling weakly at his sides. Geldion waded in, fist balled over the hilt of his dirk-turned-sword, and slammed Kelsey in the face, and Kelsey toppled. Geldion's soldier hit the elf again, on the back of the neck as he rolled, and Kelsey knew no more.

"MICKEY!" Diane's call was purely frantic. She moved beside Gary and helped him back to his feet. The realization of what had just happened stunned Diane; in the space of a few minutes so many men lay dead or wounded on the floor.

So many men, and Kelsey.

And Diane did not like the prospects now facing her as a grim Geldion and his soldier came out from under the loft and steadily advanced.

"Mickey?" she called again.

"I think he's gone," Gary answered. He nodded to the door. "The two that were fighting each other ran out—probably chasing Mickey."

"Well, imposter, what have you to say for your treason?" Geldion asked, drawing them from their private conversation.

"Nothing, to you," Gary spat back.

"But I am judge and jury," Geldion calmly explained. With no response apparently forthcoming, the Prince began to laugh aloud, a wicked laugh indeed.

He stopped abruptly, studying Gary's wounds. "See to the woman," he told his soldier. "I will settle the lie of the spearwielder, the imposter hero who claims the defeat of the dragon Robert."

"I did kill Robert," Gary insisted.

Geldion laughed again. "Then a mere Prince should pose no difficulty for you."

Driven by a sense of honor, Gary nudged Diane aside. She stared at him, somewhat disappointed, and thinking his honor misplaced. He was still holding the long spear in only one hand, his other arm too weak to do much more than help guide the weapon's swipes.

He was surely going to get himself killed, Diane decided, but she couldn't spend too much time thinking about that now, not with the club-wielder, a powerfully built man, his smile more filled by gaps than stained teeth, steadily approaching.

She readied her own club, putting her feet wide apart, feeling her balance. In stalked the soldier, casually snapping off a series of blows. Diane blocked and responded in kind. Each hit sent a shock wave along her arms, but she stubbornly held on, her confidence returning, her survival instincts washing away her fears.

But then the man's club hit hers down low, near the handle, and hit, too, Diane's lead hand. Her fingers went strangely numb, a wave of pain rolled up her arm, and the man's next solid hit knocked the club from her hand.

And he was still smiling wickedly.

GELDION showed Gary, and that legendary spear, great respect for the early passes of their fight. The Prince could see the fatigue and the pain in Gary's eyes and in his every movement, and the dislocated shoulder was evident enough.

Geldion did not think that there could be much power behind the spear pokes and swipes, but he had no intention of learning the truth firsthand—obviously this badly wounded man had found enough power to knock two of Geldion's men from the fight already. So the Prince would play defensive, would bide his time and let exhaustion force that heavy speartip to the ground.

Geldion's logic was obvious to Gary as well, and he tried to conserve his energy as much as possible. But that was no easy task with Diane in a fight against a trained soldier barely twenty feet away.

"Shall you watch her die?" Geldion asked, smiling wickedly.

Gary saw the bait for what it was—but could not ignore the image Geldion's words had conjured in his mind. He roared in protest and started ahead.

No, young sprout! came the sobering cry in his head.

Geldion sidestepped the awkward attack and slapped at the speartip, knocking it farther aside. Gary was already backpedaling, though, and the Prince got no clear strike.

"Easy," Gary whispered over and over to himself. He needed to keep his control.

He looked over his shoulder, though, ready to explode, when Diane cried out.

SHE took the only course left open to her.

She ran.

Diane cut around a hay bale, sensed her enemy's movement and reversed direction, coming back out the same side as the soldier circled the other way. He was still on her heels, though, and his swishing club clicked off her ankle and nearly tripped her up.

"Mickey!" she called, but the leprechaun was nowhere about. She went under the loft, cut around another bale, and came right back out. She hopped over the man she had clobbered with the hay bale and nearly tripped again as the semiconscious soldier grabbed at her ankle.

Off balance, head low, she cut a straight line across the barn, past the man Mickey had tricked into the shackles, past the beaten TinTamarra, hanging limp at the end of his chains. The eager Connacht soldier came in close pursuit, ignoring the pleas of his trapped comrade, pushing the hanging elf roughly aside.

He did not notice that TinTamarra was watching him under half-closed eyelids, and his surprise was complete when the elf's legs came up suddenly and wrapped about his neck, pulling him off balance.

Diane heard the commotion and dared to look back—just in time to see the soldier snap his club up above his head for a solid hit on TinTamarra's chest. Still the stubborn elf held on, and the man hit him again, and lowered his club to begin a third strike.

Diane barreled into the soldier, wrapping him in a tight bear hug, pinning the club down low. The soldier and Diane pitched right over, but held fast in the grasp of the elf's strong legs, they did not fall all the way to the floor. They hung there, weirdly, the soldier's neck twisted and his air cut off.

GELDION saw the turn of events by the shackles and pressed furiously, his magical dirk/sword throwing sparks whenever it struck the metal tip of Cedric's spear.

Gary matched the Prince's intensity, though the effort pained him greatly. He swiped with the spear, accepting the jolt as Geldion's sword connected, and when the Prince sidestepped one thrust and rushed in, Gary promptly retreated, turning as he went.

He crashed into one of the barn's supporting beams.

Gary, and Geldion too, heard the crack as Gary's shoulder popped back into place. Nausea and agony swept over the man; he thought he saw Diane, entangled with the soldier and the hanging elf. But the dazed Gary couldn't be sure of what he saw at that awful moment.

He thought the floor was up in his face, thought one of the barn's walls was falling outward.

He heard the ring as Geldion's sword slashed the speartip once again, saw the sparks igniting.

But they, too, were tilted weirdly, falling and spinning like all the world.

THE man went limp under her. TinTamarra, his energy expended, let go, and Diane pulled herself from the pile. She knew that Gary was in trouble, knew that she had to help, and so she got right back to her feet and turned about, nursing her swollen hand but stubbornly searching for a weapon.

The soldier's club was not far away, but Diane found suddenly that she had no time to even go for it. Geldion's sword slashed across, connecting solidly on the shaft of Cedric's spear. The weapon flew out wide, out of Gary's grasp. He caught it with his other hand, winced with the shock of pain, then grabbed it again.

But his grip was reversed, his defensive posture shattered, and Geldion, sword up high, surely had him.

"Gary!" Diane cried, running desperately, reaching into the belt pouch Mickey had given back to her in Tir na n'Og, looking for anything that might save the moment.

Geldion snapped his head around, shifted as though he would strike Diane down first. His sword remained up high, at the ready, and Diane's hand came up as well—to block, the Prince figured.

She pushed a little button on the strange black box she held, and there came a flash, the likes of which the startled Prince Geldion had never before witnessed. Blinded and thinking some evil sorcery had befallen him, Geldion stumbled backwards, and Diane, ever the opportunist, rushed into him, both her hands locking desperately on his weapon arm.

Geldion caught his balance quickly and pushed back, whipping his arm about to pull it loose. He grabbed a handful of Diane's thick hair and tugged viciously.

"Gary!"

Diane's cry seemed distant, but her husband did not miss its intensity. He fought through the nausea and the dizziness, forced his eyes to focus, and jabbed straight out with the butt of the spear, popping the Prince in the side of the head and sending him and Diane tumbling to the ground.

Diane hung on like a pit bull, and to her surprise, Geldion let go of his sword, which immediately reverted to its dirk form. She understood when she looked up—to see Gary standing over the man, speartip pressed to Geldion's throat.

TWELVE

As the Gentle Rain from Heaven

DIANE had never seen Gary's face so twisted with rage. He meant to finish Geldion—she knew that he meant to plunge the spear deep into the helpless Prince's throat.

"The quality of mercy is not strained," she said suddenly, grabbing at a desperate thought.

Gary glanced sidelong at the unexpected remark, and his sudden confusion halted his progress. A small line of blood began to run from the side of the penetrating speartip. "Shakespeare?" he whispered incredulously.

"It droppeth as the gentle rain from heaven," Diane stubbornly went on, closing her eyes and trying to remember the lines. "Upon the place beneath: it is twice blest; it blesseth him that gives and him that takes." She looked up and relaxed a bit, seeing that Gary had eased his grip on the spear.

"'Tis mightiest in the mightiest!" came a cry from the door. All three, Gary, Diane, and even Geldion, turned to see Mickey enter, disheveled and banging the dust from his tam-o'-shanter. "And suren it becomes the throned monarch better than his crown." The leprechaun paused to take in the scene, then nodded in satisfaction. "Yer father might be taking a tip from the Bard," he remarked to Geldion.

"The Bard?" Diane whispered, trying to sort through the illogic. She turned a confused glance on Gary. "How does he know about Shakespeare?"

Gary mulled it over for a moment, then chuckled aloud, remembering what Mickey had told him about others of his world passing over into Faerie. Mickey had claimed that J.R.R. Tolkien had obviously come over, else where would he have learned so wondrous a tale as *The Hobbit*? Could it be that some of Shakespeare's work, possibly something like *A Midsummer Night's Dream* was more than an imaginative piece of fiction?

"Don't ask," Gary said to Diane, remembering that they had more important matters to tend to. Gary looked fearfully to the area under the loft, where Kelsey had struggled to prop himself up on his elbows. Never relinquishing the trapping pressure of the spear on the Prince, Gary continued his scan, all about and back to the door, where Mickey was straightening his disheveled and dusty clothes.

"Where have you been?" the man demanded.

"Them two was better at seeing through things than I figured them to be," the leprechaun explained casually.

"And where are they now?"

"One's down the well, th'other's running back for Dilnamarra," Mickey replied. "And I'm thinking that we should be on our way."

By this point, Diane had retrieved the key and let down the wounded Tin-Tamarra.

"What are ye meaning to do with him?" Mickey asked Gary, indicating the Prince.

"I guess he's coming with us," Gary replied.

"Kill him," came a reply from under the loft. Kelsey limped out, one hand pressing tight against his lower back. "Geldion would have shown us no mercy, and deserves none! We are wounded and weary, and will not have an easy time of getting back to Tir na n'Og with him in tow."

It was truly a horrible moment for Gary Leger. Kelsey's logic was solid, but Gary couldn't imagine finishing off the helpless Prince. Yet what might Gary do if Kelsey decided to walk over and cut Geldion down? He looked down to Diane, whose expression was unyielding.

"Don't you dare," she warned.

Gary growled in frustration, retracted the spear, and roughly reached down and pulled the much smaller Geldion to his feet. "Not a bit of trouble from you," Gary snarled into the Prince's face.

Gary looked over to see Kelsey glaring at him. The elf said nothing, though, just moved to the pile of equipment and once again began donning his suit of mail.

Gary pushed the Prince past him, prodding him for the door, but suddenly Kelsey was there, his sword snapping to a stop just an inch from Geldion's already bleeding throat.

"No!" Diane and Gary said together, thinking that Kelsey would kill the man.

In response, Kelsey held up a curious bandolier, strung one end to the other with hammers.

"Geno," Gary whispered, recognizing the belt.

"Where is the dwarf?" Kelsey demanded.

Geldion smirked as though he had no idea of what Kelsey might be talking about.

Kelsey belted him across the face.

"I ask you only one more time," Kelsey said sternly, his voice deathly even and controlled. "I will have an answer, or I will have your head."

"When did the Buldrefolk become the concern of the Tylwyth . . ." Geldion began obstinately, but his words ended in a groan as Kelsey slugged him again.

"Stop it!" Diane demanded, coming up beside them, dragging TinTamarra, who was leaning heavily on her shoulder.

Gary held her back, knowing Kelsey better than she. He understood the unlikely friendship that had developed between the elf and Geno, and knew that neither he nor Diane could stop Kelsey in this matter. Geldion would speak, or Kelsey would kill him.

The Prince stared long and hard into Kelsey's golden eyes, matching the elf's intensity. Then Geldion nodded to the side, to the area under the loft. "In a hole," he spat. "Where dwarfs belong."

Kelsey moved under the loft and soon found the wooden slats of a trap door, pinned under a huge cask of water. With great effort, the elf picked the cask up on its edge and rolled it aside—and found that the trap door had been chained and padlocked three different ways. Not waiting to see if Geldion could be coerced into producing any keys, Kelsey called to Gary to give him the mighty spear. Diane immediately had a sword poised near the Prince, and with a nod to her, Gary moved under the loft and handed over the spear. Three hits later, all the chains were free.

Gary took note of the elf's frantic movements, further confirmation of the bond that had been forged between Kelsey and the surly dwarf. Kelsey grabbed the rope for the trap door and took a deep breath to steady himself—like Gary, he feared that Geno would be in tough shape, perhaps even already dead.

Up came the door—Geno was nowhere to be seen.

Kelsey dove down to the floor for a closer look, but the pit was only a few feet deep and a few feet wide, and encased in bare and solid stone. A bit of water had gathered at the bottom of the hole, but it was only an inch or two deep, and concealing nothing but more stone.

"He is not in here!" Kelsey growled at Geldion.

The Prince seemed honestly perplexed. "Impossible," he protested. "The pit is solid stone."

Kelsey and Geldion kept up their banter, accusations flying fast from the angry elf. Gary joined in as well, even promising Geldion severe consequences if he did not produce the dwarf.

Mickey was not so judgmental, though. More wise in the ways of the Buldrefolk than the others, and more wise in their tricks, Mickey believed that Geldion's incredulity was sincere. He calmly walked under the loft and pushed past Gary and Kelsey, peering knowingly into the hole.

"Come along, Geno," he called softly, tap-tapping the stone along the pit's side with his huge pipe. "We've not the time for games." Mickey's face brightened an instant later, when he noticed a small crack running along the wall of the pit. He tapped his pipe in that spot and called for the dwarf again.

For a moment, nothing happened, and then suddenly the ground began trembling so violently that Gary thought they were in the midst of an earthquake. Across the barn, near the opposite wall, the flooring planks broke apart and the earth erupted—and out hopped Geno, covered in dirt, his wrists and ankles tightly and heavily shackled, though he had bitten through one of the wrist chains and had done considerable damage to the other.

He shook his head, launching a spray of sand and roots, and spat out a stream of munched pebbles.

Then he spotted Geldion, and no chains in all the world could have held him back. He half ran, half hopped across the barn, bearing down on Diane. To her credit, she held her ground until the very last moment, then fell aside. Geno leaped high into the air, tucked his stubby legs under him, and slammed down atop the Prince.

Kelsey was on him in an instant, Gary and Diane helping as much as possible. The elf finally wrestled Geno off Geldion, a break in the action long enough for Gary to reason with the dwarf that Geldion would make a valuable prisoner.

Geno stood trembling and staring at the battered Prince, on the very edge of an explosion. "Get these off," he growled, lifting his shackles toward Geldion.

The obstinate Prince snorted and turned away.

Geno rolled his tongue around in his mouth, digging out another pebble he had pinched between his cheek and gum. He spat it with the power of a high-end BB gun and it bounced off the back of Geldion's head, nearly laying the Prince out flat.

"I told you to get these off," Geno said as the outraged Geldion spun about. "Now do it," the dwarf warned, "or my next spit-stone will be a piece of your crunched skull."

Not a person in the room doubted Geno's claim.

It was Mickey who relieved the tension, the leprechaun, an expert lock-picker if ever there was one, rushing over and quickly freeing the dwarf of the shackles.

"Don't ye kill him," Mickey whispered to Geno as he worked the locks. "He's the treasure that'll stop the war."

Kelsey apparently did not agree. As Mickey freed the dwarf, the elf stalked over to Geldion, his sword dangerously close to the Prince's neck.

"Easy, Kelsey," Gary remarked. "We need him."

Kelsey turned to Gary, his expression both angry and incredulous. "You have taken command of the actions of the Tylwyth Teg?" the elf asked.

Gary thought the question utterly stupid, and was too surprised by it to answer.

"You have become quite the hero," Kelsey remarked.

Gary winced and Kelsey turned away.

"I do all right," Gary answered suddenly, to Kelsey's surprise, and to his own. The elf stopped but did not give Gary the consideration of turning to face him squarely. "I've more than my share of luck and better friends than any man deserves!" Gary answered anyway.

Kelsey remained silent and still for a moment, then walked away. Gary didn't know what to think. He understood that Kelsey was frustrated and afraid—afraid for Tir na n'Og and all his world.

Diane was at Gary's side then, her arm in his, lending him support.

By the time they had donned their armor and left the barn, two more of the Connacht soldiers were up and in tow. Kelsey forced Geldion to carry the wounded TinTamarra, and Geno walked only a stride behind the Prince, telling him how much he liked the Tylwyth Teg, and promising him all sorts of pain if the elf should die.

Kelsey led them to the west, farther from Dilnamarra and farther from Tir na n'Og. They were a sorry-looking troupe, to be sure, even though Gary's shoulder, knocked back into place during the battle, was already feeling somewhat stronger. They encountered only one Connacht patrol, a group of five, who surrendered at Geldion's command (since Geno was nibbling on the Prince's ear at the time).

That night, they camped along a hedgerow. The Connacht soldiers were put in a line, with grim Kelsey and TinTamarra, who, like Gary, was fast recovering, walking a tight guard. Geldion was not with them, though. He was farther along the makeshift encampment, speaking with Diane, while Gary, Mickey, and Geno lay back on the grass not far away, staring at the stars and the occasional rushing cloud.

More than once, Kelsey came up near to the group and shot a dangerous glare Geldion's way. It was obvious to the others that the elf would have preferred to leave the Prince dead in the barn.

"Not a good time," Mickey remarked after one of Kelsey's visits, in effect apologizing for Kelsey's behavior.

"I thought he wanted me here," Gary asked.

"So he did, and does," Mickey replied. "He's just afraid, lad, and with good cause."

"What has she to say to that Prince?" Geno put in, motioning to Diane and Geldion. The dwarf had been cordial to Diane, and actually glad to see Gary again, and so his words did not sound so much like an accusation.

"She's just looking for information," Gary replied.

"Aye, that one's a thinker," Mickey agreed. "Suren she's asked me more in the short time I've known her than yerself has asked in all yer three visits to Faerie!"

"She's your wife," Geno grumbled. "She cannot be too smart."

Gary elbowed him hard in the ribs, but if the stonelike dwarf felt it at all, he didn't show it.

"I been meaning to ask ye," Mickey put in. "I heared ye calling me many the time. What made ye want to come back so badly? I mean, I've heared yer call before, now and again, but the last day, ye just wouldn't stop."

Gary, still rubbing his elbow from the contact with the dwarf, wondered how he might explain his emotional turmoil, how he might tell them about the loss of his father and his frustrations with Real-earth. These two had played such an important role in Faerie, how might Gary convey to them his sense of utter helplessness to change the bad things, in his own life and in the world around him?

As it turned out, Gary didn't have to say much. As soon as he told about his dad, both Mickey and, unexpectedly, Geno were honestly sympathetic. Geno even told the story of how he had lost his own father—to a mountain troll and an avalanche.

"But being here won't get ye away from the grief, lad," Mickey was quick to warn. "Not-a-thing can get ye from the grief."

Gary nodded, but he wasn't so sure that he agreed. He felt better just being in Faerie, despite the desperate situation surrounding him. He felt again like he was part of something larger than himself, like his potential death, or even the death of his father, was, after all, a very small part of a grander scheme. Far from making him feel insignificant, though, that knowledge made Gary feel invulnerable.

He lay quiet, looking at the enchanting canopy of Faerie's nighttime sky, looking at the eternal stars and the endless, rushing clouds.

And feeling as though he was truly a part of them.

THIRTEEN

Worth a Thousand Words

THE group got back into Tir na n'Og the next day, entering the forest far from the battle lines. All through that morning's hike, there seemed to be a measure of tension growing between Kelsey and TinTamarra. More than once, Gary saw TinTamarra turn an angry glare Kelsey's way, though it didn't seem to Gary as though Kelsey had noticed. Or at least, if the elf-lord did notice, he was feigning disinterest.

TinTamarra would not let go of that glare, though, and finally, with the safety of the thick trees all about them, the tension burst.

"You will take the prisoners, except for Prince Geldion, to the holding area, where their wounds might be tended," Kelsey informed TinTamarra. It seemed a perfectly reasonable command, spoken with all respect.

"And what, then, of the Prince?" TinTamarra retorted, his lips thin with anger.

Kelsey appeared honestly caught off guard by the sharp retort. He spent a long moment scrutinizing his fellow elf before answering. "He remains with me until I can decide what worth he might prove," he said.

"You make many decisions on your own, Kelsenellenelvial," TinTamarra replied.

"To what do you refer?" Kelsey asked, still calm, still of a mind to defuse the situation. The last thing the besieged Tylwyth Teg needed now was dissention in their ranks.

TinTamarra turned his sour expression alternately on all the prisoners, then settled it back on Kelsey. "And we left more wounded humans in the barn," he said, as though that should explain everything.

"They could not travel," Kelsey answered, missing the point.

"I think he's meaning that ye should have killed the men," Mickey interjected.

TinTamarra said nothing, but his expression confirmed Mickey's guess readily enough. To the side, the prisoners shuffled uneasily, to a man wondering if their fate suddenly hung precariously in the balance.

"That's stupid," Diane was quick to put in, pushing her way past Gary as he, more familiar with the stern and dangerous demeanor of the proud Tylwyth Teg, tried futilely to hush her.

"Why would you kill wounded men?" Diane insisted, moving near Tin-Tamarra—too near, by Gary's estimate. He went right along beside her, though, and immediately decided that if TinTamarra lifted a weapon against her, the elf would feel the bite of Donigarten's spear. Gary wasn't confident, however. The Tylwyth Teg were fast with their blades, and he sincerely feared that any counterstrike he made would be in revenge for the murder of his wife.

Still, the stubborn woman pressed on, fearless, oblivious.

"Are you no more than a murderer?" she said, and even Kelsey, who was on her side in this argument, clenched his fist.

Geno, standing watch over the prisoners, chuckled softly, thinking that the trembling elf was about to knock the woman to the ground.

"Easy, lass," Mickey implored. TinTimarra remained silent—Gary pictured a fuse burning short atop his ravenblack hair.

Diane started to speak again, but Gary hooked her with his arm and forced her away, loudly interrupting every sentence she began.

"She speaks the part of the fool," TinTamarra remarked.

"The fool that saved your life," Kelsey quickly reminded him.

TinTamarra's glare fell full over the elf-lord. "They are enemies of the wood," he said. "We will waste many warriors, having need to stand guard over the growing number of prisoners."

"What would you have us do?" Kelsey asked.

"As we always have done to enemies of the wood," TinTamarra replied grimly.

"Then we would be killing potential allies," Kelsey argued. He knew that the elf was not sharing his sympathies for the humans caught under King Kinnemore's unlawful rule, and so he tried to reach his kin on a more pragmatic level. "Many have come over to fight beside us, to fight beside the spearwielder," he reasoned. "Kinnemore's hold is not so tight, or perhaps he grasps at his army too tightly, squeezing men through his fingers. We have found allies among his ranks—was it not two Connacht soldiers who led us to the catapults? They died for our . . ."

"Only one died," Mickey corrected. Both Kelsey and TinTamarra looked at the leprechaun curiously.

"I went along for the other's ride," Mickey explained. "He got a bit o' shaking, that's all. And he's in the forest now, talking to his kin, bringing more to the spearwielder's—and the Tylwyth Teg's—side. Another week o' fighting and I'm thinking that ye'll have as many men guarding Tir na n'Og's borders as elfs."

With that said, Mickey hopped off to join Gary and Diane, who had moved some distance away. TinTamarra had no reply, to Mickey or to Kelsey.

"Bitter times," Kelsey remarked, trying to alleviate his honorable companion's obvious embarrassment. "But we must not forget who we are, and why ours is the just cause. Kinnemore will call for truce soon, by my guess. He is losing soldiers and now"—Kelsey glanced over at Geldion, looking perfectly miserable as he sat among the handful of prisoners—"he has lost his son."

TinTamarra nodded and bowed, a sign of concession, then turned towards Geno and the prisoners. Kelsey stood quietly, musing over his last words. He did indeed believe that King Kinnemore would soon call for a truce, and that truce would undoubtedly spare Tir na n'Og the scars of further war. Ceridwen was not so convinced that she could ever conquer the proud Tylwyth Teg, Kelsey knew, and so she would likely be glad just to have them out of her army's way.

For Tir na n'Og and the Tylwyth Teg, the prospects seemed bright. But Kelsey, with his increasingly worldly view, his growing compassion for those who were not of his race, truly feared that the elders of Tir na n'Og would accept that truce.

"I always wanted to meet a Prince," Diane said disarmingly. She sat down in the clover next to Geldion, who pointedly shifted and looked away.

"I've brought some food," Diane explained and held forth a bowl of porridge.

Despite his desire to remain aloof to his captors, Geldion could not ignore the offering. He hadn't eaten in nearly a day, and his stomach was surely grumbling.

Shortly after noon, the group had encountered another band of Tylwyth Teg and had separated, TinTamarra and the common prisoners going with the elfs, while Kelsey led the others on a more southerly route, towards the battlefield and the elfish leaders. The group had separated again late in the afternoon, with Kelsey, Mickey, and Gary leaving Geno, Diane, and the Prince in a clover-filled meadow, lined by a row of tall and thick pines. Twilight was upon them now, the slanting rays turning all the clover orange and casting long shadows of the western trees across the field.

"You took the food, so you have to talk with me," Diane said cheerily. Geldion kept his face low, to the bowl of porridge, but his beady dark eyes turned up to regard her from under furrowed brows.

"Don't waste your breath," Geno, a short distance away, offered to Diane. "That one has little to say that is worth hearing."

Diane thought differently. She dropped her hand into her belt pouch, feeling the snugly packed cameras and the quite remarkable picture she had slipped between them.

"What's it like to be a Prince?" she asked.

"What is it like to be a pestering wench?" Geldion answered coldly. Behind him, Geno grunted and hopped to his feet, hammers ready in his hands. But Diane scowled and waved the fiery dwarf back.

"Fair enough," she conceded to Geldion. "I was just curious about your father and your life in Connacht."

Again Geldion eyed her, but he seemed a bit less sure of himself.

"He is the King, after all," Diane went on casually, glancing all about (though in truth, her focus ever remained the Prince). "And from what I've heard, he plans to rule all the world. I though it would be wise to learn more about this man."

Geldion went back to his porridge.

"And more about his son," Diane went on slyly. "This Prince who would one day be King."

"Not while he's sitting chained in an elfish forest," Geno was happy to put in. Geldion turned a glare on the dwarf, and Diane did too, not appreciating the interruption. There was a method to the woman's remarks, a design so that she might measure Geldion's responses, whether he answered verbally or not.

"What kind of a King will Geldion be?" she asked.

The Prince snorted incredulously, and Diane quieted, considering the reaction. Was Geldion brushing off her question because he believed that he owed her, the simple pestering wench, no explanation? Or did the concept of him being King at all seem preposterous to him?

"Will he be a kind man, who cares for the needs of his subjects?" Diane pressed. "Or will he . . ."

Geldion smacked his half-empty bowl of porridge away, stopping the woman in midsentence. He eyed Diane contemptuously for a moment, then pointedly turned away.

His anger told her that her second line of reasoning was on target. Geldion did not believe that he would ever be King. But why? Diane wondered. The Tylwyth Teg would not kill him—he knew that. They would bargain with him and return him to Kinnemore when the deal was struck.

Then it was Geldion's father who would stop him, Diane realized, and she dropped her hand to that telling picture once again.

Across the way, Geno snorted loudly. "King of what?" the dwarf demanded, moving near the fuming Prince. "King of a burned-out town that was once called Connacht? For that is all that will remain when the peoples of the land rise in unison against Kinnemore!"

The dwarf's boast brought Geldion out of his silent brooding.

"Kinnemore will rule the land!" he proclaimed. "And all the Buldrefolk will be slain, or driven deep into their filthy mountain holes!"

Diane thought that Geno would surely beat the man down, but the dwarf only blew away Geldion's threat with a simple and heartfelt burst of laughter.

"Kinnemore will rule the land," Geldion grimly said again.

Geno huffed. "You are to feel the same grief as Gary Leger," he replied, and he snapped his fingers (which sounded somewhat like the report of a heavy-caliber rifle) and walked away, laughing with every step.

Geldion hurled no retorts at the dwarf's back. In the course of conversation over that last couple of days, he had overheard talk of Gary's loss, and so he understood what Geno had just implied.

It struck Diane as more than a little curious that the Prince did not seem bothered at all by the dwarf's grim prediction.

GARY, Kelsey, and Mickey returned to the small meadow the next morning. The forest was calm this day; for the first time since the taking of Dilnamarra, Tir na n'Og had not wakened to the sounds of battle. Diane took that as a good sign, as did Geno, and even Geldion seemed more comfortable.

Diane thought that the Prince appeared relieved by the apparent turn of events, and her insight was confirmed an instant after Kelsey made his announcement.

"The King will not bargain for the life of his son," the elf explained.

Geldion's expression told Diane so very much. He was crestfallen, certainly, but not surprised. Not surprised! With everything else Diane had confirmed, by Gary's tales of Ceridwen, by her own talks with Mickey and with Geldion, and by the picture in her pouch, Diane nodded her understanding and believed that all the pieces of this puzzle had fallen neatly into place.

"Then why is the forest quiet?" Gary asked Kelsey.

"The envoys have just recently returned," the elf-lord explained. "Kinnemore will not bargain for the life of his son," Kelsey said again, pointedly looking wounded Geldion's way, "but he may yet bargain. The potential for loss has grown for King Kinnemore. His army is bogged down at the edge of the forest. His fires scar the trees, but do little damage when countered by the magics of the elfish wizards. And he is losing his soldiers, by the sword and by their consciences."

Kelsey's smile was smug indeed when he looked again to Geldion, the Prince looking perfectly miserable. "Every one of the men who were brought into the forest at your side has sworn fealty to Tir na n'Og and the Tylwyth Teg. Many of my people have been slain, yet our ranks are larger now than when the conflict began. Can your father make the same boast?"

Geldion turned away, and Diane winced in sympathy.

"So the forest is quiet," Kelsey finished. "And King Kinnemore considers the options for truce."

Geno kicked hard at a small stone—which was really a large stone buried deep in the turf. The depth of the dwarf's anger became quite obvious as the rock overturned, popping up from the ground.

Kelsey understood the source of that anger. "The options presented to Kinnemore call for a complete cessation," he assured Geno. "The Tylwyth Teg have not forsaken the eastern lands. We have not forgotten Braemar and Drochit, nor the Buldrefolk of Dvergamal, nor the gnomes of Gondabuggan."

Geno nodded. He knew the Tylwyth Teg well enough, and knew Kelsey well enough, to realize that the inclusion of anybody outside of Tir na n'Og's precious borders in the bargaining was Kelsey's doing. But though Geno truly appreciated the loyalty of Kelsey, he also understood that the Tylwyth Teg would likely agree to Kinnemore's counteroffer, a set of terms that did not extend beyond the borders of the elfs' precious forest home. The Tylwyth Teg would accept any truce that saved Tir na n'Og, even at the price of the eastern lands.

Kelsey was smiling, trying to assure his dwarfish friend, but that smile was strained, for the elf, too, could not deny the aloof attitude of his people.

To Diane's relief, the others pretty much left Geldion alone after that. She feared that surely Geno might bring the Prince harm, or that, since his father would not bargain for him, Kelsey would send him away with the other prisoners. Certainly the elf had ample opportunity. Bands of the Tylwyth Teg, repositioning their forces as they awaited Kinnemore's reply, were all about the shadowy borders of the meadow, and more than one group came in to speak with Gary, the spearwielder.

Diane took little note of them, though. She again spent her time with Geldion, and noticed Gary's concerned, and perhaps jealous, glance her way more than once.

She was back with her four companions for lunch. Kelsey continued to be optimistic, as did Gary, but Mickey remained quiet (for a leprechaun) and Geno did not seem convinced that the skies of Faerie would soon brighten.

As soon as the opportunity presented itself, Diane turned the topic of conversation to Ceridwen. Kelsey didn't want to talk about the witch, Geno didn't want to talk about anything, but Gary, knowing his wife well enough to understand that she thought she was onto something important, was quickly becoming intrigued, and Mickey was willing to talk.

"I heard that she could change herself into a raven," Diane said. "And a snake."

"And anything else she's a mind to change herself into," Mickey assured her. "Not so much a trick to one of Ceridwen's powers. Ye've seen the elfish weather-magic fighting Kinnemore's fires and ye've seen a bit o' me own illusions . . ."

"She was a bit o' yer own illusions," Gary interjected, mimicking the leprechaun's thick accent, and drawing a much-needed smile from both Diane and Mickey.

"But ye should know that Ceridwen's powers are beyond both those magics together," Mickey continued, his smile vanished and his voice suddenly grave. "She's a wicked one, and not all the magic-spinners of Faerie together could break one o' her spells."

Diane nodded knowingly.

"We have heard enough of the witch," Kelsey said suddenly, sternly. All three, and Geno too, turned to him, wondering what had prompted his outburst. Kelsey started to elaborate, started to explain that talk of Ceridwen only destroyed what little morale was left, but stubborn Diane cut him short.

"Not so," she insisted. "We have not heard enough of the witch. Ceridwen, and not Kinnemore, is the key to our problems, and if I'm going to help at all, I'll need to know everything I can about her. Know your enemies—that is the greatest weapon in any war!"

Kelsey's amazed expression fast shifted into one of respect.

"She's adjusting well, lad," Mickey remarked to Gary.

"She's been hearing about Faerie for more than seven years," Gary, obviously proud of his strong wife, replied. "And she believed my stories all along."

"Sure I did," Diane added with more than a little sarcasm.

They spent the next hour discussing Ceridwen, without any further complaints from Kelsey. Then the meal was finished, and Kelsey asked Geno to accompany him to the area where the elfish elders would be gathered. It was more than a simple courtesy, Geno realized; Kelsey wanted him in plain sight of the elders if and when Kinnemore's response came. The decisions of the Tylwyth

Teg had implications far beyond Tir na n'Og's borders, and Kelsey wanted his elders to understand the weight of that decision fully, wanted them to appreciate the allies they might soon abandon.

"Wait," Diane bade them as they rose to leave. The sudden urgency in her tone startled the others, even Gary.

Diane took a deep breath and looked straight at Mickey. "Kinnemore is not Ceridwen's puppet," she announced.

No one spoke against her claim, but their expressions revealed their doubts clearly.

"I don't know that Kinnemore is even alive," Diane went on.

"I have seen the King," Kelsey argued.

"And so've I," Mickey added.

Diane was shaking her head before they ever finished. "That's not him, not Geldion's father," she replied confidently.

"What are you babbling about?" Geno, in no mood for cryptic games, demanded.

"I don't know who, or what, the King is," Diane explained, reaching into her pouch and taking out the picture she had snapped of Dilnamarra Keep's front door. "But I know that he . . . it is not human."

She held out the picture and the others crowded around. There stood the two Connacht guards, and between them their King—or at least, something dressed in their King's clothes. The face was not human, with a mouth spread from pointed ear to pointed ear, and shaggy hair everywhere, seeming to sprout even from the sides of the thing's nose.

"What the heck is that?" Gary asked, having no idea of what was going on.

Geno and Kelsey seemed equally disturbed, though whether the sight of the picture alone was the source, Diane could not guess.

Mickey, the only one who had been at Diane's side, remembered the scene when they had approached the Keep, remembered the guards and the man standing between them. And the leprechaun, with his greater knowledge of the machines of Real-earth, was not so taken aback by the mere sight of a photograph.

"What is it?" Gary asked again, more emphatically.

"King Kinnemore," Diane answered evenly.

"No, lass," Mickey corrected. "This one I've seen before, and wearing the trappings of the King don't change who and what it is."

"Who?" Gary cried, growing even more agitated by Kelsey and Geno's continued disbelief, by their blank stares and by the fact that even sturdy Geno hardly seemed able to draw his breath.

"Ye've not seen it, but ye've heared it before, lad," Mickey answered. "Suren it's the wild hairy haggis."

FOURTEEN

What Price Victory?

FLAMES sprouted from every tree, lifting their hissing voices in defiance of the drenching rain. All the edge of the forest was in turmoil, men rushing about, fires leaping high, bowstrings humming, as King Kinnemore gave his answer to the call for peace.

Far from the brutal fighting, Prince Geldion sat despondently, his suspicions of his father's feelings for him apparently confirmed. Few prisoners sat in the field near the Prince, most of the soldiers having sworn fealty to the other side. Even now, many of Geldion's men were into the battle, fighting for the Tylwyth Teg, fighting against his father. It was, perhaps, the most bitter pill the troubled Prince had ever swallowed.

And so the fighting that day was even more confusing, with elfs battling men, and men battling men.

Diane, too, was at the front, simply refusing to be left behind again. She rode a white mare beside Gary and Kelsey, the elf leading a wild rush along the length of the battlefield, shouting for men to desert their unlawful King and come to the call of the spearwielder, the new Donigarten. In his shining suit of mail, atop the great stallion, the mighty spear raised high above him Gary Leger certainly looked the part. But he did not feel the part, did not feel like the reincarnation of that legendary hero. Far from it.

Gary had seen battles in Faerie before, had seen Geldion and a host of his knights battle a sea of goblins in Cowtangle. Indeed, Gary had been in battles, had killed the knight Redarm in single combat. And he had seen atrocities in his own world on the increasingly graphic evening news, footage of war-torn countries and of the troubles in the cities of his own land. None of that prepared him for this vicious day in Tir na n'Og. The simple fury of the fight, the echoing cries of the dying, the ring of steel against steel, so commonplace that it sounded as one incessant and grating whine, assaulted his sensibilities. He gritted his teeth and rode on, determined to see it all through. This was not the time for weakness, he knew, though it truly revolted him that, in this time of battle, compassion and weakness were apparently one and the same.

Diane was similarly horrified. She had brought both her cameras along, thinking to chronicle the battle. She took only one shot with the Polaroid, though. After that, she used the Pentax, knowing that she would not have to view the result of her handiwork for a long time, not until she and Gary got out of Faerie, at least, where she might get the film developed. That camera became Diane's salvation that horrible morning. Truly a paradox, it made her feel as though she was making an important contribution, while at the same time the camera allowed her to distance herself from the horrible scene. Somehow, watching a man cut down through the eye of a lens was not the same as witnessing it without the transparent barrier.

The fighting went on all morning. With Kelsey leading, cutting a swath through enemy ranks, and with a growing group of Connacht turncoats swelling in the elfish ranks. Gary saw little personal fighting, Diane none at all. But they both were surely a part of that battle, as inevitably scarred as those who limped away from the action covered head to toe in blood—be it their own or the blood of slain enemies.

"We claim victory this day," Kelsey declared long after the bows had stopped humming and the swords were put away. The wails had not ended, though, cries of men and elfs grievously wounded, many still in the scarred area as Tylwyth Teg patrols cut their way through the destroyed tangle, using the screams to guide their steps.

"The enemy has been driven back to the fields, far from Tir na n'Og's borders," Kelsey went on determinedly, though it seemed to all who could hear that the elf-lord wept beneath his stern façade.

Gary nodded grimly, though Diane looked away. She had not learned to accept what must be in Faerie.

Geno, who had spent the day with Mickey as the sole guards over the prisoners, offered no response to the news of victory. The mountain dwarf was untrained in forest fighting, yet tough enough (and deadly enough with those flying hammers!) to keep the score of men on the field in line.

He had been up front for some time now, and had seen the field and heard the results. More than three hundred Connacht soldiers lay dead in the woods, another fifty had been taken prisoner, and three score more had come over to the elfish ranks. But the price had been high. Nearly a hundred Tylwyth Teg were dead or wounded so badly that they would see no more fighting, and the southern border of Tir na n'Og, beautiful even to the dwarf who lived among the great boulders of Dvergamal, would be decades in recovering from the deep scars.

By all accounts, the elfs had scored a victory by a margin of four to one, but

Kinnemore could spare four hundred much easier than the Tylwyth Teg could spare one hundred. Kelsey claimed victory, yet his people had surely been decimated, their ranks nearly cut in half.

Kelsey's enthusiasm at his proclamation could not withstand Geno's silent appraisal of the battle. The elf understood Geno's stake in the outcome of the fight for Tir na n'Og, and the dwarf's grim expression spoke volumes.

Kelsey nodded and departed. A new envoy from Kinnemore was expected, now that the wicked King had made his statement with fire and sword. The elf took with him Diane's revealing photograph of their nemesis, and also took with him a grim determination. Kelsey had come to see the world as a larger place than Tir na n'Og. He believed in his heart that the Tylwyth Teg held responsibility for their neighbors' well-being.

But Kelsey realized the devastation of this day, understood that this continuing battle was taking a brutal toll on both sides, and on the forest that served as the battlefield. Kinnemore was losing many good warriors, and was losing precious time while the news of his march inevitably spread to the eastern lands. The longer the King remained bottled up at Tir na n'Og's border, the better prepared his future enemies would become. Even worse, Kinnemore was losing men to desertion, was breeding enemies among his own ranks. That he could not afford, any more than the Tylwyth Teg could afford a prolonged defense.

Kelsey knew what would soon happen, knew that Tir na n'Og would likely see no more fighting, but whatever relief he felt for his kin and his home could not diminish the pain in knowing what would likely befall Braemar and Drochit, and all the folk of the east.

The very next day, the elfish elders signed a truce with King Kinnemore, a pact that included the return of Prince Geldion and any other prisoners.

Kelsey had argued vehemently against the truce, had even revealed the photograph to the elders. They were more than a little suspicious of its origins, since the amazing reproduction was a magic they did not understand. But even conceding Kelsey's point that Kinnemore was not who he appeared to be, was more a creature of Ceridwen's control than they had believed, they would sign the truce and secure the borders of Tir na n'Og.

Let the war for Faerie be fought around their borders, so the elfish elders proclaimed, and if Kinnemore should win out, then so be it. The Tylwyth Teg would survive; Tir na n'Og would endure.

To Kelsenellenelvial Gil-Ravadry, elf-lord and he who reforged the legendary spear of Donigarten, friend of dwarf and gnome, of leprechaun and human, that did not seem enough.

———

IT took a great effort by Kelsey and Gary, and more than one of Mickey's fine tricks, to keep Geno off Geldion's throat when Kelsey announced the truce. Diane remained at the Prince's side throughout the struggle, shielding him and talking with him.

"Is there so much hate in you?" Kelsey asked the dwarf, the elf's body stiff and straining and his heels digging deep ridges in the rain-drenched turf as the growling Geno bulled on.

"Have you forgotten the pains this miserable Prince has brought to us?" the dwarf replied. "Have you forgotten the fight on the field south of Braemar, where my kin were cut down by Geldion and his soldiers?"

Kelsey had to nod in reply, but he noted something else in Geno's stern tone, something more calculating. The elf smacked the dwarf hard to temporarily break Geno's momentum, then hopped back, standing resolute in the dwarf's path.

"Is that it?" Kelsey said evenly, and the surprising question did more to slow Geno than the slap.

"Is that what?" Geno demanded.

"Are you angry at Prince Geldion for what has occurred, or do you seek a solution now through murder?"

"What are you babbling about, elf?" Geno huffed, but the dwarf, obviously caught off his guard, stood still, gnarly hands on hips. "Give him a weapon, then. I'll fight him fairly!"

"Of course," Gary agreed, recognizing Kelsey's logic. "You want to kill Geldion now to destroy the truce. If Geldion doesn't come out of Tir na n'Og, Kinnemore will renew the fighting, and the Tylwyth Teg will be forced back into the war."

Geno turned a seething glower upon Gary, but he had no answers to the charge. He looked to Kelsey, and saw sincere sympathy in the elf's golden eyes.

"Prince Geldion will be returned, as the elders of the Tylwyth Teg have agreed," the elf said solemnly.

Geno sent a stream of spittle splattering off Kelsey's soft leather boots. "I should have expected as much from a bunch of elfs," the surly dwarf grumbled, and he turned away.

Gary did not miss the clouds of pain that crossed over Kelsey's fair face.

"My people have suffered greatly," Kelsey said, aiming the remark Geno's way. The dwarf turned on him sharply, Geno's blue-gray eyes unblinking. The expression alone rebutted Kelsey's point, said clearly what the elf, in his heart, already knew: with the Tylwyth Teg out of the fighting, the suffering would be greater for those races still standing opposed to the merciless King of Connacht.

"Did ye show 'em the lass's picture?" Mickey asked, more to break the tension than in any hopes of a resolution.

Never taking his eyes from Geno, Kelsey nodded. "They did not know what to believe," he explained, and he recounted all the doubts of the elfish elders.

"But ye're believing," Mickey reasoned.

Again without taking his stare from Geno, the elf nodded. "And though my people are out of the war, Kelsenellenelvial is not."

That proclamation did much to soften the surly dwarf's glare.

"Then where do we go from here?" Gary asked, a perfectly reasonable question. "To Braemar, to wait for the new battles? Or back into Dilnamarra, where we try to kill Kinnemore?"

"Not an easy task, if Diane's picture tells the truth," Mickey reasoned.

Kelsey was in full agreement. He remembered the arrow he had put into Kinnemore, a shot that would have killed many men, or at least taken them out of the fighting. Kinnemore, Kelsey recalled, had been more angry than hurt—if hurt at all.

"To the Craghs," Diane answered unexpectedly, coming over to join the group. All eyes, even Geno's, turned to regard her. "Did I pronounce that right?" she asked.

"It makes sense, doesn't it?" she reasoned against the silent stares. "If King Kinnemore is the haggis, then the haggis must be King Kinnemore."

"Unless Ceridwen merely used the haggis as a model for a transformation of the King," Kelsey reasoned, but Mickey was backing Diane's logic on this one.

"The haggis is older than Ceridwen, by all accounts," the leprechaun put in. "And ever filled with mischief. Me own guess is that Ceridwen would have found an easier time in switching the two than in trying to copy that fiend."

"Exactly," Diane agreed. "And if we go and get the haggis—King Kinnemore— we might be able to do something about it."

The others had been to the Crahgs and had heard the shriek of the wild hairy haggis, and not one of them, even Mickey who agreed with the reasoning, seemed excited about the prospect of hunting the thing.

"It won't be as bad as you think," Diane assured them, her smug tones telling Gary, who knew her best, that she had a secret. "If the haggis is Kinnemore, the real Kinnemore, he won't be anxious to attack his own son."

Kelsey nodded and even smiled at the reasoning, happy to grab at the offered chance, until he understood the implications of what Diane was saying. His own son, she had said. Did this foolish and ignorant woman expect Prince Geldion to travel along beside them?

"Prince Geldion has already agreed to go along," Diane announced, as though she had expected Kelsey's unspoken doubts all along.

She winced as Geno's spit splashed off her shoe.

"I have agreed," Geldion called from his seat in the clover a short distance away.

"Ye're to go back to Dilnamarra," Mickey said. "As is decided in the truce. If ye do not, then Tir na n'Og'll be full o' fighting again on the morrow."

"And so I will go back," Geldion replied evenly. "I will go back and see this monster, that has stolen my father's throne. And then I will leave, explaining that I must scout the eastern road before the army moves on. We will meet in Cowtangle Wood three days hence."

The friends exchanged doubting expressions. They had all dealt with Geldion in that very same forest—Gary, Kelsey, and Mickey had been chased through Cowtangle on two separate occasions by Geldion and his men. They seemed to come to a silent agreement, looking at each other, inevitably shaking their heads.

"He has nothing to lose!" Diane interjected, understanding where the tide was flowing. "Nothing to lose and everything to gain." She looked back to the seated Prince and nodded, and he nodded back to her. "He will be there," Diane asserted, mostly to her husband. "Alone."

Gary paused a moment to consider the claim, to consider all their options. "Cowtangle Wood," he finally agreed, ignoring the skeptical stares of Kelsey and Geno. "In three days."

"Two days," Mickey corrected. "We've got little time before Ceridwen comes free o' Ynis Gwydrin."

Again Geldion nodded. "Then get me back to Dilnamarra quickly, elf-lord," he bade Kelsey. "My King"—his voice was full of biting sarcasm—"will demand a full report, and Cowtangle is a hard ride."

Kelsey looked to Geno, apparently the only one left supporting his doubts. But the dwarf only shrugged as if to say, "What else can we do?"

Kelsey and Geldion soon departed, and Diane rubbed her hands together eagerly, thinking she had solved the puzzle. Mickey and Gary did not doubt her reasoning, but did not seem so elated.

They had been to the Crahgs, the home of the haggis, before.

FIFTEEN
Too Hot to Handle

GARY leaned the huge shield, Donigarten's shield, against a tree and looked anxiously back to the west, towards Dilnamarra. Gary normally wouldn't have taken the bulky shield, for fighting with it and the great spear was no easy feat. Mickey's offhanded remark that "It'd take a wall stronger than Donigarten's own shield to stop a charging haggis" had prompted Gary's decision, much to the chagrin of the sentient spear.

Dost thou remember thy battle with crahg wolves, young sprout? the spear called incessantly in his mind, and Gary suspected that the spear's reversion to the older dialect was its way of acting superior to him: The spear was referring to a battle Gary had fought in the eastern reaches of these same Crahgs, when a host of wolves had come down after the companions. That had almost been Gary's final battle, mostly because he kept getting tangled up with the long spear and heavy shield in trying to keep up with the darting movements of the swift wolves. *Dost thou remember that this very shield almost sent thee spinning to thy doom?*

Forget the damned wolves, Gary telepathically answered. *We've got a long way to go before I start worrying about crahg wolves!*

The sentiment was true enough. Here they were, still well within the borders of County Dilnamarra, with a hostile army barely a day's march away. And by all reports, the Connacht army would soon be marching down the road from the west, towards Cowtangle. Kinnemore was held up in Dilnamarra, tending to the many wounded and regrouping his forces after the troubles of the battle for Tir na n'Og.

But the King and his men would come soon, Gary knew. Several times this day, he had viewed clouds of dust—small ones, from individual riders, he presumed. The truce had been signed two days before, and, as agreed, Gary and the others had traveled to Cowtangle, about thirty miles east of Dilnamarra, to await Prince Geldion's appearance.

"He is not coming," Geno griped, and not for the first time. "Unless he is at the lead of a cavalry group. Or maybe he is already here, hiding in the woods, waiting in ambush!"

Kelsey seemed similarly cynical, but Mickey, ever the optimist, tried to keep their hopes up, and Diane flatly rejected Geno's assessment.

"Prince Geldion will be here," she asserted every time the dwarf grumbled. "The truth about King Kinnemore wounds him more than anything, and he hates that truth more than he hates you."

Geno didn't show any sign that he was convinced. Nor did the dwarf concede his surly mood when Kelsey jumped up, fitted an arrow, and drew back on his bow. The elf stood perfectly still and silent, and the others, trusting in his keen woodland senses, followed his lead. Suddenly his bow came up, but as the others scrambled for weapons and position, Kelsey eased the string back—and Prince Geldion walked into their encampment, leading a lathered gray stallion.

The small man seemed badly shaken, his oily hair sticking out in back in a sharp cowlick, as though he had spent all the day nervously running his fingers over his scalp. Not only his horse was lathered in sweat; the Prince had been riding hard.

"Who did you bring along?" Geno, demanded, not loosening his grip on his hammer a bit.

"You are confused, good dwarf," Geldion replied sarcastically. "This is a horse, not a companion."

Gary wisely bit back his chuckle, remembering that Geno rarely appreciated sarcasm. He heard Mickey cooing softly in Geno's ear, trying to ease the volatile dwarf's hammer down low to his side.

"The army is not far behind?" Kelsey reasoned.

"They will leave in the morning," Geldion answered. "Though scouts have come as far east as Cowtangle. Kinne . . ." He caught himself and looked to Diane, frustration evident on his angular features. "The King," he corrected, spitting the word derisively, "will take his time on the road to Braemar and Drochit, even pausing long enough to send a line around the eastern end of Tir na n'Og, just to make sure that the Tylwyth Teg mean to keep their bargain. Also, he wants to bring some of the smaller hamlets, such as Lisdoonvarna, under his control before he gets to the larger towns in Dvergamal's shadow."

"Foolish," Kelsey remarked. "If Braemar and Drochit are taken—and together they could not resist the army of Connacht—then the smaller hamlets will fall without bloodshed."

"Kinnemore is running shy," Geno reasoned. "His army took more of a beating on the edge of your forest than he, and they, expected. They need to roll over a couple of smaller, defenseless towns to regain their confidence."

Kelsey agreed with the grim assessment.

"The Connacht army will not crush the towns," Geldion put in angrily. "Even more than military confidence, the King needs for the army to believe in the justice of his cause again. We . . . he lost nearly as many to desertion as to wounds in the battle for the forest, and the King knows that he will lose many more if the army perceives the campaign as unjust."

"Not bad having an ear at Kinnemore's side, huh?" Diane asked slyly, aiming the remark mostly at Geno and thinking herself quite clever.

Geldion didn't seem to appreciate the comment, though, and neither did the dwarf.

"I guess that makes you one of those deserters you were talking about," Geno said to the Prince.

"The King is not Kinnemore, so I've been told," Geldion replied. He put a cold look on Diane, as if he was fearful that all of this was an elaborate ruse.

"And I do not believe that I have been deceived," Geldion declared firmly, though his dangerous expression hardly matched that claim. "Thus, I am no traitor to the crown. If Kinnemore was King, and he told me to go to war with the Buldrefolk, I would gladly kill a hundred of your kinfolk."

Geno snorted, half in humor, half in rage.

"I'm thinking that we should be going," Mickey quickly and wisely interjected. "We've a five-day ride to the Crahgs, and an army on our tails."

The group was silent for a long and tense moment, Geno and Geldion locking stares and the rest looking from one to the other, wondering which would strike the first blow. But despite their obvious hatred for each other and their surly dispositions, both Geno and Geldion were pragmatists. The mission before them was more important than their personal squabble, and so they helped break the camp and load the mounts. When the group exited Cowtangle sometime later, out the wood's southeastern end, Geldion rode up front beside Kelsey, with the elf's white Tir na n'Og stallion far outshining Geldion's gray. Next in line came Gary and Mickey, riding the same horse, another of the enchanted forest's tall white stallions (the leprechaun tucked in neatly at the base of the creature's powerful neck), and Diane, on a small and muscled black-and-white mare. Geno took up the rear, walking his brown pony far behind the others, grumbling to himself every step of the way.

"Suren it's to be a long ride," Mickey remarked, nodding towards Geno.

"I don't think so," Diane replied. "Prince Geldion is not really a bad guy—I figure that he's had more pain over what the King has become than any of you."

Gary snickered somewhat derisively. Diane hadn't been with him on his first journeys through Faerie; she hadn't witnessed Geldion's narrow-eyed viciousness or been chased long days by the relentless Prince. She hadn't witnessed Geldion's attack against the men of Braemar and Drochit on the eastern fields, or his presiding over the attempted execution of Baron Pwyll. Even if Diane was totally correct and King Kinnemore had been replaced by Ceridwen with the haggis, Prince Geldion's actions over the last few months were certainly not above reproach, and his loyal-little-son excuse echoed weakly at best.

"You don't know Geldion as well as you believe," Gary said to her.

"Nor Geno," Mickey remarked with a resigned sigh. "Suren it's to be a long road."

Actually, both Gary and Mickey were surprised at how calmly and uneventfully the next five days passed by. With news of war, the roads were deserted, and few traveled anywhere near to the Crahgs in any case. Kelsey and Geldion carried on a running conversation day to day. Gary was truly surprised that the usually judgmental elf could apparently so readily forgive the Prince, considering the recent devastation to Tir na n'Og's sacred border, but when Diane and Mickey put things in a different light for him, that amazement fast shifted to approval.

"He's thinking of the future," Diane reasoned. "What happened at Tir na n'Og wasn't Geldion's fault, but Geldion will have a lot to do with whatever might happen next."

"Aye," Mickey agreed. "Kelsey's putting aside what came before—how could Geldion have known that his father was not his father?"

"I don't know that he deserves a second chance," Gary stubbornly argued. "You remember the chase through the swamp."

"I remember it all better than yerself, like it was yesterday," Mickey said, subtly reminding Gary that while, by Gary's clock, those events had occurred years ago, a span of only a few weeks had passed in Faerie. "But these are dangerous times, lad, and I'm not one, nor is Kelsey, to push away a helping hand."

"Even Geno seems better with the Prince," Diane remarked.

"Hasn't spit on his shoes in two days!" Mickey added hopefully. "And I'm willing to take the dwarf's word that the time when he bumped Geldion into the embers was an accident."

Gary didn't openly argue, but his doubting expression told Mickey that he wasn't as certain of Geno's claim on that smoky occasion. Still, the young man had to admit that things were going better than he had expected when they had left Cowtangle. Geldion had done nothing to provoke any scorn. Far from it, the Prince was going out of his way to excuse Geno's subtle attacks, even while he was patting out the smoldering embers on his scorched behind.

"Prince Geldion has the most to lose," Diane reasoned.

"Geno could lose his home," Gary argued. "And his kin."

"But not his heart," Diane replied.

Gary accepted the logic. This entire episode, all the way back to Kelsey's quest to reforge the spear of Donigarten, and even before that, must now come as a bitter pill to the Prince. On those previous occasions he had been following the will of his Father and King, so he had thought, despite the fact that he apparently believed in his heart that course to be immoral.

Geldion had been deceived into immoral action, and for a man of honor (if the Prince was indeed a man of honor), that could be a more painful wound than any a sword might inflict.

Though they had another half day of riding, the Crahgs were in sight by this time, rolling hillocks, some shrouded in clouds, others shining green under the light of the sun. In looking at them, even from this distance, Gary remembered the paradoxical feelings the place had evoked, a feeling of alluring and tingling mystery, and also one of chilling terror. Mostly, Gary remembered the pervading melancholy, the dreamy landscape that could lure a man off guard to the very real dangers of the place.

With grew effort, they coaxed the horses past the flat few crahgs. Geno wanted to leave the mounts altogether. He suggested many times that they tether them in a copse of trees and pick them up on the way out, but Kelsey would hear nothing of it. The wild hairy haggis would not leave the Crahgs, but crahg wolves certainly would—and the beasts were known to have a particular liking for horseflesh.

Still, less than two hundred yards from the flat fields and first mounds that marked the western border of the Crahgs, the companions were walking, not riding, pulling their skittish and sweating steeds along behind them. The day was fast fading into twilight, and so Kelsey led them up the side of one medium-sized hillock, a hike of about a thousand feet through thick and wet grass.

The evening grew dark and close about them, and a chill wind came up, biting through their cloaks. Kelsey insisted that they light no fire, and none disagreed. The elf did pile kindling in the center of the camp, and placed some lamp oil and a flint and steel in easy reach beside it—just in case. But Diane in particular wasn't thrilled with their choice of campsite, and wondered why, if they couldn't light a fire, they hadn't found a sheltered vale, or a cave perhaps to spend the chilly night.

"It's the crahg wolves," Gary explained to her, wrapping her in his arms to ward off the cold. "Their front legs are longer than their back, so they don't go uphill very well. if they can't get above their prey, they won't usually attack."

"They will attack," grumpy Geno was quick to put in, and he threw a glare at Kelsey (who was paying no attention). "If they catch the smell of those horses."

With that, the elf turned about, facing Geno squarely.

"But their eyes are usually turned down the slopes, not up," the dwarf conceded, seeing Kelsey's scowl. Geno's blood was up, but he realized that if a fight came, his best ally would likely be Kelsey, and he needed no open arguments with the elf at this point.

"Let us hope that this will be our only night in the Crahgs," Geldion said, and even Geno nodded at the sentiment. "Kelsey said that you would call to the haggis," the Prince remarked to Mickey.

"And so I already am," the leprechaun explained. "As soon as we set the camp, I put some o' me magic into the hill. Nothing'll set a haggis to running like the noise o' working magic. If the beast is anywhere near the western side, we'll likely catch sight of it tonight or tomorrow."

"I still don't know how we're supposed to catch the thing," Geno grumbled.

"If the haggis is Kinnemore . . ." Kelsey began.

"The haggis is Kinnemore," Diane promptly corrected. "And he'll be tamed by the sight of his son."

Geno didn't seem convinced. He picked up a fair-sized rock and bit into it, but his expression soured and he tossed the remaining piece of stone away.

Nor did Gary or Kelsey, or even Mickey, seem convinced. Gary remembered the creature's curious shriek, an ear-splitting cry that sent chills along the marrow of his bones, that stole the strength from his knees. And Mickey remarked more than once that illusions had little effect on the likes of a wild hairy haggis. Only Geldion held out beside Diane's reasoning, and Gary, who felt keenly the loss of his own father, sympathized with the Prince's need to hope.

And so they spent the bulk of that night, huddled against the wind, sitting in a circle as though the light and warmth of a campfire was between them. The horses nickered nervously a short distance away, and stomped their hooves and banged against one another whenever the piercing howl of a crahg wolf cut through the stillness of the night air.

But mostly, it was quiet and it was cold, luring Gary into his dreams.

GARY felt a tapping on his face and opened his heavy eyes. Diane was in front of him, breathing rhythmically. Asleep, and apparently he had been asleep as well. The tapping continued, and it took the groggy man a few moments to understand that it had begun to rain, lightly but with big drops.

It was still dark, though the sky had lightened considerably above the rim of the eastern horizon, a lighter gray area reaching a quarter of the way up into the sky. Around the dozing couple, the camp was stirring. Gary saw sparking flashes as Kelsey struck steel to flint, lighting the piled kindling.

Diane stretched and yawned and came awake as the oiled kindling caught and threw out a soft light, the flames hissing against the press of rain.

"We're thinking it's the haggis," Mickey whispered, moving near to the pair.

Gary and Diane pulled themselves to their feet, immediately recognizing the leprechaun's serious tones. The horses were crowded together, and though the light was meager at best, thick lather glistened on the sides of the nervous animals, mixing with the streaking droplets of rain. The couple from the other world could feel the tension in the air, a tangible aura, a taste on their lips.

"It is the haggis," Gary whispered, and Diane didn't doubt him.

The hillock was too quiet. Even the horses made not a sound. Geno threw himself to the ground suddenly, putting an ear to the soft turf. Almost immediately, the dwarf's face crinkled with confusion.

"What's it saying?" Mickey asked.

Geno shrugged.

"Who is he talking to?" Prince Geldion demanded.

"The ground," explained the leprechaun.

"The ground?" both Geldion and Diane said together.

"Dwarfs can do that kind o' thing," Mickey replied.

"Be quiet!" Kelsey demanded in a harsh whisper, and Geno accentuated the elf's command by hurling a piece of sod the companions' way. As luck would have it, the flying divot struck Gary, the only one who hadn't said anything.

Geno lifted his head and looked curiously back to the turf, then turned his head around and firmly planted his other ear into the wet grass.

"What's it saying?" Mickey asked again.

"I do not know!" the flustered dwarf admitted. "It's screaming at me—I have never heard the ground so emphatic—but I cannot make out a single word!"

"Perhaps it is the rain," Kelsey offered, but Geno scowled at him.

Gary and Diane, standing side by side, each lurched to the side suddenly in opposite directions, as some borrowing thing plowed between them, just under the ground, making a straight run for the prone dwarf, and for the fire, which was sputtering between it and Geno.

"Geno!" Kelsey called in warning.

Flaming brands and lines of orange sparks went flying up into the night sky. Beyond them, the dwarf lifted and turned his head curiously, then soared into the air as though he had been sitting in the basket of a catapult, spinning out of sight into the dark sky. A short distance farther along, across the top of the hillock where the slope descended once more, there came a tremendous, ground-shaking explosion, and out popped a hunched and hairy form.

"*Ee ya yip yip yip!*"

Diane felt her bones ringing with vibrations; Prince Geldion grabbed his stomach as though he would throw up, and Gary Leger, having heard the cry of the wild hairy haggis before, clenched his fist and firmed his jaw, determined to fight away the dizziness and the terror.

Kelsey grabbed up his longbow and rushed about, trying to follow the creature's path. Gary and Diane scrambled for their own weapons, Gary scooping up the spear and Diane hoisting his large shield.

Now is the time for heroes! the proud spear screamed in Gary's thoughts.

"I never would have guessed," Gary whispered sarcastically.

They caught a glimpse of the creature, running clockwise around the fairly uniform slope of the hill. It seemed little more than a large ball of fur, the size of a curled-up man, except that one side of this hairy sphere was cut, practically halfway across, with the widest maw Gary had ever seen, with teeth that looked like they belonged in the mouth of a great white shark. Most curious of all, the creature's left arm and leg were longer than its right limbs, so it was perfectly level as it ran along on the uneven crahg!

"*Ee ya yip yip yip!*" it wailed, and black spots appeared before Gary Leger's eyes. He looked to Diane for support and saw that she was swaying, grabbing at her ears.

Geno landed with a thump and a groan, and bounced back to his feet, pulling out a hammer.

Kelsey cut across the top of the hillock, angling to intercept the haggis, but the beast disappeared suddenly, as abruptly as a fish going under the water.

A mound rolled up onto the hillock's top once more as the creature tunneled as fast as it had been running. The elf leaped to the side, but Geno, still trying to get his bearings from his unexpected flight, never saw the danger coming. Up the dwarf went again, cursing his rotten luck. He tried to turn so that he could launch his hammer towards the running mound, but it had happened too fast, and when he threw, he was already spinning back around.

The hammer shot out to the side, cutting the air right between the wide-eyed, horrified faces of Gary and Diane.

The turf exploded again on the side of the crahg as the haggis came back above ground, and Prince Geldion was there to meet the creature.

"Father!" he yelled, and felt heavy feet run straight up his legs and up his chest. He cried out and tried to throw himself backwards, only then realizing that he was already lying prone on his back, sunk several inches into the soft turf.

The haggis was long gone, taking up its clockwise, circling run around the side of the hillock again. *"Ee ya yip yip yip!"*

Geno landed with a thump and a groan, and bounced back to his feet, pulling out another hammer.

The poor horses kicked and scattered, thundering down the hillside. In the growing gray light of the impending dawn, Gary spotted his stallion, cutting across the path of the fast-running monster.

He started to cry out for the horse, but the words stuck in his throat as the haggis intercepted, barely seeming to shift its angle, moving so brutally fluidly that Gary hardly realized it had leaped off the ground. He heard the impact, though, a sickly, slapping sound as the haggis plowed into the horse's side.

The stallion stopped abruptly and stood perfectly still, and the haggis ran on around the curving mound. Then, to the amazement and horror of all looking on, Gary's stallion fell in half.

Geno pitched a hammer, perfectly leading the fast-running monster and scoring the first hit. The haggis never slowed.

Outraged, Kelsey again took up an intercepting route, but wasn't quite quick enough, and the haggis ran past him and out of his reach before his sword completed its downward cut.

Geldion, pulling himself up to his elbows, saw the creature completing its circuit, bearing down on him once more.

"Father," he said weakly, and he wisely fell back into the Geldion-shaped hole in the ground. The haggis ran right over him, blasting the breath from his lungs and knocking him in even deeper.

Geno and Kelsey scrambled wildly; Gary and Diane simply tried to get their bearings on the dizzying creature.

"Ye got to anticipate the thing's moves!" came a suggestion from high above. Gary looked up to see Mickey, the leprechaun catching the first rays of sun, floating under his umbrella about twenty feet above the top of the hillock.

"Only place to watch a haggis fight," the leprechaun said weakly.

Geno closed fast on the running haggis. He pitched another hammer, but the creature cut an impossibly sharp turn and dove underground.

"Stonebubbles," the dwarf grumbled resignedly as the mound rushed under him, and then Geno was flying again.

Kelsey, off to the side, quickly calculated the haggis's exit point and ran with all speed across the mound, his elfish sword gleaming in the morning light.

"*Ee ya yip yip yip!*" came the bone-shaking shriek as the haggis changed tactics and direction, bursting up out of the ground atop the hillock and bearing down suddenly on Gary and Diane.

Gary's only thought was to save his wife—and her only thought was to save him. They turned on each other simultaneously and slammed together as each tried to push the other from harm's way. Gary was much heavier (and heavier still because of the metal armor and shield), and it was Diane who went flying.

Gary nearly tumbled to the ground, as surprised by Diane's movement as she apparently had been by his. He kept the presence of mind to pivot, though.

Brace! came the sentient spear's warning cry in his head.

Gary lifted the spear, trying to put it in line, and fell aside. The tip only grazed the rushing haggis.

"*Ee yaaaa!*" it wailed, seeming for the first time as though it was in pain.

Geno, landed with a thump and a groan, and bounced back to his feet, pulling out another hammer

The haggis went over the lip of the hillock—and to everyone's amazement, especially poor Gary's, came right back along the exact angle at which it had departed, but now underground.

"Sonofabitch!" stubborn Gary growled, and he planted his feet widely apart, lifted the great shield as high as he could, and slammed its pointed bottom into the turf, sinking it in several inches.

"Uh-oh," he heard Mickey remark from above.

Gary braced his shoulder hard against the shield and peeked around it, his eyes widening in shock as the haggis burst out of the turf, running, flying, right for him.

There came a blinding flash—even the haggis seemed to flinch.

"*Ee ya yip yip . . .*"

Slam!

Gary knew he was flying, felt the motion and heard the whistle as the air blew through the slitted faceplate of his great helm. He knew, too, that his shoulder hurt again and it felt as if something hard was biting on his arm and side.

He tumbled completely around, his helm falling free. He saw green, shining grass in the morning light, glistening prettily with the wetness of the light rain.

That pretty grass rushed up and swallowed him.

SIXTEEN

Resilience

IT was still raining, and that pitter-patter on his face again brought Gary's conscious mind whirling back from dreamland. He stirred and tried to open his eyes, felt a dull ache throughout his entire body.

From somewhere not so far away, he heard the ring of a dwarfish hammer.

Waves of agony rolled up his left arm, accompanying each note. Gary half screamed, half gasped and tried to roll away, his eyes popping open wide. A strong hand clamped hard on his chest and held him still.

"What are you doing?" the suddenly wide-awake Gary demanded. He managed to turn his head to the left in time to see Geno's hammer go up high once more, then come crashing down, out of his view, ringing against metal. The waves turned Gary's stomach and sent the world spinning dizzily before his eyes. He tried to scream out, but found no breath for it.

Up again went the grim-faced dwarf's hammer.

"No!" Gary protested.

Then Diane was there, gently easing Geno aside (though the dwarf kept his hand firmly on Gary's chest and would not let him turn) and putting her face close to Gary's.

"He has to," she tried to explain.

"What? What . . . is . . ." Gary stammered between gasps.

"It's your shield," Diane went on. She eased Geno's hand away from Gary's chest so that Gary could roll over enough to take in the scene.

Gary's gasps fell away to silence, his breath gone altogether as he regarded his shield, the shield of Donigarten, the strongest shield in all the world. Fully a third of it was gone, the metal ripped away, and what was left had buckled around Gary's arm, bent like the aluminum foil Gary might use to wrap the remains of a Thanksgiving turkey. Gary realized then that, while his previously injured shoulder throbbed with pain, he felt nothing at all along his arm.

Nothing at all.

His gauntlet was off and he stared hard at his unmoving left hand. It didn't look real to him, not at all, resembling the lifeless limb of a mannequin, except that it was so pale that it appeared blue.

"If we cannot get the shield off soon, you will lose your arm," Kelsey said grimly.

"Good shield," Geno remarked, eyeing the flattened end of his ruined chisel—the third chisel he had destroyed in the last fifteen minutes.

Gary was silent for a long moment, considering Kelsey's grim words. He rolled flat to his back again. "Get it off," he said. "Just get it off."

Diane shifted over to be close to her husband, while Geno shrugged and gladly—too gladly, Gary thought—moved back into position.

Again and again, the dwarfish hammer rang out, accompanied by Gary's increasing growls. Finally, after five more minutes that seemed like five days to poor Gary, the dwarf grunted triumphantly and tossed the destroyed shield aside. Geno was far from done, though. Next he went to work on the arm plates, of Gary's armor, twisting and turning brutally, loosening straps and every once in a while giving a solid hit with that hammer and chisel.

Then it was over and Gary lay flat in the rain, closing his eyes and concentrating against the gradually receding pain. Kelsey wrapped his arm in something soggy, which Diane explained as a healing poultice, and Gary only nodded, though he hardly comprehended anything at that moment.

Only the pain.

"Never seen a hit like it," he heard Geno mumble.

"I telled ye the haggis was one to be feared," Mickey answered.

"It wasn't the haggis," Diane insisted.

On cue, all eyes turned to Geldion, who had seen the creature up close. I know not," the Prince admitted helplessly. "If that . . . thing was my father, then it did not recognize me."

"It wasn't the haggis," Diane said again.

Gary had heard that tone before, and knew that his wife had something tangible up her sleeve. He forced himself up on his good elbow, and studied Diane's smug smile.

Gary remembered that last moment before his collision with the beast, the blinding flash . . .

"You took a picture of it," he said to Diane, his tone making the remark sound like an accusation.

Diane chuckled and produced the Polaroid snapshot from her pouch, handing it to Kelsey. The elf said nothing out loud, but his expression spoke volumes. The photograph was passed from hand to hand, from Kelsey to Geno to Mickey.

"Kinnemore," the leprechaun remarked, handing it to Geldion. The Prince's knees almost buckled and he stared at the picture for a long, long while.

Gary felt tingling needles in his arm a bit later, and could move his fingers once more. Diane showed him the picture and explained to him what had happened.

Gary saw the creature clearly in the photograph, a hunched and hairy thing, its left arm and leg nearly twice as long as its right limbs. But the face was not as Gary had seen it. Rather than the hairball with a wide, stretching mouth, it was clearly the face of a man, though still with a mouth that reached from ear to ear.

Gary saw himself in the photo too, peeking around the shield at the flying thing, wearing the most profound expression of terror he had ever seen. Like a missile, the haggis had slammed the shield, Diane explained. And had bitten the bottom piece right off, as Gary had gone flying up into the air.

Apparently the creature had been hurt by the impact, though. With Gary out of the fight and Geldion trampled into a muddy trench, it had almost evened the odds, yet instead of turning back after the others, it had burrowed straight down into the crahg, keening wildly all the while.

"We got back all the horses," Diane went on, and then added in a lower tone, "except yours."

Gary grimaced, remembering the gruesome attack.

"Then we got out of the Crahgs," Diane finished. Gary propped himself up higher to get his bearings. He saw the rolling hillocks a short distance away, and by the position of the sun, a lighter gray area in the heavy sky, he knew that most of the day had passed.

"How's your arm?" Diane asked.

Gary flexed the limb, clenched and opened his hand a few times, and nodded. His shoulder was still quite sore—all his body ached as though he had been in a car wreck—but he felt as though he could go on, knew that he had to go on in light of the photographic confirmation of the haggis's true identity.

He motioned to Diane to help him to his feet.

"What's next?" he asked hopefully of the others.

Kelsey, Mickey, none of them had any answer, and Geldion's responding stare was cold indeed.

"We know now that the haggis is truly the King," Gary reasoned, using that simple logic to try to force them from their helpless resignation.

"Unless your wife is a witch," Geldion retorted suspiciously, "and her magic a deception."

Gary turned a smug smile on Diane. "Sometimes," he answered. "But the pictures show the truth."

"A lot o' good that'll do us," Mickey put in.

"We can't give up," Gary said.

"Maybe we could use the pictures to convince the Connacht soldiers," Diane reasoned. "Prince Geldion could take them back to the army."

Both Kelsey and the Prince were shaking their heads even as she spoke.

"I have come to trust Gary Leger as I would a brother," Kelsey explained. "And thus, to trust in you. Yet, my own doubts about your magic remain. I have watched you with your flashing charm . . ."

"Flashing charm?" Diane asked.

"The thing ye called a camra," Mickey explained.

"And yet I still am not certain of its paintings," Kelsey finished.

"You are asking that I tell loyal and professional soldiers to desert the King they have known all their careers," Geldion agreed. "I could never convince them with such meager evidence."

Diane look to Gary and shrugged, her hands, each holding one of the revealing photographs, held wide in disbelief. "Meager evidence?" she whispered.

"You're looking at things from the point of view of our world," Gary explained knowingly. "We know what a picture is, and we know how to test it for authenticity. But here, the 'camra' is just another form of magic, and from what I've seen, most of the magic in Faerie is illusion, a leprechaun's tricks. Mickey could produce two pictures that look exactly like the ones from the Polaroid in the blink of an eye."

Diane looked to the leprechaun, and at that moment, Mickey's pipe was floating in the air before his face, lighting of its own accord, despite the continuing rain. The woman gave a loud sigh and looked back to Gary, seeing things in the proper perspective.

"Then we just have to go back and catch the haggis," Gary announced, as though it was all a simple task.

Words of protest came at him from every corner, strongest from Geno (no surprise there) and from Kelsey. Gary eyed the elf skeptically, not expecting such a vehement argument, until Kelsey, in his angry raving, mentioned the dead horse. The Tylwyth Teg were protective of their magnificent steeds, and Kelsey had lost one already to the wild beast.

But Gary remained determined against the tide. "We have to go back," he said firmly. "We'll never stop the war now if we don't catch the real King Kinnemore and reveal Ceridwen's deception."

"And the war will go on without us when we are lying dead in the Crahgs," Geno answered.

Gary started to respond, but fell silent. The dwarf was right—all of them were right. They had met the haggis and had been run out. If not for Cedric's shield, Gary would have shared a fate similar to the one his horse found. Despite his determination, a shudder coursed along his spine as he pictured himself lying in half atop the wet hillock.

But they had to go back—that fact seemed inescapable. They had to catch the haggis and prove the truth of Ceridwen's deception, or all the land was doomed.

Gary pondered the dilemma for a moment, then snapped his fingers, drawing everyone's attention.

"I saw a movie once," he began, "or maybe it was a cartoon."

"A what?" Mickey asked.

"Or a what?" Kelsey added.

Gary shook his head and waved his hands. "Never mind that," he explained. "It doesn't matter. I saw this show . . . er, play, where a monster was too strong to be held by anything, even steel or titanium."

"What's that?" Mickey asked.

Gary was shaking head and hands again before the leprechaun even got out the predictable question. "Never mind that," Gary went on. "The monster was too strong, that's the point. But in this movi . . . in this play, they caught the monster, and held it, with an elastic bubble."

"A what kind of bubble?" Mickey asked against Gary's shaking head and limbs.

"Never mind that," Gary huffed.

"It might work," Diane agreed, following the reasoning perfectly. "But how are we going to get something like that?"

Gary was already thinking along those lines. "Where's Gerbil?" he asked.

"In Braemar," Mickey replied.

Gary abruptly turned to Geno, his voice filled with excitement and hope. "If I give Gerbil something to design, you think you could build it?"

Geno snorted. "I can build anything."

"On to Braemar!" Gary announced and took a long stride towards the horses.

None of the others took a step to follow, all looking skeptically at Gary.

"Trust me," Gary answered those looks.

Mickey, Kelsey, and Geno glanced around at each other, silently sharing memories of the last few weeks. Gary's ingenuity had gotten them off of Ceridwen's island; Gary's quick thinking had allowed them to escape Geldion's troops in the haunted swamp; Gary's ingenuity had brought about the fall of Robert.

They broke camp and headed out for Braemar, Gary and Diane sharing Kelsey's mount, the elf riding behind Geldion on the gray, and Mickey propped against the neck of Geno's pony.

SEVENTEEN

ACME School of Design

DIANE stood wide-eyed, her mouth hanging open. She had been introduced to not one, but two, unusual characters upon their arrival in Braemar. She had met her first gnome, Gerbil Hamsmacker, as expected, and the three-foot-tall, pot-bellied creature was pretty much what Diane had envisioned, even down to his ample beard, orange turning to gray, and sparkling blue eyes. He talked the way Diane thought a gnomish inventor should talk, with long, profound pauses, followed by bursts of rapid sentences all run together, where listeners would then have to sit back for a while and sort them all out. Gerbil was obviously thrilled to see Gary and company, and talked wildly about the shot at Buck-toothed Ogre Pass, the gnome-built cannonball that had toppled mighty Robert and had ensured Gerbil a place of the highest respect—post-mortem, of course—among his colleagues.

Soon after meeting up with his friends, Gerbil called another friend out to meet the companions, one they hadn't expected to see out of his home in Dvergamal, and it was the sight of gigantic Tommy One-Thumb that had so unnerved Diane. His face was childish, dimpled cheeks and a continual smile, and it seemed to fit the kindhearted giant's demeanor despite the fact that Tommy was nearly twenty feet tall, with a foot that could crush a full-grown man flat and hands that could wrap about a human skull as though it was a baseball.

It didn't take long for Tommy to come to like Diane, and vice versa.

But there was little time for pleasantries in Braemar. The town was prepared for war, with most of the farmers from the surrounding fields, a host of dwarfs, and even a contingent of gnomes from faraway Gondabuggan, on hand. More tents were in and about the town than buildings, and the tips of old swords and makeshift spears, pitchforks and huge bardiche axes dominated the scenery in every direction, farmers-turned-soldiers marching in ragged formation.

The friends were well known in Braemar—and so was Prince Geldion. Every smile that turned Gary's way or Kelsey's way inevitably bent down into a profound frown at the sight of the Prince, the man who, in the eyes of Brae-mar's populace, had accounted for more than a few widows and orphans. He wasn't set upon, no one even challenged the fact that Geldion openly wore that infamous dirk of his, but that was only because of the respect the Prince's com-panions had rightfully earned.

Kelsey realized how uncomfortable the situation was, though, and he quickly arranged for a meeting between himself, Geldion, and Lord Badenoch, who ruled Braemar and was among the most respected men in all the eastern region.

The others were invited along as well, but Gary, seeing the necessity for all speed, would hear nothing of it. He needed Geno and Gerbil (and he wanted Mickey along), and asked for ink and parchment and a quiet place where they might be alone. They were granted all their requests without question and wound up in an abandoned and ruined farmhouse on the outskirts of the town. The place had been razed in the last dragon raid on Braemar, right before Gary had lured the wrym into Dvergamal and the gnomish cannon had taken Robert down, and still smelled of soot, but it was light enough in there, since the thatched roof had been vaporized by Robert's deadly breath.

And so the group went to work, with Gary relaying his ideas to Mickey, who produced illusionary images of them on a makeshift table in the middle of the room. As soon as he caught on to Gary's general ideas, Gerbil took over the con-versation with Mickey, fine-tuning the basic design into a workable and build-able contraption. All the while, Geno grunted and nodded, scribbling on the parchment, listing the materials and equipment he would need and often inter-rupting the gnome—whenever the excitable inventor began getting carried away with elaborate and unneeded accessories. Outside the structure, Tommy hovered over them, peeking in over the skeletal stone walls (and often blocking their precious light!).

They got flustered many times, argued more than once, especially Geno and Gerbil. Geno wanted a simple haggis trap, something they could construct in a couple of days; Gerbil's first few designs would have taken a year to build and an army to move. The pragmatic dwarf had the full support of Gary and Mickey, though Gary was truly intrigued by some of the gnome's outrageous designs, and so Gerbil was put under wraps.

The gnome offered up more than a few "Oh pooh"s and at one point stood glaring at the others with his fists tucked tight against his hips and his lips pressed tight into thin lines. But eventually they came to an agreement on the design, the pragmatic friends granting Gerbil one or two of his most easily con-structed innovations. Next came a materials list, composed by Geno, and then they were off, scattering to the four corners of Braemar in search of the items and a forge.

LORD Badenoch was a quiet man, a stately leader of experience and even temperament. Those qualities were put to the test indeed when Prince Geldion entered the man's study!

"He comes not as a prisoner," the Lord remarked, and his face went suddenly stern, grayish blue eyes narrow and unblinking. Badenoch was tall, nearly as tall as Gary Leger, with broad shoulders and perfect posture. His dark brown hair showed signs of gray at the temples, but he did not seem old or frail. Far from it; it was often whispered across Faerie's hamlets that if Kinnemore could be overthrown, Lord Badenoch should be appointed King.

Diane thought him an impressive and handsome man, a combination of vitality and experience befitting a leader. There was a dangerous quality to him, as well, one that seemed on its very edge now, with his most hated enemy standing barely ten feet away.

Geldion, so often placed in a defensive situation, did well to bite back the sharp retort that came to mind. Neither did he match Badenoch's imposing stare, standing quietly to the side and letting Kelsey do the explaining.

"He is not here as a prisoner," the elf answered firmly, "but as an ally. We have new information concerning our enemy . . ." He looked to Geldion and the Prince nodded. "Our common enemy," Kelsey explained to Badenoch, "King Kinnemore of Connacht."

"If Kinnemore has shown himself as our enemy, then he has done so through the actions of his son," Badenoch promptly reminded. The Lord, too, looked to Geldion. "The people of Braemar and of Drochit, and the Buldrefolk, have not forgotten the battle, Prince Geldion," he said grimly. "If more of Kervin's sturdy folk were about in Braemar this day, you would not have made it to my quarters alive."

"Geno Hammerthrower supports our plan," Diane interjected, though she knew that it was not her place to speak. Badenoch's superior gaze fell over her, and she blushed and averted her eyes.

"This is Diane," Kelsey said. "Wife of Gary Leger, who journeyed with him to aid in our cause."

"She is a fighter?" Badenoch asked, and his tone showed no disrespect, for despite the suit of fine mesh armor the elves had given to her and her size (which was large in a land where the average woman barely topped five feet), she did not hold herself as a warrior.

"She is a thinker," Kelsey corrected.

"It was her magic which showed me the truth about my father," Geldion added.

"A witch?" the Lord asked.

"A thinker," Kelsey reiterated. "With a bit of magic about her, no doubt." He looked to Diane and smiled, and the woman, feeling more than a little out of place, truly appreciated the support.

Kelsey's ensuing nod had Diane reaching into her pouch for the revealing photographs, the picture of the haggis-turned-King near Dilnamarra Keep and the one of the King-turned-haggis atop the crahg.

Neither the pictures nor the continuing assurances of Kelsey and Diane, nor Prince Geldion's diplomatic attitude, did much to convince Badenoch of their perspective on the situation. Even if he agreed that Kinnemore and the haggis had been switched, which he did not, he saw little chance that they might gain anything by hunting the King-turned-monster.

Over the last few weeks, though, Kelsey and Gary Leger, Geno, Gerbil, and Mickey had certainly earned Lord Badenoch's trust and respect. There was even a giant walking free in Braemar, trusted despite the reputation of his race simply because he was known as a friend of these companions.

"I do not agree with your assessment," Badenoch announced after mulling over all the information that had been presented to him, after all the pleas and assurances. "Nor do I agree with your apparent trust of this man." Once again, for perhaps the twentieth time in the short conversation, Badenoch and Geldion locked dangerous stares.

They would have liked nothing more than to be alone, Diane realized, to complete their battle and satisfy their mutual hatred once and for all. If Geldion was truly convinced (and Diane believed that he was), then he and the Lord were on the same side in this conflict, but there remained great animosity between the two.

"And I have no men to spare for your desperate plan," Lord Badenoch added, still eyeing Geldion.

"We have asked for none," Kelsey replied.

"Then what do you ask for?" Badenoch said, seeming for the first time a bit flustered. "Then why have you come to Braemar? Why have you brought Prince Geldion before me?"

"To inform you of our designs," Kelsey answered. "The haggis, pretending to be Kinnemore, will soon march east with his army, and battle will likely be joined."

Badenoch grimaced but did not even blink. It seemed to Diane that he had known this already, but hearing confirmation from Kelsey was painful to him nonetheless.

"And the Tylwyth Teg will not come to your aid," Kelsey went on, and now it was the elf who seemed pained.

"I have heard word of the truce," Badenoch replied grimly.

"Not all of Tir na n'Og agree with it," Kelsey said.

Badenoch nodded—that much was obvious just from the fact that Kelsey was now in Braemar.

"I wanted you to know," Kelsey went on. "To know of our plans and to know that I and my companions will not desert you in this dark hour."

"But you will not be there when the battle is joined," Badenoch reasoned. "Your fine sword will play no part, nor will the presence of the spearwielder, whose appearance was said to have made a profound impact on the Connacht army as it battled for Tir na n'Og. Is Braemar any less deserving than your elfish home?"

Kelsey sighed deeply. "I must return to the Crahgs," he explained. "As Gary Leger must. If we are right, we may yet avert this tragedy."

"And if you are wrong?"

"Then we'll return," Diane said firmly. "And we'll fight beside you." She paused and flashed a wry smile, then pointed to Prince Geldion. "Even him," she said. "And more than a few of Kinnemore's soldiers will come over to our side with Prince Geldion among our ranks."

Geldion did nothing to affirm the claim, and proud Badenoch did nothing to acknowledge it. Diane remained solid in her determination, though, and both Kelsey and Geldion were silently glad she had spoken the words.

Kelsey looked to Geldion suddenly, wondering if it might serve them all better if the Prince remained with Badenoch.

"We need him to tame the haggis," Diane remarked, understanding the elf's look.

Kelsey nodded, and realized anyway that leaving Geldion in Braemar might not be such a good idea.

"You may take what materials you need, Kelsenellenelvial," Lord Badenoch decided. "I owe you and your companions that much at least. And as for you, Diane, wife of Gary Leger." The proud Badenoch paused and looked intently at Diane, and she rocked back on her heels, intimidated, expecting to be scolded.

"I pray that you may return to Braemar on a brighter day," Badenoch finished. "All of Faerie owes your husband a great debt, and I would be honored if we might meet when times are not so grave." He finished with a curt bow, and Diane, overwhelmed, had no reply.

The three left Badenoch's quarters soon after, and on Kelsey's orders, the elf thinking it wise to keep Geldion as far from the activity as possible, headed for the lonely farmhouse away from the bustle of Braemar.

Gary, Mickey, and Tommy joined them later in the day, reporting that Geno had secured the forge and most of the materials and Gerbil had nearly completed the final designs.

For the road-weary companions, that night and the next came as a welcome reprieve, a time to brush the dirt from their cloaks and allow their tired bodies some much needed rest. But the reprieve was physical only, for none of them could put the coming trials out of their minds, could forget the sheer wildness and ferocity of the haggis and the fact that a hostile army was even now marching their way.

Geno and Gerbil worked right through the night, right through the next day and the night after that. Gerbil made the designs and explained the concepts, such as how to bend the pounded wire into a spring, and Geno, who had well earned his title as the finest smithy in all the world, only had to be told once. When dawn broke on their third day in Braemar, the two half-sized companions joined the others at the farmhouse and announced that the haggis trap was completed.

"Then we're off," Gary was happy to say.

"Just one problem," Geno replied smugly, and even Gerbil seemed at a loss.

"How are we to carry the thing?" the dwarf asked. "It weighs near to four hundred pounds and is too bulky to be strapped onto a horse."

"Oh, good point," Gerbil groaned, and that groan became general.

"Could build a skid for it," Geno went on. "But that will take another day— make it two days because I need some rest!"

The groan went up a second time.

"We're not having two days to spare," Mickey reasoned.

Gary alone was smiling, and eventually everyone focused on him. "Tommy will carry it," he explained when his mirth drew all eyes his way.

A brief moment of doubts and arguments ensued, particularly from Geldion, who hadn't quite gotten used to having an eighteen-foot-tall giant along. But the complaints quieted soon enough, the others realizing that they had few options, and even proud Kelsey had to admit that having powerful Tommy around might not be a bad thing when facing a wild hairy haggis.

They went to the rebuilt Snoozing Sprite tavern for breakfast—all of them, even Geldion, though Tommy could not fit inside and had to take his meal out on the porch. Then they retrieved the haggis trap, and while Gary's eyes lit up as he regarded a tangible material manifestation of his theory, Kelsey and Geldion looked on doubtfully, not knowing what to make of the curious thing.

Its metal frame was box-shaped, thick rods forged together and supported at each corner by metal joists, and supported diagonally on three sides, corner to corner, by crossing rods. Inside this open frame was a second structure, a jumble of wires, metal rods and springs—more springs than Diane had ever seen together in one place! A springloaded plate completed the picture, on the front and open end of the contraption. Geno took special pride in this feature, for he had designed and added a particular action to the fast-opening plate.

He nodded to Gerbil and the gnome produced a curious tool, some sort of wrench, and made a simple adjustment to a lever on the side of the box. Gerbil then stepped aside and Geno moved over and grabbed the spring's lever. "Just let the little hairball come at us underground," the dwarf remarked and tugged the lever.

The whole contraption jolted hard as the edge of the faceplate slammed straight into the ground, diving deep beneath the surface.

"Boom!" Gerbil explained happily, clapping his plump little hands.

Gary cupped his hand, blew on his knuckles, and rubbed them across his chest. Diane held back her remarks and let him bask in the glory—even to doubting Kelsey and Geldion, this thing looked like it might actually work.

Lord Badenoch was gracious enough to part with a fine pair of horses, and a pony, for Gerbil decided that he had to go along as well, to see how his design worked out in actual application. Tommy had no trouble in keeping up, even with the bulky box on his shoulder and another sack Geno had given to him tucked under his other arm. The road out of Braemar was clear, with no sign of Kinnemore's army yet apparent, and the group made fine progress back to the Crahgs. The weather was an ally, too, fine and clear and with a comfortable breeze blowing off the Dvergamal peaks.

None of them needed to be reminded that the fine weather would also facilitate Kinnemore's march towards Braemar, and all the way around Dvergamal's southernmost peaks, they kept looking back to the west, looking for a telltale cloud of dust.

It rained on the second day, but the clouds flew away on the third, and by late that afternoon they came again upon the Crahgs. Gary sat atop a brown stallion staring long and hard at the ominous mounds, a look of obvious dread on his face.

"It will work," Diane, on her Tir na n'Og mount at his side, insisted. "The trap will catch the thing and then we'll prove that the haggis is really King Kinnemore."

"And th'other way around," Mickey, tucked in his customary spot against the neck of Gary's horse, added.

"The trap will work," Geno put in, and Gerbil's head bobbed frantically in agreement.

Logically, Gary didn't disagree, but that did little to calm the dancing butterflies in his stomach. He looked from one companion to the others, settling his gaze on Diane.

"It will work," she whispered determinedly.

"Then how come I feel like Wile E. Coyote?" Gary asked, and kicked his horse into a trot to catch up with Kelsey and Geldion.

EIGHTEEN
Frenzy

THEY went atop the same hillock where they had encountered the haggis previously. Again, fortunately, no crahg wolves or any other monsters were about to challenge them.

"The dragon was flying back and forth on this side o' the Crahgs not so long ago," Mickey reasoned, trying to explain the unusual calm in the dangerous region. "Robert probably sent all them wolves running to the east, deep in their hills."

It was a cheery thought—somewhat. None of the others, certainly not Kelsey, Geldion, or Geno, feared crahg wolves or anything else the Crahgs might throw at them, with the exception of the one beast they had come to catch.

The sun was nearly down as they sorted out their encampment. Kelsey tethered the horses closer to the group this time, while Geno, with help from Tommy, moved about securing the perimeter of the mound. The giant carried the large sack, and took a sheet of metal, perhaps three feet square, from it every few feet. Following Geno's instructions, Tommy jammed the sheets into the soft turf, and the dwarf pounded them the rest of the way down.

"Let the little hairy bug come burrowing at us underground," the dwarf said wickedly and smacked his hammer on top of the next plate in line.

Twilight turned to darkness and the howls of distant crahg wolves came up.

All in the camp were nervous; not one of them fostered any thoughts of trying to sleep. Kelsey and Geldion looked to Mickey often, their expressions reflecting their increasing impatience.

Mickey walked all about the mound's top, whispering enchantments under his breath, sending his magic deep into the soil that the wild hairy haggis might hear it clearly. The leprechaun wasn't thrilled about summoning the beast, of course, but his pragmatic side told him that the sooner they encountered the haggis, the sooner they might be out of the Crahgs.

The moon was full and high above them; the calls of the wolves had increased tenfold, and had come closer, sometimes seeming as if the strange-looking canines might be all about the base of the mound.

"Are we to fight a haggis, or all the creature's minions?" Geldion asked nervously after one particularly vocal stretch.

"Let the stupid doggies come up," Geno retorted sharply, his tone revealing his tension. He stalked to the edge of the mound and howled, and when a wolf howled in reply, somewhere in the thick darkness below the mound, the dwarf let fly a hammer, spinning into the night. "Stupid dogs," Geno muttered and walked back toward the middle of the encampment.

Geldion kicked hard at the soft turf in anger, expecting a thousand crahg wolves to rush up in answer to Geno's attack.

"Easy," Mickey said to the Prince, and to all the others. "The wolves'll not come up, not when the haggis is about. We're too much for them, and they know they'll find much carrion after their wild leader's done his work."

"Well put," Geno grumbled sarcastically.

"I mean that's what they're thinking!" Mickey corrected. "How can they be knowin' that we've a trap . . ."

"*Ee ya yip yip yip!*" The cry buried the leprechaun's thoughts and brought a shriek from Gerbil, and the gnome threw himself face down on the ground.

"What was it? What was it?" he squeaked from under his elbow.

"*Ee ya yip yip yip!*" the cry came again, and the horses nickered and banged together, and Geno hopped in circles, a hammer in each hand, and Tommy, poor Tommy, trembled so badly that he looked like a willow tree caught in the eye of a tornado.

"*Ee ya yip yip yip!*"

"Where is it?" Kelsey demanded, running about and trying to get his bearings on the obviously nearby monster. The haggis's cry echoed off every hillock, resounded a hundred times and filled all the air about them.

Gerbil got back to his knees. "Indisputably incredible," the gnome announced.

"What?" Gary demanded.

"That cry!" the gnome said happily, all his fears apparently washed away. "That cry! Oh, how perfect!"

"Duh?" said Tommy, and Gary and Diane agreed wholeheartedly.

"*Ee ya yip yip yip!*" came the wail.

Gerbil hopped up and down, clapping his plump gnomish hands. "I must find a way to reproduce that!" he squealed. "Yes, in a bottle or a beaker." He looked directly into the blank stares of Gary and Diane. "That sound will keep the rodents from Gondabuggan. Oh, I will get my name on the Build-A-Better-Mousetrap plaque!"

"The Build-A-Bet . . ." Diane stuttered.

"Don't ask," Gary warned, knowing they had no time for one of Gerbil's gnomish dissertations.

"*Ee ya yip yip yip!*"

"There's the bug!" Geno yelped, pointing a hammer over the mound's southern edge. The dwarf growled and fired, then stamped his foot in frustration as the haggis dove underground and the hammer bounced harmlessly away.

Up the hillock the monster charged, churning the ground above it. Full speed, right into the buried metal plate.

The entire mound jolted as though a bomb had gone off, and then there was silence.

Geno hopped up and down and punched his fist into the air in victory.

But then the ground churned atop the mound, on the other side of the plate.

"Duh?" Geno blubbered, sounding a lot like Tommy. Suddenly the dwarf was flying again, spitting curses through every somersault.

Gerbil was fast to the trap, and Tommy too, the giant working to shift the cage in line and Gerbil ready with the faceplate lever.

But the haggis turned abruptly, rushing to the side, towards Kelsey and Geldion. It burst free of the ground and leaped, flying between the two.

Kelsey spun to the side, sword in hand, and snarled as he began his vicious cut.

His arm had barely begun to come around when Geldion intercepted, throwing all his weight against the elf and knocking Kelsey to the ground.

"Father!" he cried after the beast.

The haggis hit the ground and disappeared so quickly that it seemed as if the creature had dived into a dark pool of water. Impossibly quick, too, was its turn, for it came up right under the startled Prince Geldion's heels, launching him into a forward roll.

Geno bounced down, right back in the thing's path. The dwarf's eyes popped wide and he shrieked and dove aside, but reached out with one hand as the haggis zipped past.

"Got you!" Geno cried, his iron grasp locking onto one of the haggis's legs. But the dwarf's triumph turned to horror as he bounced off behind the wild thing, his "capture" not hindering or slowing the haggis one bit.

"Duh, hey!" Tommy cried, throwing his hands in front of him as the haggis went airborne. The next thing the giant knew, he was laid out flat in the grass, watching the pretty stars and moon, his chest throbbing.

The haggis bounced high after slamming the giant, and plunged down for another underground dive, Geno in tow. The haggis was bigger than Geno, but it was sleeker, and better prepared for its tunneling swim.

The dwarf grunted and ate dirt, and hung in place, his legs and feet the only thing visible above the ground.

And the haggis tunneled off for the edge of the mound, and smack into another of the buried plates, jolting the mound so fiercely that Diane found herself suddenly sitting.

The creature's tremendous momentum took out the side of the mound's lip, and the haggis, suddenly above ground and holding a dented and torn metal plate, sat perfectly still for a moment, apparently stunned.

It shook its shaggy head, its ample lips batting loudly, then let loose another of those bone-shivering wails and ran off into the night.

"There it goes!" Gary called, thinking the encounter ended.

"Here it comes," Mickey corrected, floating up above the camp under his umbrella. "The thing's making straight for the horses."

"Tommy!" Gary called, grabbing at the heavy trap, trying to drag it in line with the approaching beast. Tommy was still staring at the stars and would be of no help. Kelsey came to Gary, as did Geldion, and the three managed to slide the trap across the grass.

Up the hillock came the haggis, diving underground again and speeding right for yet another of the buried plates.

"Brace!" Mickey warned, but the haggis skidded to a stop right before the plate and popped above ground, gently hopping over the devious barrier.

"*Haaaa, hahahahaha!*" it chided. Its wild eyes darted all about. It looked to the horses and a long tongue flopped out of its mouth, dragged on the ground before licking the thing's lips. Then it seemed even more eager as it regarded the floundering Geno, half-buried.

"*Ee ya yip yip yip!*" it shrieked and disappeared underground, making straight for the dwarf.

Diane was there first, and Gerbil rushed beside her, each taking one of Geno's large boots under their arms and pulling hard. Both flew over backwards, Diane clutching the boot, and it took her a moment to realize that she didn't have the dwarf with her.

She looked back to see the haggis bearing in, the helpless Geno's toes waggling in the air.

"Geno!" she and Gerbil and all the others cried. Sword in hand, Kelsey rushed across, and a horrified Geldion followed, calling for his father, trying anything to calm the monster.

The haggis slammed in; the dwarf grunted and his legs stopped kicking. Then the haggis popped out of the ground, still on the same side of the dwarf, its tongue hanging low and a sour expression on its contorted features.

"*Blech!*" it groaned and again its wild eyes darted side to side, searching for a meal.

Gary heard a whinny right behind him and he turned, then fell away in surprise, seeing a fat pony right where the trap had been sitting.

"Bait it in, lad," Mickey implored him.

The pony-cage whinnied again.

Kelsey charged and cried out, bringing his sword to bear. He hit nothing but air and grass, though, for the haggis took to tunneling again.

Prince Geldion went for another spinning flight as the hungry haggis sped underneath him, bearing down on the fattest prize of all.

Gary jumped out in front and to the side and plunged Cedric's spear deep into the ground, and the haggis, feeling the strength and remembering the cruel weapon from their last encounter, surfaced and rushed over the angled shaft.

"*Ee ya yip yip yip!*" it cried triumphantly, lifting from the ground, flying for the heart of the fat pony.

Flying straight into the spring and wire cage.

Over and ever the heavy cage rolled, off the side of the crahg, settling a dozen feet below the lip.

Triumphant cries became a wail of disbelief as Mickey floated down and yanked the lever, closing the trap's door.

Gary was the first down the hillock, with Geldion and Diane coming fast behind.

"I never knew that Wile E. Coyote hunted the Tasmanian devil," Diane remarked, taking Gary's arm, and the analogy seemed accurate enough, for the haggis went completely berserk, pulling and slamming, biting at the wire and clawing at the thick support beams. Its frenzy stood the cage up on one end, despite Gary and Geldion's efforts to hold the thing steady, and it seemed as if the creature would surely break free.

Tommy came bounding down, but even his great and powerful arms could not hold the cage in place.

"It's not to hold!" Mickey cried.

"Talk to it!" Diane pleaded with Geldion.

The Prince dove to the ground near the cage. "Father!" he called over and over, to no apparent effect.

"Father!"

The haggis stopped its kicking suddenly and focused on the Prince. A hopeful smile widened across Geldion's face, and he unconsciously leaned nearer to the cage.

The haggis's right arm tore through the mesh and clawed out at Geldion's face, coming up just a few inches short.

"No, I am Geldion!" the Prince protested. "Your son!"

The haggis retracted its arm and a curious expression crossed its face.

"It's trickin' ye!" Mickey warned, but too late, for Geldion, hoping against all reason, again leaned in and the haggis launched its left, and longer, arm and hooked him around the back of the head.

Geldion felt his cheekbone crack under the pressure as the beast hauled him in tight against the side of the cage, but that was the least of his worries with the monster's snapping maw barely inches from his face!

"Stop!" Gary commanded, and he accentuated his point with the point of a spear, sticking the creature in the forearm.

The haggis let go of Geldion and went berserk again, slamming the cage all about.

"I said stop!" Gary roared, prodding at the beast.

"Don't kill it!" Diane yelled, at the same moment that a pained Geldion called for Gary to stick the spear right through the thing's heart.

Gary could hardly aim at any particular point on the spinning ball of hair. Suddenly the creature twisted about, its hands locked around the spear's shaft.

Be strong, young sprout! the spear cried in Gary's mind, and it seemed to the man as though the weapon was terrified.

Gary tried to hold on, but his shoulder ached as though it would pop out of the socket once more, and he got hit more than once in the face from the spear's whipping butt end.

A blast of magical energy exploded from the speartip and the haggis fell away, dazed, all its hairs dancing up on end.

Gary prodded the spear in tight against the thing's chest. "I said stop!" he growled, poking hard. The haggis sat perfectly still, and slowly, Gary retracted the spear.

"*Ee ya . . . Ee ya,*" the haggis began chanting quietly (quietly for a wild hairy haggis). The creature's wild eyes closed tight, and it swayed back and forth.

"What's it doing?" Gary asked, freeing the spear from the last of the cage's entanglements and withdrawing it altogether.

"Might be that it's . . ." Mickey began, his explanation interrupted by the sudden renewal of howls.

"Callin' the wolves!" Mickey finished. The leprechaun nodded to Tommy, and the giant hoisted the heavy trap. The haggis immediately went into its frenzy again, but Gary poked the spear through the side of the cage and the enchanted weapon issued another stunning blast.

Atop the hill, they found the others, even Geno, to their profound relief, the dwarf standing dazed, his left arm reaching across his chest to hold his other, injured limb tight to his side. Gary had never seen the sturdy dwarf so shaken, a point heightened considerably as the dwarf rocked back and forth unsteadily on his large bare feet.

Geno growled repeatedly upon seeing the haggis, but he made no move towards the beast.

"*Ee ya,*" the haggis crooned softly. "*Ee ya.*"

"We're off and running fast," the leprechaun said to Kelsey, and a few moments later, they were indeed, with Geno and Gerbil setting the pace, and Kelsey and Geldion taking up the sides and rear, weapons drawn in preparation for any pursuit. Gary and Diane rode on either side of Tommy, Diane talking to the giant, offering him whatever comfort she might, and Gary ready with the spear, prodding the haggis whenever it got too excited.

The wolves did come to the creature's call, dozens of them running in packs to the sides of the speeding group. But crahg wolves were not fast runners (unless they were coming down a hill), certainly not as fast as ponies and horses, and one very frightened giant!

One time a group did get in front of the troupe, but Geno blasted through, and Kelsey and Geldion were up in an instant, the Prince hacking away and the elf setting his deadly bow to action.

The end of the Crahgs was soon in sight, with no resistance between the friends and the open plains beyond, and their escape seemed inevitable.

Apparently it seemed that way to the haggis as well, for the beast went into such a frenzy as they had never seen before, so wild that Tommy tipped over sideways in trying to hold the pitching cage. Gary prodded the creature several times; the spear let off blast after blast of energy. But the haggis would not relent in its insane thrashing.

"Do something!" Geldion pleaded.

"I designed the cage to hold!" Gerbil insisted.

"I built the cage to hold!" Geno added, but neither of the two seemed overly confident in the face of the haggis's incredibly fierce display.

Diane came to understand. "It doesn't want to leave the Crahgs," she reasoned, slipping down from her horse and going as close to the cage as she dared.

"It has no choice in the matter," Kelsey said coldly, and Diane jumped as a rope fell over her shoulder. She looked back to see the other end fastened to Kelsey's steed.

"Tie the cage off," the elf instructed.

Geldion tossed a second rope over and motioned for Diane to tie it to the other side. They were off again soon after, the cage bouncing behind the pulling horses, with Tommy behind the cage, trying to keep it as steady as possible.

It seemed fitting that the dawn broke just as they crossed between the last two Crahgs, and the companions' fleeting moment of hope was torn away by the most agonized and horrifying cry any of them had ever imagined, the scream of a thousand cats dropped into boiling water, of a thousand souls banished to eternal Hell.

"*Eeeyaaaaaa!*"

NINETEEN

A Ray of Light among the Clouds

FROM a high ridge a few miles to the west of Braemar, Lord Badenoch watched the dawn spread its fingers of light beyond him and across the rolling fields, the sun reaching out to the west. Scores of crows and larger vultures hopped and flitted about, from one corpse to the next.

So many bodies.

Battle had been joined the day before, with Badenoch's forces out on those same fields, hidden behind stone walls or within the many dotting corpses of trees, waiting for the Connacht army's approach. There was no doubt of King Kinnemore's intent; many people, including Kelsey's band, had ridden into Braemar with news that Kinnemore marched east for conquest.

And so Badenoch and the militia of Braemar, along with a small contingent of dwarfs and gnomes, had gone west to meet the invaders. Kervin's dwarfish folk and the gnome designers had worked through two days and nights preparing the battlefield, concealing deadly pitfalls, and laying lines of pickets that could be raised quickly by a single crank.

They had met the enemy head on, with the element of surprise on their side, for Kinnemore hadn't expected the men of Braemar to come out so far from their sheltered mountain dells and meet them in the open fields, where the larger Connacht form held so obvious an advantage. Kinnemore's first ranks hadn't even sorted out the curious sound, the hum of so many bowstrings, before the rain of arrows decimated them. Panic hit hard in the ranks, surprised soldiers at first scattering every which way. When one group had sought shelter behind a stone wall, they had found many more soldiers waiting for them there, poised on the other side of the stones.

The Connacht soldiers were not inexperienced, though, and after the initial shock, they had regrouped into their battle formations and roared across the battlefield, as Badenoch had expected all along.

But something was missing in the Connacht force, Badenoch realized—that element of discipline that had earned them their reputation as the finest army in all the land. They charged as a horde of animals, a bull stampede, straightforward and wild.

In reflecting on it now, in looking down at the corpses strewn across the fields, the Lord of Braemar understood what had been missing. The Connacht army was without the binding presence of Prince Geldion, their undisputed field commander for the last several years. King Kinnemore was likely struggling with too many duties (not the least of which was answering to Ceridwen!), and his field generals, each trying to fill the void left by Geldion's absence, each trying to win the utmost favor of the King, were reportedly fighting among themselves. Badenoch had even been given information indicating that some generals were being executed in the Connacht camp.

At least there was one good point in Prince Geldion's apparent change of heart, Badenoch thought. The Lord of Braemar still did not trust Geldion, and certainly he had no love for the man. All of his encounters with Geldion before the Prince had so unexpectedly shown up in Braemar with Kelsey had been unpleasant and, lately, openly confrontational.

Badenoch looked to his left, to the sparkling snake of a small stream winding through the thick grass. Many soldiers had died there in a group, their right flank terribly exposed when the dwarfs had come out from behind a ridge. Had that flank been left exposed on purpose? the Lord of Braemar wondered. Had one of Kinnemore's generals allowed the slaughter merely for the sake of making a rival commander seem a fool?

The thought sent a shudder along Badenoch's spine; the whole scene sent a shudder along Badenoch's spine. Living in the shadows of wild Dvergamal, the middle-aged man had fought many battles, but he had no taste for war. His heart ached and more than a few tears washed from his experienced eyes, tears for his men who had died the previous day, for the handful of dwarfs and gnomes who would not return to their distant homes. And tears for the Connacht soldiers, helpless misinformed pawns of a ruthless King. Badenoch hated battle even when it was a fight of self-defense against evil goblins or mountain trolls, even when it was necessary.

And the Lord of Braemar never considered battle, man against man, to be necessary.

He had to suffer his emotions alone, though, for his force could not afford to perceive any weakness within him. Despite the slaughter of the previous day, with well over a hundred Connacht soldiers cut down as compared to only two score of Braemar's soldiers, Badenoch could hardly claim victory. The traps were all gone now, along with the all-important element of surprise. The pickets were blunted by bodies, and in the end it had been Badenoch, and not Kinnemore, who had been forced to withdraw. The Braemar force had given several miles in exchange for a new battlefield, one that Kinnemore and his soldiers were not now familiar with, one that would put the defenders on the higher ground in the foothills of Dvergamal.

Their next retreat—and Badenoch fully expected that there would indeed be another retreat—would put them all the way back into the village of Braemar, with their backs to Dvergamal's towering mountain walls.

And where from there? the beleaguered Lord wondered. Kervin of the Buldrefolk had offered refuge in the mountains, an invitation Badenoch believed he would ultimately be forced to accept. But that refuge would cost his people their homes and their way of life, would separate them from kinfolk across the land, in County Dilnamarra and even in Connacht, and would turn farmers into hunters. And what peace might Dvergamal offer to the weary folk of Braemar? Kinnemore would send scouting forces into the mountains after them and Ceridwen, when she was free of her isle, would surely give them no rest.

Badenoch looked far to the south, to the distant end of the rugged Dvergamal line. Around that bend, farther to the east, lay the mysterious Crahgs. Somewhere around that bend, Kelsey and Geldion and Gary Leger and their companions hunted for an answer to this unwanted and evil conflict.

Badenoch shook his head and straightened in his saddle, firming his jaw. No more tears washed from his eyes. The Lord of Braemar could not hope for any easy resolution. He had to act based on what he saw before him; had to prepare for this day's battle, and the next.

They would hit at Kinnemore again, and then fall back to Braemar, and from there, Badenoch had to admit, to himself at least, they would accept Kervin's invitation and slip into the mountains, would realign their lives to fit in with the new and harsh realities of Ceridwen's impending reign.

Better that than the price of all their lives should they stay in Braemar. Better that than swearing fealty to Ceridwen's murderous puppet.

THE wild hairy haggis wailed and wailed, kicked and bit at the wire netting until its limbs and mouth bled in a dozen places. Gary's prodding with the spear did nothing to calm it; Geldion's words to soothe his transformed father only sent the beast into greater tirades.

Gerbil and Geno hopped about the cage, inspecting the joints, and both of them shook their heads more than once and wore worried expressions upon their faces.

"It's in pain," Diane observed. She looked back to the row of Crahgs, realizing that the creature's agony had started the moment they had left the hilly domain. Diane remembered what Gary had told her about his imprisonment on Ceridwen's isle, how the witch had cast a spell to keep them in place, to make the surrounding lake as acid to them should they try to leave. Was a similar spell the cause of the haggis's torment? she wondered, and Mickey seconded her guess a moment later.

"More evidence of Ceridwen's spellcasting," the leprechaun said, looking to Kelsey. "If the witch put Kinnemore in the place o' the haggis, then she'd be wanting him to stay in the Crahgs."

Kelsey, too, looked back to the rolling hillocks, his expression grave. He also remembered the imprisonment on Ceridwen's isle, and the spell the witch had used to bind them. The named price of breaking that spell was his very life. What good would King Kinnemore be to him and to the goodly folk of Faerie dead? he wondered and looked back to the cage, where the haggis continued its wild frenzy.

The sun was up in full by this point and the haggis seemed to like that fact as little as it liked being out of the Crahgs.

"Kill it," Geno said to Gary, motioning to the spear. "Just kill it and be done with it!"

Yes, do, young sprout, agreed the sentient spear.

Gary took a deep breath. He feared that he would have to do just that. If the haggis broke free of the cage (and that was beginning to look more and more likely with each passing second), it would probably kill half of them before running back to its hilly home. The thought of stabbing the caged and helpless creature repulsed the young man, though. By all the evidence, this was Faerie's rightful king and no monster. Even worse, this was Faerie's greatest hope for peace, and killing Kinnemore now would do little good for the land.

Gary growled and pushed the spear into the cage.

"No!" Diane cried, but when she moved near him, Geno caught her around the waist and easily held her back. Geldion rushed for Gary as well, but the powerful dwarf's free arm hooked him and stopped him in his tracks.

The haggis twisted and kicked to keep the spear at bay, but finally Gary had the thing pinned, the spear's powerful tip pressed against its belly.

Zap it, like you did to the men in the barn, Gary's thoughts said to the spear.

Plunge me home, the spear replied. *Vanquish the beast!*

"Zap it!" Gary growled and gave the handle a shake.

The ensuing jolt pushed the haggis halfway into the mesh. Gary prodded the spear ahead, keeping pace, keeping the tip pressing on the beast. It looked at Gary curiously now, its hair standing on end, its fingers and toes twitching from the electrical blast.

"*Ee ya yip yip . . .*" the creature started to wail, and the spear promptly zapped it again.

Then the haggis was calm, suddenly, whimpering and trembling but no longer in its frenzy.

"You're not going back to the Crahgs," Gary said to it calmly. "You're going home, back to Connacht."

The haggis snarled, but the snarl turned into a whimper quickly, the battered creature granting the speartip a great deal of respect.

Geno let go of both Diane and the Prince, and Geldion moved to the side of the cage nearest the trapped haggis and began talking to the creature once more. Gradually, with the haggis seeming under control, Gary eased the speartip away from it.

He looked around to his friends, to Geno, and the dwarf was shaking his head doubtfully.

"That thing starts jumping about again and you kill it," the dwarf ordered. "The cage will not take much more of the beating and I'm not fond of the idea of a haggis running free among the group!"

Gary looked to Kelsey and to Mickey, both of whom seemed in complete agreement.

Geldion's cry startled them all, made Gary clutch tightly to the shaft of the spear. The Prince was not calling out in distress, they soon realized, but in surprise, and when he fell back from the side of the cage, the others began to understand the source.

The face of the haggis seemed less hairy, with clumps of hair falling out before their hopeful eyes. Also, the creature's eyes seemed not so wild, not so animalistic.

"Kinnemore," Diane and Mickey whispered together.

Suddenly, the creature went into its frenzy once again, kicking at the cage near Geldion's face and sending the Prince sprawling backwards. Gary was on it in an instant, his spear prodding through the mesh. The spear loosed a jolt of its stunning energy, then a second, but the haggis ignored them, too consumed by its pain. It thrashed and threw itself against one side of the cage repeatedly, weakening the integrity of the supporting beams.

Tommy grabbed at the iron box, trying to lend it some support, but a haggis arm tore through the mesh and clawed at him.

"It will not hold!" Geno and Kelsey cried. The elf drew out his sword, Geno took out a hammer, and Gary shifted the angle, lining the speartip up for a killing strike.

As the tip neared the beast, though, it suddenly calmed, looking more confused and scared than angry.

"Easy, lad," Mickey implored.

Then the haggis began to jerk violently, and Gary retracted the spear, lest the creature impale itself. It let out a bloodcurdling shriek, a cry of sheer agony, and the companions looked on in disbelief as the haggis went through a series of convulsions and contortions. Bones crackled and popped as the creature's arms shifted, one shortening, the other lengthening until they had become the same length. Then its legs went through a similar realignment. The edges of its wide lips retracted and its face reformed, soon appearing more human than beast. Hair continued to fall from its face and body.

Then it was done, and in the cage, in the place of the wild hairy haggis, sat a naked man of about fifty years, a haggard look on his face and his gray hair standing about in a wild tangle. Deep scratches covered his body, especially on his arms and legs, and his fingers and fingernails were caked with dirt and dried blood from his frantic burrowing.

Prince Geldion fell to his knees and could hardly talk; Gerbil fell all over himself fumbling with his keys to unlock the cage, and Kelsey rushed to get a blanket from his saddlebags.

The cage was too battered for the door to be simply unlocked and pulled open, and Geno had to hammer at the thing for several minutes before freeing the confused and haggard King.

Kinnemore came out and stood straight for the first time in many years, his eyes wide with confusion, his limbs trembling. He wrapped himself in the offered blanket, seeming a dirty hobo awaiting the next train. Gary and Diane looked at each other, neither of them prepared for this pitiful sight. So stood Faerie's King, but could the man even talk?

"We'll stop at the nearest farmhouse," Mickey reasoned hopefully. "And find some clothing more fitting the man. And then we'll get him straight away to Braemar, for a meeting that's long overdue."

Kinnemore looked at the leprechaun and blinked, but said nothing.

TWENTY

When the King Comes Calling

FLAMES licked the side of the Snoozing Sprite tavern from a dozen different fires. Men and women, even children, scrambled about Braemar, buckets in hand, battling valiantly against the continuing hail of flaming arrows. The grating scraping of steel against steel cut the air as battle joined in a pass west of the town, and the watchman on a ledge along the mountain wall east of Braemar cried out that Kinnemore's army was in sight, to the west, to the south, and to the north.

Lord Badenoch looked forlornly at the one apparently opened trail, a narrow pass running east out of Braemar, deep into the towering peaks of the mighty Dvergamal range. His army had been backed into the town, chased across the foothills by Kinnemore's superior forces. Even dug into the high ground, the militia of Braemar and the handful of dwarfs and gnomes that fought beside them could not resist the overwhelming flood of Connacht's army.

They had been forced to break ranks barely minutes after battle had been joined, and Badenoch had declared the fight a rout and had told his men to run with all speed back to Braemar, and to gather together their families and their goods.

Badenoch knew that they could not hold the town from Kinnemore. He and his people would have to take up the offer of Kervin the dwarf and go into Dvergamal. At least, that is what the Lord of Braemar expected that most of his people would do. He would not force their loyalties in this matter. Those who wished to go into Dvergamal would be welcome; those who preferred surrender to Kinnemore would not be judged, at least not by Badenoch.

It all seemed a moot point now, though. Unexpectedly, King Kinnemore had chased Badenoch's retreating force right through the night, and the break of dawn had brought the assault in full on Braemar. Now the Lord knew that he would need to leave a strong contingent of warriors behind, to block the eastern pass and keep Kinnemore at bay. Braemar would lose many men this day, and Badenoch fully expected that he would be among the fallen. And he would lose his village, precious Braemar, to Kinnemore's fires. Tears welled in his wise eyes as he looked upon the scrambling throng of the bucket brigade, people fighting to save their homes.

Fighting an impossible war.

"Tell them to stop," the Lord said to one of his nearby commanders. "Go among the people and tell them to waste no more energy battling the fires. We must be away, on the trail before it is too late."

"It is already too late," came a gruff, but not unsympathetic, voice from the side. Badenoch turned to see Kervin and three other dwarfs rounding the corner of the building behind him, their faces more grim than usual.

"Kinnemore has men on the trail," Kervin explained. "He knew that you would try to run and so he sent riders along the passes north and south of the town."

"How many?" Badenoch asked.

"Enough to hold us at bay until the main force closes on us from the other side," Kervin assured him.

"How do you know this?" the Lord of Braemar demanded accusingly, his voice full of anger. "My watchmen have said nothing . . ."

"The stones told him," answered one of the other dwarfs, and Badenoch quieted, knowing then that Kervin's information was indisputable.

There would be no retreat into the mountains; Kinnemore had them surrounded. Badenoch looked all about helplessly, to the people still battling the flames despite the protest of his commander, to the soldiers running in from the western pass, many of them wounded and all of them carrying the unmistakable look of defeat. How far behind was Kinnemore's army? the Lord wondered.

"Dear Kervin," Badenoch said, his voice barely louder than a whisper. "Then what am I to do?"

"Stonebubbles," Kervin replied under his breath. He sent a stream of spittle to the ground. "Surrender," he said firmly.

Badenoch widened his eyes in surprise, never expecting to hear that word from one of the sturdy Buldrefolk.

"I see few options," Kervin went on determinedly. "They will soon close over us and that monster King will slaughter every person in the town. For the sake of your children, and the helpless wounded and aged, offer your surrender to King Kinnemore."

Badenoch paused for a long moment, contemplating the advice, knowing in his heart that Kervin was right. "What of the Buldrefolk?" he asked. "I doubt that Kinnemore would even accept your surrender, and even if he did, you would be speaking for only a handful."

Kervin snorted, as though the entire line of thought was absurd. "My kin and I will stand beside you—for the time. But we'll offer no surrender to King Kinnemore, not a one of us. He will allow us to go back to our mountain homes—and the gnomes to go to theirs—or we will fight him, every step." Kervin chuckled and spat again. "It will take more than a king's army to keep a dwarf out of Dvergamal!" he insisted, and his wide smile brought a small measure of comfort to the beleaguered Lord of Braemar.

Badenoch nodded appreciatively at his bearded friend, but his answering smile lasted only the second it took the Lord to remember the grim task ahead of him. Kervin's judgment was right, Badenoch knew, though the admission surely pained him. If the stones told the dwarf that soldiers were blocking the eastern pass, then the war had come to an abrupt end. The folk of Braemar could not afford a prolonged battle, could not afford any battle at all.

Badenoch motioned to his commanders, all of whom were listening intently to the conversation with the dwarfish leader. "Coordinate the firefighting," Badenoch explained. "Perhaps the King will accept our surrender and allow us to keep our homes."

In truth, Badenoch had given the commands only to keep his people busy, only to keep them from dwelling on the impending defeat. He doubted that Kinnemore would show much mercy, and knew that he, long a thorn in Connacht's side, would surely be replaced—as Baron Pwyll of Dilnamarra had been replaced.

Badenoch hoped that he would face his death bravely.

THE real King Kinnemore was not as tall as the imposter haggis, but still he towered over Gary, and with the exception of Tommy (of course), Gary was the tallest of the group. He was twice Gary's age, but held himself straight and tall, his expression firm yet inquisitive. He used Kelsey's fine-edged sword to shave, leaving that telltale goatee, and though his clothing remained ultimately simple, it seemed to Gary that this man was indeed a King.

The troupe made fine progress away from the Crahgs, with Kinnemore taking Diane's horse and Diane accepting Tommy's invitation to ride on the giant's shoulder. Gerbil was a bit upset that his cage had to be left behind, but Kinnemore promised the gnome that he would be given all the credit he deserved, by his gnomish kinfolk in Goodabuggan, and by Connacht.

Truly King Kinnemore was in good spirits, ultimately relieved to be finished with his years of torment. His body was sore in a hundred different places, from the transformation and the years of living as a wild beast, but his mind was as sharp as ever, and his determination was plainly splayed across his handsome and strong features.

"I never forgot my true place," he explained to them all. "Even at those times when the savage instincts of my trappings overwhelmed my conscious decisions, I never forgot who I was."

"Even when you split Kelsey's horse in half?" Geno had to ask, just to put a typically negative dwarfish spin on all that had occurred.

Kinnemore took the remark lightly, with a resigned smile, then put a plaintive look upon his son, a look that tried pitifully to apologize for all the lost years. "And I never forgot my son," he said, nearly choking on every word.

Geno, still no fan of Prince Geldion's, wanted to interject another sarcastic remark. He looked at Kelsey before he spoke, though, and the elf, somewhat sharing the dwarf's feelings, recognized the look and gave a quick shake of his head. And so Geno let it go, figuring that both Kinnemore and Geldion had been through living Hell.

Kinnemore rode beside Geldion, talking, always talking. When they made camp, the King listened to Kelsey and to Mickey, both complaining about the reign of the imposter king, a reign of terror during which every village of Faerie, every hamlet and every secluded farmhouse came to despise the name of Kinnemore. Mickey talked of impossible tithes demanded by Connacht, and of the edicts that declared magic, all magic, the work of evil demons; Kelsey talked of the seclusion of the Tylwyth Teg, of how in recent years, the elfs had come to remain mostly within their borders and had worked hard to keep any who was not Tylwyth Teg out of Tir na n'Og. Geno spoke similarly of the situation concerning the Buldrefolk, though the taciturn dwarf wasn't saying that the new developments, the heightened seclusion from the humans, were a bad thing, and Gerbil explained that the gnomes of Gondabuggan had long ago forsaken the kingdom altogether.

King Kinnemore sat quietly and listened through it all, obviously pained, then turned to Gary and Diane.

"And what of you two?" he asked. "What of the spearwielder and the woman who figured out Ceridwen's most devious riddle?

Gary and Diane looked to each other and shrugged, not knowing what they might add to the conversation.

"There's not much from Bretaigne," Mickey explained. "The lad and lass're a long way from home."

Kinnemore accepted that readily enough. "And glad I am that you are a long way from home," the King said. "All of Faerie's peoples owe you their gratitude."

"All but Ceridwen," Gary remarked.

"Indeed," agreed the King. "And when this is done, you shall be properly rewarded, and Ceridwen properly punished."

"Just put things back together the way they belong," Diane was quick to respond, echoing Gary's sentiments exactly.

"Indeed," the King said again, and he was pleased.

Gary snapped his fingers suddenly, drawing everyone's attention. "Give him the armor and spear!" he said excitedly, pointing to the King.

Young sprout! the sentient weapon protested.

"Geno can fit it to him," Gary went on, ignoring the whining weapon. "Let Kinnemore look the part of King—that will put the Connacht troops behind him."

None of the others seemed overly exuberant at the suggestion—especially Geno, who wasn't thrilled at the prospect of trying to realign the tough metal. The dwarf had needed the flames of a dragon's breath, after all, to forge the metal of the spear. Kinnemore shook his head doubtfully through it all, and held his hand up repeatedly to stop Gary from going further with the reasoning.

"You are the spearwielder," Kinnemore declared. "And the wearer of Donigarten's armor. And from what my son tells me, you have earned the right many times over."

Gary glanced sidelong at Geldion, surprised that the man would show him any respect at all.

"You are the spearwielder," the King said again, determinedly, "and though you owe your allegiance to a far-off kingdom in the land beyond the Cancarron Mountains, I ask of you now that you remain for the time in Faerie, at my side."

Gary found that his hands were trembling.

"As my champion," Kinnemore finished.

Gary nearly swooned. Once again, he felt as though he was part of something much larger than himself, something eternal and important. He looked around to see Kelsey, Geno, and Gerbil all nodding solemnly, and understood then that he could do much to help the causes of their respective people. Prince Geldion, too, was nodding his head, putting aside his own ego for the sake of a battered kingdom. Whether or not he could defeat Gary in single combat was unimportant at that time; Geldion had witnessed his own normally loyal soldiers converting to their enemy's cause in the name of Sir Cedric, and he had personally counseled his father to name Gary as champion of the throne.

And then Gary looked to Tommy and Mickey, and to Diane, all beaming—especially Diane—understanding the honor that had just been given to him, sharing his moment of glory.

"I'll do my best" was all that Gary could think of in reply.

Kinnemore nodded and seemed satisfied with that; then he rose and walked away from the firelight, motioning for his son to follow so that they could continue their private conversation.

Gary feared that he would be too excited to sleep, but he did drift off, and slept more soundly than he had in many nights.

TRUMPETS heralded the approach of the giant King as he rode triumphantly into Braemar, flanked by a score of armored knights. The pennants of Connacht and Dilnamarra waved in the morning breeze, one on either side of the King, and Lord Badenoch shuddered to think that the flag of Braemar would join that procession when Kinnemore turned north, towards the smaller village of Drochit.

The people of Braemar lined the wide street, cheering as they had been instructed, though halfheartedly, to be sure. Connacht soldiers filtered through the throng, prodding any who did not seem excited enough.

Both Badenoch and Kervin were waiting for Kinnemore in the center of the town, on the wide way between the central building, called the Spoke-lock, and the Snoozing Sprite. They said nothing, silently watched as Kinnemore rode a complete circuit of the town, smiling smugly and turning his head slowly from side to side to survey his newest "loyal" subjects

Then Kinnemore was before the Lord of Braemar and the leader of the dwarfish contingent.

"I am not pleased," he said from high on his horse.

Badenoch did not reply.

"Your mere presence here wounds me, good dwarf," Kinnemore went on, revealing that his displeasure was not with the Lord of Braemar—at least, not entirely. "I should have thought that you and your kin would have come into the town at the side of the rightful King of Faerie."

"We were already here," Kervin replied sarcastically, "and saw no point in going out just to turn around and come back in."

Kinnemore's features; crinkled into a scowl, and a low, feral snarl escaped his tight lips.

"We figured that you would be coming in soon anyway," Kervin went on easily, ignoring the glares of the armored knights, almost wishing that one of those smug humans would make a move against him.

"So be it," Kinnemore remarked, his grim tone hinting that there would be consequences for the actions of Kervin's dwarfs, and for Kervin's treasonous words.

"And what have you to say?" Kinnemore asked Badenoch. "To attack your King out on the field."

"To defend against an invading army," Badenoch corrected.

"Invading?" Kinnemore echoed, seemingly deeply hurt. "We marched to celebrate the dragonslaying, an event worthy of . . ."

"Then why is Baron Pwyll of Dilnamarra not among your ranks?" Badenoch dared to interrupt.

Kinnemore grinned evilly. "The Baron was delayed in Dilnamarra," he replied.

Badenoch slowly and deliberately shook his head, knowing full well that what he was about to say would ensure a noose about his neck. "Baron Pwyll was murdered in Dilnamarra."

"How dare you make such a preposterous claim?" Kinnemore balked.

"Your own son made such a claim!" the flustered Lord of Braemar retorted.

Kervin sucked in his breath; he did not think that so wise a thing to say, and even Badenoch, as soon as he had finished, realized how foolish he had been to reveal that Geldion had been about.

Kinnemore trembled; again came that animallike snarl. He calmed quickly, however, and painted his disarming smile back on his face. "You have spoken with Prince Geldion?" he asked.

"We have heard about the events in the west," Badenoch replied cryptically. "We know that Dilnamarra was overrun, that Tir na n'Og was besieged, though the army of Connacht was handed a stinging defeat at the hands of the proud Tylwyth Teg."

"That is not true!" Kinnemore roared, and he seemed to Badenoch as a spoiled child at that moment, a brat who had not gotten his way. Again he composed himself quickly.

"You should be more careful of your sources of information, Lord of Braemar," the King said. "False information can lead to rash, even fatal, decisions."

Badenoch squared his shoulders and did not justify the remark with a reply.

"So be it," Kinnemore said at length. He nodded to his left, and ten knights obediently dismounted, their armor scraping and clanking noisily. Kervin tightly clutched the axe hanging on his belt.

"Good dwarf," Kinnemore said, noticing the move, "you and your people are without guilt."

"We were on that field," Kervin boldly pointed out.

"You were misinformed," the King reasoned. "By a treasonous lord."

There, he had said it, plainly, and though the proclamation surely stung Badenoch (and condemned him), he was glad that it was finished, glad that the gloating King had put things out clearly on the table.

Badenoch relaxed, even turned to smile at Kervin and to put a calming hand atop the volatile dwarf's shoulder as Kinnemore's soldiers surrounded him.

Kervin returned the look, but the dwarf was not smiling. The only thing stopping him from cutting down the nearest guard was the knowledge that Badenoch had tried to calm him for more than his own sake. If Kervin started something now, then surely his rugged dwarfish kin would join in, and probably half of those men loyal to Badenoch as well. When it was over, Kervin realized, and Badenoch obviously realized, most of Braemar's men, and a good number of the town's women and children as well, would be dead.

So Kervin held his place and his temper. Badenoch was taken away in chains and King Kinnemore addressed the crowd, telling them that they had been deceived, but that he was here now, and peace would prevail and all would be put aright.

As much as the weary folk of Braemar wanted to believe those words (at least the part about things being put aright), not a face in town brightened with false hope.

"THEY are in Braemar," Gerbil reported to the group, except for Prince Geldion, later that morning. The gnome, an expected and not out-of-place visitor to these eastern parts, had been riding alone, up ahead, visiting the area farmhouses (though most were now empty). "Word spreads that Badenoch has surrendered."

"Stonebubbles," Geno grumbled.

"A wise move," Mickey remarked. "Be sure that all the town would've been laid to waste if he did not."

"Stonebubbles!" Geno growled again.

"That could make our course easier," Kelsey reasoned, and Kinnemore was nodding his agreement.

"We know now where to find the imposter," said the King.

"But how to get in to him?" asked Diane. "If Kinne . . . if the haggis is in Braemar, then all the town will be surrounded by his army. I'm not so sure that they'll be willing to believe that you're really the King."

Kinnemore nodded to the east, where a lone rider could then be seen, fast flying for the group. "That will be the job for my son," he reasoned. "By all accounts, he is still the commander of the Connacht army, second only to the imposter. Let us see if Prince Geldion is worthy of his heritage."

Diane studied the King hard at that moment, soon coming to realize that Kinnemore did not, for the moment, doubt his son. She was glad for that, for Geldion's sake and not for her own.

"The haggis is in Braemar," Geldion said, bringing his mount to a fast stop before the others. "And Badenoch has surrendered."

"So we have heard," Kinnemore replied.

"Badenoch is in chains," Geldion went on. "And word has it that he will be executed at sunset."

"Big surprise," Mickey remarked.

"What about Kervin?" Geno asked.

Geldion shrugged. I heard nothing," he honestly answered. "But if the dwarf is still in Braemar, then know that he is not in good spirits!"

"How shall we get in?" Kinnemore asked abruptly, directing the question to his son and reminding them all that they hadn't the time to sit and talk. Even at a swift pace, they would not make the village proper before midafternoon, and if they encountered any delays, then Badenoch would be hanging by his neck.

"I doubt that I will be able to talk us all into Braemar," Geldion, who had obviously been planning that very job, answered. "Not the giant, certainly, and the dwarf and elf . . ."

"All of us," Gary interrupted grimly.

Questioning looks came at him from every side, even from Diane.

"All of us," he said again, not backing down an inch. "We have been through this together, and so together we'll see it through, to the end."

"But lad," Mickey quietly protested.

"Use your tricks," Gary demanded of Mickey. "And you," he added to Geldion, "use your mouth. Tommy's been a horse before, and so he'll be a horse again," he said, referring to the time when Mickey had made Tommy look like a mule so that he and Geno could deliver the reforged spear and armor to Dilnamarra inconspicuously.

"And you'll be more believable," Gary added to Geldion, "if you're surrounded by soldiers when you escort the spearwielder into Braemar."

"Human soldiers," Geldion corrected, eyeing Kelsey and Geno doubtfully.

"So they'll appear," Gary replied without missing a beat. "As will your father. The haggis does not know what happened to you."

"So we're hoping," Mickey interjected. Gary turned to the sprite, seeming unsure for the first time since he had begun laying out his plan.

"We're not for knowing what Ceridwen's seen, lad," the leprechaun explained. "And what she's telled to her haggis lackey."

"Then we'll have to take that chance," King Kinnemore unexpectedly answered. "The plan is sound, so I say." He looked around at the troupe, affording them the respect they so obviously deserved. "And what say you?" he asked of them all.

"Lead on, Prince Geldion," said a determined Kelsey. "And quickly. Lord Badenoch is too fine a man to share Baron Pwyll's undeserved fate."

Geno grumbled something (certainly less than complimentary) under his breath, but then nodded his agreement.

They were off in a few moments, after the leprechaun worked a bit of his magic, with Diane riding Tommy, who now appeared as a plow horse.

They encountered soldiers an hour later, the back ranks of the Connacht army, settling in for their stay on the fields to the west of Braemar. Whispers went up all about the newcomers, concerns for the appearance of the spearwielder, and more than one soldier eyed the group intently, fearful of a leprechaun's tricks, perhaps. But not a man would openly oppose Geldion, and he and his escorts were allowed passage.

"Do you know the commander of this brigade?" Kinnemore asked his son quietly as they made their way through the large encampment. The wise King was thinking that perhaps the time had come to enlist some allies. Even if they got into Braemar unopposed, convincing the army that he was the real King, and their leader an imposter—and the haggis, no less—might not be an easy feat. The prospect of a battle within the town seemed plausible.

"Roscoe Gilbert," Geldion replied, and he paused and eyed his father, coming to understand and agree with the logic. "I have trained with him on occasion."

Kinnemore nodded and Geldion broke away from the others, trotting to the nearest campfire to enquire of the field commander's whereabouts.

"Thinking to make some friends?" Mickey, sitting invisibly on Gary's mount right beside the King, asked.

Kinnemore, eyes steeled straight ahead, nodded slightly.

The group did not pass all the way through the encampment unopposed. A line of cavalry galloped around them and stood to block them with Prince Geldion and an older warrior, Roscoe Gilbert, sitting directly before the riding King.

Kinnemore eyed the man directly and slipped back the hood of his traveling cloak.

Gilbert did not blink.

"An incredible tale," the soldier said a moment later, his tone showing that he was not convinced.

"A true tale," Gary replied boldly.

Gilbert turned a nervous glance up and down his ranks. He knew that many of the Connacht soldiers had deserted back near Tir na n'Og, swearing fealty to Sir Cedric. And now the spearwielder was here, right in his midst, with a tale to turn all the world upside down.

"And you have nothing to lose by escorting us," Gary went on, "and everything to lose by not."

"What say you, Gilbert?" Kinnemore asked bluntly. "Do tales of Ceridwen's troublesome interference so surprise you?"

They were off at a swift pace soon after, Geldion and Gary flanking Kinnemore, Diane at Gary's side, and Roscoe Gilbert at Geldion's side. At Kelsey's insistence, Mickey let the illusion drop then, showing the elf, dwarf, and gnome as they truly appeared (though Mickey kept up Tommy's façade, knowing that the sight of a giant would unnerve the sturdiest of soldiers in the best of conditions).

They swept through the next encampments without incident and without delay, Roscoe Gilbert and Prince Geldion bringing even more soldiers into their wake. By the time they crossed the western pass, moving into Braemar proper, few Connacht soldiers had been left on the field behind them.

Predictably, the entourage attracted quite a bit of attention as they approached, and most of the people were out and about anyway, since sunset drew near. Angry whispers filtered through the crowd; more than one fight broke out, but the Connacht soldiers were too numerous for the poorly armed citizens of Braemar to do anything to prevent the impending hanging.

Those people didn't know what to expect—certainly nothing good—when Prince Geldion and some of Kinnemore's field commanders swept into the town. The presence of Kelsey, Geno, and Gerbil, who were all known to them, and of the spearwielder and his wife, whom they considered to be allies, brought mixed reactions, some wondering if the time had come for hope, others thinking that their supposed friends had either been captured or had gone over to the undeniable flow of Kinnemore's tide of conquest.

Kervin, standing by the tree designated as the spot for the hanging, and Badenoch, even then being led out of the Snoozing Sprite's wine cellar, his temporary dungeon, did allow themselves a moment of hope, for they alone among Braemar's populace knew of the mission to the Crahgs.

The imposter King, standing with his knights in a glade beside the Spokelock, to the side of the hanging tree, did not know what to make of the entourage, did not know why Geldion would ride in beside the enemy spearwielder, let alone in the presence of Kelsenellenelvial Gil-Ravadry, that most hated elf-lord.

But Geldion did come in, directly, his newfound friends in his wake and his father, hidden beneath the cowls of a traveling cloak, at his side. Geldion walked his gray right up before the imposter, the Prince's eyes unblinking.

The imposter looked from Geldion to Gary, let his gaze linger long over this man who had become such a thorn in his side, this man who had banished Ceridwen, the imposter's mentor, to her island. Then he looked back to Geldion, trying to find some clue about the unexpected arrival. Why had Gary Leger come openly into Braemar? And why were so many of Kinnemore's own field commanders, and the Prince of Connacht, lined up behind the man?

He waited a long while, but Geldion said nothing, forcing him to make the first move.

"So you have returned," the imposter said at length, indignantly. "I had wondered if you were dead out on the field."

"Not dead" was all that Geldion replied through his clenched teeth.

"Then what is this about?" the imposter demanded. "Have you brought the spearwielder and an elf-lord into my fold?"

"Or have they brought me into theirs?" Geldion said, voicing the imposter's unspoken thought.

"What is this about?" the imposter demanded again, a feral snarl accompanying the question.

"It is about the rightful King of Connacht," said the tall hooded man seated between Geldion and Gary Leger. "And it is about an imposter, a beast tamed by Ceridwen and put in the rightful King's stead." He reached up to clasp the sides of his hood and began slowly drawing it back.

"Kill them!" the haggis roared. Knights bristled; there came the ring of many weapons pulling free of their scabbards.

The friends held calm, kept their composure, and that fact alone bought them the needed seconds.

King Kinnemore pulled the hood from his face. Gasps arose from those close enough to view him, nearly an exact likeness of the man he faced, and whispers rolled out from the glade, down the streets and through every house.

"I am Kinnemore," said the rightful King.

"By whose word?" demanded the imposter. His voice broke as he spoke, guttural grunts coming between each word. Diane and Gary watched him closely, as did Mickey and the others, noticing that his beard seemed suddenly larger and more wild.

"By my word!" King Kinnemore said forcefully, rising tall in his saddle and turning all about so that all near to him could hear clearly the proclamation, and see clearly the man speaking the words. "Trapped by Ceridwen these last years in the body of a beast." The rightful King settled in his saddle and squarely eyed the imposter, who was grunting and wheezing, his mouth widening to the sides.

"While the beast sat on my throne," Kinnemore declared. "While the beast led my kingdom to ruin!"

The knights in the glade escorting Lord Badenoch did not know how to react; none of the soldiers, even those who had come into town in the friends' wake, knew how to react. The battle became, so suddenly, a personal duel between these two men who seemed, physically at least, so much alike.

The hush held for several long seconds, no one knowing where to begin or who should begin.

"Long live the King!" proclaimed Lord Badenoch and he pulled free of the soldiers holding his arms (and they were too overwhelmed to try to stop him) and lifted his chained hands in defiance. "Long live the rightful King of Faerie!"

The imposter tried to say, "Kill him!" but the words came out only as a growl, that same feral, uncontrollable snarl that the true Kinnemore had known all too well in his years romping about the Crahgs. There could be no doubt anymore; the imposter's beard had widened, encompassing all of his face.

He shrieked in rage and pain as his body twisted and cracked, Ceridwen's enchantment stolen by the truth, stolen by the appearance of Faerie's rightful King. The soldier nearest to him made a move, but the haggis slapped the man, launching him a dozen feet across the glade.

Fully revealed, the creature whipped back and forth, eyes wild, maw dripping drool.

Cedric's spear took him cleanly in the breast.

He staggered backwards, clutching at the weapon's shaft, growling and whimpering. Then he fell to the grass and lay still.

No one moved, no soldier put his weapon away, and all eyes turned to Gary Leger, the spearwielder.

The moment was stolen an instant later, when the haggis leaped up and tossed the bloodied spear aside. *"Ee ya yip yip yip!"* it wailed, and all covered their ears—and all in the creature's path fell away in terror as it rushed from the glade, and from the town, down the western pass and farther, running to the southeast, towards its hilly home.

"Tough little bug," Mickey remarked dryly.

"Long live the rightful King of Faerie!" Gary cried, sitting tall atop his stallion. He slid from his mount, recovered the spear, then fell to his knees before the mounted King, bowing his head.

That was all the folk of Braemar, and the weary men of the Connacht army, needed to see. The cry went up, from one end of town to the other, along the mountain passes and through every encampment.

The cry went up for King Kinnemore, for Connacht.

And for peace.

TWENTY-ONE
Head On

GARY walked quietly, inconspicuously, down the western trail leading out of Braemar. He had left his armor back in town, glad for the reprieve, glad to be out of the suit, and back there too, talking and singing in the Snoozing Sprite, were Diane and Kelsey, Geno and Gerbil, and all the others. Even without the remarkable armor, Gary was recognized by every sentry he passed and by everyone else walking along the road, most heading back into Braemar for the celebration. Gary's size alone marked him clearly, for the only man in Braemar as large as he was King Kinnemore himself.

The gentle folk granted Gary his privacy, though, only nodded and offered a quick greeting, and soon he was off the main trail, walking down a narrow and rocky path that seemed no more than a crevice cutting between the foothills.

Around a sharp bend, he came into a sheltered dell, almost a cave beneath a wide overhang, where Mickey was waiting for him.

"You asked me to come here to tell me that you were leaving," Gary remarked, having long ago recognized the sprite's intentions.

Mickey shrugged noncommittally. "Would ye have me stay, then? Be sure that all in the town're dancin' and playin', and wouldn't their party be greater if they catched a leprechaun in the course?"

"Kinnemore and Badenoch will grant you your freedom," Gary reasoned. "They owe you that much at least."

Again the leprechaun shrugged. "I been too long with humans," Mickey muttered. "Too long in tricking them and too long in dancing from their greedy clutches. And too long working to set aright things that aren't truly me own concern. I'm back for Tir na n'Og, lad, back to me home that's no longer pressed by an army.

"And so I've asked ye to come out," Mickey went on. "Ye should be thinking of yer own home now."

Gary looked around, a hint of desperation in his darting eyes. Mickey was right, it seemed, but it had all ended so suddenly with the revelation of the true King, that Gary hadn't emotionally prepared himself for returning to Realearth. Not yet.

"Ye fought the war and now ye're wanting to enjoy the spoils," Mickey reasoned.

Now it was Gary's turn to simply shrug.

"Is it over?" he asked plaintively.

Mickey sighed—it seemed that the leprechaun, too, was somewhat sorry the adventure had apparently come to an abrupt end. "All the folk will rally about the rightful King," Mickey reasoned. "Even Prince Geldion and Badenoch have seen it in their hearts to end their feud."

"I do not believe that it is over," came a commanding voice from behind. The two turned to see King Kinnemore walking around the bend.

"You followed me," Gary remarked.

"I do not think it is over," the King said again, ignoring the accusation. "Not with a witch soon to be coming out of her hole."

"Oh, she's coming out," Mickey agreed. "But not with much behind her. Ceridwin's power's in those she tricks to being allies, and she's to find few in these times. All the humans'll be together with yerself returned to the throne, and even the elfs and dwarfs'll come to yer call if ye're needing them."

Gary was hardly paying attention to any of it, still perplexed by the appearance of the King. "Why did you follow me?" he asked bluntly, as soon as he found a break in the conversation.

Kinnemore turned a disarming smile his way. "Because I knew the sprite would not remain," he answered. "And I know that you need our good Mickey to return to your own home."

Both Gary and Mickey turned up their eyebrows at that proclamation. As far as they knew, only Mickey, the pixies, Kelsey and Geno, and a few other of the Tylwyth Teg knew of Gary's true origins, with everyone else merely thinking that he had come from the far-off land of Bretaigne.

"I guess he's the King for a reason," Mickey said dryly.

Kinnemore chuckled at that. "I had many dealings with Bretaigne in my first years on the throne," he explained. "Before the witch interfered. I know a Bretaigne accent, and know, too," he added, looking straight at Gary, "when I do not hear one."

"Fair enough," Mickey admitted.

"And I have entertained visitors from your world before," Kinnemore went on. "Thus I know that you may soon be returning, and thus have I watched closely your every move, even following you to this place."

"To say goodbye?" Gary asked.

"To ask that you remain," the King replied. "For a time."

"Oh, here we go again," Mickey whispered under his breath as Gary squared his shoulders and assumed a determined expression.

"The witch will soon be free," Kinnemore declared. "And she does indeed have allies," he added, shooting a quick glance at Mickey. "The mountains of Penllyn hold goblin tribes and great clans of mountain trolls."

"She'll not come out with them," Mickey reasoned. "Not in an open fight. Never has that been Ceridwen's way."

"Perhaps not," the King conceded. "But Robert is no more, and the witch will not surrender her designs."

"You want to go after her?" Gary stated as much as asked, his tone skeptical and bordering on incredulous. Gary had been to Ynis Gwydrin before, and the memory was not a pleasant one.

The King didn't flinch a bit as he slowly nodded.

"Oh begorra," Mickey muttered.

"Now would seem the time," Kinnemore said. "Ceridwen and her powers are locked upon an island, and our army is already assembled on the field. We can deal Ceridwen a blow from which she will be years in recovering, cripple her to the point where her mischief will not be so great."

"Why're ye needing Gary Leger?" Mickey wanted to know.

"We are not," Kinnemore replied to the sprite, though he never took his unblinking gaze off Gary. "But would it not add to the legend? And would not the presence of the spearwielder serve well the morale of the soldiers? Do not underestimate the power of emotion, good sprite. Why, after all, did Ceridwen try to prevent the reforging of Donigarten's spear?"

"Now, how're ye knowing all of this?" Mickey asked.

"I guess he's the King for a reason," Gary answered, mimicking Mickey's earlier tones.

"She feared the emotions inspired by the reforged weapon," Kinnemore said, answering his own question. Again he put an admiring look directly at Gary Leger. "And rightly so, so it would seem."

Gary held the King's gaze for a long moment, then turned to regard Mickey, the leprechaun sitting on a stone and shaking his head, and lighting his long-stemmed pipe.

"I want to stay," Gary said.

"I knew ye would," Mickey replied without hesitation.

"And you, too, I ask to come along, good sprite," Kinnemore said. "And by my word and Gary Leger's arm, not a man will bother you."

"It's not the men I'm fearing," Mickey whispered under his breath, thinking of the huge mountain trolls, and worse, of the witch herself, as mighty an enemy as could be found in all of Faerie. Despite all of that, though, Mickey knew that Kinnemore's reasoning was sound. Robert was gone, and without the dragon to balance the power, they had to work hard and fast to keep Ceridwen in check.

Mickey just wanted to know why he, a carefree leprechaun used to romping in the secluded meadows of a sylvan forest, kept getting caught up in the middle of it all!

———

GARY knew that there was something big, probably a mountain troll, crouching around the tumble of boulders. When he paused and concentrated, he could hear the monster's rhythmic breathing, barely perceptible against the steady breeze that blew over Penllyn this day.

The armored man turned back to his companions and nodded; the four of them, Gary, Diane, Tommy, and Mickey, had played out this same routine three times already in the five days of fighting since the Connacht army had entered the mountainous region around the witch's island home.

Diane, more than any of them, held her breath now. She still hadn't quite gotten used to the spectacle of a mountain troll. They weren't nearly as big as Tommy, only twelve feet tall, but they looked like the stuff of the mountains that gave them their name. Their skin was a grayish color, sometimes tending towards brown, and their heads were square, faces flat, like a big slab of stone. They wore little clothing, and needed no armor with their thick skin; and whatever hair they had, on top of their heads, across their massive chests, or anywhere else, typically stuck out in clumps, like small bushes among the rocky sides of a mountain. No, trolls weren't as imposing as Tommy, and certainly the spectacle of the giant had somewhat prepared Diane for the enemies she was facing now, but she doubted that she would ever be comfortable seeing one of the dirty monsters, even a dead one.

Gary rested back against the stones and took a deep, steadying breath. He lifted his mighty spear in both hands, took another breath and adjusted his too-loose helmet, then rushed around the bend, shouting wildly.

The troll leaped out at him, club in hand, but the man, expecting the resistance, had already begun to backpedal.

Around the bend came the pursuing troll, and its square jaw surely drooped open in surprise when it found an eighteen-foot-tall giant waiting for it!

Tommy's uppercutting fist had barely begun its ascent when it connected squarely on that jaw, and by the time the troll broke free of the giant's swinging arm, the dimwitted evil brute was several feet in the air, and rising as rapidly as the fist. The troll slammed down against the rounded top shoulder of the boulder tumble, cracking its thick head, and slid slowly down the side, unconscious at least, and probably dead.

"There's another one, lad!" Mickey squealed from his high perch on a ledge against the mountain wall behind the main group.

"Behind you!" Diane added, rushing to Gary's side.

The young man spun on his heel, thrusting desperately with his spear, scoring a solid hit in the rushing troll's belly. The brute roared in agony, but could not stop its charge, further impaling itself, and running Gary down.

Tommy turned to try to catch his tumbling friend, but Mickey yelled again, and the giant spun back just in time to take a hit from yet another troll's whipping club. Tommy grunted, not really hurt, and responded with a punch that crushed in the troll's face.

But two more trolls stood behind that one, each delivering a solid whack against the giant's thick arm. And another troll came in from the back side of the boulder tumble, bearing down on Diane, whose short sword surely seemed shorter still facing the likes of a twelve-foot-tall, nine-hundred-pound troll!

Diane shrieked and stabbed, scoring a glancing hit. Her heart stopped as the troll's great club swished across, but to her ultimate relief (and amazement) the monster somehow missed her cleanly. Not stopping to consider her fortune, she struck again, and a third time, each stroke of her elfish blade drawing a line of red blood on the massive creature's torso.

The troll responded with its club, and again missed badly. It snorted in disbelief and kicked with its huge boot—and missed again, overbalancing in the process so that when Diane wisely snuck in under the high-waving foot and jabbed at the knee of its lone supporting leg, the monster fell heavily to the stone.

Diane rushed around near the monster's head, slashed at grasping troll fingers—which, for some reason that Diane could not understand, were grasping at the empty air three feet to her left—and dared to dive in close, poking hard at the fallen behemoth's throat.

She scored a single hit, and dove away desperately as the suddenly wheezing monster began to thrash and kick. The troll grasped at its torn throat, bubbles of blood and spittle coming out through its fingers. Its shin slammed against a boulder and sent the stone flying; its foot slammed straight down, cracking the stone beneath it.

"More, lass!" Mickey called above the tumult, and Diane nearly fainted away when she looked back around the boulders to see half a dozen more mountain trolls rushing down the path behind the boulder tumble, bearing down on the group. She called for Gary, and saw that he had slipped out from under the dead troll, but was working hard (and futilely) to free up his impaled spear.

Diane looked to Tommy, just as the giant caught a handful of troll hair in each massive hand and, ignoring the clubs pounding hard against his sides, slammed the brutes' heads together with a resounding *crack!*

Diane winced as Tommy slammed the heads together repeatedly. The clubbing stopped after the third or fourth smack; the heavy clubs fell to the ground.

"Six of them!" Mickey called.

"Run away!" was Gary's sound advice. He finally tore free the spear, but slipped on the wet, gore-covered stone, falling hard to his back.

Diane was beside him, helping him, urging him to his feet.

Trolls swarmed about the boulder tumble, spiked clubs in hand, with only poor Tommy to block their way.

Tommy, and a hail of arrows.

Horns sounded from every trail, and scores of Connacht soldiers, led by Prince Geldion, followed the volley, shouting for Sir Cedric at the top of their lungs.

It was over before Gary had even found the opportunity to strike another blow, all six of the new trolls joining their five comrades in death.

"How did you know?" Gary asked Geldion when all had settled.

"Credit the King," the Prince explained. "He did not approve of your little band running off to fight on its own."

"We've been doing that since the war began," Diane interjected.

"So my father knows," replied the Prince, "and so, he believes, does Ceridwen. The witch understands the implications of the war, and knows that the spearwielder is an important target. He would not let you go out on your own, though you believed that to be your course."

"Thank him for us all," Diane remarked.

"I guess he's the King for a reason," both Mickey and Gary said together, sharing a knowing wink.

Gary looked at the fallen trolls—nearly a dozen more in this encounter alone. And similar battles were being waged all across Penllyn, with Kinnemore's army, bolstered by Lord Badenoch and the forces of Braemar, rousing the trolls and goblins from their filthy mountain holes, scattering them to the wastelands to the east, and killing those that did not flee. By all reports nearly five hundred mountain trolls had been slain, and perhaps ten times that number of goblins, the unorganized and chaotic tribes proving no match for the teamwork of the skilled and trained soldiers.

In five short days, the heart of Ceridwen's ragtag forces had been torn out of her mountain stronghold.

Gary wished that Kelsey might have witnessed this. And Geno! Yes, he decided, the sturdy dwarf would have liked to walk over the bodies of so many dead trolls and goblins. But neither had chosen to make the trek to Penllyn, not now. Kelsey was off to Tir na n'Og to report on the monumental happenings and to advise his elders in their dealings with the rightful King, and Geno had simply decided that he had been too long from his forge and his backlog of work.

They would have enjoyed this rout, Gary knew. They would have applauded every battle, knowing that the land of Faerie would be a better place when Penllyn was purged.

And so, with grim satisfaction, Gary Leger looked over the newest battlefield, and Ceridwen looked over Gary Leger, the frustrated witch fuming, feeling positively impotent. She could not yet go free of her island, could not even send forth her magic to aid the monsters in the mountains. And the one contingent of monkey bats she had sent flying out from Ynis Gwydrin had been met by a seemingly solid sheet of arrows, most of the strange-looking monsters falling dead in Loch Gwydrin before they had even cleared the lake.

She had lost Kinnemore, and had lost her hold on Connacht and the army that came with that hold. And now, before her very eyes, the remnants of her last force, the mountain trolls and goblins that she could always manipulate or force under her control, were being swept away.

Positively impotent.

It was a feeling that the mighty witch did not enjoy.

"Geek!" she screamed, and the spindly-armed goblin, who had been standing only a foot behind the witch, jumped so violently that he left one of his shoddy boots sitting in place on the floor.

"Yesses, my Lady," he grovelled, falling to his knees and slobbering kisses all over Ceridwen's beautiful shoes (and at the same time, trying to quietly manipulate the boot back on his smelly foot). The goblin had been beside "his Lady" for many years and knew that this was no time to give Ceridwen any excuse to vent her rage.

The witch pulled her foot from the goblin's spit-filled grasp, retracted the leg, and kicked Geek hard in the face.

"Thank you, my Lady!" he squealed, and she kicked him again, closing one of his eyes.

"Did you send my messenger?" the witch demanded.

Geek looked at her quizzically—and promptly got kicked in the face a third time. Of course he had sent the monkey bat—Ceridwen knew that he had sent the monkey bat!

A single thought overruled the goblin's confusion: No time to give her an excuse!

"Yesses, of yesses!" the goblin squealed. "It flied off last night, it did! It should be close to Giant's Thumb . . ."

"Oh, shut up," Ceridwen grumbled and kicked the goblin square in his smiling face one more time.

"Yesse . . ." Geek started to reply, but he wisely realized that answering that command was directly contrary to that command. With a whimper, he rolled out of kicking reach and cowered on the floor. After a few minutes he dared to look up again, and saw his Lady standing by the tower's window, staring out to the east, to the mountains and beyond.

Ceridwen was more calm then, finding a measure of composure in the knowledge that she was not sitting idly by, that she was at least taking some action to aid in her cause.

But even then, standing safe in the bastion of her evil power, a castle that she had owned longer than the memory of any living man, the witch realized that she might be playing her final card.

AT the end of that fifth day, bold King Kinnemore set his camp on the very banks of Loch Gwydrin, in plain sight of the witch's crystalline castle. Assured by Mickey that the witch could take no personal actions, magical or otherwise, beyond the boundaries of her place of banishment, the King, still carrying the scars of outrage from his years running wild in the Crahgs, thought it fitting to push the witch to the edge of her sensibilities, to taunt her in every manner that he could find.

To that end, he set his soldiers to singing, loud and clear, the ancient songs of proud Connacht.

Diane was charmed by the magical sight of Ynis Gwydrin—and the witch's castle was truly an enchanting vision—but Gary Leger, who had been to that island and that castle, was not alone in his trepidation of simply being in view of the place.

Even Mickey, who constantly assured Gary that the witch was fully bound to her island, seemed on the edge of his nerves. So great was their fear of the witch that Gary and the other soldiers were honestly relieved each morning when they left the encampment, and the sight of Ynis Gwydrin, and went into the mountains to hunt giant trolls.

Those trolls were getting harder to find, and by the third day of the Loch Gwydrin encampment, the eighth day of the assault on Penllyn, only a single small skirmish occurred, and that with a handful of goblins that surrendered before the Connacht bows thrummed from the release of the first arrows. That same day, when the sun was at its highest point, King Kinnemore declared Penllyn secured.

"And a good thing," Mickey remarked to the King shortly thereafter. "The witch'll be walking free in just two days, by me guess, and we'd be a smarter bunch to be gone from the mountains before she can start her mischief."

"Off and running," Gary agreed.

King Kinnemore said nothing, just turned a longing stare out towards the crystalline castle. In ages past, Ynis Gwydrin had been the seat of goodly power in Faerie; Kinnemore's own ancestors had presided over their kingdom from the place that Ceridwen now called home.

"Don't ye even be thinkin' it!" Mickey spouted, recognizing the gaze, and the wish behind that gaze. The leprechaun's outburst brought a number of looks—Geldion's, Gary's and Diane's included—sharply on him. One simply did not talk to a King that way!

But Kinnemore gave a short laugh and nodded his head in agreement. "We came to Penllyn to cripple the witch," he said. "To steal her means of mischief, or at least, to steal the army she might conjure to deliver that mischief. Penllyn is secure, excepting the island fortress, and Ceridwen will be a long time in recovering from the wounds we have inflicted."

"And from the alliances you have forged," Gary put in.

Again, King Kinnemore nodded his head in agreement, then, to Gary's profound relief (and the leprechaun blew a sigh, as well) the King gave the orders to break down the camp.

The tents were almost down by midafternoon, and the four friends hoped that they would get several hours of marching before setting the next camp (though Tommy, who had spent many fairly good years serving Ceridwen on Ynis Gwydrin, looked to the isle more than once, his expression almost homesick).

Geldion came to the group then, his face grim. "Lord Badenoch rode in," he explained, "just a few minutes ago. He sought a private audience with my father."

"Are ye feeling left out?" Mickey asked, not quite understanding the Prince's sour expression.

"There are rumors that an army approaches from the east," Geldion explained. "A vast host. Robert's old minions, come to the call of Ceridwen."

"Lava newts," Gary whispered.

Diane eyed Gary, and then Geldion, nervously. She remembered Gary's tales of the dragon's mountain castle, of the lizardlike guards that served and protected mighty Robert.

"We will hold the mountains against them," Geldion said determinedly. "Our position is one of strong defense."

"For a day and a half," Gary put in.

"Until the witch flies free," Mickey added grimly.

TWENTY-TWO

Preemptive Strike

GARY, Diane, and Mickey were beside King Kinnemore, Geldion, and Lord Badenoch before dawn the next morning, on a high plateau that peeked through the towering mountains and afforded a view of the eastern plains.

The sun broke the horizon in their eyes, dawn spreading its lighted fingers across those plains, but all the companions saw was a dusty haze, and a darkness so complete beneath it that seemed as if a foul lake or a great, black amorphous blob was rolling out towards them.

"Thousands," King Kinnemore remarked, and for the first time, he seemed to doubt the wisdom of coming to Penllyn.

"Tens of thousands," Badenoch corrected. "Eager to serve a new leader, eager to anoint Ceridwen as their god-figure."

"We could fight a retreating action out of Penllyn," Prince Geldion offered. "Nearly half our force is mounted, and should be able to flank any spurs of lava newts that rush out to challenge our flight."

"And then where?" the King asked. "Back to our homes? Back to Connacht and Braemar? Which town will Ceridwen likely strike against first?"

"Braemar," Badenoch was quick to put in, for his village was the closest to Pennlyn, with the exception of Connacht itself.

"Connacht," Kinnemore corrected. "Ceridwen is outraged. She will come straight for the throne, straight for my heart."

"Connacht's high walls will . . ." Geldion began, a snarl of determination accompanying his words. But Kinnemore cut him short with an upraised hand.

"Connacht's high walls will offer little protection against the witch's magic," the King answered. "Ceridwen will open the holes through which her wretched army might flow."

"We will kill five newts for every man!" Geldion promised.

"And even so, it would seem that we would still need ten times our number of men," the King answered. But Kinnemore, despite the grim words, did not seem despondent, seemed, in his own way, at least as determined as his volatile son.

"What are you thinking?" the perceptive Diane asked him bluntly.

"Ceridwen comes free tomorrow," Kinnemore replied. "Today she remains on her island." He looked directly at the woman, the set of his eyes showing that he spoke in all seriousness and with a clear mind. "Her small island."

"Oh begorra," they heard Mickey grumble.

That clued in Gary to the leprechaun's suspicions, a guess that he shared. "You're going after her," he said to the King, his tone making the statement sound like an accusation.

Kinnemore didn't flinch. "My son will command . . ."

"I'm going with you!" Geldion interrupted.

Kinnemore paused for a long moment and studied the Prince. Geldion had been fiercely loyal all his life, even against his own better judgment, because he had believed that the haggis was truly the King. Kinnemore had heard this above all else when his field commanders and old friends spoke of his son. It wouldn't be fair now, Kinnemore realized, to force Geldion to remain behind, even if he believed that Geldion was the best choice to handle the impending battle with the lava newts.

He bobbed his head, just slightly, and Geldion returned the nod.

"Lord Badenoch," the King said, turning the other way to face the proud man, "it would seem that I am without a commander."

Always conscious of protocol, the man did not verbally respond, just came to a straighter posture.

"And so I give you the command of Connacht's army," Kinnemore went on. "And in the case that we do not return, I give to you the crown of Connacht. Wear it well, good man, for if we do not return, then surely your first days as King will be filled with difficult decisions."

Badenoch unexpectedly shook his head. "In this I must refuse," he answered, and more than King Kinnemore gasped in surprise.

"You have a commander," the Lord of Braemar explained. "And though I applaud Prince Geldion for wanting to accompany you on this most important mission, I fear that his judgment is skewed, and his wisdom is altogether missing."

"You speak words that could be considered treasonous," Kinnemore replied, but there was no threat in his inquisitive tone.

"So they would be, if they were not true," Badenoch said. "The mission to Ynis Gwyndrin is of utmost importance, but so too is the coming battle. Our armies must fight well now or be destroyed, and scattered from the moun-

tains. While flattered by your confidence, I must admit that I am not qualified
for what you have asked. I have never directed a force a quarter as large as the
army of Connacht, nor am I familiar with the training and tactics of your
soldiers."

"Surely there are commanders . . ." Kinnemore began to reason, but Badenoch was adamant.

"I have witnessed your army in action without the leadership of Prince Geldion," he firmly replied. "They were not an impressive force."

"I wish to go to Ynis Gwydrin," Geldion said through gritted teeth, for he
could see that his chance to accompany his father was fast slipping away.

"Yet you are needed here," Badenoch answered. "To direct our combined
forces in a battle that might well determine the future of our land. I understand
your preference, and applaud your loyalty and courage. But you are a Prince of
Faerie, and if you are ever to properly ascend to your father's throne, then you
must learn now that your personal preferences are of little consequence. To be
a leader, Prince Geldion, means to understand the needs of your subjects, and
to put those needs above your personal preferences."

Gary, and everyone else, gawked in disbelief. Lord Badenoch had just put
this tentative and so new alliance to a difficult test by speaking to, scolding,
Prince Geldion publicly. But the Lord of Braemar's words had been honest, and
undeniably wise, and even Geldion, showing no outward signs of any impending explosion, seemed to understand that.

King Kinnemore started to respond, but paused and put a thoughtful look
over his son.

Geldion glanced around to all his companions, his expression revealing
that caged and hungry look that had typified the volatile Prince's behavior for
the last few years. That expression changed to resignation, though, and then to
open acceptance. Gary, and especially Diane, saw that clearly, saw that Prince
Geldion had just passed the first true test of this new kingdom.

It seemed to Diane that at that moment, the boy-Prince had become a
rightful heir.

"With your permission," Geldion said to his father, "I will excuse myself
from the trip to Ynis Gwydrin. I will do as you first instructed me, and lead our
forces to victory over the invading lava newts." Geldion paused and glanced at
Badenoch, who was trying to remain regal, but could not completely mask his
widening and approving smile.

"Fare well, my father," Geldion said, fighting hard to keep his voice from
cracking. "And, I pray you, keep safe."

"Here it comes, lad," Mickey whispered as both Geldion and Kinnemore slowly turned Gary's way.

"I'm going with you," Gary, the King's appointed champion, remarked before Kinnemore could even ask.

"And I am, too," Diane promptly added.

Behind them, Mickey groaned, and Gary smiled, knowing that the sprite, too, would accompany them. Gary had come to fully understand Mickey McMickey, and he had confidence that the loyal leprechaun would stick by his side through any darkness.

Kinnemore accepted Gary's offer with a determined nod, then looked from the man to his wife.

"She goes," Gary said, his even tone offering no chance for debate.

Again the King nodded, and thought that Gary's trust in his wife was a very special thing indeed.

The encampment near Loch Gwydrin bustled with activity soon after, the soldiers putting down their weapons and taking up hand axes, pegs, and ropes. Tommy was most effective, running from the sandy banks repeatedly, returning each trip with an armful of huge logs that could be cut and strapped together into barges.

Gary, ordered by Kinnemore to keep his armor buckled on, Diane, and Mickey remained with the King during the construction, leading silent support to the determined yet obviously troubled man. Kinnemore had little to say those hours, even when Diane proclaimed that his son would one day make a fine King.

Mickey wasn't so sure of that; neither was Gary, who had seen the other side of Prince Geldion, but neither said a word to contradict the claim and both hoped that Diane was right.

The boats were completed soon after noon, a flotilla of fifteen barges that could each carry between seven and nine soldiers, in addition to those rowing. They were squared boats, just strapped logs, really, but Gwydrin was not a large lake and the isle, nestled in the shadows of towering cliffs, was only a few hundred yards from the shore.

Kinnemore quickly determined his forces. It would take four men to properly navigate each raft, and all but one of the barges would return to this bank, ready to ferry more men across if the need arose or if they could be spared by his son. That would put approximately six score soldiers on Ynis Gwydrin with the King and his champion—or champions, because Diane was playing the role as well as Gary. Kinnemore picked the leaders of that small force from the few friends he remembered from the days before Ceridwen had stolen him away, the few soldiers who had been strong enough to remain in their beloved army despite the unruly reign of the haggis. The King, in turn, let these leaders select the men who would accompany them, and then the rest of the boat-builders, some three hundred soldiers, were dismissed, to return to Prince Geldion for further orders.

It was all done quickly and efficiently, without a hitch—except for one.

Tommy put a perfectly plaintive look over Gary, the giant understanding that none of the barges would support his bulk. Tommy had walked across this lake before (once even carrying Gary and his companions), but even the not-so-bright giant seemed to understand that he would not be allowed to go this time.

"You have to get back to Prince Geldion and Lord Badenoch," Gary said cheerily, trying to put a positive spin on things. "They'll welcome your strength in their fight!"

Tommy shook his head. "Tommy go back to the island with you," he replied. "Tommy wants to see the Lady again."

The giant's tone made Gary and Mickey exchange nervous stares. Ceridwen had not treated Tommy badly in his years on the island, had served somewhat as a surrogate mother to the orphaned giant, and if Tommy held any remaining loyalty to the witch, he would surely make King Kinnemore's mission more difficult.

"Tommy remembers," the giant said determinedly. Again Gary and Mickey looked to each other. "Tommy remembers what the bad lady did on the one mountain."

"The one mountain?" Diane asked.

"Giant's Thumb," Gary explained, and both he and Mickey were more at ease then, knowing that if they could not convince Tommy to remain behind, the giant would at least be a complete ally in this venture, even if their goal turned out to be the death of Ceridwen. Ceridwen had turned on Tommy, had nearly killed them all on the slopes of Giant's Thumb, before Gary had put the mighty spear into her belly, banishing her to Ynis Gwydrin.

Still, Gary thought it important to convince Tommy to go to Geldion and Badenoch. The powerful giant would no doubt be much more helpful in the coming large-scale battle than in the tight confines of the witch's castle.

"You can't even stand straight in most of the rooms," Gary reasoned. "If you go with us to the island, you'll have to just wait outside the castle while we go in after Ceridwen."

The giant's expression became an open pout.

"But if you stay here," Gary continued hopefully, "you'll be able to help out in the fight. And they'll need you, Tommy."

The giant continued to pout as he considered the words. "Tommy does not like his choices," he remarked at length.

"Neither did Geldion," Diane put in. "He wanted to go along with his father, but he knew that it would be better for everyone if he stayed behind. That's what we have to do now, Tommy. Think what's better for everyone."

The giant stubbornly shook his head, but in the end, he agreed, and after pushing off all of the barges (and what a fine start that was towards the island!), Tommy waved goodbye to Gary, Diane, and Mickey, gave a determined nod, and followed the departing soldiers into the mountains.

PRINCE Geldion sat atop his horse, the same gray he had used on the two trips to the Crahgs, on a high ridge at the head of a valley that opened up to the fields east of Penllyn. When he and Badenoch and their closest advisors had first come to this spot, after Geldion had left his father, Geldion had thought this a magnificent view.

Soon after, all he could see was the encroaching doom, the lava newt army swarming across the fields like the shadow of a dark cloud.

"Too many," Badenoch whispered at his side.

Geldion eyed the Lord directly.

"I agree that we must catch them between the spurs, in this same valley," Badenoch went on. "But I fear that they are too many to even fit into this valley."

Prince Geldion couldn't find the conviction to disagree. His first plan of defense for Penllyn had been simply designed. They would try to lure the lava newts into the mountains through a few select areas, most notably the valley before him, where the defenders might concentrate their form enough to stall any advance. To that end, Geldion's cavalry and a single, imposing giant were even now slipping out of the mountains south of the approaching force in an attempt to strike at the lava newts' southern flank. By all accounts, the lava newts were running and not riding, and thus should pose little threat to the swift force, for the soldiers were not out to engage on any large scale, only to herd.

Prince Geldion was betting that the lava newts, so anxious to get to Ceridwen, thinking that they would do better against horsemen in the rough mountain terrain than on the open fields, and thinking that they would do better to avoid the giant at any cost on any terrain, would hardly slow to deal with the minor inconvenience of the cavalry. Likely, their forces would slowly shift to the north, putting them more in line for the rocky spurs and the valley, the designated killing field.

All reports thus far showed that Geldion's guess appeared to be on the mark. The lava newts were sliding inevitably north, giving ground to the cavalry and running with all speed from Tommy. That gave little measure of comfort to the tactical-minded Prince, though, for he feared that Lord Badenoch's assessment that, like a flood, the newts would simply swarm over the hills, through all passes, guarded and unguarded, might prove painfully true.

"Every group is ready, my Prince!" one of Geldion's advisors said determinedly, and Geldion nodded, not doubting the discipline of his warriors, or of those men from Braemar.

"Then tell the archers to bend back their bows," Lord Badenoch replied, and motioned back towards the eastern end of the valley, where the lead runners of the lava newt force had nearly entered.

They spotted the cavalry contingent a moment later, tiny figures out on the wide field, working hard to keep the line shifting. Horsemen rushed in and out for quick hits and quicker retreats. Geldion (and the others too) winced as one horseman rode down a newt too far out from the line. But the soldier's horse tripped up as it pounded over the fallen monster, and though the man managed to keep his seat and keep the horse upright, the stumble cost him precious moments. Before he could bring his mount back up to a gallop, a group of newts rushed over him and, by the sheer weight of numbers, brought him down. Other horsemen tried to get in to help their fallen comrade, but they were inevitably driven off by scores of the vicious lava newts. Tommy rushed in and scattered the newts, but the soldier was lost by that time.

Crying out in their hissing voices, beating their clubs and swords against shabby shields, a huge bulk of the lava newt force thundered into the valley.

Badenoch looked to Geldion, but the Prince sat calm. "Let them come," Geldion said softly, more to himself than to the Lord, trying to keep his calm and his patience.

Half the valley was full of newts, and lines of the lizardlike humanoids filtered up the rocky spurs, and no doubt along many of the trails north of this position.

Still Geldion waited. Their moment of complete surprise would be short; the Prince knew that he had to make it as effective as possible.

Most of the valley was filled with darkness. Lava newts flowed out from many angles, along climbing trails, most of which led nowhere.

Finally, Prince Geldion nodded and the soldier to his left put a horn to his lips and blew a single, clear note.

Up came the roar of the Connacht and Braemar forces. The humming of half a thousand bowstrings echoed from the mountainsides, and a wall of arrows cut the air with a great rush and whistle.

The newts continued to pour into the valley; screams of pain grew around their hissing war chants. Arrows flew as thick as locusts, and few answering shots came up from the valley floor.

Along those trails exiting the valley that did not abruptly end, the leading newt soldiers found themselves suddenly in combat—and usually in the worst possible attacking position along the ledge. Ringing steel joined the thrumming of bows, and screaming newts plummeted from high ledges, crashing in among the dead on the valley floor.

In all their years, in all their battles, neither Geldion nor Badenoch, nor even the professional soldiers flanking them, had ever seen such a massacre. The devastation was horrendous, the valley floor fast blackening with the writhing forms of dying newts. In one section along the southern wall, Geldion's soldiers even set off a small avalanche, crushing a hundred newts under tons of rock.

But a thousand newts swarmed over that area immediately after the tumble had ended.

All across the valley, and in those passes to the north, the line of the invaders seemed endless, two replacing every one that died, and four to replace those two after that. The archers continued to rain devastation on the newts, while those soldiers holding the strategic ledges methodically cut down their opponents one after another.

Even so, the newts made progress to complete the filling of the valley. Even so, every time a soldier on any ledge was defeated, valuable, critical ground was lost. And those newts that had gotten into the foothills along the northern passes were coming fast, flanking the defenders.

It went on for a solid half hour, lava newt bodies piled high, but the tide began to shift, the ratio of losses began to even out.

"Well fought," Lord Badenoch remarked to Prince Geldion when the two came to a new vantage point, one farther back as all of the Connacht army had been pushed. Geldion studied the older man. Badenoch's sentiments seemed true enough, but the man's tone revealed a sense of utter hopelessness.

"I know how you are feeling at this moment," the Lord of Braemar explained. "For I felt the same when my army came out onto the fields to battle the forces of Connacht. The tactics were impressive, and we have killed the newts at ten to one, or more. But they, and not we, have the soldiers to spare."

The grim words rang painfully true to Geldion as he looked down at the now-distant valley, its floor writhing with the black mass of lava newts who had not yet even seen battle. All along Penllyn's eastern edge, north, and even south of the Prince's position, was now in the hands of the enemy.

Geldion looked over his shoulder, back to the west, to the higher and still-open trails filled with defensible positions. But Geldion's expression was not a hopeful one, for he feared that he and his soldiers would soon have nowhere to run.

TWENTY-THREE

Terms of Surrender

THEY were met on the beach of Ynis Gwydrin by the witch's ragtag island forces, goblins mostly, but some other races, including more than a few humans who had spent years in Ceridwen's captivity and did the witch's bidding only out of fear of reprisal. Undisciplined and untrained, the island defenders went in a mob towards the first barge that skidded aground near the beach, swarming like ants, and those soldiers on that barge were sorely pressed.

But the soldiers of the other craft, including Gary and Diane, came ashore with relative ease. Mickey used his tricks to aid in the confusion near the first barge, making men appear where they weren't and sending goblins splashing to the surf after wild swings that hit nothing but air. And Gary led the charge of the Connacht infantry, all of them calling, "Yield to the spearwielder!" with every running step.

They formed into a wedge as they cut into the island mob, with Gary at its tip. Donigarten's spear flashed every which way, cutting down goblins. As the monstrous ranks parted, Gary came upon a human soldier, a filthy wretch of a man.

But a man nonetheless.

"Yield!" Gary screamed, jabbing the spear's deadly tip near the man's belly. "Yield!" Gary desperately hoped the man heeded the command, desperately hoped that he would not have to kill another human. His sigh of relief was sincere when the enemy threw down his makeshift club and fell groveling to his knees, whispering "Sir Cedric" repeatedly.

The wedge cut on, soon linking with those soldiers caught on the barge. The witch's forces swarmed around the lines, hoping to encompass the entire group, but as they went wide of the Connacht soldiers, they presented wonderful targets for the battery of archers waiting patiently further down the beach.

By the time the goblins had passed that rain of arrows, the back edges of the wedge had come together, turning the formation into a defensive diamond, and though Ceridwen's forces still outnumbered and had surrounded the invaders, the skilled Connacht troops were now fighting back to back, with no weaknesses in their line.

Gary, still the spearhead of the group, swung them about and pressed in from the beach, and like the prow of a fast ship, that corner of the diamond sailed through the sea of enemies.

"Above!" came more than one cry, and one Gary recognized as Diane's voice. All those soldiers, Connacht and island forces alike, who were not engaged looked up to see a black swarm coming out one of the crystalline castle's high towers, a line of monkey bats, screeching and beating their leathery wings. Even worse, out the castle's main door came two huge shapes, mountain trolls, armored head to toe with heavy metal plates over their thick hides and carrying swords taller than Gary, with enchanted, glowing blades as wide across as a strong man's leg.

The Connacht soldiers closest to the trolls rushed in fearlessly, scoring vicious hits with their fine swords. But the weapons seemed puny things next to the brutes, and were turned aside by the two-inch layer of metal armor.

The trolls swept across with their huge swords, cutting through shields and armor and men alike, cutting a swath of devastation in a single swipe.

Gary understood his duty here, knew that he alone carried a weapon that might get through the trolls' plated armor. He broke from the formation, running across the sand—and those minor island troops that saw him coming worked hard to get out of his way!

You must not let them maneuver about you, the sentient spear telepathically instructed. *Position, brave young sprout, will see us through!*

Gary didn't consciously answer, but was nodding his agreement as he came up on the first troll. He swerved far to the side and winced as the troll slashed its sword, sending an unfortunate Connacht soldier flying through the air. Then Gary came in hard, jabbing the spear against the side of the troll's leg. Sparks flew as the speartip connected on the heavy armor plating, and as Gary had expected (as Gary had prayed!), the mighty spear, the most powerful weapon in all the world, poked through.

The troll roared; its leg buckled sideways. It didn't tumble immediately, but roared again in absolute agony as Gary yanked the spear back out and ran on, out of the stumbling thing's reach.

Back near the water, Diane, standing with a handful of infantry as guard to Kinnemore and to the archers, heard the cry and noticed Gary's daring actions. Her heart skipped more than a few beats as she watched her husband rush around the wounded troll, cut between it and its other gigantic companion.

"Mickey!" she called, hoping the leprechaun might in some way help, but when she turned, she saw Mickey behind the battery of kneeling archers, as intent as they on the approaching flock of monkey bats.

As one, the archers fired, and so did the leprechaun, casting a spell to make every arrow appear as ten. Barely a dozen of the three score monkey bats took any hits, and only half of those were fatal, but all of the group went into a frenzy, dodging illusory and real bolts, slamming against each other, and spinning desperate maneuvers from which they could not recover.

The archers quickly readied and fired again, but before their next volley was even away, Mickey's continuing line of arrow images had the monkey bats scattering. A few more took hits and tumbled from the sky; the rest broke ranks and flew off in every direction available to get them away from Kinnemore's nasty soldiers.

THE wounded troll tried to turn about as Gary darted behind it, and that movement, pivoting on its torn leg, brought a resounding crack as the monster's knee snapped apart. Down it went in a spinning tumble, dropping its sword and clutching at the leg. A swarm of Connacht soldiers, following the lead of the spearwielder, of their King's champion, fell over it, hacking mightily and mercilessly.

Gary, bearing down on the next troll, hardly noticed the brute behind him, had his focus straight ahead. He clutched the spear in line, one hand balancing the shaft, the other near the weapon's butt end, and put his head down as though he meant to run the weapon through this troll's leg as well.

Up went the troll's sword and the beast lurched forward, bending to cleave the puny charging human in half. More than one soldier coming behind Gary cried out, thinking the man surely doomed, but Gary skidded up short and straightened suddenly, and his back hand rushed forward, hurling the spear straight for the most dumbfounded expression Gary had ever seen.

The troll cut across with its sword, trying to parry, and for a moment, Gary thought it had somehow knocked the spear aside. But when it all sorted out, there stood the beast, somehow still clutching its sword, hands out wide, and with the back portion of the spear's shaft protruding from its neck, angled up under the brute's chin.

The sword fell to the sand and the troll reached up with both hands behind its square head, weak fingers grasping at the spear's other, more deadly end.

It fell forward, and Gary did well to scramble out of its way.

The fight was over in the span of a few minutes, with dozens of goblins and a few of Ceridwen's men lying dead in the sand, many more of the humans huddled on the ground in surrender, and many more of all the monsters and humans running wild, scattering in terror along the beach.

It took Gary and a half dozen men a long time to shift the dead troll about so that Gary could pull free his bloodied spear, and by the time he had the weapon back in his grasp, Diane, Kinnemore, and Mickey were again at his side.

The King said nothing, but his admiring expression showed that he had gained new and greater confidence for this man he had named as his champion. Gary knew that Diane, too, was proud of his actions, but her sour look only revealed her disgust at the carnage on that bloody beach, and at the pieces of gore that Gary had to wipe from his magnificent weapon.

The skilled Connacht soldiers soon had the beach, all the way to the crystalline castle, fully secured, with an area set up for their wounded, and another for the prisoners.

King Kinnemore gathered his leaders together and bade them to sweep the island clean of opposition. Then he hand-picked a group of soldiers to accompany him and Gary (and Diane and Mickey—and the leprechaun wasn't too thrilled about that!) into the castle to parlay with the witch.

Kinnemore allowed Gary the honor of rapping on the huge doors of the castle, and Gary wisely did so with the butt end of his spear. Sparks flew and a minor explosion erupted as the weapon connected with the door and Gary was thrown back several steps and would have fallen to the seat of his pants had not two Connacht soldiers caught him by the arms and held him steady.

"A minor trap," the embarrassed man said, and he was glad that he wore the great helmet so that the others, particularly Diane and Kinnemore, could not see that his hair was standing on end.

With a determined grunt, Gary went back to the door and pounded it again, even harder. "Little witch, little witch, let me in, let me in!" he called in his best big-bad-wolf voice. He turned to Diane and winked through the faceplate of his helm. "Ceridwen doesn't have any hairs on her chinny-chin-chin," he said, trying to make light in the face of his true fears.

Those fears were fully revealed when the door unexpectedly swung open, and Gary jumped right off the ground and gave a yell.

Geek the spindly-armed goblin stood eyeing the man curiously.

"We have come to speak with Ceridwen!" King Kinnemore declared, stepping past his unnerved champion.

Geek nodded stupidly. "The Lady will see you," the goblin announced, and his confident, evil chuckle—even though he was so obviously vulnerable and overmatched—made more than a few soldiers look to each other nervously, as did Gary and Diane and Mickey, all wondering if they were walking right into the proverbial spider's web.

But in went King Kinnemore, fearlessly, and the others were obliged to follow.

THE Connacht and Braemar armies fought well, continuing the slaughter that had begun between the rocky outcroppings of the great spurs on the eastern edge of Penllyn. But the vast lava newt force could not be stopped, made its inevitable way to the west, taking one trail after another and pushing the defenders back on their heels.

Geldion and Badenoch each saw fighting that afternoon, each bloodied their weapons and took many minor hits. Most devastating was Tommy One-Thumb, the giant pounding away whole groups of lava newts at a time. But when Geldion and Badenoch came upon Tommy, sitting behind the lip of a high ridge overlooking Ynis Gwydrin, they knew that the giant, like an honest reflection of their entire army, was nearing the end. Tommy was truly exhausted, and his resigned look spoke volumes for the Prince and the Lord of Braemar, who knew that they could not win.

Gradually the human army had contracted, coming together on a high and flat plateau in north central Penllyn. The well-organized lava newts were all about them, particularly on the lower fields to the north, preventing them from fleeing the mountains and running back to their towns.

Prince Geldion blamed himself, thinking that he should have hit at the newts repeatedly, but with the ultimate design of fleeing the mountains.

"We could not afford that course," Lord Badenoch promptly reminded him. "The mountains offered our best defense, better than the walls of Connacht."

"And how many soldiers will run free of Penllyn?" Geldion asked sarcastically. "And what shall Connacht, and Braemar, do without their armies when the witch comes free?"

With no comforting answer, Badenoch shrugged and eyed the black host encircling his force, the ring growing ever tighter.

The lava newts continued to show skill and discipline. Those on the east, west and south of the plateau dug into defensive positions, for the trails were narrow and treacherous from those approaches, and easily defended by the soldiers on the higher ground. The host in the north gathered in increasing numbers, filtered together in a vast swarm. Their run to the plateau was open, though uphill, and the human defenders would be hard pressed by lines a hundred abreast.

Like a thunderstorm, the lines broke, and with a singular, hissing roar, the lava newts rolled towards the cornered humans.

"Fight well," Badenoch said to Geldion, and from his tone, the Prince understood the further implication: Die well.

KING Kinnemore knew nothing of the battle as he walked along the maze of the crystalline castle's winding and mirrored corridors. The lava newt force would be held at bay on the eastern edge of Penllyn, so he hoped, and thus he had devised the terms of surrender, including the reversion of Ynis Gwydrin to the rightful King of Faerie.

With their common understanding of the powerful witch, Gary and Mickey thought the King's plan grandly optimistic and based on presumptions that simply did not hold true where wicked Ceridwen was concerned. Neither said anything, though, or showed their fears, for Kinnemore was more determined than any person either of them had ever seen.

And he was the King, after all.

They met Ceridwen in a bare, octagonal room, its walls, floor and ceiling mirrored so that it took each of them several moments to get their bearings. The witch, beautiful and terrible in a black silken gown, seemed completely at ease, standing barely a dozen feet from her greatest adversaries.

"You know why we have come," Kinnemore said to her, his voice steady. If the King was intimidated, nothing he did, nor the tone of his voice, revealed it.

Ceridwen cackled at him.

"Your surrender will be accepted!" Kinnemore demanded. "The truth is known, evil witch, throughout the land. And ever was the truth your greatest bane."

Again the witch cackled hysterically. "The truth?" she chided. "And what do you know of the truth, foolish man? Is it not true that your pitiful son is even now being overrun in the mountain passes? That your pitiful army, so undeservedly proud, is now in full flight from a host of lava newts that have come to my call?"

Both Gary and Diane eyed the witch curiously, then looked to each other. Beyond what Ceridwen was actually saying, which was disturbing enough, the witch's lips seemed to be moving out of synch with the words, like a badly dubbed movie.

"What do you know of the truth?" the witch boomed in a voice that was not Ceridwen's, in a voice that was powerful and deep, grating and demonic in its pure discord.

Kinnemore began to reply, but the words were caught in his throat as the witch began to change. A third arm, black and scaly, burst from the creature's chest; writhing tentacles grew out of her hips, slapping the floor at her sides.

"What do you know?" the beast roared again, from a head that was now monstrous, fishlike, with a gaping, fanged maw and needle-sharp spikes prodding from the forehead.

Kinnemore fell back a step, Mickey whined, and Gary and Diane couldn't find the breath to utter a sound. Neither could the five escorting soldiers, though they remained loyal enough to their King to draw out their swords.

"Be gone!" the King managed to call to his escorts, but when he and they turned about, they found only another unremarkable mirror where the door had been.

"That might be a bit harder than ye think," Mickey whispered.

GELDION centered his front line, arrows flying over his head from behind, cutting devastation into the lava newt ranks. The Prince only shook his head, for the black tide was barely slowed, the monsters merely running over their dead and wounded without regard.

A hundred feet away, Geldion could see their slitted, reptilian eyes, gleaming eagerly, immersed in the thoughts of the killing that would soon begin.

But then another volley of arrows hit the lava newts, a greater volley than had come from behind Geldion, and this one coming, not from in front of the approaching horde, but from the west!

"Tylwyth Teg!" screamed one soldier, and it was true. Riding hard along the western trails, their white mounts shirting in the light, their bows humming in their hands, came the minions of Tir na n'Og. Behind them charged the remaining men of Dilnamarra, a group whose eyes were set with such determination as can only be inspired by great sorrow.

And from the north, from behind the horde of lava newts, came a second force, a greater force, such a host of Buldrefolk as had not been seen outside of Dvergamal in a dozen centuries. Geno Hammerthrower and Kervin were at their lead, and beside them, Duncan Drochit, and behind him, the brave soldiers of the town of the same name.

Great gnomish war machines rolled across the rough ground to either side of the dwarfish force, hurling stones and flaming pitch and huge spears into the midst of the suddenly scrambling lava newts.

Prince Geldion did not miss the moment. "Ahead!" he cried to his men. "Fight well!"

Lord Badenoch echoed that call, and this time, there were no dire, unspoken implications in his exuberant tone.

Kelsey, his bow spewing a line of arrows, rode hard and fearlessly. Unlike in the battle of Tir na n'Og, the elf saw a definite end to this fight, a conclusion from which all the goodly peoples of Faerie would benefit. He had left Braemar hopeful, but with the knowledge that the witch would soon be free and the misery could certainly begin anew. To Kelsey's surprise, he had found a host of elves marching east on the road outside of Dilnamarra, along with the remnants of Dilnamarra's militia and those soldiers the phoney King Kinnemore had left behind to guard the town. The word of the imposter haggis and the return of the true King had spread faster than Kelsey's ride, and already, the people of Faerie had seen the opportunity presented them.

And so the elf had been thrilled, but not truly surprised, when his force had swing to the south, a direct line towards Penllyn, and had found another army—the men of Drochit, a strong contingent of gnomes from Gondabuggan, and a force of sturdy dwarfs five hundred strong—marching south from the Dvergamal line, paralleling them on their way to Penllyn.

The lava newts were not nearly as chaotic and self-serving as the goblins and trolls and, under the guidance of iron-fisted Robert, had trained for large-scale battles. But now they were caught by surprise, nearly surrounded and with death raining in on them from the front, from the side, and from behind. They tried to swing their lines about, to regroup into tighter defensive formations, but they were too late, and the elfs and dwarfs, gnomes and humans fell over them, cutting their force piecemeal.

Many numbered the dead of the men that bloody day. Many elfs, who should have seen the dawn of centuries to come, would not, and many of the sturdy Buldrefolk were taken down, but not a one before he took down a dozen newts with him. The only unscathed force was that of the gnomes, and not a single name would be added to the plaque of *Fearless Gnomish Fighters,* as with all gnomish awards a posthumous honor, from the fabled battle of Penllyn. The lava newts did not know what to make of the huge gnomish war machines, and kept clear of them. The closest any gnome came to serious injury was when an upstart young female by the name of Budaboo strapped flasks of volatile gnomish potions around her waist and, desperate to get her name on that plaque, and perhaps even to win the posthumous Gondabugganal Medal of Honor, launched herself from the basket of one catapult. Budaboo had the good fortune (or misfortune, from her perspective) of sailing into an area near a friendly giant with soft hands, and Tommy promptly caught her and carried her back to safety. Later tales of the battle claim that Budaboo's ensuing, "Oh, pooh!" was heard above the clamor of the fighting, above the trumpets and the cries.

None of Gary's friends fell that day. Among them, only Geno took any hits at all, and the dwarf, with his typical stoicism, shrugged the wounds away as inconsequential. And when the battle was ended, the lava newts were scattered and beaten. The call of Ceridwen had been silenced by the thunder of armies joined.

TWENTY-FOUR

At the Heart of Darkness

THE thing was huge, half again taller than Gary and as wide as three large men. Eight limbs, all dripping slime, protruded from it: two scaly legs, four long arms ending in clawed fingers, and two tentacles, waving teasingly, with suction rings along their length and tipped by a cudgel of thick bone. Was it a creature of the water, or of the earth? Gary wondered, trying to find some perspective, trying desperately to put this most awful sight in a proper viewpoint. The monster's wide mouth gulped in air, but below the face, where the torso widened, were rows of slitted gills, and, though this room had been dry, a large puddle grew around the feet of the monster.

"Not water," Gary whispered to himself, shaking his head. He had met a demon before, in this very castle, and had defeated the creature, but that fact did little to bolster Gary's confidence now.

Courage, young sprout, the sentient spear, sensing the man's failing sensibilities, imparted.

"Not water," Gary whispered again, and he ignored Diane's ensuing question at his side. He watched another ball of slime elongate to hang low on the creature's forward arm, then splatter to the floor. This was a creature not of earth and not of water, he decided, a creature of sludge, of the eternal torments of Hell or the Abyss, or some other awful place.

Gary was not the first to muster the courage to charge. Two of the five soldiers who had accompanied him and the King to this room burst from the line, crying for their King and waving their swords.

A tentacle whipped across low, catching one man on the side of the knee and dropping him to the floor—where he hit the slippery slime and slid in close to the monster. Before he could even shift his body around, the fish-demon slammed a heavy foot atop him and ground him mercilessly.

The other soldier stumbled in the slime, but held his balance and even managed a swipe with his sword. The weapon hit the creature's arm, but did not bite deeply, sliding down the slimy limb. A clawed hand caught the man by the wrist and jerked him forward.

Where the monstrous maw waited.

In charged Kinnemore, Gary, and the other three soldiers. Diane drew out her small sword, but hesitated, understanding that they would need more than simple weapons to win out. She glanced all about the room, searching for a door, searching for a clue, and noticed Mickey, shaking his head helplessly and fading away into invisibility.

The monster kicked the man under its crushing foot aside, and he slid all the way across the room to slam hard into the base of one mirror. The other man, his shoulder torn away, was thrown to the side, where he fell without a sound, too far gone to even cry out in agony.

Both tentacles met the charge. One hit a soldier on the side of the face, and he went down, his consciousness blasted away. The other whipping limb took out the feet of a second man, then continued on into Gary.

Gary had seen it coming, though (mostly because the first victim had cried out as he tumbled away), and he dropped to one knee and angled his spear in front of him to catch the brunt of the blow. He had been stopped, but with a deft shift of his weapon, he made certain that the dangerous tentacle stayed with him and could not impede his other companions.

The left only King Kinnemore and a single soldier moving in close to the monster. As its front limb reached out for them, both scored solid hits with their swords, and the arm dropped free to the ground, where it writhed of its own accord in the slime.

On charged the two, between the fish-demon's side arms. The King's sword slammed hard against the thing's gill, opening a new and deeper slit. An arm clamped around him, though, and hugged him tight, and he worked desperately to keep the chomping maw from his face and neck. He looked back for his accompanying soldier, but saw the man stopped cold, for the monster had grown a new limb, where the arm had been severed—and this one more resembled a spike than an arm, a spike that impaled the surprised charging man!

Gary worked the spear fiercely in front of him, twisting and turning to keep the tentacle from retracting so that it might strike at him again, or strike at the man lying stunned on the ground not so far away.

Then Gary's breath was stolen away as the second tentacle smacked hard across his back, a blow that he believed would have cut him in half if he had not been wearing the armor. He felt himself sliding inevitably backwards as the second tentacle, its suckers clinging fast to his armor, moved away. As soon as he broke clear of the first, Gary kept the presence of mind to jab ahead with his spear, snagging it and pulling it along, as well.

"I'm with ye, laddie!" Mickey cried, coming visible right beside Gary, stabbing at the tentacle locked on the man's back with a puny knife.

"Use your tricks!" Gary yelled, stunned to see Mickey in a physical fight.

"And what use might they be against a demon?" Mickey asked sarcastically. The leprechaun's undeniably sharp knife dug in again on the tentacle, but Mickey seemed to Gary to be a tiny mouse nibbling a fat length of hemp rope.

Gary called to the man on the floor, told him that his King was in dire need. But the man could not rise, could not find his sensibilities enough to even know where he was.

That left Kinnemore battling alone in close, smacking his sword wildly against the fish-demon's head and torso, though the weapon, fine as it was, seemed to have little effect. The monster spat forth a line of slime, right into the King's face, blinding him. And then Kinnemore was yelling in agony, for the slime was based in acid.

Diane went down to her knees at full speed, slid across the wet floor as though it was ice, with her sword pointing straight ahead and angled up, braced in both arms. She hit the fish-demon in the armpit, the elfish sword plunging in right up to its hilt.

A hot green liquid spewed from the wound, and Diane wisely fell back. Her eyes widened in horror as the hilt of her sword fell to the floor, and she found that the blade had been melted away.

The fish-demon was fully capable of fighting multiple battles. Though it roared in pain from Diane's solid hit, and though it was still engaged with King Kinnemore, its tentacles worked in unison against Gary, pulling in opposite directions, one secured to Gary's back (and seeming hardly to notice the leprechaun's repeated strikes), the other tugging at the impaled spear.

"Hit it!" Gary screamed to his weapon, fearing that the spear would be pulled from his grasp. The spear complied, sending a burst of energy from its tip into the tentacle.

Gary inadvertently punched himself in the chin, under his great helm, as the tentacle whipped in a frenzy. He somehow managed to hold on, though, and the spear blasted again, and a third time. The tentacle danced wildly, but without control, its muscles reacting to impulses that did not emanate from the fish-demon's brain.

Gary heaved up with all his strength, then reversed his grip and slammed spear and tentacle against the floor, the sharp edge of the mighty spear cutting through and free of the monstrous limb. Then Gary spun about, knocking Mickey face down in the slime and jabbing hard at the second tentacle, scoring a brutal hit.

"Ye're welcome," Mickey muttered dryly.

The fish-demon wailed and hurled Kinnemore to the floor, where he lay crumpled in the slime. Diane, weaponless, thought of going for his fallen sword, but discounted that avenue and grabbed the King by the collar instead, tugging hard. Surprisingly, the King resisted, even slapping Diane's hand away. Half-blinded by the acid, battered and bleeding in several places, Kinnemore went for his sword.

He forced himself to his feet, coming up right in line with the fish-demon's maw, and managed a solid slash across that wide mouth, taking out two fangs and sending lines of bright blood into the creature's mouth.

The maw snapped forward; Kinnemore snapped his sword in line to block and scored a wicked hit.

But that blade wouldn't stop the powerful monster, and as it broke through, teeth gouging into Kinnemore's chest, only Diane's tug at the King's back stopped him from being bitten in half. Both Diane and the King fell back, and so did the fish-demon, for the sword was stuck painfully into the roof of its mouth.

Diane found her breath hard to come by as she looked around at the King's garish wound. Kinnemore smiled weakly at her, as if to say that it was worth the attempt, then slipped from consciousness. Diane couldn't secure her footing on the floor, but the slime worked in her favor, allowing her to drag the King quickly.

Soon she passed Gary, who was still hacking away, and Mickey joined her, and together they got back to the place where they had first entered the room.

Gary regained his footing and, finally free of the sticky tentacle, covered the retreat. He struck repeatedly with the mighty spear, at the tentacles, at a reaching arm, at the bulk of the beast whenever it ventured too near. Still, Gary didn't see where he and his friends might ultimately run. Diane searched frantically along the spot where they had entered, but it seemed just a mirror now, with no handles or hinges.

Not so far away, one of the soldiers started to rise.

"Stay down!" Gary cried to him, for the man was obviously dazed and in no position to defend himself.

The soldier apparently did not hear, or did not comprehend the meaning, for he continued to rise, and almost made it up to his feet.

Almost.

The fish-demon whipped a heavy tentacle across, the bone cudgel slamming the rising man on the back of the neck and launching him into a flying somersault. He flew into the nearest mirror and crashed right through, falling into a shallow alcove amid the shards of crumbling glass. He continued to groan and to stir a bit, but could not begin to extract himself from that mess.

Overwhelmed by rage, Gary charged ahead, thrusting the spear in vicious and effective overhead chops. As with Diane's sword, the mighty spear plunged into the monster's torso, but the spear, unlike the sword, could not be damaged, could not even be marked, by the green acidic gore.

Gary blindly struck repeatedly, growling every time his weapon hit something substantial, but soon his fury played itself out. He had backed the fish-demon halfway across the room, but now it was the creature that was advancing. Gary slashed the spear across in front of him, parrying the lunging limbs and the prodding spike.

There were too many angles, though, too many limbs and weapons from this unearthly beast. Gary saw a tentacle soaring at him from the left, down low, noticed out of the corner of his eye the other tentacle, fast flying in from the right, up high.

"Oh, no," he muttered, and he jumped and tried to curl into a ball, feeling like a double-dutch rope skipper on the local playground.

He got clipped on the heel and the opposite shoulder, the momentum of the heavy blows sending him into a double spin, sending his loose-fitting helmet flying away, before he crashed down to the floor. He heard Diane calling, heard Mickey calling, but all he saw was the fish-demon leering, smiling at him as it began its advance once more.

Gary fought to regain his footing, tried to rationalize that the fight was going better than he could have hoped, that he had scored many serious hits on his monstrous opponent.

But when Gary looked to those wounds for encouragement, his heart fell away, for all the wounds were fast mending, closing right before his eyes.

He muttered a hundred denials in those next few seconds, a hundred pieces of logic that told him this could not be. But it was, and his words were truly empty. Gary was still muttering when he felt the butt of his spear tap the mirror at his back, when he noticed Diane and Mickey flanking him, their expressions as hopeless as his own.

Reacting on pure survival instinct, Gary spun and slammed the spear into the mirror. The glass broke apart but though the companions had entered through this very area, they found no door behind the break, just another shallow and unremarkable alcove.

"Search it!" Gary cried to Mickey and he spun back, whipping his spear across just in time to deflect a tentacle swipe from the closing monster.

The fish-demon roared and charged suddenly, and Gary and Mickey and Diane all cried out, thinking their doom upon them. Simply because she had nothing else to possibly do, Diane lifted the Polaroid and snapped a picture—and the blinding flash stopped the fish-demon in its slimy tracks.

Gary didn't miss his one chance. He leaped out from the wall and plunged the spear deep into the monster's chest. The fish-demon fell back, off the tip, and responded with a tentacle clubbing that staggered Gary and almost knocked him from his feet. The monster was in a slight retreat, though, giving Gary the time to recover.

He heard a winding noise then, and turned to accept the other flash, the one that could be fit atop the Pentax, from Diane. He saw that Mickey was in the newest cubby by then, but the sprite was shaking his head, finding nothing that gave any clues to a door.

Full of determination, but not of hope, Gary advanced on the monster. One of the other soldiers was up again, wounded but willing to fight, and with sword in hand. He and Gary shared a nod, then advanced.

A tentacle slammed the soldier, but he caught it and went with it, holding fast with one hand while hacking away with his sword.

Gary spun to the other side, his spear intercepting and driving away the second tentacle, and then he charged straight ahead and scored again with yet another solid overhead chop.

"How many can you take?" Gary snarled defiantly at the fish-demon and struck again, then leaped back and twisted frantically to avoid the rushing monster and its front limb that had become a deadly spike.

He avoided the hit, but lost his footing, slamming heavily to the floor. And when he managed to look up, there was the demon's maw, barely a foot away, too close for him to bring the spear to bear. Gary didn't know if the "ready" signal was lit on the back of the flash or not, and didn't have the time to look. He just thrust the small box forward and pushed the button.

The flash did fire, and the fish-demon bellowed and fell back, allowing Gary to scramble to his feet. The spearwielder backpedaled, and winced as the outraged monster gave a tremendous snap of its engaged tentacle that sent the poor soldier spinning across the room.

Then Diane was beside Gary, though he was far from Mickey and the fallen Kinnemore. She had no weapon, though.

Just a photograph, a picture of the room that revealed, in the light of the flash, a slender silhouette behind one of the mirrors.

Gary lifted the spear over his head, prepared for the fish-demon's final charge, the one he knew he and Diane could not hope to stop.

On came the beast; Diane stuck the picture in front of Gary's face.

It all happened too fast for Gary to truly sort it out, but the one thing he held above all was his trust in Diane, and when she called for him to "Throw the spear!" he understood her meaning perfectly.

With a primal scream, Gary shifted and heaved the spear to the side of the demon, past the demon. It hit a mirror and dove right through, and cracks widened around the hole. Shards of glass fell clear, and there, in the alcove, stood a stunned Ceridwen, Donigarten's spear deep into her chest. She grasped at its shaft and tried to scream, but no sound would come past her trembling lips.

Gary and Diane were watching the fish-demon, though, and not the spear's flight. The monstrous beast bore down on them, seemed to fly straight for their hearts. They huddled together and cried out, certain that their death was upon them. But like the mirror covering Ceridwen, the fish-demon suddenly split apart into black shards and fell away to nothingness.

And then the room was strangely quiet, eerie, with Gary and Diane standing at each other's side, holding each other, in the slime and the gore and the devastation.

"The laddie got her again!" yelled Mickey McMickey, the most welcome voice and words that Gary Leger had ever heard.

TWENTY-FIVE

The Torch Is Passed

"NAME her place, lad!" Mickey called excitedly. "Send her away before it's too late."

Gary was mesmerized by it all, by the so sudden shift in the events about him. He gawked at Ceridwen, her form becoming an insubstantial shadow, fading around the spear (which was stuck fast into the wall behind her).

"Name her place!" Mickey cried again. "If ye do not, then she'll be bound again to Ynis Gwydrin, bound again to this very castle, and the fighting will begin anew!"

That grim possibility shook Gary from his daze. He thought for just a moment. "Giant's Thumb," he announced in a loud and clear voice. "I banish you to Giant's Thumb, evil witch, where you shall remain for a hundred years!"

Mickey nodded, but his cherubic smile was short-lived. There was a hoard of treasure in Giant's Thumb, the leprechaun realized, a hoard that, with Robert dead and the lava newts away to Penllyn, was all but unguarded. The leprechaun gave a resigned sigh, admitting to himself that Gary, with his limited knowledge of Faerie, had chosen well. The lad had indeed beaten the witch again, stuck her with the only weapon in all the world that could hurt her.

But whatever feelings of victory Gary, Diane, and Mickey might have felt were washed away as soon as they considered the room about them. Two of the five soldiers lay still in pools of blood, one of them obviously dead and the other three, even the one who had stood to fight beside Gary in the final moments, grievously wounded.

So was King Kinnemore, his face burned, one arm broken, and a deep wound in his chest.

The defeat of the witch also returned the door to the strange room, and Gary ran off to gather the other soldiers together, to find help for the wounded, and to find news of the fight in the mountains. Diane and Mickey remained behind, and Diane knew enough about first aid to realize that King Kinnemore was in a very bad way.

PRINCE Geldion bit back tears and bravely firmed his jaw as he knelt beside the cot, staring at his father.

Kinnemore managed a weak smile and lifted a hand to gently stroke his son's cheek.

"'Tis not fair," Geldion whispered. "I have only recently found you."

"What is fair?" Kinnemore replied between shallow breaths. "Better this fate than what I was presented. Better that I have lived to see my kingdom restored and to see what a fine man my son has become."

Geldion's eyes misted at that. "I wish to know you," the Prince protested. "I wish to know your joys and your sorrows. To learn from you."

Kinnemore slowly shook his head. "You do, my son," he whispered.

"I am not ready . . ."

"You are," the King interrupted forcefully, and the exertion cost him his strength. He fell deeper into the cot, his muscles relaxing for a final time. "You are," he whispered, barely audible, "my son."

Gary and Diane, Mickey and Kelsey and Geno, and all the leaders, dwarf, elf, gnome, and human, gathered in the anteroom to the King's chambers (in what had been Ceridwen's chambers when the witch ruled Ynis Gwydrin) when Geldion came out.

"The King is dead," the Prince said quietly, though his expression had told all before he ever uttered the words.

Gary looked all around, not knowing what to expect. Would Geldion become King? Would Badenoch and Duncan Drochit, and particularly the Tylwyth Teg, accept this man who had been so complete an enemy?

"A fine man was your father," Kelsey offered, and he privately nodded to Gary. "Let none question his wisdom or his courage."

"To King Kinnemore," Lord Badenoch said, drawing his sword and lifting it high in salute, a movement that was repeated all about the room.

Diane saw her opportunity and did not let it pass. She wasn't sure of Faerie's customs in this regard, but guessed that it was pretty much along the lines her own world in ages past. She moved beside Geldion, took his hand and lifted it high. "The King is dead," she proclaimed. "Long live the King!"

There ensued a moment of the most uncomfortable silence, even Geldion seeming confused as to how he should proceed, as to whether anyone would second Diane's bold claim.

Gary put a stare over Kelsey, green eyes matching gold, the man silently reminding the elf how crucial this moment might be for all the land. Whatever Kelsey's feelings for Geldion, whether or not the elf was convinced that this man should rule, the Connacht army would surely remain loyal to Kinnemore's son.

Kelsey returned Gary's stare for a long moment. "Long live the King!" he said loudly, shattering the silence, and more than one person in that room, new King Geldion included, breathed an honest sigh of relief.

The first days of the new King's rule met, and even exceeded, the hopes and expectations of the leaders of the other towns and races. Geldion proclaimed that Ynis Gwydrin, and not Connacht, would become the new seat of power, and that the island, and all of Penllyn, would be open and welcoming to any of Faerie's men, elfs, dwarfs, and gnomes.

To Lord Badenoch, who had been perhaps Geldion's staunchest detractor, the new King offered the Dukedom of Connacht, and when the Lord, loyal to his dear Braemar, politely declined, and when Duncan Drochit, equally loyal to his own town, also declined, Geldion begged that both men provide a list of candidates who might properly fill the most important position. It was an offer that surely brought the confidence of many camped in Penllyn, including the Tylwyth Teg, all glad to know that the new King would not put a puppet in Connacht's seat.

That only left one position open, and Gary Leger alone was surprised by Geldion's next offer.

"Your friend, Baron Pwyll, died a hero," Geldion said to Gary one night on the quiet beach of Ynis Gwydrin. The lights of a hundred campfires flickered in the distance, on the shore across the still water.

"Aye," agreed Mickey, the leprechaun standing at Gary's side and doodling in the sand with his curly-toed shoe.

When Gary did not reply, Diane hooked her arm in his, offering him support.

"The people of Dilnamarra have come to expect excellence from their leader," Geldion went on. "The good Baron . . ."

Gary's skeptical stare stopped Geldion momentarily, reminded the new King that he and Pwyll had not been the best of friends while Pwyll was alive.

But Geldion nodded in the face of that doubting expression, and silently admitted the truth. Things had changed, so it seemed, and Geldion pressed on. "Perhaps Baron Pwyll's detractors were misinformed," he admitted. "No man has known a finer moment than Baron Pwyll. He stood on the platform in Dilnamarra, surrounded by enemies, and spoke the truth, though he knew the words would bring about his death. I pray that I might find such courage should the occasion arise. I pray that I might be as much a hero as Baron Pwyll of Dilnamarra."

The sentiments seemed honest enough, and Gary found himself placed in the middle of a test, much as Kelsey and the others had been placed when Diane had first proclaimed Geldion as King. Gary let go his anger then, completely, and put aside his judgments. Through all the turmoil, Geldion had been loyal to his father, or to the monster he had believed to be his father; in remembering his own dad, how could Gary honestly claim that he would have done differently? And now Geldion had lost his father, as Gary had lost his, and the new King was standing strong and honestly trying to do what was right.

Gary's glower faded away.

"I am in need of a Baron," Geldion went on, seeming to understand that he had gained Gary's confidence. "A man who will command the loyalty of the beleaguered people of Dilnamarra. A man who will guide the rebuilding of the town after the grave injustices they have suffered."

For the first time, Gary understood what was coming.

"I offer Dilnamarra to you, spearwielder," Geldion said firmly. "To the slayer of Robert, the man who has acted on behalf of Faerie's goodly folk in all his days in the land. I offer it to you and to Diane, your wife, she who solved the riddle of the haggis and saved Faerie from a darkness more terrible than any the land has ever seen."

Gary and Diane looked to each other for a long, long while.

"They'll be needing some time," Mickey whispered to Geldion, and the two slipped away, leaving the couple alone on the dark and quiet beach.

HE thought of the good he might do, the improvements to the political system and the general welfare of the common people. He felt like an American colonial, who might bring the idea of democracy to a world full of kings, who might draft a document based on his own Constitution. He and Diane could stay for a few years, perhaps, then return to their own world, where by that world's reckoning they would only have been gone a few days.

How tempting was Geldion's offer, to Gary and to Diane.

Then why? Gary wondered when they were back in a glade in Tir na n'Og just a couple of weeks later, waiting with Mickey and Kelsey for the pixies to come and begin their world-crossing dance. Why were they going back?

Both Gary and Diane had come to the same conclusion, separately, that they could not, should not, remain in Faerie. For all the thrills it might offer, this was not their world, not their place, and they both had families back home. And they had been summoned by an even more insistent call, a call that emanated from their own hearts. Gary had come to terms with the loss of his father now. In the fight for Faerie, in what he had seen pass between Geldion and Kinnemore, the young man had come to remember and dwell on not his father's death, but his father's life. He had come to terms with mortality, and knew then how to beat the inevitable. His answers would not be found in Faerie, but in his family.

Gary and Diane had decided that the time had come for them to have a child, and they could not do that in Faerie—how could they go back to their own world and possibly explain the new addition?

So it was not with heavy hearts that Gary and Diane said their goodbyes to Geno and Gerbil and Tommy at the border of Dvergamal. And it was not with heavy hearts that they stood now in Tir na n'Og, waiting to go home.

"Ye're sure, lad?" Mickey asked, drawing the man from his private contemplations.

Gary could tell from Mickey's tone that the sprite approved of the decision. The leprechaun had hinted several times during their journey back to Tir na n'Og that too much needed to be done in Gary's own world for him to even think of staying to help with Faerie's problems. Indeed, Gary got the distinct impression that if he remarked that he had changed his mind now, Mickey would likely try to steer him back towards his original choice. Kelsey seemed in full agreement. As much as the elf had come to trust and love Gary, and as much as he had already come to respect Diane, Kelsey still thought of them as outsiders, as people who belonged to another place.

"It's been an amazing few . . ." Gary stopped before he said "years," remembering that, by Mickey's terms, all of this incredible adventuring had occurred in just a few short months. "It's been an amazing few months," he corrected with a private chuckle. "So how many others have come over for a similar experience?"

"Faerie's always wanting another hero," Mickey explained cryptically.

"So is my own world," Gary replied. He looked at Diane and shrugged. "Not that I'm anything special back there."

"It's a tough place to get noticed," Diane agreed with a resigned smile.

"But we have to go back," Gary asserted to Diane and to Mickey. "I'd be willing to return—we both would—but let's keep it one adventure at a time."

"It's more mysterious that way," Diane explained. "If we stuck around long enough for the people to get to know us, they'd probably become a bit disenchanted."

Gary, Diane, and Mickey shared a chuckle at the self-deprecating humor.

"I do not believe that," Kelsey interrupted, the elf's tone even and serious. "Their respect would not lessen with familiarity."

Gary, who knew Kelsey so very well, understood how great a compliment the elf had just given to him and his wife. He turned to Diane and she was nodding, fully comprehending.

That satisfying moment was lost when the melodic call of pixie-song wafted through the night air. As one, the companions turned to see the ring of glowing lights, Gary and Diane's ride home.

With a nod to Mickey and Kelsey, and not another word, for they both knew that if they dragged this out, they would not have the strength to continue, the two walked over and stepped in.

"Remember, lad and lass," they heard Mickey call, his voice already sounding distant, "the bridges to Faerie are in yer mind's eye!"

Then they heard the surf pounding below them, and awoke in the early morning hours amid the ruins of a castle in a lonely place on the Isle of Skye known as Duntulme.

Epilogue

"THE bridges to Faerie are in your mind's eye," Gary muttered.

Diane looked up from her book. "What?" she asked, putting her mouth close to Gary's ear so that he could hear her over the drone of the 747's engines. As usual, the two found themselves sitting over a wing, with no view and the loudest noise.

"What Mickey said," Gary explained. "The bridges to Faerie are in your mind's eye. What do you think that means?"

Diane sat back and folded her book on her lap. She hadn't really considered the leprechaun's parting words in any detail, too consumed by the journey back to her own world and by the implications of all that she had witnessed. Like Gary on his first journey, like any who had gone over to Faerie, Diane found the foundations of her own world, and of a belief system that had guided her through all her life, severely shaken.

"Mind's eye?" Gary whispered.

"Maybe Mickey was saying that the bridges remain, and you'll be able to see them," Diane offered.

Gary was shaking his head before she ever finished. "Mickey's been saying that the bridges are lessening—look at the woods out back of my mother's house. That place was a bridge to Faerie, once upon a time."

Gary sank back into his seat, his expression sour, lamenting.

"Maybe the bridges are what Mickey was talking about when he said that your world, that our world, needed fixing," Diane offered.

Gary looked at her quizzically, doubtful but intrigued.

"Really, do you think you can make some major changes in the course of our world?" Diane asked. "Five billion people in structured societies—what, are you going to become President or something?"

Gary started to say, "It could happen," but realized that he was beginning to get more than a little carried away. In Faerie, he was the spearwielder, the wearer of Donigarten's armor, champion of a King. In this world, he was Gary Leger, just another guy going about his life, trying to get along.

"So what do you think he was talking about?" Gary prompted, thinking that Diane had a better grasp than he did on the reality of it all.

"The bridges," Diane decided after a short pause. "Mickey laments the passing of the bridges, and he wants you to make sure that they don't all go away."

"That would make our world a better place," Gary quietly agreed, resting back more comfortably in his seat. Diane smiled at him and went back to her reading.

A few minutes later, Gary popped forward, drawing Diane's full attention. "That's it!" he said excitedly, and too loudly, for he noticed that several nearby passengers had turned to regard him. He huddled closer and spoke more quietly as he continued. "We can show them," he said. "We can tell them and we can show them, and we can make them understand."

Diane didn't have to ask to figure out who this "them" that Gary was talking about might be. He was speaking of the general populace, speaking of going public with their adventures, perhaps even with the pictures of Faerie that Diane had brought back with her. Her doubts were obvious in her expression.

"We've got the proof," Gary went on undaunted. He nodded to Diane's travel bag, the one holding the cameras and the revealing film.

Diane looked there, too, and shook her head.

"They're unretouched Polaroids," Gary protested.

"Of what?" Diane asked bluntly.

Gary mused that one over for a moment. "Of the haggis," he said finally. "We've got a picture of the haggis in the King's clothes."

"That should get us on the cover of one or two tabloids at least," Diane replied sarcastically. "Maybe even on a daytime talk show, right next to the London werewolf."

Her sarcasm was not without merit, Gary fully realized. The most remarkable pictures they had were shots that could be easily faked, were images that didn't even compare with the ones in the lower-budget science-fiction movies.

"Mickey wouldn't have said it if he didn't have a reason," Gary huffed, growing thoroughly flustered. "There's a key to this somewhere. I know there is."

"Your imagination," Diane answered suddenly.

Again Gary looked at her quizzically.

"Your mind's eye, don't you see?" said Diane. "The bridges to Faerie are in your mind's eye."

"We didn't imagine . . ."

"Of course not," Diane agreed before Gary could even finish the argument. "But maybe what Mickey was talking about, maybe the reason we're losing the bridges to Faerie, is because we, as a world, are losing our ability to imagine."

"The bridges to Faerie are in your mind's eye," Gary uttered once more, the words coming clear to him then.

Diane leaned in close and whispered into Gary's ear. "And maybe we can open up someone else's mind's eye," she said.

Gary knew what she meant, had the answer sitting in his desk drawer in his apartment in Lancashire, Massachusetts, in the form of a book written by a man who had opened up Gary Leger's imagination. Maybe, just maybe, he and Diane could do the same for some other potential adventurer.

It was a seven-hour flight back to Boston's Logan Airport, and by the time the 747 touched down, Gary had the first chapter plotted and ready for the keyboard.

R. A. Salvatore was born in Massachusetts in 1959. His love affair with fantasy, and with literature in general, began during his sophomore year of college when he was given a copy of J.R.R. Tolkien's *The Lord of the Rings* as a Christmas gift. He promptly changed his major from computer science to journalism. He received a Bachelor of Science Degree in Communications from Fitchburg State College in 1981, then returned for the degree he always cherished, the Bachelor of Arts in English.

Salvatore's first published novel was *The Crystal Shard* in 1988. Since that time, he has published numerous novels, including the *New York Times* bestselling *The Halfling's Gem*, *Sojourn*, and *The Legacy*. He is best known as the creator of the dark elf Drizzt, one of the fantasy genre's most beloved characters. More than three million R. A. Salvatore novels have been sold with many translated into different languages and audio versions. He makes his home in Massachusetts with his wife and their three children.

Visit the author's website at www.rasalvatore.com.